# THE NEXT GENERATION®

# STAR TREK
## THE NEXT GENERATION ®

**THE GENESIS WAVE**

**John Vornholt**

SCIENCE
FICTION

Book One Copyright © 2000 by Paramount Pictures. All Rights Reserved.
Printing History: Pocket Books Hardcover November 2000

Book Two Copyright © 2000 by Paramount Pictures. All Rights Reserved.
Printing History: Pocket Books Hardcover April 2001

First SFBC Science Fiction Printing: June 2001

Published by arrangement with:
Pocket Books
A division of
Simon & Schuster Inc.
1230 Avenue of the Americas
New York, New York 10020

ISBN 0-7394-1843-2

Visit our website at *http://www.sfbc.com*
Visit Pocket Books's website at *http://www.simonsays.com/startrek/*

PRINTED IN THE UNITED STATES OF AMERICA

# Contents

### THE NEXT GENERATION®

*For Ruth, who has saved us many times!*

# one

Waves lapped delicately at the blue pebbles and copper-colored sand of the lagoon, while ferns waved in the scented breeze. Their slender branches traced ripples in the tide pools, while sleek, black shapes teemed in the deepest part of the lagoon. Beyond the shore stretched an endless turquoise sea filled with whitecaps, dancing to the music of the waves. Heat and light radiated from the red midday sun, bathing the quiet seascape in a golden halo.

The sun felt good on the old woman's wrinkled skin. It seemed to penetrate into her aged bones and joints, making them feel good, too. Her hair was white and thinning, but it had once been vibrantly blond, matching her square-jawed Scandinavian face. She covered her eyes with a spotted hand and squinted into the glare, noting only a whisper of clouds in the azure sky.

The old woman bent down and ran her hand through the copper sand—it felt like a combination of bath water and hot ashes. With fingers that were spotted with age but still nimble, she probed the granules until she uncovered a tiny filament, no wider than a hair. Patiently she kept digging, ignoring a twinge of pain that rippled from her back down to her thighs. The glitches of advanced age were old acquaintances at this point in her life. She was 135 years old. Or was it 136? She often lost track in this sunny paradise, where every day was much like the day before.

The longer she kept digging, the older she felt, but her careful labor was slowly rewarded. One by one, she collected more fibers, stretching them across her palm, careful not to uproot them from the underground connectors. Her digging didn't stop until she had unearthed seven of the delicate filaments, and she hunched over to study them more closely.

"None of these are damaged," she said with relief, sinking back on her haunches. The woman recalled how fierce the storm had been last night, knocking out their sensor array. By midmorning, the sky over the island had reverted back to its usual crystal clarity.

"Sometimes this place is almost too sunny," the old woman complained. "It's not exactly the real world."

No one agreed or disagreed. The breeze whispered a reply, saying it didn't matter one whit, because the great work of her life was behind her. The old woman sighed at her foolishness and replanted the delicate fibers in the sand.

She stood up, groaning at the creak in her back. "I should take my medicine." Then she quickly added. "Computer, erase that last sentence from the log."

"Sentence erased," repeated a tinny voice coming from the combadge on her white jumpsuit.

The old woman snorted a laugh. "Is anybody really *listening* to me? Does anybody *care* that I've turned this entire beach into a giant solar-energy collector? And I did it without upsetting the ecosystem. Is everybody in the Federation just trying to humor an old lady?"

Once again, no one answered, except for the gentle lapping of the waves. The computer back in the lab was simply capturing her remarks in a log, to be transmitted to her correspondents in other locations. She missed having live colleagues around. Oh, they came to visit every so often, but they seldom stayed for long. They were intimidated by her bodyguards and her monastic lifestyle, neither of which was her choosing. Over the years, she had come to accept her quiet life until it had become the norm.

The old woman could travel if she wished, but it was too difficult taking her entourage with her. As the years passed, she traveled less and less. Her isolation in the watery expanses of Pacifica wasn't due to her experiments—it was necessary for that other part of her life, the part which often dominated. The old woman was a prisoner of the past, still suffering from acts of pride, ambition, and selfishness.

On days like this, it seemed as if her punishment and grief would be endless—as endless as the turquoise sea that surrounded her. Of all her grievous mistakes, the worst was leaving her son behind in that terrible place. The bloodstains from the past could never be cleansed, not by all the waves and torrential rain in the universe.

*Why leave my island?* thought the old woman bitterly. *I have no one out there, no one who cares about me. It's not respect or love my keepers feel for me—it's fear. I'm valuable because I have a secret.*

*They'll be glad when I'm gone. . . . Then they can stop protecting information they don't even want to know.*

"Dr. Marcus?" asked a helpful male voice.

She whirled around to confront Ensign Martin Dupovitz, the youngest and newest member of her four-person security detail. "Don't sneak up on me like that!" she snapped, instantly regretting her hasty reaction.

"I'm . . . I'm sorry, Doctor," stammered the lad. In this setting and his gold-hued Starfleet uniform, he looked like some exotic waiter at a beach resort. "You sounded distressed over the comlink, and you were . . . talking to yourself."

"I was not talking to myself," insisted Carol Marcus impatiently. "I was making a log entry . . . talking to the computer."

"Of course, Doctor," answered Martin, trying not to sound condescending, but failing. "It's just that—with our sensor array down—we have to be extra careful."

"Go ahead and call me Carol," said the old woman, trying to muster some of the personality that used to charm the Federation Council and young suitors, such as James T. Kirk. "We don't stand on formality around here."

Martin lowered his eyes and kicked at a blue pebble in the sand. "Well, I prefer to maintain a professional demeanor, Dr. Marcus. I want to get good reports from Commander Quay'to—"

"So you can get out of here all the sooner," replied Carol, finishing his thought. He looked at her, abashed, having been found out.

"Don't worry about it," she said warmly. "Everybody leaves here eventually—we haven't lost an officer yet. And it's not so bad. The scuba diving is quite good, and so is weather watching. You don't know anything about solar flares, do you?"

The young man shook his head. "No, that's not my field of study. I have a black belt in karate, and I'm rated for tactical weaponry."

"Hmmm," said Carol with mild disapproval, having never liked the militaristic side of Starfleet. "What exactly do they think is going to happen to me out here? It's been ninety years since . . . the incident . . . and no one has come after me yet. Someday I'm just going to blurt out everything I know, and you people can spend eternity guarding *each other!*"

Martin blanched and took a step back. "Please, Dr. Marcus, it's not my job to question orders. And I don't want to know *anything* about what happened to you—or why you're here. All Starfleet says is that you have to be protected, and I'm here to do that job."

The old woman gazed wistfully at the pastel ocean. "I used to think that children would read about me in their science classes, maybe in their history classes. But, no. They wiped all traces of my early work from Starfleet records. Some people have duplicated small parts of it by accident, but not the way I did it. Nobody will ever learn about me. It's all too dangerous . . . too controversial. There are too many curious parties."

Martin shifted his feet uncomfortably. "They tell me your solar-energy experiments are very important."

"Glorified make-work." Marcus sniffed. "Oh, I've made some strides here, but hundreds of others could have done the same thing. My *real* work—no one else could have done that but me. And David." Her voice faltered and cracked at the mention of her son. He had been about the age of this young officer when he was brutally murdered.

"I'm sorry," said Martin. "But with respect, Doctor, I still don't want to hear about it."

"You won't." With effort, Carol mustered a smile. "I've kept my secrets this long. I think I can keep them a little while longer. There's nothing left of that other project, except for what I carry up here." She tapped her forehead.

"We'll protect you," vowed the young man. "Even the president of the council doesn't have around-the-clock security like you do."

"I know," said Marcus with a trace of melancholy. "If your professional demeanor permits it, could you please offer an old woman a steady arm for the walk back to the lab?"

"Certainly, Doctor." Gallantly the officer extended a brawny arm, and she grasped it with relief. It was difficult breaking in these new bodyguards, only to lose them quickly if they showed any ambition or skill. How many hundreds of security officers had drifted through her life in the last ninety years? What did they think about their time spent with the Mystery Woman of Pacifica? Maybe all they remembered was the endless sea and the searing sun, which could be exhilarating and sedating at the same time.

In the first years of her banishment, she had gotten too friendly with a few of her guards, believing that she had a right to still live a normal life, despite everything that had happened to her. That had been a mistake, which had cost the career of a man she loved. Or thought she loved. The truth was, she had been grasping for tenderness and forgiveness in the wake of David's death and the spectacular destruction of Project Genesis. Jim Kirk had disappeared again, and there was no one to console her while they erased her life's work from recorded history.

If it had been tough for her, it had also been tough on her guards.

She remembered the despondency of the officers assigned to protect her during the Dominion war. They craved to be on the front lines—in the action—not beachcombing with a strange old lady. They could see her solar-energy research, but they didn't know why she should be valuable to the Dominion. In the end, Pacifica had avoided attack, but that only made their incomprehensible assignment seem more futile. Even now, she often overheard hushed conversations, discussing transfers. As a lot, Starfleet officers weren't happy sitting around on the beach.

How many times had she wanted to burst into their midst and tell them to go away? Just to leave her alone! But she had learned to play her role as well. It was a role scientists had played throughout the ages—the outcast who possessed forbidden knowledge.

As Dr. Marcus and Ensign Dupovitz walked from the beach toward a cluster of low-slung, green buildings, she admired the natural beauty of her island. Massive yellow succulent plants covered the ground, and they sprouted ten-meter-high pistils of a flaming burgundy color. Brilliantly colored insects, as big as birds and shaped like dragonflies, darted among the pistils in their furtive mating dance. Behind the row of buildings, giant ferns and trees towered into the sky, waving their wispy branches back and forth to the buzzing harmony of the waves and insects. Clumps of purple labano fruit hung from the trees in her orchard, and the bohalla bushes were in bloom with waxy lavender buds. Everywhere there was abundance and the sweet smell of the ocean.

That was all she had wanted to create with Project Genesis— beauty and life. Even now, it seemed a noble dream to turn barren matter into a thriving paradise that could rival this one. Of course, that was in a perfect universe, where people thought of progress and altruism before they thought of weapons and revenge. After years of reflection, Carol had come to admit to herself that she had been naïve those many years ago. No one had been prepared for Genesis to be a success, least of all her.

Yet ultimately it had been a failure . . . a planet formed from a nebula . . . erratic and unstable. *And I sacrificed my son trying to find out why,* thought Marcus miserably. *If only I had taken David home with me, instead of letting him go back there! If only I had told him to stay with his father . . . go anywhere, do anything but that!*

The toe of her boot hit the first step of the walkway, and she was jolted out of her melancholy. Now Carol was glad to be holding onto the ensign's arm, and she tightened her grip to steady herself.

He looked at her with concern, and she managed a smile. "I'm all right," she assured him. "You know us absent-minded scientists—can't walk and think at the same time."

Martin lowered his voice to say, "I don't understand why you have to live way out here. I think we could protect you in a rural town or a space station, someplace like that. And you could still do your experiments."

"Trust me, Martin, I deserve to be here." She patted his arm and started up the winding walkway. "Besides, I work best away from prying eyes—I hate interference. But I'm sure you would prefer to be out there in space, zooming around. I hate to tell you though, space travel is usually more boring than this island."

The young ensign smiled and was smart enough not to argue with her. They climbed the hill to the entrance of the compound, which required them to pass through a security gate in an electrified fence about eight meters high. Carol Marcus straightened her spine and peered into the retina scanner, trying not to blink her tired eyes. After a moment, the computer voice announced, "Carol Marcus, identity verified. You may pass."

"Thank you," she drawled. The woman stepped through the fence and waited while the young ensign completed the security procedure. While she stood on the short sidewalk between the fence and the first building, she noticed something odd on the ground. It looked like a sprig of moss, and she bent down to pick it up.

The waxy, gray sprig was unlike any vegetation she had ever seen on the island, and she studied it closely, trying to identify the plant. It looked something like mistletoe. "Is everything okay?" asked Martin.

"Except for this," she answered, holding up the sprig for him to see. He looked at it and shrugged blankly.

"Maybe somebody was planning a Christmas party," said Marcus with a smile. She dropped the sprig into an empty pocket on her jumpsuit and stepped toward a double door, which slid open at her approach.

Followed by Ensign Dupovitz, Carol Marcus strode into the common room of the Big House, as they called it. The Big House was really the dormitory where she lived with her four bodyguards. Other buildings housed her laboratory, their security and communication center, the water purification plant, a small infirmary, and equipment storage. All of their electricity was generated by various solar-energy collectors, and they had much more than they needed. Microwaves dispersed some of the excess power to nearby islands.

In the common room, Commander Quay'to and Lieutenant Jaspirin were seated at a card table, playing a game of three-dimensional chess.

They looked up from their game at the new arrivals, feigning disinterest. Although they tried not to act like zealous babysitters, her protectors were nervous whenever she was out of their sight. This was doubly true with the sensor array down. The old woman had long ago ceased to be annoyed by their constant attention, but her guards still went out of their way not to appear overbearing.

Quay'to was a Zakdorn with an impassive, scaled face. A brilliant tactician, she seldom lost at three-dimensional chess unless she was badly distracted. Marcus could tell from the pieces she had lost to Jaspirin that she was not playing her best game.

"The beach hasn't washed away, has it?" asked Jaspirin, a Tarkannan whose red uniform was beginning to bulge a bit around his waistline. He seemed to be enjoying the leisurely life on the island more than any of his fellows.

"No, it's still there," answered Marcus, sitting down at the dining table to catch her breath. "How is the array?"

"Wilson's working on it," said Quay'to. With a swift movement, she made a decisive quadruple jump spanning three different planes of the chess board and capturing three of her opponent's pieces.

Jaspirin stared at her in mock shock. "Commander, I resent that move. I think you were setting me up."

"Not at all," replied the Zakdorn. "I merely saw an opening I hadn't noticed before."

"Do you want me to take a look at the array?" asked Carol helpfully.

Quay'to shook her head. "No, that's not necessary. We've got a repair crew on the way—they should be here by tonight. In the meantime, Wilson is trying to rig together something with the tricorders—at least we can have short-range sensors." The studious calm in the Zakdorn's voice barely masked her annoyance at this interruption in their routine.

"If we don't get another storm," said Martin Dupovitz, glancing out a window.

"Can't do anything about the weather," remarked Jaspirin, "although everyone keeps trying."

Carol smiled to herself, thinking that she had once been able to do a great deal about the weather. But that was in the past, in another lifetime. She rose slowly from her chair, feeling a twinge of pain in her lower back. Weariness overcame the scientist, reminding her that she had awakened well before dawn, fretting over the possibility of the storm damaging her experiments. In the end, it had turned out to be just another beautiful day on Pacifica.

"Is there anything on the local dish?" asked Jaspirin, glancing at a nearby viewscreen. "When are the yacht races from Pacifica Prime?"

"Not for another six months," answered Quay'to, pointing to the chess game. "Your move."

Carol Marcus yawned broadly and made a decision. "I'm going to take a quick nap."

"Go right ahead, Doctor." The commander nodded her approval, then went back to her chess game.

"We'll have lunch ready for you when you wake up," promised Martin.

Marcus nodded gratefully at the young ensign. One of the happy prerogatives of old age was that one could take a nap whenever one felt like it, without eliciting any resentment. She caught the three of them watching her as she made her way to her quarters; they were undoubtedly relieved that she would be inactive for a while.

Lying in her bed felt as luxurious as lying in a weightless mud bath on Rigel II. Marcus felt all of her worries and pain melting away as her body sank into the mattress. Faintly she could hear the gentle lapping of the waves, lulling her into tranquility. She also heard the muffled voices of her guards, greeting Wilson, who had just joined them in the common room.

*I don't know when I've ever been so tired*, Carol marveled to herself. She must have slept, although she wasn't sure. All she knew was that a strange mist seemed to enter her bedroom, filling it with shadows. Everything became deathly quiet, except for the rhythmic hush of the waves, and her body felt paralyzed, but comfortably so.

Then a warm hand touched hers, and the mattress dipped as someone alighted beside her. Stirring gently from her dreamy reverie, Carol Marcus looked up to see the most wonderful sight in the whole world: *David!* Her son's angelic face was framed by unruly blond curls, and he smiled at her with those delicate dimples and intense brown eyes. How all the girls, young and old, had loved to run their fingers through those curly locks of his.

"David," rasped Carol with tears brimming in her eyes. She lifted a trembling hand to touch his face, certain there would be nothing to feel but an old woman's illusion. To her astonishment, her hand touched real flesh, and she ran her fingers over his nose, mouth, and eyes.

"David . . . you . . . how?" she sputtered.

"Don't worry about that now," cooed David, cupping her hands in his. "The universe is full of strange and wondrous things. I'd like to show them to you, Mother. Are you ready to leave this pointless life behind and come with me? Father is anxious to see you, too."

"Jim?" she asked in astonishment. "But he's dead. *You're both dead!*" Carol shook her head and screwed her eyes shut, not wanting to consider the obvious. "Or maybe I'm the one who's dead."

"Even in death, there is life," said David, grabbing her slender shoulders and pulling her into a sitting position.

"I killed you!" said the old woman, weeping. "I left you behind!" She buried her face in his gray tunic and sobbed loudly, inconsolably. David stroked her matted ivory hair, the child comforting the mother.

Suddenly Carol looked up in a panic, certain that her loud crying would bring all four bodyguards running. She gazed out the open door toward the common room and saw Martin lying on the floor and Quay'to slumped in her chair.

"What's the matter—"

David touched her lips, silencing her. "Nothing is the matter . . . not anymore. It's taken me a long time to find you, Mother, but now we're going home."

"Home!" said Marcus with a gush of emotion. "Yes, home. Do you mean—"

David nodded happily. "Yes, back to the Regula I lab—to finish your work."

The old woman gulped and looked at him with a combination of joy and disbelief. She didn't feel dead, so she had to be dreaming. But if this was a dream, it was an exceedingly cruel one, because she couldn't stand to be torn away from David again.

He smiled with understanding. "I know you have questions, but you've just got to accept what is. I'm here, you're here, and we can be together just like always. We can start over, do it right. Just come with me . . . and trust. Will you do that?"

Carol nodded, tears of happiness streaming down her face. "Oh, yes, David! If you forgive me—"

"I forgive you, Mother. We'll never be apart again. Come along— Father is waiting." He smiled radiantly and wrapped his arms around her. From the corner of her eye, Carol saw the mists and shadows creeping back into the room, and she had a momentary lapse of doubt. *This can't be happening!* David's solid arms reassured her, and the old woman surrendered to her bliss. Her consciousness seeped away until all she felt was oblivion.

# two

"The yacht races on Pacifica came to an exciting conclusion today," said the sportscaster on the audio feed, his voice wafting across the open-air market, along with the smells of a hundred different foods and perfumed oils. Everywhere signs proclaimed "Happy Terran Day," a celebration marking the day when the first human colonists had arrived on Seran to join the Camorites, Deltans, and other species. Aurora Square was filled with shoppers and revelers, picking up fresh produce, spices, gifts, and tasty delicacies for the holiday dinner.

The announcer went on, "With fireworks in the sky and a grand flotilla on the waves, the winners were honored today on Pacifica. A Bynar catamaran, the *Gemini*, won for the second year in a row in the freestyle category. A replay will be broadcast at twenty-two hundred hours on the All-Sport video transponder."

"I'll have to try to catch that," said Mikel Gordonez as he hefted a melon from a nearby stand and sniffed its dewy freshness. "I'll come back to the club tonight and watch it with the boys."

Leah Brahms lifted her blue eyes from a selection of squashes and tubers and looked curiously at her husband. Gray-haired, paunchy, Mikel was twenty years older than she, and he sometimes treated her like his subordinate, which she had been at the Theoretical Propulsion Group. Lately Mikel had been coming to the planet's surface almost every night, frequenting his athletic club.

She couldn't help herself—she had to ask, "Why would you want to watch a yacht race from the other side of the quadrant? You never pay any attention to the yacht races here."

"This is the Pacifica Invitational," he protested. "It's famous. All the other ones are just . . . the minor leagues." Mikel scowled and walked away from her. "If you don't want me to come to town tonight, just say so."

Leah followed him through the throng, brushing her chestnut-colored hair out of her eyes. For years, she had worn her hair long, usually pinned up in a bun, but now it was cut short. Mikel hated it. Although she was determined not to fight with him, she was equally determined to make her case. They had a ton of work left to do, and he acted as if they were on vacation.

As Leah charged after her husband, she realized that she didn't want to start an argument in public, surrounded by hundreds of residents of the capitol city. Leah Brahms and Mikel Gordonez were respected scientists, known to everyone on the planet as the landlords of Outpost Seran-T-One. Fighting in public wouldn't win them any friends, and they needed friends now that a vote on their funding was coming up before the council. They had enough enemies already.

She didn't want to blame Mikel for all of their problems, but his attention had been drifting for some time, from both the research and her. Even now, her husband strode through the crowded market ten paces ahead of her, oblivious to her struggle to keep up. She was carrying all of their purchases, an armful of bundles.

*Stop!* she wanted to scream, but she didn't. Leah was always the one who worried about appearances, the one who kept quiet when people were watching. She could be outspoken and opinionated on her own turf, but she maintained decorum when it came to the two of them. Where he was frivolous and childish, she was serious and adult. Where he was a people person, she was a techie. They were a good partnership on the face of it, but she still didn't understand him. *Why does he want to watch a yacht race when we're in the middle of running tests?*

*He's just trying to get away from work*, she concluded. *Or me.*

Leah didn't know everything in life, but she knew that Mikel couldn't get away from her. They worked together all day long, and their names were linked on hundreds of papers, proposals, and studies. It was impossible to tell where her life ended and his began. Colleagues and customers depended upon them—escape wasn't an option.

Finally Leah Brahms slowed down, took a deep breath, and paused to look at the colorful booths and luscious wares for sale. It had been Mikel's idea to come shopping in the market today, not hers. Leah had to admit that she seldom took time to admire the pottery or smell the bread pudding. *Maybe I should be the one who changes*, she thought with a start. *Maybe I should watch yacht races.*

A Deltan woman walked by, pushing a double stroller containing two beautiful, dark-haired children. Leah was suddenly aware of the laughter and gaiety of children all around her, running through the square, chasing their hoops and robotic pets.

*It would have been different if we'd had children*, thought the scientist. *Never had time*, came the familiar reply. She was still young enough, just approaching forty, and she could attempt it yet. But Leah didn't know whether having a child would balance her life and help the marriage or put undue stress on everyone. She knew that Mikel would be horrified at the idea.

The truth was, she didn't have as many other interests and people in her life as she should have. Everything revolved around work, even her marriage, which probably made her boring. She didn't work very hard at her marriage either, except to stay monogamous when confronted by the rare temptation. There had been moments of unwanted attention, such as Geordi La Forge's crush on her. At least that was over, and they had become friends. But who could make time for romance, with a husband or anyone else?

*Yes, I'm boring*, she decided. *If I'm boring to myself, what must I be to Mikel?*

A gangly Camorite bumped into her, and he politely nodded his plume of yellow hair. "Excuse me. Happy Terran Day."

"Yes, it is!" Leah replied cheerfully. She gazed up at the indigo sky, ablaze with the brilliance of a double-star system. There was a slight chill in the air, but midyear was coming soon with its dry, warm weather. All around them towered shimmering skyscrapers and sinewy monorails, stretching into the depths of the metropolis. Two joyous children cut through the crowd, waving streamers over their heads. A flotilla of hot-air balloons floated overhead, affording scores of Serans a lofty view of the festivities. On a glorious day like this, what was the point of fighting?

She tapped her combadge. "Brahms to Gordonez."

His voice didn't sound happy when he answered. "What are you doing? I'm ten meters away from you."

"Yes, and you're going to stay ten meters ahead of me unless you slow down. I just wanted to catch up with you." She cut through the crowd and bumped into him before he had time to react. After a grin, she said, "Brahms out."

He looked down at her, suppressing a smile despite his anger. "Listen, why don't you come with me to the club tonight? We'll watch the race together. You don't get out of the lab enough."

"All right, I will," she answered. "Here, help me carry this stuff."

While Mikel gaped at her, she shoved packages into his arms. "Are you kidding?" he asked.

"No, I'm not kidding," she said. "You have to help me carry this stuff."

"No, do you really want to go to the club with me tonight?" Suddenly he sounded doubtful.

"Yes, already—I'm going." Leah was more resolute than ever, because she sensed an odd reticence on his part. Mikel had asked her to go to his club many times before, but she had never said yes. Maybe she should have gone with him before now.

"Are we about done shopping?" asked Mikel, swiftly changing the subject. "Have we got enough for that special dinner tonight?"

"I think so. If not, we'll make do." But Leah suddenly felt a sort of panic, realizing that the entire day would be lost to shopping, cooking, eating, watching yacht races, and who knew what else? That was the problem with having a life—work always suffered.

"Let me just check in," she said, tapping her combadge. "Brahms to Outpost Seran-T-One." She tried to ignore the way Mikel smirked and rolled his eyes at her attention to duty.

"Henricksen here," came a high-pitched, harried response. "Is everything all right, Doctor?"

"Yes, it's all right with us," answered Brahms, speaking above the din of the crowd. She knew every nuance of voice and mannerism in her assistants, and she sensed that Ellen Henricksen was upset. "What's wrong up there?"

"It's nothing we can't handle."

"Go ahead and tell me," said Leah Brahms. "I'll find out sooner or later."

"Well, it's the test site—" began the worried assistant. "The Civil Guard showed up an hour ago, and they've held up our tests. Paldor is trying to talk them out of it, but they won't budge. They say we're not allowed to use radiation with any of the local subjects."

"What?" demanded Mikel angrily, yelling over Leah's shoulder. "That's the whole point of it! What's the matter with those rubes?"

Leah looked around at the crowd in the marketplace, wondering how many had overheard Mikel's remark. A few people glanced their way, but most were worried about holiday preparations and getting the last bit of Saurian sylph butter.

"Maybe we should go there," concluded Leah. "We're done here, anyway. Get ready to receive us."

"Paldor didn't want to call you," whined Ellen miserably. "We can handle it. *Really* we can!"

"We're on our way." Leah gripped her husband's hand and was soon dragging him and all their packages through the crowd, headed toward the outskirts of the square. She kept glancing at the signposts overhead, trying to find one which indicated a transporter kiosk. Mikel kept barking about "superstitious locals" and "bureaucrats on a power trip," but Leah did her best to ignore him.

Finally she located a transporter kiosk in the corner of the square, but there was a line of about twenty Serans waiting to get in. On a normal day, there wouldn't be anyone waiting, but this was hardly a normal day.

She hated doing it, but she had to pull rank. "Get out your I.D. card," she told Mikel.

He smiled slyly as he pulled the card from beneath his tunic and let it dangle from the cord around his neck. "They're going to hate you."

"I don't care." Leah whipped out her own badge and waved it at the people in line as she plowed past them. "Medical emergency! Coming through! Medical emergency! We need to use the transporter."

The Serans eyed their packages and attire doubtfully, as if thinking they didn't appear to be on any kind of emergency. Nevertheless, the customers at the front of the line stepped back to allow Leah and Mikel to enter the kiosk first. Such was the power of the Science Service badges they wore, which marked them as members of the elite on Seran.

Leah stamped her foot impatiently as she waited for the force-field to clear, then she charged inside the circular room and took her place on the transporter platform. The interior of the kiosk was hardly any bigger than a Jefferies tube, and Mikel struggled to drag all their packages inside. "Hurry up," she urged him.

Breathing heavily, the gray-haired man finally took his place beside her on the platform. He looked ruefully at her. "Did anybody ever tell you that you're a slave driver?"

"All the time," answered Leah, knowing it was the truth. She had driven herself and others mercilessly all her life, and she had never learned how to relax. The current emergency probably wasn't much of one, but it had served the purpose of ending their brief shore leave before it became uncomfortable. She glanced at Mikel, who was busy keeping all the packages in his hands. She had never thought that he could hide anything from her, but maybe he wasn't as predictable as she thought.

The most disturbing part of this realization was the fact that it meant so little to her. As usual, her worry was for the work—always the work. Today they were testing the prototype of new, vastly improved radiation suit.

"Destination?" queried a polite computer voice.

"Outpost Seran-T-One," she answered. "Authorization code: five-zero-eight-one-nine."

"Prepare to energize."

Leah stared straight ahead, waiting for the familiar tingle to grip her spine. The sensation quickly faded, as the walls of the kiosk morphed into a shadowy cargo bay inside the largest of Seran's eight moons. The hidden outpost had been built as a Starfleet observation post over two centuries ago on the edge of Federation space. After observing the planet for thirty years and finding no high-level life, Starfleet issued permission to colonize. The Camorites had been first, followed by Deltans, Saurians, and others. In time, Federation borders had moved a bit closer to the center of the Milky Way, and the Federation had turned the outpost over to the science branch.

Leah stepped off the transporter platform, feeling a bounce in her step from the decrease in gravity. Mikel stumbled off the platform and promptly dropped all of their packages. Before Leah could help him, doors opened at the end of the bay, and Ellen Henricksen rushed toward them, bounding in the low gravity like an ostrich.

Ellen waved a padd over her head. "I've got the site permissions, environmental studies, and waivers right here!"

"Thanks," said Leah, taking the handheld device from her. She glanced guiltily at Mikel, who was chasing a rolling melon across the cargo bay. "Ellen, could you please round up the food for us and start dinner, as best you can."

Ellen flapped her long arms helplessly. "I guess so." She was a good kid, but just a kid, and this was her first real job since leaving the Daystrom Institute. Leah was often inclined to cut fellow Daystrom graduates more slack than the others. Ellen bounced over to the transporter console and busied herself checking coordinates.

Mikel stood up, rubbing his back. "Something tells me that tonight will be another meal from the replicator."

"Not if I can help it," vowed Leah. "Did we do the maintenance on the shuttlecraft?"

"Did the maintenance," answered Mikel, "and we're going to need it tomorrow."

"Let's settle this bit with the Civil Guard once and for all." Leah Brahms climbed back onto the transporter, her jaw set resolutely. She looked expectantly at Mikel, who wasn't moving quickly enough.

With a shrug, he dutifully followed. "They probably resent the fact that we're working on a holiday."

Leah shook the padd at him. "These people know they have no authority, they just want to meet the ones in charge. If they had left us alone, the test would be done already."

"The more tests, the better," said Mikel, snidely repeating a familiar litany. "We'll set them straight. Energize, Miss Henricksen."

"Yes, Doctor." The young woman plied the controls with authority, and Leah again felt the tingle of the transporter beam. A moment later, she and her husband materialized in a meadow on the outskirts of the capitol city. A muddy stream ran through the middle of the field, and tiny yellow flowers sprinkled its banks. The city and its monorails were nestled in the foothills beyond, looking like strands of pearls strewn among green velvet. On the jagged horizon rose the Tinkraw Mountains—shrouded, snow-dusted peaks which guarded the glistening city.

Sixteen tall coral pillars stood in the center of the meadow, forming a circle around a clearing. The pillars had been built to resemble the fertility temples of the Deltans, so as not to disrupt the natural beauty of the meadow. But this was no temple—it was a monitoring station. The pillars housed test equipment, scanners, monitors, forcefield generators, and a particle accelerator. What had once been a remote area was getting more popular all the time, with a couple dozen people in attendance.

In the center of the pillars stood what appeared to be a white sculpture representing a humanoid. This stoic figure was the center of attention, with people milling around it. As Leah and Mikel strode toward the gathering, she could see that the bulky radiation suit was empty. Standing beside it was a young Deltan woman wearing an oversized robe and a chagrined expression.

Their assistants, Paldor and Gershon, were arguing vociferously with about twenty members of the Civil Guard, as denoted by their distinctive purple sashes. On a peaceful planet with no standing police or army, the Civil Guard was a volunteer organization that enforced laws. Sometimes they couldn't resist meddling.

At their approach, the warring parties broke off from each other and charged the new arrivals, waving their hands. Leah started to say something, but Mikel's voice boomed over her head. "I'll thank you to stop harassing my technicians! We've got all of our permissions, and this site has been cleared for these tests. Unless you're standing right on top of the emitter, it won't be any more dangerous than getting an X ray!"

"That's what I've been telling him!" bawled Paldor, a chubby Tellarite with a piglike snout, bristly orange beard, and shock of orange hair.

A tall, plumed Camorite approached Mikel, looking very grave. He was also armed with a padd full of data, so Leah handed her padd to Mikel. The Camorite spoke with authority. "According to common ordinance six-three-seven-point-nine, this facility is not to be used for class-three experiments on an official holiday when local citizens are endangered by their presence in the area."

Mikel turned to Leah and grinned triumphantly. "You see, it *was* because of working on a holiday." His expression grew somber as he turned back to the Civil Guard. "Okay, then no locals will be endangered, because we'll keep them away. We'd like to start by keeping *you* away, so please leave."

The Camorite craned his scrawny neck and looked at the Deltan shivering beside the radiation suit. "*She* is a local, endangered by your experiments."

Mikel sputtered indignantly, "But . . . but surely that doesn't mean we can't *hire* people as subjects! We have to collect data with a variety of different—" He caught sight of one of the Civil Guards touching the radiation suit, and he rushed toward him, waving his arms like a madman.

"Get away from there!" screamed Mikel, startling the man. "Get away! *Shoo!*"

The scientist hugged the hard-shelled suit as if it were a long-lost friend, then he gently wiped a smudge of dirt from the curved faceplate of its built-in helmet. "Do you know what this equipment is going to do? It's going to save hundreds of lives—maybe the life of *your* son or daughter. With this, starship engineers won't have to risk their lives trying to save the main engines. In this suit, they can work in the middle of a distressed warp core, surrounded by antimatter leaks, and they'll be safe. It's got medical monitoring, life support, a communications array, and phase-shifting."

Leah cringed. The phase-shifting technology was supposed to be a secret, because they had cribbed it from the Romulans without their permission. Even though it had only the standard shielding and reflective materials, what made the suit special was its interphase generator. An oscillating temporal displacement allowed the wearer to be effective in a dangerous environment but slightly removed from it as well. On a much larger scale, the Romulans used the same technology to cloak their ships.

Mikel pointed to her. "My wife here has spent her whole life designing warp engines and propulsion systems, only to see how dangerous her creations became when things went wrong. So she did something about it—she invented this suit. We have to test it under every known condition, including planetary atmosphere, before we can present this prototype to Starfleet. Every day we delay, lives are at risk."

The head of the Civil Guard scoffed. "Self-important, aren't you?"

Bounding on his feet beside her, Paldor could stand no more. The Tellarite's orange hair stood on end, and he wrinkled his snout and puffed out his chest. "No, that would be *you*, Sir, delaying our work over a *technicality*! This test is perfectly safe, and we need a female subject."

"This is Terran Day," complained one of the human members of the Civil Guard. "Have some respect for our heritage."

The Tellarite snorted loudly, and Leah Brahms laid a calming hand on his beefy shoulder. "Don't fight with them, Paldor. Go back to the base and relieve Ellen—send her down here. Then we'll have *two* females to finish the test, and none of them will be locals."

The feisty Tellarite wrinkled his nose with distaste. "But that's giving into them! There's a principle involved here."

"There's work that's not getting done," answered Brahms curtly. "Electricity always takes the path of least resistance, and so do I. Now get going."

"Yes, Doctor." Paldor bowed politely to her, then swiveled on his heel and marched out of the clearing.

"And see if you can do something with the food we brought home!" Leah called after him. She had a lot more faith in Paldor's cooking than in Ellen's, which was the main reason she had sent him back. The Tellarite waved to her as he strode beyond the pillars into the open meadow. He was still walking when the transporter beam whisked his molecules away.

Mikel continued to argue with the Civil Guard, while extolling the virtues of the radiation suit. But that was Mikel, thought Leah with quiet frustration: *Always so stubborn.* Once the argument became about winning the argument, then all was lost. Leah couldn't think that way. What was the point of winning an argument if it meant wasting time and losing an opportunity?

She approached the Deltan woman who had volunteered to be their subject. "Thanks for sticking around, Margala, but this isn't going to work. Go ahead and enjoy the holiday—we'll pay you for your trouble."

"Are you sure?" asked the woman hesitantly.

Leah nodded, and the young subject hurried away before she could change her mind. Then Leah unsnapped the collar of her tunic and began to take off her clothes.

Mikel and the Civil Guard stopped their pointless conversation to stare at her. "What are you doing?" asked Mikel.

"I'm getting into the suit," answered Leah. She looked pointedly at their tormentors. "After you leave, there won't be any more locals to endanger."

The popinjay with his yellow plume and purple sash looked stunned that he could be dismissed so easily, while a grin spread across Mikel's face. "Yes, take your posse and go bother somebody else. We've got work to do."

After Leah began to remove her trousers, most of the Civil Guard turned on their heels and politely wandered off. Their spokesman flashed a scowl at Leah, but he eventually turned and strode away, too. Within a few minutes, there was no one left in the meadow except for Leah, her husband, and three technicians. That number swelled to four when Ellen Henricksen walked into the group.

"Where is everybody?" she asked puzzledly. "I thought we had a standoff here."

"Nope," said Mikel, proudly hugging his wife. "Leah took care of them. Are you really getting into that thing?"

"For the first trial," she answered. "Then Ellen is going to take over for me." The young woman gulped upon hearing that she would be a guinea pig, too.

"Are you sure?" For the first time, Mikel sounded a little nervous as he considered his wife donning the imposing suit during live radiation tests.

"I was the first one to wear it, remember?" Leah took off her pants and handed them to Mikel, having stripped down to her conservative underwear. She wasn't overly modest in front of this group of people, with whom she lived and worked in close confinement, but she didn't linger in the chill air. She opened the back of the suit like someone cracking open a giant lobster claw, then climbed in.

Leah mashed her forehead against the clear faceplate as she shoehorned her limbs inside; her grunts echoed loudly in her own ears. The gel interior of the suit molded to the contours of her body, shrinking or expanding as needed. The arms and legs retracted slightly, because she was smaller than the Deltan. Settling into the suit felt like entering a cocoon or jumping into the water—it was alien, disconnected from reality. In the fingers of the gloves, she found the controls, and she turned the suit on.

The upper right corner of the faceplate illuminated, giving her a reflective viewscreen full of instructions. Then she heard a slight whirring noise as the opening in the rear sealed itself tightly. It tickled when the interior molded itself to her buttocks, but that was over in a moment.

Leah felt a flash of claustrophobia when she realized she was completely encased, but she tried to breathe evenly and relax. Although space travel was her business, the scientist didn't have much cause to wear protective suits, even ones she designed. She tried to tell herself it was no different than wearing a cleanroom suit and hood, although it was completely different. Those lightweight suits were designed to protect the environment from the wearer, not the other way around.

Her uneasiness quickly passed when she remembered all the resources at her disposal, resources she had made sure to include. Leah often imagined the suit as a wearable escape pod, with its own life support, communications, and computer. It contained enough food and water for three days of moderate exertion. She tapped her little finger upward, activating the medical artificial intelligence.

"Systems are normal, Dr. Brahms," said the suit, recognizing her physiology. "Your pulse rate is elevated thirty-two percent from the rate on your last examination. Would you like me to administer a mild sedative?"

"No thanks," answered Leah with a smile. Maybe the suit was a little *too* friendly.

The next voice to cut in was Mikel's. "Are you all right in there?" She glanced up to see him striding toward her, adjusting his communications headset.

"Just fine," she answered, giving him a thumbs up. It felt cumbersome to move around, but there wasn't anything anyone could do about that in normal gravity. In microgravity, the suit could float free or be anchored in any number of positions by embedded magnets. She had tried to think of everything, but it was still daunting to consider the conditions under which the suit would be used. The engine room in chaos, ruptures in the hull, life support failing, core meltdown imminent. But in this suit, an engineer at least had a chance of staying at his post and doing some good.

Leah looked around at the brilliant blue sky, lush green meadow, and short-sleeved workers, thinking this really wasn't much of a test. Oh, well, Starfleet wanted to see results under every possible condition, including picnic weather.

"Your medical data is coming through," said Mikel's voice in her ear. "Just relax, Hon."

"Okay." Leah took a deep breath and shook her arms, which barely moved inside the constrictive suit. "Shall I put on phase-shift?"

"Let me get the gel-pack reading first," answered Mikel, who stepped behind one of the picturesque pillars surrounding the clearing. "Yes, power levels are normal. Go ahead."

Leah knew the power levels were good, because she could see the readout reflected on her faceplate. But she said nothing. In production models, phase-shifting would be automatic, coming on as soon as the suit was activated. In the prototype, it had to be activated manually for testing purposes.

"Computer, phase-shifting on," she ordered.

"Phase-shifting on," answered a voice matter-of-factly.

The lack of any sort of sensation startled Leah, considering that she was wavering in and out of the temporal plane. Here—not quite here—back and forth like a sine wave. In instances when she was present in the real world, she could interact with objects, and those instances blended together to form coherence. It was like a bad singer who used vibrato to make sure she hit the right note at least some of the time.

"Before we go live," said Mikel, "let's do some dexterity tests. Logs are recording. Okay, Ellen, toss her the ball."

The young woman picked up a colorful play ball and stepped closer to the immobile white figure. "Five years at the Daystrom Institute to toss a ball," muttered Ellen with a smile. Her voice sounded tinny and distant, even though she was only four meters away.

"Ready?"

Leah Brahms nodded, and Ellen bounded forward, tossing the ball with both hands. As it floated through the air on a high arc, the sky above them completely changed colors, shifting from a pale blue to a vivid green. Leah took her eyes off the ball to watch something curious on the horizon. A flaming curtain swept over the distant mountains, throbbing and mutating as if distorted by heat. The snowy peaks erupted in fury, disappearing into rolling clouds of ash and steam. And the ground trembled.

In the peaceful valley, buildings and monorails writhed like snakes on fire, and the city was consumed by the flaming green embers. A squeal sounded in her ears, and columns of readouts on her faceplate began to scroll at a madcap pace. Leah thought there was a malfunction in her suit, and she let the ball bounce off her chest and land at her feet.

As the ball hit the ground, it exploded, and the soil under her feet began to twist and churn. Leah looked up to see the ungodly wave pass over Ellen Henricksen. Caught in midscream, her skin flared like fire and turned a mottled green before it liquefied. Tissue dripped off her skeleton, which became brittle and crumbled, and her body contracted into a brackish, quivering puddle.

Eyes agape, Leah looked up to see Mikel stagger toward her, the gruesome transformation already ravaging his body. The squeal in her ears might have been his screams as his body contracted into a lumpen mass.

"No!" she yelled in panic. "Mikel! I'm hallucinating! Help me—"

Leah staggered to stay on her feet, because the ground was still erupting, shooting geysers and flaming green embers. *This isn't real, is it?* She clomped forward, trying to reach her husband, but there was no trace of him in the churning, twisting inferno.

All across the planet, millions of souls died the same ignominious death, as their flailing limbs were sucked into the seething morass. Towering mountains and tiny pebbles all crumbled into molten, fiery sludge. The seas erupted and boiled, shooting monstrous plumes of steam into the mottled skies. The wind roiled, and great forests of trees flew through the air like so much burnt kindling. The atmosphere became a choking, blood-streaked miasma, and the entire planet throbbed like a sun going nova.

# three

Leah Brahms gritted her teeth and tried to hold onto her sanity as the ground convulsed all around her. She looked for the remains of her husband and friends, but their bodies had been absorbed in the cataclysm. Khaki clouds swirled in the sky, quivering vines shot from the ground, and obscene, wormy life-forms writhed in the detritus of a planet in agony.

She sniffed back a wad of mucus and tears, staggering to stay on her feet in the bulky radiation suit. Readouts on her faceplate screen were back to a semblance of normal, although she and the suit were the only things unchanged on the churning landscape. *The moonbase!* she thought in panic. *It might be all right.*

Trying to remain calm, she used the glove controls to turn on the comm system. "Leah Brahms," she said shakily, "to Outpost Seran-T-One."

Certain there would be no response, she jumped when Paldor's voice responded loudly in her ears, "Doctor! Doctor!" gasped the Tellarite. "We've lost contact . . . what's happening down there?"

"They're dead . . . all dead," she rasped. "I'm only alive because I'm in the suit." As slimy grubs tried to wrap around her foot, Leah stepped back and shook them off, suppressing her revulsion.

"Dead," muttered Paldor in disbelief.

With effort, Leah shook off grief and despair long enough to keep thinking. "What hit us? Did you see anything on sensors?"

"I didn't see anything before, but I see it now," answered Paldor. "An energy wave of some sort. It's past Seran . . . on its way to the moon!"

"Beam me up! Now!" shouted Leah.

She waited, while the ground continued to spew forth obscene, writhing life-forms unlike anything she had ever seen, even in her nightmares. Monstrous stalks and vines sprouted into the swirling sky, towering above her like prehistoric beasts. "Get me out of here!" she shouted.

"I can't," he answered. "There's something wrong . . . I can't get a lock!"

Leah tried to remain calm, even as slimy tentacles and vines curled around her feet, trying to absorb her into the mad convulsions of the planet. The wave might be causing interference, but their comm signal was strong.

"Maybe it's the phase-shifting," she said evenly. "I'll turn it off."

"But you might—"

There was no point thinking about what might happen, because she knew she couldn't stay here. With a gulp, Leah flicked off the interphase generator and held her breath. Although the soil continued to mutate beneath her feet, she found that she could still escape from the twitching slime, but the soles of her feet were starting to smolder. Leah yelled, "Now try it! Hurry!"

She would try to remember that the wave's effect, awful as it was, apparently did its damage and left. As her encased body escaped from the graveyard of her husband and friends, Leah made a desperate vow. She had to stay alive long enough to warn others of this cataclysmic disaster.

When she materialized in the cargo bay, she found Paldor running around, stuffing tins of food into a shoulder bag. "The wave will be here in a few seconds!" he shouted.

"Direct-beam us to the shuttlecraft! Punch it in, and get up here!"

Nostrils flared, eyebrows bristling, the Tellarite rushed to the transporter controls and entered the coordinates. Then he leaped onto the platform, moving swiftly for a big fellow. A moment later, they were deposited inside the roomy cabin of a type-8 personnel shuttle-craft. Leah needed the extra space in order to thrash about in the bulky suit until she got her bearings.

Paldor immediately rushed to the controls. "Should I start the ignition sequence?"

"Yes, and start the sensors and video log!" responded Leah, even though Paldor was hardly a shuttlecraft pilot. She pressed the escape button, opening the suit with a pop, then she pried her sweaty body out. As Leah tumbled to the deck, she heard the faint whine of the impulse engines powering up. "Open the space doors!"

Paldor did as he was told, opening the launch doors. Through the black expanse of space, they could see a rippling green wave reaching toward them.

"Oh, Mizerka!" cried the Tellarite, gaping at the awesome sight. Leah dropped into the seat beside him and punched the thrusters. They were both thrown back in their seats as the sleek shuttlecraft zoomed toward the hangar doors. The craft raked the doorway on its way out, shearing off a shielding cowl and a subspace dish. But the dent in the door didn't matter, because the entire moonbase was consumed in hellish green flame a second later.

The shuttlecraft banked away from the shimmering curtain as it rippled across the moon, turning pitted rock into living tissue, pulsing with freakish energy. Explosions ripped the planetoid, and the resulting clouds were also consumed in the churning maw. Leah watched this remarkable transformation in her viewscreen, as she pushed the shuttlecraft to top impulse speed. Even with her grief and shock, the scientist in her wanted to understand this phenomenon. What kind of alchemy turned a peaceful planet into a seething quagmire in a few seconds?

They were still outrunning the unknown wave, but not by much. It seemed to pick up speed as it left the devastated planet and her moons for the vacuum of open space. At the very least, it wasn't diminishing in size or force.

"Getting ready to enter warp drive," she said.

"Yes, warp!" agreed the Tellarite, nodding his approval. "Good idea."

Leah punched in maximum warp for the shuttlecraft, and they soared away from the solar system. For the first time, she sat back in her seat and paused to take stock . . . and reflect.

Paldor cleared his throat. "Are you sure . . . I mean, there's no way—"

"They're all dead," she answered numbly. "All dead." Like a robot, Leah rose from her seat and went to the locker, taking out a standard blue jumpsuit. She pulled the clothing over her shivering body, hoping it would staunch the chill, but it didn't.

Leah sniffed, thinking about the mate she had loved, and taken for granted. Mikel was gone now, and it was too late to do the things and say the things she should have said. He was struggling to get back to her when he died, even though she was the only one who was safe. Just like that, everything in the universe could be turned upside-down, until nothing mattered but a moment's worth of survival.

"What *is* that thing?" grumbled Paldor, studying the scanner readouts. "I've never seen anything like it. It must stretch across a hundred thousand kilometers!"

"I don't know what it is, and I've seen it up close." Leah sighed and looked gratefully at the radiation suit that had saved her life, functioning just as it was supposed to. But her survival was small consolation, unless it served a larger purpose. "We've got to warn the Federation."

"That won't be easy," said the Tellarite, working the board. "Our communications are out. Probably from that launch . . . it was a little rough."

Leah nodded solemnly and stared out the window at the endless starscape, looking slightly blurred and unreal at warp two. She could feel a tightness under her eyes where her tears had dried. How could something as vast as space be vulnerable? Yet it was. How many planets, stars, and moons would be consumed by the relentless force behind them?

"The distress signal may still be working," said Leah hopefully. She took her seat at the pilot's console and brought up a damage report. She had never claimed to be the greatest shuttlecraft pilot—Mikel did most of the flying—and she needed more practice. She would get that now.

"You know, there are a lot of my people in this part of the quadrant," said Paldor, wrinkling his snout.

"A lot of everybody's people." Brahms studied her readouts and made sure they were headed into the heart of the Federation. Then she began calculating how she could coax a little more speed from the shuttlecraft. "We'll keep running until we find somebody," she promised.

"Or until it catches us," muttered the Tellarite.

Ship's pipes sounded softly in the bowels of the *Enterprise*-E, noting the end of the second watch in main engineering. Geordi La Forge looked up from a display of schematics, adjusting his perception to deal with ambient light instead of digitized images. He checked the chronometer over the door to make sure it was time to quit, and it was. Not that Commander La Forge kept regular hours as chief engineer of the *Enterprise*, but he had to make sure that he scheduled time for other pursuits. If not, he was prone to workaholism. He rubbed his eyes, something he could do now that he wore ocular implants instead of a VISOR.

Geordi glanced around the bustling engine room. Nearly twice as big as the old one on the *Enterprise*-D, it had multitiered access points to the warp drive, a dozen control rooms, twenty workstations, and three master situation displays. But he still missed his old engine room, with its tight corners, bright lights, and cramped displays. This room was more efficient and ergonomically correct, but it lacked that homey feeling of a place that had been wrecked, repaired, and refitted many times.

Montgomery Scott had once told him that he felt the same way about the engine room on the first *Enterprise*. There was something about your first command that always stayed with you.

He heard the distinctive squeak of Data's footsteps a moment before he heard the android's clipped voice. "Geordi, you asked me to—"

"I remember," said the engineer with a smile. "Time to knock off. Thanks for reminding me."

The yellow-skinned android nodded thoughtfully. "I, too, am leaving engineering. The lateral arrays and the torque sensors appear to be operating within accepted parameters."

"That's what I tried to tell the captain," said Geordi, lowering his voice. "But he still thinks he can hear the torque sensors go out of alignment."

Data cocked his head. "His hearing did improve during the time we spent with the Ba'ku."

"Yes, but that was months ago, and we're back to normal now. At least, *I'm* back to normal now. Aren't you?"

Data considered the question. "As I am a unique being, there is no 'normal' to which I may compare myself. As for appearing normal, you almost always appear normal to me."

"I think that's a compliment," said Geordi with amusement. Then he frowned and looked back at his friend. "Exactly when are the times I *don't* appear normal?"

"When you are trying to make small talk with a suitable, available woman."

"Okay," muttered Geordi irritably. "We don't need to get *that* specific." He moved quickly to the exit, acknowledging the nods from his subordinates, many of whom had just come on duty. "Lieutenant Keenayle, take over."

"Yes, Sir," answered the white-haired Argelian, snapping to attention. "Computer, log Commander La Forge off duty. Direct hails to me."

"Change in command noted," answered the computer.

The door slid open as La Forge strode into the corridor, followed by Data. To his relief, Geordi saw that there was no one around, and he could talk freely to his best friend. "I guess you mean Dolores Linton."

"Yes," agreed Data, "Mission Specialist Linton. At the reception, I skillfully drew you into our conversation, turned the topic to one of mutual interest to both of you, made a witty parting remark, then left. What more could I do?"

Geordi scowled and looked around again to make sure they weren't being overheard. "Okay, so I froze and didn't know what to say. *You* were programmed to make small talk; some of us weren't so lucky."

"I have adjusted my programming over the years," replied Data as if confiding a secret. "As I was originally programmed, I was deficient in conversational skills. Standard replies often do not fit the context or the occasion, so I made a conscious effort to improve my programming."

"And you're saying I haven't?" snapped Geordi, realizing it was true.

"Specialist Linton is only going to be onboard for sixty days," observed Data. "As they say, you should move with alacrity."

La Forge groaned. "Maybe the problem is that I'm getting romantic advice from an android."

"If you prefer Commander Riker—"

"No, no," sputtered Geordi. "I couldn't take a single one of his lines and make it come out right. I can't smile like he can."

"But you also have dimples."

"That's not the point." Exasperated, Geordi stopped at the turbolift door and folded his arms. It took a few moments for the door to open, and when it did, Mission Specialist Dolores Linton stood inside the lift all alone. She was a few years younger than Geordi and quite a vibrant woman; stocky and muscular, she looked as if she could break him in half. He had no problem believing that she was a geologist who spent her life hiking and climbing.

"Specialist Linton," said Data cheerfully, as he grabbed Geordi's arm in a viselike grip and ushered him inside. "We were just discussing you."

"Oh, you were?" she said warily.

Geordi tried to wave off this conversation or find some way to escape from the turbolift, but the door closed behind him. "Level ten," he muttered to the computer.

"Level six," said Linton.

"Bridge." Without mercy, Data plowed onward. "Yes, Commander

La Forge was saying that he planned to come to my violin recital at twenty-two-hundred hours, and he wondered if you would enjoy it."

"Yes, I love violin music." Linton glanced politely at Geordi, but her eyes returned to Data. "What are you playing?"

"Bach's Sonata in G Major, on baroque violin."

"Oh," she said, sounding impressed. "Are you using real gut strings?"

"Yes, I constructed them myself according to seventeeth-century techniques."

Geordi tried to figure out how he could enter this conversation, but the turbolift door opened before he did. He did manage to say, "I'll pick you up at your cabin fifteen minutes before."

"Thank you, Commander." At least she was polite, if totally uninterested.

On his way out, Geordi whispered to Data, "You still need work." The android gave him a quizzical expression, but the engineer had left the lift.

As the door shut behind him, La Forge breathed a sigh of relief. He knew his friend was well-meaning, and he had certainly spotted an area that needed improvement. But Geordi had been trying to improve his love life since he was a teenager, with very little success. He could be perfectly okay around women once he got to know them, but making small talk with strange women was beyond his ken. He probably could have taken advantage of his position to woo the young engineers under him, most of whom were unattached, but that wasn't his style.

*No, being a lonely nice-guy is my style*, he thought ruefully.

After a slow stroll down the corridor, Geordi stopped at the entrance to his quarters and touched a panel to identify himself and open the door. He stepped inside a friendly suite of rooms that were decorated in the earth tones of Africa—dark green, rust, red, and yellow. There were masks from Africa, but Geordi's art collection was eclectic, reflecting his taste in modern sculpture and mixed-media works made from a variety of materials. Their tactile and infrared qualities were as important to him as the way they looked to others.

The sofa, tables, and chairs were homey and comfortable, because Geordi wouldn't put up with furnishings that weren't functional. The room was soothingly dark, because he didn't need visible light to see. But he left minimal lights on for any guests who might accompany him. *Always hopeful*, thought Geordi, chuckling to himself.

Although he had just left a bank of viewscreens in engineering, he went immediately to his desktop terminal and sat down in his old armchair. "Computer, check new messages, personal file." He loosened his collar and put his feet up on a hassock.

"Twenty-two new messages," said the computer dryly. His compact viewscreen gave him a page of headings, and he read them over, amazed that he had fallen so far behind in his correspondence. He found that he had missed a meeting of the Physicists Society, failed to respond to two invitations, including one from Data for tonight's recital, and had ignored a great many polite queries for papers or engineering advice. But he would make it up to his friends. Which apology should he issue first?

Geordi kept scrolling down until his implants caught a name that stopped him cold. *Leah Brahms.* It was probably a thank-you note for the gift he had sent, but any contact from Leah was a major occasion, even if it left him feeling like an also-ran. He said hoarsely, "Computer, play message nineteen."

La Forge sat forward in his chair as Leah's angelic face and form appeared on the screen, surrounded by the jumbled accoutrements of her laboratory. There was something new—a hulking white form loomed behind her, looking like an abominable snowman about to attack. Geordi also liked her short haircut, because it finally let her delicate cheekbones stand out. Now that Leah was older, her face had more character and less of that cherubic baby fat that had made her seem so young for her wisdom.

"Hi, Geordi," she said cheerfully. "I've just got to tell you about the new project we've been working on—and thank you for sending the fresh kiwi! I know we can replicate it, but it's not even close to the same."

Another person strolled through the background then stepped out of the frame. "Is that Geordi?" asked a male voice. "Tell him to send more kiwi. And guavas!"

*Her husband*, thought La Forge with a pang. Mikel was always in the background, and Geordi could never quite get a clear picture of him. He knew he worked with Leah and handled most of the political and paperwork aspects of the operation, but La Forge had a hard time imagining Leah needing anyone's help. She had started to explain about the radiation suit standing behind her, but he had been so lost in his own thoughts that he didn't catch it.

"Freeze playback," he said.

Now Leah Brahms was frozen on the screen, looking both radiant and excited, her delicate hands hovering in the air, trying to explain her enthusiasm. This frozen image, in all its glory, told Geordi all he needed to know about his love life. Not only had he made every possi-

ble wrong move with Leah, including turning her into a holodeck character, but he had fallen hopelessly in love with her—a married woman!
It sounded like something Reg Barclay would do.

*There you have it, as many boneheaded mistakes as one fool can
make.* Geordi shook his head, realizing he had only himself to blame.
He persisted in comparing every woman he met to Leah Brahms, an
exercise in futility if there ever was one. Maybe he could move on in
that part of his life, if he could just get over her.

With determination, he had maintained a long-range friendship
with Leah by concentrating on their mutual interests instead of his feelings, which he kept hidden. This piecemeal friendship over hundreds
of parsecs was better than nothing, and he felt as if he had to prove to
her he was an okay guy, after the rocky start to their relationship.

It had not been *this* Leah which had gone to the beach with him
and held his hand under the palm trees. No, that had been a dream
from a holodeck, created to help him solve a problem—only to create
a bigger one. *This* Leah was a real person with a husband and a busy
life that only peripherally included him. Still she was here in front of
him, talking to him; that was consolation enough for the moment.

"Rewind and resume playback," said Geordi, paying attention this
time. Yes, the radiation suit sounded fascinating, and it was exactly the
kind of thing that would challenge her mind. When she talked about
the interphase generator, he felt a shiver, because he'd had personal
experience with that Romulan device.

"But keep that hush-hush about the phase-shifting technology,"
she said in a sly aside. "We don't really have permission from the
Romulans, but I've always been good at reverse engineering. I think
that with the Alliance, maybe we can get permission after the fact."

"We'd better!" said the disembodied voice of Mikel, somewhere
in the background.

"Anyway, it's worked in all the trials, and we're doing more
today," concluded Leah. "I really feel happy about this project,
because it's going to do some good and save lives. So take care,
Geordi. Keep the *Enterprise* running. And thanks for all the kiwi!"

Her beaming face blinked off the screen, taking part of his heart
with it. "End transmission," added the computer.

La Forge sat back in his chair, wondering what he would say to her
in reply. As always, it would be carefully worded to be innocuous.
"Computer, record reply to message nineteen."

"Begin when ready."

Geordi plastered a smile on his face. "Hi, Leah . . . and Mikel. I'm
glad you like the kiwi. When you've been around the fleet as long as I

have, you learn how to pull a few strings. Everything is fine here on the big E, and we're almost back to full staff again. We're supporting a geological survey on Itamish III to see if it's stabilized enough to support a mining colony. It beats fighting a war. It's been months since we've had any real excitement, but nobody's complaining. Uh, Data has a violin recital tonight."

He twisted his hands, trying not to get tongue-tied. "I'm going to try to go to more conferences next year. Maybe I'll bump into you somewhere or other. I'll send you a schedule. Good-bye, Leah. End transmission." He cringed as soon as he signed off, wondering if he had sounded too forward. Meeting her at a conference somewhere was probably *his* fantasy but not hers.

"Message sent, delayed subspace relay," said the computer.

Geordi tried to shrug it off, because, after all, Leah already knew he was a hopeless goof. *I should just forget about her and never see or hear from her again*, he decided, knowing he would be better off. But he wouldn't do that, because he didn't have a lot of sense where Leah was concerned.

The off-duty engineer went on to answer a dozen more messages and do a little technical reading. He was thinking about getting a quick bite to eat when his terminal beeped at him.

"Message undeliverable," said the computer.

"Which message?" asked Geordi.

"Reply to message nineteen, Leah Brahms at Outpost Seran-T-One. Outpost not responding."

Now Geordi sat forward with interest. "That can't be—we've got a million relays out there. Why isn't the outpost responding?"

"No response from sector 4368."

"No response from the entire sector?" asked Geordi incredulously. "What is the explanation?"

"None reported."

"Keep trying," said the chief engineer, rising to his feet. He fastened the collar of his tunic as he strolled toward the door. It looked like his free time would include a trip to the bridge.

# four

A grizzled old Klingon sat alone at a table in the back of a dark tavern, staring into space. He had wild salt-and-pepper hair that tumbled past his shoulders, craggy forehead ridges split diagonally by an old scar, eyebrows that bristled like weeds, a broken nose, and a pointy white beard, streaked with black. But the most frightening thing about him was his blurry eyes, which stared straight ahead in abject terror.

With a twitch, the Klingon broke out of his fearsome reverie and realized where he was. He quickly grabbed a mug studded with *targ* knuckles and drained it lustily, letting half of the amber liquid course down his beard. Without warning, the Klingon pounded his fist on the table, shaking the whole establishment. "More ale!" he roared.

Fortunately, the dim tavern was mostly empty, except for two lovers giggling in a corner booth and a drunk Tellarite sleeping at the bar. The customer at the bar woke up and blinked, as Pasoot the bartender scurried from behind the counter, hefting another huge mug of foaming ale.

"More ale!" thundered the voice, shaking the glasses hanging above the bar.

"Coming!" shouted Pasoot, weaving gracefully among the empty tables and chairs. Pasoot was also a Tellarite and a large one, but he had learned to negotiate the tavern furniture like a ballet dancer.

"Here you go!" said Pasoot, presenting the mug he had specially ordered for this customer. "Anything else, Sir?"

"No," muttered the Klingon in a guttural voice, again staring straight ahead. "You didn't see it coming, did you?"

"See what?"

The elder's eyes blazed. "The green fire . . . it eats *everything*!

Then there's the lava and the geysers . . . and the wind . . . that awful wind—"

"Uh, didn't see it today, Sir," answered Pasoot cheerfully. "The weather looks nice outside. You sure you don't want some skull stew?"

The Klingon laughed insanely for a moment, then grew somber once more. "Go away," he grumbled.

Pasoot didn't wait to be told twice. He grabbed the empty mug and scooted across the room and back behind the bar.

His other customer was now awake and indignant at the loud-mouth who had woken him up. "Who's he?"

Pasoot whispered, "The Klingon consul. Drunk again as usual."

"He's in shameful condition," sniffed the Tellarite, his speech slurred.

Pasoot considered that for a moment, then shook his head. "Not for a Klingon. He's pretty peaceful for a Klingon. I used to serve a lot of them, and believe me, we could do worse. He's quite reasonable when he isn't getting nostalgic."

The Klingon muttered into his mug of ale, "Don't leave them! No chance . . . not with the lava—"

"What's he yelling?"

"I don't know . . . it's this kind of nightmare he has. Something about the 'green fire eating everything.' Then he talks about the lava and the wind. Always with the wind."

"The wind! The wind!" roared the Klingon.

Pasoot nodded sagely. "See what I mean."

"Why do you put up with that?"

"Because he's my best customer." The bartender picked up a glass and thoughtfully dried it with his towel. "I guess I feel sorry for him, because he must have messed up really badly to be sent to Hakon. In fact, a Klingon that old should either be a general, an ambassador . . . or dead."

He prodded his indignant customer. "So are you going to order another drink, or are you just going to complain?"

Before the tipsy Tellarite could reply, the outer door opened, and a ray of light sneaked into the darkness. The sunlight realized it didn't belong and quickly vanished, but a young Tellarite female was left in its wake. She was short and shapely, and her bristly hair was a rich auburn shade, not the orange of most males. She peered around the tavern, squinting into the dim light.

"Is he here?" she asked irritably.

"I don't know who *he* is," said the drunk at the bar. "But *I'm* here, and I'm all you need."

She wrinkled her snout. "Just tell me, Pasoot, is he here?"

"Maltz? Yes, he's way in the back." The bartender pointed with his towel. "He must be asleep, or else you'd hear him."

She snorted and put her hands on her hips. "Do you know how to sober up a Klingon?"

"Well, you can always impugn their honor, but I wouldn't recommend it." With a sigh of resignation, Pasoot finally moved from behind the bar. "Come on, Solia, I'll help you."

They warily approached the rear table, where the Klingon was indeed sleeping and snoring harshly, his face immersed in a puddle of spilt ale. Pasoot asked, "What's the emergency?"

"A trade delegation from the neutral worlds has landed, and they're demanding to see somebody important," answered Solia.

"And *this* is the best you could do?" asked the bartender, shaking his head.

"A Klingon is always impressive," answered Solia, looking doubtfully at her charge. "Well, almost always. My orders are to bring him to this reception."

Pasoot shrugged. "I guess we don't have a lot of local celebrities. Okay, but I'm only going to do this once."

The bartender leaned over the fallen Klingon and said sharply, "Officer Maltz, to your feet! The enemy is near! *Jagh! Jagh!*"

The old Klingon lumbered to his feet, looking startled and wary. "It was that madman, Kruge, who got us captured! I could not do . . . Huh? Where am I?"

"Hello, Consul Maltz," said Solia soothingly, taking his arm and snatching his cloak from the back of his chair. "If you'll come with me now, we'll get you ready for your reception. More food . . . and *drink!* Come on."

Brave soul that she was, Solia dragged the stumbling, muttering Klingon out of the tavern into the blazing light of day. Pasoot could only shake his head and say to his other customers, none of whom were listening, "I have a bad feeling that old guy is not going to live long."


"But I tell you, Dr. Brahms, we can't let them all die!" whined Paldor, his snout flaring. The Tellarite sat in the cockpit of the shuttlecraft, banging on the star map on his console. "This Tellarite colony is right in the path of that thing back there, and we have time to go warn them. Besides, you say you want to get word to *somebody* in the Federation."

Leah gulped, although she kept her hands firmly on the controls, wondering how far the big Tellarite would go to save his people. They still hadn't made their communications system work, although Leah thought the distress signal was getting out. Yes, they had to stop somewhere, but was this it?

"How much time do we really have?" she asked.

"I can't tell." Paldor shook his bushy head with frustration. "Its speed is variable, depending on how many solar systems and dust clouds it has to chew up along the way. Now that I know what to look for, I think I can spot it on sensors. At warp speed, we were traveling about three times faster, so I'm sure we've gained some time on it. Come on, Dr. Brahms, we've got to stop running and start *warning!*"

"Okay," said Leah, "you made your point. Do you think you can make your people believe their whole planet is in imminent danger of being destroyed?"

"What choice do we have?" asked Paldor grimly.

Leah nodded and glanced at his map. "Okay I'm changing course for—"

"Hakon in the Hivernia System," answered the Tellarite with relief. "Thank you, Dr. Brahms."

"You're going to do something for me," she replied. "You'll find isolinear chips in the media drawer."

"Okay," said the Tellarite, opening the small drawer and finding the compact storage devices. "What should I do with them?"

"Transfer all the data we've collected, plus your thoughts and recollections—anything you can think of—onto an isolinear chip. We've got to make a record of what we've seen . . . in case something happens to us."

"But how will we protect the chip?" asked Paldor.

"The same way I was protected—we'll put it into the suit." She glanced back at the radiation suit, hulking silently in the rear of the craft.

"Okay," said the Tellarite, inserting a slim rectangular device into the computer. "How would you describe the changes that this mysterious energy wave made to the planet?"

"Mutagenic, radical," answered Brahms with a shiver, trying not to visualize what she had seen all too closely. "Matter seems to be reorganized into an entirely different substance, but it's also alive. You saw what it did to the moonbase."

"Let's hope we get to Hakon in time," said the Tellarite, frowning so deeply that his bushy eyebrows knitted together.

"Let's hope somebody listens to us," added Leah.

\*    \*    \*

Dressed in a laboratory gown and wearing rubber gloves, Captain Jean-Luc Picard carefully washed the clump of rock and sand with water and a small brush. He made certain to stand over the strainer, so that any small material which fell off would not be lost in the flow of water. It was meticulous work requiring patience, but it was also oddly satisfying. The captain of the *Enterprise* liked working with his hands, and he could be infinitely patient when dealing with antiquities.

It helped, too, that he was in a lab full of people doing the same work. Although he wasn't entirely sure what he was doing, there was plenty of expert help with whom to consult. Plus he felt useful when he saw the small piles of shells, fossils, and mineral specimens he had gleaned from the fist-sized chunks of river bottom in his basket.

He felt a presence looming behind him, and he turned to see the mission commander, Itakva Gedruva. Professor Gedruva was a Tiburon, so she had the dignified, bald head and enormous, leaf-shaped ears of her species.

"Thank you, Captain, for volunteering to do all this work," she said gratefully. "We normally have a hard time finding volunteers to clean and sort samples."

"Think nothing of it," said Picard magnanimously. "I enjoy working with antiquities. You can ask my crew; I welcome any mission that gets me poking around in some old dig." He lifted a delicate bit of rock that was full of clam-shell imprints. "How old do you think these fossils are?"

"I would guess the carbon dating would show them to be half-a-million in terran years," answered the professor. "Thus far, we haven't been surprised, but maybe you'll find an arrowhead and shock us."

"That would be shocking, wouldn't it?" asked Picard with amusement. Then his expression grew thoughtfully serious. "But what do you think happened to life on Itamish III? It was on track to be a garden planet, wasn't it?"

The elderly Tiburon shook her enormous ears. "We have theories, but we don't know exactly. That is what we hope to find out, to try to prevent it from happening again. Life is so delicate, Captain Picard. You realize that after you sort through the bones of a few hundred planets where life used to thrive and does no longer."

"Professor!" called someone else at a nearby table.

"Excuse me, Captain." With a polite nod, the mission commander was gone, leaving Picard to continue brushing and washing.

He was just starting to remove the clay from a new sample when his combadge chirped. "Bridge to Picard," said the familiar voice of Commander Riker. With gooey, gloved hands, the captain couldn't touch his combadge to answer it, and he had to set down his material and tools, remove a glove, and open his gown.

With relief, he finally answered the hail. "Picard here."

"I'm sorry to bother you, Captain," said Riker, "but we've got a situation."

The captain knew his first officer well enough to realize that he wouldn't interrupt his free time unless it was important. He was also not going to come out and say what it was when he could be overheard. Riker was confident enough to deal with almost anything on his watch, so this had to be something well beyond the scope of their peaceful mission.

"On my way," said the captain, rising from his stool. He removed his other glove and his lab gown, shrugging helplessly at Professor Gedruva. Her brief smile told him that she quite understood the requisites of command.

A few moments later, he strode onto the circular bridge of the *Enterprise* and looked curiously at the clutch of senior officers gathered around the tactical station: Riker, Data, and La Forge. Neither Data nor La Forge were supposed to be on duty, yet both of them were poring over data.

"Status?" he asked Commander Riker.

"As Mister La Forge discovered, we've lost contact with almost an entire sector of Federation space, 4368. That's fairly close to us, toward the center of the galaxy."

Picard frowned. "What about ships in the area?"

"We've tried, but we can't raise any ships, outposts, or any relays out there. Unaffected areas nearby don't report anything amiss."

Data looked up from the tactical station. "The communications blackout spans several inhabited solar systems, and there was no advance warning. Starfleet can offer no explanation."

"You can't raise anyone at all?" asked Picard incredulously. He knew that region of space, and it was one of the sleepiest, most peaceful parts of the Federation, far removed from the Demilitarized Zone and sites of recent conflicts.

La Forge lifted his head up. "We think we've found a faint distress signal, but that's it. We can't even get a signature from it."

"Can you read me the last message from Starfleet?" asked Picard.

"Yes," said Riker, leaning over the small terminal built into the arm of the captain's chair. "Communications outage in sector 4368 confirmed, reason undetermined. Unable to reach other ships in area, so no ships dispatched at present time. *Enterprise*, use captain's discretion to investigate, but please advise of decision. Signed, Admiral Nechayev."

Picard rubbed his chin thoughtfully, well remembering one of the more prickly members of the admiralty, Alynna Nechayev. It was odd that she should be involved in such a day-to-day matter, since she was usually more concerned with counterespionage tactics and secret missions. She had spearheaded their espionage efforts against the Maquis, Bajoran terrorists, and Cardassians, for instance. Not that those situations didn't call for extreme tactics, but Picard still felt guilty over having recruited Ro Laren, Sito Jaxa, and others for such dangerous missions, many of which had not ended well.

The captain couldn't help himself—whenever Admiral Nechayev was involved, he felt the warning hackles rise on the back of his neck. He said nothing to any of his subordinates, but they knew. After all, they had seen the admiral chew him out for one of their risky failures. All of this was just one more reason to take "captain's discretion" very seriously. He had a strong feeling that Nechayev wanted the *Enterprise* to go but wouldn't come out and say so.

"We're trying to get a fix on that distress signal," said La Forge. "It's moving, and there's interference in the background—like solar flares or something."

"If you do get a fix, use it for a course setting," ordered the captain. "Otherwise, pick an inhabited planet. Maximum warp. Alert Starfleet of our intentions."

"Yes, Sir," answered Riker, his voice showing no surprise. "We've got to pick up a few people on the planet. Do you want me to tell the team that we're going to have to postpone our current mission?"

"No, I'll tell them," said Picard regretfully as he moved to the turbolift. "Get us moving as fast as you can."

"Thank you, Sir," added Geordi La Forge, sounding as if the engineer had a personal interest in sector 4368.

"Keep trying to raise them," ordered the captain. "I don't want to waste our time on a wild-goose chase."

# five

A dry wind crackled across the baked-clay walls and rambling, earthen dwellings of Patoorgiston, the capital of Hakon's sole inhabitable continent. The hand-molded walls had wide arches every twenty meters or so, and inside the arches were clay pots full of flowers and candles, swaying in the searing breeze.

Most of the dwellings were two story and looked like children's blocks, piled one upon another. The upper levels were smaller, allowing the outer edge of the lower roof to be a balcony. Children played fearlessly on these narrow labyrinths, which were connected by ladders and stairs; the Tellarites had good balance and seldom had accidents despite their bulk. Although the earthen houses looked similar in color and shape, they were distinguished by curtains, banners, and laundry in large, bright plaids, flapping from every window and balcony.

The inhabitants themselves wore these same kind of brilliant, often clashing squares of color as they bustled up and down the rambling streets. Some of them rode solar-powered, two-wheeled scooters, which breezed along the bumpy thoroughfares, narrowly missing the pedestrians. The Tellarites were vocal, and their loud voices carried on the wind, which was hot and dry, just the way they liked it.

Every so often, a face appeared in the crowd which did not have orange hair and a prominent snout, but the outsiders were few in number. Most of them were headed toward the only four-story building in town, the Cultural Affairs Center, which was a hub of interplanetary commerce. A bushy crown of salt-and-pepper hair towered above the Tellarites, Ferengi, Valtese, and the rest of the pedestrians. He was the lone Klingon, and the others gave him and his handler wide berth.

"We're almost there," said the cultural affairs attaché, Solia, guiding the grizzled Klingon down the walkway.

Maltz squinted into the bright sunlight, thinking that if he had any *klin* at all, he would shake off this simpering flunky and crawl back into a dark tavern. But that old call to duty still stirred him, even though everything he did in this post was pointless. Most days he felt like a sideshow attraction. *Look at the Klingon! Hakon is important enough to have one of its very own.*

Maltz couldn't believe it had taken them this long to walk a few blocks, but he hadn't been paying attention. It seemed it was now afternoon, and he had left home that morning, hadn't he? His keeper must have led him on a merry stroll, trying to sober him up. Well, it hadn't worked! He was still drunk.

He looked down at the small figure holding him up. Well, she was small for a Tellarite. The Klingon knew he ought to take her in his arms and protect her, instead of the other way around. But he was beyond offering protection to anyone, including himself. Now he had to be guided around like an old fool, propped up against the wall to be admired like the relic he was. Maltz was old enough to remember fighting against these people on a daily basis, before the Khitomer Accords. How had he turned from a proud warrior to a broken-down souvenir for the conquering enemy?

"When did we lose?" he muttered.

"What did you say, Consul?"

"When did we *lose!*" he thundered. "When did a pack of puny do-gooders take over our lives and our heritage and turn us into *diplomats?* A whore you dress up and show off for dinner—not a warrior. But this is what I've been reduced to by the Federation."

Solia laughed nervously as she tried to ignore the stares of passersby. "Why, Sir, you haven't lost anything. The Klingon Empire is still as powerful and respected as ever. You're her representative—you should know."

"Yes, I know very well," grumbled Maltz. "The niceness and even-handedness of the Federation has spilled over, infecting us. There is no way to die with honor anymore." He swallowed hard and rasped, "No way to redeem myself."

"Now, Sir, you can't blame every misfortune in life on the Federation."

Maltz laughed harshly. "In my case, I can. Although I should blame Kruge as much as Kirk."

"Kruge and Kirk?" asked the young Tellarite doubtfully.

"Before you were born," snapped the Klingon with a derisive snort. "That was when the captain of a starship was a force unto himself, a sovereign with no equal. It's not diplomats and massive fleets who decide history, it's out there . . . where two captains meet in the eye of the storm!" He shook his head miserably. "And destroy my career."

"I'm sure it's not that bad," replied Solia briskly, her patience running out at the same time the assignment was mercifully coming to an end. "We're here. Now watch it, because there are some steps."

Maltz finally had enough of this simpering lackey. He straightened his cloak and yanked his gleaming chain-mail sash across over his gaunt frame. Then he leaped up the stairs to the landing. "I can make it from here. There must be some other infants somewhere who need your attention."

"I'm sure," she answered with a smile. "Straight ahead to the reception desk and sign in with . . . Consul Maltz!"

But the Klingon was already headed toward the refreshments, his nostrils flaring at the smell of food. With a few long strides, he was across the lobby and into the ballroom, where a gathering of notables from the city and many surrounding planets were enjoying the hastily assembled soiree. Tellarite servers bustled among them with steaming trays of food and tinkling glasses of blue Saurian ale. The old Klingon skidded to a stop and licked his cracked lips.

A Tellarite waiter passed by with a tray full of fluted glasses containing the bluish liquid, and Maltz quickly seized him. "Don't be in such a hurry."

"Of course, Sir!" said the young Tellarite with a trace of awe and fear in his voice at being waylaid by a Klingon. He started to offer a glass to the dignitary when the Klingon grabbed the whole tray of glasses.

"Get another one," he grumbled. "I'm thirsty."

The Tellarite nodded and hurried off, while Maltz looked around the demurely decorated ballroom. From a nearby serving table, he grabbed a vase full of flowers, dumped the flowers and the water under the table, and began to pour the contents of the fluted glasses into the vase. When he was done, he finally had a warrior-sized receptacle that fit his hand, and it was already full of ale.

As he mingled among the crowd, looking for servers with food, Maltz heard a voice call, "And there he is! Maltz, our esteemed Klingon representative!"

The old warrior froze in his tracks and slumped his shoulders. He knew that voice—it was Bekra, the Capellan consul and self-appointed social director of the diplomatic community. Maltz turned around to face the elaborately dressed consul and his retinue, softening his scowl to a mild frown. On his head, Bekra wore a conical turban the shape of a tornado, and its rich fabric trailed seamlessly into his bejeweled turquoise jumpsuit.

"Consul Maltz," said Bekra, sliding unctuously toward him. "We have some distinguished visitors from the Neutral Worlds. They're making a swing through the Federation colonies, discussing trade opportunities. We're so glad you could come on such short notice."

"I would not miss it," grumbled Maltz, taking a long drink of ale as he surveyed the half-dozen newcomers to their midst. A grinning Orion, plus two unsightly Talavians, a bug-eyed Dopterian, a sinewy Mikulak, and a green-skinned Rutian. Bekra assigned them all names as he introduced them, but the names flew right out of Maltz's head the moment he heard them.

"Pleased to meet you," he grumbled, mustering very little sincerity.

"Does the Klingon Trade Council do much business here on Hakon?" asked the Rutian, whose long, stringy hair had more streaks of white than Maltz's.

The Klingon dug deep in the recesses of his memory for an innocuous response. "We would like to do more, which is why we are all here, right?"

"As you know, the Klingons require more security controls than are typical," said Bekra, the know-it-all. "Consul Maltz spends a great deal of his time checking to make sure that all the conditions are met."

"Yes, I do," lied the Klingon, who rubber-stamped everything that crossed his desk. He took a long swig of ale and wiped the excess from his beard with the back of his gauntlet. "How long are you staying on Hakon?"

The Orion answered, "Long enough to see what the populace needs, and what they have to offer in trade."

Bekra broke in, "The locals manufacture a natural cloth here that is unlike anything else in the Federation. It's strong, tough, resistant to mildew, and—"

He went on, but Maltz managed to corral a passing waiter and confiscate about half a tray of truffles. He tuned out the conversation while he ate, but he caught the Orion looking intently at him. He wasn't surprised when the visitor sidled up to his elbow a moment later.

"There's something familiar about you," said the Orion in a low voice. "Maybe it's that scar. Have we met before?"

Maltz tapped the crooked dent in his forehead ridge and peered down at the snaggletoothed trader. "I have met a lot of people," he said warily. "And my memory is not so good."

"I'm sure of it." The Orion tugged thoughtfully on a giant earlobe as his beady eyes studied the Klingon's face. "What did you do during the war?"

"That is none of your business," answered Maltz defensively.

"He was right here with the rest of us," said Bekra. "Sweating it out."

But the Orion was shaking his finger and smiling with satisfaction. "Yes, I remember it now. I never forget a face, especially not a distinctive one like yours! It was probably thirty years ago, when I was in the prison supply business."

"I am not interested," grumbled Maltz. Actually he had no idea what the Orion was about to say, but he truly didn't want to hear anything about his past, whether it was factual or not.

"You were a bounty hunter."

Now the Klingon's stomach heaved, and he felt the bile of almost a century of dodging the past come surging up his throat. Maltz gripped his larynx and caught the bile before it spilled out, then he caught the snide Orion by the throat and lifted him off the tiled floor.

"Yes, I have been a bounty hunter," he snarled, "and worse than that. But I have never been a freeloader who drifts in here out of nowhere expecting to be wined and dined for free!"

"Maltz!" shouted Bekra with alarm, trying to pry his grip from the gagging Orion. "Set him down!"

It was then the Mikulak and the Dopterian attacked Maltz, with the Mikulak wrapping long tentacles around his neck, while the shorter Dopterian punched him rapidly in the stomach. The Klingon had to drop the Orion, but he smashed his vase over the Dopterian's head, coating the bug-eyed creature in blue ale. Then he grabbed the tray of truffles and smashed the Mikulak into submission, while he laughed with delight.

The two Talavians tackled Maltz from the rear and propelled him into a serving table, which crumpled under their weight, spilling punch and desserts over all of them. The melee continued on the floor in a churning heap of limbs and foamy punch. Maltz was all elbows, fists, and hobnailed boots, smashing anything that came within range.

*Ah, it felt good to fight!* There were no friends or enemies, just the enemy—he had to silence them all! Maltz barely noticed when three beefy constables rushed in from the street and joined the fray.

"Cowards!" he roared.

The old Klingon was still hollering and kicking when the exasperated constables leaped to their feet, drew phaser pistols, and shot him with pinpoint blue beams.

*Peace at last*, thought Maltz as his body stilled and consciousness drifted away.

"Geordi," said Data, tapping his friend on the shoulder. He kept his voice low in the efficient hum of activity on the bridge. "I must speak with you."

"Just a minute," answered the engineer impatiently as he gazed at his readouts. "The long-range sensor scan is just coming in, and it's pretty bizarre. I can't figure out what's going on out there."

"We should know in twelve hours and forty-five minutes," said the android. "Meanwhile, I have a recital to perform, and you have a date."

Geordi scowled and finally looked up from his console among the circle of stations on the *Enterprise* bridge. Commander Riker was conferring with the officer on the conn, probably refining their course setting. "Can't you pick her up?" whispered Geordi. "She's interested in seeing *you*, anyway."

The android leaned closer. "We are enroute at maximum warp, and your concern will not make us reach Outpost Seran-T-One any faster."

Geordi blinked at his friend, feigning ignorance. "What do you mean . . . Seran-T-One? Why there?"

"Is that not where Dr. Leah Brahms lives?" asked Data with sympathy. "In addition, every long-range scan you have done has been centered on Outpost Seran-T-One."

Geordi smiled, thinking that Data didn't miss much. "Okay, so I'm worried about her. Do you think we'll get back to the bridge fairly soon?"

Data cocked his head thoughtfully. "I will play the violin six percent faster and cut out my curtain call."

"Okay, it's a deal." Geordi rose from the station and crossed the center clearing to Commander Riker. "Sir, Data and I will be back in a little while."

"Get some rest," suggested Riker. "We'll let you know if we find out anything of interest, but I kind of doubt it. Data, sorry I'll miss the show."

The android nodded with tacit understanding, and he waited by the turbolift until La Forge caught up. The two of them boarded the lift and went hurtling down to level six, where there was a wing devoted to guest quarters, close to the main shuttlebay for convenience sake.

For once, Data didn't practice his small talk, and Geordi was grateful for the silence. The engineer tried to tell himself there were a million logical—or even implausible—reasons for the communications to be out while the population was still fine. They weren't at war, and there hadn't been any unusual activity reported by any of the posts or settlements. Still, he had seen enough in his twenty years in Starfleet to be worried about things that weren't seen or reported.

He parted company with Data and quickly found the corridor devoted to guest quarters. Normally Geordi would have been nervous, but he had so much on his mind that this date seemed like an afterthought. He chimed her door and waited.

When the door opened, Dolores Linton was standing about a meter away from him, an intense look in her sultry eyes. She was dressed in a formfitting black evening gown that a regular crew member wouldn't have dared to wear. A slit up to her thigh showed her muscular legs, while the sleeveless gown revealed an impressively developed upper body, too. Geordi could see an aura of vibrant energy about her, and he sincerely regretted that he would have to shortchange her on this date.

"Hello," he said, trying to muster as much charm and enthusiasm as he could under a cloud of worry. "I'm sorry I'm a few minutes late."

"Don't worry about that. Come in." With a firm grip, she took his arm and pulled him into the small single quarters. The room was cluttered with climbing gear, collection boxes, chemicals, stasis bags, tricorders, and other tools of her profession, and there was barely room to stand.

The geologist put her hands on her hips and demanded. "Okay, what is the deal with them canceling our mission?"

Geordi was caught off guard by this topic of conversation, but of course that had to be a big disappointment to the visiting team of specialists. Plus they probably hadn't been told very much about the circumstances.

"Well, it's only been postponed while we check something out," he answered. "This kind of thing happens, especially to the *Enterprise*."

"What are we checking out?" she asked bluntly.

"Loss of contact with a sector not far from here." He shrugged. "It will probably turn out to be nothing, and we'll only lose a couple of days. Are you ready to go see Data perform?"

"Looking forward to it," she answered, taking his arm and gazing at him with those disconcerting dark eyes. "In fact, I have a lot of free time now, so tell me about everything there is to do on the *Enterprise*."

"Well, we have a large library, an exercise facility, recreation room, and holodecks, although you need a reservation for those." The door opened, and they strolled into the corridor.

"Holodecks aren't my cup of tea," said Dolores, shaking her medium-length brown hair. "I prefer real thrills and real fresh air. Please don't tell the ship's doctor, but I suffer from a bit of claustrophobia. I'm always glad to get out of these tin cans and back to solid ground, even if it's a Class-H planetoid."

"A Class-H planetoid?" asked Geordi, only half-listening.

"You're a million light-years from here, Commander," said the woman with bemusement. "Usually when I wear this dress, I have my date's undivided attention."

"I'm sorry, really," he stammered. "I have to admit that I'm concerned about this detour we're taking, because I have a good friend who lives out there. I'll be happier than anyone when we find out it's nothing."

She nodded sympathetically. "By the worry lines on your face, I think it must be a lady friend."

"No, Leah is a . . . a fellow engineer." Geordi lowered his head and plowed down the corridor, embarrassed by the direction of the conversation. Dolores Linton seemed to be one of those people who said anything she felt like saying. Maybe that was a luxury enjoyed by those who flitted from one place to another, disappearing in the wilds for weeks at a time.

"This way to the turbolift," he said, motioning to the color encoded lines which ran the length of the corridor.

"Oh, there's a turbolift down there?" remarked Dolores in amazement. "I didn't know. I get so lost on ships. When you caught me today, I was just riding around on the lift, seeing how many decks there were. I've been on a lot of space stations smaller than this vessel. Seriously, Commander, if you get any free time at all, I'd love a tour of the *Enterprise*. Might as well, if I'm going to spend some time on shoreleave."

"We'll see," he answered with a half-smile. "And call me Geordi."


"You had to go and smash up the Cultural Affairs Center," said a chiding voice, followed by tongue clicking. "You're going to get a nasty bill."

"Aarghh," murmured the Klingon as he shuddered awake and stared at a brown ceiling carved with thousands of chit marks. With a grunt, Maltz swung his legs over the edge of the bed and finally succeeded in sitting up. "I thought I was dead."

"You sound disappointed," said Consul Bekra, standing outside a holding cell in an earthen room with a low ceiling and no windows. A shimmering force-field guarded the cell door.

"I am," grumbled Maltz.

"Come on, it's not that bad." The Capellan chuckled with amusement. "You'll be glad to know, none of our guests were seriously injured, and I think they relished the opportunity to tangle with a Klingon. At least you lived up to your advance billing. Not everything in life does."

"I'm gratified the tourists were happy," rasped the old Klingon. "How long do I have to stay in here?"

"You know how it works—you have to see the magistrate." Bekra stepped away from the wall and walked toward the door. "I'll do what I can to move the process along."

"Thanks."

"Hey! Hey, out there!" The Capellan stood by the door, trying to attract someone's attention to let him out. He finally gave up and turned back to Maltz. "Is it true you were once a bounty hunter?"

"Yes," muttered the Klingon. "I thought somebody would kill me back then, too. But nobody ever did."

The outer door suddenly opened, allowing more light and a cacophony of voices to flood into the quiet holding cell. It sounded as if a full-scale melee was taking place in the waiting room. Maltz tried to ignore it and concentrate on his thumping headache, but the voices were too loud and insistent. A Tellarite constable dressed in a red-and-white plaid uniform ducked into the room, looking as if he were trying to escape from the racket.

"What is going on out there?" asked Bekra.

"Two people have landed in a damaged shuttlecraft," answered the constable. "They're claiming that some kind of strange energy wave destroyed Seran and is coming after us."

"An energy wave destroyed a whole planet?" asked Bekra doubtfully. "Did they say what it was?"

The Tellarite shrugged. "Something about a green fire consuming the planet, turning it into sludge."

Maltz gasped and nearly fell out of his bed. "What!" he shouted, rushing the door. "What did they say *exactly*?" In his enthusiasm, he got too close to the door, and the force-field shocked him, hurling him to the floor.

"Careful there!" called the guard angrily. "You just sit tight until the magistrate gets here."

"I've got to see those people!" shouted Maltz desperately. He staggered to his feet, careful not to trip the force-field again. "Please, Officer, you've got to let me see them."

"You're in enough trouble already," scolded Bekra. "Would it help if *I* talked to them?"

The constable shrugged. "Well, they are asking to speak to important people, but we don't know what to tell them. They claim we haven't got any time, that we have to evacuate the planet." He snorted a laugh. "As if we could."

"Please!" roared the Klingon. "I know what they're talking about. Let me see them!"

With a scowl, the angry guard pushed Bekra out the door and slammed it shut behind him. Maltz could still hear muffled voices, but he couldn't hear any specifics. He howled like a wounded animal and dropped to his knees, beating his fists against his craggy skull.

"Listen to me!" he moaned. "I knew someone would use the device again . . . I *know* what it is!"

But no one was listening.

# six

"Listen! Listen to me, please!" begged Leah Brahms, pushing up the sleeves on her jumpsuit and leaning over the amber desk to stare at an enormous Tellarite. She still couldn't believe this quaint hovel was the regional police station. "You've got to get ready to evacuate," she told them. "How many space vehicles have you got?"

The chief Tellarite raised his beefy hands and smiled condescendingly at her. According to a plate on his desk, he was a proctor. "Now you listen for a second . . . what did you say your name was?"

"Dr. Leah Brahms," she answered impatiently for the nineteenth time. "I'm in the Science Service, I was once in the Theoretical Propulsion Group, I run the lab on Outpost Seran-T-One." With a lump in her throat, she corrected herself. "I mean, I *ran* it before it was totally destroyed about fourteen hours ago."

"That's what we're trying to ascertain," said the proctor importantly as he shuffled papers and motioned to his confederates. "We've got to discover the facts in the matter. So far, the only fact we know is that the two of you landed in a shuttlecraft, which isn't all that unusual."

Leah turned with exasperation to her colleague, Paldor, but the Tellarite was in shock. He'd had no idea that Hakon was such a sleepy backwater of a place, where no one would pay any attention to their anguished cries of warning. She could see from the despair on his face that he realized all of these people were going to die, and no doubt the two of them as well.

"Paldor," she said, trying to wake him from his reverie. "Tell them it's true! That a destructive wave is coming."

"Huh?" he said, blinking at her like a person coming out of a trance. "All they have are farms and a small village. They haven't got any labs here."

"A subspace radio," she told the officer at the desk. "There's got to be *some* way for you to contact other planets. Try contacting Seran, where we came from." She snapped her fingers. "Or better yet, let us try to contact Starfleet! We've got to warn the rest of the Federation."

Several of the smug constables chuckled at her earnestness. "We don't have any reason to contact other planets from this station," said the proctor slowly, as if talking to a child. "The spaceport probably has that capability. So do the ships in orbit."

"The spaceport!" exclaimed Leah, clinging to any semblance of advanced civilization in this provincial hamlet. "Yes, how can we get there?"

"It's about forty kilometers on the outskirts of town," explained the constable, pointing out the window at a row of mudflats.

"They can't help you," said a cultured voice coming from behind Leah. She whirled around to see an elegantly dressed Capellan; he shook his lofty turban sadly. "The spaceport is nothing but an automated system to handle our freighter and passenger traffic, which isn't much."

"Who are you?" asked Brahms, hoping he was the mayor or someone of enough rank to get things done.

"Capellan Trade Consul Bekra, at your service," he answered with a smart bow.

She gripped his turquoise collar, which brought a grimace of distaste to his dignified face. "Listen, Bekra, you've got to believe me—everyone on this planet is going to *die!* Do you understand me?"

"Do you have proof of this?" he asked gravely.

From the pocket of her jumpsuit, Leah removed an isolinear chip, which she waved in his face. "I've got this and another copy back in our shuttlecraft. But this is raw data—sensor readings, vidlogs, and recollections—you'd have to spend some time analyzing it. And you don't *have* any time."

"Let me see that!" ordered the constable, reaching across his desk and snatching the isolinear chip from her fingers. "You say this contains evidence?"

"Not evidence . . . data!" The human rolled her eyes in exasperation. "No crime's been committed—this is more like a natural disaster, I think. Do you have someone who can analyze our data?"

"We've got our medical examiner and the professors at the agricultural college," said the constable proudly. "First thing in the morning, we'll take this to them and—"

"No, no!" shouted Leah, balling her hands into fists and shaking them at the dense constable. "You're not listening to me! You won't be here 'first thing in the morning.' This entire planet will be pulverized into something . . . some kind of new life-form. You, your wife, your kids, your friends—"

"Now, you listen to *me!*" roared the proctor, jumping to his feet and shaking a beefy fist at her. "Around here, we don't tolerate people creating a public disturbance, and you're doing just that. We're a simple people—we don't look kindly on doomsday cults. We've got a sensor warning system in place from the war, and it hasn't put out so much as a *peep.*"

"This is pointless," said Paldor, shaking his head miserably. "You're all doomed."

"That's quite enough of that!" bellowed the belligerent chief. As his fellows moved from behind the counter and surrounded them with a bulky phalanx, the proctor pointed toward the door. "Now get out of here, both of you. We've got your data, and we'll study it. And don't leave town."

"Come along," said the Capellan, putting a protective arm around Leah Brahms. She was so disillusioned—and fearful—that she let the consul lead her out of the building into the street, where the cheery sunshine did seem to belie their dire warnings. The weather had been just as beautiful on Seran seconds before the ungodly fire scourged everything, she recalled. How much time did they have? Hours? Seconds?

Paldor stumbled after Leah and bumped into her. "I'm sorry, Doctor. You were right—we should have kept running."

She turned again to the popinjay in his conical turban. "Have *you* got a ship, some way we can contact the Federation? Or at the very least some equipment, so we can repair our shuttlecraft?"

"Speaking of which, I should get back to the shuttlecraft," said Paldor, rousting himself from his stupor. "I'll keep our sensors running."

"Stay in contact via combadge," ordered Brahms, "and be ready to beam me back." Intellectually, she knew she had to fight through the locals' ignorance and make them understand, but part of her just wanted to get the hell out of there. Most of her reasons to live were gone, but the urge to save herself was still amazingly strong. Some internal motor wouldn't let her stand still and have that nightmarish wave strip her flesh off her bones.

"You're in charge, Doctor," Paldor gave her a grave bow, acknowledging that he had been wrong. He was also assigning his life to her hands, a fact which weighed heavily on her.

"I'll do what I can," she promised. "Go on."

With a nod, the Tellarite scurried off, glancing suspiciously around him. And well he might, because it looked as if the constables had been watching them from the station. Two of them took off in pursuit of Paldor, rushing right by Leah and the Capellan consul.

"Your ship," she told the Capellan. "We've got to contact somebody."

"All I've got is a shuttlecraft, too," he answered apologetically. "It doesn't even have warp drive, I'm afraid, but there is a subspace relay to my homeworld."

"Will they believe me?"

"Even if they do, what can they do to help?" asked Bekra rhetorically. "They're two thousand light-years away. You know, this planet *does* have sensors. If there was anything—"

"It's not like anything we've seen before," cut in Leah, shaking her head. "I've got to make *somebody* believe."

The Capellan grimaced. "Well, there is somebody who might be inclined to believe you, but he couldn't do much to help you either."

"Why is that?" she asked impatiently. "Who is this person?"

"Another consul. A Klingon. Unfortunately, he's a prisoner in the station we just left."

She blinked at the stranger. "Why should he believe me? Is he a scientist?"

"No, but he's old, and he's seen many things in his life. He thinks he's seen this energy wave of yours—I've heard him talking about it." The diplomat shrugged. "Then again, he may be insane."

"If he's seen what I saw, he has every right to be insane." Leah shuddered and looked back at the station, wondering if anything she could do on Hakon would make any difference. Evacuating entire planets on the spur of the moment was not going to work, not unless she had the whole Federation behind her. To get support, she needed more information. If there was any chance to find out more about that awesome force, she had to take it.

"Can we see this Klingon?" she asked.

Bekra sighed, as if realizing he was getting himself deeper into a quagmire. "You'd better not be getting me into trouble. I have to work with these people."

"Believe me, by tomorrow, that will be the least of your worries." Leah fixed him with a doleful stare.

The Capellan took her elbow and guided her back toward the station. "I wish I weren't starting to believe you, because you're frightening me."

"So far you're the only one." Leah Brahms made a concerted effort to soften her expression as they reentered the two-story police station. The half-dozen Tellarite officers in the waiting room regarded them warily as they approached the desk, and the big proctor snorted and tugged on his bristling orange beard.

"I thought I told you to leave?" he said gruffly.

"Our visitor . . . she thinks she may know Consul Maltz," answered Bekra quickly.

The big Tellarite smiled and glanced at his fellows. "She thinks she knows Maltz? Why does *that* not surprise me?"

"Listen," said Bekra, leaning across the desk and lowering his voice, "when the magistrate gets here, I'll make it easy on everyone by vouching for Maltz and paying any fines."

"Oh, he's not getting out of here so easy," said the proctor with satisfaction. "He attacked three constables and tore up a peaceful gathering. I've got a dozen witnesses who say it was his fault, and we'd like to teach that big oaf a lesson."

"I doubt if he even knew he was fighting three constables," answered the Capellan. "Can't you let her see him for a moment? I'll go with her."

"Why should I?"

"Because I'd be willing to take Maltz away from here," answered Leah forcefully. "Take him clear off the planet, out of your hands."

The Tellarite considered that for a moment, then pointed a chubby finger at her. "You'd better not get him riled up." He motioned to one of his underlings. "Let them in. Ten minutes, no more."

"Yes, Sir." A constable motioned to them, and Leah and Bekra dutifully followed. He opened a door, and they entered a room that seemed even more clammy and oppressive than the waiting room, due to its windowless, earthen walls. It was unusually cool in here, too, and Leah shivered and hugged her arms. The four small cells were all empty, except for the one on the end, wherein stood a tall, wild-eyed, bushy-haired Klingon, glaring at them.

He was grizzled and old, but he also looked defiant and vibrantly alive, like a wild animal kept in a zoo. The Klingon cautiously approached the door, shimmering with a force-field barrier, as Leah Brahms warily approached him.

"Did you see it?" he rasped.

"What is it?" she asked dubiously. "Describe it."

His big hands gestured in the air and his eyes blazed with the remembrance of a tale he had been told, or perhaps a tape he had seen. "It sweeps across the land like a burning curtain, ripping up every-thing. But it leaves new life—strange life—growing in its place. There are geysers, a terrible wind, mountains shooting up, awful things . . . growing in the muck."

"Yes! Yes! What is it?" she gasped. At last she would know that nameless force that killed her husband and colleagues.

The Klingon glanced suspiciously at the Capellan, who was lean-ing against the wall near the door. "I should not tell you. Your own government considers it top secret."

Leah gaped at him. "Are you telling me that *we* invented this thing? That it's *artificial?*"

"Is it a weapon?" asked Bekra, suddenly interested.

"It did not start out that way," the Klingon answered enigmatically. "You say, they set it off on Seran?"

"Nobody set it off . . . I don't think." Leah shook her head, unable to believe this explanation. "What you described sounds right, but this was an energy wave—moving through space. It hit Seran and all of her moons, and it's coming right this way, expanding as it goes."

"Moving through space," said Maltz, scratching his long white beard. "Maybe they improved it."

"Who is *they*?" demanded Leah. "Who controls this thing?"

"You do!" growled the Klingon. "You are the only ones who know the technology."

Leah's shoulders slumped, and the scowl returned to her face. "You're wrong. Nobody would unleash this against their own people. Like they say, maybe you *are* crazy."

The old Klingon howled with laughter, then he held up a tri-umphant finger, his eyes blazing. "I know the code word—what your people called this device many years ago. The Klingon High Council has our reports, but we never learned how to make it. All this time, I have *feared* it would be used again, and now it has."

"Ridiculous!" snapped Leah, marching toward the door. "Get me out of here, Bekra. He is mad."

"Mad?" said the Klingon, stifling a laugh. "Such great power you have never seen, have you? Such a force for change you have never seen. It takes matter and *guts* it, leaving behind something chaotic and loathsome."

Leah turned again and stared at the wild Klingon. If he hadn't seen it, then he had seen something eerily close. But the notion that this horror might be an invention fostered by her own government—a weapon—was repulsive in the extreme.

The door opened, and Maltz yelled one more thing. "How much time do we have?"

"A few hours," she answered, pausing in the doorway. "Maybe ten. Maybe one."

At that, the Klingon grew somber and gaunt, and Leah could see desperation and fear working in his rheumy eyes. It was the same desperation and fear that she felt churning in her stomach. She didn't want to believe him any more than the Tellarites wanted to believe her, but at that moment, she feared the old Klingon spoke the truth.


"The performance was lovely," gushed Dolores Linton, shaking Data's outstretched hand. The android was dressed in tuxedo and tails and looked very dapper, thought La Forge. Despite the high spirits at the end of the performance, most of the audience dispersed swiftly from the Antares Theater on deck fifteen. It was as if everyone realized their mission had assumed an element of the unknown, and they had better stay close to their posts.

Geordi wanted to escape quickly, too, but Dolores Linton wanted to stay behind and congratulate Data. To people who had never heard the violin played to weeping perfection, a performance by Data was sheer magic. Geordi was fortunate enough to have heard him play many times. Although he wanted to get back to the bridge, he couldn't deny his friend a chance to hear a new fan tell him how wonderful he was. Geordi tried not to fidget, but the recital had lasted longer than he expected. Plus Data had been forced to take a curtain call, captain's prerogative.

"And your sustains are sublime," said the vivacious geologist as she studied Data's hands. "Your finger strength must be phenomenal. I bet you could do anything you wanted to do with these hands."

"When I first started," said the android, "I broke many strings. The fragility of the violin is a large part of its appeal."

"Yes, you have to handle fragile things with care," replied Dolores, gently stroking Data's palm.

"You should see his paintings," added Geordi, just trying to enter into the flow of the small talk.

"I would like to," answered the geologist, sounding in awe of the android.

"Another time," replied Data with a pointed nod to Geordi as he withdrew his hand and backed off.

Thankfully, there were only a handful of well-wishers left, and Geordi could edge toward the door without feeling guilty. "I'd like to give you that tour I promised," he began slowly, "but we don't know what we're getting into."

"Duty calls," said Dolores, shaking her pert brown hair and flexing a sizable bicep. "I really appreciate your bringing me to hear Data play. I wouldn't have come otherwise. I probably just would've sat in my room, stewing over the messed-up schedule."

"What is our delay going to mean to you?" asked Geordi as they strolled down the corridor.

"We were already on a tight schedule, and if we can't get done with Itamish III in eight weeks, then the team is going to have to delay another start. Then another. And we're booked a year in advance." Dolores smiled and batted her eyes playfully. "We're real popular."

"I can see that," said Geordi, reaching the turbolift and holding it for her. They stepped inside, and he added, "We hardly ever know what we're doing two months from now, or even two days from now. We're always in scramble mode."

The turbolift door shut, and Dolores said, "Level six." Then she turned to Geordi and smiled warmly. "Thank you for a great evening."

"I'm sorry it has to end so soon," he answered apologetically.

"Does it have to end so soon?" Dolores asked pointedly. "I heard them say that we're not going to reach the area for about ten hours."

"Uh, yes," stammered Geordi. "That's true." The door opened, and Dolores gave him a sly smile and stepped out. La Forge took a gulp of air and followed the sauntering figure in the skintight black dress.

She led the way to her quarters, letting him trail along behind her like a puppy dog. Since he didn't know what to say to her, he didn't catch up until she had reached her door. Then she turned to him, not with a sultry look but with doe-eyed sympathy.

"You know," said Dolores softly, touching his cheek, "there's something very appealing about a man in love . . . with someone else." She raised an eyebrow. "I hope she's worth all the anguish you're going through, worrying about her. Good night, Geordi. Thanks for the lovely evening."

Her hand touching his cheek wasn't exactly a kiss, but it felt like one as she pulled her fingertips away.

"I could check with the bridge," said Geordi uncertainly.

"Good night. Just don't forget my tour." With a whoosh of the door sliding shut, Dolores Linton was gone.

Geordi immediately hit his combadge. "La Forge to bridge."

"Riker here," came the answer.

"Have there been any developments?"

"Well, one small one," answered the first officer. "In addition to the other distress signal, we're now picking up a Capellan distress signal from a planet named Hakon. We're changing course now, because it's not much out of our way."

"Changing course?" asked Geordi with alarm. "I thought we were headed to Outpost Seran-T-One." He began charging down the corridor.

"It's on the edge of sector 4368," answered Riker. "There isn't a lot of traffic out here, so we've got to follow these distress signals, now that they've converged. They're our only clue that something's wrong."

La Forge bit his lip, knowing that he couldn't argue with his superior, and Riker read the silence perfectly. "Don't worry, Geordi, we'll find out what's going on. I've got Data on ops running ten times as many scans as you can, and I really don't need you on the bridge. Isn't there somewhere else you can go?"

The engineer stopped and looked back down the corridor at Dolores Linton's door. He took a deep breath and finally said, "I promise I won't pace too much."

"Okay, see you on the bridge. Riker out."

His brow furrowed with worry, the chief engineer strode toward the turbolift. He could almost hear Data berating him for his hapless handling of Mission Specialist Linton. This was all just one more reason to regret his obsession with Leah Brahms, an obsession Data could never understand.

# seven

"Here's your shopping list," said Leah Brahms, handing a padd to her comrade, Paldor, who stood outside the open hatch of the shuttlecraft. "If we can get these parts, I think we can fix the comm array."

Looking dismayed, the young Tellarite glanced at her and then at the gawkers who surrounded the vacant field where they had landed. Three of them were constables in red-and-white checked uniforms, and he lowered his voice to say, "I don't know where to begin. I doubt if they have *half* this stuff."

"Come on, they're your people, and you wanted to come here," Leah reminded him, instantly regretting her testiness. "It may be a farming community, but they're still part of the Federation. Ask around. I saw some sophisticated gear for monitoring the weather, so they must have antennas and dish arrays. We've also seen replicators."

"And money? What am I supposed to use for money?" asked the Tellarite skeptically.

Leah pointed to the screen of the handheld padd. "I have a blank purchase order right there on behalf of the Science Service. They should honor it anywhere in the Federation."

The Tellarite's orange beard bristled. "But this hasn't been requisitioned. That's illegal."

"You and I are probably already presumed dead," said Leah through clenched teeth. "Chances are we're really going to be dead unless we get some help. Now get me the stuff on that list."

"Yes, Doctor," said the Tellarite, recoiling from her gaze. He took a few steps from the shuttlecraft but turned back to her, pain etched in his small, black eyes. "I can't stand to talk to them . . . knowing they're all going to die."

"I know it's hard," admitted Leah. "Maybe your calculations were wrong, and it'll miss here."

"No," said Paldor grimly. "But even if they believed us, I don't know what they could do on such short notice."

"Just get our stuff," ordered Brahms, growing exasperated. She didn't want to be cold to the plight of these people, but she had seen her husband and friends perish in the consuming flame. Strangers were important, but she had no emotions left to grieve for them. Maybe living their last day in ignorant bliss instead of panic was a blessing.

"I'll be back as soon as I can," said Paldor. He hurried off, taking with him two of the constables, who followed at a discreet distance.

Leah couldn't worry about that now, because her associate's departure would finally let her try something she'd been eager to do. She hurried back into the shuttlecraft and shut the door behind her, blocking out the prying eyes surrounding the field. Then she sat at the pilot's console and ran a sensor scan of the constable station a couple of blocks away. She wanted to see if she could locate the Klingon in his cell, or at least find the force-field that marked his door. Then she would get a lock on him with the transporter.

No such luck. Surrounding the entire station was a dampening field, making it impossible to beam people in or out. These folks weren't the hayseeds they appeared, and she had to forget about pulling off a painless jailbreak. Although the dampening field worked against her, it wouldn't do anything to stop the monstrous force headed their way.

It would, however, keep her from getting easy access to the Klingon and whatever he knew. So all she could do now was watch the sensors and the darkening sky, wondering how much time they really had left.

Maltz paced in his cell, suddenly more sober than he had been in the last fifty years. All he knew was that he had to get out of this place and help that poor, deluded human. He should have helped her more when she was standing in front of him, but if she persisted in thinking it was a natural disaster, then she was a bigger fool than those fat constables. They had to be honest about what they were fighting. Like most objects of true horror, the Genesis Device was artificially designed.

But who had control of it now? Who had turned it into an energy wave that could sweep across space? One thing was certain: he wasn't

going to get any answers sitting in this cell. He had to get out of here—
or he'd be left to die like a caged animal.

Unfortunately, Maltz knew how long it took to roust the magistrate, if they even knew which bars to search. He glanced around at the
brown earthen walls and shimmering force-field, realizing he had to
arrange his own release. The Klingon had thought about breaking out
of here before, but his rashness was always tempered by the knowledge that he would have to deal with these people the next day. Now
there would be no tomorrow.

Although they had taken his knife, they had left him with his cere-
monial chain-mail sash, not knowing what a treasure trove a Klingon's
sash could be. He surveyed the room again, thinking those rustic walls
and ceiling could house video-log equipment. But he decided that even
if they were recording him, he was the only prisoner, and they probably weren't paying very much attention. Besides, he would look as if
he were repairing his clothing, and it certainly needed it, after that
brawl.

Maltz removed his sash at the same time that he removed his
cloak. He wanted to look as if he were just getting comfortable,
preparing to stay for a while. He sat on his cot and hunched his broad
back, trying to shut off their view, while he turned over his sash and
unsnapped the back lining. From hidden crevices and folds, he drew
forth his arsenal: three small throwing daggers, a garrote and fishing
line, a stiletto, a vial of deadly poison, a vial of acid, a wad of gel
explosive, knuckle armor, lockpicks, sewing kit, Klingon communicator badge, and five strips of latinum.

The last object he withdrew was a small signal mirror, only it
wouldn't be used for signaling today. Carefully he returned all the
other objects to their hiding places, except for the explosives, the mirror, and the armor to fortify his knuckles.

Maltz palmed these objects while he put his cloak and sash back
on. Then he strolled over to the door of his cell and bent down, as if
fixing something on his boot. In his experience, every force-field had
blind spots near the edge, between the field emitters. These blind spots
were only a few centimeters across, which didn't do a normal-sized
person a lot of good. But Maltz also knew that a force-field wall was
actually thousands of criss-crossing beams, and that a beam reflected
back onto itself caused all sorts of havoc.

Using his knuckle armor, he slowly pushed the mirror across the
floor, probing for a blind spot between the emitters. The mirror
bounced off the shimmering barrier a few times, but each time he

caught it in midair and patiently tried again. Finally he succeeded in slipping the reflective glass under the pulsing shield, and he gave a satisfied grunt. Now penetration in the right spot would change the direction of the beams just enough that they would strike the mirror on the floor and be deflected upward. When that happened, the force-field would be attacking itself.

He couldn't conceal what he would do next, but if he moved quickly enough, perhaps his jailers wouldn't notice. He ran to his cot and grabbed his threadbare mattress. Holding it in front of him like a battering ram, the Klingon gritted his teeth and charged the door of his cell. The mattress hit the force-field and was propelled back into his face, but the Klingon kept charging forward as a lightning bolt rippled across the doorway. With a burst of smoke and sparks, the force-field imploded, and the shimmering curtain blinked erratically. Maltz's momentum carried him and the mattress through the opening into a heap on the floor. He was free—then a siren screamed directly over his head.

Maltz leaped to his feet, slipping the knuckle armor over his fist just as the outer door opened. The first one through happened to be the haughty proctor, and he received a crushing blow straight to the snout that sent him reeling into the wall. Before the big Tellarite even hit the floor, the Klingon had ripped the disruptor from his holster, and he sent a wild beam streaking through the outer doorway—just to keep the others at bay.

Maltz quickly slammed the outer door shut and propped the Tellarite's unconscious body against it. He chuckled at the shouting and commotion outside in the waiting room, and he ignored them when they began to demand that he give himself up.

"You can't get past us!" they shouted.

He had no intentions of going past them. Gingerly, he retrieved his mirror from the doorway of the cell, which was attempting to return to normal. With his newly acquired disruptor, he drilled a small hole about waist-high in a wall which abutted the outdoors. The Klingon stuffed his tiny wad of gel explosive into the hole he had made, then stepped back. With steely-eyed fearlessness, he adjusted the disruptor to maximum and blasted the charge he had planted.

The resulting explosion rocked the neighborhood and sent a cloud of dust and debris spewing twenty meters into the air. It also blew open a hole in the wall about a meter across, through which staggered a bedraggled Klingon, his clothes and facial hair still smoldering. With shouts and whistles, concerned citizens began converging on the smoky site, and Maltz had to shake himself off and run for it. He covered his head with his cloak, hoping no one would be able to give a good description of him.

As he rounded a corner and dashed down a side street, Maltz tried to figure out where he could go or what he could do. He had to find the strange woman and her shuttlecraft, that much was sure. But he didn't know where she was, and he couldn't very well start asking; in fact, he had to stay out of sight, if possible. The constables would really be after him now.

As the Klingon staggered into the shadows and slumped behind a trash vaporizer, he remembered someone who knew where she was. His old colleague, Consul Bekra. If he knew the Capellan, he was probably taking measures to save his own skin. That would mean a trip to the hangar where he kept his shuttlecraft.

"Urgh, why don't I have a shuttlecraft like everyone else?" muttered the old Klingon. He knew the reason—they didn't trust him with one.

Maltz unfolded the hood from his cloak and pulled it over his head, hoping to hide his head ridges and shock of hair. But he glanced at himself in his signal mirror and realized it wasn't enough, so he took the sewing kit from his sash. Using a pair of small scissors and the mirror, he clipped off most of his distinctive beard and moustache. A lot of it was singed, anyway, and it wasn't hair that made a Klingon.

Now when he looked at himself in the mirror, he looked sufficiently different to fool people at a glance. With a groan, Maltz dragged himself to his feet and wrapped the cloak around his gaunt frame. He had a long walk through back streets to reach the shuttle hangar, but at least the sky was darkening. Soon it would be night on this part of Hakon.

Rubbing her arms in the suddenly chill air, Leah Brahms stepped out of the shuttlecraft and looked at the crimson clouds backlighting the skyline. Light shifted on the earthen walls of the rustic dwellings, making them look like an eroded slope deep in the desert; and for the first time, Leah appreciated the naturalistic architecture. However, she wasn't too thrilled about the idea of night falling in this quaint village.

That was silly, because the awful force which chased them moved almost too swiftly to be seen. Still, she didn't want it to sneak up on her in the darkness. With a gulp, the scientist stepped closer to the open hatch of the shuttlecraft, so that she could hear the sensor alert she had programmed. Once the wave came within sensor range, they would only have a few minutes. How many minutes, it was anyone's guess.

A furry animal about the size of a goat strolled through the vacant lot, a bell ringing from its collar. It stopped to consider her for a moment, then shook its bell and walked on. She had noticed a decline in the presence of the onlookers, who had probably gone home to eat the food she smelled wafting on the breeze. The police presence was still high, hovering around six or seven ever since that explosion an hour ago. No one had explained what the explosion was about, but it had obviously cast suspicion upon the doomsayers.

Leah figured even more constables were following Paldor, who had yet to return from his shopping trip. This was bad, because she didn't know if they could effect repairs before they had to run for it. The Tellarite had checked in via combadge to say that he was making progress, albeit slowly, but that wasn't much consolation. She still couldn't do anything but wait, and Leah had never been good at waiting.

Leah glanced inside the shuttlecraft at the radiation suit, hulking silently in the rear. She didn't want to put it on again, but that gnawing, mindless drive for survival was urging her to don the suit. But to put on the suit meant that she had given up and was willing to watch another planet die. Besides, she needed full dexterity to pilot the shuttlecraft, because if they lost the shuttlecraft, there would be no escape at all. No way to warn anyone else. At the moment, the shuttlecraft and the data they had collected were more important than anything.

*I'll have enough warning*, Leah told herself, not really believing it was true. She stepped inside the shuttlecraft and shut the door, blocking out the crimson sunset that was bathing the mud-colored street in a warm glow.

As Maltz pushed open the window, which he had unlocked with his lockpicks, he could smell the scent of something burning. Choking smoke didn't fill the cavernous shuttlecraft hangar, but he could see light at the far end of the building, silhouetting a dozen boxy shuttlecraft. In fact, that was the only light in the whole building, now that night had fallen. He sniffed again, deciding that *something* was burning at the far end of the building.

As he stalked through the dark hangar, moving from one shuttlecraft to another, the Klingon drew his disruptor from his belt. There were windows on every wall, but the only light came from a work light hanging in the far corner, illuminating a shuttlecraft with its hatch open. It looked like somebody was packing to leave.

He drew closer, keeping to the shadows. To no surprise, it was the Capellan consul, Bekra, and he was burning papers, transparencies, and isolinear chips in a trash receptacle, where he had a considerable fire going. Bekra wasn't dressed in his usual finery, but instead wore a simple black jumpsuit as well as his ubiquitous turban. Duffel bags and boxes of gear sat outside the hatch, ready to be loaded into the waiting shuttlecraft.

"Going somewhere?" asked Maltz, stepping out of the shadows. He kept the disruptor trained on his old colleague.

"Ahh!" shouted Bekra with alarm, having been taken by surprise. He squinted into the wavering light, uncertain who the hooded visitor was. "Is that you, Maltz?"

The old Klingon scratched the stubble on his chin and grinned. "Makes me look younger, I think."

The Capellan laughed nervously. "You don't need that weapon, my old friend. If you want to escape with me in my shuttlecraft, that's no problem. But I have to warn you—I don't have warp drive. I'm thinking that if I leave now, I can get out of the path of that thing . . . if it's really out there."

"It is really out there," said Maltz, stepping toward the small bonfire. "What are you burning up in that can?"

"Oh, nothing of interest," said Bekra, edging toward the open hatch of his shuttlecraft.

"Stop there," ordered the Klingon, aiming his weapon at the Capellan's chest. "Just so you know, I never set weapons to stun. So who have you been spying for all these years?"

"Spying?" Bekra forced a laugh. "You are getting melodramatic in your old age."

Maltz smiled wistfully and kicked the trash can over, spilling its flaming contents on the floor of the hangar. Hoping he was distracted, Bekra bolted for the hatch of his shuttlecraft, but Maltz drilled him in the leg, shearing it off just below the knee. Howling with pain, the Capellan dropped to the floor and writhed, gripping his burnt stump.

He screamed incoherently, while Maltz carefully picked through the smoldering debris.

"I always suspected you," said the Klingon. "Too much brains for this post—you had to have ambitions."

"The first-aid kit!" sputtered the Capellan, twisting in agony.

"You will not die," said the Klingon, scoffing at him. "Unless I have to shoot you again. Now who do you spy for?"

Without warning, the windows all around the enormous hangar

imploded, showering them with debris; and a ferocious wind ripped half the corrugated roof off the building, revealing a blazing field of stars in the sky.

The wind churned through the metal cavern, whipping the burning embers from the fire into a glowing funnel cloud. Maltz rocked unsteadily on his feet, while Bekra cried out with fear and rolled under his shuttlecraft.

"The wind!" roared Maltz, holding his ears and gaping at the hole in the roof. *"The wind!"*

# eight

Leah Brahms felt the shuttlecraft shake as if it were being vandalized by a mob of hooligans. That was her first thought—that the citizens of Hakon had attacked her for some stupid reason. She punched her board to open the hatch, bolted to her feet, and charged outside, ready to give them hell. Instead she was met by an icy blast of wind—so frigid, it was like being in the Antarctic. It staggered her, and she felt the skin of her face stiffening. She looked up, expecting to see the worst, but the starlit sky was so brilliant that it was like viewing it from space. The distant moon seemed to have a strobe light on it.

She had heard of it getting colder at night in some places, but this was ridiculous. As she shivered and tried to stand her ground in the freezing wind, she noticed that the Tellarites and constables were also running for cover. Their vacant lot was suddenly deserted, and there was a frightened buzzing sound, as if the populace were crying with alarm. This wasn't normal weather.

She ducked back inside the shuttlecraft and shut the hatch, at the same moment that her sensor alarm went off. Without even checking what it was, Leah started the transporter sequence to lock onto Paldor's combadge and bring him back to their tiny refuge, which was shuddering like a grass shack in a hurricane.

The Tellarite appeared on the small transporter pad at the back of the craft, his arms full of dishes and electronic parts, which dropped to the deck as he shivered uncontrollably. "What's . . . happening?" he asked, barely getting the words out.

Leah studied her readouts, and her eyes grew wide with fright. "Oh, my God! The wave attacked the sun first, and it's eating its way around it. This solar system could be without a sun!"

"Will we start to go out of orbit?" asked Paldor, dropping the rest of the spare parts and dashing up the aisle.

Leah shook her head in frustration. "Who knows? The sun should maintain its mass, and it might even remain a star—but what kind of star? Anyway, it will hit us soon. We've got to get out of here."

"But all these people!" said Paldor.

"If you want to stay here and die with them, get out now," said Brahms coldly. "Otherwise, sit down and prepare for launch."

His face ashen, the Tellarite slid into his seat beside her. But he didn't do anything to prepare for launch; he just stared at the blank front screen, weeping. Leah put everything else out of her mind as she plotted a course for the heart of the Federation and set the computer to work on compensating for the wind.

Moments later, the shuttlecraft roared out of the vacant lot, streaking over the tops of the earthen buildings, which were already beginning to crack and fall apart from the extreme cold and gravitational changes. In a panic, people rushed into the street, only to be blasted by the wind and flying debris. There wasn't anything anyone could do for them now, thought Leah grimly.


"I feel alive!" bellowed the old Klingon, shaking his fists into the savage wind as it wreaked havoc in the shuttlecraft hangar. Nothing was left of the roof, and the air was cold and bracing, like a firm slap to the face. Maltz stood tall against the debris which pelted him, shouting down the wind.

"Yes, you Genesis Wave . . . you're a worthy adversary! Come and get me."

The wind was trying to get him, but he wouldn't go down without a fight. His jaw set with determination, Maltz strode toward the shuttlecraft just as a blue phaser beam streaked past him, tearing a hole in his cloak. He ducked down and zigzagged in a crouch, dodging streaks as Bekra continued to shoot wildly at him. Maltz finally reached the injured Capellan and kicked the phaser out of his hand.

"Stop being a pet Q!" shouted the Klingon over the din. "I hate these Federation toadies and all they stand for, so I do not care who your masters are! But you tell me what you have done, or I will leave you here. Understood?"

"Romulans," said Bekra, lowering his head. "I send dispatches to the Romulans. It started out innocently enough, when I—"

Maltz smacked him across the face, setting off another round of whimpering. Then he spit on the Capellan and said, "Romulans! I should kill you, anyway. But you brought the human to me, and she gave me the warning."

The old Klingon pointed a crooked finger into the howling wind. "Somewhere out there is an enemy worse than any we have ever faced. To have unleashed this weapon on us . . . they are worse than the Borg or the Dominion."

But Bekra was too busy whimpering and clutching his cauterized stump, so Maltz heaved a sigh, grabbed the injured consul, and threw him into his own shuttlecraft. He threw in a few of his bags and boxes for good measure, but he left most of them behind.

The Klingon climbed aboard the shuttlecraft and sat at the controls, cracking his knuckles. He had flown similar vessels many times—there was nothing to it. Most shuttlecraft hadn't changed much in a hundred years, and this one in particular looked old-fashioned. Maybe Bekra wasn't as important as he thought he was, having only this pathetic vessel with no warp capability.

He went into a vertical launch and zoomed straight up through the torn roof of the massive hangar. Paying no attention to the instruments, the Klingon punched the membrane board repeatedly until he got the craft to keep going up. There was no subtlety in this launch—it was thrusters blasting against the monstrous wind, with the craft straining and creaking to gain every centimeter in altitude. Finally they broke through the stratosphere of the planet into calm sailing, spiraling upward at a breakneck speed.

As they reached their maximum impulse speed, which was more suited to continent hopping than solar-system hopping, he turned on the sensors to take a look around.

The first thing he picked up was a distress signal about four thousand kilometers ahead of him, and he locked onto the signal and used it for a course heading. Ignoring Bekra's moans and heartfelt pleas for assistance, Maltz opened several Federation frequencies and broadcast on all of them.

"Hello, fellow shuttlecraft," he said jovially. "This is Consul Maltz and Consul Bekra on Bekra's shuttlecraft. We have escaped from the planet, but we do not have warp drive."

"That's too bad," came the woman's unfriendly response, accompanied by static. "The wave is working its way through the sun in this solar system, and we don't have a lot of time. I may save your worthless hides, but you'll have to play by *my* rules."

The Klingon grunted with distaste at having to be tactful to a human. "You could put a tractor beam on us, and both ships could go into warp."

"Listen to me, Maltz—I'm the only one who has warp drive, so your shuttlecraft is worthless. Unless you'd care to face that demon behind us, you'll do exactly as I say. I've got shields up, and I'll leave you here unless you give me your word that I'm the commander."

The Klingon clenched his teeth and grunted, although his admiration for this human woman had soared tremendously.

"Take the deal!" rasped Bekra, writhing on the deck.

"I agree," said Maltz, bowing his head and slamming his fist to his chest. "I pledge to follow your command if we unite crews. But I must report to a Klingon base as soon as possible."

"Fine with me," answered Leah. "I think it's a little grandiose to say we're 'uniting crews,' but—" Her voice broke up in a crackle of static.

"We have interference," said Maltz.

After several moments of useless noise, her voice came back forcefully. "I've stopped. We only have short-range communications, and the anomaly is affecting it. Lower your shields and prepare to transport."

"All my gear . . . my records," said Bekra, suddenly alarmed at the finality of what they were doing.

The Klingon scowled as he punched the board. "Your deeds in the next few days will mean more than anything you've done before. We're going to go down in history, my friend . . . if there is any history after this."

One at a time, their bodies turned into shimmering columns of suspended molecules, only to disappear entirely, while the empty shuttlecraft hurtled toward its doom.

Captain Picard paced within the circle of workstations on the bridge of the *Enterprise*, trying not to show his concern. They weren't making any headway—this process was moving too slowly over too vast an area. They were on the defensive, waiting. And he never liked to wait.

La Forge looked up from his engineering console and said, "Captain, the planet Hakon is sending all kinds of distress signals and subspace chatter. Something must be happening there."

"I concur," said Data on ops. "We are picking up unusual readings from solar system SY-911 on long-range sensors. It appears the sun in that solar system is in distress."

"Distress?" asked Captain Picard curiously, taking a step toward Data's station. "It is going nova? Dark corona syndrome?"

Data shook his head. "No, Sir. The sun appears to be decreasing rapidly in temperature and size—among other radical changes. It is oscillating and emitting variable gravity waves and solar winds, which must be affecting the planets in the solar system. These readings are troubling, because there is no recognized phenomenon that would cause them. One thing is certain—unless the inhabitants of Hakon have a reliable shelter system, they are not going to survive the drastic changes in climate."

Picard gritted his teeth and looked at the concerned faces all around him. "How many inhabitants?"

"Eight million, Sir, most of them Tellarites," answered Data. "The colony was settled on agrarian principles and has relatively small population centers spread out over one large continent."

"Captain!" called La Forge with urgency in his voice. "Most of the messages from Hakon have now stopped, although we're still getting distress signals from a few ships in the area . . . freighters and shuttlecraft."

The captain stepped toward the tactical station, where a pale Antosian, Ensign Coltak, busily worked the board. "Did you try to answer their hails?"

"Yes, Sir," answered Coltak, sounding frustrated, "but they haven't responded. There's a great deal of interference, but we captured what we could before the channels went dead."

"ETA, Mister Data?" asked Picard, helplessness gnawing in the pit of his stomach.

"Two hours and twenty-three minutes before we reach the solar system," answered the android.

Picard's shoulders slumped as he turned toward the tactical station. "Mister Coltak, it would appear that we have time to view some of those messages from Hakon. Maybe we can get an idea what we're facing."

"A thing that can blight a star," answered the Antosian in amazement as he studied his readouts. "I'm sorry, Sir, I'll start isolating the messages."

"That's all right, Ensign," said the captain, knowing how he felt.

A few moments later, the main viewscreen blinked on, showing what appeared to be the interior of a spaceport. A few panicked people dashed across the screen, covering their heads from flying debris. The walls and ceiling of the building appeared to be crumbling all around them, and wind ripped the furnishings. Finally a frightened Tellarite staggered in front of the chaotic scene; although he was large, he was shivering uncontrollably, and Picard could see his icy breath.

"Dispatcher Makolis from Cloud Spaceport on Hakon . . . calling whoever's out there!" shrieked the Tellarite, his voice barely audible over the ferocious din. "Something is happening . . . strange weather, without warning. Help us, please!"

The distraught Tellarite went on, begging futilely for help, but Picard barely listened, he was so deep in thought. "They did have warning," he said to himself. "Somebody went all the way there from Seran to warn them, but it didn't do any good."

Suddenly a mass of debris fell upon their poor commentator, and the screen went blank. "Bringing up another one," said Ensign Coltak without comment.

Now they saw a Ferengi on the bridge of his vessel, gripping the captain's chair as his ship was rocked back and forth by some mysterious force. His eyes were wide with fear as he stared down at them from the viewscreen. "Mayday! Mayday! Captain Baldoru on the freighter *Rich Prize*, and we're under attack!"

One of his crew members shouted something to him, and the Ferengi seemed to reconsider, despite the obvious pounding his craft was taking. "We're not under attack, but . . . we don't know what it is. Temperatures falling, gravity fluctuating—it's some kind of natural disaster! We've got to try to lift off the planet." He waved frantically at his subordinates. "Eject cargo!"

There was a flurry of activity and barked orders as the frightened Ferengi crew tried to get their launch together. Picard felt his hands balling into fists as he watched the dramatic effort, because he had a bad feeling it was not going to turn out well.

"Full thrusters! Manual launch at one-quarter impulse." The Ferengi captain looked with hope and confidence at his helmsman, who intently worked his board. Interference streaked the image on the viewscreen, and the freighter shuddered mightily as it tried to lift off. Picard imagined that they were on a giant outdoor landing pad, thrusters lifting them upward like a big helicopter.

"Stabilizers weakening!" yelled the ops officer.

"Divert emergency power to shields," ordered the captain.

Picard drew a sharp intake of breath, thinking that *he* would divert all power to thrusters. They were either going to get off the ground or they weren't—worry about damage later. "Altitude," he said softly, rooting for them.

"We're hitting solar winds!" called a voice a second before the image on the viewscreen disappeared in a slash of static. Just before the scene faded to complete darkness, they heard the screams of the Ferengi crew, forming a dissonant chorus of death.

Silence commanded the bridge of the *Enterprise* for several seconds until Ensign Coltak softly asked, "Do you want to see more, Captain?"

Picard shook his head grimly. "Not at the moment. Even though someone went to Hakon to warn them, the message never got through."

"These records are consistent with the expected results of a failing sun," said Data. "Which should not have happened in this solar system for another three billion years."

"What could transform a star like that?" asked Geordi, peering at his readouts. "It's still there—it hasn't been blasted apart—but it's a lot different. A yellow giant turned into a red dwarf."

Data cocked his head curiously. "Long-range sensors show another planet in that system which does not match the description we have for it. SY-911 Alpha, closest planet to the sun, is supposed to be Class-H, but now it is Class-L, bordering on -M. It has an oxidizing atmosphere that it never had before."

"Are you sure about that?" asked Picard doubtfully. "Could it be an error in the readings?"

"Possibly," admitted the android, "but the data from the sun appear to be consistent with what we have seen on Hakon. I agree, these readings are so unusual as to be questionable."

"Forward all of this data to Admiral Nechayev," ordered Picard. "Maybe she can make something out of it."

"Let's do a long-range scan of Seran," said La Forge, grimly plying his console. "We'll see if we get more weird readings."

Weird readings or not, thought Picard, there were beings out there dying by the millions, perhaps the billions. Not just highly intelligent beings but animals, birds, fish, microbes—ecosystems vanishing in the blink of an eye. It would be nice to pin it all on interference and erroneous sensor readings, but in his mind he could still hear that Ferengi crew screaming.

# nine

From the cockpit of her shuttlecraft, Leah Brahms looked around at her motley crew, consisting of a Tellarite who would not stop crying, a Capellan who was suddenly missing a leg without any explanation, and a grizzled Klingon who hummed happily to himself as he gazed out a side viewport. Maltz seemed more clean-cut, too, and a few years younger, although his regal clothes were a wreck.

She had let everybody just find a seat and get comfortable while she plotted the course of the deadly wave. *Straight into the Federation, just like us. Only it's expanding and going faster, and we're not.* Without explaining it to anyone, Leah put the shuttlecraft into warp drive.

"How fast is her top speed?" asked Maltz, recognizing the change.

"Warp two, although I can get it close to three if I override our safeties." Leah wasn't eager for any conversation when her own thoughts were so heavy, but she recognized the need to communicate with this pathetic lot of survivors. "Paldor, will you do some first-aid on Consul Bekra? He's being stoic, but I think he's in pain."

The Tellarite sniffed and let out a sob that got caught several times in his throat. "Can you believe it? All of them *dead*. And us helpless! Oh, what was I thinking?" He began to blubber anew.

"We're all suffering," said Leah through clenched teeth, "but we've got a job to do—"

"What?" shrieked the Tellarite. "Flying somewhere else where they won't believe us . . . or move quickly enough? So we can watch this happen all over again!"

Behind them, Maltz muttered, "We've got to find out who set it off."

"What does he mean?" asked Paldor in confusion. "Who set *what* off?"

His turban askew, Bekra shifted in his seat and let out a groan. "Maltz has a theory that this is some sort of weapon. He has talked about a similar thing in the past." The Capellan grimaced. "I could use some of that first-aid, by the way."

When Paldor didn't move, Leah sighed wearily. "Maltz, can you pilot this shuttlecraft?"

"Aye, Captain," answered the Klingon, rising to his feet. "They're all the same. You learn one ship—you learn them all. I once knew a handful of humans who figured out how to fly a bird-of-prey."

"You really don't have to do anything," said Leah. "We're on course under computer control. Just watch the readouts for anything unusual."

"What about me?" asked Paldor, sounding hurt. "I could do that."

"When you get yourself together, maybe you will." Leah rose to her feet, feeling the lack of sleep and the overabundance of adrenaline and grief. She grabbed the first-aid kit from the locker and sat down to minister to Bekra's burnt stump of a leg.

"How did this happen?" she finally asked.

The Capellan grumbled, "I lost an argument to somebody who was a better shot."

Leah glanced pointedly at Maltz, sitting in the pilot's seat, but the consul's face remained stoic. She prepared a hypospray. "This will kill the pain."

"I'm going to need a lot of it to kill *all* the pain," replied the Capellan with a grim smile.

"I hear you," answered Leah softly. She put gloves on her hands and took a prepared dressing and a tube of antibiotic ointment from the kit. Thankfully, she wouldn't need the medical tricorder or surgical tools, because the wound had been cauterized by the disruptor.

"What about *this* planet?" asked Maltz from the front. "Pelleus V. It is on our way, and they have thirty-four million inhabitants. We could be there in six hours."

"You weren't supposed to do anything but watch the readouts," answered Leah testily.

"That planet isn't even in the Federation," said Paldor, glancing over his shoulder.

The Klingon scratched the white stubble on his chin and chuckled. "So you can let them *die* if they are not in the Federation? Hmmm, you people are more practical than I thought."

"We're doing the best we can!" snapped Paldor. "How would *you* save them?"

"I was only looking for a Class-M planet where we could set down and fix the communications array," answered Maltz. "We need to get help. It just so happens that the nearest place is inhabited; and by the graph you are running, I can see it is in the direct path of the wave."

"I saw the planet," answered Leah Brahms as she finished dressing Bekra's wound. "You should get some sleep," she told the Capellan.

"Thank you, I'll try," he promised.

The scientist stood and went to the cockpit, motioning Paldor to get up so that she could take the copilot's seat. She needed help, and this old Klingon seemed the most sane, competent, and energetic among them. Sobbing and grumbling, the Tellarite squeezed past her to get to the back of the craft, and Leah slid into the seat he had vacated.

She looked at her new first officer and lowered her voice. "If you were me, what you would do?"

Maltz scowled. "You cannot land on a strange planet and expect them to voluntarily leave their homes at a moment's notice—due to a threat you can't explain. That is, if they even have a way to leave. We need help. Where are the vaunted reinforcements of the Federation?"

"It hit too suddenly," Leah answered defensively, "and we lost a lot of ships during the war. Plus I hate to tell you, but this is a forgotten corner of the Federation. The wars, the wormholes—all of the action has been up by the zones. There aren't a lot of settlements this close to the middle of the Milky Way."

"But many settled worlds lie in the path of this thing," observed Maltz, pointing to his screen. "If I'm not mistaken—expanding on your chart—one of the targets is Earth."

"Earth?" asked Leah, leaning closer to the gaunt Klingon. She hadn't seen the latest updates on the computer projections, but Maltz had figured them out rather quickly. She had to go to three other screens to verify his quick analysis. Yes, it seemed, Earth itself was in the path of this awful scourge.

"You know better than I do where Earth is," remarked Leah.

He shrugged. "In my day, all of us learned those coordinates in basic training. We had to have some place to attack on the simulators and war games."

"Right," answered Leah dryly. "Exactly how many humans have you killed?"

The old warrior wrinkled his jagged brow. "Not enough, I can tell you. Had I killed just a few more, I would not be in this place." With a grunt, he pointed at the screen. "The enemy is going to cut a streak through the Romulan Star Empire, too. I also know those coordinates."

Bekra suddenly sat up, not sleeping as peacefully as he appeared. "Did you say the Romulans will get hit, too?"

"This is only a projection, but you can see its path widening through the Neutral Zone." The Klingon sighed and sat back in his seat. "It looks like you are going to need a lot of help to fight this thing."

"Are you ever going to tell us who built it, and what you think it is?" asked Bekra.

The Klingon shook his head forcefully. "No. I will know the right person to tell, and it will have to be someone who can verify what I say. No one on this ship can do anything but doubt my sanity. Now, do we change course for this planet . . . Pelleus V?"

Reluctantly, Leah Brahms nodded. "Yes."

"Doctor, you are making the same mistake I made," protested Paldor from the back.

"She is the captain—it is her mistake to make." The Klingon narrowed his eyes at the Tellarite. "If you want to debate that point, you can take it up with *me*. Now all of you sleep—I will inform you when we get there."

Leah nodded gratefully and rested her head on her arms, which were folded across the console. In a matter of seconds, she was asleep where she sat, her fate in the hands of the grizzled old Klingon.

In a sumptuously appointed stateroom on the namesake *Sovereign*-class flagship, the *U.S.S. Sovereign,* the gray-haired admiral turned off her viewscreen and lowered her reading glasses. In her sharp green eyes was an emotion seldom seen there—fear. She had witnessed many extraordinary events in her long career, but nothing like these reports and fragments from the *Enterprise.* It was hard to believe that this bitter fruit had been planted only six months ago. Someone had been busy making use of what they stole.

She tapped a companel on her desk. "Nechayev to bridge."

"Captain Tejeda here," came a prompt response. "What can I do for you, Admiral?"

"Set course for solar system SY-911 in sector 4368. Maximum warp."

"Sector 4368," repeated the captain, sounding a bit doubtful as to what could be important there. "That will take us about thirty-three hours. What kind of mission should we prepare for?"

"When you need to know, I'll tell you," answered the admiral in a tone of voice that brooked no discussion. While most people were in awe of veteran captains of great starships, Nechayev treated them like underlings. It kept them from getting too full of themselves and reminded them that they were only links in a chain.

"Yes, Sir," responded Captain Tejeda, properly chastened. "Should we alert Starfleet of our change in course?"

"I'll do that," she answered. "But you can alert the *Enterprise* that the *Sovereign* is en route to their general position, and tell them to keep sending me raw data."

"Yes, Admiral."

"Nechayev out." Taking a deep breath, the weary admiral activated her terminal one more time. "Computer, send a secure message to recipients list 'Nechayev Priority One.' "

"What is the password?" demanded the computer.

"Tulip bulbs in spring," answered Nechayev grimly.

"Proceed," suggested the computer.

"Tulips are blooming again sooner than expected," said Nechayev, her mouth feeling dry now that the dreaded words were finally out. "Weeding will require all hands. Blooms must be seen to be believed. Yours truly—A."

She closed her eyes. "End message. Send it."

"Message sent," the reasonable voice of the computer assured her.

Now a large part of the fleet was going to be mustered under some pretext and sent to the afflicted area. Other than seeing for herself how bad it was, there wasn't anything else she could do. But knowing that didn't ease Nechayev's mind—her response still seemed inadequate.

She told herself, *I have the best ship in the fleet on it, the second best coming for backup, and all the others getting ready to come. I'm hitting it with both barrels.* Unfortunately, she couldn't block out the knowledge that she had nothing in her arsenal which could stand up to what she feared was out there.

"If only I could see him once in a while," said Beverly Crusher, her watery blue eyes staring at a beige bulkhead. "At least . . . if I could get some kind of sign that he's okay, I'd feel better."

"Wesley is with extremely advanced beings," said Deanna Troi, leaning forward in her chair. The dark-haired Betazoid pushed the teapot and cup across the elegant coffee table in her office, but Beverly wasn't paying any attention to it. "I'm sure the Traveler is taking good care of him," the counselor continued, "but I'm not so sure they have the same sense of time we do."

"But why Wes?" asked Beverly, shaking her auburn hair with frustration. "There are billions of other humans—he could have taken anybody!"

The counselor smiled sympathetically. "Wes has a gift, and the Traveler got to know him. I think he chose well, too, because your son was bored with so much in Starfleet. He had basically mastered this job while he was still in high school. He was ready to move on."

"I know, but sometimes . . . it seems like he's dead." The distraught mother rose to her feet and paced the confines of the nondescript office. "I don't want to stop him . . . his development. But, dammit, I want to know where to send a birthday card! Is it too much to ask that he make contact with his mother?"

Troi sighed, thinking it was always hardest to make a good friend face harsh reality. "The Traveler said he was taking Wes to another plane of existence, so we have to assume that contact is difficult. He's your ambassador to a race that is light-years ahead of ours. We don't begin to understand how they get around."

"They have incredible powers," agreed Beverly, half in pride and half in fear. "I just want a sign that he's okay."

Troi's combadge sounded a second later, and she listened with relief to the interruption.

"Picard to Troi."

"Yes, Captain, Troi here."

"I'm sorry to interrupt your appointment. Is Dr. Crusher with you?"

"Yes, Sir."

"I need you both in transporter room two," ordered the captain. "We've made contact with a shuttlecraft of survivors who escaped from Hakon, and they may be injured or traumatized. We don't want to prolong their ordeal, but we do have to find out what they know. Their shuttlecraft is damaged, so we're taking them on as passengers."

"We're on our way. Troi out." The counselor rose from her chair and moved toward the door, stopping when she realized that Beverly was still in her seat, gazing at the bulkhead.

"You know," said Deanna softly, "we can send for a different medteam. I'll tell the captain you weren't feeling well."

"No," replied the doctor, rising to her feet and pushing back an errant strand of red hair. "I need to go and do my job. You're right—if I'm not going to hear anything, then I'm not going to hear anything."

"Are you sure you're okay?"

Beverly waved her off. "Yes, you go on. I'll pick up the medteam on the way."

Troi nodded and strode through the door into the corridor. She wished she could do more to comfort her friend, whose life had often been one of sacrifice, but she couldn't bring herself to worry about someone as competent as Wesley Crusher. Then again, she wasn't his mother.

After a quick trip in the turbolift, Deanna reached the broad corridor outside transporter room two at the same time that Captain Picard, Data, and La Forge came from the other direction. Of the three of them, only La Forge looked pleased, as if he were about to meet a friend coming for holiday. Both he and Data were carrying padds.

The door slid open, and the captain motioned her inside the transporter room. "We don't know what condition they'll be in. Tell me, Counselor, what do you know about our latest mission?"

"Commander Riker has told me a few things," she replied. "I know there have been a series of unexplained disasters."

"That's putting it mildly. Unfortunately, we don't know much more than that. At least we're close enough now that we can help." Picard gazed at the transporter operator, a tall, blue-skinned Andorian named Tyriden. "Do you have a lock on them?"

"Yes, Sir. Four in total."

The doors opened again, and Beverly Crusher entered, leading a fully equipped medteam of five people. The captain smiled warmly at her for a moment, and she smiled back, then he motioned to the transporter operator. "Energize."

"Yes, Sir."

In a shimmering curtain of light, four bedraggled survivors appeared on the transporter platform. Two of them instantly collapsed, and Beverly and her team rushed forward to help them. All were male, and all were Tellarites, except for one, who appeared to be a Centaurian from his regal dress.

The most startling reaction was from Geordi La Forge, whose eager expression turned downcast and puzzled. He busied himself making entries on his padd, but Troi could tell that he was disappointed over the appearance of these survivors. Maybe he was expecting somebody else.

The healthiest of the Tellarites charged off the platform and gripped Captain Picard in an embarrassing embrace. "Oh, thank you, Captain! Thank you!"

Deanna rushed to aid the captain, pulling the overly grateful survivor away. "What happened to you?" she asked.

"Who knows?" he exclaimed. "We're a surveying team. One moment, we're laying out the boundaries of a wildlife refuge, and the next minute the trees are blowing over! And it's hailing and sleeting! We were able to take off, but not before a tree limb struck our craft. Then we hit a meteor shower on our way out—we were lucky to make it to warp."

"What did you see or get on your sensors?" asked Picard. "Anything unusual?"

"Nothing until we got into space," answered the Tellarite. "But we heard others on the emergency channels, and we saw what was happening to the sun." He buried his snout in his hands and began to weep.

"We ran for it," said the Centaurian defensively. "Is that so bad? Maybe I should've kept a video log, but I didn't."

"You weren't the shuttlecraft that came from Seran to Hakon just before this happened?" asked La Forge, stepping forward.

"No," said the Centaurian. "I'm their pilot, and it was strictly a day trip. We all left our families behind. Are they—"

Deanna hurriedly took his arm. "Before we deal with that, we'd like our medical personnel to take a look at you. The important thing is that you did right to get out of there."

"We've got to go back for them!" demanded the Tellarite, fighting through tears. Suddenly he grabbed the Centaurian pilot and shook him by the lapels of his flashy uniform. "I told you we had to go back for them!"

Troi and Picard reached in to try to pull the Tellarite off, but he was as big as both of them put together. Fortunately, Dr. Crusher made a timely arrival with a hypospray, getting the big Tellarite in the neck. A second later, he released the pilot, who dropped to the deck, coughing.

The big Tellarite stood as still as the bearded statue of an old general, but Crusher was able to move him toward the door. She motioned to her team to follow. "Let's all go to sickbay, shall we? Ogawa, Haberlee, I think everybody is ambulatory. Let's just walk."

"Beverly, will you need me?" asked Troi with concern.

"Not right now. I think we're looking at some sedation, rest, and a physical. I'll let you know." Under the doctor's direction, her team conducted the survivors from the transporter room. They looked more shell-shocked than anything else.

"They look like refugees from the war," said Troi, watching the last one exit.

"I was thinking the same thing," agreed Picard. "They *are* refugees. Unfortunately, there are only a handful, and they don't know anything."

"We've got to keep looking for the rest of the shuttlecrafts and freighters," insisted La Forge. "One of them came from Seran to Hakon to warn them, but we lost its signal when all hell broke loose. There was also the Capellan shuttlecraft that put out an early distress signal—"

"The Capellan shuttlecraft has been destroyed," said Data matter-of-factly.

"Are you sure?" asked Geordi in a hoarse voice.

The android nodded. "Yes, I was about to ask Commander Riker to continue tracking it when it disappeared."

"What destroyed it?" asked Picard, the frustration evident in his voice. "If it was safely in space, it couldn't have been the effects of the sun."

"That is unknown," answered Data. "It would appear the Capellan shuttlecraft did not have warp drive, and it remained in proximity to Hakon, where sensor readings have been unreliable."

"When you get back to the bridge, set course for solar system SY-911," ordered the captain. "Maximum warp."

"But, Sir!" pleaded La Forge. "If this mystery shuttlecraft is trying to warn people—and they know where to go next—we should keep looking for them. They manage to stay just ahead of this . . . trail of disaster."

"Get moving, Data." The captain nodded, and the android hurried off. Then Picard put his hand on La Forge's shoulder and said softly, "I know you have a personal interest in this. Since you have the opportunity, I wish you would take a moment to talk to Counselor Troi about it."

La Forge hung his head, knowing he had lost the argument, and the captain went on, "You've been on duty for about twenty hours straight, which I didn't deny you, because you discovered these irregularities. But now you need to talk to Counselor Troi and sleep."

The captain's lips thinned. "I'm afraid this is going to be a long haul. We can't go chasing after every small craft from Hakon, and we have to accept the fact that Seran and Outpost Seran-T-One are in the damage zone. What we need most are answers and firsthand observation."

"Yes, Sir," answered Geordi, trying to get control over his emotions.

The captain strode away, leaving La Forge and Troi alone in the transporter room. Even the operator was behind the platform, his head in an access panel.

"I still think we should track down that shuttle," insisted Geordi in a whisper. "Somebody out there *knows* what's going on—or at least where this thing is headed. We've got to find them. If I were really being selfish, I would want to go to Seran."

"Who's on Seran?" asked Deanna, moving toward the door.

"Remember Leah Brahms? We talked about her."

The counselor nodded sympathetically. "You really cared for her, didn't you? I'm sorry, Geordi."

The engineer swallowed hard, and she could see moisture in the corners of his opaque eyes. "I just can't believe that she could be gone . . . just like that. I mean, I knew she was married, but somewhere in the back of my mind, I always thought that someday there might be a chance—"

"Oh, Geordi," said Troi hoarsely, squeezing his shoulder. "I keep thinking that we've had these great lives aboard the *Enterprise*. We've had more adventures than anyone should have in ten lifetimes, but we've missed out on the ordinary parts of life. Sometimes I wonder how many of us could even have a normal relationship in an artificial world like this." She motioned around at the sleek, empty corridor.

He cleared his throat. "You and Will—"

"It's taken us a dozen years to be comfortable with each other in this small town we call the *Enterprise*." She gave him a wry smile. "You fell in love with the most brilliant woman you ever met, only it was on a holodeck. I sometimes think we should all be committed to a mental institution, considering what we've been through."

"You're just trying to cheer me up," said La Forge, "and I'm not buying it. Forgetting Leah, who is probably dead . . . we're up against something that's wiping out stars, planets, and nebulas like they're piles of dust! We don't even understand what it's doing to them, and now we're flying straight into the teeth of this thing."

"Okay, so you depressed me," admitted Troi. "And there are going to be a lot more refugees, like those people in sickbay."

"They're the lucky ones," said Geordi.

# ten

Leah Brahms rustled in her sleep, muttering to herself. Finally she lifted her head groggily from the instrument panel and looked around the cramped shuttlecraft cabin. "Oh," she groaned, rubbing her head. "It's true."

"What is true?" asked the old Klingon sitting beside her.

"I had a dream that all of this *was* a dream . . . or rather a nightmare." She massaged her dry, cracked lips. "But, no, it's all true, isn't it? The thing behind us . . . it's still there."

"There is always an enemy," said Maltz with a shrug. "Sometimes it's boredom, but not today." He pointed to the back of the craft, where the Tellarite and the Capellan were sleeping among their luggage and the hulking radiation suit. "What is that unpleasant-looking device back there?"

"Oh, you mean the radiation suit?" Leah smiled despite her gloominess. "That suit saved my life. None of us would be here without it."

"It survived the wave?" asked Maltz, sounding impressed. "Can you do a space walk in it?"

"That's not what it's designed for, but you could. You would be using only half its capabilities."

The Klingon sat forward eagerly. "I have been looking at the parts you collected for your comm array, and I think we can repair it easily. The space walk should take no more than half an hour." He quickly added, "I can do it."

"No," said Leah forcefully. "I'll do it. I know the equipment better than you do."

"But the captain should not be at risk," grumbled the Klingon. "It should be someone expendable—what about Paldor?"

"Me!" squeaked the Tellarite, suddenly awake. "You want *me* to go outside and fix the shuttlecraft? I wouldn't even fit inside that suit. Are you sure we have to do this now?"

"Yes, because we need help." The old Klingon lowered his voice. "The first thing a captain should learn is this—when you are outnumbered, get help. If we do not, the next planet will be Hakon all over again."

"Listen to him," said a voice from the back. Leah turned to see Consul Bekra sitting up, trying to adjust his ornate turban and his bandaged stump. "We have to spread the word as fast as we can. A few hours could make a great deal of difference."

"Even if it means our lives?" asked Paldor in disbelief. "We don't know how far ahead of it we are, or how long it will take to fix the array. Dr. Brahms is not a welder by trade."

"That's enough, people. I don't know if we have enough time for this repair, but we sure as hell don't have time to argue about it. Besides," Leah added with a smile, "molecular bonding is easy, even for humans. We have everything we need in our supplies."

With a sigh, the engineer stood up and began removing her jumpsuit, which she had meant to change, anyway. If she were smart, she would just put the radiation suit on and leave it on, but she didn't want to be the only eyewitness survivor again. "Keep us on warp until I'm ready to exit the ship," she ordered. "I want as much distance between me and *it* as possible."

The young Tellarite began to weep all over again, and Leah surprised herself by grabbing his loud plaid shirt and shaking him. "Get ahold of yourself, Paldor! We don't have the luxury of grieving . . . not right now. I need you to help me get this suit ready, and monitor me . . . like we do in the tests. Get up!"

She yanked him to his feet, where he struggled to stand at attention, while bravely sniffing back tears. Behind her, she heard Maltz give a low chuckle.

"Now you are getting the hang of it," said the Klingon with satisfaction.

"Slow to one-quarter impulse," ordered Captain Picard as he hovered behind the young Bolian on the conn. He peered at the viewscreen with concern, not because he saw something which looked amiss; on the contrary, this part of space looked oddly tranquil, considering what it had gone through. Even the radically altered sun of system SY-911 looked like a natural part of the starscape when viewed from the safe distance of two million kilometers. At least Picard hoped this was a safe distance.

"Mister Data, where do we stand?"

"I would advise that we stop here," answered the android. "Radiation is very high in a field of particles about a hundred thousand kilometers from our position. This area also has trace readings of almost every element known to science, including organic components. I would almost conclude that a massive fleet of starships moved through here, expelling waste as they went, except we know that did not occur. Some extraordinary event has taken place, although I am unable to say what it was."

"Full stop," ordered the captain, concerned that they knew so little about this deadly menace. "Data, prepare three probes. A solar probe for the sun and two class-1 probes—one for Hakon and one for the planet with the strange readings."

"SY-911 Alpha," concluded Data, working his board with fingers moving so swiftly they were a blur. "Targeting probes."

"Launch when ready," ordered the captain.

"Probes launched."

On the viewscreen, the torpedoes streaked from the *Enterprise* across the peaceful starscape until they disappeared among the distant stars and the pulsing red sun. The transformed sun glowed with a brilliance that dared them to do something about it.

The turbolift door opened with a whoosh, startling the captain from his troubled reverie. He turned to see Counselor Troi enter the bridge, and he asked, "How are our passengers?"

"They're all sleeping now," she answered, "but we've got a lot of work to do. They're going to ask me what the chances are of going back to their homes. Will we mount a rescue effort, or at least recover the bodies?"

"I hope to know soon," answered Picard. "We've sent out probes, and we're trying to gather information. There's something destructive out here, but we don't know much about it."

"Captain," said Data from the ops station, "the first probe should be reaching the particle field. Peculiar."

"What is it, Data?"

"The probe ceased transmission." He worked his board furiously. "In fact, both probes have ceased transmission since they entered the particle field just ahead of us." The android looked up with concern. "I suggest we put up shields."

"Shields up," ordered Picard without a moment's hesitation.

"Shields up!" echoed the officer on tactical.

"What's the threat?" asked the captain.

Data shook his head. "Some sort of energy wave is following the deuterium trails of the probes—right back to us."

Picard looked up at the viewscreen to see two thin ripples—like green lightning bolts—come tearing from the darkness, headed straight toward them. "Brace for impact," said Data.

The captain wasn't expecting much of an impact since they had their shields up, and he wasn't disappointed. He felt nothing, although it was disturbing the way the mysterious strands seemed to remain attached to the ship, trailing off into the distance like giant vines.

He was shocked a moment later when the ship's alarms sounded, and the bridge went automatically to emergency lighting and Red Alert. "Hull breach on decks eleven and twelve," said the voice of the computer.

As he worked his console, Data added, "To be specific, the forward launch tubes."

"Our shields—" started Picard.

"Ineffective," answered Data.

"Conn, take us out of here, reverse course, full impulse," ordered Picard, striding to his command chair.

"Yes, Sir."

"Repair crews have been dispatched to the forward torpedo room," reported Data. "It was running under automated control—no casualties reported."

"Let's see what it's like. On screen." The captain sat stiffly in his chair, his brow furrowed, as the scene overhead switched to the cramped, elongated torpedo room. Torpedoes and probes were stacked top to bottom in robotic racks, ready to be moved into place, and rails ran the length of the deck, leading to the launch tubes. But the bank of launch tubes were gone—instead there was an amorphous green glow around a jagged hole which opened to the darkness of space. And the pulsing hole seemed to be growing larger.

The scene turned hectic a moment later when a team dressed in environmental suits charged in with fire extinguishers and foam guns blazing. They instantly attacked the breach, some of them erecting temporary force-field barriers, while the others battled the oddly glowing flames.

"I have isolated their audio," said Data. Suddenly, they heard a feminine voice saying, "What is that stuff? It's not working . . . it's not containing it! Kipnis, get a tricorder reading."

"Working on it, Sir." A moment later, his voice croaked when he said, "It's organic! Protomatter. It's eating through the hull . . . like acid!"

"Aagghhh!" screamed another voice. "It's got me! It's all over me! I can't get it off!"

Now there was real bedlam as a panicked officer staggered back from the breach in the hull, plowing through his coworkers trapped in the narrow room with him. He swatted and beat himself as if he were on fire, but Picard could see only a bit of the glowing vegetation on him. Anguished screams rent the air, and more of the repair team seemed to fall victim, scratching and clawing themselves. They began to tear off their environmental suits.

His jaw clenched, the captain rose from his chair. "Mr. Data, seal off the forward torpedo room."

"Yes, Sir." The android calmly worked his board. "Sealed off."

When some of the panicked repair crew tried to escape to the corridor, they realized they were shut off, and their screams became more urgent and frightful. Meanwhile, the cancerous hole in the hull kept growing, and the distraught workers scrambled and clawed over one another to get away from it.

"Patch me into them," ordered Picard. Data nodded to him, and he went on, "This is the captain. We are facing a quarantine situation in your position. Try to remain calm." He motioned to Data to cut off the transmission, then he said grimly, "Prepare to jettison forward torpedo module."

Deanna Troi sprang in front of him. "But, Sir, there are ten crew members trapped in there."

"We'll get them back," vowed Picard, "but we can't let that thing reach the main hull. Data, jettison the forward torpedo module."

"Yes, Sir."

On the viewscreen, the crew trapped in the torpedo room suddenly became weightless, and their panicked thrashing increased as they floated helplessly. With a jarring shudder, clamps released and powerful thrusters shot the entire module away from the Saucer Module of the *Enterprise.* One of the most dangerous parts of the ship, loaded with armaments, the torpedo module was designed to be ejected if its contents proved unstable. But it was never meant to be jettisoned with people in it.

"Patch me into them again," ordered Captain Picard, straightening his tunic. The image on the viewscreen was now obliterated by static, although the desperate struggles of the crew were plain to see . . . or imagine.

"Captain," said Data, "life support is failing in the module."

"Prepare to transport them," ordered Picard. "Data, can we surround the transporter room with a containment field?"

"That is inadvisable," answered the android. "If our battle shields had no effect on the intruder, we can assume our force-fields would not either."

Helplessly, the bridge crew gazed at the viewscreen, where the new image was more disturbing than the one inside the torpedo room. The trapezoid-shaped module was now misshapen and throbbing, which had to be an optical illusion, thought Picard. It hardly seemed possible that thick bulkheads could twist and mutate like that, no matter what power they were under. "Am I patched in?"

"Yes, Sir."

He stuck his jaw out. "This is Captain Picard to the members of the repair crew in the torpedo module. We're working on a way to rescue you from—"

"Captain," said Data, "the comlink has gone dead. No lifesigns either."

"Keep recording this," ordered Picard with a scowl, pointing to the abomination on the viewscreen. "But take us back another million kilometers, half impulse."

"Yes, Sir," answered the Bolian at the conn.

Feeling weary and saddened, the captain slumped into the captain's chair. Deanna Troi joined him in the center of the bridge, her face drawn with shock, and she lowered her head. "You tried, Captain. It all happened so fast—"

"You always think a miracle will happen . . . but sometimes it doesn't." The captain's gaze finally focused on the face of his longtime comrade. "I had to protect the ship."

"Yes, you did," agreed Troi. "You undoubtedly *saved* the ship."

Picard pointed to the ops station. "Data, make sure you send copies of this data to Admiral Nechayev. How much longer before the *Sovereign* is here?"

"Sixteen hours at our present position," answered the android, "although we could meet her sooner by backtracking."

"As long as we're collecting useful information, maintain position," said the captain. "I have to make a shipwide announcement."

He pressed a companel on the arm of his chair, and his voice reverberated throughout the ship. "Captain to all hands. I regret to announce that all members of the repair crew who answered the emergency in the forward torpedo room have been lost. There was a breach in the hull and a threat to the ship, for which we had no defense. So I made the decision to jettison the torpedo module.

"We will now all observe a moment of silence for our fallen comrades, who risked their lives many times on our behalf. Today they died valiantly on our behalf." Picard stood still for a moment, his hand resting on his chest, wishing there was more he could tell them about the peril which claimed their shipmates' lives.

"There will be an announcement about a memorial service later," he concluded. "That is all."

Picard slumped back in his chair and stared at the molten green object on the screen, an object which had once been part of his ship. Had they been able to observe this phenomenon without losing any lives, it would have been fascinating. But now it was just disgusting and frightening. "It almost looks alive," he said to no one in particular.

"It *is* alive," agreed Data. "The mass which was formerly the torpedo module has generated into simple life-forms, which continue to evolve."

"What do you mean, evolve?" asked Deanna Troi.

"Single-celled animals are in a rapid state of growth," answered the android, "forming more complex creatures as they develop. It is like a hundred million years of evolution condensed into a few minutes. Without firsthand observation, I cannot be more specific than that."

"We're not getting any closer," vowed Picard. "I feel rather helpless just sitting here, but without more information, we can't do anything." He tapped his fingers nervously on the arm of his chair. "What *is* that thing?"


After floating in space for a while, cut off from her sullen crew inside the shuttlecraft, Leah Brahms began to relax and enjoy the excursion outside the ship. She was fairly dexterous, often wielding a soldering iron or a laser torch in her normal routine, and installing the makeshift comm array was just construction on a bigger scale. The work would have gone faster if she'd had real Starfleet-approved replacement parts, but she didn't. So she had to do some drilling, bending, and creative kludging, with advice from Maltz and Paldor. She soon discovered that she knew as much about the comm system as either one of them.

Fortunately, her radiation suit had been designed with the

expressed purpose of doing manual repairs, and the gloves worked well. Also she was able to kneel on the outside of the boxy shuttlecraft, using the magnetic fields on the suit. Handling the bonding gun was no problem, and Leah found the repetitive manual labor to be soothing. At least it felt as if she were *doing* something, rather than running for her life. Or mourning.

"How much longer, Captain?" came Maltz's gravelly voice over the intercom. He didn't sound frightened, exactly, but there was an urgency in his voice.

"It *might* work now," she said. "But if we want clean subspace on all channels, we'll have to get the signal preprocessor and the Doppler compensator working. But . . . what's the matter?"

"Do you remember that big asteroid belt we passed a while ago?"

"Yes," she answered, a sudden fear gripping in her stomach.

"It's gone!" cut in Paldor's voice. "And there's something that looks like a new planet in its place."

"I think I've done enough for now," said Leah, stuffing her floating tools and extra parts into a large net bag. "Reel me in. And make it quick!"

# eleven

Geordi La Forge dragged himself out of his bed at the first alarm, still groggy from a deep sleep. As quickly as possible, he dressed in his uniform and was about to dash out of his quarters when he was stopped by Captain Picard's shipwide announcement. He didn't know offhand who was on that repair team, but he was sure there were people who had served with him in engineering, maybe some who currently served there. Despite the tragedy, it sounded like the *Enterprise* had dodged a bullet.

La Forge finished buttoning his collar and stepped toward the door, waving his hand at a panel to open it. He was so busy charging ahead that he nearly plowed into Dolores Linton, who was in the passageway just outside his door.

"Oh, my gosh, Geordi!" she exclaimed, grabbing him in a forceful hug. "I'm so afraid."

"It's okay," he said, returning the embrace and drawing some strength from her warm body. Her voluminous dark hair smelled fragrant and clean as it billowed just centimeters from his nostrils. He finally whispered hoarsely, "It sounds like the danger is over."

"But all those people!" She pulled slowly away from him and gazed at him with her sultry eyes. "How many?"

"In a crew like that, probably ten." He shook his head and felt guilty for having slept so soundly while the ship was in turmoil. He would hear the whole story later, but probably not from Dolores. "What were you doing out here?"

"I was pacing around," she admitted, straightening her khaki jumpsuit and looking ready to climb mountains that didn't exist on the

*Enterprise.* "I don't really have any place to go—no station. I learned from the computer that you were off duty, and I was coming down here to bug you when the alert happened. I'm sorry if I behaved unprofessionally. I've been known to act very cool when there's a rockslide or a mudslide. I just feel a little helpless inside this ship."

Geordi gave her an encouraging smile. "We'll look out for you. But it's too bad you couldn't have picked a quieter time to travel with us." He stepped away from her, anxious to get to engineering.

"Are you still off duty?" she asked, following him down the corridor.

"Well, technically, yes. But we've just had a hull breach and casualties—and we've lost a chunk of the ship. I think I'd better check on things in engineering."

She smiled wistfully. "I was just going to ask if you wanted to have breakfast. It is breakfast time for you, isn't it?"

"Yes it is," he admitted, still moving to the turbolift. "Let's have a late breakfast in two hours. I'll give you that tour of the ship I promised. Meet you back here?"

"All right," answered the muscular brunette, mustering some bravado.

*Maybe she is interested,* thought Geordi as he dashed into the turbolift, *but her timing is nearly as bad as mine. It must be tough to be a passenger during a crisis like this, with nothing to do but sit and hope for the best.*

"Main engineering," he said to the computer. The turbolift had barely begun moving when his combadge beeped. "Bridge to La Forge," came the familiar clipped tones of Captain Picard.

"La Forge here," he answered. "Is everything all right?"

"As well as can be expected. I'm sorry to disturb you on break, but I doubt you were sleeping any longer."

"No, Sir, I'm on my way to engineering." The turbolift door opened, and Geordi stepped into his familiar workplace. It was bustling, the Red Alert having drawn plenty of hands to their posts. At the same time, the mood was subdued and somber after the tragedy.

"You might want to come to the bridge," said the captain. "We think we may have found your mystery shuttlecraft. They're broadcasting information about the nature of this disaster."

"I'm on my way. La Forge out." He glanced at the duty commander, Krygore, and waved. "I have to go to the bridge. Is everything under control?"

"We didn't take any damage," answered the dignified Kerelian.

"But I guess there's nothing left of the forward torpedo module. The casualty list is just coming in. What's out there, Sir?"

"We don't know . . . yet. I'll look at the list on the bridge." With a troubled sigh, Geordi stepped back into the turbolift. "Stay alert down here."

"Yes, Sir."

A few moments later, he stepped off the turbolift onto the bridge, where it was also somber. The viewscreen was full of startling images: an entire planet wilting under vivid green flames; a shimmering curtain sweeping across space; a moon ripped apart by what looked like solar flares. The images were followed by columns of raw data, moving so swiftly that only Data could keep up with them.

"Where is that coming from?" asked Geordi.

"It's from Seran," answered Picard gravely. "We also saw images from Hakon which confirmed our fears about what happened there. Who knows how many planets and stars have been destroyed in between?"

"Can we talk to these people?" asked La Forge, stepping closer to the screen.

"We can't contact them at the moment," said the captain. "They're using all their bandwidth to broadcast raw data on every channel. It's gone through one cycle already. We're on course to intercept them."

"In approximately two hours," added Data. "Based on this new information, we are taking an elliptical course to stay out of the way of the phenomenon."

"Do we know who they are?" asked Geordi.

Data shook his head. "No. From the warp signature, it appears to be a type-8 shuttlecraft, but I am assuming their communications equipment is damaged. They appear to be on course for the inhabited planet, Pelleus V, which could indicate that Pelleus V is in danger."

"What else do thay say?" asked Geordi, leaning over his friend's shoulder.

"The most interesting thing is what they do *not* say," answered the android. "They claim to have more information—of a sensitive nature. And they do not identify themselves."

"Do you need help analyzing this stuff?" asked Geordi, sitting at an auxiliary console near his friend.

"Your perspective would be welcome," answered the android.

"What is their speed?" asked Captain Picard.

"Approximately warp three."

La Forge gave a low whistle. "Wow, that's fast for a type-8 shuttlecraft. They must have their foot to the floor."

Data cocked his head. "I fail to see how having their feet on the floor would make them go faster."

"It's an old analogy," answered Geordi. "It means they're not taking any precautions. They probably overrode the safeties."

"That is inadvisable," said Data with concern.

"Not when that thing is chasing you," concluded Captain Picard, gazing at the awesome destruction on the viewscreen. "Let's hope we reach them before *it* does."

"We need to get out of its path!" shouted Paldor, leaning uncomfortably over Leah Brahms' shoulder.

Leah tried to remain calm while she got a course correction from the computer, but panic had begun to sink in among her ragtag crew.

"We have to come out of warp to change course," she patiently explained. "It's right behind us—we don't know how far."

The Tellarite pressed forward, his ample stomach pushing the back of her head. "It can't take more than a few seconds. Maybe you can swing around a celestial body—"

"Will you back off!" she yelled at him, planting an elbow in his midsection.

The obstinate Tellarite pushed forward even more, which was a mistake. Maltz jumped to his feet, planted a fist in Paldor's chest and knocked him backwards; he sprawled in the aisle, bumping into Bekra's amputated leg. The Capellan groaned with pain, and Paldor shrieked as he thrashed about on the deck.

"The captain said to back off," explained the Klingon simply. "I will put you out the airlock next time." He sat down at the co-pilot's seat and continued to monitor the sensors.

Paldor jumped to his feet and sputtered in anger, shaking his fist. Leah tried to ignore him to concentrate on the job at hand. As long as they kept moving in their current course, she didn't think the wave could catch them, unless they stopped. If they changed course, they might flank the wave and get out of its path. Then they would be safe, but that was risky. They had estimates but no real idea how much the wave had expanded in girth, and if it caught them . . . there weren't any second guesses.

They continued to broadcast raw data on all channels, which had been Maltz's idea. He also suggested that they keep the information anonymous, so that everyone could take it at face value. As their projections increasingly showed, this was not just a Federation problem, and they didn't want it to sound that way.

From the corner of her eye, Leah saw Bekra motion to the Tellarite, and they were soon conversing in urgent whispers. Neither one of them liked the Klingon very much, but his lively presence was like a tonic to Leah, reminding her that there was nothing pretty about commanding a ship in the middle of a crisis. This desperation must have been what it was like for Geordi when he created a duplicate of her on the holodeck to consult with. A person could get crazy trying to operate under such stress, searching for a solution while death hovered all around. Leah suddenly had a great deal more compassion for Geordi and spacefaring engineers.

"Maintain course for Pelleus V?" asked Maltz, breaking into her troubled thoughts.

"Yes," she answered decisively. "And keep the message going out. Do you think it's getting through?"

The Klingon scowled, "If it isn't, it's not for lack of trying."

Suddenly the blackness of space lit up as if a thousand flares had gone off, and something streaked past their window, rocking the tiny ship. Leah had her hands full trying to control their rapid drop in speed, but she finally stabilized the small craft.

"That brought us out of warp," reported Maltz.

"What was it?" wailed Paldor behind them.

"A comet?" asked Bekra.

"No," answered the old Klingon. "Offhand, I would say it was a warning shot across our bow."

"From where?" asked Leah.

"Right there." Maltz pointed upward as a massive golden warship cruised overhead, blocking out the starscape. "I think we had better stop broadcasting and put on local two-way."

"Go ahead," rasped Leah with a squeak in her voice.

"We haven't got time for this!" shouted Paldor. "Unless they'll take us on board. Tell them to take us aboard!"

"Shut up," said Maltz as he fooled with his instruments. "Here we go. Let's see what they have to say."

After a screech of static, a deep voice which sounded stiff and mechanical came on the comlink. "Unknown spacecraft, you have entered Pellean space. Pelleus V is not a member of the Federation, and entry to the Pellean Principality is restricted. Please turn around and go back the way you came."

"We can't do that," said Paldor with alarm, echoing all of their thoughts.

"Come to a complete stop now," ordered the voice. Leah quickly obeyed him and brought the shuttlecraft to a full stop. But her eyes were on the sensor readings, and so were Maltz's. Although they couldn't pick up the exact location of the wave, they were learning to recognize the kind of incredible damage it left behind.

With anger and fear in her voice, she pressed a panel and responded. "Listen, we are running from a terrible energy wave that has already destroyed half a dozen solar systems. Millions of people on Seran and Hakon are dead, and *we're* going to be dead unless we both get out of here."

"Turn around and go back the way you came," ordered the stiff voice.

"Let me talk to him," said Bekra, sitting forward in his chair with effort. "After all, I'm a diplomat."

Maltz laughed. "It will not do any good. I ran sensors, and I do not see any life-forms on that whole ship."

"You mean, it's automated?" said Leah in amazement and distress.

"They're claiming an awfully big chunk of space," said Bekra indignantly.

"I heard they wanted a buffer zone during the war," said Maltz. "The Federation was in no position to contest them, so they took it. Maybe they decided to hold onto it. *Now* might be a good time to try that course change we talked about."

"Okay," said Leah, working her board. "I want to skirt around their territory. I'll try a bearing of two-seven-zero and see if they let us get away with that." She piloted the shuttlecraft straight down, but the massive starship swiftly followed and barged in front of her, forcing her to stop.

"Insufficient," said the voice. "Resume bearing one-eight-zero or equivalent."

Bekra spoke up. "We're diplomats! This is Consul Maltz, and I'm Consul Bekra. There's been a terrible disaster, and your planet is right in the path of it. Escort us back to your leaders so we can talk. It's urgent!"

"Leave now!" ordered the voice. "Or we will put a tractor beam on your vessel and escort you from our space."

"I'm reversing course," said Leah, her heart thumping rapidly in her chest.

"Are you crazy?" shouted Paldor. "That's suicide!"

"No," she answered evenly, "suicide would be letting that big drone get a tractor beam on us. We'll stay on impulse."

"Then what will we do?" asked Bekra.

"I'll let you know when we get to that point." Leah Brahms swallowed hard, wishing she had a hologram of Captain Picard to consult. She glanced at her copilot. "Are they following us?"

"No," answered Maltz.

"That's good." Leah breathed a sigh of relief, and she peered into the endless distance. Only it didn't appear so endless today, with a glowing, spiral cloud blocking out the center of the starscape.

"What's that out there?" she asked. "A nebula?"

"No, not a nebula." Maltz stared intently at his instruments, then back at her. "It is moving rapidly toward us—at warp speed."

"Oh, no," whispered Leah. She heard Paldor wail in alarm, then Bekra and Maltz began arguing about who was at fault for their being here. But the din in the shuttlecraft seemed to float over her head, and she felt as if she were back inside the radiation suit, removed from everything around her, concentrating only on the mission. Right now, the mission was to make a decision.

The right decision.

# twelve

Without giving it a moment's thought—because she didn't have a moment—Leah reversed course again and slammed the shuttlecraft into warp two. Zooming into an elongated streak, the tiny craft hit warp just as a fiery green curtain wiped across their position, its fingers licking and lapping like solar flares. Ahead of them was a huge Pellean warship that was programmed to keep them from entering its space, which they did, anyway.

"Shields up," said Maltz with a wide grin. He shook his fists at the enemy and roared, "*qatlho*! It is a good day to die!"

"Speak for yourself!" exclaimed Paldor, slumping into his seat.

"At least we spread the alarm," muttered Brahms, hoping against crushing reality that it would do some good. Maybe the old Klingon was right, and it *was* a good day to die. Leah felt weary and miserable enough to die, but the old urge for self-preservation kept the adrenaline flowing, making her work to stay alive.

"Maltz," she asked, "do you think they'll fire another warning shot or go straight for us?"

"Perhaps they will be stupid enough to give us one more chance." Suddenly the darkness in front of them erupted with a blaze of light, and the little ship was jolted hard. Once again, they spun out of warp.

"Unknown spacecraft, you have entered Pellean space," said the cold voice. "Pelleus V is not a member of the Federation, and entry to the Pellean Principality—"

Leah slammed the ship back into warp—this time warp three. Worrying about the safeties didn't seem to be a high priority under the circumstances. She was hoping they would underestimate her speed just enough to miss.

"Come to a complete stop now, or we will fire," warned the Pellean ship.

She increased their speed five percent just as another volley lit up the darkness and jarred them—but it didn't bring them out of warp.

"Ah, bad shots," said Maltz, rubbing his hands together with delight. "If I had just *one* aft torpedo, I would get them off our tail for good!"

"We've got warp-equipped sensor probes," said Leah.

Maltz scowled. "Sensor probes? What good is that?"

"They don't know they're sensor probes." She looked pointedly at the Klingon.

"Yes, Sir." The Klingon punched his board with enthusiasm. "I launched them all!"

"All two of them." She gave him a wry smile.

After studying his readouts for a few moments, the Klingon grinned and banged his fist on his console. "Well done, Captain! They are coming out of warp . . . taking evasive maneuvers. Humans are so devious." It almost sounded as if that were a compliment.

"Have we escaped them?" asked Paldor eagerly.

"I doubt if it will be that easy." As the Klingon continued to study his board, his expression drooped like his old moustache. "No . . . now they are powering up phasers."

"They can't miss with those, can they?" asked Leah with a gulp.

"Not at this range. Brace for impact!"

In the next instant, the tiny shuttlecraft was shaken like a rabbit in a wolf's mouth, and they were all dumped out of their seats, while lights in the cabin flickered and sparks spewed from the rear.

"There go the shields!" said Maltz over Paldor's screams and Bekra's groans. "The next shot, and we're space dust. It has been a pleasure serving with you, Captain!"

Leah dragged herself back into her seat. "Do we still have warp?"

Maltz rose to his knees to look at his console. "Yes."

The mechanized voice broke in. "You will cease hostilities, or we will destroy you. Prepare for our tractor beam to—" The voice suddenly became strangled and distorted, until it turned into a shrieking whine. Both Leah and Maltz stared at their screens, and they could see the ungodly curtain sweep over the golden starship, turning it into a lumpen mass.

"Full warp!" shouted Leah, working her console. The scorched shuttlecraft shot into space just as the fingers of the shimmering green curtain lapped at its stern.

\* \* \*

"We are entering Pellean space," reported Data from the ops station on the bridge of the *Enterprise*. "We should have been hailed by now."

Geordi looked up from his console to watch Will Riker pace in front of the viewscreen, which showed what looked to be a peaceful stretch of space. The reality was far different, thought the engineer, because somewhere out there was a murderer, killing on a massive scale.

Captain Picard was getting some much-needed rest, and Riker was in charge. "What's the protocol with the Pelleans?" he asked.

Data cocked his head. "According to our treaty with them, we are not allowed to enter their space unannounced. If we are not hailed, we are to wait until we are met by an escort."

"There's no time for that," muttered Riker. "But we don't want to rush into an ambush either. Conn, slow to impulse but maintain course. Data, what's on long-range scans?" Geordi could see impatience etched on Riker's face, plus blotches of heated blood vessels under his skin, even if his tone of voice was relaxed.

After a moment, the android reported, "It would appear that Pelleus V has undergone the same sort of disaster and transformation that we have seen before. The particle field is also in evidence, as well as other indicators."

Riker pounded a fist into his palm, and La Forge knew how he felt. Once again, they were too late. An entire civilization—a billion souls—had vanished from existence along with every other form of life on the planet. They were one step behind this monster, and the only ones who were ahead of it had gone silent again.

"How is Paul Revere?" asked Geordi.

"Paul Revere?" queried Riker. "What's he got to do with it?"

Data spoke up, "That is Geordi's nickname for the mysterious shuttlecraft which has been trying to warn planets in this sector. We have been unable to identify it, other than that it is of Federation design and probably from the planet Seran. They are the ones who furnished us with the data you saw."

"And the captain's orders are to find them," added Riker, "not wait here for an escort who will likely never show up. So what is Paul Revere's position?"

"We are still picking up a faint distress signal from the other side of the Pellean solar system," answered Data. "But since they are no longer broadcasting on all frequencies, I cannot be one hundred percent certain that it is the *same* shuttlecraft."

"It's worth a try," said Riker. "Keep after them."

"Setting a course at warp speed is going to be tricky," broke in Geordi. "We've got to avoid the energy wave, which seems to be expanding."

"Data, you take over the conn," ordered Riker. He nodded gratefully at the resident helmsman. "Sorry, Mr. Bollinger, but we need the best pilot we've got. You take ops."

"Understood," said the bald-headed Brekkian. Neither he nor Data had to move from their seats, because with a push of a button, the functions of their consoles were switched. Data was probably watching everyone's readouts, anyway, thought Geordi.

After a few dizzying moments of working his board, Data reported, "Course laid in. I suggest a maximum speed of warp 4, which will give me time to make needed course corrections to avoid the anomaly. I estimate we can intercept them in one hour."

"Sir," broke in the young Benzite on tactical, "I've received a message from the *Sovereign*." Now she had the attention of Riker, Data, La Forge, and everyone else on the bridge. With a slight tremor in her voice, she went on, "They want to know why we keep changing our position. It's making it difficult for them to rendezvous with us."

Riker stroked his clean-shaven chin for a moment, then said, "Tell them that Pelleus V appears to have been destroyed, and now we're on a rescue mission."

"Before you send that," said Geordi, cutting in, "can I make a suggestion?"

"Go ahead," answered Riker, "but make it good."

The engineer spoke quickly. "We've got a Stellar-class shuttlecraft that can catch them as well as the *Enterprise* can, under these circumstances. Why don't Data and I go chase them, and you stay here and wait for the admiral?"

Riker snapped his fingers and pointed to the turbolift. "Get going. I'll contact the captain and try to have his permission by the time you get to the shuttlebay."

La Forge and Data bounded out of their seats and rushed for the turbolift as relief personnel took their stations. It was a long shot, thought Geordi, and maybe a waste of time; but he couldn't sit around and do nothing while the people who had risked their lives to save others were in danger.

He and Data were soon speeding through the Saucer Module en route to the main shuttlebay. Data was unusually quiet, and La Forge noticed an electromagnetic haze around his friend, indicating a high degree of processing.

"What's the matter?" he asked.

"The nature of this threat has me puzzled," answered the android. "It defies most of what we know about natural science."

"Then it's *unnatural* science," said Geordi as the turbolift door opened.

"Artificial," concluded Data, cocking his head. "Manufactured. This theory supports the facts, yet it raises even more questions."

"I know somebody who has the answers," said Geordi, striding ahead of him through the cavernous main shuttlebay. "Paul Revere."

"You seemed convinced of that, yet they may prove to be nothing more than frightened refugees."

"I don't think so." La Forge strode past the front row of shuttlecraft nearest the launch doors, ready for immediate launch. He stopped at the biggest, sleekest, and newest craft, named the *Balboa*. "This one?"

"It's checked out, ready to go," said a voice behind them. They turned to see Chief Halstert, a curmudgeonly, gray-haired human who ran the shuttlebay like his own fiefdom. He practically lived in the place. But since he had been on duty for four years, no one had stolen a shuttlecraft—a new record.

"Commander Riker called down and said you were cleared to launch," reported the chief. "The Stellar-class is a real sweetheart, but watch your range if you spend a lot of time in warp. Good luck—I don't think I'd want to get to close to that thing."

"We intend to keep a safe distance," answered Data, stepping through the hatch into the cabin of the shuttlecraft.

"Thanks, Chief." With a wave, Geordi followed his friend onto the craft. He saw Halstert turn and jog away from them, seeking the safety of his observation booth. He must've remembered how quickly Data prepared for launch.

Less than a minute later, the great launch doors opened, and the doorstop-shaped *Balboa*, sporting twin warp nacelles, streaked into space.

The wind chimes tinkled merrily as a southernly breeze blew across the porch, bringing with it the sweet scents of lilac and honeysuckle, plus the gay laughter of children. Carol Marcus couldn't see the children, but she was certain they were out there . . . just beyond the high hedges and pink bougainvillea. She rocked contentedly on the old porch swing, watching the hummingbirds flit around the honeysuckle bushes, and she remembered sucking the nectar from those same sweet blossoms as a kid.

It was wonderful how little the old family home had changed over all these years. She vaguely remembered her parents selling it, but that couldn't be—or else they couldn't be here now. She must have been mistaken about that, but then so many things had been hazy lately. The present was incredibly vivid, but the past was like a book she had read years ago and only partially remembered.

Carol knew one thing—it was good to be on vacation after all the hard work of the last few months. When she looked at it, though, the work hadn't been that hard, thanks to her brilliant helpers.

She heard the screen door open with a creak, then slam shut, followed by footsteps crossing the porch. Carol recognized the sure footsteps right away, and she looked up to see Jim Kirk, holding a frosty glass of iced lemonade. When he gave her that winning smile, he looked impossibly handsome—about twenty-six years old with sandy hair and mirthful brown eyes. He was dressed in a tight-fitting gold lieutenant's uniform, just as he had been the day she first met him.

Jim touched her shoulder, and the old electricity still coursed between them. "I brought you a lemonade," he said.

"Thank you, Darling." She canted her head upward and closed her eyes, letting him kiss her longingly, yet gently. Finally Jim pulled away, still smiling at her with those dazzling dimples.

"Drink up," he suggested. "You must be thirsty."

"I am," she decided all of a sudden. Carol took a sip of the lemonade, and it was oddly flat, not having the usual biting tang she remembered. Then she took another sip, and it tasted much better—more lemony.

"How is that?" asked Jim with concern.

"Fine," she answered brightly. "It would be just perfect if David were here. When is he coming?"

"I talked to our son this morning," answered Kirk, "and the tests are going very well. He thinks he'll be able to join us tomorrow."

"Wonderful!" said Carol, clapping her hands together. "You can stay longer, too, can't you?"

"Of course, Sweetheart," he answered, kneeling in front of her and taking her free hand in his.

"Don't you have to report back to the *Farragut*?"

"No, I'm on special assignment," answered Jim. "Taking care of you is my only priority."

"And Genesis," she added.

"And Genesis," he agreed. "I haven't worked on it for as long as you and David, but I feel it's my baby, too."

"Well, it has changed so much, hasn't it?" she answered proudly. "The new delivery system . . . the carrier wave . . . the experimental life-forms. It means so much to me that Genesis is on the front burner again." "But still a secret," Jim reminded her. "Not that you would ever tell anybody." He gently rocked her in the swinging porch chair, his voice taking on a soothing tone. "Nobody will know, not after you managed to keep it a secret for so many years. You are amazing."

"I was bursting to tell someone," said Carol with a yawn.

Jim gently took the glass of lemonade from her hand. "Honey, I can see in your eyes that you look a little tired. Don't feel that you have to stay awake on my account. You could take a nap right here on the porch. There's no one around—no one to worry about. Go ahead . . . sleep."

"Yes, I could," rasped Carol, immense drowsiness overcoming her. "Why not?"

He touched her forehead, and his hand felt as cool and dry as the breeze. Carol took his hand and held it to her face as she drifted off to sleep, the happiest woman in the universe.

Maltz grumbled and cursed in Klingon for several seconds, then crawled out from under the instrument panel and looked forlornly at Leah Brahms. "It's not going to work . . . we're still leaking plasma, and I can't fix the comm system."

Paldor and Bekra crowded around the cockpit of the shuttlecraft, shooting questions at the Klingon, but he ignored them while waiting for Leah to respond. In desperation, she finally turned to the Capellan and the Tellarite and shouted, "Be quiet! I can't hear myself *think*!"

Chagrined, Bekra retreated and hopped one-legged back to his seat, but Paldor pressed forward. "What's going on? We've got a right to know!"

Maltz growled and looked about ready to throttle the annoying Tellarite, but Leah put a calming hand on his shoulder. "It's okay. We have to face the truth."

She took a deep breath and turned to her shipmates. "It's like this—we already had damage, and we took more damage from the Pellean attack. We're leaking plasma, which means our fuel is going to run out sooner than expected."

"How soon?" asked Paldor.

"That depends whether we want to keep life support going."

"You mean, we can fly farther if we're all dead?" asked Bekra snidely.

Leah sighed. "I guess that's not an option, is it? I'd say we have twenty minutes . . . half an hour at the most."

"That does it!" shouted Paldor angrily. The Tellarite began to pace, making the cabin of the shuttlecraft seem even more cramped. "You should have listened to *me*! I never wanted to go to Pelleus V. I wanted to get out of the way of that thing! Now we don't have enough fuel to get out of the way—it's just going to eat us alive . . . like it did all the others!"

Maltz countered, "No, you will be spared that, because I am going to kill you!" The Klingon jumped to his feet and lunged for the Tellarite, but the big humanoid threw himself over a row of seats and crouched in the back.

"That's enough," snapped Leah, grabbing Maltz by the sash and pulling him gently back to his seat. "We're not going to spend our last few minutes bickering—we're going to find a way out. If we don't, we'll join lots of other good people."

"We're not all going to die," said Bekra with a sneer. "*One* of us is going to live."

The Capellan pointed to the hulking white radiation suit in the corner, and everyone's eyes followed his gesture. After a moment, Paldor timidly asked, "How will we choose who lives?"

"It's not *my* suit," said Maltz. He looked pointedly from Bekra to Paldor. "Not yours either."

Leah couldn't help herself—she laughed out loud at the absurdity of this argument, and the three males stared at her as if she were insane. Under their gaze, her deranged laughter trailed off. "I'm sorry; I lost it there. One of you can have it. I lived through seeing my husband and colleagues all die, and I'm not going to do *that* again. Besides, judging by how quickly we've been rescued so far, whoever is in that suit is just going to float in space for a few days longer before he dies, too."

"Still, it's a chance, isn't it?" said Bekra. "That's all we've been doing for the last day, trying to turn disaster into a fighting chance."

Leah nodded sadly, unable to argue with that. "Make sure you keep the isolinear chip in the pocket, so in a thousand years when they find your mummified body, they'll know what killed you."

"I think I should wear the suit," declared Maltz. "I need to tell someone what I know about this weapon."

"Why don't you tell me?" suggested Bekra. "Then I could wear the suit and survive."

"What about *me*?" wailed Paldor indignantly. "I work with Dr.

Brahms, so I should be next in line. I'm also the youngest of everyone here. Most of my life is ahead of me."

Maltz grinned and slammed his fist into his palm. "What do you say we fight to the death for the honor? That way, even the losers will benefit from a valiant death. Come on, I will fight both of you at once!" He crouched down, waving his arms.

"Maltz, there's not enough room in this shuttlecraft for a brawl to the death," said Leah with disgust. "It's my invention, and I'll choose. Paldor is the youngest, and he already knows how the suit works. I haven't got time to train one of you."

The Tellarite leaped to his feet and rushed forward. "Oh, Dr. Brahms, thank you very much!" he gushed. "I won't forget this . . . or you."

"You have to get the suit on," she pointed out. "And it wasn't designed for someone your size."

"I'll get in," promised the Tellarite, rushing to the back of the cabin and starting to strip.

With a scowl, Maltz dropped into the seat beside her. "I can't believe you let that . . . that nuisance save himself."

"I'm still going to try to save us all," answered Leah.

Without warning, a beep sounded on her console, and the computer voice broke in, "Plasma injectors are depleted, and deuterium reserves are low. We are now operating on emergency gel-packs. We will come out of warp in one minute."

"Hurry!" shouted Leah. "The leak was worse than we thought!"

Grunting and groaning, Paldor tried to shoehorn himself into the hard-shelled suit, but he ended up crashing to the deck in a heap. Grumbling and cussing, Maltz rose to his feet and tried to help the Tellarite get into the armor. Having to keep her eyes on her instruments, Leah couldn't really watch them, but she heard howls of pain from Paldor.

"Keep going!" insisted the Tellarite through clenched teeth. "I'm almost in!"

"You people are fools!" shouted Bekra. "I should be the one who lives!" The one-legged Capellan suddenly lunged out of his seat, tackling Maltz and knocking Paldor over. The scene was surreal, although Leah only caught glimpses of it, with Maltz and Bekra grappling in the aisle while Paldor wrestled with the radiation suit. It looked as if the brawl to the death had broken out after all.

Maltz finally clawed his way to the top position, and he slugged the Capellan into unconsciousness. Without a word, the Klingon staggered to his feet and went back to helping Paldor, but the ruckus had cost them precious seconds. Paldor whimpered anxiously as he tried again to get into the suit.

With a low whine, the shuttlecraft dropped out of warp and began cruising at impulse speeds. Leah wished she knew some Klingon curses of her own, because she was all out of tricks. She fought the temptation to look for the wave, because she knew it was out there, churning through the heavens, bearing down on them.

She had a strong urge to call for help, which was futile, because all she had was local short-range communications, hardly better than a combadge. Still she opened up her comm channel and shouted, "Mayday! Mayday! We're out of fuel. We need help!"

"Maintain position," came a calm male voice, breaking through the crackle of static. "Stand by to transport."

"What?" she asked. No one else was paying the slightest attention, with Bekra sprawled unconscious on the deck and Paldor and Maltz still struggling to squeeze the Tellarite into the radiation suit. Maybe she had imagined that calm, efficient voice answering her hail, but it gave her the spark of hope she needed to keep thinking.

She stopped the shuttlecraft and checked her long-range sensors, certain the wave must be right behind them. Half-a-million kilometers away, there was nothing but the kind of destruction they had seen before, so it was almost on top of them. Behind her, she heard a howl of victory as Maltz finished fastening the back of the suit, encasing the Tellarite inside.

Brahms quickly hit her combadge. "Paldor, don't turn on the phase-shifting yet."

"Why not?" he demanded nervously.

"Because—" She felt a familiar tingle along her spine, or maybe it was delirium. "We're being rescued!" she cried.

Leah closed her eyes as her body was whisked away, and she didn't open them until she felt a deck under her feet. She looked up to see an angel with gleaming white eyes and outstretched hands, swooping in to catch her. Not only that, but he was an angel she *knew*. "Geordi!" Leah gasped with delight as she tumbled into his arms.

"Leah!" he shouted deliriously. "You're alive!" He gripped her and hugged her ferociously.

"More coming though!" called that calm, efficient voice.

Geordi immediately pulled her away from the small transporter platform, which was inside another shuttlecraft. She found herself weeping with relief, unable to do anything but shuffle along the aisle, going where he led her.

He guided her gently into a seat and grinned. "We'll talk in a second. The others—"

"Go, go!" she cried, anxiously gripping his arm. "Tell your pilot to go, too. There's no time to waste!"

# thirteen

Geordi had to use every ounce of discipline and sense of duty in his being to pull himself away from Leah Brahms. Then he heard a clomping sound, and he turned to see a grizzled Klingon step off the transporter.

"At last you showed up," grumped the Klingon. "I am Maltz."

"Pleased to meet you," said Geordi, shoving past him to catch an injured man who staggered off the transporter platform. The man, a Capellan by the look of him, shot a glare at the Klingon as Geordi lifted him into a seat. He noticed that the Capellan's leg had been amputated at the knee and was freshly bandaged.

"The next one is a big one!" warned Maltz.

That was an understatement, decided Geordi, when an enormous being encased in white armor arrived on the transporter pad, thrashing around and filling up the rear of the shuttlecraft. Geordi rushed to calm him and keep him from breaking anything.

"Now!" called Leah. "Get out of here!"

"Very well," answered Data. He worked his instrument panel, and the shuttlecraft jumped into space.

"Here, I will get him out." The old Klingon stood at Geordi's side, and he waved through the faceplate at the inhabitant of the bulky suit. "He is a nuisance named Paldor, and that other one is a traitor named Bekra." The Klingon pointed to the surly Capellan. "You seem to know our captain."

"Captain?" said La Forge, glancing at Leah. "You got promoted?"

She shrugged. "It was my shuttlecraft."

La Forge knew he should take statements and get particulars from everyone, but only one person on the vessel commanded his attention.

Since the Klingon seemed to know how to extricate the Tellarite from the suit, Geordi gave in and rushed to Leah's side.

"I . . . I just can't believe you're alive," he said, unable to stop grinning.

"That makes two of us." She looked beaten down, depressed, and he could guess why.

"Are you two the only ones who got away?"

She nodded and sniffed back the tears. Knowing Leah, this was probably one of the few times she had allowed herself to cry. "It was . . . It was horrible. I'd be dead, too, except for the radiation suit."

"I'm sorry," said Geordi, glancing behind him. The Tellarite was nearly out of the suit. "Yes, I remember the radiation suit from your last message. In fact, that's when we knew something was wrong." He quickly told her about his reply getting bounced, initiating the investigation which had brought the *Enterprise* here. But he could tell that she wasn't listening—she was in shock, grief-stricken, and exhausted. Soon she would have to describe what she had seen, but he wasn't going to make her do it now.

"I'm just glad that *you* were Paul Revere."

"Pardon me?" she asked with confusion.

"That was our nickname for you when we didn't know who you were." He patted her on the shoulder. "I know you've been through a lot, but you're all right now."

"No," she said, shuddering. "As long as that thing is out there, we're not all right. Everyone on Earth—"

"Earth?" echoed Geordi with alarm.

Data spoke up, "Which one of you claims to have secret information about this anomaly?"

"That would be me," said the gray-haired Klingon haughtily. "It is a weapon." He drew a bit closer to Data and peered curiously at him. "What kind of creature are you?"

"I am not a creature at all—I am an android."

"Are there many like you?"

"No." Data shook his head.

"Good." Maltz sat down beside him at the copilot's seat and studied the readouts. "Hmmm, this is a nicer shuttlecraft than she has. What ship did you say you were from?"

"The *Enterprise*. My captain would like to speak with you."

"I am sure he would," said the old Klingon with satisfaction. "The sooner, the better."

While Data contacted the ship, Geordi leaned forward to listen, but he discovered that Leah was asleep on his shoulder. So he sat still and listened, as did everyone else on the shuttlecraft. He could tell from the rapt attention that the Tellarite and the wounded Capellan were giving to Maltz that they also believed he knew what he was talking about.

"This is Captain Jean-Luc Picard of the Federation starship *Enterprise*."

The old Klingon lifted his stubbled chin and declared, "I am Maltz from the House of Grokan, formerly Klingon consul to Hakon. I have heard of you, Captain Picard. They say you respect our traditions."

"I do," replied the captain. "I would like to share a bottle of bloodwine with you, but right now we have more pressing matters. Do you know the origin of this destruction?"

"I do," said the old Klingon. "But are *you* the right one to tell?"

"Why is it such a secret?" asked Picard.

"I don't know—*you* tell me," said Maltz, holding up his palms. "This is the Federation's secret."

Frustrated, the captain scowled. "Listen, I'm about to meet with an admiral, and if you know anything that might be pertinent, it's your duty to tell me. If you don't, I have to conclude you're a *'yIHmey SurghwI'.*"

Maltz bristled and bolted upright; then he seemed to relax once again. "An admiral, eh? Listen, Picard, if this admiral seems to be hiding something from you, not being honest about what *they* know, all you have to do is say one word. That word is 'Genesis.'"

"Genesis?" asked Picard doubtfully. The word stirred a vague memory. Could this old Klingon mean *that* Genesis? If so . . .

Maltz nodded to himself, and there was a genuine look of fear in his eyes. "When I get to your ship, I will talk with you and your admiral. In the meantime, you could learn much armed with that word."

The Klingon sat back in his seat and made a regal motion to cut off the transmission. Data tapped his panel and said, "Captain, Dr. Leah Brahms is with us, and she believes Earth is in danger."

Picard nodded grimly. "We're working on those projections. We'll see you at the rendezvous. *Enterprise* out."

It suddenly became very quiet inside the shuttlecraft as everyone realized that *they* were safe but billions of people were not. But they had rescued four souls who would have been dead otherwise, and maybe one of them possessed the key to fighting this menace.

La Forge looked down at Leah, who was sleeping deeply, her head resting on his shoulder. He planned to live through this crisis, but if he had to die right this moment, he'd be a happy man.

*   *   *

Captain Picard rose slowly from his desk in his ready room, his lips thinning with distaste at the idea that Starfleet might know more about this peril than they let on. It was not beyond them to keep secrets, as he had learned recently. Nevertheless, Admiral Nechayev had always been straight with him, often brutally honest, in fact. When she had a dirty job for him, she told him it was a dirty job. If his crew would face extreme risk, she told him so.

His door chime sounded. "Come!" he said.

Will Riker poked his head in. "I thought you would like to know," said the first officer, "Admiral Nechayev is on her way up from the transporter room."

"We're meeting here?" asked the captain, slightly surprised. "Very well. How many aides does she have with her?"

"None," answered Riker. "It's just her."

Hmmm, thought Picard. It was odd that their conversation was to be private when they had so much they should be doing. He decided to follow the old Klingon's advice and look for other signs of secrecy.

"Stick around, Number One," he said. "I'd like you to sit in."

"Fine, Captain." Riker stepped inside, allowing the door to shut behind him. "We're running projections based on our new data, and it doesn't look good."

"Is Earth in its path?"

"It could be," agreed Riker with surprise. "How did you know?"

"One of the people on the Paul Revere shuttlecraft was Leah Brahms. She told Data that Earth was in the path."

"Leah Brahms," said Riker with a slight smile. "I bet Geordi is happy."

Another chime sounded at the door, and both Riker and Picard snapped to attention as the captain said, "Enter."

The door opened, and in walked a slight woman with grayish-blond hair, a cranberry uniform, and a bar on her collar with five pips. Alynna Nechayev was not the kind of woman you'd pay much attention to if you passed her on the street, but you couldn't get around her in Starfleet. If you were an enemy of the Federation, she would have your head on a platter, and she was not above fighting dirty.

"Admiral," said Picard, mustering a smile.

"Captain Picard, Commander Riker," she acknowledged. "I hope I haven't interrupted you during a briefing, but we haven't got much time."

Picard nodded. "I was hoping Commander Riker could sit in with us and be—"

"Out of the question," snapped Nechayev. "We're tying to avoid a panic, so our plans have to remain secret for the time being. I'm sure you understand, Commander."

Riker raised an eyebrow that made it clear he *didn't* understand, but he still moved toward the door. "I'll keep you posted, Captain," he said on his way out.

*Okay*, thought Picard, *two more strikes against full disclosure*. After the door shut, he motioned the admiral to a guest chair while he went behind his desk. Despite his intentions to let Nechayev do most of the talking, Picard found himself speaking up. "I don't see how we can keep this a secret. We have to muster fleets of ships, evacuate dozens of planets, convene a meeting of the council. Whatever it takes."

"I don't want to dampen your enthusiasm," said Nechayev, "but we don't know the first thing about this phenomenon."

"Haven't you been looking at the raw data we sent you?" asked the captain. "Do you mean that nobody in Starfleet has formed a theory about what this thing is?"

"Yes, there have been theories," admitted Nechayev. "But if you asked ten different scientists, you'd get ten different answers. Meanwhile, Captain Picard, I don't appreciate your tone of voice. We're all working just as hard as we can to react to this crisis—putting out incomplete and false information won't help the situation."

Picard screwed up his courage and said the magic word: "Genesis."

Nechayev's poker face didn't change, but she did flinch for a moment. A blush came to her face as she considered what to do with the word, and she shifted in her chair. *Damn if the old Klingon wasn't right*, thought the captain.

She finally asked, "What makes you mention Genesis? It is just a . . . space legend."

"A certain old Klingon we rescued," answered Picard. Since that was the only fact he knew for certain, he hoped he could bluff the rest of the way. "So if the Klingons know Genesis is not a myth, why don't your veteran captains know?"

"I doubt if every Klingon knows about it," answered the admiral. "There might be a few—"

"His name is Maltz," said Picard.

Nechayev nodded with the grim certainty of a bridge player who has just realized that she can't make her contract. "Then you might as well hear our side of it, too. Read this and tell me what you think we ought to do." She opened a small utility pouch on her belt and pulled out an isolinear chip, which she handed to Picard.

With that, the admiral rose from her seat and started for the door. "We'll talk later, Captain. Although you may be angry at me now, you'll see that these decisions were made many years ago."

The captain also stood, hefting the purple storage chip in his palm. Nechayev's somber, almost defeated attitude was more disturbing than anything else he had seen that day.

"Admiral, what makes you so certain that thing out there *is* Genesis?"

"You'll read a lot about Dr. Carol Marcus in those documents," said Nechayev. "She was kidnapped six months ago, by parties unknown. We've been expecting something like this ever since, because she's the only one who knows how to build it. After you digest that, you won't be in the dark anymore. I'll be on the *Sovereign*."

Picard nodded, feeling more troubled than ever. So this was some kind of dangerous technology which the Federation had failed to protect properly. He couldn't help but wonder why they had built it in the first place.

# fourteen

After Admiral Nechayev left the ready room, Captain Picard sat with trepidation at his desk and inserted the isolinear chip into his computer terminal. Figuring he might need some soothing music, he requested a Beethoven sonata to play softly in the background. Then he leaned forward to read the documents given him by Admiral Nechayev.

## THE GENESIS REPORT

CLASSIFIED TOP SECRET
by Executive Order of The President
of The United Federation of Planets
18 December 2286
(Stardate 8399.4)

SECURITY CLEARANCE
LEVELS 9 AND HIGHER ONLY

Unauthorized access punishable by mandatory life imprisonment

## GENESIS REPORT—SUBJECT INDEX

01.00 TECHNICAL EVALUATION—03 November 2286
(Stardate 8411.2)
*Dr. Carol Marcus, director, Project Genesis*

**01.00  PROJECT GENESIS—TECHNICAL EVALUATION**
*Dr. Carol Marcus, director, Project Genesis*
Regula I Space Laboratory

Transmission Received via Secure Subspace Channel Zed-328
03 November 2286 (Stardate 8411.2)


## 01.01  PROJECT OVERVIEW

Project Genesis was a scientific research program whose goal was to develop a process whereby uninhabitable planets could be transformed into worlds suitable for sustaining a variety of life-forms. The project began its preliminary research in August 2270, under my direction, as a purely voluntary effort by more than a dozen scientists from throughout the Federation.

The first challenge of the project was to harness the power, and control the behavior, of a wide variety of subatomic particles. The second, and far more daunting challenge, was to prevent the premature degradation of matter generated by the matrix. Because of the extremely high energy level of a Genesis Wave reaction, the strong and weak nuclear forces essential to normal subatomic cohesion are annihilated. Controlling the behavior of subatomic particles was only the first step; we next needed to isolate the Genesis Effect from external particles in order to effect the renormalization of covalent bonds.

Numerous new technologies were developed to isolate the reaction matrix from such hazardous particles as various colors and flavors of quarks, bosons, muons, gluons and assorted high-energy/low-mass cosmic particles. The greatest threat was the spontaneous appearance of quark strangelets, which initiated near-instantaneous and total annihilation of the matrix. (Refer to Starfleet Research & Development briefing 478594 for a complete catalog of the Project Genesis Subatomic Bestiary.)

In July 2272, we succeeded in directing the behavior of several types of fermions by altering their quantum states through the use of a Heisenberg compensator coupled with a quantum flux capacitor. The Heisenberg compensator and quantum flux capacitor also served to isolate the matrix from external particle interference, and consequently became the first integral components in the Genesis Matrix Generator.

Once it became possible to direct the behavior of subatomic particles, the next step in the development of Project Genesis was to create the Genesis Matrix, which would serve as the quantum-level template to guide the reassembly of high-energy particles into cohesive matter and renormalize their strong and weak nuclear forces.

The Genesis Matrix was crafted to simulate the geophysical structure, topography, environmental chemistry and organic ecosystems of a range of Class-M planets suitable for humanoid life, although the matrix could theoretically be reprogrammed to generate the full range of planetary types and simulate various alien organic ecosystems. These mutagenic changes are permanent.

From July 2272 to October 2282, we conducted numerous controlled experiments in our laboratory on Deneva, applying the Genesis Matrix to various types of inanimate matter, at varying energy levels. Despite some early setbacks that caused the reformed matter to disintegrate within minutes, a reformulation of the matrix in 2283 by my son and colleague, Dr. David Marcus, succeeded in long-term stabilization of matter reorganized by the Genesis Matrix.

In November 2283, it became evident that continuation of Project Genesis would require a level of funding, technological resources, and manpower that my private scientific consortium was no longer able to provide. In order to continue our work to its logical conclusion, a research grant proposal was made to the United Federation of Planets' Department of Science. Funding and official assistance was secured in March 2284, and Starfleet made available the services of the *Starship Reliant* and her crew, and relocated our team to the Regula I Space Laboratory, in orbit above the Class-D asteroid Regula, in the Mutara Sector.

Development of the planetary delivery system and the high-power Genesis Wave generator was completed at the Regula I Space Laboratory in February 2284, at which time a first-generation Genesis Device prototype was constructed. The first device was designed for a low-power, limited-range-of-effect detonation within a confined space. On March 3, 2284, at our request, the Starfleet Corps of Engineers began to excavate an underground facility within the Regula asteroid, which we confirmed was composed only of inanimate matter. The *Starship Reliant* was tasked with finding a planet devoid of all life, in a suitable orbit for a Class-M world, on which to test a full-scale Genesis Effect. The excavation of our underground test site took the engineers ten months to complete.

In January 2285, after the sealed underground space had been sufficiently hollowed out and was confirmed to be free of gaseous particles, we initiated our first field test of the Genesis Matrix. The test was an unqualified success and transformed the lifeless, vacuum-sealed underground cavern into a thriving primitive organic ecosystem that required only the addition of artificial sunlight to sustain itself. New plant forms evolved at a dramatically accelerated rate within the new environment, a consequence that had not been anticipated during development.

Although the test versions of the Genesis Matrix included no templates for eukaryotic life-forms, they could conceivably be added in future versions of the matrix; however, given the rapid evolutionary rates of plant species within the matrix, such a course of action might be inadvisable, depending upon the genetic complexity of the animal species. Plankton and krill might prove relatively stable, whereas higher-order forms might not.

## 01.02 THE MUTARA NEBULA DETONATION

The final intended phase of Project Genesis was to await *Starship Reliant's* discovery of a suitable test planet for the final prototype test. However, this effort was sabotaged by the actions of Khan Noonien Singh, who on March 22, 2285, hijacked the *Starship Reliant*, stranded most of her crew on Ceti Alpha V, and on March 25, 2285, stole the Genesis Device from our underground facility, where we had hidden it for safekeeping. Khan detonated the Genesis Device on March 26, 2285, in the Mutara Nebula.

## 01.03 THE GENESIS PLANET

The detonation of the Genesis Device within the Mutara Nebula resulted in the formation of the Genesis Planet from the cloud of stellar and planetary debris of which the nebula was composed. The planet coalesced within hours into a primordial sphere of molten rock approximately .47 times the mass of Earth, but with a variable gravity field of .78-G to 1.36-G. Because of its low total mass and accelerated subatomic reaction rate, the planet cooled and formed a solid crust over its mantle and molten core in less than 26 hours. Plant lifeforms evolved almost immediately and spread quickly across the planet surface.

During the weeks following the formation of the Genesis Planet, erratic weather systems developed, and the planet's crust became increasingly fragile and susceptible to geothermal stressors. Alien microbes introduced into the planet's ecosystem by a soft-landing Starfleet torpedo casing, used as a burial container, evolved rapidly into eukaryotic forms, including complex invertebrate animal forms.

The planet's subatomic bonds destabilized rapidly, and finally disintegrated altogether on April 29, 2285, resulting in its explosion.

A posthumous report filed by Dr. David Marcus revealed that the planet had destabilized because he had used protomatter, an energy-rich but notoriously unstable form of matter, to energize the Genesis Wave. He had used protomatter because it was the only way he could generate an initial energy burst of sufficient power to sustain a global imprinting of the Genesis Matrix. His use of protomatter was not revealed in any of his earlier documentation, leading to the regrettable conclusion that all experimental data for Project Genesis generated after 2282 are inaccurate, fraudulent or suspect.

### 01.04 FINDINGS & RECOMMENDATIONS
Because of the clearly unstable results produced by the Genesis Device, the process is unsafe for the creation of habitable worlds, rendering the technology worthless for rapid terraforming.

Because of the inherently dangerous and unpredictable nature of protomatter, the Genesis Device is not reliable enough to be repurposed for military applications, which would in any event be unethical and in violation of the Federation charter; because the Genesis Wave would replace a living world's ecosystem with one generated by the Genesis Matrix, any use of this device on a living world could be described only as genocide.

For the above reasons, and because of the flawed and unethical research methods used to develop the Genesis Device, my formal recommendation to the Federation Council is that all research into Project Genesis' continued development be terminated immediately and permanently. This concludes my report.

*Dr. Carol Marcus*

### 02.00 STRATEGIC EVALUATION
*Commander Stephen J. Klisiewicz, Starfleet Intelligence*
San Francisco, Earth
Received via Encrypted Internal Channel 423-Sierra
09 November 2286 (Stardate 8420.1)

### 02.01 CIVILIAN APPLICATIONS
After evaluating the continued stability of the Genesis Cave within the Regula asteroid, this office has concluded that Project Genesis is stable at low-power levels when applied on a small scale. Although the technology has clearly proved too unstable for large-scale terraform-

ing efforts, it continues to be a promising technology for rapidly establishing sustainable food sources in remote locations. Extrapolating from the volume of transformed matter in the project's Phase Two experiment, we believe the Genesis Effect could safely be applied to many underground locations, as well as on large asteroids or very small moons located in favorable orbits.

## 02.02 SCIENTIFIC APPLICATIONS

Despite the late-phase failure of the Genesis Device prototype and Dr. Carol Marcus' understandable concerns regarding Dr. David Marcus' falsification of critical data, we believe there is still substantial scientific merit to continuing research into the Project Genesis technology. The ability to reorder subatomic particles into animate matter is one that, if it could be harnessed at much lower energy levels, could yield near-miraculous discoveries in medicine, materials fabrication, and agriculture and aquaculture.

Although the energy requirements of the process currently are far too high to risk exposing living subjects to its effects, we believe that within two centuries discoveries spurred by Project Genesis research could lead to cellular-regeneration matrices that would permit the near-perfect repair of all cellular damage. Such a discovery would, in essence, allow organic sentient beings to achieve lifespans so greatly extended that they would effectively become immortal.

On a more immediate level, a technology that could transform raw energy into living plant and animal matter would revolutionize our food-production methods and represent a quantum leap forward from our current food-replication models.

## 02.03 MILITARY APPLICATIONS

Despite the obvious, sheer power of the Genesis Device as a weapon, this office concurs with Dr. Marcus that it would be unethical, immoral, and a violation of Federation and interstellar law to pursue any development of the Genesis Device for military purposes. Furthermore, because of the instability of protomatter, it would be unsafe to transport it as part of a live ordnance system aboard a Federation starship.

There is a serious risk, however, that foreign powers might seek to replicate Genesis Device technology and employ it against the Federation.

As a weapon of mass destruction, the Genesis Device would be one of the most lethal systems ever devised. It most likely would be deployed as a torpedo launched from a starship, from a range of not more than 1 A.U., assuming the device is used in its current configuration. Because of the payload of protomatter located in the device's core, it would be unsafe to fit the torpedo delivery system with an anti-matter-based propulsion system capable of warp-speed travel, because the proximity to the warp drive's subspace field would catastrophically destabilize the protomatter, resulting in premature detonation. This lack of warp capability significantly reduces the threat of interstellar deployment of the device. (This assessment will need to be revised if, at some future time, a means is found to shelter the protomatter core from the subspace field without compromising the functioning of the system.)

Another distressing possibility would be a limited-range Genesis Device, such as the one used inside the Regula Asteroid, reduced in size to fit inside a scanproof diplomatic courier container or ship's hold. Our preliminary simulations indicate the Genesis Matrix could be reprogrammed to create a micro-ecosystem of virulent airborne and waterborne genetic pathogens that could swiftly grow and "infect" an entire biosphere, ultimately killing or replacing all life-forms on the planet.

The Genesis Effect for such a weapon could initially be of very low power, perhaps low enough to evade detection by existing planetary sensor nets. More important, the Genesis Device could be programmed to spontaneously tailor its pathogens to the environment in which it is detonated, creating a universally lethal effect in microseconds without requiring any prior research into the target's genetic code.

## 02.04 POTENTIAL COUNTERMEASURES

Unfortunately, short of destroying a Genesis Device before its detonation sequence is triggered, there currently are no known methods for shielding a ship or planet from the Genesis Effect. We are researching a system that would create an energy wave whose signature is the perfect inverse of the Genesis Wave, as a potential negation method, but because of the Genesis Device's tremendous energy level and uniquely complex wave signature, there has been no success with this method as of this time.

## 02.05 FINDINGS & RECOMMENDATIONS

Contrary to Dr. Marcus' suggestion, which we believe to be inspired by her grief over the recent death of her son on the Genesis Planet, we feel that Project Genesis has enormous potential civilian, scientific, and military applications, and requires further top-secret research within Starfleet Research & Development.

In addition, the very real risk of this technology being acquired or independently duplicated by powers external to the Federation make it imperative that our knowledge of this technology be complete and accurate. We must not let others turn our own science against us because we are too morally repulsed to look beyond the horrors of the device's failures to see its full potential.

*Commander Stephen Klisiewicz*


## 03.00  POLITICAL EVALUATION
*Xev Chiana, Secretary of State, United Federation of Planets*
Paris, Earth
Received via Encrypted Internal Channel 719-Kilo
16 December 2286 (Stardate 8426.9)


### 03.01  DIPLOMATIC RAMIFICATIONS
The political fallout in the wake of the detonation of the Genesis Device in the Mutara Nebula can best be described as "disastrous." Aside from the expected howls of alarm that immediately were logged by the Klingon and Romulan ambassadors to the Federation, protests were declared in the Council Hall by several Federation Council representatives, including those from Deneva, Cestus III, Argelius and Mars.

Despite numerous efforts at political rapprochement with both the Klingon and Romulan governments in recent years, their ambassadors' filibusters in the Council Hall were met with little concern and silenced for the most part by Federation Ambassador Sarek of Vulcan. Despite the Klingon Ambassador's insistence on referring to the device as "the Genesis Torpedo," Ambassador Sarek made a compelling argument for the nonmilitary nature of Project Genesis.

Most of the protests entered into the record by Council representatives stemmed from their desire to distance themselves from what they perceived to be the development of a weapon of mass destruction. Ambassador Arwen of Mars, however, criticized the technology because of her mistaken perception that the Genesis Effect was designed to generate only Earthlike environments. After a detailed technical briefing by Dr. Carol Marcus, the Martian ambassador withdrew her protest.

The Klingon High Council and Romulan Senate, meanwhile, continue to demand that the Federation disclose the technical specifications for Project Genesis in order to, as they stated in a joint briefing, "maintain the balance of power in the quadrant."

In response to unambiguous refusals of their requests by the Federation President, the Klingons have threatened to resort to "more forceful means" and reportedly are tripling energy production output on the Klingon Homeworld's moon, Praxis, in anticipation of a military buildup.

The Romulans, for their part, appeared to take the President's refusal in stride, but since that meeting long-range sensors have detected a marked increase in activity by Romulan starships on their side of the Neutral Zone.

Starfleet Command has reported that the additional vessels and personnel required to police both the Klingon and Romulan borders simultaneously is presenting enormous logistical difficulties and is reducing the fleet's ability to enforce the law and conduct routine patrols within Federation territory. Consequently, Admiral N.J. Weiland of Starfleet Operations is recommending that Starfleet temporarily shift its focus from constructing Starbases to enlarging the fleet, in the interest of interstellar security.

### 03.02  PACIFICATION OF FEDERATION RIVALS

In order to mollify representatives from the Klingon, Romulan, Gorn and Tholian governments, the Federation Security Council officially interdicted the Genesis Planet on March 28, 2285 (Stardate 8201.5), restricting all traffic in the Mutara Sector and prohibiting all starships from approaching to closer than 10 A.U. from the planet. Only preauthorized Starfleet research vessels were permitted to approach and orbit the planet.

A Klingon bird-of-prey, captained by Commander Kruge, ambushed the Federation science vessel *U.S.S. Grissom* in orbit over the Genesis Planet on April 28, 2285, and also contributed to the destruction of the hijacked Starfleet vessel *U.S.S. Enterprise*. Kruge and his crew murdered Dr. David Marcus on April 29, 2285, on the Genesis Planet in a failed effort to obtain scientific data about Project Genesis. Kruge and all but one member of his crew, Second Officer Maltz, perished on the Genesis Planet when it exploded. Their bird-of-prey subsequently was commandeered by Captain James T. Kirk and his expatriate crew, who took the stolen vessel to Vulcan for a three-month period of exile, before returning in the vessel to Earth.

The official position of the Klingon High Council was that Kruge acted alone and in defiance of explicit orders not to violate Federation space, in an effort to enhance his political standing in the Klingon Empire by acquiring "the secrets of Genesis." The Klingon High Council denied any prior knowledge of Kruge's intent and disavowed any involvement in his actions.

In the interest of diplomacy, the Federation Security Council has chosen not to seek reparations for violations of the border treaty, the destruction of the starships *Grissom* and *Enterprise*, or the murder of Dr. David Marcus. Similarly, the Klingon High Council has withdrawn its demand for the immediate return of the bird-of-prey stolen by Captain Kirk and his crew, choosing instead to view its capture as "spoils of war."

Further protests, however, have been filed by the Klingon High Council following the August 7, 2285, full pardons of Kirk's crew and the dismissal of all charges against Kirk himself (except for one charge of disobeying the orders of a superior officer), and their subsequent assignment to active duty aboard a newly commissioned *Starship Enterprise*, under Kirk's command. The Federation Council has taken the Klingon government's protest under advisement.


**03.03  THREAT OF EXTERNAL DUPLICATION**
In response to the very real risk that a foreign power—such as the Klingon Empire, Romulan Empire, or Tholian Assembly—might choose to develop its own Genesis Device for less noble purposes than peaceful terraforming, the Federation Diplomatic Corps has undertaken a major treaty initiative in an attempt to prevent the proliferation of this dangerous technology.

The Tholian Assembly has willingly entered into negotiations to suppress the technology, most likely because they expect to be technologically unable to duplicate the Genesis Effect for at least twenty-five years, due to their technological emphasis on adapting to new planetary environments through enclosed shelters due to the extreme conditions on their homeworld.

The Romulans so far have declined to sign the treaty unless they receive additional territorial concessions by the Federation along the Neutral Zone. Federation Ambassador Liz Braswell currently is developing a counterproposal that would concede no territory directly to the Romulan Star Empire but would extend the area of the Neutral Zone deeper into Federation space.

The Klingons, naturally, are resisting all attempts at diplomacy,

demanding instead the surrender of all Project Genesis technical specifications and Genesis Device schematics, and refusing to consider
any treaty that requires a ban on weapons development.

### 03.04 FINDINGS & RESOLUTIONS
Weighing the political stability of the Federation and Alpha Quadrant
against both Dr. Carol Marcus' concerns and Starfleet's strategic
desires, the prudent course of action appears to be to cease all public
research into Project Genesis and to halt all Federation-funded
research of the technology until the political climate becomes more
conducive to diplomacy.

Starfleet Intelligence has been issued an Executive Order from the
Federation President to initiate long-term covert operations within
Klingon and Romulan territory to detect and actively sabotage any
efforts by those entities to develop their own Genesis Devices.

Future inquiry into the applications of Project Genesis will be
conducted under Level 9 Security Protocols by Starfleet Research &
Development. Project Genesis data and technology are hereby classified as Level Ten munitions, and any publication, duplication, transmission, or possession of said data; or creation, possession, shipment,
sale, or transfer of an active or inactive Genesis Device, or any of its
primary components, by any unauthorized person(s) or agency will be
prosecuted as treason (for Federation citizens) and espionage, and in
all cases shall be punishable by a mandatory sentence of life imprisonment in solitary confinement, with no possibility of parole.

### 03.05 ADDENDUM—FINAL DETERMINATION
By agreement of all the parties to the Genesis Nonproliferation Treaty,
all records, materials, schematics, mock-ups, and logs of Project Genesis are ordered destroyed, and active research is hereby terminated.

*Xev Chiana*

### 04.00 PROJECT GENESIS—A REASSESSMENT
*Lt. David A. Mack, Starfleet Research & Development*
New York, Earth
Report filed via Encrypted Internal Channel Alpha-5C
12 May 2374 (Stardate 53303.4)

## 04.01 INTRODUCTION

Officially, only anecdotal evidence exists about Project Genesis, although enough people are familiar with its controversial history to have kept unofficial records and theories, especially of related technologies that might someday be applied to a rebirth of Genesis. Non-Federation powers have tried to duplicate the efforts of Dr. Carol Marcus and her team, to no avail. This document is merely meant as an assessment of where Project Genesis now stands in its development cycle, because this technology is too dynamic to be ignored.

## 04.02 RECENT DISCOVERIES REGARDING PROTOMATTER

Pioneering work performed at the Vulcan Science Academy by Dr. Temok and at the Daystrom Institute by Dr. Glenn Hauman indicate that the instabilities in protomatter are the result of interactions between its subatomic constituents and a nine-dimensional 5/2 spin variant on the quark strangelet, which Temok and Hauman have agreed to dub a "changelet."

Changelets affect the strong nuclear force in the covalent bonds of protomatter, and are able to breach the dimensional gap because of natural fluctuations in the fabric of space-time. According to Dr. Temok, because changelets are extradimensional, they are extraordinarily massive when compared with other subatomic particles. They appear to have a mass of approximately 21.9 GEv, placing them beyond the threshold of the gravitational constant.

Because of their already precarious position in the space-time continuum, changelets become volatile in the presence of subspace fields, which further warp the fabric of space-time, thereby permitting the negatively charged changelet to interact directly with the densely clustered protons of protomatter. The result is a catastrophic, chain-reaction annihilation of protomatter into high-energy photons.

According to Dr. Hauman, the tendency of protomatter to violently collapse in the presence of a subspace field can be counteracted through the application of a stasis field generated by a quantum flux capacitor and a Heisenberg compensator working in tandem. The compensator deflects space-time distortions from the protomatter, and at high-enough power levels can actually stabilize protomatter by suppressing microdimensional ripples in its subatomic structure that promote interaction with changelets. The quantum flux capacitor prevents subatomic constituents of protomatter from slipping through microdimensional fractures and encountering changelets.

## 04.03  A NEW THEORY ON THE COLLAPSE
## OF THE GENESIS PLANET

It has always been accepted that the Genesis Device had a protomatter core; both it and the Genesis Matrix were stabilized by a Heisenberg compensator and quantum flux capacitor. Although the two components had been used by the Marcus team only to guide the subatomic reassembly of the target planet in accordance with the Genesis Matrix, the device's compact design necessitated that the protomatter core be contained within the stabilization field.

Conventional wisdom has always blamed the planet's rapid disintegration on David Marcus' use of protomatter; our new research refutes that. Based on our study, we have concluded that the device in fact was remarkably stable, and that its results would also have been stable had the device been deployed in the manner for which it was designed.

Dr. Carol Marcus' own briefing to the Federation indicated that the Phase Three test of the device was intended to be carried out on a lifeless planetoid or small moon. We are confident that if the device had been detonated on an appropriate target—i.e., a lifeless small moon or asteroid in an appropriate orbit for sustaining a Class-M planet—it would have produced a stable, organically rich, and eminently habitable planet. (Our findings are supported by the continued stability of Project Genesis' thriving underground ecosystem within the Regula asteroid.)

Because the device was triggered in a diffuse nebula of highly charged gas and radioactive debris, the result was a highly unstable planet. Instead of transforming a solid-core planetoid already in a stable orbit, the Genesis Effect was forced to create from loose debris an entire planet with little-to-no inherent gravitational impetus to orbit its star. Furthermore, the newly formed Genesis Planet was subject to highly erratic gravitational fluctuations caused by its situation between two gas giant planets, resulting in its greatly accelerated rotation rate and a variety of severe atmospheric anomalies, which were required by the matrix to sustain a Class-M atmosphere at a less-than-ideal distance of 1.93 A.U. from a yellow dwarf star.

Those factors, coupled with the fact that the Genesis Wave was overextended because of the vast amount of energy needed to build a new planet from gas and dust, left the Genesis Effect incomplete. The final phase of the Genesis Effect, in which the strong and weak nuclear forces are renormalized at the subquantum level, never took place because the formation of the new planet prematurely depleted the reaction's energy.

Drs. Temok and Hauman concur with our assessment and are prepared to demonstrate to the Federation Security Council that Project Genesis is a successful, viable terraforming technology, and could be a potentially decisive weapon against the Borg if its inherent tactical weaknesses can be remedied.

## 04.04 PROPOSAL FOR DESIGN UPGRADES

The original Genesis Device was intended to be delivered to its target as a slow-velocity torpedo released from a starship. The original research team omitted warp propulsion systems from their prototype designs because they were unnecessary during the test phase. Later evaluations of the project's military applications concluded that because the Genesis Device contained protomatter, it would not be safe to equip it with a warp drive because the subspace field would cause the protomatter to detonate.

We believe the stabilizer field for the Genesis Matrix renders its protomatter safe for transport; we therefore can devise a number of methods for protecting the protomatter payload from subspace disruption while enabling the Genesis Device to be economically deployed across intermediate interstellar distances.

First, we can produce a more compact design, at roughly 45 percent of the mass of the original device, by employing more-advanced isolinear processors and ODN circuitry. Second, we can add an additional layer of duranium shielding around the Genesis Matrix core without compromising the effectiveness of the device. Third, we can install a Mark X warp coil and antimatter core in the rear half of the casing, enabling the device to sustain a velocity of warp seven for up to ninety-two hours. Last, we can adjust the warp-field geometry to envelop the device payload without putting undue stress on its core stabilizer.

## 04.05 KEEPING PROJECT GENESIS FROM THE BORG

Although use of the Genesis Device as a weapon is strictly prohibited by the Genesis Nonproliferation Treaty, the Borg are not signatories of that document, and keeping Genesis from them is a more pressing concern.

If the Borg were to capture Genesis Device technology, they would be able to equip it with a transwarp conduit generator, duplicate it, and send one to every Federation planet, instantly transforming them all into Borg homeworlds.

Unless a Genesis Device can be kept from Borg detection, it will be a devastating tactical alternative. Because of these possible consequences all efforts must be made to prevent their acquisition of the Genesis technology.

## 04.06 EXTERNAL POWERS DEVELOPING GENESIS TECHNOLOGY

Thanks to aggressive covert operations during the past century by Starfleet Intelligence, no other major Alpha Quadrant power has succeeded in developing a working Genesis Device. The Klingons' attempt to develop the technology as part of a military buildup is believed to have been a contributing factor in the June 2293 explosion of the moon Praxis, which caused massive environmental damage to the Klingon Homeworld.

The Romulan Star Empire withdrew from direct confrontation with the Federation following the Tomed Incident in 2311, and for nearly thirty years no Romulan vessels were detected within twenty light-years of the Romulan Neutral Zone. It is believed that the Romulans chose to pursue an aggressive expansion policy into the Delta Quadrant, and curtailed their investigations into the Genesis Effect in favor of rapidly building and deploying new starships.

The Tholian Assembly appears to have abided by the terms of the Genesis Nonproliferation Treaty.

Unconfirmed reports indicate the Cardassian Union flirted with a Genesis Device-like technology, but abandoned the research following a catastrophic accident at their key research facility. The official statement from the Cardassian Union blamed Bajoran terrorists for the explosion, but data from long-range sensor arrays indicate the explosion signature was consistent with a massive, uncontrolled protomatter detonation.

New reports, however, indicate that while the major governments of the Alpha Quadrant don't appear to be developing Genesis Device technologies, there are several terrorist factions and criminal organizations seeking to develop the technology privately. Among the organizations suspected of trafficking in protomatter with the intent of developing weapons of mass destruction are the Orion Syndicate and the Black Company, a large and well-equipped private mercenary corps.

A protomatter-based weapon also was employed by the Dominion in an unsuccessful attack on Bajor's primary star. In the aftermath of the collapse of Dominion forces in the Alpha Quadrant, other Dominion-crafted protomatter weapons might have fallen into the hands of black marketeers. Such weapons could be transformed into crude Genesis devices with the addition of a basic Genesis Matrix Generator and two components found in all transporters: the Heisenberg compensator and the quantum flux capacitor.

## 04.07  FINDINGS & RECOMMENDATIONS

Because the Genesis technology is, in fact, stable and safe, it would be an ideal tool for rapid terraforming. However, to avoid the political furor that accompanied the first use of the device, such a visible display of its capabilities is not advisable.

Its use as a military technology continues to be expressly forbidden by the Genesis Nonproliferation Treaty, and it is in conflict with the essential tenets of the Federation charter. Its use as a weapon also poses the unacceptably high risk that the technology will be acquired by powers hostile to the Federation—most notably, the Borg.

However, the failure of so many other parties to develop a working Genesis Device suggests that Dr. Carol Marcus has depths of knowledge unknown to both our own scientists and theirs. Including her in further research, while she is still alive, would be crucial to success.

The recommendation of this office is that further research and development to seek methods for using the Genesis Matrix to direct the creation of animate matter from raw energy, for the pursuit of peaceful applications for the fields of medicine, agriculture, and aquaculture, is tempting but inadvisable

*Lt. David Mack*

# fifteen

Captain Picard took a deep breath and rose from his desk, the ramifications of what he had just read still sorting themselves in his brain. Now he knew why Admiral Nechayev seemed so subdued—she was frightened, much more frightened than the Dominion, Cardassians, or Maquis had ever made her. And why not? In brilliant phosphors, his screen said there was no way to stop the Genesis Effect, and the basic components were off-the-shelf commodities.

Over the years, Picard had heard rumors of Genesis but had dismissed them as exaggerated tales or a theoretical technology. But it seemed that Genesis was all too real.

Picard paced his ready room, hands behind his back. The documents mentioned torpedoes as the delivery system, but this was no torpedo barrage they were facing—this was an energy wave, sweeping across space and expanding as it went. The documents said that ignition of this device caused an energy wave which swept across a planet, causing the mutagenic changes. It was plain to see that someone had perfected the device to work without the torpedo. They were deploying the wave itself—indiscriminately across the vastness of space.

*But who? And why?* Picard pushed a hopeless sigh through his clenched teeth, realizing that the answer was depressingly simple. *Conquer all the planets you want without risking a single casualty, and do it instantly! Not only will everything be just the way you like it when you get there, but there won't be any annoying locals to bother you.*

The captain tapped his combadge. "Picard to bridge."

"Riker here."

Picard crossed to his computer screen and entered a command. "Number One, I'm going to send you some reading material. Read it and disseminate it to the senior staff; send it to the *Balboa* as well. Add to the message that Dr. Carol Marcus was kidnapped six months ago. This concerns the current crisis, so tell everyone to start thinking. When Data and La Forge return, the senior staff will have a briefing."

"Yes, Sir," said Riker. "Got it. Anything else?"

"As soon as I can reach the admiral," said Picard, "I'm going over to the *Sovereign.*"

Onboard the shuttlecraft *Balboa,* Data read the missive from the *Enterprise* in a matter of seconds, then recapped it orally for the others. From the sour looks around him, Geordi decided that all of them were getting sick to their stomachs hearing this, especially the old Klingon. When Data mentioned that Maltz was in the file, he perked up a bit, but then his gaze grew distant as he relived his own nightmares of Project Genesis.

Data concluded by saying that Dr. Carol Marcus had been kidnapped, which seemed to bring the mystery full circle. Sitting beside the engineer, wrapped in a blanket, Leah Brahms shivered, and Geordi resisted the temptation to wrap his arm around her.

Leah shook her head. "Maltz told me that *we* had invented it, but I didn't believe him. This Genesis sounds exactly like what I saw on Seran, down to the rapid growth of new life. I can only tell you . . . if you are on the rock which gets chewed up by this thing, you don't view it so benignly. Whoever tried to keep Genesis a secret was on the right track—they just didn't work hard enough."

"What goes around comes around," said Geordi softly. "You think you can bury a thing—forget about it—but you never can." He was thinking of his feelings for Leah as much as the promising invention turned deadly. He gazed at the slight woman curled up beside him. Her hair plastered limply to her head, grief etched in her face, and her clothes soiled and torn, Leah Brahms was still beautiful.

"It must have been awful down there," said Geordi sympathetically, unable to find the right words. "I'm truly sorry about Mikel and your team. I can't imagine—"

She gently touched his arm. "Let's hope you'll never be able to imagine it. Nobody deserves to die like that . . . in sheer terror . . . your body convulsed in pain."

Leah shivered and lowered her eyes. "You never got to know Mikel very well, but he really liked you, Geordi. I would tell him all the places you went, adventures you had, and I think he lived vicariously through you. I know I did." She swallowed hard. "We often talked about signing aboard a research vessel, but it was just one of those things we never did."

"All of this is very touching," said a snide voice behind them. "But is the Federation going to do anything about this?"

La Forge turned to see the Capellan, Bekra, looking expectantly at him. "Do you have any ideas?" asked the engineer.

"Yes." The Capellan pointed to the radiation suit. "This thing saved *her* life, and it could save everyone's, if we had enough of them."

Leah gave a hollow laugh. "The plans and components are all gone . . . lost with everything else on Seran. I'm sure I could duplicate it, but it would probably take me a few weeks—and we don't have that. It also depends upon Romulan phase-shifting technology, which is better than my poor imitation. We need to consult directly with the Romulans."

From the copilot seat came a hearty laugh. "We've got somebody who can talk to the Romulans for us." He pointed at Consul Bekra, and the Capellan shifted uneasily under the scrutiny.

Leah ignored him, and her eyes stared straight ahead. "That's not the worst of it," she rasped. "Even if you could survive when the Genesis Wave swept over your planet, you wouldn't want to live in what was left behind. You wouldn't want to be there for ten seconds."

"I agree," muttered the old Klingon.

"However," said Data from the cockpit, "somebody must plan to live on the altered planets, or else why go to the trouble of terraforming them?"

"Maybe they just don't like the Federation," said Maltz. "There are plenty of species who don't."

"We've got to find the ones who did this," said Leah softly, "and kill them."

"Yes!" agreed Maltz heartily. "A blood oath. Kahless, give me the strength to be there with you, Captain, when you rip out their hearts."

"Thank you," said Leah grimly. "That would be good."

Conversation inside the shuttlecraft trailed off after that, as the pall of death haunted their journey back to the *Enterprise*.

"The Stellar Cartography room," said a young ensign, pointing toward double doors at the end of the corridor. "The admiral is in there."

"Thank you, Ensign," replied Captain Picard. Since the *Sovereign* was the model for the *Enterprise*, he could have found the right room without any difficulty, but protocol demanded the escort. "You have a fine ship here."

"Thank you, Sir," answered the young man, snapping to attention. He remained at attention until Picard strode through the doors at the end of the corridor.

The Stellar Cartography room of the *Enterprise* had been turned into a war room, with the positions and courses of hundreds of ships outlined on a sweeping, three-dimensional, holographic star chart. The image rotated slowly, updating constantly, showing fleets of ships converging on their position. Admiral Nechayev stood in the midst of the three-dimensional rendering, pointing out vessels to an aide, who made notes on a padd.

Picard waited patiently while the admiral finished her task; then she stepped down from the holograph and shook his hand. "Thank you for coming, Captain Picard. You see, we haven't been totally inactive—we've got portions of five fleets coming and more in reserve. Of course, a lot of these ships are freighters, passenger ships, and such. The official story is that we're evacuating planets because of a plague."

"I told my senior staff the truth," answered Picard, "and I let them see the documents."

Nechayev scowled, and her eyes narrowed upon the captain. Her aides cast their eyes down and tried to look busy. "You had no authorization, no right . . ."

"I don't believe we can fight this thing unless we're totally honest about what it is. And to do that my entire crew needs to know about Genesis."

"What you believe, Captain, is not the issue. And be assured I will deal with this willful breach of security after this is over," she said angrily. But then her bright eyes filled with resignation. "For the time being, though, a more important problem remains: Just how are we going to fight it?"

"I don't know, but even if you had ten times as many ships on that map, we could only evacuate a small fraction of the people in danger. I don't want to spend all day playing God, trying to decide who lives and who dies."

"Nobody wants to do that," snapped Nechayev, "but until we have a workable plan, evacuation is the only alternative."

Picard gaped in disbelief. "You would abandon Earth to this monster?"

"We're not sure Earth is in danger yet," said Nechayev defensively. "We have to collect more data."

"What about the Romulans?" asked Picard. "We've got to tell the Romulans, because it's going to hit them, too."

The breath went out of Nechayev, and her shoulders slumped perceptibly. "If you read the documents, you know we're prohibited by treaty from even discussing Genesis with anyone else. Starfleet has stuggled for years to keep Genesis under wraps. I violated seventeen regulations just showing those documents to *you*."

Picard's lips thinned. "If nothing else, those papers show that this has been a poorly kept secret. I need to be able to discuss this matter freely with my staff and other experts."

She turned her back on him and stepped once again into the revolving holographic map. Now her aides were nowhere to be seen. "So, Captain, you're saying you'll continue to disobey *my* orders and a treaty signed by all the great powers of the Alpha Quadrant in order to do whatever you see fit."

"I've proven I'll go to great lengths to save Earth," answered Picard.

The diminutive admiral froze in her tracks, apparently making up her mind about something. Then she turned to him with a tired expression on her pinched face. "Now I have to cover for you and give the order for *everyone* in the fleet to be told about Genesis. That's all right—it's better that *I'm* in the brig than you."

Picard smiled slightly, hoping that was a joke. "Under the circumstances, you couldn't get in trouble for this, could you?"

"I'm in considerable trouble already," answered Nechayev with a sigh. "I was in charge of the security for Dr. Carol Marcus. My career is basically over after this—win, lose, or draw."

"That's not fair," said Picard with all sincerity. "You've always had the tough assignments."

Nechayev flashed him a very brief smile, then resumed her all-business demeanor. "I see from your reports that you suffered some casualties."

"Yes, ten crew members lost when we had to jettison the forward torpedo module. Now I understand what was happening to it . . . and what would have happened to the ship."

"That was quick thinking, Picard. I know it wasn't easy."

The captain nodded slowly, grateful for the acknowledgment from someone who did know. "We're having a memorial service at twenty-three hundred hours. It would be an honor if you could attend."

"Certainly, Captain. Afterwards, I would like to see those projections which show that Earth is clearly in danger. We haven't been able to project that far from the data we have."

"For that, we're relying mostly on Dr. Leah Brahms and the survivors from the first planet hit, Seran. Brahms has been observing it and tracking its course the longest."

Nechayev nodded, her brow furrowed in thought. "Yes, she's the one who lived through it—in a phase-shifting radiation suit. Has fate given us one tiny piece of good luck in all of this destruction?"

"The suit's aboard our shuttlecraft," said Picard. "With her permission, we can take it, dismantle it, and start replicating it. It will be slow going, but—"

"Yes, do it." Admiral Nechayev walked back into her revolving hologram of fluorescent starships streaking across a three-dimensional star chart. "Now you've got to leave me, Captain. I've got to officially break a ninety-year-old-treaty as well as commit treason. I may hold off on talking to the Romulans until we hear the whole story."

Picard cleared his throat. "We supposedly have a Romulan spy coming on board, one of the refugees."

Nechayev scowled. "Alliance or not, they still have more spies in our midst than anyone else. I may need help dealing with them. See you at the memorial service."

"Yes, Sir," answered Picard, hurrying out the door. His escort was still in the corridor outside, waiting for him.


The shuttlecraft *Balboa* swooped through the launch door into the main shuttlebay like a bat returning home to its cave. When the craft set down and Data stilled the engines, a sigh or relief echoed inside the small craft. The *Enterprise* wasn't solid ground, but it was the closest thing to it, thought Geordi; and these people had been put through the wringer. His first priority was to get Leah Brahms settled into her quarters with a regimen of food and rest.

He would probably ask Counselor Troi to see her, because she needed help in dealing with her grief. He was troubled by her talk of killing her husband's murderers, although that was probably a normal reaction under the circumstances. However, he knew that Leah had a temper and a lot of determination. After all, she had raced the Genesis Wave through light-years of space, trying to warn as many people as she could. Geordi had been the focus of her anger, and he knew it was a force to be reckoned with.

He wondered how well Leah would be able to continue with her life, providing any of them got out of this alive. He had tried not to think of her as single and unattached, but it was impossible not to when she was so alone. But Geordi vowed to himself not to complicate her life or make her more unhappy than she already was. He just hoped he didn't get weak and tell her how he really felt.

When the shuttlecraft hatch opened, La Forge was a bit surprised to see Commander Riker waiting for them, along with a security team. They didn't have drawn weapons and obvious uniforms, but he recognized the personnel. Not far away stood another clutch of people, Dr. Crusher and a small medteam. One by one, they filed off—Leah Brahms, La Forge, Consul Maltz, Consul Bekra, and Paldor. The Tellarite lent support to the one-legged Capellan, and they seemed to have become allies. Data was last off the craft after shutting down the *Balboa*'s systems.

"Welcome aboard the *Enterprise*," said Riker. "I'm Commander William Riker, first officer. We know you've been through a lot, and we were thinking that you might like to rest before we debrief you."

"I can rest in Sto-Vo-Kor!" growled Maltz, putting his hands on his hips. "How do we get this big ship turned around and find out who is responsible for this?"

"We're working on that," answered Riker. "We've got a fleet of ships trying to surround this wave, which we think is conical in shape and expanding. Once we get its dimensions, we can triangulate its source."

"We had the same trouble," agreed Leah. "You would need a fleet of ships to measure it." She staggered a bit on her feet, and La Forge propped her up.

"Commander," said Geordi, "I think Dr. Brahms needs to get some rest. Does she have quarters assigned to her?"

"Stateroom 1136," answered Riker. "But I have a quick question for you, Dr. Brahms. The captain would like to know whether we can take your radiation suit and try to replicate it. We promise not to damage it, although we'll have to take it apart."

"Go ahead, if you think it will do some good," answered Brahms wearily.

"Thank you. It's good to have you onboard. Please don't keep Mr. La Forge for long, because he has a staff meeting right now."

"I won't," agreed Leah.

Geordi nodded and quickly ushered his charge toward the door. As they left the shuttlebay, he heard Dr. Crusher ask if anyone needed medical attention, and both the Capellan and the Tellarite demanded it. He didn't really care about what happened to anyone else at the moment, because his entire focus was on Leah.

So once again, he didn't see Dolores Linton until they ran into her in the corridor. "Geordi!" she exclaimed, grabbing his arm. "You're back! Is everything okay?"

"Dolores," he said, flustered to be standing between the two women. "What are you doing here?"

"Well, after you stood me up—"

Geordi banged his palm on his forehead. "Oh, I'm sorry, I forgot all about our date."

He looked at Leah with embarrassment, but she was smiling at his dilemma. *She probably thinks that Dolores is my girlfriend*! thought Geordi with alarm.

"It's all right, I know you're busy," said the geologist cheerfully. "I looked you up and found out you had left the ship again; then I found out when you were due back."

The door opened again, and the medteam walked out, with Bekra on a gurney and Paldor limping beside him. They were followed by the Klingon and an entourage of security officers sticking close to him. Two more crew members carried the radiation suit, and Riker and Data were the last ones out of the shuttlebay.

Riker looked at La Forge with a frown. "You're still here? We've got that staff meeting, so we'll have to find somebody else to take Dr. Brahms to her quarters."

"I'll take her there," offered Dolores Linton brightly. "I haven't got anything better to do."

Geordi wanted to object, insisting that it was *his* job to protect Leah, but he couldn't make a scene in the hallway, surrounded by people. Besides, Dolores Linton didn't have anything better to do. "Number 1136," he said.

Riker smiled charmingly at the bubbly young lady. "Thank you very much, Miss—"

"Dolores Linton, geologist with the mission that's on hold." Dolores turned to Leah Brahms and smiled. "So you lived! That's great. Geordi was very worried about you."

"I bet." Brahms smiled wanly, while La Forge wanted to crawl into a hole. "Go on," Leah told him softly. "I'll see you later."

Geordi just nodded blankly, reluctant to be parted from Leah, especially when he didn't know what Dolores would say about him. Nevertheless, with Riker and Data looking expectantly at him, he knew where his duty lay. He nodded at his commanding officer and the three of them strode off down the corridor.

The android slowed down to let La Forge catch up with him. "It appears that you are making headway with Mission Specialist Linton," he said.

"Data!" exclaimed Geordi, shocked. "We're right in the middle of a crisis—I'm not thinking about that."

The android cocked his head. "But I have noticed that humans often experience their most intense love affairs in the midst of a crisis."

"Commander Riker, what did you do with the old Klingon?" asked Geordi, pointedly changing the subject.

Riker smiled. "He wanted to talk to somebody, so I sent him to see our ship's counselor. Let Deanna find out his state of mind. We already know he's the only Klingon survivor from the first appearance of Genesis, but we don't know how much good that will do us. What about the Cappellan? Is he really a spy for the Romulans?"

Geordi shook his head. "He never denied it whenever Maltz accused him of it."

"Maybe they'll both be useful," said Riker with a heave of his broad shoulders. "One thing for sure, we need all the help we can get. Now that you're back, the *Enterprise* and the *Sovereign* are headed in tandem to the next planet in danger—Persephone V."

"I know some people who retired there," murmured Geordi.

"Half of Starfleet is retired there," said Riker, stopping at the turbolift door. "Now they're all going to have to be evacuated. Being ex-Starfleet, maybe they'll obey orders and will do what they're told."

The door opened, and the commander stepped inside, shaking his head. "I can't believe that we invented this device, and now we're fleeing in the face of it. Somebody is grabbing whole solar systems without firing a shot, and we feel good if we save a few lives before we run like rabbits. Where does it end?"

"When we stop running," answered Data, drawing the logical conclusion.

# sixteen

"Sorry I'm late," said Deanna Troi, rushing into the observation lounge and seeking an empty seat at the conference table. Will Riker smiled warmly at her, and she gave him a fleeting smile. Also in attendance were Data, Geordi, Beverly, and, of course, Captain Picard.

"We've just been going over what we know about the Genesis Wave, which isn't nearly enough," said the captain, tight-lipped. "How is Consul Maltz?"

"He seems fine," she answered. "He's perfectly lucid, and he knows all about Dr. Carol Marcus and the original Genesis Project. He's an old-fashioned Klingon from another era—the kind you don't see much anymore. In fact, he kept asking me why we're not doubling back to Seran to get revenge."

Picard answered, "Admiral Nechayev has sent a small task force of *Defiant*-class ships to try to find the source. What else did our guest say?"

"He has a lot of respect for Leah Brahms and says that she's the one who saved them. He also says we should use the Capellan to contact the Romulans. He insists that Bekra is a spy."

The captain scowled and said, "We still don't know what to tell the Romulans. The admiral thinks we'll have the wave's course fully plotted by the time we get to Persephone V. Gearing up for this has been like gearing up for another war, only we don't know where the front is."

He paced in front of a cabinet full of gleaming models of other ships which had born the name *Enterprise*. "In the meantime, we're pursuing a few courses of action on our own. Commander Riker is spearheading an effort to replicate as many of Dr. Brahms' radiation

suits as we can. Our thinking is that our people on the surface of Persephone V may have to stay until the last second, evacuating people. If
we don't get them out in time, this will give them a chance to survive."

He continued around the table. "La Forge and Brahms will work
on a way to expand the phase-shifting technology in her suit—maybe
there's a way it can protect more than one person at a time. Data is
going to work on a plan to stop the wave permanently, and Dr. Crusher
is studying the biological data to see if we can lessen the effect of the
wave, or reverse it."

"You'll need live samples for that, won't you?" asked Troi.

"I would settle for tricorder readings," answered Crusher.

"That's another use for the radiation suits," said Riker with a
smile. "We can stick it out long enough to get tricorder readings."

"We?" asked Deanna doubtfully, not liking the idea that Will
would be wearing one of those suits. "What's my assignment?"

"Your job," answered the captain. "This ship will soon be full of
traumatized evacuees. And I want you around whenever I speak with
either Consul Maltz and Consul Bekra."

"Yes, Sir."

Riker cleared his throat and tapped his chronometer. "Captain, it's
time for our memorial service."

"Yes," said Picard with a sigh. "Let's adjourn. After the service,
we all have plenty of work to do, but don't forget to eat and rest. Dismissed."

While the others filed out of the room, Deanna hung back to wait
for Riker. She lowered her voice to ask Will, "You're not planning to
hang out on a planet in one of those suits, are you?"

"It will probably be Data," answered the first officer, "although he
shouldn't be down there alone. We'll see."

"I know you're a thrill-seeker," she said, "but you don't need to
stand up to this."

"We need to stand up to it eventually," answered Riker, ending the
conversation on an uneasy note.

Two minutes later, the same group from the briefing room filed
into the Antares Theater, a small amphitheater on deck fifteen where
Data had performed a few nights earlier. The hall was already starting
to fill up with somber crew members, many of whom would normally
be sleeping this shift. Deanna Troi doubted whether anyone was finding it easy to sleep these nights.

There was a podium center stage and a lone drummer with a snare
drum; he was one of Will's musician friends from his jazz band. The
commander waited patiently while the crowd settled down and late-

comers straggled in. Riker opened his handheld padd and set it on the podium. Most of the audience were seated, but Deanna remained standing in the back with her captain.

There was a slight commotion and an uplift of voices around the main door, and she turned to see Admiral Nechayev rush in. Nechayev strode immediately to Picard's side and greeted him with a nod. On stage, Will wisely decided to wait a few seconds longer.

"Hello, Captain," said the admiral. "I'm glad I'm not late."

"Thank you for coming," replied Picard. "I was going to say something, but we would be honored if you would say a few words."

"I will," she answered bluntly.

When the audience had quieted again, Riker began speaking, his deep voice carrying over the crowd. "I would like to read the names, ranks, and accomplishments of our fallen shipmates in RC Three."

Accompanied by drum rolls, he read basic data about each of the dead, and Deanna recalled similar ceremonies during the Dominion war—mass funerals, no time for individual ones. When he was finished, Will looked at the captain, who nodded toward Admiral Nechayev.

"We are honored to have Admiral Nechayev onboard to speak to you." Riker nodded to the drummer, and the two of them relinquished the stage.

The stiff-backed, gray-haired woman tugged on her jacket and lifted her chin, showing off all her bars and pips as she strode toward the podium. The audience hushed as she turned to face them, except for a few scattered sniffles and sobs.

Her expression stoic, Nechayev began, "I didn't know your ten shipmates who perished, but I can tell you a great deal about them. They were selfless, devoted, loyal, well-trained, and courageous. I'm sure they weren't any more perfect than the rest of us—but when your ship was threatened, they never thought twice about risking their lives to save yours.

"We who serve in Starfleet are the front lines of the Federation, the first ones to confront threats and enemies. Yet among us is a front line—*our* first line of defense—and that is our repair and rescue crews. We all know that space is not a natural environment for our species. The only thing that stands between us and disaster is our repair crews. Their work is largely unsung, but they have saved more lives than all the admirals, doctors, and diplomats put together."

She nodded at a tearful crew member in the front row. "It's all right to cry, because your survival is a testament to their bravery. Now you need to make the most of it. We've been through wars and catastrophes before, but none of them was as devastating as the threat we face today. We must all take inspiration from those we mourn, because now *we* must be the first line of defense for all the worlds that are in danger."

The admiral took a breath and lowered her head. "I would like to observe a few moments of silence for our fallen shipmates. Not only for them—but also for the millions of innocent beings who have perished from this awful onslaught. May they all rest in peace according to their beliefs."

As the theater stilled, Deanna Troi bowed her head. She wanted to meditate, but her troubled mind wouldn't let her. She kept worrying that this was only the beginning of something much worse.

Less than seven hours later, Deanna Troi walked numbly down a corridor crammed with evacuees. They sat propped against the bulkheads, looking sullen and dispirited; a few of them barely moved their legs, forcing her to step over them. Most of these displaced people were older humans, although there were children and representatives from almost every species in the Federation. When it came to lovely shore-leave planets, Persephone V was almost as famous as Pacifica, although its greater distance from Earth made it more of a retirement colony.

"Commander!" called an older man jumping to his feet. In his desperation, he gripped her arm. "You've got to help me! I'm Captain Kellman, retired, and my daughter, Amy, is still down on the planet. She was camping in the Cosgrove Wilderness on the South Continent. I keep asking them to look for her, but nobody will help me!"

Troi slowly extricated her arm from his grip. "I'm sorry," she said. "We've got to evacuate the urban centers first—get as many people as we can. And we can't change our orbit to search for people, because the whole effort is coordinated—"

"Damn you!" shouted someone behind her. "Have you been down there? The whole thing is *un*coordinated. It's chaos!" There were grumbles of agreement up and down the corridor, and many of the strangers—who would have been dead without their intervention—began to complain.

Deanna wanted to run screaming from all of this, but she knew it was her job to listen to these unfortunate souls and let them blow off a little steam. But there were so many people—the entire ship was filling up with them—and she couldn't do any more than briefly wander among them. She could organize group therapy sessions and memorials, but she had no idea how long they would be onboard the *Enterprise*. They could be off-loaded to the nearest Class-M world that had been spared. The captain had been right—she didn't need any extra assignments, because her own job was overwhelming.

When Deanna tried to move on, Captain Kellman stepped in front of her, blocking her way. The old gray-haired autocrat was used to commanding people and having them do what he wanted. "Listen," he said desperately, "just give me a shuttlecraft, and I'll go get my daughter."

"Only the captain—"

"The captain is in hiding!" bellowed another man. "Where is he? Let him come down here and explain to us what's happening. He's a coward!" There were shouts of agreement.

"What *is* this thing that's supposed to hit the planet?" demanded a woman.

All of a sudden, there was a cacophony of noise as a dozen people bombarded her with questions and complaints. Backed up into a corner, Deanna considered calling for security, but she remembered that every security officer was busy—either on the planet surface or protecting the transporter rooms and crucial areas of the ship. Both the shuttlebay and bridge were under heavy guard while the ship bulged with ten thousand extra people, expected to go much higher.

They pressed her against the bulkhead, peppering her with demands. Captain Kellman was right in her face, insisting they give him a shuttlecraft. She could sense their panic rising, along with her own. Finally Deanna Troi exploded and gave Kellman a firm push in the chest.

"Step back and maintain order!" she bellowed. "I don't care if you were all *admirals*—I am an active-duty officer on a mission. You will maintain order, or I'll have you thrown into the brig! Is that clear?" She didn't mention that the brig was probably already full of evacuees.

Kellman gulped and stepped back. "Yes, Sir." The others followed his lead, looking chastened and depressed. A scowl firmly set on her face, Deanna shoved her way through them. She *was* on a mission, but it had nothing to do with rescuing people from Persephone V. The only one she was trying to rescue at the moment was her beloved, Will Riker.

She continued down the crowded corridor, eyes straight ahead, trying to ignore the pleas and questions of the evacuees. The way they littered the hallway and the vacant looks on their faces reminded her uneasily of the Borg, who had once taken over these same passageways.

Moving briskly, Troi finally reached transporter room one, which was guarded by three security officers wearing riot gear and carrying phaser rifles. It almost seemed as if the *Enterprise* had been overrun by intruders, and in a way it had been.

The security officers acknowledged her, and one of them pressed a panel to open the door for her. She strode into the transporter room, half-expecting it to be jammed with evacuees, as it had been earlier. Instead there were only three people there now: Will Riker, Data, and the transporter chief, a dour Andorian named Rhofistan. Both Will and Data were dressed in T-shirts and underwear, nothing else. Three hulking white radiation suits, replicas of Leah Brahms' prototype, stood on the transporter platform, looking like snowmen about to transport to the North Pole.

"Deanna!" said Will nervously. "What are you doing here?"

"You don't have to be an empath to know what I'm doing here," she answered. "I don't want you going down there, Will . . . trying to live through that thing."

"There is risk involved," admitted Data. "But we need tricorder readings and observations taken at close range. Plus we need a greater understanding of how the phase-inversion avoids the mutagenic effects."

"Data, I don't mind if *you* go down there. Just be careful." Troi walked over to Will and took his hands, gazing at him with her sultry brown eyes. "It's you, *Imzadi*. I lost you before, and I don't want to do it again. I know you're in charge of this operation, and you could send somebody else."

He enveloped her in his brawny arms and pulled her toward him. "I'll come back to you, I promise. We've tested these suits under a simulation, and they work fine. Dr. Brahms showed us the controls, and there isn't time to train anyone else. Besides, everyone else is busy."

"Okay, then I'll go with you." Troi pulled away from him and stepped upon the transporter platform, taking her place beside one of the hulking suits. "You have an extra."

"A spare," answered Riker, "in case something goes wrong."

"I thought you said they were working perfectly."

"You can help me get into it," said Will, leaping onto the platform and standing behind the suit. "We added a tricorder to all the other hardware, and it's automatically activated to record when we put on the phase-shifting."

"You know, it's supposed to be crazy down there," she said worriedly.

"I know."

Troi hugged him ferociously, not completely understanding why she was so concerned about *this* mission. Maybe it was seeing so many distraught people worried about their loved ones down on the planet. Their emotions had affected her. Or maybe it was the awful nature of this Genesis Wave, which moved so swiftly and so devastatingly. There was no defense against it—raw survival was the best one could hope for.

She heard a cracking sound, and she turned to see Data opening the back of his suit. As gracefully as if he were putting on his pants, the lanky android slipped into the imposing case. Then Data stuck an arm out at an impossible angle—as if he were double-jointed—and reached behind him to close the rear clasps.

"I think I'll need your help," said Riker with a smile as he pulled away from her. "I'll be back, *Imzadi,* I promise."

Data pointed to the transporter operator, and his voice was amplified from inside the suit. "Actually whether we get back or not all depends on you, Chief Rhofistan. We will only have ten seconds after the Genesis Wave hits before the ship has to go to warp. If we are not recovered by then, there may be no way to recover us."

"Thanks for bringing that up," said Deanna dryly.

"I'll get you back," promised the Andorian in a deep voice, his antennae shooting to attention. Thoughtfully, he considered his readouts. "We have approximately two hours before the wave hits. The question is where to set you down to do the most good. A shuttlecraft evacuation site in the capitol city of Carefree is requesting more personnel to deal with the crowds. Should I set you down there?"

"That's fine," answered Riker. He looked warmly at Deanna. "Time to put me in my shining white armor."

"You always wear that." Deanna kissed him one last time, pulling away from his lips very reluctantly. "I knew you were the guy in the white armor."

With her help, Riker managed to squeeze into the bulky radiation suit, and Troi fastened him in. The suit was a marvel of technology, and she wanted to believe it would work flawlessly. Unfortunately, she knew it was a hurried replication of a prototype, which depended upon an imitation of Romulan technology.

Riker's amplified voice boomed from inside the suit. "Chief, enter your coordinates." Troi took that as her cue to step down from the transporter platform.

"Coordinates entered," said the Andorian.

Riker finally stopped fidgeting in the bulky suit, and he stood as still as Data, making them look like two identical golems.

"Energize," ordered Riker. The gleaming white suits evaporated into swirling columns of charged particles, and the transporter platform stood bare.

"All right," said Chief Rhofistan, "now I have to get back to the evacuation."

Deanna looked at him, shocked. "You're not just watching them?"

"I can't. There are too many people to rescue. I'll shut down operations here before it hits—to pick them up on sensors. Could you please tell the officers outside that we're starting evacuations again?"

"All right." Troi walked uneasily toward the door of the transporter room, a knot twisting in her stomach. So many people were in danger—death was all around, and so were terror and fear. It was hard for her to separate her emotions from all of theirs, especially when she reached the corridor, where dozens of eyes looked up to her for hope, insight . . . a miracle. She put a pleasant look on her face and grabbed the first likely conversational group she saw, about seven or eight people.

"Come on, all of you," she said with a brave smile. "We're going to talk among ourselves about what's happening. I'll tell you what I know, but then I've got to move on to other people. I just want to get you talking."

# seventeen

When Will Riker materialized in a large public square, surrounded by glittering, blue skyscrapers, a bottle pelted him, bouncing off his radiation suit. He looked at Data, who stood only a few meters away, and the android was in a crouch, fending off two brawlers who had rolled into him. Unruly lines snaked around the numerous sculptures and benches in the square, as people huddled with children and oldsters, wondering if there was any way to get farther along in a queue that seemed to have no end.

As he looked around, Riker discovered they weren't even in the busiest part of the square; that was sixty meters away, where Starfleet officers were trying to load two shuttlecraft. Other officers were attempting to push back the crowd and make room for a third shuttlecraft to land. To complicate matters, Starfleet wasn't the only outfit loading vessels in the packed square. A few intrepid entrepreneurs had opened up shop and were taking on passengers . . . if the price was right. It was bedlam.

Riker stared incredulously as one private shuttlecraft, which looked to be a six-seater, boarded about a dozen passengers. When they tried to lift off, desperate people in the crowd jumped on the landing rails of the craft and hung on. The crowd screamed and ran for cover as the distressed shuttlecraft bobbed and weaved over the mobbed square. Two of the people hanging from the rails dropped off, causing more pandemonium in the fearful crowd. Its thrusters roared, but the shuttlecraft swooped out of control, carrying too much weight.

Riker glanced over at Data, who was still busy trying to break up the fight. For some reason, the android's actions infuriated the crowd around him, and several of them attacked him, jumping on his back and legs. This had no effect on Data, who merely brushed them off as if they were lint, but more of the rioters pressed around him, trying to see what was happening with this strange apparition in white armor.

Suddenly everyone in the square screamed at once, and Riker looked up to see the stricken shuttlecraft veer straight into a skyscraper. The blue building shattered like glass, and a fireball roared from the crater, showering half the crowd with debris and flaming embers. Erupting in howls of panic and fear, the crowd ran in every direction.

The security detail near the shuttlecraft were soon firing phasers on the horde, and the officers tried to fall back to the refuge of their ships. *They'll abandon the square!* thought Riker. *Plus all these beings— thousands of them—and they don't know that Data and I are here.*

A mad rush of people suddenly plowed into the commander and knocked him off his feet. He rolled over in his bulky suit and tried to stand up, but people were pushed on top of him by the panicked crowd. Riker feared he would be trampled in the stampede, but he heard a voice in his helmet, telling him calmly, "Activate phase-shifting."

Breathless, Riker echoed the words, "Computer, activate phase-shifting!"

At once, the crowd no longer plowed into him but seemed only to glance off, and he was able to stagger to his feet. Pushing his way through the throng, Riker sought refuge behind a statue of a historical figure mounted on what looked like a giant ostrich. Data moved swiftly to his side, wrapping an arm around him and bucking him up.

"This is worse than I expected," said the android, his voice sounding unruffled yet overly loud in Riker's headgear. "I suggest we seek refuge in one of the buildings and report back to the ship. I also want to perform diagnostics on the suits to see if they have been damaged."

"Good idea," said Riker with a nod. As they lumbered off, he couldn't help but look in the direction of the Starfleet shuttlecraft, where the scene was getting ugly. With a roar of thrusters, one of the shuttlecraft managed to take off, scorching a dozen onlookers in the effort. However, the second shuttlecraft was overrun by rioters, who climbed on top of it, trying to pry their way inside. The third shuttlecraft, which had been circling overhead, simply sped away, not risking a landing.

Abandoned, the small cadre of security officers fell back from the angry mob, shooting phasers as they went. It looked as if they had no escape.

"They need help!" said Riker with alarm. "And the shuttlecraft . . . that crowd is going to smash it to pieces."

"This evacuation process does seem to be ill-advised," agreed Data. "However, we do not have any weapons, and crowd control is not our primary mission. We must leave."

"You're right." Riker felt the android grip the arm of his suit and guide him through the surging crowd. Although they were a strange sight, there was nothing on the prototype suits to mark them as being Starfleet. In this surreal scene—amidst riots and shuttlecraft wreckage—two people in white armor had a kind of logic.

As they reached the sidewalk outside the square, Riker turned back to look. He was greatly relieved to see swirling transporter beams where the beleaguered officers had been battling the crowds. They had been rescued, probably by the shuttlecraft which had fled. He saw the mob pull people out of the grounded Starfleet shuttle, while others desperately tried to take their places. At the same time, other rioters swarmed on top of the craft, ripping it apart.

"The security detail was rescued," said Riker, "but that shuttlecraft is history."

"We have two hours," said Data with a puzzled tone to his voice. "Had the crowd allowed us to proceed, we could have taken the majority of them."

"I'm afraid when people panic, they don't think that rationally. If this is happening all over. . . . This is a nightmare."

"Apparently we no longer have the problem of convincing people this is a real threat," observed Data.

Without really paying much attention to where they were going, the commander followed Data into the lobby of a grand hotel. The scene here was also chaos, with clothes and litter strewn everywhere, and people rushing madly through the plush lobby. There was a clutch of people kneeling in a corner, and they seemed to be praying. A desk clerk stood behind the counter, pointlessly operating his computer and dealing with customers in line.

Riker was aghast. "There is no way we were ever going to rescue more than a fraction of these people, even if everything went smoothly."

The android nodded his headgear. "We were unprepared for a catastrophe of this magnitude. We must reconsider the evacuation option."

"So far, it's the *only* option," grumbled Riker.

A small, purple-skinned Saurian staggered in front of them and regarded them suspiciously. He curled his beaklike mouth and asked, "Heeeey, what are you two dresshhed up for?"

"His slurred speech indicates he is intoxicated," observed Data.

"No kidding." Riker pushed a button on his helmet, and his voice boomed out into the lobby. "Do you have a room here?"

"Yesshh," answered the Saurian proudly.

"Can we borrow it?"

He looked curiously at the two people in the weird suits and shook his bulbous head. "Takes all kindsss. Sure . . . here's the chip." The Saurian produced a smaller version of an isolinear chip and handed it to Riker. The commander studied the entry key and read the number "219."

"Thank you." Riker started off, but he felt a bit guilty. "Do you have any way off this planet?"

"Sure I do!" The little Saurian proudly produced a flask and took a long drink; then he staggered off, weaving his way through the trashed lobby of the elegant hotel.

"If this were not so tragic, it would be fascinating," said Data.

"Let's take the stairs." Riker pointed to a sweeping staircase that dominated the rear portion of the lobby. He lumbered up the plushly carpeted steps and proceeded into a corridor. After checking numbers on room doors, he was glad to find that the Saurian's room was here on the second floor, and they had to climb no higher.

The hotel room turned out to be a fairly good observation point, with a balcony looking down on the chaotic square. Riker walked to the balcony and gazed at the panicked crowd below, surging from one end of the square to another. Statues had been toppled in the rioting, and the Starfleet shuttlecraft lay on its side, having been pushed over.

Persephone V had always had a reputation as one of the most peaceful planets in the Federation, thought Riker ruefully. It was supposed to be a sanctuary from the rat race, where crime was almost nonexistent. So were police, apparently. In the center of their capitol, there was no local help in crowd management. Maybe the local authorities had cast off their uniforms in hopes of getting out sooner. Probably all the important authorities—who might have been some help here—were already aboard the armada orbiting the planet.

"Commander, should I report to the captain?" asked Data.

"Go ahead," answered Riker glumly. "And don't spare him the gruesome details."

Bad news continued to pour in. Captain Picard paced the bridge of the *Enterprise*, reading the latest projections for the Genesis Wave's course. It was strongly suggested that the wave would strike Earth and the heart of the Federation before cutting a wide swath through the

Neutral Zone and the Romulan Star Empire. They only had about six days before it entered Earth's solar system.

After a consultation with Admiral Nechayev, he had to talk to Consul Bekra immediately, but he couldn't leave the bridge during the evacuation of Persephone V. It was going badly, except for the million or so lucky ones who had been saved. "Disaster" was not too strong a word, judging by reports like the one he had just received from Data. They were doing the best they could, but the task of rescuing ten million people at short notice was just too daunting for the Federation alone.

A shortage of planning time had resulted in breakdowns and panic in a variety of locations. The main square of Carefree was one of the worst places, but there were other sites that had been abandoned, too. At this rate, the fleet wouldn't even meet their worst projections for the rescue mission. For every life they saved, five would be lost.

Filled ships were already going to the next planet, too. Unless they did something, there would always be a next one. The *Enterprise* was fully occupied with transporter evacuation, and he couldn't divert a single crew member to the mess in Carefree. He already had two on the surface that he would rather have back. If Riker and Data wanted someplace to observe the worst of the disaster, they were getting it.

Picard heard the turbolift whoosh open, and he turned to see Counselor Troi and Consul Bekra enter. The Capellan was limping slowly on a new artificial limb, and the scowl had deepened on his face.

"Captain!" called Bekra, moving more quickly. "I simply must protest. I was very comfortable in the private room I had, but now there are *six* people in there with me! In a room intended for *one*."

The captain cleared his throat, attempting to hide his annoyance. "There will probably be a few more people in your quarters by the end of the day. I'm sorry, but we have to squeeze as many people onto the ship as we can."

The Capellan sniffed and looked around. "It's quite roomy up here on the bridge. Tell me, when are we going to be dropped off somewhere else?"

"I haven't gotten my orders yet," answered Picard curtly. He looked at Deanna Troi, who seemed to be at a loss to help him. In fact, she looked haggard and exhausted.

"Let's step over to this auxiliary console," said the captain, leading the way to an isolated workstation on the outer ring. Despite his limp, Consul Bekra kept up with him. "You seem to be adapting to that prosthetic device," said Picard.

"Do I have much choice?" asked the Capellan. "I must say, your Dr. Crusher is very skilled, but I intend to press charges against that crazy Klingon . . . after this is all over."

The captain lowered his voice to say, "We have a serious problem. Our latest projections say that the Genesis Wave will pass through Romulan space, as well as the heart of the Federation."

Bekra shifted his eyes and looked at Troi. "You brought me here under false pretenses."

"I said the captain wanted to meet you," answered Troi wearily. "You've met. Now will you help us?"

"What makes you think I have any influence with the Romulans?" asked Bekra snidely.

"Listen," whispered Picard, "at this point, I don't care about anything you've ever done before in your life. If you want a full pardon, Admiral Nechayev will give you one. We need you to contact the Romulans—using any means you desire—and tell them the truth. Tell them what you've been through and what's happening here. We're going to contact them through official channels as well, but we wanted them to have outside verification from . . . somebody they trusted."

"They may already know about this," said the Capellan.

"They may," conceded the captain, "but we can't take that chance. We have to make sure they know. This auxiliary console has been configured for subspace communications, and I don't think you'll have any trouble operating it. We're just going to walk away, and nobody is going to watch or record what you're doing here. Feel free to contact your homeworld, too, if you like, but . . . you know what you have to do."

Consul Bekra considered Captain Picard for a few moments, then he finally nodded. "I wish to leave this ship as soon as possible. My friend, Paldor, also wishes to leave."

"We'll let you off at the nearest opportunity, when we let off the evacuees," answered Picard. "There will never be any record of our conversation."

"All right," said Bekra, looking away from them. "Leave me now."

Picard motioned to Troi for her to follow him. When they had gotten out of earshot, he whispered, "Do you think we can trust him?"

She nodded. "I believe so. I have been sensing that he had something to hide, but his mental defenses let down when he agreed to help."

"You look tired," said the captain.

"Please don't tell me to sleep," she cautioned him. "Will is down on the surface in one of those suits, and my cabin is full of refugees. Unless you've got a cot in your ready room—"

"I'm afraid not," said the captain with a wry smile. "I agree, there's no rest at the moment. Thank you for your help, Counselor."

She shook her head doubtfully. "We need a lot of help."

"I know."


Geordi La Forge paced the gleaming confines of the radiation lab on deck seventeen, feeling guilty that he had all this space to himself when the ship was crammed to the airlocks with evacuees. He hoped he wouldn't be alone much longer, because Leah Brahms was supposed to be working with him. She was late for their first shift together, which made him pace all the faster.

This situation—the two of them working alone together in a crisis—was uncomfortable like the circumstances under which he had fallen in love with Leah. Of course, that had been a simulation on the holodeck. The radiation laboratory was the same kind of close, isolated environment, removed from the rest of the ship. Geordi wasn't worried that *she* would be distracted by this—after all, the real Leah Brahms hadn't been on the holodeck—he was worried about his own feelings spilling out.

She's a widow, he reminded himself, and she's just lost everything she has in the world. . . . More than anything, he had to respect her right to privacy and grief during this tragic time. She needed a friend right now, not more complications. In many respects, he felt guilty about even making her work on this assignment, but her radiation suit was the only object to withstand the Genesis Wave so far. And she was the only person to have lived through it.

La Forge had one of the replicated suits in the lab, and he had started to study it while he waited; but he wasn't quite sure what he was looking at. What they needed were a couple of Romulan engineers who knew this phase-shifting like he and Leah knew warp engines. He could make educated guesses, and Leah had done more than guess— she had put it to use—but they had no design notes or schematics. Even Leah's records were all lost on Outpost Seran-T-One.

With a whoosh, the door to the lab opened, and Geordi turned eagerly to see his fellow engineer walk in. She was dressed in a gray engineer's jumpsuit borrowed from his department, having arrived with only the grimy clothes on her back. She looked determined and alert, if not happy to be there. Once again, he thought about how much he liked the short, chestnut-colored hair framing her angelic face, and he gave her a warm smile.

The smile faded almost immediately from his face when he saw another figure stride through the door behind her. It was the old Klingon, Maltz, and he cast a fishy eye in Geordi's direction. There was something proprietary in the Klingon's rheumy gaze, as if he considered himself Leah's protector, or at least her chaperone.

Seeing Geordi's surprised expression, Leah patted him on the shoulder. "It's all right—I told Maltz he could come along to help us. He's seen it, too."

"I must do *something*," grumbled the old Klingon. "They filled up my cabin with more derelicts like me, and it got depressing. We can not run from this enemy—we must go down fighting it!"

"Uh, yes," agreed Geordi, "but our particular mission is to find a way to let more people survive the wave."

Leah shook her head grimly. "I'll help you do it, but you won't want to live on one of these planets after you're done."

"That's just it," said Geordi excitedly. "Now we've got some really good long-range scanner data from the affected planets. They may not be pleasant—borderline Class-L—but they are livable, with thin oxygen and native plant and animal life. By replanting and standard terraforming, we can probably get them back to what they once were."

Leah shivered and looked down, and Maltz's attention seemed far away, as if dealing with an old memory. Geordi quickly added, "Both of you saw these planets when they were still forming, before the radical changes were over. The new Genesis Planets look like they're going to be stabilizing quite nicely."

Brahms turned away, and La Forge felt a pang of guilt about having been so blunt. Of course, one of those planets was Seran, where her husband and friends had been absorbed into the new ecosystem. He appealed helplessly to her. "I didn't mean anything by it . . . I was just trying to explain—"

Maltz laughed out loud and shook his head. "This is why humans are so pathetic. In trying to look on the bright side all the time, they ignore the obvious danger. Do you not see? These worlds are being terraformed to the specifications of the new owners, and they will come to claim them."

"But it won't be as easy if there are *living* people on the planets," countered La Forge. He held up his palms, beseeching Leah to forgive him. "I'm sorry, I didn't mean to be so blunt—I wish you didn't have to be here. We're just trying to save lives as best we can. We haven't got enough ships to evacuate everyone—this current mission is a mess. We need shelters that work, and we need them right now."

The woman turned around and gazed at him; her brown eyes were moist from tears, but her jaw was set in firm determination. "All right, I'll help you, but we need a lot of stuff. Start making a shopping list."

"I will," answered Geordi, snapping to and grabbing a padd. "What do you need?"

"We need those big interphase generators the Romulans have."

"Okay," said La Forge doubtfully. "That's going to be hard. We don't have that technology."

"Call up Admiral Nechayev," said Leah. "Have her contact the Romulans. Without those big generators—the kind they use to cloak their *newest* ships—it won't work. If we can get a few, we can replicate them like we did with the suit, but we need those to stand a chance."

"Where is this admiral?" said Maltz, balling his hands into fists. "I will deal with her."

"No, I'll get on it," promised Geordi, rushing to a communications console. "What else?"

Leah stroked her chin thoughtfully. "I'll also need data on how deep into the crust of the planet the Genesis Effect goes. Maybe all we need to do is dig holes deep enough to protect the inhabitants. I know a certain geologist who's not doing much, and she'd be willing to help us."

"The more the merrier," muttered Geordi under his breath as he worked the console.

"What did you say?" asked Maltz suspiciously.

"Um, just talking to myself." Geordi went back to carefully wording a message to Admiral Nechayev and Captain Picard.

"I really like Dolores," said Leah. "I approve."

Geordi wanted to correct her impression of him and the visiting geologist, but he was done looking like he still had a thing for Leah, even if he did. He kept his attention on his work. "While we wait, you can bring me up to speed on this technology. I'd like to see how it works in the suit."

"All right," answered Leah, sitting on a stool. For the first time, she looked around the sumptuous laboratory with its miniature clean room, test chambers, and racks of test instruments.

"It has running water, too," said Leah with a wry smile. "Say, I might just move in here. There's a lot more room here than in my quarters. What do you say, Maltz?"

"Typical Federation decadence," the Klingon said, his body language at odds with his disdainful tone as he stretched out on the roomy deck. "You do your research and save your lives, while I save my strength to take lives. We will go back and kill the ones who are doing this. Right, Captain?"

"I'll be there." Leah winked at Geordi as if she were humoring the old warrior, but there was a spark of excitement in her eyes. She added, "To at least one person in the universe, I'm a captain."

"That's great," said Geordi, mustering some enthusiasm when all he felt was hopelessness. "I thought that maybe we could use a protomatter beam, so I installed one in Test Chamber Two."

"Dangerous," said Leah, frowning at the idea.

"I know, but we need it to simulate the wave in tests, don't we?"

"You want to recreate the wave?" she asked incredulously.

"Not the mutagenic part, just the energy wave that is carrying all this information."

"He is right," said the Klingon, lying on the deck, his eyes still shut. "The original Genesis Device used a detonation to expand, turning into a wave as it moved outward, circling a planet. Someone must be projecting this wave from a fixed point—a space station. It is probably hidden and hard to reach."

"A task force has been sent to look for the source," added Geordi.

The Klingon growled. "They do not know what they are looking for, do they? I understand this enemy—I knew it would come looking for me again someday, and it did. When you finish saving lives, we shall go kill it. Wake me then, Captain."

"Okay, Maltz," said Leah Brahms without a trace of humor in her voice.

"I don't much like waiting for the end of the world," muttered Will Riker. The commander sat on the edge of his bed in a strange hotel room, wrapped in a blanket; it was getting cold, and he was only wearing underwear. The climate controls in the hotel had ceased working, to go along with all the chaos in the streets. But why try to save energy now—when this world would soon be gone, replaced by something else?

"It is difficult to watch this world die," allowed Data, "especially with so little dignity." The android unplugged his tricorder from a jack on the back of his radiation suit, apparently finished with his diagnostic routines. "Both suits are still functioning within normal parameters."

"That's good," said Riker, rising to his feet. "Because I'm going to put mine back on."

"We have approximately twenty-two minutes," observed Data. "We should be receiving new projections from the transporter room very soon, and the evacuation will be over."

"Ending with a whimper, not a bang," said Riker. He stood and walked toward the balcony door, careful not to step into view, because vandals had been throwing bricks earler. All of the glass was smashed. Nevertheless, he could gaze down into the square, which echoed with plaintive voices, begging to be saved.

For the last hour, people in the square had been disappearing in random clusters, rescued via transporter beam from ships in orbit. Now thousands of residents were standing around, lifting their arms to the heavens, beseeching the fickle gods of far-off transporters to save them. Some danced; others sang, wept, or did whatever they thought might get them noticed, although both they and Riker knew it was a random process. At least somebody was doing something for the people stranded in the heart of Carefree.

"When it hits," said Riker, "I don't want to be inside this skyscraper. I want to be down there." He pointed to the square.

The wind shifted, and a whiff of something acrid hit Riker's nostrils. He looked up just as the sprinkler system in the ceiling of the hotel room came on, blasting everything with a dense spray of water and chemicals. Smoke was seeping through the closed door from the hallway. Data immediately rushed into action, grabbing the radiation suits, but even the android couldn't move quickly enough to keep them from getting drenched. Plus there was nowhere in the room to hide from the cascading liquids.

The chemicals burned in Riker's eyes, but he still managed to grab one of the suits and haul it out onto the balcony. From there, he could see that the hotel was on fire several stories overhead, where columns of black smoke curled into the sky. Riker glanced into his suit to see that it had gotten wet inside, and he also realized that they couldn't get out the doorway. It was about twelve meters straight down to the sidewalk, and that looked like the way they would have to leave.

He was jostled when Data joined him on the balcony, dragging his armor, and it suddenly became very crowded out there. "I'm considered aborting this mission," murmured Riker. "I just have a bad feeling . . . too many things going wrong."

Data cocked his head. "Transporters on the *Enterprise* will be occupied for another ten minutes and twenty seconds. Most of the rescue ships have already departed, although a few still remain in orbit. This would not be an opportune time to seek assistance."

Riker glanced down at the square and saw that the mob was

milling around, arguing disgruntledly among themselves. The random transports seemed to have ceased, and so had the momentarily happy mood. Now a feeling of desperation was setting in.

"We need to get down," said the commander.

"I will jump down, and you can throw me the equipment."

Riker nodded, and Data bounded over the wrought-iron railing as easily as if he were stepping over a curb. The android made a perfect two-point landing and looked up to the human—at the very instant that an explosion blew the room door open. A fireball roared from the hallway through the room, hurling Riker and the radiation suits over the railing.

# eighteen

Deanna Troi stopped in the middle of her sentence, her finger in the air, and she couldn't remember what she had been saying to the group of evacuees gathered in her office. She had an overwhelming premonition—a certainty—that something had happened to Will.

Troi looked at the chronometer over her door and noted that they were only about fifteen minutes away from the expected arrival of the wave—and their departure soon after. She knew the radiation suit was supposed to be foolproof, but so many things had gone wrong today that she couldn't rest easy for one second. She had been worried about Will before, but now she was terrified.

Patients were bombarding her with questions, but she shoved her way through them, saying things like, "We'll talk about that when I get back. Have strength! Maybe your loved ones are on another ship. We'll get lists of names as soon as we disembark."

Finally she broke out of her office into the corridor, which was hardly any better. Her shoulders and forearms were bruised from having to shove her way through the crowds which clogged the corridors of the *Enterprise*. But she lowered her head again and plowed through the dispirited, disgruntled throng. This time, Deanna was more determined than ever, because the worry for Will had turned into abject fear.

Only one turbolift was open now on this whole deck—to keep the evacuees from moving around the ship. All of them had heard about how wonderful the accommodations were in the lounge, the theater, the holodecks, or some other leisure area, and they didn't want to stay in a packed corridor. She wondered how they would like it if they knew the *Enterprise* wasn't leaving orbit until the last possible second.

Troi was slowed down by the milling crowds, who glared suspiciously at her, knowing that she had free run of the ship. But today free run of the *Enterprise* was not what it used to be; she almost looked fondly back to when it had a skeleton crew. Impatiently, Deanna tapped her combadge and said, "Troi to Riker."

After several seconds of silence, she tried again. "Troi to Riker."

A chime sounded, followed by the computer's voice. "Commander Riker is not responding."

Her jaw set firmly, Troi lifted her elbows and jabbed her way through the crowd, shouting, "Out of my way! Emergency!"

Deanna finally reached the turbolift, where the hectored guard was busy arguing with refugees. She noticed that he now had his phaser rifle leveled for action rather than slung over his shoulder, as she had seen him last time. Upon noticing her, he slapped a panel to call the turbolift for her.

"I have to go with you!" shouted a woman, chasing after Troi.

"Let me see the captain!" shouted someone else. "You don't understand—"

The counselor hated having to turn a cold shoulder to their fervent pleas, but they were safe—and Will was not. When the turbolift door opened, she dashed inside, leaving the guard to fend off the evacuees who tried to follow her. He snapped and barked at them, using his rifle to push the mob back. Deanna was grateful when the door finally shut, leaving her alone in the conveyance. It seemed oddly peaceful inside the cocoon of the turbolift.

"Transporter room two," she ordered, hoping to get as close as possible.

When the turbolift door opened at her destination, an armed security officer tumbled backwards into Deanna, pushed by a surge of refugees trying to get on. Operating instinctively, Troi picked up the man's phaser rifle and quickly fired a shot over the crowd's head. That stopped them for a second, long enough for her to make sure the phaser was set to stun. When the horde pushed forward again, she drilled a big Ardanan in the front row, and he tumbled across the threshold of the turbolift, unconscious.

"Back off!" she shouted. "Make way! That's an order!"

She wanted to see how far this mutiny would progress—if it even was a mutiny. The sight of the ship's counselor wielding a weapon and firing at will into the crowd did have an effect, and they finally made a slight path for her.

Before she left the turbolift, Troi bent down to make sure the security officer was all right. The young ensign seemed groggy but coherent. "Can you get to your feet?"

"Yes, Sir."

"I'm keeping your weapon," she told him. "I want you to call for backup on this deck and get yourself to sickbay."

"Yes, Commander," he answered. "Thank you."

Phaser rifle leveled in front of her, Troi strode off the turbolift, motioning people to get out of her way. "If necessary, we won't hesitate to use force to maintain order!" she shouted.

Most of the panicked crowd backed away from her, but a few distraught evacuees regaled her with queries and demands. "My children are in school!" shouted one worried man.

"All your questions will be answered," she told them. "Now let us do our jobs and rescue as many of you as we can. If you cause us to delay, maybe *your* loved one is the one we'll miss. Get out of the way!"

Moving steadily down the jammed corridor, Deanna finally reached the transporter room, where there was now only one security officer on guard. Since the door was open, she could see why—the other two officers were busy trying to move people off the transporter platform and out the door. But where exactly these new arrivals were supposed to go was hard to tell.

She muscled her way into the transporter room, shoving people out of the way with her phaser rifle, until she reached the operator's console. The tall Andorian was busy working his instruments, bringing groups of eight haggard evacuees in at once. The security officer moved them off the platform just as another wave took their place.

"Chief Rhofistan," she said, "have you heard from the away team? Riker and Data."

"No," he answered, never taking his eyes off his instruments. "I'm due to pick them up exclusively in another two minutes."

"I think they're in trouble," said Troi. "They haven't answered my hails."

"Maybe they're out of their suits for some reason," said the Andorian. "Their only communications systems are inside the suits."

"They're not wearing their combadges?"

"No, that signal wouldn't get through the shielding in the suits. Excuse me, Commander." The transporter operator had to ignore her while he brought up another group of dazed survivors. Deanna spent those few precious seconds looking around the crowded room, and she finally found what she was looking for. Discarded in the corner was the third radiation suit, the spare one.

When the transporter chief looked up again, she asked him, "Do you have two spare combadges?"

"Sure." From a drawer, he fished out two standard combadges and handed them to her. They usually kept a few spares on hand to give to passengers to make it easier to lock onto them with the transporter.

"I'm going to put on the extra radiation suit and go down to the surface," she told the chief.

He raised a snowy white eyebrow, and his antennae twitched for a moment. "Are you sure that's advisable?"

"No, but I'm doing it anyway. Set me down exactly where you set Riker and Data down. But do what you can to get all three of us." Troi hefted the phaser rifle. "I think I'll take this with me, and my combadge."

"The combadge won't do you any good inside that suit," said the transporter chief. "But I'll route your communications through. Are you staying to take the readings?"

Deanna swallowed dryly. "Let's say for the sake of argument, I am."

"I have to turn off the phase-shifting a split second before I transport you," said Rhofistan. "I'll control that from here, but I didn't want you to be surprised. The suit checks out—you're good to go."

Having helped Will into his armor only a couple of hours ago, Deanna remembered fairly well how to get into it. First she stripped off everything but her undergarments; then she cracked open the back and climbed in. Troi was unprepared for the way the gel material molded itself to her body, but the disconcerting sensations soon passed—to be replaced by the strangeness of being encased in the bulky cocoon. Good thing I'm not claustrophobic, she thought. In fact, Troi was reminded of the meditation chambers on Betazoid—hardly bigger than coffins.

One of the security officers helped her close her rear clasps, then he went back to work. "One more group to bring up," explained the transporter chief, his voice booming in the headgear.

Deanna waited impatiently inside the armor, listening to her own labored breathing and thumping heart. Finally the last group of refugees arrived and stepped numbly off the transporter platform. Troi tried not to think about the ones waiting in line behind them—the ones who would not make it to safety.

As security officers tried to deal with the new arrivals, Troi lumbered onto the platform and situated herself on the pad. She knew time was running out—she could see it in the anxious faces of the security detail and the transporter chief. If she had any sense at all, she wouldn't be doing this, but she had never had any sense where Will Riker was concerned.

With a wave of her phaser rifle, she ordered, "Energize."

A moment later, Deanna Troi materialized in the middle of a huge public square, filled with people, trash, and the wreckage of a couple of shuttlecraft. She instantly whirled in every direction, looking for Will and Data, but she couldn't see them in the mass of people rushing to and fro.

Then she remembered that she had a tricorder, sensors, and all kinds of goodies built into this suit. Of course, she didn't have any training in using it, but she assumed its computer would take orders.

"Computer," she said, "locate any radiation suits like this one."

"Please clarify the request," answered the computer.

"Activate comlink. Troi to Riker. Troi to Data!" She waited, but her hails met with stony silence. Before she could think of another order to give, her attention was distracted by columns of dark smoke spewing from one of the glittering skyscrapers bordering the square. *I need to find some kind of high ground*, thought Deanna, *so I can see over all these people.*

As she lumbered along, wielding her phaser rifle, Troi got a few blank stares, but most of the inhabitants were lost in their own worlds. Unless they were in denial, as a few jovial souls were, they were facing death for the first and last time in their lives. She could feel the fear and desperation—it was as palpable as the dark smoke that hung in the sky.

She jumped when she heard a voice in her headgear. "Chief Rhofistan to Troi."

"Troi here," she answered, relieved that the transporter operator was keeping tabs on her.

"I just wanted to let you know that we've stopped evacuations, and we're on Yellow Alert. The captain has given word that we should be ready to pull out any second."

"But I haven't found them yet!" she said with alarm.

"You know we can't stay here," said the chief. "After it hits the planet, we only have ten seconds before it reaches the ship. I'm under orders to get you after six seconds, even if we can't find the other team."

"All right," rasped Troi, knowing it would do no good to argue with him—he had his orders. Captain Picard had already shown that he was prepared to sacrifice lives to save the *Enterprise* and all aboard, even if that meant losing his first and second officers.

How could she find them in all this chaos? She suddenly realized that she had the equivalent of a signal device in her hands, and Deanna pointed the phaser rifle toward the sky and sent one brilliant streak after another into the sky. Many of the startled inhabitants shrunk away from the strange white golem who was blasting off a phaser as if it were New Year's Eve, but she didn't care about that. She *wanted* to cause a commotion and attract some attention.

It seemed like forever that she wandered in the square, shooting her phaser, but it was only a couple of minutes. Finally, a figure came bounding toward her across the park, leaping over people's heads. His leaps were so huge and effortless that he looked like a man jogging on Earth's moon. Troi stopped firing, knowing it could only be one entity—Data. He wasn't wearing his radiation suit.

"Counselor Troi," said the android, bounding to a graceful stop. "I am surprised but gratified to see you."

"Where is Commander Riker?" she demanded.

"He was injured in that fire." Data pointed to the black smoke spewing from an elegant skyscraper. "He is conscious now but unable to walk. I believe his leg is broken. The problem is that our radiation suits were also damaged, and we were unable to contact the ship."

A voice burst into her ears over the comlink in her headgear. "Picard to Troi."

Deanna held up a finger, motioning Data to wait. "Troi here, Captain."

"You're on the planet surface?"

"Yes, Sir."

"The wave is moving faster than we anticipated. You have less than two minutes. We can't seem to contact Riker and Data."

Troi took a deep breath and looked around the dying city. In this suit, it would take her two minutes to walk across the crowded square to reach Will, and probably another minute to get out of the suit. So she made a difficult decision. "I'm staying on the surface to take readings, but I've got combadges for Riker and Data. Beam them up now, but don't forget *me*."

"We won't, Counselor. Good luck. Picard out."

She turned to Data, about to explain, but the android was holding out his palm. "My hearing picked up the conversation. You are very brave, Commander."

"Just get Will to safety," she said as she handed over the two extra combadges. "How do I work this suit?"

"Say, 'Computer, phase-shifting on.' Tricorder operations are automatic." With that, the android turned and bounded off, leaping twenty meters at a time, sailing over the desultory crowd.

"Computer, phase-shifting on," ordered Deanna. She held her

breath, expecting some change, but nothing felt different inside the suit. Deanna had a moment's panic that the phase-shifting wasn't working, and she would be dead with all of these poor, dispirited souls.

"Computer, what is the status?" she asked with a gulp.

"All systems functional, interphase mode activated," answered the computer. "For a Betazoid, your vital signs are quite elevated, indicating severe stress or illness."

"Never mind about me; I'm okay." She had more pressing concerns. Every passing second, more people were staring at her in curiosity and anger, and they were coming closer. Troi lifted her phaser rifle and leveled it at the crowd, thinking that the weapon seemed lighter and more slippery than it had before.

"Hey, you got any more of those suits?" asked one older man, who might have looked distinguished if his shirt weren't torn and his nose weren't bloody. "We could use some more suits like that."

"Yeah!" called a Coridan female. "When are they going to start beaming us up again?" A crowd was starting to gather around the strange, armored figure. They had nothing else to do, thought Troi, but wait for their own deaths and harass her.

"Go ahead and use that phaser on me!" demanded one old, gray-haired Argelian. "I don't want to live through this thing, if it's as bad as they say. Shoot me!"

"Kill me!"

"Me, too!"

Although they were menacing her, Deanna's heart went out to these distraught beings, many of whom were retired Starfleet officers. She wanted to bring them as much comfort as she could, but she was one person, surrounded by hundreds.

In a raspy voice, she spoke, and her amplified voice boomed from the suit. "Are any of you former Starfleet?"

"Yes, me! Me! Here!" Hands shot up all around her, and there was a glimmer of hope in their vacant eyes.

"I have to take tricorder readings," she said. "That's why I'm down here in this getup. I need people to do a little crowd control for me—to keep the curious away."

"But what about *saving* us?" they demanded. "Aren't there any more rescues?"

"Starfleet officers," she said. "Do you remember the oath you took to help others? To do as you were ordered? You can't worry about yourselves when you have your duty to perform. Your actions will help to save others in the path of this disaster."

She had shamed them—or at least stunned them—into a few moments of silence and retrospection. The Coridan female suddenly dropped to her knees and began to wail. "It's coming! We're all going to die!"

Deanna wasn't sure what was coming, but the sky over the town square began to darken, shifting from a pale blue to a putrid green. Screams and gasps rent the air, and people began to run, colliding into each other. Complete strangers gripped each other in terrified embrace, and there was a trembling deep in the ground.

She turned to see mirrored skyscrapers, framed by a beautiful aurora, quivering like an optical illusion. The whole city looked like a sidewalk baking in the summer's heat. Gulping down her fear, Troi gazed upward and saw a searing green curtain envelope the buildings. The mirrored surfaces throbbed, then exploded into clouds of smoke and molten debris.

The pavement heaved under her feet and crumbled to dust, and the people around her shrieked their last, as the unholy flame swept over them. Before Troi's horrified eyes, their bodies broke down into basic components—blood, organs, bones. Their death throes and anguish were mercifully short. Her stomach lurched; bile shot up her throat as she watched living beings seep into the ground, joining a seething miasma of twitching new life.

Readouts on her faceplate began to scroll at a blinding pace, and Deanna panted in fear. Her mind was convinced that the awful transformation was happening to *her*, even if her body was still encased in the magical armor.

She finally controlled her fear long enough to gape at the awesome transformations. The urban jungle had become a *real* jungle, with twisting vines, sky-high trees, and rudimentary forms of animal life writhing in the muck. Troi hoped the built-in tricorder was recording all of this, because she would never remember half the things that happened in a split second.

"Phase-shifting off," said the computer's voice, which was eerily calm. As her feet began to smolder and sink in the mire, Deanna screamed. Then she felt the comforting grip of the transporter beam, and a second scream died in her throat.

She staggered off the transporter platform convinced that her suit was on fire, and it was. A team moved in with extinguishers to put out the embers, while strong hands unsnapped the back of her suit and grasped her torso.

Effortlessly, Data pulled her out of the burning suit and deposited her in another pair of strong arms—Will's. She hugged him desperately, sobbing with relief and pent-up fear. *"Imzadi,"* he said warmly. "It's all right—you're safe."

It took her a moment to realize that Will was standing on crutches, and Dr. Crusher hovered nearby, ready to aid her, too. "Are we getting out of here?" she asked hoarsely.

"We're already in warp drive," answered Chief Rhofistan from the operator's console. "The tricorder data appear complete. Mission accomplished. Congratulations, Commander Troi."

She nodded wearily, and Will gave her an extra hug and a proud smile.

The transporter chief added, "I'm patched into the video log from the bridge. Would anybody like to see what's happening to the planet?"

"No, no!" barked Deanna quickly. "I've *seen* what happened to the planet—I don't ever want to see that again."

She shivered and gazed at Will, who conducted her from the transporter room, limping on his crutch. *We survived this one,* Deanna thought gloomily. *At least some of us did.*

# nineteen

On the edge of the Neutral Zone, four mighty starships rested motionless in space, their curved noses pointed toward one another like a flock of vultures gathered around a carcass. Green-hued and lit stem to stern like floating cities, the Romulan warbirds sparkled more brightly than the stars around them. Tiny support vessels flitted between the massive ships, refueling and exchanging crew, and they looked like remoras tending a school of sharks.

In his quarters, Commander Jagron of the warbird *D'Arvuk* stood perfectly still while his valet straightened his regal dress uniform, complete with padded shoulders, rich embroidery, and elaborate belts crossing his chest. He couldn't fathom the reason behind this hastily called gathering of every warbird in the sector, but he wasn't going to quarrel with the directive. The Praetor himself was due to meet with them—a great honor.

Jagron was young for a Romulan commander, the equivalent of captain; he had only had his command since the Dominion war, when his commander had fallen in battle. The young centurion had picked up the command staff and had turned the tide against a Breen ship, disabling and capturing it. Of course, all the Breen crew had vaporized themselves, since they never allowed themselves to be captured. Jagron had moved swiftly up the ranks after that, gaining command of this D'deridex-class warbird, but he had ambitions beyond the command of a single vessel.

Despite his relative youth and a family background of low nobility, Jagron looked every centimeter the part of a Romulan commander. He was tall and slim, handsome in a hawklike way, and arrogant to a fault.

"That's enough fussing," he said, brushing off his valet's hands and straightening his own stiff collar. "It's just a meeting."

"But with the Praetor, Sir," said the old valet in hushed tones. "And the Proconsul."

"Yes," replied Captain Jagron with a frown. "All this firepower . . . for what?"

"You'll know soon, Commander."

Still frowning, Jagron strode from his quarters down the hallway to the transporter room, where he was met by his top aides, Centurion Gravonak and Intelligence Officer Petroliv. The tall and stately Petroliv was also his lover, but they had taken considerable pains to hide that fact from the rest of the crew. They always treated each other with cool professionalism.

"My Liege," said Gravonak, bowing like the toady he was.

"Are we still in the dark about the reason for this gathering?" asked Jagron as he strode into the transporter room.

"Not entirely," answered Petroliv. "We're sure it has something to do with the massive fleet movements we've been observing in the Federation."

"Movements *away* from the Neutral Zone," added Gravonak, sounding displeased that, unlike his colleague, he had nothing new to report.

When they reached the transporter platform, all three of them climbed aboard. A very nervous transporter operator cleared his throat. "I'm sorry, Commander Jagron, but the protocols call for every commander to bring *one* aide, no more."

Centurion Gravonak folded his hands in front of him, as if expecting the intelligence officer to step down. Commander Jagron gazed from the stuffy first officer to his beautiful intelligence officer; he had already made his decision, but he wanted to make it look as if he were deliberating.

"Gravonak, return to the bridge."

"Sir?" asked the centurion as if he hadn't understood. But Jagron was not going to humor him with another request. He simply motioned to the transporter operator, who sent the commander's molecules and those of his lover into the bowels of another warbird only five kilometers away.

They were met on the *Terix* by Commander Tomalak, who smiled pleasantly at the new arrivals. An old veteran, Tomalak could afford to be more personable than the usual Romulan commander. He had seen almost everything in his long and distinguished career, and he never let you forget it. Jagron respected, envied, and hated Tomalak, but he was never anything less than cordial to the venerated commander.

"Welcome aboard, my young colleague," said Tomalak, grasping Jagron's shoulder. "You're the last one—even the Praetor was here before you."

Jagron shrugged, not explaining that he had planned it that way. "Are we supposed to be guarding the Neutral Zone or sitting around in a conference room?"

"You're jaded at rather a young age," observed Tomalak with amusement. He led the way out the door. "The Praetor and the Proconsul—this is undoubtedly the most important meeting you've ever attended."

Jagron motioned to his intelligence officer, Petroliv. "Why could we bring only one aide?"

"Apparently the number of people who are allowed to know about this will be kept small."

"Do you know?"

Tomalak stopped and shook his head, a scowl on his craggy face. "No. And I don't remember ever hearing of a similar meeting in all my decades of service."

They said no more until they reached the briefing room, which appeared to be a small classroom near a row of laboratories. A large viewscreen dominated one wall of the room. Already seated were two more commanders, Horek and Damarkol of the *Livex* and the *G'Anohok* respectively, plus their aides. The Praetor and the Proconsul were not in evidence.

After a few quick pleasantries, Tomalak said, "Our most distinguished guests will be joining us soon. They wanted us to watch some video logs first. I am told these were sent to us by the Federation." After finding a seat, he said, "Computer, begin playback."

Jagron had never pretended to have seen as much in his life as Tomalak and these veteran captains had seen, but his jaw was hanging open a few seconds into the presentation. In one harrowing scene after another, they watched as an eerie wall of flame destroyed planets, moons, stars, nebulas, cities, mountains, skies—everything that stood in its way. "Destroy" was not quite the right word, Jagron decided, because planets and suns were left in the wake of this awful wave. But they were drastically altered.

When the horrendous images finally ended, a Romulan scientist came on the screen to explain what they had just witnessed. Although Commander Jagron didn't understand half of what he said, he grasped the gist of it perfectly well. A secret Federation weapon, which had been outlawed by every power in the Alpha Quadrant ninety years ago, had been unleashed in a new attack. This mass destruction was happening in the Federation right now. The only thing which had stood up to it so far was phase-shifting technology copied from the Romulan Star Empire.

The image of the scientist blinked off, leaving a blank screen and equally blank expressions among the audience. "That's not the worst of it," said a voice behind them. Jagron turned to see the round face and pudgy body of Proconsul Woderbok, head of the Senate. "If the Federation cannot contain this Genesis Wave, it will cross the Neutral Zone and strike deep into our territory, endangering dozens of inhabited worlds."

"No," whispered Commander Damarkol. She might have once been beautiful, but now the commander was gray and wizened. "How can they do this to us? What's the matter with those fools? Can't they control their own weapons?"

"Apparently, they don't know who unleashed this attack," answered the Proconsul, "or who perfected the Genesis Device to be employed in this manner." He went on to explain about Dr. Carol Marcus and her abduction.

Commander Horek sneered in disbelief. "How do we know this is even *real*? Maybe it's some kind of trick to make us move our fleets . . . or abandon our worlds."

"It has been verified by one of our operatives in the area," answered the Proconsul, "as well as our own long-range sensors. Believe me, we *wish* this was a hoax, because the reality of it is staggering."

Commander Tomalak looked ashen. "What are we supposed to do?"

"You will receive your orders from the highest source. Please rise for the Praetor." Everyone in the briefing room jumped to their feet, and the stocky Proconsul stepped back from the doorway to allow a bent, gray-haired man to enter. He wore the regal charcoal and lavender robes of state, bedecked in elaborate insignias, medals, and ribbons, all of which connoted this order or that society. Although the Praetor was elderly, a spark of anger and intelligence burned in his hooded eyes.

"Sit down, Commanders," said the Praetor in a gravelly voice, and they all did so. "If it were only the Federation in danger, we would do nothing to help these pathetic fools. However, this may be the gravest threat our empire has ever faced. I am ordering you to go to the coordinates which are being sent to your bridges as we speak. Proceed at maximum warp—you will receive free passage through the Federation. If hailed, just use the code word 'Genesis.' Upon reaching the Starfleet vessels *Enterprise* and *Sovereign*, you are to hand over your interphase generators to their scientists."

Commander Damarkol opened her mouth as if she wanted to speak, but she held her tongue, apparently realizing she would be interrupting the Praetor. Commander Jagron now saw the need for all this firepower. If anybody other than the Praetor had ordered them to go into Federation space and relinquish their interphase generators—the guts of their cloaking systems—they would have resisted. When the news came from their supreme leader, they all realized how truly grave this crisis was.

"In short, you are to assist Starfleet in any way they see fit to use you," rasped the Praetor, the mealy words twisting his lips into a scowl. "You're only the advance party. The Third Fleet is being mustered as we speak, but the Federation is in dire need of our technology now. We are in dire need of your courage. Go with the speed of the bloodhawk. You are dismissed."

They stood again as the Praetor shuffled out of the room. Tomalak sighed and said, "If the *Enterprise* is on duty, that's a small token in our favor."

"We should have destroyed the Federation years ago," muttered Damarkol, striding out the door.

Horek sneered. "Those fools. They set out to do terraforming and end up creating the most horrendous weapon in the galaxy!"

Jagron didn't trust himself to say anything profound, so he kept his mouth shut. From the corner of his eye, he saw the pudgy Proconsul motion to him. "Stay a moment, Commander Jagron. I have news from home."

This seemed odd, but Jagron kept an indifferent look on his face while the others, including his intelligence officer, filed out of the classroom.

It wasn't until the door shut that Proconsul Woderbok stepped closer to him. "You're looking well, Commander."

"A message from home?" asked Jagron doubtfully.

The Proconsul snorted a laugh. "I sincerely doubt if I know any of your family. You're not of the same bloodlines as the others. Why, you're almost a commoner."

Jagron maintained his stoic expression, because this was hardly news. There was some reason why the Proconsul wanted to see him. And why he needed him.

"You're not of noble birth," said Woderbok, "but you have distinguished yourself by your actions. This mission is one more opportunity for you to take the initiative. There's something that needs to be done, and I can't ask one of the others to do this. In fact, I can't ask *you* to do it."

Jagron nodded. "You want me to steal this Genesis Device."

The Proconsul smiled, increasing his double chins. "Hypothetically, if someone were to come into possession of such a device, it couldn't be known to anyone. He would have to cover his tracks and make sure no one knew, especially not the Federation. He would have to take full responsibility, if caught."

The pudgy man drew closer, his voice a whisper, "If this person were successful in smuggling the device back to *me* . . . well, the stars are the limit for a young man with such initiative. He would have backing from the highest levels."

"I can't even tell the other commanders?" whispered Jagron.

"No. Their careers are on the downward path—they have no ambition beyond sitting in their command chairs. They would argue with me. Or you. They don't understand that this Genesis Wave makes their mighty warships obsolete. I need somebody who will be *bold*—with no thoughts of treaties or alliances."

Commander Jagron shook his head slowly, running through the possible pitfalls in this risky plan. "It may be hard to hide it from the other commanders, and I won't fire on them."

The old politician smiled and put his hand on the commander's padded shoulder. "You leave that to me. Copy me on your dispatches, and I'll know when the time is right to *withdraw* the others and leave you in a position to snatch the prize. And the glory."

Jagron tried not to smile, but the corners of his mouth tilted slightly upward. He was already one of the youngest commanders— maybe he could be one of the youngest senators.

"Maybe we'll have ill fortune, and you'll never get an opportunity to grab it," said the Proconsul with a shrug. "So be it. However, a rich future awaits us if we're successful. As you have seen, Genesis means food for multitudes, a convenient way to terraform planets, and a painless way to destroy our enemies. It would be a shame if the only ones to possess this technology were the Federation."

"Besides," said Jagron, "they used our phase-shifting technology without permission."

The old Proconsul laughed. "Yes, Commander. As usual, right and justice are with the Romulan Star Empire."

\*    \*    \*

Captain Picard and Admiral Nechayev stood on the observation deck of Starbase 393, watching a stream of refugees disembark from the *Enterprise* and file down the extendable docking port into the space station. The *Sovereign* was docked at another pylon, disgorging its passengers as well. The starbase was beginning to look like a Paris tube station during rush hour, except that the people milling about had no place to go.

Picard had never seen the admiral so despondent, not even after other missions had gone awry. Although she tried to mask her feelings, Nechayev looked about ten years older, and there was a sadness in her eyes that he had never seen before. Normally she was the type who could give a suicide order, lose all hands, and never show a scintilla of regret. But the Genesis Wave had Admiral Nechayev gazing deeply into her soul.

"I can't say I'm sorry to see the evacuees go," remarked Picard, just trying to make conversation. "But we can be justly proud of all the lives we saved."

"What about all the lives we *didn't* save?" she muttered. "Did you read the final casualty reports from Persephone V?"

"No. I didn't see much point in it."

"You're wise, Captain. I wish I hadn't read them." Nechayev rested her elbows on the railing and looked down at the sea of people below them. "We lost more people in three minutes than we lost during the entire Dominion war."

"Don't be too hard on yourself, Admiral; we did all we could do."

She gave him a withering glare. "*You* may have done all you could, but I didn't. It's not that I didn't move quickly enough once I knew the threat was real. I did. But I erred six months ago when I didn't make full disclosure about the abduction of Carol Marcus. I should have put Starfleet on alert right then and there."

"If you're going to have twenty/twenty hindsight," said Picard, "we should have handled Project Genesis differently ninety years ago. We should have known that we couldn't sweep technology like that under the carpet."

Nechayev narrowed her gaze at him. "We were virtually at war with the Klingons back then. We were trying mightily to keep the peace with a stubborn, hostile power. You and I know how difficult that is—we failed with the Cardassians. So we appeased everyone and hushed it up. As with most appeasements, it only delayed the inevitable."

"Speaking of Klingons," said Picard, "I kept Consul Maltz on board at Leah Brahms' request. He might also be helpful in dealing with the Klingons when they arrive. Plus we kept the specialists we had on board from our aborted mission. They're proving to be helpful."

"That seems like a long time ago, doesn't it? When it's only been a few days." The admiral rose to her feet and stuck out her chin. "The Klingons have started arriving, and they're taking over much of the evacuation. But we have to find someplace to make our stand."

"I agree," said Picard. "We can't keep running, saving a fifth of the population here and there. Once we get the interphase generators from the Romulans, Brahms and La Forge think we can arrange shelters big enough to protect large groups of people and animals. Our latest long-range scans show that the planets revert to a livable state sooner than we thought."

"The task force has already skirted around Seran," said the admiral, lifting her chin. "Soon we'll have another front. Maybe they can find the source of the wave . . . and shut it down."

Picard nodded, unable to add anything to that fervent hope.

# twenty

Captain Landwaring of the *Defiant*-class starship *Neptune* peered curiously at the dark boulders, debris, and dust cluttering his viewscreen. According to the charts, this was the Boneyard, a vast asteroid field—the remains of some cataclysm when the universe was new. It had never been explored, except with sensors, because it was too dangerous. There were trillions of rocks in there, ranging in size from Earth's moon to the tiniest dust particle. With the naked eye it was impossible to pick out much detail—it looked like an avalanche frozen in midfall. Landwaring did notice several large asteroids that were shaped like rubber dog bones.

According to the latest projections, *this* was ground zero—where the Genesis Wave began. Of course, here the wave was hardly bigger than a laser point and undetectable by their sensors. It was nothing like the destructive force it became light-years from here.

The five *Defiant*-class vessels had small crews but the speed and firepower of much larger ships. To do a physical search of the Boneyard would take them a lifetime. They had come fully armed, ready to fight to the death with a ruthless adversary—and all they found was a galaxy's biggest rock pile.

The *Neptune* observed the Boneyard from a cautious distance of two hundred thousand kilometers. Even so, the captain felt inexplicably nervous.

"Probe three reporting back," said his ops officer, a young blond woman named Herron. "No life-forms reported, although there are amino acids, proteins, and other building blocks."

"That kind of residue is commonly associated with the wave," said his science officer, Mitchell. Normally the *Neptune* didn't have a science officer, but on this mission it did. So far, the mousy fellow hadn't been much help.

"That residue often occurs in regular space dust, too," said Ensign Herron.

"What about signs of a power source?" asked the captain. "Electrical interference? Fluctuations?"

"All over the Boneyard," answered the ops officer, shaking her head. "Half of those rocks must be magnetically charged, and the other half are kelbonite, which distorts the readings. There could even be fake, hollow asteroids in there—we couldn't spot them with a few probes."

"It's a good haystack in which to hide a needle," conceded Landwaring. "Is anybody here a hunter?"

No one volunteered to have ever been a hunter, and the captain went on, "Sometimes you have to flush the game," he explained. "You know, fire a couple of wild shots and see if you can roust anything from the brush."

"I advise against firing willy-nilly into there," said the science officer.

"Why?"

Mitchell hemmed and hawed for a second then came up with, "Well, you're liable to send that debris flying in all directions."

"And so would a wandering comet or a meteorite," answered Landwaring. "If you have a better idea of how to proceed with our search—the fastest way possible—I'm listening."

The science officer hung his head. "I know these are dire circumstances."

"They sure are," said Captain Landwaring. "Tactical, open up a secure channel to the task force."

"Yes, Sir," answered the bald-headed Deltan, working his board. "Channel open."

"To all ships in Task Force Javelin," began Landwaring, stepping behind the tactical console. "I've decided to fire a brace of torpedoes into the Boneyard, to see if we can stir anything up."

The captain reached over the Deltan's shoulder to enter a target, his best guess. "We're transmitting targeting information to you. On my mark, fire torpedoes in firing pattern delta nine. Remember that we can't fire and forget. We have to change position—just as we did with the probes—because the Genesis Effect has been known to follow the deuterium trail back to the firing ship. Rendezvous thirty thousand kilometers dead to port. Keep all logs running, and look for anything . . . I mean, *anything*. Landwaring out."

He nodded to the Bajoran male on the conn, Jorax. "Set new course. Be ready to go to full impulse as soon as we launch."

"Yes, Sir."

On ops, Ensign Herron said, "Captain, all ships report targeting complete, per your orders."

"Course is set," repeated Ensign Jorax with a nervous glance over his shoulder.

It was clear that none of the crew would care to have his job at the moment, thought Landwaring. While they were groping around here for answers, whole worlds were being lost forever.

"Alert the task force. Hold for my mark." The captain lifted his hand, then brought it down decisively. "Fire."

"Torpedoes away," said the Deltan, looking up at the viewscreen, where two streaks of light shot outward from the ship, headed toward the asteroids.

"Going to impulse power," said Jorax on the conn. The image on the viewscreen blurred and took a few moments to refocus as the *Neptune* sped away. They had done this routine so many times with the earlier probes, their actions were almost automatic.

Seconds later, they had stopped and were again watching the endless, ageless sprawl of debris called the Boneyard. Without warning, ten violent eruptions tore through the asteroid field, like a string of firecrackers going off in a pile of dirt. Rock and debris were blasted outward and inward, turning the targeted area into a ricocheting demolition derby.

A minute later, it was relatively peaceful again in the Boneyard, except for slowly expanding clouds of dust and clumps of debris hurtling outward.

"Anything on sensors?" asked Captain Landwaring, leaning over Herron's shoulder.

She frowned curiously at her readings. "I'm detecting vegetable matter."

"Vegetable matter?" asked Landwaring curiously.

"It's true," said the science officer, Mitchell, who peered at his own readouts. "But it looks old. Probably lichens on the rocks, still there from eons ago when this field was a living planet."

The ops officer suddenly sat up. "There's something metallic out there, Sir! It appears to be spherical in shape."

"Spherical?" asked Landwaring. "You mean, as if it were manufactured?"

She nodded her head. "I've isolated it—I can put it on visual."

"Do it." The captain folded his arms and gazed expectantly at the viewscreen overhead. Thus far, they'd had nothing of interest to look at, and he was eager to see this metallic sphere which had lain hidden inside the Boneyard for who-knew-how-many years. When the image cleared, he gasped with surprise. It looked like a charred, dented escape pod, revolving slowly as it sped through space.

"What's the size of that thing?" he asked.

"It's approximately four meters in diameter," answered Mitchell. "There are no lifesigns on board, and it doesn't seem to be producing any power. But I am picking up a bit more of that vegetable matter. Maybe it's old foodstuffs."

"Conn, take us within a hundred kilometers of the sphere," ordered Captain Landwaring. "And get a tractor beam on it. Just to stop it. Don't bring it aboard. Keep shields up as much as you can."

"Yes, Sir," answered Jorax, working his console.

While he was doing that, the captain prowled behind the row of secondary stations. "Tactical, what are the other ships reporting?"

"Same thing we're seeing," answered the Deltan. "That sphere is the only thing of interest."

"I'm locked on with tractor beam," said Jorax on conn. "The sphere has stopped moving."

It had even stopped revolving as it hung in the darkness of space, bathed by the eerie glow of their tractor beam. Landwaring peered curiously at the relic on the viewscreen and ordered, "Tell the other ships to converge on our position. Shields up."

He wanted to believe that this find was significant, but there were plenty of logical explanations why an escape pod had become lodged inside an asteroid field. After all, they didn't call it the Boneyard for nothing.

"Mitchell," he said to the science officer. "I want you to do an EVA inspection on that object, while we take another look around for anything that got shaken loose. Take the shuttlepod. Herron will pilot for you."

The young science officer gulped. "You want me to go outside and do a hands-on?"

"Yes," answered the captain in his coldest tone. "You can start earning your keep around here."

"Come on, Sir," said Ensign Herron, pointing to the door. "I'll be right there in the shuttlepod."

"Sapor, take the conn," ordered Landwaring, motioning to the auxiliary consoles where relief personnel were waiting. "Come on, let's move quickly," he said. "They're not paying us to sit on our hands. While we're messing around here, that thing is eating its way through the Federation."

The shuttlepod was the smallest self-propelled vessel to carry Starfleet markings, except for one-person escape pods. The clunky little craft didn't have warp drive, and its range was limited, but it was all they had room for on the *Neptune*. Nevertheless, Eileen Herron liked piloting the little sprite, and she was the best on the ship.

Peter Mitchell sat down beside her, wearing a thin, low-pressure environmental suit, and he gave her a pout that was part disdain and part fear. "I shouldn't have to do this. Don't we have security officers or something?"

"You know, science officer isn't a desk job out here," answered Eileen. "And the *Neptune* isn't a big cushy starship. We have a small crew, and everybody has to do as many jobs as they can. Besides, we don't know you, and the rest of us have been through hell together. So you have to prove your mettle."

"Prove my mettle," echoed Mitchell doubtfully. He hefted an armful of tricorders, tools, drills, and sample bags. "Okay, let's do it. At least I get to ride in Eileen's Buggy."

"Oh, you heard them call it that," said Herron with a grin. "Nobody can touch me in this thing. How close do you want me to get?"

"How long is the tether?"

"We usually do fifty meters."

"Okay, make it thirty. Then I can get all the way around it."

"Hold on." The ensign applied thrusters, and the shuttlepod shot out of a small opening in the underbelly of the *Neptune*. With a few quick, sure maneuevers, Herron homed in on the aged sphere floating in space. The closer they came to it, the more it looked like space junk, although it appeared mostly intact. She was amused at how it seemed to be about the same size as the shuttlepod, although of a completely different shape.

She applied reverse thrusters then looked at her instruments with a smile. "Thirty-two meters away. Is that close enough?"

"Good flying," muttered Mitchell, peering at the sphere which filled the main viewport. "I don't see why we can't bring this thing onto the ship for study at our leisure."

"Just make a quick appraisal of it," said Herron impatiently. "Take some readings, a core sample, a few souvenirs—just do your job. I don't think anyone will be shocked if it doesn't have anything to do with why we're out here."

"I know what to do," Mitchell said huffily. "Prepare to open the hatch." He put his helmet over his head, and Herron helped him tighten the seals. Both of them checked the readings on the tether.

"Go get 'em, Tiger," she said with a thumbs-up. The pilot grabbed an oxygen mask from a panel overhead and put it over her face. Then she belted herself into her seat. Force-fields would keep most of the atmosphere inside the shuttlepod, but it never hurt to be safe.

"Ready?"

He nodded, and she cracked the hatch open. With a whoosh, a bit of the air flew out, and Mitchell fumbled anxiously in the sudden weightlessness. Finally he managed to extricate himself from his chair and float out the open hatch. He quickly attached his tether.

Once the science officer got hooked up, he oriented himself fairly well. Taking a small harpoon gun from his bag of tools, he shot a grappling hook at the sphere. On his first attempt, he hit the relic and got a solid hold with the molecular bonding. After tugging hard on the rope, he set out, pulling himself easily hand over hand in the microgravity of space, his tether trailing behind him.

From her pilot's seat, Ensign Herron shut the hatch, having decided that the mission was going smoothly so far. On her instrument panel, she saw that Mitchell's vital signs were a bit elevated, but that was normal. Checking her sensors, she concluded that this part of space was about as boring as it got, even if the source of the Genesis Wave lurked nearby. With no sign of the deadly weapon, it felt as if they were the victims of some mass hoax.

Gazing out her viewport, she noticed that Mitchell had reached the mysterious sphere and was taking tricorder readings. Then he moved very close to the relic, as if he were listening to something inside. Or perhaps he was trying to read markings on the hull. Herron thought about asking Mitchell what he was doing, but she didn't want to interrupt him. He obviously wasn't having any difficulty with his assignment. In fact, he moved around the sphere touching and feeling its surface as if he knew its intimate workings.

Then he astounded her by pulling or pushing something that opened a hatch. At any rate, a dark cavity suddenly appeared on the surface of the sphere, and Mitchell stuck his hand into it.

Now Herron got on the comlink. "Mitchell, what are you doing?"

"I've got to go inside," he replied insistently. Without any further leave, the science officer popped into the sphere and was gone.

She hit the comlink again. "Shuttlepod to *Neptune*."

"Go ahead," said Landwaring. "How's it going?"

"Well, Mitchell is being awfully brave," she reported. "He just went inside the thing."

"Really," said Landwaring, sounding impressed. Then he grumbled, "I didn't clear him to do that. Can you see anything?"

"It looks awfully dark in there, Captain." Herron shook her head. "I'm only thirty meters away, and it doesn't look like anything but space junk to me. I don't see how this could be connected to the Genesis Wave."

"Do you think we could beam it aboard?" asked the captain.

"Only if we took it apart, and I don't know if it would be worth the effort. This old museum piece will still be here if we need it later."

There was movement around the pod, and a helmet emerged, followed by the rest of the environmental suit. The ensign sat up in her chair. "He's coming out."

"Reel him in," ordered Landwaring. "Unless there's something pertinent we should investigate, I want you to get back here."

"Yes, Sir. Shuttlepod out." The ensign gave two taps on the companel. "Herron to Mitchell, I'm going to bring you in. All right?"

The hooded figure waved to her and hefted what looked like a bag of old leaves. Slowly he removed the grappling hook from the sphere. Herron activated the winch to retract the tether; then she put on her oxygen mask. The ensign watched with amusement as Mitchell's body drew closer; he looked like a kite floating at the end of its string.

A few seconds later, she sprang the hatch, and the suited figure climbed back into the shuttlepod. His movements stiff and jerky, Mitchell deposited his equipment and samples behind the seats; then he settled into his chair. His chest went up and down in the suit as he caught his breath. Herron knew what it was like to readjust to gravity, so she let him have his moment of reorientation.

Finally, Mitchell removed his helmet and smiled at her, looking somehow more at peace and more handsome than he had before. This trip had been a confidence builder for him, she decided.

"Is there anything unusual?" she asked. "Anything we should report back to the ship before we leave?"

"No," he answered, staring straight ahead. "It's dead. Really old. I don't think this escape pod, or small craft, was ever manned. Maybe it was released by mistake."

"What's that stuff in the bag?" asked Herron, glancing behind the seat. Now that she saw the dried plant life at close range, it looked dirty and gray, like old clumps of Spanish moss or mistletoe. "Are you sure we should bring it back to the ship?"

Mitchell gazed meaningfully at her, his words calm and soothing. "It's inert, and it's probably the only thing that will tell us the age of this craft. It's definitely not Federation. It must have been a survival pod of some sort, because they had a kind of hydroponic growing system. That's the remains of it, a plant that's been dead for a long time. It's no more harmful than your grandmother's pressed flower collection."

She blinked at him, amazed. "How do you know about my grandmother's pressed flower collection?"

He shrugged. "Every grandmother has a pressed flower collection. So did mine." He boldly touched her arm. "It's just one more thing we have in common."

Herron knew she should slap him, but the move had caught her by surprise . . . and in an oddly receptive mood. In fact, her skin seemed to burn where his mere fingers touched it, even through a heavy glove. Why had she never noticed how desirable he was?

"What do you say to calling the captain, and telling him that neither one of us feels well. We're both going to need to go lie down in our quarters."

She smiled slyly and punched her companel. "Shuttlepod to *Neptune*."

"Landwaring here," came the response.

"There's nothing major to report," said Ensign Herron, gazing at the handsome man beside her. "Mitchell just says it's real old and real dead, so we're on our way back."

She coughed and tried to sound sick. "But I don't feel well, and neither does Mitchell. We're going to need to go to our quarters and lie down when we get back."

"What's the matter?" asked Landwaring with concern.

"I don't know, maybe it's something with the air in the shuttlepod. It got a little thin when we opened the hatch. It's all right now. I'll run diagnostics when we get back."

"All right," said the captain begrudgingly. "I guess you've both earned a rest, but don't expect it to be a long one. Sometimes an EVA can leave you a little nauseous."

"I'm sure that's it," answered Herron, barely containing her excitement over being alone with Mitchell. "Shuttlepod out."

# twenty-one

Maltz snored peacefully in a corner of the radiation laboratory, snuffling and grunting to himself, while Geordi La Forge and Leah Brahms poured over equations and charts on their situation monitors. These documents represented the release patterns, speeds, and trajectories of the Genesis Wave once it hit a planet, and it couldn't be more devastating. They continued to sift through data gleaned from Commander Troi's jaunt on Persephone V, and it felt as if they needed months to get a hold on this thing, when all they had was hours.

La Forge couldn't help but glance at his beautiful colleague every now and then, just to make sure she was really here beside him. It wasn't that she was a distraction—her presence was more reassuring than anything else. If the universe could drop her here beside him, then maybe it wasn't as cruel as it seemed to be at the moment.

However, Geordi didn't care much for her Klingon chaperone. He understood survivors' syndrome and how the two of them might have bonded in that shuttlecraft, but he was still a little jealous. Leah and Maltz were a crew, albeit tiny, but he wasn't part of it.

Still he and Leah worked as smoothly together as they ever had, in reality or simulation. She was immersed in the task at hand, and Geordi was basically assisting her. He was in awe of her intellect and drive, although the urgency of the situation made the atmosphere around the lab unusually grim.

Other teams on nearby ships and elsewhere in the Federation were wrestling with the same problems. Some of them reported different solutions or variations on the phase-shifting plan. Since the Romulans were already on their way with the interphase generators, it was definite that phase-shifting would get the first trial under fire. The irony was that Leah had created the vaunted radiation suit, but she didn't have a lot of faith that the same technology could protect thousands of people at a time. Despite her dedication and hard work, it was clear that she would have preferred to be with the task force that was hunting down the perpetrators of this horror.

While Leah continued poring over equations and charts, La Forge checked on dispatches from Data. In addition to his bridge duties, the android was sifting through incoming correspondence from their colleagues. He rejected the preposterous and unworkable, and the stuff that just rehashed what they already knew, forwarding anything he thought might be helpful. Unfortunately, that wasn't a lot.

As Leah had surmised, the Genesis Effect only extended a certain distance into the crust, since it retained its terraforming characteristics and was programmed to move fast over a planet that met the right criteria. This had brought many suggestions for using mines, caverns, underground storage tanks, missile silos, and the like for shelters. Unfortunately, the wave triggered earthquakes and volcanic eruptions as a side effect. Plus it wasn't always predictable how deeply into the crust it went. It was probably dependent upon the composition of the bedrock.

The effect on stars, nebulas, and miscellaneous objects in space was more devastating and unpredictable, resulting in total reconfiguration. Even in Leah's radiation suit, Geordi wouldn't care to be caught in a starship when that wave hit it. Oddly enough, despite the horrendous upheaval, a suitable planet was the safest place to be.

"Anything new?" asked Leah, glancing at him from the corner of her eyes. Although she didn't appear to be paying that much attention to him, she always seemed to know exactly what he was doing.

"No," he answered glumly. "A correspondent from Alpha Centauri would like us to put everybody in transporter suspension while the wave passes through."

"That would work, except how do you protect the transporter stations themselves?" She shook her head glumly. "Unless we stop the wave itself, we're just killing time . . . along with a lot of planets."

"But the same technology saved you," said Geordi, hating to sound like a broken sound chip.

"Oh, it may save *lives*, but if you think you're going to save anybody's *home* with this, you're sadly mistaken. You're still going to have to evacuate these people."

"If we can evacuate them at a normal pace, that might not be such a bad trade-off." La Forge took a deep breath and tried to tone down his rhetoric. "If I've learned one thing in my decade on the *Enterprise*—if you can't do anything else, you buy time."

Brahms closed her eyes and rubbed her forehead. "I'm sorry, Geordi—I don't know why I'm so negative. Well, I do know why, but I'm trying hard *not* to deal with it."

"If you want to talk, I'll listen. Or you could see our counselor."

"I've seen your counselor, and she has enough patients to last her a lifetime. Every day, we pick up more."

"We're letting them off, too." La Forge shook his head in exasperation. "I don't know what to tell you. The loss of a spouse . . . that's something I've never gone through. It must be awful."

"I didn't love him anymore," she said softly, as if admitting it for the first time.

"What?" asked Geordi hoarsely.

"I mean, he was a huge part of my life—my husband, my colleague, my partner—but he felt more like a partner than a husband. And I think he was seeing somebody else." Leah sighed and looked down. Now her short brown hair framed a face that had lost its cherubic innocence; it was an adult's face full of character and experience.

"He certainly had the opportunity," she said with a disdainful laugh. "Because I let him go his own way whenever he wanted. I just didn't care enough."

Geordi didn't trust himself to say anything, or even make a sound, so he just nodded slowly. He wanted to take her hand and assure her that she never needed to lack for love as long as he was alive, but he wasn't courageous or uncouth enough to do it.

Leah sniffed and rubbed her nose. "Now that he's gone, of course, I see all the good about Mikel. And the bad. I see my life for everything it was, and everything it wasn't. I need to try harder at living—to balance myself with work. I can't think of any other reason why I was spared."

Trembling, Geordi extended his hand and was about to reach for hers, when the door whooshed open. The old Klingon was instantly on his feet, brandishing a knife. "Who goes there?"

It was Dolores Linton, dressed in work overalls. She stepped sheepishly into the lab and glanced warily at Maltz. "Hi, Leah. You asked me to come at noon?"

Brahms dabbed a sleeve at her eyes and jumped to her feet. "Dolores! Thanks for coming. Is it that late already? I had forgotten what time it was."

"It happens." The geologist shrugged cheerfully. "Hi there, Geordi. You still owe me—"

"I know." He waved helplessly at her. "I heard you were heroic on the lines in Persephone V."

She smiled. "I used to be a bouncer. That's how I put myself through the academy."

Brahms made the introductions. "Consul Maltz, this is Mission Specialist Linton. She's on our side."

The Klingon nodded.

Leah motioned Dolores over to the situation monitor and tapped her finger on the screen. "We've got a lot of geology data, but we're not exactly sure what we're looking at. In open air, the interphase generators should work against the wave, and I'm not sure how far either one of them extends into the ground. I don't want it to come up through our feet and get us."

"Interphase generators?" asked Dolores.

Geordi jumped to his feet. "We really should spend some time bringing Dolores up to speed on the plan."

Maltz laughed out loud, and everyone turned to look at the grizzled old Klingon. "What is to explain? Throw down some sneaky Romulan devices, and hope for the best! This is just the kind of reaction you would expect to get from the Federation."

"We've sent a task force to Seran," said Geordi defensively.

The Klingon waved derisively and sat down, having said his piece.

Dolores Linton glanced around at the desultory expressions in the room and put her hands on her hips. "When was the last time any of you were out of this room?"

"Um—" Leah shrugged and looked at Geordi, who also shrugged.

"That's too long," insisted the geologist. "It's lunchtime, and the ship is relatively clear of refugees. I say we talk over food."

"Good idea!" barked Maltz, headed for the door. "We need our strength to confront the enemy. Have you ever tried rokeg blood pie, Mission Specialist Linton?"

"One of my favorites, Consul Maltz." She stepped back to allow the lanky Klingon to exit first, and he seized the honor.

"Oh, great," muttered La Forge to himself, "a double date."

"Pardon me?" asked Brahms, moving toward the door.

The engineer cleared his throat. "Nothing. I thought you were getting somewhere . . . talking about your feelings. Then we got interrupted."

"I wasn't getting anywhere," she answered. "Besides, this isn't the right time to dwell on personal issues, is it?"

"No," said Geordi quietly. "I suppose not."

\*　\*　\*

A padd in his hand, Captain Picard paced across his ready room, reading the reports from another world that had fallen, Sarona VIII. It could have been much worse. Although the Klingon fleet showed up with less than eight hours to spare, they had very efficiently saved four million lives, killing a few dozen rioters in the process. Unlike Starfleet's rescue attempts, they reported no sites abandoned or overrun.

"Maybe we've found the right party for that job," Picard muttered to himself.

His handheld device beeped, picking up an intraship transmission from the bridge. He glanced at the padd and saw that it was a coded message from Admiral Nechayev. It read simply:

"We stand at Myrmidon. The Romulans will meet us there at fifteen-hundred hours. Need-to-know basis at present."

Picard nodded to himself, half-expecting this news. Myrmidon was moderately populous—almost fifty million—and it would be hit in about twenty-six hours according to their forecasts. That would be cutting it close, but wherever they tried to mount this operation, it would be cutting it close. This information was on a need-to-know security basis, and he knew someone who needed to know.

He tapped his combadge. "Picard to Mot."

"Mot here!" said his favorite barber. "What can I do for you, Sir?"

"Can you come up to my ready room for a moment?"

"A trim, Sir? A shave?"

"No, you don't need to bring anything with you. It's not business. Picard out." Mot was the unofficial head of the Bolian contingent on the ship, which hovered between ten and twenty in number at any given time. He had gone home at the height of the Dominion war, but he had come back to the *Enterprise* a year ago to reestablish his business.

The blue-skinned humanoids with the bifurcated ridge in the center of their faces were some of the most personable, loyal, and competent members of his crew. Picard would gladly take more Bolians aboard the *Enterprise*, if he could find them.

Myrmidon was a good choice. Although not the Bolians' ancestral homeworld, it was declared their spiritual home five hundred years ago—after an ancient artifact, the Crown of the First Mother, was discovered there. A former paramour of his, Vash, had tried to steal the relic, so Picard knew all about it.

The Crown of the First Mother bore a striking resemblance to the royal jewelry depicted in the Orezes Codices, the Bolians' most sacred text. Its location and rediscovery also fit in with the origin stories and predictions. After numerous archeological expeditions to Myrmidon, the Bolians found they had much in common with a long-dead race who used to inhabit the planet, the Bolastre. There were intriguing indications of a common ancestor.

Although the artifact was never proven definitively to be related to the Bolians, they were very happy to accept Myrmidon as their main religious shrine. It was a beautiful planet, by all accounts, and Bolians had relocated there in record numbers until now there were almost fifty million inhabitants. It was all about to tumble down—sacred archeological sites and modern cities alike. He only hoped their new plans wouldn't result in a worse disaster than they had already witnessed.

His door chimed, jarring him out of his worries. "Come."

Mot bustled in, and he was his usual jovial self in the face of what must be considerable personal anguish. The portly Bolian snapped to attention. "Good afternoon, Captain. Mot reporting."

The captain put his hand on the blue-skinned barber's shoulder and said, "You haven't asked for any favors, Mr. Mot, but I know you must be thinking about Myrmidon. You have family there, don't you?"

The smile vanished, and the barber gulped. "Yes. My parents, in fact. Almost all of us on board have relatives there. We have big families."

Picard nodded sympathetically. "Keep this under your hat, Mr. Mot, but Myrmidon is where we're making a stand. We're going to try the phase-shifting plan there."

The barber put his hands together in applause. "Oh, thank you, Sir! Thank you!"

"Don't thank me, thank Admiral Nechayev. But we're keeping this on a need-to-know basis for the time being. I think all the Bolians on the ship need to know."

"I agree," said Mot with relief. "But why the secrecy?"

Picard leaned forward, his voice low. "I'm not the admiral, but I know she's concerned about how some of the past evacuations have gotten out of hand. We don't want to raise anyone's hopes, because there may be extenuating circumstances. We might not be able to pull it off. As soon as possible, we'll alert the populace and the rest of the crew."

Mot nodded thoughtfully and cast his eyes downward, increasing his double chins. "Thank you, Captain, for telling me. However, I should warn you—my people believe strongly in assisted suicide."

"Yes, the double-effect doctrine. I'm familiar with it." The captain frowned deeply, not having considered this complication. That was all they needed—mass suicides—as they were trying desperately to save lives.

"Any act that relieves suffering is acceptable, even if that act has the effect of causing death," said Mot. "The philosophy and history behind it are very complicated, but that's the kernel of it. We're a very religious species."

"Understood," said the captain somberly. "I may need your help to convince your people that the Genesis Wave is a swift way to die, with very little suffering. So even if things go wrong—"

"Is that true?" asked the Bolian.

"It's definitely swift," answered Picard with a pained expression. "Your remains become fused with the surrounding earth. There's no way we can measure the suffering, but if you knew it was coming—"

"Count on me, Captain," said Mot, sucking in his stomach and sticking out his chest. "I won't let you down."


"Okay, Geordi, let's do it again with the same modulation," ordered Leah Brahms. "But see if you can get everything lined up this time."

She peered through a shaded, triple-paned window into the dimness of the test chamber, where La Forge was tending the equipment. He wore goggles and a lightweight environmental suit, although force-fields were supposed to offer protection, too. The shielded chamber was about ten meters long, which was big enough for their immediate purposes. Once they reached Myrmidon and got their hands on the large generators, they could test their plan under the real conditions.

This experiment was simple but crucial. They were shooting a narrow beam of protomatter at a beaker full of organic material, which was protected by the tiny interphase generator pulled from Leah's radiation suit. She wanted to see exactly how the Genesis Wave, as represented by the beam, managed to "miss" the material. With each variation of the test, Geordi changed the modulation of the interphase generator, trying to find the perfect setting. The generator had originally been optimized to avoid fatal varieties of common radiation found in an engine room. It had worked against the Genesis Wave, but there was room to tweak it.

It was Geordi's job to set up the various components of the experiment—the beaker, target, generator, and beam emitter. Each time, he dutifully lined them up along a guide beam that represented the stream of protomatter, but he wasn't doing a very good job. Occasionally the protomatter beam missed by enough to throw off the results. The beams were always absorbed harmlessly into a damping field at the other end of the chamber, but it was time-consuming to keep running the experiment over and over again.

"I swear," said Geordi, his voice going over the comlink, "something keeps *bending* those beams each time."

"What?" asked Brahms. "The beam can't be affected until it gets in range of the phase-shifting. Look, I know we're all tired, and it's hard to keep doing this—but we've got to bear down."

"I *am* bearing down," murmured La Forge helplessly. He snapped his fingers, or at least tried to in the bulky suit. "Maybe it's the force-fields. I should turn them off for one test, and see if it's any better."

"Then you'll have to get out of there each time," said Brahms with an impatient sigh. "It will slow us down even more."

"Humor me," insisted Geordi. He rechecked all his calculations and ran his ocular implants along the guide beam. When he was satisfied that everything was in readiness, he shuffled out of the test chamber and quickly sealed the hatch.

"See, it only took me a few seconds to get out," he said, panting. La Forge stepped in front of Brahms, taking over the control panel and making a slight adjustment. "Okay, force-fields off."

"Computer," said Brahms, "log test one-hundred-thirty-seven." She pushed a panel, and there was a bright flash and a clicking sound, which quickly subsided.

She bent over her readouts. "Hey, not bad. Right on target. Maybe we can make an engineer out of you yet, La Forge."

"Thanks," he replied with a weary smile. Geordi was about to say something else, when his combadge chirped, sending the thought scurrying from his mind.

"Bridge to La Forge," came the captain's voice.

The engineer quickly pulled off his helmet. "La Forge here."

"We've just entered orbit around Myrmidon," said the captain. "And the Romulans and Klingons are already here. I'd like to have yourself, Dr. Brahms, and Consul Maltz as part of the greeting committee. To answer questions."

"Yes, Sir," answered La Forge, looking sheepishly at Dolores Linton, who had taken over the situation monitor. The geologist shrugged, as if to say she would keep on working.

"We're not going to have much time to make ourselves presentable," said Geordi.

"This isn't a reception—it's a briefing session. I'll come by to get you. Picard out."

"Now it gets interesting," said a gravelly voice. La Forge turned to see Maltz grinning as he ran a sharpening stone over the long center blade of his three-bladed knife. Then he stuck the *d'k tahg* in its sheath and straightened his gleaming sash. The old Klingon looked better prepared for this meeting than the rest of them, because he'd had the presence of mind to get new clothes from a replicator.

"Let's get it over with," said Leah Brahms, leading the way out the door.

# twenty-two

Captain Picard led his considerable entourage into the Saucer Lounge on the *Enterprise*, the only room big enough to handle the surprising crush of people. The lounge was the observation deck at the widest part of the Saucer Module. It had a broad expanse of windows, showing endless space on the starboard side and a beautiful yellow-green planet on the port view. Myrmidon was a planet with large continents and vast webs of rivers and deltas. One emerald river snaked around most of the planet at its equator—that was the Mother Vein, according to their charts.

This gathering looked suspiciously like a reception, thought the captain, instead of the briefing he had envisioned. There was a large contingent of Klingons—a dozen or so—who were busy raiding the food and drink. At least that many Romulans stood in haughty isolation, reading handheld devices and conversing in low tones among themselves. There were also plenty of Starfleet officers and local Bolian dignitaries, not to mention the servers. To Picard's observant eye, the beefy young servers looked like security personnel, ready for a scuffle to break out. Admiral Nechayev was nowhere to be seen.

Oh, well, he supposed they all had to get acquainted, providing they did it quickly. Right now, the room was big enough that the various groups could ignore each other, except for the blue-skinned Bolians, who were eagerly making friends wherever they could. The captain looked back at his party to make sure they were accounted for. There was Commander Riker, Counselor Troi, Commander La Forge, Dr. Leah Brahms, Consul Maltz, and Mr. Mot, the barber.

The only one who even seemed remotely glad to be here was the old Klingon, who bounded in front of the captain. "I am taking my leave, Sir, to report in. I may be reassigned, but I would like to stay aboard your vessel until that happens." He glanced pointedly at Leah Brahms.

"Certainly, Consul, you're always welcome."

The Klingon strode off, waving his hands as if he were greeting old friends, although his fellow Klingons regarded him warily. Maltz paid them no mind as he began to introduce himself in loud tones.

Riker grinned. "Captain, I think I know one of those Klingons. Can I go over?"

"Go ahead, Number One." He turned to his staff. "All of you, feel free to mingle."

"I'll just see how my people are holding up," said Mr. Mot, puffing out his chest bravely.

"Captain Picard!" called a stern male voice.

The captain whirled around, expecting to see an admiral with some complaint to air. Instead he saw the regal gray uniform of a Romulan commander, topped by a craggy face etched with cruelty but also honor and intelligence. It was Commander Tomalak, an old adversary from numerous encounters, none of which had proven fatal. He was accompanied by a much younger commander—a tall, thin, cadaverous sort.

"What is going on here, Picard?" asked Tomalak. "Can't you people be trusted with your own toys?"

The captain scowled and lowered his voice. "Believe me, I never believed in Project Genesis until now. Our intentions were good, but we failed to foresee the consequences."

The old Romulan nodded sagely. "Now that sounds like the Federation we know and love. Captain Picard, this is a rising star in our fleet, Commander Jagron of the *D'Arvuk*."

Picard shook the hand of the hawk-faced Romulan. "It's a pleasure."

"The honor is all mine," said the young commander with a polite nod, his alert eyes never leaving Picard's face. "Your career is the stuff of legends."

"That's because the Federation writes most of the legends," said Tomalak with a sneer. "Although in this case, the legend is more notorious than proud. I don't think our alliance is going to last very long if this disaster destroys several of our worlds."

"It's not going to get that far," vowed Picard, although he didn't know how were going to stop it before then. "When do you turn over your interphase generators to us?"

"Your efficient Admiral Nechayev has us dismantling them right now," answered Commander Jagron. "How can you possibly replicate enough?"

"Apparently, there are a lot of facilities on the planet," answered Picard, hoping that was true.

The noise level of the conversation trailed off, and Picard saw several Starfleet officers hurry toward the door. He turned to see Admiral Nechayev stride into the sumptuous lounge, accompanied by her padd-carrying staff. She looked charged with energy, which was a welcome change from the last time he had seen her, and he wondered if she had gotten good news from the task force.

The small woman stopped in the center of the lounge and said loudly, "Honored guests, generals, captains, commanders, thank you for attending this gathering. In the days to come, there won't be much time to get to know each other or share a convivial drink, so make the most of it. In twenty-four hours, the beautiful planet floating beneath us will be transformed forever. But it will still be here, and so will *we*. This time, we will not retreat!"

This sentiment met with shouts of approval, especially from the Klingon contingent. Picard glanced at Leah Brahms, who shook her head and looked very troubled. She said something to La Forge, and the two of them moved away from the crowd to continue their conversation in whispers.

Nechayev continued, "Our Romulan allies are contributing the most important part of our new defense, and we can't even begin to express our gratitude to them. Our Klingon allies have proven themselves to be the champions of the rapid evacuation. They have already saved three times as many lives as Starfleet itself has been able to save. In this operation, they will provide logistical support. We also have representatives from Myrmidon herself, and we welcome the chance to hear their concerns."

The admiral motioned to the Romulans. "Some of you are still reading data sheets about the Genesis Wave. If any of you have any questions, please don't hesitate to ask myself, my staff, or our experts: Dr. Leah Brahms and Commander Geordi La Forge."

That rudely interrupted the private conversation of La Forge and Brahms, and they nodded hesitantly at the crowd of hard-bitten Klingons and Romulans.

"I have a question!" growled a stocky Klingon, striding forward. "Why do you not eliminate the beasts who are doing this to you?"

"We're trying," answered Admiral Nechayev. "We've dispatched a task force of five *Defiant*-class starships to locate the source, but so far they've been unsuccessful. I assure you, General Gra'Kor, we have talked about opening another front against our unknown enemy. If we continue to be unsuccessful, I will be happy to give you that assignment."

The Klingon grunted with satisfaction and looked at his aides, who also seemed satisfied with this response.

Captain Picard felt a light tug on his sleeve. He turned to see Counselor Troi, who leaned close to whisper, "I don't believe she's being entirely honest."

"Really?" whispered Picard. He listened more closely to what the admiral had to say, but she went on to simply recap much of what he already knew.

Finally Nechayev grabbed a filled glass from an aide, held it aloft, and concluded. "Although the impact of the Genesis Wave has been tragic, it has brought the great powers of the Alpha Quadrant together in acts of bravery and altruism. We will never forget your courage under these trying circumstances. We salute you, our allies."

"Hear! Hear! Bravo!" and similar calls echoed throughout the lounge. No one was more appreciative than the Bolians in attendance.

While conversational groups formed all over the room, Nechayev turned to address her aides. Her instructions sent most of them scurrying off, then she motioned to Picard. "Captain, could I see you for a moment?"

"Certainly," he said, taking his leave from Commanders Tomalak and Jagron. Deanna Troi stepped in to keep the Romulans occupied.

Admiral Nechayev led him along the observation window until they were far away from anyone else's hearing. Picard realized he was about to be told a confidence, and he could guess what it was.

"Something wrong with the task force?" he asked softly.

"How did you know that?" Nechayev stopped to stare at him with frank amazement.

"I have a Betazoid on staff. What happened to them? "

"We've lost contact," said the admiral glumly. "They stopped checking in about eight hours ago, and they haven't answered our hails either."

"Where were they? Is there any sign of them on sensors?"

She kept her voice low. "Not now. They were investigating a large asteroid field called the Boneyard, where we *think* the wave might originate. We haven't seen any sign of them since, but with all the space traffic . . . our tracking systems are overloaded. Everybody with a spacecraft is flying it, making an escape or picking up passengers."

The diminutive admiral sighed. "I suppose it's good that the private sector is starting to kick in. I hear Earth is beseiged with Ferengi vessels, offering expensive passage out. Of course, the Ferengi would pick the richest, most populace planet, and give themselves plenty of time."

The captain nodded gravely, still troubled by the news that the task force not had only failed, they had disappeared. "What are we going to do about the missing ships?"

"All of our forces are committed here," said Nechayev, motioning toward the yellow-green planet shimmering below them. "Or they're involved in other evacuations. We're facing a ruthless enemy, and they're not going to make it easy for us. If we don't hear soon, I'm going to give the Klingons this information. Maybe they can spare a ship or two. There's really no time for us to question our strategy now—we'll have to leave that to the survivors."

Her stern expression softened into thoughtfulness as she gazed out the window at the endangered planet. In a confidential tone, she added, "I have something else to tell you."

"Yes, Sir?"

"I'm going to stay on Myrmidon with the populace during the . . . transformation. A show of confidence."

"Sir?" said Picard, trying not to sound alarmed. "Is that really necessary?"

"I think it is," answered Nechayev. "We have to be able to show our confidence in order to win their confidence. We have plenty of technicians who must stay behind, too, and I want to show camaraderie with them. Besides . . . I have to do it for myself. If I can live through this, I'll be able to convince others that they can live through it. That there's hope."

"How will you get off the planet . . . afterwards?" asked the captain.

"Our scientists think the Romulans can cut through the wave in a cloaked ship and beam us off Myrmidon. If they can't or won't, I'll have to wait several days until the effect diminishes. It's not a perfect plan."

"But it is a noble gesture. Perhaps I should . . ." he began.

"Don't even think about it, Picard," she answered curtly. "Although I'm going to make a call for Starfleet volunteers to stand with me, I really don't want a horde of people. Besides, you have to make sure the *Enterprise* survives. If I don't get out, my aides will put through a field promotion for you—to admiral—so that you can take over this operation. That won't be doing you much of a favor, of course. For that, I'm sorry. But you're here, you're able, and you know as much about it as anybody."

"Admiral, eh?" said the captain distastefully. "I can assure you, we will do everything in our power to make sure you survive and get back to your desk as soon as possible."

"I'm certain," said the admiral with a fleeting smile. "Just don't volunteer when I make my call. That's all, Captain."

"Thank you, Admiral." The captain stepped away from the observation lounge window to allow others access to Admiral Nechayev. Despite the massing of ships and the arrival of allies, he was worried. The disappearance of the task force showed that their mysterious enemy was more formidable than they imagined.

Admiral Nechayev appeared energized by her plan to risk her life in solidarity with the people, and she was sure of her reasons. But Picard could see the disaster in the making. If admirals and dignitaries died horrible deaths—not to mention fifty million Bolians—then confidence in Starfleet would disappear. The rest of the evacuations would be more insane than they were now. Picard would be left to oversee a chaotic stampede stretching halfway across the quadrant, plus the destruction of more planets and billions of people, including Earth. And the ultimate enemy would remain anonymous and untouched.

*We have to succeed on Myrmidon*, he told himself in no uncertain terms.


Will Riker did indeed know one of the Klingons at the reception, from having served with him aboard the *Pagh*. Dermok was now first officer on the *Jaj*, and the two of them relived old times. The other Klingons bombarded Maltz with questions, but the old warrior held his own, sounding alert and arrogant. When Maltz began to sweep his hands through the air and gruffly relate his tale, Riker and his friend had to stop to listen. No one could ignore a Klingon in full storytelling mode.

First came his heroic escape from Hakon, complete with jailbreak, Romulan spy, and the Genesis Wave bearing down on them. In a hoarse whisper, Maltz told about their final contact with the Pelleans—a mighty, spacefaring race who were now gone forever. He praised the young human who had saved him to spread the alarm, Dr. Leah Brahms.

"Saved by a human!" said General Gra'Kor with a sneer. "You still have much to answer for, Maltz."

Steel and a hint of madness glinted in the old Klingon's eyes. "What do you mean by that?"

The stocky general growled. "I mean, you and that idiot, Kruge, let the Genesis Device escape our grasp when you had the chance to seize it! And protect it. You let a bird-of-prey be captured and piloted by a ragtag band of humans. You haven't tried hard enough to get to *Sto-Vo-Kor.*"

There were audible gasps, and the other Klingons moved away from Gra'Kor and Maltz, who proceeded to size each other up. For the first time, Riker realized that it was no accident that Maltz had been living on Hakon—he was an outcast.

The old Klingon finally laughed—a howling, roaring shriek that sliced through the genteel conversation and brought every eye to him. He finally sneered in the general's face and said, "Is that the best you can do? That insult is ninety years old, and I hear it every day of my life."

Maltz pounded his chest. "I *know* I am going to *Sto-Vo-Kor,* because I have sworn a blood oath against this cowardly weapon and the demons who unleashed it."

"*Qapla'!* y*Intagh!*" cheered the younger Klingons, catching Maltz's infectious spirit.

Maltz drew his *d'k tahg* and pointed it menacingly at the general's ample stomach. "So if you stand in my way, you will either get killed, or you will usher me to *Sto-Vo-Kor.* I do not care. I have been alive long enough. This beast has come after me *twice*—wrecking my career each time—and this time I intend to finish it!"

Now every one of the Klingons was cheering Maltz and slapping him on the back. General Gra'Kor grinned and pounded the old warrior's shoulders with his beefy fists. "I misjudged you, Maltz. I will sing your praises at the High Council! Nothing will stand in the way of your blood oath. What will you require?"

"A ship," said Maltz boldly.

Gra'Kor nodded. "Will you be captain?"

"No, I have a captain—a partner to my blood oath. I am content to be first mate."

"Getting a ship may take some doing," said the stocky Klingon, tugging on his beard. "Ships are scarce at the moment. But I will do what I can. In the meantime—"

"I would like to stay on the *Enterprise.*" Stealing a glance at Riker, the old Klingon leaned forward and said, "They need a Klingon to keep reminding them of what is important. They think it  is saving lives, and I know it is taking lives."

"Well said!" barked Gra'Kor, lifting a mug of ale. "We drink to your success! *Qapla'!*"

Maltz nodded and sheathed his knife, tears filling his rheumy eyes.

Riker had the feeling it had been a long time since a gathering of his fellows had praised the old Klingon.

"Leah, please!" insisted Geordi in a tight whisper. "You can't leave now." He pulled her away from the dignitaries in the Saucer Lounge and hustled her along the starboard window, hardly noticing the beautiful starscape.

"I'm going to leave as soon as this operation is over," she said fiercely. "That's only twenty-four hours from now."

"But why?" asked La Forge, certain he was sounding shrill and possessive. But he couldn't let her walk out of his life without a fight, even if he couldn't tell her why.

Leah sighed with exasperation. "Because my life's been destroyed, because I don't know what I'm doing, because I'm not a member of your crew. All those things, Geordi. I know you're being sweet—wanting to give me a new place to call home—but I'm not ready for that. I just need to wander for a while. I think I should tell the captain."

"But we need you," insisted Geordi, hiding much more than those four words conveyed.

"Why?" Brahms shook her head and gazed wearily at him. "If this idea works, anyone can set it up. If it doesn't work . . . Well, I'm not sure I can save the Federation single-handedly. I don't want that responsibility." She started walking off.

"But if there's a new idea . . . one that works better?" begged Geordi, grasping for words that would keep her beside him.

"I'll see you in an hour on the surface," said Leah Brahms. She turned and strode quickly from the Saucer Lounge. Several pairs of eyes watched her go, including Captain Picard, who pointed to her and said something to his Romulan companions.

La Forge turned back to the observation window, gazing at the endless vista of space. To his bionic vision, darkness was mostly coolness, and this space looked as chill as the emptiness in his heart.

# twenty-three

For an hour, Deanna Troi wandered the streets of Neprin, the most populous city on Myrmidon. It was a glorious city—with towering triangular and conical shaped buildings, many of them constructed with the widest part of the triangle at the top. The smaller buildings were almost all domes, either geodesic or smooth, with breathtaking inlaid mosaic that sparkled in the sun. There was not a single conventional box-shaped building in sight. Not surprisingly, blue was a favorite color, and the Bolians seemed to have discovered more shades of blue than anyone else in the galaxy. The architecture reminded her of the stylishness that the Bolians exhibited in everything they did.

Interspersed tastefully among the buildings were small, parklike areas. At first, Deanna thought these parks were decorated with strange, bulbous statues. But upon closer inspection she realized the "statues" were in reality gigantic vegetables up to four meters tall and shaped like artichokes. Citizens often stopped during their travels to cut off a bit of the giant plant to eat as they walked, although Deanna did not partake.

She was supposed to be interviewing the residents, gauging how much work Starfleet would have to do to convince them to stroll into a building or an empty field and calmly watch the Genesis Wave roll over them. But she couldn't bring herself to talk to the Bolians, who gazed upon her Starfleet uniform as they might gaze upon a figure in a dark hood, carrying a sickle. Her presence represented the destruction of everything they knew, plus the loss of their greatest religious shrines. Many of them were still in denial, going about their regular business. Others flashed her furtive glances as they scurried away, probably to catch a shuttlecraft or transport off the planet.

Ferengi and Bolian hawkers stood on the street corners, offering

passage off Myrmidon for exorbitant prices. A thousand strips of latinum seemed to be the going rate. Although Deanna hadn't dealt much
with money, she knew that was a lot.

"Starfleet's plan is a hoax!" one of the hawkers shouted loudly.
"There's no way to survive this thing. Look at what happened on
Persephone V! Their plan is unproven and risky!"

Troi thought about stopping to refute his claim, but their plan *was*
unproven and risky. So she walked on, feeling terrible about her cow-
ardice. She couldn't bear to speak to the Bolians, because when she
looked at them, all she saw was death. It was the same horrible death
which had claimed millions on Persephone V. She could envision their
bodies being ripped apart, screams still frozen on their lips, as their
flailing limbs sank into the churning morass this planet would soon
become.

With a start, Deanna realized that *she* should really be under a
counselor's care herself, after what she had witnessed. But there
weren't enough counselors to go around.

Feeling despondent, she continued to walk down the sidewalk,
gazing at the magnificent buildings, none of which would be here this
time tomorrow. She shuffled past one of the geodesic domes, which
was covered in a mosaic of inlaid gold, and a kindly voice said, "My
child, rest a moment. You look weary."

Troi stopped and turned to look at an older Bolian woman standing in the doorway of the domed building. She was dressed in flowing
blue robes, like some kind of cleric, and the counselor realized that she
had stumbled upon a place of worship. A sign over the door said it was
the "Sanctuary of the First Mother."

The woman looked so kind and helpful that Deanna felt her reticence to speak slipping away. "Hello," she said, "I'm with the fleet
that's orbiting the planet."

"I assumed as much," said the old Bolian with a smile. "You look
particularly upset, when *we're* the ones who should be upset."

"But you're smiling," said Deanna in amazement.

"Yes, because I can gaze at the Crown of the First Mother whenever I want. I know this awful scourge will not destroy us."

"But—" said Deanna helplessly.

"Come inside, Child, and cast off your bonds of worry." The old
woman took her hand and gently pulled her inside the beautiful dome.
"What is your name?"

"Deanna Troi. I'm a counselor. . . . I help people."

"That's wonderful," replied the old woman. "Then we're in the
same business."

"And your name?"

"Just call me 'Mother,'" she answered with a smile. They walked slowly through a vestibule which was lined with beautiful murals depicting an archeological dig and the discovery of Myrmidon's most famous relic. Deanna saw the story unfold as they strolled through the vestibule—first the discovery, then the mass pilgrimage, ending with the construction of this great city and others. The last murals showed happy Bolians dancing and feasting under flowered garlands, with a blazing golden crown.

Instead of being consoled by these vivid images, Troi was only more distressed. Centuries of joyous work and progress were about to vanish in a matter of seconds, and there wasn't anything any of them could do about it.

Pushing open a pair of gold-inlaid doors, Mother led the way into a vast sanctuary, which was filled with Bolians on their knees, muttering prayers aloud. All of them faced a small cabinet, which was lit by its own internal fires. Overhead, the inside of the dome seemed to sparkle with an unearthly light, and Deanna realized it was sunlight filtered through a clear ceiling. It seemed as if the entire room was suffused with a holy glow.

"Is that really the Crown of the First Mother?" asked Troi in a hushed voice.

The woman smiled wistfully. "I'd like to think it is, but I don't know for sure. There are sanctuaries like this all over the planet, and one of them contains the genuine relic. The rest contain copies identical of the original. We did this to thwart thieves, but it has been a blessing in disguise, allowing every citizen to feel as if he has personal contact with the greatest of our treasures. Shall we move closer?"

Troi nodded, and Mother led her down an aisle of worshipers to stand at the side of the case, so they wouldn't block anyone's view. Deanna peered inside at an unexpectedly simple piece of golden jewelry, which had the same triangular motif she had seen in the Bolians' architecture; each of the crowning points was an upside-down triangle. Whoever had made the copy—if this was a copy—had done an excellent job, because the relic looked as old as the universe but undiminished in beauty.

"Now do you feel peace?" asked Mother.

Troi shook her head. "I wish I could say I did. But, Mother, I've seen the Genesis Wave. I know what it can do."

"Faith can conquer mountains," said the woman. "I heard a human say that once."

*The Genesis Wave can also conquer mountains*, Deanna thought glumly. She looked around, realizing that the domed building was about the size of a standard starship; then she suddenly had an idea. "Tell me, is the sanctuary always as crowded as this?"

"Yes, and I expect it to get more crowded as the day goes on," answered the holy woman. "No offense, Deanna Troi, but our people place more faith in the power of the Crown than in all the might of Starfleet."

"Maybe they have the right idea," said Troi, hope stirring in her heart for the first time. "Do you have the locations of all the sanctuaries like this on the planet?"

"Yes, in my office, on the computer."

"I need that information right now," said Troi.

Will Riker gazed with satisfaction at the platform in transporter room two. Every spot on the pad was occupied, not by a person but by a complex machine about two meters tall, with emitters, injectors, nozzles, and power taps all over it. In addition to those eight interphase generators, another dozen waited in the cargo area, and the transporter chief and cargo handlers were beaming them down to the surface as quickly as the replicators could produce them.

"Everything going as planned, Chief?" he asked.

"Yes, Sir," answered the dour Andorian. "This is the last batch consigned to the planetary factories—all the rest are headed to the sanctuaries."

"Great. Let me know when you're done with the generators, and we'll start sending down crates of gel-packs. Keep up the good work."

Riker strode from the transporter room, headed to the forward torpedo module, which was being replaced with spare parts contributed by other ships in orbit. He didn't think they would need quantum torpedoes, because they hadn't done any good so far against the Genesis Wave, but he was determined to replace the module while they had the chance. Something told him this would not be the end of their battle with their unknown foe, and he wanted to be ready.

"The power source is going to be our biggest problem," said Geordi La Forge, gazing at a field of gigantic vegetables that would serve as their testing ground. "I don't know if the gel-packs can handle the surge."

"Of course not," sneered a senior Romulan engineer whose name was Duperik. "I could have told you that."

"Then why didn't you?" asked Leah Brahms impatiently.

"This was *your* idea," said the Romulan. "Nobody consulted us until just now. These generators draw a lot of power, which is their biggest flaw. If we could erect your shelters near power stations—"

"We could," answered Brahms, "but then we would have to protect the power stations as well, and we can't protect all the underground cables and transformers. One breakdown along any of the lines would kill us." She groaned with exasperation. "How many more hours?"

"Twenty," answered Geordi, checking his chronometer. "We only have to maintain power for the first onslaught of the wave, about ten minutes. Let's run the test, and see how long the gel-packs can power it."

He waved to the dozen or so technicians who were assisting them, one of whom was Dolores Linton. "Start the monitoring equipment. Check the power couplers. Get the emitter and the dampening field ready."

For several minutes, there was frantic activity in the field, as the technicians double-checked the various pieces of equipment. Their test was a larger version of the test they had run aboard the *Enterprise* in the chamber. Two interphase generators and their power packs had been set up in the center of the field, which was a bit less than one hectare in size. They assumed they could cram almost sixty thousand people in an area this size—and many more if they used buildings of multiple stories. Two generators were being used, with the second one intended as a backup in case the first one failed.

They would measure how far the protective phase-shifting field extended and how effective it would be in guarding the giant vegetables from the protomatter beam. Geordi knew it was awfully late in the process to see whether this plan would work, but this was the first chance they'd had to try it. If the test failed . . . He didn't want to think about that, because they didn't have a backup.

While the Romulan was checking one generator, La Forge was checking the other, when he felt a comforting hand on his shoulder. He looked up, hoping it was Leah, but instead it was Dolores Linton, smiling at him. He felt a pang of guilt, because he'd been awfully cavalier about her feelings for him. But he resented the fact that Leah thought the two of them were involved. Nevertheless, he reached up and squeezed her hand warmly.

"You know, you don't have to be here," he said.

"What?" said Dolores cheerfully. "Do you think I'd miss a chance to get off that ship onto solid ground?"

Geordi smiled. "Maybe if I ever gave you that tour of the ship, you'd appreciate it more."

"Maybe." Dolores glanced over at Leah Brahms, who was some distance away, tinkering with the protomatter emitter. "Leah told me that she's leaving . . . and that I should take care of you."

La Forge grumbled and turned back to his work. "Is that so?"

"It's too soon for her, Geordi. Too much has happened. Besides, she doesn't realize how you feel about her."

"I know," he said, grabbing a spanner from his tool belt and making a slight adjustment. "I've been a perfect gentleman."

"Yes, and some of us are getting a little annoyed about that."

He turned to look at her, and Dolores was gazing hard at him, having made a joke that wasn't a joke.

"Okay," he said boldly, "when this is all over, a tour of this ship it is. Starting with my quarters."

"That's more like it!" replied the geologist enthusiastically. "Now save the day, will you?" Dolores squeezed his shoulder one more time and walked away.

La Forge watched the muscular young woman's easy stride, wondering what on Earth was wrong with him. It was a good thing Data wasn't here to see how inept he was—he'd never hear the end of it. Yes, he was still carrying a torch for a traumatized widow who seemed to prefer the company of a grizzled old Klingon. But then, it was a torch he was used to carrying.

A few meters away from him, the Romulan finished his adjustments to the second interphase generator, and he stood and walked over to La Forge. "I'm still not sure it will work, but you might as well try it."

"Thanks for your vote of confidence." Geordi was finished, too, having set the device to the optimal settings they had discovered in the lab. On the edge of the field, a transporter beam deposited half-a-dozen swirling columns of light, who formed into half-a-dozen Starfleet officers, one of whom was Admiral Nechayev.

"The brass is here," said La Forge, motioning to Duperik to follow him. He and the Romulan walked up to the admiral and her aides, several of whom looked frightened to death.

"Is everything in readiness, Commander?" asked the admiral solemnly.

"Yes, we were just about to do our first test."

The admiral frowned and looked at her chronometer. "You're a bit behind schedule."

La Forge didn't argue with her, or mention that the schedule was absurd—along with this whole idea. Instead he clapped his hands loudly and yelled, "Come on, let's do it! Everyone to their places!"

A ring of technicians formed around the estimated area of protection, and all of them were manning tricorders, monitors, or remote controllers. "Ready?" called Geordi.

All around the field, assistants acknowledged that they were ready, and La Forge nodded to the Romulan. "Activate generator number one."

Duperik pressed his control device and reported, "Phase-shifting activated. Power levels holding steady."

Nothing in the field looked any different to normal sight, but Geordi could see the oscillating ripple of wave after wave of energy pulsing outward. Some of the huge vegetables seemed to quiver, like asphalt in the summer sun.

He pointed to Leah on the emitter gun. "Give it the protomatter. Begin countdown. All monitors on!"

Brahms shot a narrow beam into the rows of giant vegetables, and it seemed to pass right through half-a-dozen of them before terminating in a dampening field on the other side. Geordi kept his eyes on his chronometer, because there wasn't any doubt that the phase-shifting would cover the distance for a short period of time. The question was whether the gel-packs could power the generator long enough to brave the worst of the Genesis Wave's effects.

La Forge saw a couple of the technicians in the circle move forward, as if the field were shrinking. He sidled over to the Romulan and asked in a whisper, "Is power holding steady?"

"No," answered Duperik. "The power has dropped by twenty-two percent, but the generator is still working. We make good equipment, don't we?"

"There are still five minutes left to go," said Geordi worriedly. The last thing he wanted was for this test to be a failure—in front of the admiral. "Activate the backup generator."

"Are you sure?"

"Yes."

The Romulan engineer did as he was ordered, and the test continued. "Are you planning to use two generators at each site?"

"I don't know yet," answered Geordi, his eyes on his timepiece. "Maybe backup gel-packs would be better. We'll have an engineer at each site."

"Not a Romulan engineer, you won't," said Duperik pointedly. "We're not staying around for this fiasco."

"Just keep that to yourself," whispered Geordi.

The minutes seemed to drag by, but the giant, artichokelike vegetables were suffering no ill effect from the protomatter beam. Geordi barely breathed until he was finally able to shout, "Time! Stop protomatter!"

Leah Brahms turned the emitter off and stood at attention, gazing at the azure sky as if her mind were light-years away. Everyone else shouted with joy, congratulating each other with hugs and slaps on the back.

Admiral Nechayev actually cracked a smile as she walked over to La Forge. "Well done, Commander! This means we can approach the Bolians with confidence and go to the next stage. Our latest plan is to use their religious sanctuaries as shelters, because they seem to be flocking there anyway. Send your settings and results to the *Sovereign*, so that we can distribute them to all the teams."

"Yes, Sir," answered Geordi, wishing he felt more confident than he did. He stole a glance at Leah Brahms, who was slowly walking toward them. Her face was a stoic mask, but he could see the fear in her dark eyes.

Nechayev was still holding court. "This also allows me to put out a call for volunteers among Starfleet officers—to stand with us here on Myrmidon."

"With *us*?" asked La Forge hesitantly.

"Yes," answered the admiral. "My aides and I are staying here with the populace. This will reassure them of our faith in the plan."

Now Geordi knew why her aides had looked so frightened when they first arrived. They were going to voluntarily remain on the planet and endure the Genesis Wave.

"Admiral," said Leah Brahms, "I would like to leave immediately. My work is done—I can't do anything else here."

"Certainly, Doctor. You can return with us to the *Sovereign* right now."

Geordi's heart sank to the bottom of his heels upon hearing Leah say she was leaving. Now it was definite. Without thinking, except that he wanted to make her feel as badly as he felt, he blurted out, "Admiral, I'd like to volunteer to stay with you on Myrmidon."

"Geordi!" said Leah, aghast. "Are you crazy?"

"Doctor, that will be enough," snapped Nechayev. She turned to La Forge with gratitude and respect on her usually stern face. "That will mean a lot to everybody if you stay, Commander."

"Then *I'll* stay, too," said Dolores Linton resolutely.

Now it was Geordi's turn to look aghast, but he couldn't very well berate her for doing what he was doing.

"Tell us your name." Nechayev nodded to one of her aides, who had already entered La Forge's name on his padd.

"Dolores Linton, mission specialist, geology."

"Ah, yes. You should be on Itamish III. Hopefully, we can get you back there without delay when this is all over. Your bravery will not go unnoticed."

Nechayev motioned to her entourage. "We'd better get back to the ship, because we have a lot to do. Dr. Brahms, you're with us." She tapped her combadge. "Nechayev to *Enterprise*. Seven to beam up."

Leah gave Geordi a final look, and it was hard to tell whether she was angry or mournful over his rash decision. She just shook her head and gazed solemnly down at the ground. In a swirl of glittering molecules, the admiral, her entourage, and the love of his life were gone.

*Will I ever see her again?* wondered Geordi. If he were a betting man, he wouldn't have bet on it.

The engineer sighed and looked at Dolores, standing resolutely beside him. "You didn't have to do that," he whispered.

"Neither did you." She mustered a brave smile. "I told you, I'd rather be on solid ground, even if it's not so solid. Besides, the test went great! What could go wrong?"

"I'm going to make sure nothing goes wrong," vowed La Forge. He tried not to look at the Romulan engineer, who was shaking his head as if the people in Starfleet were absolutely insane.

# twenty-four

On the bridge of the *Enterprise*, the mood was somber as they listened to a fleet-wide message from Admiral Nechayev, calling for volunteers to stay on Myrmidon and tough it out. The admiral could be persuasive, thought Will Riker, but not persuasive enough to convince him. It helped that she had specifically asked for no more than one or two volunteers per ship.

When the message was over, he looked at Captain Picard and asked, "What do we do if we get volunteers?"

"We let them go," answered Picard from his command chair. "One or two at the most. But I'm under orders *not* to volunteer, and I hope none of my senior staff do either."

"You knew about this?"

"I'm afraid so," said the captain grimly.

"At least it sounds like she wants to keep it to a small number," said the first officer. "Do you think some of our Bolians will want to stay?"

"I don't know," answered the captain. "Although we haven't been ordered to take any evacuees, I intend to make an exception for Mot's parents and other family members of our crew."

"That is odd," said Data, seated in his usual post at the ops console. "A Starfleet vessel has just come out of warp twenty thousand kilometers from here—"

"Why is that odd?" asked Riker, glancing at a viewscreen that was full of Starfleet, Klingon, and Romulan vessels. They were lined up in orbit like hover-taxis waiting at a spaceport.

"It is the *Neptune*, *Defiant*-class. She is part of Task Force Javelin, which has been reported missing."

Now Captain Picard whirled around in his seat and stared at the android. "Are you sure about that?"

"Yes, Sir. Warp signature matches. Here is the ship on visual." The viewscreen overheard switched from a view of ships in orbit to a single, squat starship floating in space. Its running lights blinked oddly, as if shorted out, and there were scorch marks along its hull.

"Hail them." Picard jumped to his feet and peered at the image on the screen. "Tactical, get me Admiral Nechayev."

"She's already on the comlink, Sir."

Picard nodded and pointed to the screen, where Nechayev's dour face appeared. "Hello, Admiral," he said. "Did you see who just arrived?"

"The *Neptune*," she answered. "You had better take a closer look, Captain."

Picard turned curiously to Data, who shook his head. "They do not answer our hails. Sensors show no lifesigns onboard. Their shields are up, which may be affecting our sensor readings."

"A ghost ship?" asked Riker in amazement. "How did they know to come out of warp right here? Who set the course?"

A troubled scowl on his face, the captain turned back to the admiral. "Did you get that, Sir?"

"Our sensors show the same thing," answered Nechayev. "We can get the override codes and turn off the shields from here, but I'd like the *Enterprise* to investigate. If the *Neptune* is spaceworthy—and she just came out of warp—we have to fly her out of here. You know what will happen if we leave her behind. If she can be saved, assign a skeleton crew and tell them to await orders."

"Yes, Sir," answered Picard. "What about possible survivors? The other missing ships from the task force?"

"All hell is going to break loose here in seventeen hours," answered Nechayev grimly. "We can't worry about anything else but Myrmidon. I'll inform our allies, although they have their hands full. That reminds me, Captain—I'm going down to the planet now . . . for the duration. It's time to muster support among the populace. Contact the *Sovereign* if you need me, and they can patch you through."

"Yes, Sir."

Nechayev glanced at the readouts on her terminal. "We've already got two volunteers from the *Enterprise*, so you're off the hook. That would be Commander La Forge and Dolores Linton, who are already on site."

"Geordi La Forge?" asked Riker with surprise. "He volunteered?"

The admiral nodded. "I'm sorry if the request wasn't put through officially, but Commander La Forge volunteered personally to my face. I couldn't say no. It was very brave of him, and it's gone a long way to calming fears down there. Give me a report on the *Neptune* as soon as you can. Nechayev out."

The captain took a deep breath and let out a sigh, while Riker stomped across the bridge. "What was La Forge thinking? Did anybody—" He stopped and rubbed his forehead, realizing there was nothing anybody could do.

"Number One, you and Data are on the away team," said Picard, getting back to business. "You'd better take Dr. Crusher, too. Tell her, it's likely the crew is dead, but she should be prepared for casualties."

Riker nodded. "I'll put Krygore in charge of engineering."

"Good choice," said the captain.

Data bounded out of his seat and started for the turbolift, with Riker following. At the turbolift door, the first officer stopped and turned around. "Captain, if the *Neptune* is shipshape, Dr. Crusher would be a good choice to command her. I'll put together a decent crew for her."

The captain scratched his chin thoughtfully. Riker figured he might appreciate an excuse to get the doctor out of harm's way. Deanna would also be a good choice, but she was already occupied on the planet's surface.

"I'll consider it," answered the captain. "Let's find out what happened to the ship first. Conn, set a course for the *Neptune*, half-impulse, and take us within five kilometers."

"Yes, Sir."

Riker's eyes drifted to the viewscreen, where a scorched starship floated in the blackness of space, its shields and running lights flickering eerily.

Pulling the strap of her medkit over her shoulder, Dr. Beverly Crusher charged down the corridor on her way to transporter room two. She was relieved that she could still move freely in the corridors, since the *Enterprise* had been spared from picking up evacuees on Myrmidon. Although most of the populace was supposed to stay on and brave the Genesis Wave, many thousands were being evacuated on the support ships. But the *Enterprise* had been held in reserve for other jobs, such as this investigation of a deserted ship. After abandoning whole worlds right and left, it almost seemed quaint to be worried about one little ship.

When she reached the transporter room, she found Riker and Data already waiting for her. "Hello, Doctor," said the first officer, checking his tricorder. "Ready for a little jaunt off the ship?"

"Just when I finally get sickbay empty," said Crusher in mock anger, "and you give me something else to do. Did we run out of security officers?"

"Yes, as a matter of fact," said Riker. "They're all down on the surface."

"What's the story with this ship?" asked Crusher.

"The *Neptune* has been missing for almost thirty hours," replied Data. "It was part of Task Force Javelin, and its last known whereabouts were near Seran, the first planet stricken by the wave."

"So what is it doing here?"

"Exactly," answered Riker. "We're not picking up any lifesigns, but you never know. It's a small ship, so it shouldn't take much time to explore."

"Which is good," added Beverly, "since we don't have much time."

Riker led the way onto the transporter platform. "If it's spaceworthy, we have to fly it out. You may end up in the captain's chair before the end of the day."

Crusher said nothing, but the prospect of having her own ship in the middle of this crisis wasn't all that unappealing. She was feeling a little frustrated in sickbay, where the action had fallen off considerably since they had unloaded all of their evacuees. So far, her review of the biological data collected on Persephone V hadn't borne any fruit, and it felt as if she would need weeks to understand what was happening to these planets.

Riker motioned to the tall Andorian on the transporter console. "Have you got the coordinates, Chief?"

"Yes, Sir," answered Rhofistan. "I'm putting you on their bridge."

"That's fine. Are their shields down yet?"

"Just went down."

Crusher looked puzzledly at the first officer. "There's nobody on this ship, but it has shields up?"

"Just one of many mysteries," answered the commander. He motioned to the transporter chief. "Energize."

A few seconds later, their swirling molecules coalesced on the bridge of the *Neptune*, which was deserted as expected. Beverly looked around, thinking that it reminded her of a smaller version of the bridge on the old *Enterprise*-D. Although no one was here, most of the consoles blinked and beeped as if they were functioning, and the viewscreen showed a disconcerting view of the *Enterprise*-E, sitting just off port.

While Data consulted his tricorder, Riker strode to the ops console and checked the readouts. "I want to see if there's any record of someone setting a warp course and then beaming off just before it engaged."

"Is there?" asked Beverly.

Riker pressed the membrane keypad several times and shook his head. "No. All the logs for the last two days have been wiped."

Data peered intently at his tricorder. "There are still no signs of life, but there is inert organic matter scattered throughout the ship."

"Organic matter?" asked Riker.

"Vegetable matter," answered the android. "Perhaps foodstuffs. There are only three main decks—this one, an upper deck for crew quarters, and the engine room below. I suggest we split up."

"All right," agreed Riker, "but let's use the Jefferies tubes, in case there are malfunctions we don't know about. Data, you take the engine room. While you're down there, take a look at the warp and impulse engines and see if they're in good shape."

"Yes, Sir." Data immediately strode toward an access panel at the rear of the bridge and opened it with an effortless tug. As if he were leaping down a manhole, the android took a single step and was gone.

"Doctor, why don't you take the crew quarters?" said Riker. "You can check on sickbay, too, and see if it's functional."

"They have a sickbay on this little ship?" asked Crusher, impressed.

"I'm going to check out the shuttlebay," said Riker, heading after Data. "I want to see if they've still got their shuttlepods. Let me know if you see anything unusual."

"Yes, Sir." A moment later, Beverly Crusher was alone on the deserted bridge of the *Neptune*, and her footsteps clacked as loudly as gunshots as she walked across the deck. It wouldn't be a bad ship to command, she decided, although she would like to know what happened to the previous captain and crew.

Slinging her tricorder and medkit over her shoulder, the doctor descended into the Jefferies tube. After finding a junction that curved upward, she climbed for several meters until she reached an access panel, which she pushed open. A moment later, Crusher was standing in a nondescript corridor with doors lining only one side. Something smelled funny—like spoiled food.

Consulting her tricorder, Crusher homed in on the strange smell and found a mound of leaves rotting in an open doorway. At least it looked like leaves, or maybe the remains of an old Christmas tree. Tricorder readings couldn't identify the pile any better than her eyes could, and Beverly stepped over it to enter the crew quarters.

There was nothing unusual in the simple stateroom, which was obviously meant to be shared by two crew members. She walked over to a desk and looked at the collection of framed pictures, depicting two human children and two elder adults. The adults in the pictures were no doubt the children's grandparents, but where were the parents? The eerie quiet of the ghost ship was beginning to get on her nerves, and Crusher found herself talking aloud, just to hear a voice.

"Where did everyone go?" she asked the pictures on the desk, but their smiling faces divulged no secrets. Beverly opened a desk drawer and found a clean, pressed uniform inside.

"This is all wrong," she muttered.

She was startled by a rustling sound—like leaves stirred by a breeze—and she whirled around to see a shadow pass the open doorway. Gripping her tricorder, Beverly dashed out of the room into the corridor, expecting to see the owner of the shadow.

But there was no one there.

"Now this is getting to me," said Beverly, shaking her long, auburn tresses. "I'm imagining things."

Deciding to concentrate on the job at hand, Dr. Crusher went swiftly from one door to another, opening each and peering inside the simple quarters. Five staterooms she checked in quick succession, discovering nothing except that the *Neptune* normally had a crew of about ten.

She made a left-hand turn in the corridor and strode down a long passageway with no doors. She skirted around another pile of dried leaves, but otherwise found nothing of distinction in the doorless passageway, which ran along the stern of the ship.

Rounding another corner, Beverly found a door marked "Sickbay" and another door marked "Replicator Room." In between them was what looked like a small lounge with tables and chairs. Resting on the tables were glasses and plates, which contained half-drunk liquids and half-eaten food.

"Whatever happened, they cleared out quickly," she told herself.

Without warning, she heard the rustling again, and Crusher whirled around. Her hand crept to the butt of her phaser, and her senses were acutely on edge as she listened to the silence of the ghost ship. Only it wasn't silent—she heard a voice whisper:

"Mother."

Crusher charged into the hallway again, only this time she wasn't certain that her senses had been reliable. Nobody on this dead ship was going to call her mother. Only one person could do that. . . .

Her eyes lit on the door marked "Sickbay," and she knew she had to check that out. In fact, she had an overpowering urge to go in there, at the same time that she had an overpowering dread. Crusher's hand hovered over her combadge, ready to call Riker. But what would she tell him? That she was spooked and kept hearing voices?

"Get a hold of yourself," grumbled Beverly. With determination, she slapped the panel on the bulkhead and opened the door to sickbay.

Once she stepped inside, all of her irrational fears seemed to vanish. Maybe it was the familiar surroundings. They had only two beds, but the biofunction monitors, diagnostic instruments, and operating equipment looked to be the latest design. But with a crew so small, they probably wouldn't have a real doctor, just a medic and an Emergency Medical Hologram.

"Hi, Mom," whispered a voice.

Beverly whirled around to see her son, Wesley Crusher, standing four meters away. She felt light-headed from the shock of seeing him and began to stumble. He rushed to catch her, and she swooned into his comforting arms.

"Wesley! Wesley!" she gasped, touching his face and tousling his hair. Tears filled her eyes, because he hardly looked any different from when she had last seen him. "I can't believe it's *you!*"

"I've come a long way to help out," he said with a broad smile on his face.

"Jean-Luc will be so glad to see you. Everybody will—"

He lifted a finger and touched her lips. "No, Mom, this has to be our secret for a little while."

"But . . . But why?"

Wesley looked at her as if *he* were the parent, explaining a difficult concept to a child. "Like I said, Mom, I came a long way, and I'm not supposed to be here. I can't stay long, because my time with the Traveler is not over. Besides, the last thing we need now are more distractions. There will be time to make my presence known . . . after this crisis is over. In the meantime, I can help *you.* And you will need it."

Beverly nodded, unable to think clearly. After years of being separated from her only child, she wasn't going to do anything to drive him away. *He's not a mere human anymore*, she told herself, *he has godlike powers.*

"How did you get here?" she muttered. "What happened to the crew?"

He wrapped her in his arms and gently stroked her hair, and all of her questions and concerns evaporated. She hadn't remembered Wes being so affectionate before, but she wasn't going to complain. It had been an awfully long time since her tiny family had been whole.

Her combadge beeped, and it was like a far-off alarm waking her from a dream. Wesley gave her a sly smile as he pulled away, and he held his fingers to his lips. *Our secret*, he seemed to say.

Her voice was a hoarse whisper when she answered, "Crusher here."

"Are you all right, Doctor?" asked Riker.

"Yes, I'm just a little winded."

"We haven't found anything of interest, except for a bit of trash on the floor. How about you?"

She looked up, but Wesley was gone. Beverly felt a twinge of panic, fearing that his sudden appearance had been the delusions of a heartsick, overworked mother. Then Wes stuck his head in the door and waved, as if to say, *I'm really here*!

Beaming with happiness, she mustered her confidence and said, "I don't see anything wrong with this craft. Tell Captain Picard that I'd be glad to be acting captain of the *Neptune*."

"That's good," answered Riker, "because Data reports that the ship is fully functional. But I would really like to know what happened to the crew."

"I'm sure we'll find out in time," said Beverly. She was bursting to tell him—or anyone—that Wesley was back, but she had to respect her son's wishes.

"Okay, you sit tight," replied the first officer. "As soon as the captain signs off, I'll muster a crew and send them over. I'll try to find people with experience on this class of vessel."

"Don't worry, Will, I'm sure I'll be just fine." It was the truth, because she had never felt more at ease in her entire life.

# twenty-five

Mot sat on the porch of his parents' small, cylindrical cottage overlooking the banks of the Mother Vein, Myrmidon's largest river. The distinctive yellow-green river cane, which towered several meters into the air, waved gently in the breeze. The river was so wide that the bank on the other side wasn't even visible. A distant sailboat plied the purple water, bouncing over choppy waves as it struggled against the current. Mot could identify with the sailboat, because that's how he felt struggling against the current in a river that was way too big and too deep.

He had delayed coming to his parents' home in order to go to the nearest city, Genroh, with a contingent of Bolians from the ship in order to convince the authorities to back the Federation plan. Mainly, they wanted access to their factories and replicators, to make interphase generators. They hadn't met with resistance exactly—it was more like a slowness to act. Bolians were a peaceful, spiritual, and optimistic people. Misfortune was something which only struck those who somehow deserved it, like the boisterous Tellarites. The people on Myrmidon clearly didn't deserve it. Besides, this was their spiritual home—a holy place—and it couldn't be destroyed without reason. Either the outsiders were mistaken about the Genesis Wave, or it was the will of the First Mother.

Unfortunately, there was no way Starfleet could demonstrate the horror of the Genesis Wave, and there was no way for the populace to get a taste of it before it actually hit. By the time they knew how bad it was, they would be dead.

The door creaked open behind him, and he turned to see his mother walk out, carrying a plate of his favorite treats, *bazoban* bars.

He mustered a smile for his parent, who was grinning broadly at him, but it was difficult to feign happiness. While she baked his favorite foods, while his father searched the closet for his favorite peg-jumping game, the minutes were ticking away. Already they had only twelve hours left, and his parents still could not fathom the seriousness of the situation.

It had been so long since Mot had seen his parents that he hadn't wanted to interject doom and gloom into their reunion, but the doom was very real. As soon as his father returned from rummaging through the closet, Mot was going to level with his parents—and force them to make a decision. He could slap himself now for not having come months sooner to visit them, but like most young people, he was selfish and wrapped up in his own life. Mot vowed never to let that happen again.

"Eat! Eat!" his mother encouraged him, shoving the plate of goodies under his nose. "It's your favorite."

"I know," he said, grabbing one of the fruity bars and shoving half of it into his mouth. Mot hadn't gotten to be as large as he was by being a slow eater. He chewed ruminatively as he watched the river flow by.

"How is that nice Captain Picard?" asked his mother.

"Fine," answered Mot. "He never complains about his haircut. Of course, he doesn't have much hair. Things have been peaceful on the *Enterprise* for many months now . . . until this."

"Your sister says she is doing well in her new position," Mother continued. "I'm certainly glad Bolarus isn't facing this problem. It isn't, is it?"

"No," answered Mot with a grunt of relief. He didn't say that their unknown enemy could always unleash the Genesis Wave again and again, until there was nothing left of the Federation but misshapen planets and old legends.

The door opened again, and his father came out with a dusty box in his hands. He looked older than Mot remembered, his once gleaming blue skin now pale and mottled. "Look, Son, I found it!" he claimed joyfully. "Your game of Tubes and Gutters! How about a quick match?"

With a heavy sigh, Mot set the plate of *bazoban* bars on the arm of his chair. "Mother . . . Father . . . we've got to talk and decide what you're going to do. You're lucky, in that you have more choices than most. Because I'm a member of the *Enterprise* crew, you can be evacuated from the planet."

His father laughed. "Leave Myrmidon? Do you know how long we worked and saved to move here? Coming here has been a dream for all of our lives, hasn't it, Mother?"

She nodded wistfully. "Yes. Nothing, except you children, has ever made us happier. Look at the beautiful view we have! Here there is enough room and land for everyone. You only have to be here for a few days to realize that *this* is truly the chosen planet."

In exasperation, Mot jumped to his feet, knocking the plate of *bazoban* bars onto the patio with a clatter. Guiltily, he bent down to pick them up, but then he realized that *he* would have to be the adult here. Mot rose to his feet, leaving the food on the floor.

"Don't pick it up," he told his mother sternly. "In twelve hours, those crumbs won't be here. That river won't be here. The cottage won't be here, and *you* won't be here. Unless you're evacuated or go to a shelter, you'll be dead. To tell you the truth, I don't even know if the shelters will work, but it's the only way we have to save as many people as possible."

The big Bolian knelt down and clasped his parents' hands. "Please! Take this opportunity to come with me back to the *Enterprise*. I don't want to call my sister and tell her that you're dead . . . and that I could have saved you, but didn't."

His mother smiled benignly. "If it's the will of the First Mother to change our world, then we will change with it."

"No!" shouted Mot. "It's not the will of the First Mother—it's a weapon! A truly horrendous weapon."

"Is there much suffering?" asked his father.

Mot well knew where that line of thinking was headed, and he wanted to head it off. "No, death will be very swift. You needn't worry about that. But the thing is, you don't have to die! If you refuse to be evacuated, will you at least go to the sanctuary in Genroh and wait there?"

The elder Bolians looked at one another and then at their little cottage, and Mot could tell they were still undecided. He screwed up his courage and added, "I'll go with you. I'll wait with you, too . . . until it's over."

"You won't leave with the *Enterprise*?" asked his father with surprise.

"Not if you're staying here."

His mother squeezed his hand. "My son, we'll all go together to the sanctuary."

With that, Mot breathed an enormous sigh of relief and wrapped his arms around both of his parents, tears welling in his eyes. At long last, when the hug was over, his father picked up the old dusty box and asked hoarsely, "Now . . . how about a game of Tubes and Gutters?"

Maltz paced the now-empty radiation lab on the *Enterprise*, which he had made his home since the ship began filling with refugees days ago. He hadn't realized that staying aboard the *Enterprise* meant staying alone, and that Leah Brahms would disappear. In fact, everybody on the ship was so busy that they were ignoring him. He thought momentarily about wreaking havoc, which would have been easy enough to do, but Starfleet was already in a more chaotic state than it had ever been. It seemed cowardly to kick them when they were down.

Besides, he might need their assistance to fulfill his blood oath. He certainly needed them to be reunited with Leah Brahms, wherever she was. The old Klingon had spent a lot of time alone in recent years, and he was content with his own company. He had also learned to be patient.

Maltz went to the replicator, wondering if it could produce a mug of ale. Finally, he rejected that idea, thinking he might need his wits about him; he settled for carrot juice, a Terran delicacy for which he had developed a taste. He was enjoying his glass of juice when the door whooshed open. In strode the tall first officer named Riker, and Maltz jumped to attention.

"You must be getting bored," said Riker.

"A bit," admitted Maltz.

"General Gra'Kor has asked for you to be reassigned to him. Are you ready to go?"

"Am I ready to go!" barked the Klingon happily. "Does a *targ* have spikes?"

Riker smiled. "Come on, let's see if we can squeeze you onto the transporter."

They exited the laboratory and strode down the corridor, which seemed oddly quiet. "Where is everyone?" asked Maltz.

"On the planet, getting ready for the wave."

"How does it go?"

Riker frowned. "All I know for sure is that there are more interphase generators down there than in the whole Romulan Star Empire. I think we'll save lives, but I wish I knew for sure."

"How much time is left?" asked the Klingon.

Riker checked his chronometer. "About six hours."

They reached the turbolift, and the first officer told the computer their destination. "Is Leah Brahms still on the planet?" asked Maltz. "No, I was told she was over on the *Sovereign*. She didn't want to stay on the planet." "She has good reason to stay alive," said Maltz darkly. "Did your task force have any success finding the beasts who are doing this?" "No," muttered Riker, "although one of the ships turned up . . . deserted."

"No sign of the crew?" asked the Klingon puzzledly.

Riker shook his head as the turbolift door opened. He strode out, and Maltz followed, smiling to himself. When vengeance would be wreaked, *he* would do the wreaking, not the Federation.

They reached the transporter room, and the cargo handlers moved aside enough boxes of gel-packs to make room on the platform for Maltz. Riker extended his hand, and the old Klingon gripped it forcefully.

"I hope you find peace," said Riker.

"I hope I find war," answered Maltz with a grin. "Tell Captain Picard he has a noble vessel and a fine crew, plus good hospitality."

"I will." The first officer nodded to the transporter operator. "Do you have the coordinates for the *Jaj*?"

"Laid in," answered the tall Andorian on the console.

"Energize when ready." A second later, the grizzled Klingon was gone.

He materialized in a much darker, smokier transporter room, where it was no less crowded. Only here it was jammed with confused Bolian evacuees, who never thought they would find themselves aboard a Klingon warship. With a few shoves and grunts, armed guards kept them moving quickly into the corridors.

"Consul Maltz," said the transporter operator. "Wait here—the general is coming."

Maltz moved out of the way and stood in the corner, waiting patiently until the stocky general arrived.

"Maltz!" Gra'Kor growled magnanimously as he strode into the room, slamming his palms on the old Klingon's shoulders. "I called in some favors. Are you ready to see your ship?"

"My ship!" echoed Maltz in an awed tone of voice. "It's been a long time since I had a ship."

"I know," said Gra'Kor, his brusque manner softening. "I'm sorry I said the things I did. A warrior shouldn't have to suffer ninety years for one mission gone wrong."

"But you were right!" insisted Maltz. "I have not tried hard enough to get to *Sto-Vo-Kor*. But now that I have another chance to face my greatest enemy, I know why I have lived so long."

The general nodded sagely. "Do you know that the Federation has failed to find the source of this scourge?"

"Yes. Fate is saving them for me."

"You have a good crew of experienced warriors," said Gra'Kor. "I tried to pick those who have had dealings with humans, but I don't know if they will follow a human female."

"They will follow this one," Maltz assured him. "What is the name of our ship?"

"The *HoS*. She is an older attack cruiser but still valiant. Her captain and first mate were promoted to larger ships, so she is perfect for your purpose. But enough talk—you must go. What is the name of the misguided human who invented this disaster?"

"Carol Marcus," answered Maltz through clenched teeth. "If she yet lives, it will not be for long." He bounded back onto the transporter pad, pushing two startled Bolians out of his way. "Thank you, General."

"*Qapla'*!" said Gra'Kor with a salute and a toothy smile.

"I will see you in *Sto-Vo-Kor*," promised the old warrior seconds before his molecules disappeared in a shimmering curtain of light.


Leah Brahms paced about three steps, then turned and paced three steps in the other direction, which was all the room she had in the quarters she shared with five Bolian evacuees on the *Sovereign*. Admiral Nechayev had treated her like a pariah ever since she came aboard, shunting her off with the refugees, who were just as miserable as she. They might have wondered what this human was doing in their midst, because there weren't many non-Bolian residents on Myrmidon. They had to conclude that she wasn't part of the rescue effort.

In their abject fear and misery, the evacuees talked very little to each other, and none of them talked to Leah. She considered speaking to them, but she didn't trust herself to say anything positive. They certainly didn't need to hear that the world they left behind, and probably most of their friends and relatives, would be reduced to sludge in a few hours. She didn't really want to tell them that she was responsible for a desperate plan which had a good chance of getting everyone on Myrmidon killed.

Now Brahms knew why Admiral Nechayev's name was spoken in

hushed and fearful tones. The woman's wrath was worthy of a wronged Klingon. Leah had been banished to this purgatory for a slip of the tongue, calling Geordi "crazy" for staying. The punishment didn't seem to fit the crime, but she had no idea how to get out of it. More than likely, she was destined to be offloaded like so much cargo at the nearest Bolian spaceport, along with the rest of the refugees. It was an ignominious ending to what she had thought was a distinguished career.

*Of course*, decided Leah grimly, *where else do I have to go? What else do I have to do? My life's over, my marriage is over, my career's over, and the only friend I have left is about to kill himself. Perhaps I should have stayed on the planet and taken my chances.*

A chime sounded at the door, and one of the Bolians said hoarsely, "Come in!"

A young ensign with a padd in his hands stepped inside and looked around. "Which one of you is Leah Brahms?"

"I am," she answered.

"Come with me, please." He motioned to the corridor, then stepped out to wait for her.

"Where are we going?" asked Leah as she followed him.

"You're being sent somewhere else." He checked his padd. "The *HoS.*"

"The *HoS*? What is that?"

"A Klingon ship." They walked briskly down the corridor, which was also packed with refugees, until they reached the turbolift.

*Hmmm*, thought Leah glumly, *I must really be in the doghouse if the admiral is shipping me off to a Klingon vessel.* She finally decided that it couldn't be any worse than being cooped up on the *Enterprise.* Nevertheless, Leah spent a few irrational moments envisioning a brutal prison ship where she would spend her final days.

Moments later, she found herself in a frantic transporter room, where Bolian evacuees were being beamed aboard while crates were being shipped off at a rapid pace. The ensign conferred briefly with the transporter chief, and they made room for her on the transporter pad.

"Are you ready?" the chief asked her.

"Whatever," she answered with a shrug. "Remind me not to run afoul of Admiral Nechayev again."

"Never a good idea," agreed the transporter chief as he plied his controls. "Energizing."

A moment later, Brahms materialized on a dark, smoky bridge, where half-a-dozen sullen Klingon warriors stared suspiciously at her.

She was about to ask what she was doing here, when the raised command chair in the center of the bridge swiveled around, and a rugged but familiar face grinned at her.

"Captain on the bridge," said Maltz.

Brahms looked around, wondering which one of them was the captain, but all eyes were still focused on her. She felt an odd mixture of dread and elation.

Maltz rose to his feet and looked down at her. "What are your orders, Sir?"

Now it was Leah's turn to grin. "You did it, Maltz! You got yourself a ship!"

"I got *us* a ship. I've already laid in a course for Seran and the suspected origin point of the Genesis Wave. I assume you will want to leave orbit immediately."

Leah hesitated, thinking about Geordi and Dolores on the planet's surface, but there wasn't anything she could do for them, short of kidnapping them. They had volunteered of their own free will, and she had now been given an opportunity to exercise *her* will.

"Yes," she said, "take us out of orbit."

When her unfamiliar crew was a bit slow to move, Leah told herself to act more like Admiral Nechayev. "Move it!" she yelled. "I've got a blood oath to fulfill!"

That made them jump, and she turned to Maltz and said, "I've got to familiarize myself with this ship. Why don't we begin with the engine room. I think I'll feel more comfortable starting there."

"Yes, Sir," answered the old Klingon snappily. "You heard Captain Brahms! Second Officer Karuk, escort the captain to the engine room and answer all her questions fully."

"Yes, Sir," said a young officer, who still looked puzzled about how he could end up serving on a Klingon vessel under a human female. These were strange times indeed.

"Don't worry," Brahms told him, "the *HoS* is going to go down in history. And in glory."

The young officer gave her a smile and nodded to his fellows, as if to say they were going to be all right. Leah decided he was awfully young to die, but millions who were even younger had already perished. At least everybody on the *HoS* would die for a purpose.

Deanna Troi nearly gagged at the musky smell of all the animals crowded into the Sanctuary of the First Mother, along with their owners and what seemed like half the city. Starfleet had been so worried about saving the Bolians that they hardly thought about saving animals, but the residents of Myrmidon were sure thinking about it, as they brought livestock and pets by the dozens. There were fur-bearing animals, milk-giving animals, primates, birds, reptiles, even insects—some of them in cages, many on leashes, and others running between people's legs. It was like a land-bound Noah's Ark.

Mother, the stocky woman who ran the sanctuary, welcomed all who came for protection, two-legged, four-legged, or six-legged. To make room, volunteers had removed the pews and every stick of furniture, except for the display case which contained the Crown of the First Mother. It was sitting in a prominent place, right on top of the interphase generator. Although people and animals were crammed shoulder-to-shoulder in every square centimeter of the domed building, Mother pushed her way through the throng, assuring everyone that they would be saved by the grace of the First Mother . . . and her Starfleet assistants.

Troi finally had to make her way outside to get some fresh air, even though there was less than an hour left before the Genesis Wave hit. To her surprise, she saw the sky had turned a salmon shade, streaked with crimson clouds. It was dusk, a suitable time for the great transformation which was about to come. The counselor was only supposed to stay for another half an hour before returning to the *Enterprise*, but it felt as if she were deserting her comrades on a sinking ship.

She toyed with the idea of gutting it out on the planet, but once again she talked herself out of it. Deanna had witnessed that awful cataclysm once, and once was enough. Besides, she didn't think she could bear to see the beautiful city ravaged, as she knew it would be. Even if millions of lives were saved as planned, Myrmidon would be changed forever.

Unable to calm her nerves, she walked briskly through the now-quiet streets, just as she had done many hours earlier. Deanna felt vaguely guilty about leaving Mother and the sanctuary, but there wasn't anything she could do there but get in the way. Her idea to use the sanctuaries as shelters had been a good one—it would work, as long as everything else worked. If the interphase generators failed, at least the people would perish in a comfortable place that gave them peace. It wasn't much consolation, but it was all she had.

As she wandered, she heard the sound of voices rising on the twilight breeze. It sounded much like the chanting and praying that was happening inside the sanctuary, but she knew these worshippers had to be outside by the way their voices carried.

Following the chanting sound, she came to one of the parks with the giant communal vegetables. Gathered in the center of the clearing was a group of Bolians numbering about thirty, and half-a-dozen others were lying on the ground, sleeping. That was odd enough to make her stop to watch the proceedings. The Bolians were passing a large horn around, drinking a dark liquid from it. With a start, Troi realized that the sleepers on the ground were not sleeping—they were *dead*. The dark liquid was poison!

Without thinking, she charged into their midst and shouted, "Stop! Stop! What are you doing?"

A large Bolian glowered at her. "This is none of your concern! Haven't you brought enough disaster upon us?"

"Go away! Leave us in peace!" shouted others.

"But you don't have to die!" she insisted. "There's safety in the Sanctuary of the First Mother. Come with me, and I'll—"

She never saw the rock sailing through the air. It hit her in the head with enough force to knock her to the ground, and Troi lay there unconscious, blood streaming from her forehead. Those bent on suicide went on with their grim task, believing they had done the Starfleet officer a favor by sparing her undue suffering.

# twenty-six

"Captain," said Data from the ops console on the *Enterprise*, "the last of the Klingon fleet is leaving orbit."

Picard looked up at the viewscreen in time to see a huge *Negh'Var*-class warship bank away from the planet and career into space, thrusters burning. The Romulan ships had pulled out fifteen minutes earlier, and the skies over Myrmidon were returning to a semblance of normal. But it was only a semblance, Picard knew, because there was nothing normal about the awesome force which was bearing down on them. Very soon those peaceful skies would turn an electric shade of green, and the fiery curtain would raze Myrmidon as it had razed every other object in its path.

"Any sign of the wave?" asked Commander Riker, pacing behind the command chair.

"Yes," answered the android as he scanned through information on his console. "The outmost planet of the solar system has already been transformed. This is only an estimate, but I would say we have twenty minutes until contact."

Captain Picard rubbed his chin thoughtfully. They had been through this before—on Persephone V—but this time it was different. This time they had hundreds of Starfleet personnel down on the planet. The *Enterprise* had contributed La Forge, Linton, Mot, and four technicians to the effort. This would be either the greatest success in the history of Starfleet or the greatest disaster.

He heard his first officer say, "Riker to transporter room two."

"Rhofistan here," came the reply.

"Has Counselor Troi come back to the ship yet?"

"No, Sir. She hasn't reported in or asked for transportation."

"Stand by." He tapped his combadge. "Riker to Troi." There was no response, so he tried again. "*Enterprise* to Deanna Troi."

Again there was no response, and Riker looked beseechingly at the captain. "Can we beam her back?"

"Go ahead."

"Transporter room two, lock onto Deanna Troi's combadge and beam her back immediately," ordered Riker.

"Yes, Sir," responded the chief's voice.

Riker looked relieved to have issued the order, until the chief's voice sounded again. "Sir, there's been a problem."

"What kind of problem?" asked Riker impatiently. "Didn't you beam her back?"

There was a pause that seemed to last an eternity, then came the response. "We beamed back the person wearing her combadge, but it turns out to be a Bolian child about eight years old."

"What?" bellowed Riker. He looked worriedly at the captain.

"Go ahead and investigate," said Picard. "But I don't want to lose anybody else. Get back here in time."

The first officer nodded and charged toward the turbolift. After he was gone, it was the captain's turn to pace nervously across his bridge. He felt like contacting Nechayev, La Forge, or somebody on the planet, but what good would that do? It was far too late for second guessing, and last-minute heroics didn't work against the Genesis Wave. From all reports, the vast majority of Bolians had either found their way to shelters or had been evacuated. They had done all they could.

Then why did he feel so lousy?

At least Picard took consolation in knowing that Beverly Crusher was safe aboard the *Neptune*, which had left orbit about ten minutes ago. He had also gotten a promise from Captain Tomalak that he would replicate and reinstall the interphase generators on his ship, so that he could use cloaking again. As soon as it was safe, the Romulan had promised to come back to retrieve the admiral, La Forge, and the others.

Still, none of it seemed to be enough.

"Data," said Captain Picard, "take over the conn. Mister Perezo, you take over ops."

Swiftly, the two officers reconfigured their consoles so that they had switched responsibilities. The captain looked at the calm, efficient android and was very glad to have him on the bridge at the moment.

He walked behind the android and bent over to whisper in his ear, "Mr. Data, I want you to get us out of here before that wave hits, and I don't care who is—or isn't—on board. Don't wait for my order. Do I make myself clear?"

Data turned to regard him with those cool yellow eyes. "Yes, Sir."

*Now*, thought Picard, *I have done all I can.*

Will Riker strode purposefully into the transporter room and looked at the chief, who pointed to a small, blue-skinned person sitting on the edge of the transporter platform. The female child was still wearing the gleaming Starfleet combadge in the center of her blue tunic. He told himself to be patient and remember that he was dealing with a child, who was probably frightened and disoriented.

He walked over and knelt down in front of her. Smiling, he pointed to the insignia badge. "That's a very pretty pin. Where did you get it?"

"I want to go home," she whined.

Riker clenched his teeth and tried to stay calm. "Listen, I'm not mad at you, but I know that pin belonged to somebody else. You can keep it, but I just want to find her. She's a good friend of mine."

"Will you take me home?" asked the child. "I miss my mother."

"Yes, as a matter of fact, I'll be glad to take you home. But I need to find my friend, too. Can you show me where you were when you found that pin?"

"I didn't find it," she answered. "My mother gave it to me."

Riker nodded slowly. Now it was making sense. Some distraught parent had hit upon a clever way of saving her child, if not herself. He clapped his hands together. "Let's go try to find my friend, and your mother."

He stood up and lifted the child to her feet, then he took her hand. "My name is Will. What's yours?"

"Dezeer."

"A pretty name," said Riker, mustering a smile. He steered her toward an empty pad. "Why don't you go stand over here, and I'll stand just over here. And the nice man will take us home."

He motioned to Rhofistan. "Do you have the coordinates where you picked her up?"

"Yes, Sir. But I'm not picking up any other life-forms around there."

"That's all right," muttered Riker grimly. "We haven't got a lot of choice." He glanced at the child to make sure she was still standing in the center of the pad, and she was. "Energize."

\* \* \*

Tricorder in hand, Geordi La Forge circled nervously around the two interphase generators he had set up in the lowest part of a dry riverbed. For at least the twentieth time, he checked all the couplers, power connections, and gel-packs. Although most of the shelters were in the religious sanctuaries, Dolores Linton had convinced them to put a few in open air. She had determined that the seasonally dry riverbeds offered the greatest chance for success—she liked the low altitude and the sandy, porous soil, which allowed for good penetration of the phase-shifting pulse.

Plus the riverbeds held a lot of beings, as demonstrated by the huge throngs of baying animals and praying Bolians. It looked like a scene from one of those old Biblical epics—with a whole nation stuck in the desert.

Geordi stopped and glanced at Admiral Nechayev and Dolores Linton, who were conferring with some nervous Bolian dignitaries. Dolores and the admiral had become fast friends in the last few hours, and La Forge figured that her career was going to take a major leap forward . . . if they survived. Dolores had been such a stalwart and cheerful presence that Geordi was beginning to feel very fond of the geologist. He hadn't stopped thinking about Leah Brahms for one moment, but he had decided that Dolores was a real keeper.

Although he had no idea where Leah was, at least she was safe. At the moment, it seemed highly unlikely that he would ever see her again. He looked up at the sky, which was just beginning to turn a rosy shade as dusk hit this part of Myrmidon. A cool breeze blew across the dry river, rustling the tall trees and grasses which grew there. It seemed altogether too beautiful of a day for this world to end.

The conference with the Bolians broke up, and Nechayev and Linton waded through the crowd to get back to Geordi's position at the generators.

Dolores lowered her voice to say, "We assured them that they were going to die quickly, and with no pain. Of course, I don't think any of us are going to die."

"We'll know soon," said Nechayev. "I've just received word that the wave is moving through the solar system and should hit here in about ten minutes. I've ordered the fleet to leave, although one or two ships will stay until the last minute. The Klingons and Romulans are already gone."

"Is the *Enterprise* still in orbit?" asked La Forge.

The admiral gave him a slight smile. "What do you think? I can always count on your captain to take the risks nobody else would."

"What are you worried about?" asked Dolores.

Nechayev sighed. "I don't know, but my career has taught me to believe strongly in Murphy's Law. Besides, we need someone to alert us when the countdown has started."

"Right." Geordi noticed that he was wringing his hands ner-vously, and he quickly dropped them to his side. With a smile, Dolores grabbed one of his hands and gripped it tightly. He could feel her pulse throbbing in his palm, and he realized that her cheerfulness was a brave act.

"As soon as we have two minutes left, we'll start the countdown," said the admiral. "I can't begin to express my gratitude for the two of you staying here. Suffice to say, it's good to be among comrades at a time like this."

There was nothing left to say, and all three of them gazed anxiously at the deepening auburn sky.


Gripping the little girl's hand, Riker tried not to drag her through the deserted streets of the capitol, but it was difficult not to hurry when time was running short—less than five minutes by Data's latest esti-mate. The Bolian child, Dezeer, was crying and fearful, and Riker couldn't blame her. He might be crying soon too if he couldn't find Deanna. It didn't help that darkness had descended on the great city, and every building and side street looked the same.

They stopped at another intersection, populated only by leaves and bits of trash which skidded along the sidewalk. "Does this look famil-iar?" Riker asked. "Is this where your mother gave you that pin?"

"I don't know," she answered, looking sorrowful.

Riker gritted his teeth. "Do you know this part of town? Please take a look around. Do you know where we are?"

Wearily, the child gazed at the triangular-shaped buildings and broad thoroughfares. Finally she nodded and pointed. "Yes. My school is down there."

"Good!" exclaimed Riker. "Now try again—do you know where your mother was going when she left you?"

Dezeer nodded. "To the park, I think."

"To a park," repeated Riker. "Do you think you could take me there? I would love to see your park."

"Where is everybody?" asked the child, puzzled.

"They're probably in the park, having a party. Why don't you take me there, and we'll have a party with your mother and all your friends."

The little girl nodded, and for the first time, she took his hand and led him down the deserted street.

* * *

"One-hundred-twenty . . . one-hundred-nineteen . . . one-hundred-eighteen . . . one-hundred-seventeen," droned the voice of the computer over the shipwide intercom. Captain Picard turned and looked at the viewscreen, where a small magenta dust cloud glimmered in the firmament. He watched, transfixed, as the dust cloud seemed to implode, forming into a gaseous ball a split second before it was obliterated completely by a seething, fiery curtain of green. Although he had seen it before, the awesome sight made him shiver. Now that the dust cloud was gone, nothing stood between the Genesis Wave and Myrmidon.

The captain tapped his combadge. "*Enterprise* to Riker."

"Riker here," came a breathless reply.

"I'm sorry," said Picard, "but we need you to return."

"Captain, we've just reached a park where there are a lot of dead bodies. I need to look through them."

"Dead bodies?"

"It must be the site of a mass suicide," answered the first officer. "Take the girl back, but give me another few seconds."

Before he could reply, Data spoke up urgently. "Captain! One of the Starfleet ships has returned, and . . . they have opened fire on the shelters!"

"What?" barked Picard. "Which ship? Hail them!"

The android looked up, a glimpse of shock in his yellow eyes. "Sir, it is the *Neptune*. Dr. Crusher does not answer our hail. I will put it on screen."

Captain Picard stared at the viewscreen, where the once-derelict ship was firing torpedoes and phasers in rapid succession. On the planet's surface, bright flashes indicated where the deadly weapons were wreaking their toll. Picard gripped the back of his command chair, hesitant to order the destruction of Beverly's ship.

"Eighty . . . seventy-nine . . . seventy-eight . . . seventy-seven," continued the computer, calmly counting down the destruction of Myrmidon and the fifty million souls who dwelled there.

# twenty-seven

The first explosion blew up a mammoth chunk of the riverbed, along with scores of innocent Bolians. There were smoke, dust, carnage, and wailing everywhere, and Geordi instinctively dove on top of the interphase generators in order to protect them. That was his first instinct, but the second one was better. Without hesitation, he threw the switch to initiate phase-shifting, even though they were over a minute early.

Then he cowered in the dirt, as the unexpected onslaught continued. Lifting his head, he squinted through the smoke and chaos to see both Admiral Nechayev and Dolores Linton lying on the ground, amidst dozens of other casualties. He fought the impulse to dash to their aid, because he had to stay with the interphase generators and power packs. As horrible as this was, the real horror was yet to come. Some of the Bolians were fleeing from the deadly explosions, running out of the field of protection. He tried to yell at them to stop, but his ragged voice was lost in screams, chaos, and explosions.

Captain Picard rousted himself from his momentary hesitation and pointed to Data on the conn. "Pursue the *Neptune*, full impulse. Tactical, target phasers on their impulse engines and fire at will."

"Yes, Sir!"

He slapped the companel on his chair, and his voice boomed over the ship. "Transporter room one, as soon as we get into range, lock onto the life-forms on the starship *Neptune* and beam them aboard. All security personnel, report to transporter room one and take the crew of the *Neptune* into custody. Use force if necessary."

*Riker*! he thought in a panic. He had forgotten about his first officer. "Transporter room two, lock onto Commander Riker and the Bolian girl right now and beam them aboard.

"Thirty . . . twenty-nine . . . twenty-eight," droned the voice of the computer as the Genesis Wave streaked ever closer.

Riker heard the explosions ripping through the city, and his small companion screamed in fear. Now he wasn't gentle at all as he lifted the girl and hauled her from corpse to corpse, looking for anyone among the bodies who wasn't Bolian.

He finally spotted her by her mane of dark hair, splayed outward from her bloody face like a black halo. Clutching the girl in one hand, he fell on top of Deanna's unconscious body, trying to protect her from the blasts. In that same instant, all three of their bodies dematerialized in the shimmering haze of the transporter beam.

Mot and his parents huddled in the vestibule of the sanctuary and tried to ignore the jostling, weeping, and wailing all around them. They could hear the distant explosions, but they couldn't figure out what they were. Mot had feared that some residents might commit suicide, but they weren't likely to blow themselves up. He also couldn't tell if the technicians had switched on the phase-shifting, but he certainly hoped so.

"Is it starting?" his mother asked fearfully.

"I don't know," answered Mot, wrapping his arms around his parents and squeezing them tightly. "Whatever happens, we'll be together."

From the vestibule, they were able to see the starlit sky through the open doorway, and Mot watched it intently. Even though it was just shortly past sunset, the sky seemed to be growing lighter, as if the sun were coming up in a roaring blaze. He watched in awe as the sky turned a mottled shade of red, then a sickly green, and then a dozen other colors in a bizarre kaleidoscope effect. The ground began to tremble, and the wails and chants increased in volume.

"Yes, it's happening!" said Mot. He kissed the top of his mother's head and then his father's. "I love you both!"

"We love you, Son!" rasped his father, burying his face in Mot's broad chest. All around them, the sanctuary shuddered, and the wind howled with an unearthly force. Mot closed his eyes and gripped his loving parents, certain that the next moment would be their last.

*   *   *

"Captain, we are leaving orbit," declared Data, taking the initiative Picard had charged him with.

On the viewscreen, the *Neptune* soared toward the planet, no longer firing indiscriminately but in flames. Their phasers had stopped the rogue ship, but there was no telling how much destruction she had wrought before being stopped.

Picard wanted to rush down to the transporter room and find what had caused Beverly and her crew to lose their minds, but he couldn't tear his eyes away from the planet. A pulsing wall of flame ripped over the yellow-green plains and the blue rivers, turning them into great pillars of steam and ash. The whole planet quivered and throbbed like a sun going nova. He tried to imagine there being hundreds of pockets of survivors, but it hardly seemed possible. It could be days before they knew how many had been saved, if any.

The last image he saw on the viewscreen was the fiery wall engulfing the tiny *Neptune* like a monstrous tidal wave crashing over a rowboat.

They had made their stand on Myrmidon, but there was no way anyone could call this a victory. In a few more days, Earth would fall, and they still had no idea *who* was doing this to them. Or how to stop it. The Genesis Wave rushed onward, undiminished, its voracious appetite still eager to consume more worlds, more solar systems, and more lives.

# Editor's Acknowledgment

The editor would like to thank David Mack, who is less fictional than some might presume, for providing THE GENESIS REPORT that makes up the bulk of Chapter Fourteen.

# THE NEXT GENERATION ®

## BOOK TWO

*For Erin, who has come to our rescue many times*

# one

Geordi La Forge had never before doubted the information his ocular implants imparted to his mind, but he could barely grasp the vivid spectrums and soaring electromagnetic pulses surging across the plains of Myrmidon. He staggered to remain on his feet in the fierce wind, which the phase-shifting did nothing to stop. The air smelled like tar, and his thumping heart told him this was not a sight that anyone should expect to see . . . and live.

Worriedly, Geordi laid hands upon the two interphase generators, each standing about two meters high, buttressed by struts and platforms. Only their phase-shifted field prevented the fifty thousand souls in the dry river bed from perishing in the holocaust.

Experienced at close range, the Genesis Wave was even more spectacular than he had been led to believe. Like a wildfire set loose in a parched forest, it ripped apart all molecules in its path and recombined them on the fly—only it moved with incredible speed. Instead of leaving spent ashes, the wave left a throbbing quagmire of new life, exploding into existence with barbarous fury. Just outside their field of protection, geysers spewed and mountains dissolved in the bubbling, churning morass. The horizon was undulating like a sine wave, and people and animals were mewling with fear all around him.

Without warning, the earth heaved under Geordi's feet, and the sand swiftly dissolved into a thick liquid. His first terrified reaction was that the Genesis Effect had reached them through the ground. But when the human didn't melt into a puddle, he figured it was liquefaction of the soil. Knowing the dissolving sand was a side effect didn't make it any less horrifying. Geordi felt as if he were slogging through molasses. He lunged for the generators and the gel packs, but the heavy equipment was also shifting and sinking into the muck. La Forge squirmed to his knees and dug a shoulder into a tilting strut to keep it level.

Now panic gripped scores of frightened Bolians in the riverbed, and many of their animals bolted into oblivion. Shrieking and wailing, the inhabitants lurched past him, hardly caring that they were all going to die if sand clogged the generators. La Forge grabbed an armful of gel packs and tried to keep them from sinking out of sight while he strained to hold the rack upright. When a distraught Bolian collided with him, knocking him into the sand, Geordi felt himself slipping downward. He rolled onto his stomach and swam over the moist sand to the generators, which he grabbed like a drowning man.

La Forge lifted his head and looked for his fallen comrades— Admiral Nechayev and Dolores Linton—but he could barely trust his vision. In every direction, there was nothing but turmoil. Despite the sensory overload, he tried to tell himself that only a few seconds had passed, and the worst of it would only last a few minutes. He would have to be patient and stay at his post with the generators, now half sunken into the sand. If the phase-shifting failed, nothing could keep them safe from the staggering forces reworking the planet.

As he hunkered down, Geordi tried to remember the strange events that had occurred just before the wave hit. Explosions had ripped through the riverbed, and they hadn't seemed accidental or part of the Genesis Effect. Geordi had seen concentrated flashes that had looked like beamed weapons to him. In the melee, Admiral Nechayev and Dolores Linton had both fallen. He had seen them on the ground, but he had stayed at his post, ignoring their plight.

*Was it self-preservation, a sense of duty, or fear that kept me from helping them*? he wondered. A howling gust of foul-smelling wind forced him to hunker down, and he tried not to be too hard on himself. He was in the middle of a world that was hemorrhaging and birthing at the same time, and the lives of a few carbon-based animals seemed to pale beside these momentous changes.

With a groan, the ground shuddered and then seemed to solidify— either that, or he and the equipment had sunk down to more solid rock. Maybe the effect was beginning to lessen, he thought with hope. Geordi looked up to see that some of the panicked inhabitants had stopped their mad flight, but many others had lost their minds entirely. In the distance, one Bolian dashed outside the protective field and dissolved like a swarm of bees breaking apart.

But most of the survivors realized that there was nowhere to run. They huddled in small groups, curled protectively over the wounded.

He still couldn't see either Nechayev or Linton, but he mustered some hope that they would live long enough for him to get help.

*Help?* he thought derisively. *Where? How?* Even if they lived through this initial phase, Myrmidon's civilization had been reduced beyond rubble to nonexistence. The churning sludge bore new life writhing in its depths, but it bore no resemblance to the sacred planet which had existed here before. All of its people's efforts paled in comparison with the throes of Myrmidon in its destruction and rebirth. He didn't want to watch the carnage, feeling shame and helplessness, but he couldn't tear his gaze away.

*We should have done better for these people than this!* he thought miserably. *This isn't survival—it's insanity.*

After a few moments, he found himself appreciating the fractured kaleidoscope in the sky, but the more he saw, the sadder he became. Although it looked as if much of the populace would survive, how could they live in this hellish place? It didn't seem possible that Myrmidon would ever revert to normal, although the spirit of a proud people like the Bolians would account for a lot. They had lived, but for what purpose?

La Forge fumbled in his belt for his tricorder, thinking that it should be safe to move around soon. If the effect was beginning to ebb, or at least enter its sustainable mode, he wanted to be ready. With reluctance, he tore his attention away from the swirling sky and writhing landscape to concentrate on his readings. The effect was lessening, but it was still too complex for the tricorder to register at all levels.

Although Project Genesis had been named for the first chapter of the Bible, this version reminded him more of the last chapter, Revelations—when the world was torn asunder in a great cataclysm . . . and the dead rose from their graves.

Captain Jean-Luc Picard rushed down the corridor leading to Transporter Room One, where Beverly Crusher and the crew of the *Neptune* were under arrest. At least he hoped they were under arrest, because their actions and treachery had endangered the entire operation on Myrmidon. The *Enterprise* had barely escaped from the Genesis Wave, because they'd been forced to disable the rogue ship. Even so, several installations on the ground had been severely damaged, and there was no telling how many lives had been lost because of the unexpected friendly fire.

The captain was hoping there would be a logical explanation, but he couldn't imagine what that could possibly be. At first, he feared the attack might have something to do with the Bolians' predilection for suicide, but there were no Bolians among the skeleton crew on the *Neptune*. No matter how he looked at it, the *Neptune*'s actions made absolutely no sense, especially coming from the one person he trusted most—Beverly Crusher.

Taking a deep breath, Captain Picard charged into the transporter room, ready to confront just about anything. The first thing he saw was a phalanx of Starfleet security officers; their broad backs were toward him as they faced the transporter platform. Their weapons were lowered, and they didn't seem unduly concerned.

Upon seeing the captain, the security detail opened a path for him, and he caught a glimpse of a shimmering force field stretched across the transporter platform. Stepping closer, Picard saw Nurse Ogawa and a medical team poised for action just outside the force field. He still hadn't seen anyone from the *Neptune,* but Ogawa's worried eyes told him where they were. Piled haphazardly like a collection of discarded dolls, Crusher and seven others lay sprawled across the transporter platform.

"Are they dead?" he asked, trying to mask his alarm with a calm tone of voice.

"No, it's like they're in a coma . . . and not breathing well." Ogawa consulted her tricorder, and Picard took a closer look at the distressed crew members. Now he could see them squirming weakly, gasping for breath even as they remained in a deathlike trance.

He looked at Ogawa, who shook her head worriedly. "They're alive, but they're dying of asphyxiation. Their lungs seem to be paralyzed. Please, Captain, won't you allow us to help them?"

Worf wasn't aboard the *Enterprise* anymore, but Picard could hear the Klingon warning him about quarantine procedures. He also knew that Beverly Crusher—the woman who meant more to him than any other—was curled in a fetal position, looking like she was on the brink of death. He would just have to count on the biofilters in the transporters to do their job.

"Lower the force field," ordered the captain, "and get them to sickbay. Let's station security in sickbay until we get an explanation."

"I don't think they'll be any threat," replied Ogawa dryly. She rushed forward with the rest of the medteam, and they quickly applied oxygen and hypos to the sick prisoners. Within a few seconds, all of them were on portable ventilators.

The captain tapped his combadge. "Picard to Riker."

"Riker here," came the response.

"I need you on the bridge," said Picard, "while I monitor the situation in Transporter Room One. How are Counselor Troi and the Bolian girl?"

"Fine. I just dropped them off at sickbay. Deanna has a concussion, but she'll be okay. I'm on my way to the bridge."

"Thank you, Number One. Picard out."

When the antigrav gurneys and more medical personnel arrived, the captain just stood out of the way with the security officers until the patients were ready to be moved. As Ogawa guided Crusher's floating gurney toward the door, the captain caught up with her.

"How does it look?" he asked hoarsely, gazing at Beverly's face, which was obscured by a respirator.

"We've stabilized them," said Ogawa, "but she's barely able to breathe on her own. Until we do complete scans, we can't say what's wrong with them. The catatonic state looks bad, but we can deal with that. I don't like their labored breathing."

The nurse brushed past him and out the door, leaving Picard in her wake, helpless to do anything more for Beverly. The condition of the skeleton crew was frightening enough, but it raised a disturbing question: How could they have flown the ship and fired weapons in that physical condition? The *Neptune* had been a ghost ship when it arrived, and it had gone down in flames, still a ghost ship.

He tapped his combadge. "Picard to bridge."

"Yes, Captain," answered Commander Riker.

"What's our status?"

"We're on course to the rendezvous," answered the first officer, "and our ETA is in four hours. Starfleet is calling the Myrmidon operation a qualified success, although there's been no word from anyone on the planet. That won't be possible for at least half an hour."

"I'll be in sickbay," said Picard. "The *Neptune* crew came aboard in poor health—comatose, having trouble breathing."

"How's that possible?" asked Riker.

"I don't know, but I intend to find out. In fact, have Data review the logs of our final encounter with the *Neptune*. Tell him to look at everything—we might have missed something while it was happening."

"We'll get right on it," promised Riker. "Will they . . . recover?"

"We don't know enough about their condition." The captain watched glumly as the stricken officers were pushed out on gurneys. Since the Genesis Wave appeared, there were always new questions, but never any answers.

\* \* \*

His legs churning through the gritty mire, Geordi La Forge threw himself onto the rack of equipment and pushed for all he was worth. Although the dry riverbed had stopped liquefying, it was still treacherous. The interphase generators lay half-buried in the grime at a dangerously tilted angle, and some of the gel packs were covered. He was afraid the delicate machines would give out at any moment.

With a glance at the horizon, La Forge could see that the Genesis Effect was lessening, or moving into another phase. Instead of undulating and mutating, the landscape was now blossoming with misshapen trees, thick hedges, and ruby-red flowers. Overgrown stands of gnarled trees sprouted like weeds across the horizon, probably fed by water in the liquefied soil.

The winds remained ferocious, whipping at the new flora like a hurricane, and the skies continued to ripple with unbridled power. Geordi began to shiver as he glimpsed snow flurries at the edge of their protective field. The survivors were relatively calm now, huddling together, shivering and staring in amazement at the evolving landscape.

With a grunt, La Forge returned to the task of pushing the main generator into a more upright position. But now the sand had coagulated around the buried struts, and the going was tougher than ever. Geordi was weakened already from his efforts, and all he got for his strained muscles was more futility.

A figure suddenly fell in beside him, also pushing and grunting against the tilted generator. With a grinding noise, the platform actually moved, and Geordi peered at his mysterious helper, who was covered with grime.

"Dolores!" he shouted with relief.

"Don't look at me," she said jokingly. "I'm a sight."

With a dumb smile, he gazed at the muscular young geologist, thinking she looked great, even though there was blood on her forehead and scratches all over one side of her body.

"I have a mild concussion, which I deserve," she grumbled. "I figured there would be a little liquefaction in the riverbed, but this whole thing is . . . beyond what I envisioned."

"It sure is!" agreed Geordi, shouting into a gust of wind. "Where's Admiral Nechayev?"

Dolores gulped and glanced over her shoulder at the huddled masses. "She's out there somewhere, but she's hurt badly. They found her a Bolian doctor. I couldn't help her. What was the deal with all those explosions?"

La Forge squinted at the swirling khaki sky. "From where I stood, it looked like an attack—a strafing run with phasers. But I can't say for sure. I'm glad you're here, so you can watch the generators while I take some readings."

"How much time is left?" she asked worriedly. "I mean, before the worst of it is over?"

"I'll try to find out." La Forge opened his tricorder, thinking that it was impossible to guess how much time had passed. With a whole world evolving from primordial ooze right before their eyes, it seemed like eons. But it had probably been only a few minutes.

He checked his tricorder and saw that almost six minutes had passed, which was something of a relief. "We're well past the halfway point."

The engineer turned and surveyed the blooming forest, then he looked helplessly at his tricorder. "These readings don't tell me much—just a lot of numbers that don't make sense. If I didn't have to stay with the generators, I'd like to chuck a rock outside the phase-shifting field to see what happens to it."

"I can do that," replied the geologist with a smile. "You stay here and watch your boxes, and I'll go to the edge."

"Not too close," warned Geordi. "Take a tricorder and don't get any closer to the edge than ten meters. Will that get you close enough?"

Dolores sniffed with pride. "I'll have you know I was regional shot-put champion in college, and I competed in the Martian Olympics, where I finished second."

"It's still dangerous," said Geordi fretfully.

"It's only a rock," said the geologist. "That's funny for a rock hound like me. After the Great Flood, Noah sent a dove to see if it was safe. But we'll have to send a rock."

She stretched her grimy legs and surveyed the sticky riverbed. It was populated by frightened, dirty clumps of Bolians, who were as much in shock as any group of survivors could possibly be. With their vacant, hopeless expressions, they looked like the homeless refugees they were.

"It will probably take me a minute to get there," added Linton, scraping the mud from the sole of a boot. "We'll try combadges, but I don't think they'll work. Just keep me in sight, and I'll wave to you if it's safe." At his worried look, she smiled and tapped the pouch on her belt. "Don't worry, Geordi, I've got my tricorder."

Unexpectedly she kissed him full on the mouth—a kiss that was warm, urgent, and gritty from sand and sweat. Dolores pulled away, grinning, and she was one of the most dashing figures he had ever seen. "Keep dinner warm." she said playfully, "I'll be back."

Geordi nodded forcefully, unable to think of anything else to say. A moment later, Dolores dashed off, her strong legs churning through the mud, and he hurriedly pulled some field glasses from his toolbox. Placing the lenses to his implants, Geordi watched the strong hiker as she wound her way between the masses of people. Here and there, she offered words of encouragement to the survivors, and she also stopped to pick up and inspect several fist-sized rocks.

All too soon, Dolores's distinctive infrared image got muddled with the others, and he lost sight of her. After making a quick inspection of the generators, La Forge went back to watching the riverbed. Although all the land looked wet and new, it was easy to see where the safety net ended and chaos took over. Their circular field was the only land in view that wasn't erupting with freakish new life. In this muddy riverbed, the old life hung on with dogged tenacity.

Another check of the equipment showed a twenty percent drop in power since the last check, and La Forge surveyed the perimeter with added urgency. He finally spotted Linton, crouched at the edge of the sand, facing a huge geyser that spewed brackish water eighty meters into the air. He assumed she had to be getting wet from the spray and wind, but she stayed in place, braving the ungodly elements.

Through his field glasses, La Forge studied the crouched figure as intently as she studied her tricorder. Finally Dolores took a deep breath and squirmed forward on her knees. With a lunge, she hurled the rock straight toward the geyser, and he could finally comprehend her logic. Because the glistening soil around the geyser was the only smooth terrain in sight, except for the riverbed, the rock was still visible. If she had tossed it anywhere else, it would have vanished in the teeming underbrush.

Although he couldn't see the rock any longer, he was certain Dolores could. Several tense seconds passed, and Geordi forced his eyes away from the figure on the periphery to check the generators. The primary generator was now down thirty-seven percent, probably because of the damaged gel packs. It they were going to get a reprieve from this calamity, now would be a good time, Geordi thought.

He heard a cry of joy that pierced through the wind, and he looked up to see Dolores running toward him, waving her hands. "It worked!" she cried. "The rock didn't change! It's all over but the shouting."

"All over?" mumbled survivors doubtfully. It was clear that misshapen plants and squirming animal life were still growing at an accelerated pace, even if the crust of the planet had stopped its upheaval. It didn't look as if anything had changed, and La Forge was hesitant to turn off the generators.

A loud clicking noise sounded, and a humming noise faded out. Geordi hadn't even noticed the hum until it stopped, and he saw immediately that the primary interphase generator had died. Seconds later, the other generator stopped too, making his decision moot. Geordi tensed, waiting for the Genesis Effect to rip through him, turning his body to sludge. But nothing happened. They had won the battle, and their prize was a chaotic, primitive planet that bore no resemblance to the sophisticated, peaceful world they had known.

Overcoming his gloom, he ran toward Dolores, and they hugged each other with tearful relief. The moment of joy ended quickly, when he had to ask, "Where's Admiral Nechayev? Can you take me to her?"

Dolores nodded her head and grabbed his hand, leading the way. They wandered among the Bolians, who peppered them with questions. Geordi found himself repeating over and over, "It's safe to leave the riverbed, but be careful out there. Stay in a group."

"Is it always going to be this chilly and damp?" asked an elderly Bolian.

La Forge shrugged. "I don't know. We'll have to learn about Myrmidon all over again."

A few moments later, they reached a clutch of Bolians and Starfleet officers gathered around a prone figure. The smile erased itself from Geordi's face when he stepped close enough to get a look at the wounded admiral. Much of Nechayev's face and left side were badly burned, and she was unconscious, breathing with a labored rasping sound. Only a few tufts of her reddish gray hair were left on her charred skull.

A Bolian doctor worked steadily on the admiral, but all he had was a first-aid kit. It was clear from the frustrated expression on his face that he wasn't happy with her progress.

"How is she?" demanded La Forge.

The doctor frowned, producing a ripple of double chins under his dour blue face. "If I had a proper medical facility, maybe I could help her. But out here . . . I'm afraid she's dying."

"Doctor!" someone else called, yanking on his shoulder. "You've got to look at my wife! Please!"

The doctor shrugged and rose to his feet. "I'm sorry, but I've done all I can for the admiral. Now I've got to look at the others—"

"Go ahead," Dolores answered with sympathy. She knelt beside the fallen officer and picked up a bloody gauze from the sand.

"All I could do was give her something for the pain," the doctor added apologetically before he was dragged off.

With moist eyes, Dolores looked up at Geordi. "If she dies, you're pretty much in charge of this entire operation."

La Forge wanted to say reassuringly that Alynna Nechayev wasn't going to die, but her gaunt visage gazed up at him, belying those words. He watched helplessly as a light snow fell on the admiral's charred face and cranberry-hued uniform.

# two

La Forge stared helplessly at the injured Admiral Nechayev, wanting to protect her from the downy snowfall. All around him in the dry riverbed on Myrmidon, survivors stirred from their traumas and tried to nurse the wounded and frightened. Geordi continued to stare at the admiral, wanting to dab at her burnt and scarred flesh, when he noticed something remarkable. Where the snow flakes fell on burnt skin, there was a foaming reaction. Nechayev was so deeply drugged that she didn't react, except to breathe a little more deeply.

"Wait here!" Geordi ordered, jumping to his feet. He dashed through the wet sand to the periphery of their protective field, about a hundred meters from the interphase generators. He could tell they had ceased operating, because the jungle of new growth was starting to encroach . . . rapidly. He skirted alongside the vines and bristling greenery, looking for a damp section where the soil was still evolving. Time was running out, because the flora, as bizarre as it was, had already started to stabilize in its new matrix.

He saw a seething hollow where it was still like a swamp, with fist-sized slugs writhing in the ooze. With a grimace, La Forge dug his hands into the primordial soup and came up with two teeming gobs of it, which he swiftly carried back through the crowds.

The refugees stumbled away from him, muttering and gasping, but Geordi delivered his precious cargo to the admiral's side and began smearing it over her burns like a medieval salve. Several Bolians fell back with cries of disgust, but Dolores leaned forward with curiosity.

"It's a good thing the doctor left before he saw this," she remarked. "I'm not sure he'd approve of whatever it is you're doing."

"It's a last resort," answered Geordi, "but still worth a try. This material is still mutagenically active at the moment. It's incredibly fertile, and it promotes new growth. So it ought to promote healing as well."

"Can we do without the leeches?" asked Dolores, wrinkling her pert nose. "Or whatever they are."

Geordi nodded and brushed off all of the squirming slugs, three of them. They should be worried about what these repulsive creatures were going to grow into, but one step at a time. Right now, he needed to save Admiral Nechayev any way he could.

"Geordi!" exclaimed Dolores. "Look!" She pointed down at the admiral's face, where the mutagenic salve was having a dramatic healing effect. Her burnt skin was regenerating with rapid cell growth, no doubt aided by the protomatter in the matrix. Whether there would be disastrous long-term side effects, Geordi didn't know, but the admiral took an untroubled breath and seemed to fall into a deep sleep.

"Now I think I'd better get the doctor," Dolores said, rising to her feet. "He might want to see this . . . for other patients."

"I'm afraid I got to the last genetically active soil," La Forge said sadly, glancing at his tricorder. "The mutagenic effects are wearing off. We got to her just in time."

"What else do we have to learn about this place?" asked Dolores Linton, gazing at the overgrown jungle of snow flurries and mist which surrounded them. "This could be a whole career, just cataloguing what happened to this poor rock."

"You're not thinking about staying here?" asked Geordi in amazement.

She shrugged. "Sure, why not? It's got to be safe. Hasn't the worst already happened? Besides, aren't you curious about this planet? This is a whole new world, waiting to be explored."

The engineer shook his head wearily. "To tell you the truth, I would just like to get back to my ship. Preferably, in this lifetime."

Dolores gave him an impertinent smile. "You're only here because you were ticked off when Leah Brahms went looking for revenge."

La Forge scowled and turned away, unwilling to admit that she was right. "All right, so why are you here?" he demanded.

"Call me old-fashioned, but in an emergency, I would rather be on the ground than in a spaceship. Besides, you looked like you needed someone to look after you."

Geordi couldn't argue with that either, but they both might live to regret their rashness. He wondered whether Leah would regret her decision, too. It was hard to find much solace in revenge. He couldn't imagine how Leah and that crazy Klingon, Maltz, were going to track down and defeat the perpetrators of this war all by themselves. They were like Don Quixote and Sancho Panza, tilting at windmills.

He finally decided that each person had to face the end on his or her own terms. What exactly had he chosen to do by staying behind on Myrmidon? At the time, it had seemed like he was confronting the Genesis Wave head-on. Now it seemed like he was hiding from it.

"You know," Dolores said softly, "we're not leaving this planet unless someone figures out a way to come back and rescue us. It makes sense to plan what we're going to do, in case we stay. I know the Romulans said they would come back to get us, using cloaking devices, but will they? Everyone out there is going to be really busy with the Genesis Wave . . . maybe forever. But here it's come and gone."

"That's a very practical outlook," Geordi said, slumping wearily into the damp sand. "I guess I should stop worrying so much about myself. We're alive, and that's as much as we could expect."

"Besides," said Dolores, sweeping her hand toward the field of demoralized refugees, "we can't leave all of them."

"Did you ever think that it might not be over?" asked La Forge. "That this is only the beginning?"

"Of what?" she asked worriedly.

"Well, someone terraformed this planet for a reason. That means someone plans to come here and use it. Who? And when? Those are the next questions to ask."

Dolores nodded gravely and sat down in the sand beside him. She gripped his hand, and wordlessly their gazes drifted to Admiral Nechayev. The injured woman was sleeping peacefully, aided by the drugs of Starfleet and the massive forces that had ripped apart the planet, and were now healing it.

In the middle of an overgrown hollow that had once been a city, the blue-skinned barber gathered his courage and rose to his feet. Mot and his parents had been sitting near the door of the sanctuary when the conflagration struck, and he had seen most of it through the doorway. He still could not believe even half of what he had witnessed, but he had waited long enough inside this lone building, protected by the interphase generators.

None of the others would move, but they hadn't seen the ground stop quaking and the skies stop churning.

"Come," he told his aged mother and father, helping them to their feet. "It's time to go out and see our new world."

The jam-packed crowd of tens of thousands, plus children and animals, all hushed at once. Crouched in the darkness, they watched to see what this fool would accomplish when he stepped into the obscene terror outside the door.

Mot touched a door handle, and it disintegrated, leaving a fine silt on his fingertips. He pushed the creaking door open, and it fell off its hinges, landing in the thick underbrush with a muffled thud. Ferns and evergreenlike plants grew in abundance, unfurling long pistils and colorful red blooms. Misshapen, twisted trees towered above them, casting cold shadows, and the air reeked of ammonia.

The ground was crawling with wormy and fishy creatures, and Mot forced himself to walk forward. He held his parents tightly, one in each arm, but he had to stop when the brush got too thick and imposing. Mot sneezed as a gust of fog swept through the hollow, and he wished he had a crate of machetes.

"Is it . . . is it really safe?" asked his frightened mother.

Mot shrugged his beefy shoulders. "Safe or not, it's all we've got."

A few hearty survivors followed them out, but they recoiled from the foreboding plant life and squirming slugs. Mot turned and looked back at the golden dome of the sanctuary. It stood amid the chaotic jungle and wispy fog like an alien spaceship that had landed in the wilderness.


Commander Jagron lifted the fluted glass of Saurian brandy to his thin lips and took a sip. His patrician nose flared slightly as the smoky solvent cleansed his throat. The Romulan officer needed the drink after viewing the logs of the disaster at Myrmidon. Despite the happy face Starfleet wished to paint upon their haphazard operation, the planet had clearly been devastated by the force called Genesis.

This was supposed to be a victory celebration, hence the brandy. But no sane person could consider the debacle on Myrmidon to be a victory. Those inhabitants fortunate enough to survive were certainly not fortunate now. They had been reduced to pathetic, homeless refugees—a drain on the Federation.

None of the other commanders in the briefing room on the *Terix* offered an immediate comment either. They quietly sipped their drinks and considered the sobering facts. After it wiped out Earth and a large chunk of the Federation, the Genesis Wave was going to cut a swath through Romulan space. Many of their colonies would suffer the same fate as Myrmidon, Seran, Hakon, and the other planets that had already perished; and there was nothing that could be done to stop it.

"We are trying to save these fools, when we should wipe them out for their carelessness," muttered Commander Horek of the *Livex*. There were nods of agreement from the other three commanders of the task force.

Indignantly, Commander Damarkol added, "How do we tell our people about this? How do we prepare them for such a disaster?"

"Everyone at home must know by now," answered Tomalak grimly. It was upon his warbird they were conferring, and he was senior among them, thanks to his considerable experience with the Federation. "We're the only ones of our people who have seen it first-hand, but a hundred of our finest ships are on their way here."

"They come only to watch more worlds die," grumbled Damarkol, a frown on her leathery face. "Even so, Genesis is an impressive achievement . . . if they could only control it. Technology like that needs a firm hand and tighter security."

"There has been too much secrecy connected with Genesis already," declared Commander Jagron. "What we need is cooperation and more information about it."

Tomalak looked at his young colleague with a wry smile. "If you think you'll get the Genesis secret from the Federation, you're wrong. They lost that knowledge when they lost Dr. Carol Marcus. Even when they had it, they didn't know what they had."

"Are you still going back to Myrmidon to rescue Admiral Nechayev?" asked Jagron.

His host nodded. "Yes. Despite their bungling, the Federation are still the ones who are most likely to find a solution. The survivors on Myrmidon have really seen the wave firsthand, and may have learned something."

"May I offer the *D'Arvuk* to go in your place?" Commander Jagron suggested, taking a sip of his brandy.

The elder Romulan blinked with surprise. "Why, that is most kind of you, Commander, considering the risk. But it was my idea, and I feel indebted to carry it out. Sort of a favor for Captain Picard."

"Why do favors for humans?" asked Horek with a disdainful sniff. "They've been nothing but a curse to us, and this is just more of the same."

"Ah, but the galaxy would be a duller place without them," replied Tomalak. "To be truthful, I don't know if I'm going back to Myrmidon at all, because I haven't gotten an answer on my request. My science officers will have to be satisfied with the long-range scans before I endanger this ship."

"After that, will you rendezvous with the *Enterprise?*" asked Jagron.

"I suppose so. They'll be at the forefront of whatever action is next. I wonder why I haven't received an answer from High Command." Impatiently Commander Tomalak moved toward the burnished conference table and ran his hand over a companel. "Commander to bridge."

"Yes, my liege," a voice answered crisply. "Centurion Londerval at your command."

"Centurion, have we received any dispatches from High Command?"

"Yes, sir, a considerable number of them," came the answer. "Subspace traffic is very high, and the encryption we must use in Federation space is slowing down our processing time."

"I don't want excuses!" barked Tomalak. "Did we receive an answer about returning to Myrmidon?"

"Yes, Commander, but I didn't feel the orders were urgent, since they don't involve us."

Tomalak scowled. "What do you mean, the orders don't involve us?"

"High Command has ordered the *D'Arvuk* to Myrmidon to rescue Admiral Nechayev, and retrieve the interphase generators. We are to await orders."

The gray-haired commander gave a sidelong glance at his young peer, and Jagron shrugged his shoulders, feigning surprise. "They probably want to send the most expendable crew of the four of us."

"I'm sure it wasn't an accident," replied Tomalak pointedly. His dark eyes drilled into the eyes of the taller officer, who blithely looked away. Jagron knew this assignment was the doing of the Proconsul of the Senate, to give him a chance to steal the Genesis technology, if an opportunity presented itself.

"You'd better return to your ship and receive your orders," said Horak.

Jagron carefully set his fluted glass on the table and turned to his host. "May I ask for the criteria your science officers have been using? I'd like to know when it's safe to proceed."

"Of course," Tomalak answered cheerfully. "I'll forward all of our data to your ship. Give my regards to Captain Picard, will you? Tell him to watch his back."

"If he hasn't learned that already, he's not worthy of his reputation," Commander Jagron replied as he strode toward the door.


Feeling frustrated, Captain Picard stepped from the turbolift onto the bridge of the *Enterprise*. He had spent almost an hour in sickbay, where no one would tell him anything about Dr. Crusher and her ill-fated crew. Finally Dr. Haberlee, a resident on the ship for less than six months, had suggested that he leave, saying they would contact him when they had results from their tests. Beverly and the others were out of immediate danger, although their long-term prognosis was still in doubt.

Commander Riker rose from the captain's chair and bounded forward to meet him. "Captain, we looked at the logs of the Myrmidon operation, as you ordered, and we found something unusual."

The first officer led the way toward Data's station, where the android was hard at work, his fingers flying over the membrane keypads. "The *Neptune* didn't go down empty-handed," said Riker.

"What do you mean?" asked Picard.

Data looked up from his readouts. "I cannot account for how this happened, which is troubling. Although all eight members of the temporary crew are accounted for, the log clearly shows that *one* humanoid life-form perished with the ship when it struck the wave."

"Why didn't the transporter room locate this person?" Picard asked, frowning at the implications.

"He was shielded by the warp core containment field," answered Data. "The log only picked him up when the warp core failed."

"Hiding?" asked the captain. "Are we talking about a stowaway?"

"That would be the logical assumption," answered the android, "except that Commander Riker, Dr. Crusher, and I searched the *Neptune* and found no one on board."

"Could he have kept hidden from us?" asked Riker.

The android frowned slightly. "I personally searched the engine room, which is the only place on a ship of that size where he could have remained hidden. The facts would indicate that I was negligent in my duty."

"I doubt that," replied the captain. "Could somebody have beamed aboard the *Neptune* when the crew went over? Or even later?"

"That theory would also fit the facts, except there is no record of any other transporter activity during that time. And none of our crew members are missing." Data cocked his head thoughtfully. "We have had many passengers on board recently, and one of them could have stowed away on the *Enterprise,* waiting for this opportunity."

"That must be it," said Riker.

Data shook his head doubtfully. "To hide successfully on both ships and to conceal transporter use—that would require detailed knowledge of Starfleet procedures and spacecraft. We would be talking about a very sophisticated provocateur."

Captain Picard scowled, not liking any of these explanations, or the questions they raised. "Something happened over on that ship—in the space of a few hours—and we're going to find out what it is. We owe it to Dr. Crusher and the others. I put them into a dangerous situation, and I feel responsible."

Riker cleared his throat and said, "The admiral ordered you to staff that ship."

"Yes, but knowing its history, we should have been more careful."

"A lot was going on at the time—you can't blame yourself." The first officer's defensive posture softened to one of sympathy. "How are they doing?"

"They're comatose, breathing artificially, surrounded by an armed security detail. It seems absurd to keep them under guard, but we're sticking to procedures until I get an explanation." The captain paced toward the command chair and circled thoughtfully behind it.

"We haven't gotten any new orders," said Riker. "Do you want to maintain this position and keep waiting for the Romulans?"

"Yes, I want to assist them when they go to rescue Admiral Nechayev and Commander La Forge."

"If they are still alive," Data added bluntly.

"Yes," admitted Picard quietly. "At any rate, we need to have a firsthand report from Myrmidon."

His combadge beeped, and a deep voice said importantly, "Sickbay to Captain Picard."

"Picard here."

"This is Dr. Haberlee. You'll be happy to know that we found the cause of the illness that's affecting Dr. Crusher and the others. It may explain their actions, too."

Picard glanced at Riker, who gave him a confident nod, as if to say that all would become clear in time. "I'm listening," said the captain.

The young doctor cleared his throat and went on, "We're almost certain that their illness is caused by some kind of fast-growing fungus that's infected their lungs and brains. We have similar fungi on Earth, like the aspergillus niger, which can live inside an old tomb or a cave for thousands of years. Histoplasmosis, valley fever—two more deadly diseases which come from fungi. This fungus is probably airborne, too, and it works fast once it hits the lungs."

Picard nodded thoughtfully. "I've read about aspergillus niger. It was thought to be the cause of King Tut's Curse, which claimed about twenty people when Tutankhamen's tomb was first opened."

"Exactly," Haberlee answered, sounding pleased that the captain understood. "It causes high fever and hallucinations. Maybe that's what killed the original crew of the *Neptune*."

"What happened to their bodies?" asked Riker.

"We're still looking into that, Commander," replied the doctor. "But now that we know what it is, we can proceed with treatment. I expect a full recovery."

"Thank you, Doctor, that's excellent news," said Picard. "I still want to talk to them as soon as possible. Now that you know what it is, maybe you can answer this question: Could those eight officers have been fit enough to fly that ship and mount an attack on the planet, just seconds before we beamed them aboard?"

After a long pause, Haberlee replied hesitantly, "I'm not sure. From what we saw, I'd have to say no, because they couldn't even stand up. But I believe they might have been weakened by the transporter beam, which threw their systems into shock. Mind you, they weren't doing well before, but they might have still been on their feet. A fungal infection can go very suddenly from the symptoms of a mild cold to a raging fever and hallucinations. It would have shut down their lungs, hearts, and brains if we hadn't caught it."

Picard nodded solemnly, trying to piece it all together. There were still gaps in their understanding, but at least two of the questions had been answered. "Are you sure that there's no danger to the crew?"

"Absolutely," answered Haberlee. "We've been keeping on alert both here and in the transporter room, scanning all the time. And we haven't found any airborne particles. The biofilter probably got any off their clothes and skin, but the fungus was too metastasized in their bodies."

Picard glanced at his strapping first officer, who looked as healthy as ever. "Commander Riker went over to that ship on the initial away team, and he didn't come down with this disease."

"There are reasons for that. Dr. Crusher and her crew got a much longer exposure than the first team, and they spent time in every part of the ship. Maybe Commander Riker didn't go where the fungus was active, or was only there a few seconds. It's like all those people who died after entering King Tut's tomb—the first ones in got a stronger dose. Plus people's bodies react differently to a thing like this. It might lie dormant in one person for years, and another person could have immunity, thanks to their genetics. Just to be on the safe side, you should send the commander down here for a checkup."

At that, the smile faded from Will's clean-shaven face, and he frowned at the captain. "I'm on my way." Squaring his shoulders, the first officer marched toward the turbolift.

"Thank you, Dr. Haberlee," Picard said. "I appreciate your quick work on this."

"My pleasure, Captain. But I should ask—we aren't going to be getting a lot of injured refugees, are we? If sickbay gets flooded again, it will be difficult to give them the proper care."

"I think we can avoid that, but I can't promise anything. The fleet is falling back to the next inhabited planet in the path of the wave, but we're staying near Myrmidon. We might have to pick up casualties there."

"Commander Riker is here," the young doctor reported. "I'll keep you informed."

"Thank you. Picard out." The captain turned to Data on the ops console. "Have you had a chance to run long-range scans on Myrmidon?"

"I have, but I have not had time to analyze the data. The computer refused to identify Myrmidon as a recognized planet, so no comparisons were possible. It classified all plant and animal life as 'unknown,' and declared the atmosphere to be highly unstable. It is essentially a class-L planet with class-M characteristics along the equatorial belt. The computer predicted there would be a moderate likelihood of intelligent life on the planet."

"That's what it seems to me," muttered Picard grimly, "a *moderate* likelihood."

For several seconds, Captain Picard stood in the center of his bridge, gazing at the tranquil darkness of space on the main viewscreen. Only it wasn't tranquil at all. In that soothing darkness lurked a monster, devouring everything in its path and leaving behind strange hybrid planets. What was the method behind all of this madness? Despite those who had always wanted to turn it into a weapon, Genesis had never been about destruction. It was always about growth and regeneration.

Perhaps Carol Marcus and her team had been arrogant to think that their vision of a useful planet was the only vision. Even a lifeless rock or dust cloud deserved its unique existence without being destroyed in the name of progress. No matter how one looked at it, the Genesis Effect was about playing God, which was always a dangerous and selfish endeavor.

*Who is playing God with us?* he wondered.

When the comlink chimed, it stirred the captain from his reverie.

"Rikcr to bridge," barked a voice, and Picard instantly recognized the urgency in Riker's tone.

"What is it, Number One?"

"One of Crusher's crew, Ensign Paruk'N, is missing."

"How is that possible?" asked the captain with concern.

"That's a good question, considering that the other seven are still unconscious. When I got here, Dr. Haberlee took me for a tour and showed me his patients. We got to the last bed, and it was empty, with blankets rolled up to look like a person."

"But the security detail—"

"Didn't see a thing. It is hectic down here, and we're hoping the video log will indicate something. Dr. Haberlee is mortified, but he needs to concentrate on his patients. I'll stay here awhile and try to sort it out."

"Good." The captain took a deep breath, fighting the temptation to rush to sickbay himself. What could he do that Riker, Haberlee, and half a dozen security officers couldn't? Faced with the Genesis Wave, they hardly needed this.

"Keep me informed," said the captain, although every time he learned something, he seemed to know less. "We'll try to find him from here. Picard out."

Studying his console, Data shook his head. "Ensign Paruk'N is not on board the *Enterprise.*"

"Go to yellow alert," said the captain grimly.

# three

Leah Brahms twisted and squirmed on the rock-hard slab upon which she was expected to sleep. The crew berths on the *HoS* were like big shelves carved into the bulkhead, and it was hard to believe that even Klingons could sleep on one. Nevertheless, three of her shipmates snored loudly in nearby berths.

As Brahms had learned, on a Klingon vessel the size of the *HoS*, even the captain didn't get a separate stateroom. She slept in the austere crew quarters along with the rest of them. This presented some privacy problems, as did the lack of other amenities on the *HoS*, but Leah was determined to fit in and earn her crew's respect. However, she had claimed an unused laboratory near the transporter room as her private lair; right now she was thinking about making a mattress from rags and hiding it down there.

As she lay on the hard berth, unable to sleep, Leah checked her chronometer. With a start, she realized that it was two hours past the time the Genesis Wave was due to hit Myrmidon. How had they fared? she wondered. Had the phase-shifting protected people on a large scale as effectively as it had protected her alone? If so, there were now millions of people who had the unique displeasure of having lived through the Genesis Wave. Leah took some grim satisfaction from knowing that she and Deanna Troi weren't the only ones anymore.

*Will any of them be driven to revenge the way I am,* she wondered. *Or am I the only one, besides Maltz, who wants an eye for an eye, a tooth for a tooth?*

There was no answer in the dreary bowels of the Klingon attack cruiser, only the chorus of snoring Klingons. Leah realized that she couldn't sleep, at least not here and not now. She rose to her feet and quickly pulled on her blue jumpsuit. She felt odd dressing differently from her crew, but she couldn't really see herself in all that stiff, garish body armor. She wasn't really a captain, except in Maltz's view, and it hardly felt as if they were part of any fleet at all. Leah felt as if she was a renegade, with allegiance to no one; her only possessions were her pain and anger.

Trying not to wake anyone, she stepped lightly from the sleeping quarters and found herself in the narrow corridor.

She chuckled at herself, her voice echoing gently in the corridor. To think that she could find and destroy the ones perpetrating the Genesis Wave, when a task force had failed, was ridiculous. But she shared a common belief with Maltz: This damnable evil had come straight after both of them, trying to crush them as it had crushed everything in their lives. But they had escaped. The enemy's plan was almost perfect, but not quite.

Nature hated perfection, so it had let them live to fight again, Leah decided. At the root, this was a battle between nature and a cold-hearted, artificial substitute for nature. Where nature moved slowly to cut down on risks, Genesis rolled with abandon, destroying the good along with the bad. That the technology had originated with her species was mortifying, but also typical . . . of humans. But they would never have used Genesis in this fashion, even if they knew how. Who would?

As Brahms walked that lonely corridor, she decided that she had to make a profile of the kind of species who would have such desperate needs—and so little regard for life—that they would unleash the Genesis Wave.

Without really knowing where she was headed, Leah rounded a corner and plowed into a hulking Klingon coming from the other direction. She bounced off a barrel chest covered in thick sashes and chain mail, and he grabbed her arm brusquely to keep her on her feet.

"Captain," grumbled the Klingon, not hiding his mirth at her embarrassment. As he let go of her arm, Leah remembered that he was the weapons master, named Gradok. Judging by the number of scars on his rugged face and his noticeable limp, she wondered how good a weapons master he could be, but she didn't say that.

"Master Gradok," she replied, "just ending your shift?"

"No, I was checking the aft phaser arrays," he said, taking a step toward her. "And where might you be headed?"

"I'm familiarizing myself with the ship," answered Brahms, taking a step back. "I should be sleeping, but I . . . just wasn't tired."

The big Klingon smiled, showing gaps in his collection of teeth.

"Our berths are not what you're used to in Starfleet, are they? You like a soft bed with a firm . . . mattress. But I could show you that a hard bunk is better. For many reasons."

When Gradok took another step toward her, Leah realized this could quickly get out of hand. She was alone with this muscular stranger in a deserted part of the ship, and *he* knew every access shaft and air lock. She could run from him, hit her combadge, and call Maltz for help; but that would make her a laughingstock. Once again, Brahms told herself to be as tough as Admiral Nechayev.

She punched him in the chest as hard as she could with the heel of her hand, knocking him back a step. "Keep your distance, Crewman! I'm not on the *HoS* for fun and games—I'm here to fulfill my Blood Oath."

Gradok blinked at her and nodded with surprise. Before he could get his momentum back, Leah spun on her heel and marched quickly toward the turbolift. This time, she was going straight to the bridge, and she wouldn't be taking any more long walks by herself in unfamiliar parts of the ship. She had always heard that being captain of a Klingon vessel was not for the fainthearted.

Brahms strode onto the bridge, where it was overly warm and smoky, but it was still beginning to feel like home. Maltz rose from the elevated command chair and motioned for her to take it, but she shook her head. Making a leisurely inspection of the manned stations—ops, tactical, and conn—Leah strolled to the most distant corner of the bridge. She motioned for the grizzled old Klingon to follow her.

When Maltz caught up with her, Leah was staring out a small triangular viewport, watching the stars streak past at warp speed. "What's the matter, Captain Brahms?" asked the lanky Klingon.

In a low voice, she answered, "Keep your voice down. One of the crew cornered me and tried to get romantic."

Maltz nearly thundered in disapproval, but with considerable effort, he controlled himself and whispered, "Who was it? I'll hang him by his heels over the warp core."

"That's why I'm not going to tell you," answered Leah. "I just wanted to know if I handled it correctly."

"What did you do?"

She told him more or less what she had done, and the old Klingon chuckled. "You handled it like a true daughter of Kahless, because you left him with his honor. And you put the emphasis on our Blood Oath and duty. That is where it should be."

"Then I won't have any more problems?" asked Leah.

Maltz scratched his white stubble and leaned against the bulkhead.

"That's hard to say. Often a female captain on a Klingon vessel will choose a consort from among the crew. But no one would be so presumptuous as to volunteer. This crew member showed a lack of respect."

"Well, they're probably still trying to figure out *why* exactly I'm captain of this ship." Leah shrugged and gazed out the viewport. "I'm still trying to figure it out myself. But I know what we want to do—what we *have* to do."

"And that is why you are the captain," Maltz answered confidently. "I would not have volunteered to be your first officer if you hadn't shown that you could lead and act quickly in an emergency. That's all anyone expects from a captain."

"That's not all," answered Leah. "They expect a captain to act a certain way—especially a Klingon captain. I've been in charge of research stations with dozens of people under me, but that was different. This is life and death, and there can't be any hesitation when it comes to following my orders."

"I will enforce your will," declared the Klingon.

"But as we've seen, you aren't always there." Brahms paced for a moment, thinking that if she had learned anything in this prolonged nightmare, it was that she couldn't depend upon anyone but herself. "My husband, Mikel, was like my first officer, and he spent a lot of time shielding me from things. And now he's not around."

"Did he die bravely?" asked Maltz.

"He died with a look of terror and surprise, not knowing what hit him," answered the engineer. "I've never seen such stark terror."

"And that is why you are here," answered Maltz through clenched teeth. "Because a death like that *must* be avenged. Trust me, this is something our crew can understand. Maybe they're not the best or the brightest in the fleet, but they have seen enough of war to know when it's serious. I'll keep an eye on them, anyway."

She turned her pale-blue eyes on the old Klingon and smiled gratefully. "Thank you, Maltz."

His aged eyes twinkled for a second. "In the meantime, if you would like me to pose as your consort, that might work to keep them in line."

Leah smiled in spite of her dour mood, "Thanks for the offer, but I want to keep it strictly business with everybody. Why don't you let them know that my mate died only a few days ago . . . that I'm still in mourning."

"I will remind them." Maltz's eyes narrowed to bloodshot slits. "Take heart, Captain—there is no cure for grief like revenge. And we're going to get the ones responsible for this, starting with Carol Marcus."

Brahms nodded and turned back to the triangular port with its view of the blurred starscape beyond. She certainly hoped the old Klingon was right, because at the moment all she felt was rage and emptiness. Maltz had a focus for his anger—Marcus, the scientist who had invented Project Genesis, the one who had been kidnapped six months ago. But Leah wasn't sure who to be mad at. That's why she needed a profile of the intelligence behind this monstrous weapon.

She looked around and spotted an unused console, blinking in readiness. "I need to do some work. Can I use this terminal?"

"Use any terminal you like—you're the captain." Maltz snapped to attention. "Do you want to check the efficiency of engineering?"

"No," answered Leah, sitting down at the console. To her lack of surprise, the seat was very hard. "I want to get to know our enemy. What are they like?"

"Despicable! Cowardly! Murderous!" Maltz started to sputter and curse in Klingon, and Brahms cut him off with a wave.

"You're right, of course," she said. "But that's only *our* viewpoint. We hate them, but what do they think of *us?* Nothing. From their actions, they think we're like the worms you crush under your feet as you walk. They don't think we or any part of our planets are worth saving. The Dominion, the Borg, the Cardassians—they all wanted to plunder and steal what we've got. Not this enemy. They don't want a single thing that we have, not even a building to live in once they get here."

Maltz stroked his stubbled chin thoughtfully and said, "They're probably not humanoid."

"Yes," agreed Leah, entering a few shorthand notes on the membrane keypad. "What else do we know?"

"They couldn't do this thing by themselves," answered Maltz, pacing rapidly. "They had to kidnap Carol Marcus and obtain her cooperation."

"They could have been planning it for years. How do you think they found out about Project Genesis, when it was such a big secret?"

Maltz stopped pacing in order to scowl and shake his head. "That could be *my* fault. I can't remember how many strangers I have told about Genesis over a mug or two of ale. I'm a fool—and all of this could be *my* doing."

"It's too late now to blame yourself," said Brahms, working her console. "Although the details were a secret, other people knew about the Genesis Planet and what happened there. All of this tells us something about the enemy. They, or their agents, are able to move among us, collecting information. And they kidnapped Carol Marcus under heavy security."

"Who would cooperate with fiends like this?" growled Maltz.

"Maybe people like you, who didn't know they were cooperating," Leah answered. "You know how the changelings infiltrated the Klingon High Council and Starfleet just before the Dominion War."

"Yes!" said Maltz urgently. "Do you think the Dominion has returned?"

"No, they couldn't have mounted an operation like this so deep in Federation space, and I heard that a changeling from the Alpha Quadrant is running the Dominion now. But that brings up a good question: How did this enemy remain hidden in the middle of the Federation?"

Maltz frowned in thought, then grinned triumphantly. "They're not humanoid, and they don't live on a class-M planet."

"Bingo!" answered Leah, her fingers flying over the keypad. "So we look for a planet like the ones that are being created with the wave. Now we know what that is, class-L, bordering on M."

The Klingon leaned over her shoulder. "Your task force thought the wave originated near an asteroid field, called the Boneyard. That's where they disappeared."

"Okay, so let's avoid the Boneyard for now—we'll look for a planet near there that fits the bill. I know exactly where it is." Her fingers never stopped moving over her console, bringing up star charts. A few seconds later, she cried again, "Bingo!"

"What does this 'bingo' mean?" asked Maltz curiously.

"It means, 'victory.' " Leah looked happy for the first time in a week as she pointed at her screen. "It also means that we have a new destination—a planet called Lomar."

"Helm!" barked Maltz. "Prepare to change course!"

Carol Marcus awoke from her troubled dream and sat up in bed, sweating and feverish. Her white-blond hair was plastered to her square-jawed Nordic face, and her blue eyes stared straight ahead. The dream—about the death of David and the awful destruction of the Genesis Planet—was the first vivid dream she'd had in months. In fact, it had been years since she'd had such a memorable dream. What did that dream mean, after so many months of tranquil bliss? She loved her life—living here on her peaceful island, going to work in the lab with David and Jim. David wasn't really dead—she saw him every day.

Still, the old woman shivered, although it had never been cold in her bedroom before. The temperature had always been just right. Carol pulled her blankets around her slight frame and lay back on her bed, trying not to be troubled by the dream, which had dredged up repressed memories. Although frightening, the dream had also been exhilarating, like an unexpectedly scary adventure. It was the first memory she'd had since returning to her work . . . that Klingons had murdered David over ninety years ago.

*This place and my new life shouldn't exist,* she told herself with awestruck realization. The joy at being reunited with David and Jim Kirk had made her overlook two troubling facts: Both of them were dead.

Carol sneezed violently, and followed it with a ragged cough. It felt like she was coming down with a cold, which might explain her fuzzy brain and grim disposition. She looked around her bedroom, a faithful reproduction of the simple, sunny room she had on Pacifica. The breeze blew through an open window, rustling the white linen curtains. In the back of her mind, the scientist had always known she couldn't be near the planet Pacifica and her Regula I space station at the same time. They were light-years apart and in different time periods—two more facts she had conveniently overlooked.

Her body feeling achy and weak, the old woman forced herself out of bed and to her feet. After casting off her blankets, she shivered as she dressed herself in her usual white scrubs and lab coat. Then she crossed to the door and grabbed the door knob, giving it a turn. Only it wouldn't turn—it was locked.

"What the—!" the old woman exclaimed. She didn't even know this door could lock! And why would it lock from the outside, turning her bedroom into a cell? That made no sense at all!

She tapped the combadge pinned to her lab coat. "Marcus to Marcus. Come in, David."

When there was no reply, she tried, "Marcus to Kirk. Jim, are you there?"

"Yes, of course I'm here," came the familiar voice with its boyish enthusiasm. "What do you need, sweetheart?"

"I need to get out of my bedroom!" she snapped, her voice sounding hoarse and raw. "I'm locked in!"

"I know," answered Jim Kirk, sounding terribly upset and sympathetic. "You don't feel too well today, do you?"

"Well, no," she admitted. "But what's that got to do with me being locked in my bedroom?"

"You're sick. You have an infection, and you've been quarantined. None of us can come into contact with you. Doctor's orders."

"What doctor? I don't remember seeing any doctor." Carol began to pace the confines of her room, growing agitated. She made a dash toward her open window, only to be propelled backward onto her bed by a force field.

"Relax, Carol," Kirk said soothingly. "He examined you while you were asleep and left some medicine for you. Just take it with the food we're transporting into your quarters, and you'll be good as new."

Carol leaped to her feet and sputtered with indignation. "That . . . that's absurd! I want to see my doctor on Pacifica. His name is—"

"No one can see you," said Jim slowly, as if talking to a child. "You're very contagious, and none of the rest of us need to be sick at the moment, not when there's so much work to do. In fact, this is going to be our last conversation for a while. Just take your medicine, eat well, and rest. Soon life will be back to normal. I promise, my love. Good-bye."

"What! Come back! How can you do this to me!" shouted Marcus, dissolving into a coughing fit. She finally had to sit back on the bed, but she continued to cry hoarsely, "Jim! David! Somebody talk to me!"

With frustration and anger, she plucked the combadge from her chest and hurled it across the room, where it skittered into a corner.

Taking a wheezing breath, Carol tried to remain upright, but all the agitation had weakened her, leaving her suddenly feeling all of her 135 years. With a tinkling sound, an elegant serving tray appeared on the nightstand beside her bed. On it was a bowl of her favorite soup, split pea, a large glass of orange juice, and a standard Starfleet hypospray.

With a snarl, Marcus gave the tray an uppercut and sent it spinning; the soup flew across the room and decorated a wall, and the hypospray clattered to the floor. Although a bout of coughing followed this outburst, the moment of insubordination felt good.

An instant later, another tray with the same contents appeared on her nightstand, and Carol wept into her trembling hands. Now she was moving from an unpleasant dream into a brutal and disturbing nightmare. Those people out there *weren't* David and Jim. Her son and his father were dead and had been dead for decades. Whoever—whatever they were—she had told them everything! They knew more about Genesis than *she* did. Worst of all, she had helped them to perfect a beamed delivery system which could span light-years.

"What was I thinking?" she rasped through her ragged tears. "I was their reference manual . . . their source material. This isn't paradise, it's *hell!*"

What everyone had feared would happen for ninety years had finally happened. An unfriendly force had seized her and had plumbed her mind for knowledge of Genesis. Her own guilt and loneliness had only made it easier for them to fool her. Anger welled within the old woman, making her more feverish and nauseated than the unknown disease. What they had done to her was bad enough, but God only knew what they had done to billions of innocent souls!

"It's my fault!" she told herself, weeping. "All my fault!"

Choking back furious sobs, Carol rummaged through the drawer of her nightstand until she found a small pair of cuticle scissors. Her first instinct was to ram the scissors into an artery and take her own worthless life. But that was the cowardly way out. She was sick and disillusioned, but she was no longer confused. The enemy was out there, somewhere beyond that door, and she had to survive long enough to defeat them. Whatever else she had done with her life— whatever opportunities she had squandered or seized—nothing mattered as much as this one moment of clarity.

"It's *not* my fault!" she bellowed hoarsely. "It's them! *Them!*"

Marcus knew that she had to grip reality and hang onto it like a life vest. Chills overwhelmed her, and so did a wracking cough—but the sickness was *good.* Somehow the illness had freed her mind . . . had given her another chance. She would take their medicine, eat their food, and get stronger, while waiting for a chance to get revenge on them. Whoever, or whatever, they were.

With firm resolve, Carol reached toward the tray on her nightstand and seized the hypospray. She lifted the device to her neck, but she paused before administering it. *What if it's the food and medicine that are keeping me under their spell?* she wondered. But that didn't make sense, because she had first seen "David" at her secure compound on Pacifica.

Then she had another worrisome thought: *These beings have exerted extraordinary control over me, and that only stopped because of my illness. What if I get well, and I'm not strong enough to resist their mind control?*

*I have to remember how much I hate them,* came the answer. *I have to remember that David and Jim are dead.*

As a little girl, Marcus had seen her mother use a trick to remember things . . . important things. She put down the hypospray and grabbed the scissors, and she cut a small slit in the hem of her nightgown. Very carefully, Marcus drew a long pink thread from the slit and wrapped it around her left finger. Using her right hand and her teeth, she tied the thread tightly, but not too tightly. Her captors would have no clue what it meant if they saw it, but she would know.

*When I see that thread on my finger, I will remember that my captors are evil . . . and that David and Jim are dead.*

Feeling faint, Carol picked up the hypospray, and she used her last scrap of strength to administer the injection to her neck. Within moments, a grogginess overcame her, and the tightness in her lungs and throat seemed to ease a little. The old woman forced herself to drink half a glass of juice, then she slumped onto her bed. Even though she was obeying their orders, she had to get well in order to resist them.

*I will remember,* she told herself. Carol Marcus gathered the blankets around her frail form and closed her eyes.

*I will remember what they did to me.*

# four

The blue-skinned child smiled as she groomed a human doll's hair, under the watchful eye of Deanna Troi. Although Dezeer had no hair of her own, she seemed to know exactly what to do with it. They were in the counselor's office, having been released from sickbay just before the crew from the *Neptune* were brought in. Troi was anxious to find out what had happened to Beverly and the others, but she also knew that she had to stay away and let the sickbay team do their job. Besides, she had head injuries from which to recover, and she was still feeling groggy, her empathic skills reduced.

She also had a new charge in her life—Dezeer—and she was going to make sure that nothing else happened to the child. Deanna couldn't remember anything about her rescue from Myrmidon, but she knew that Dezeer had saved her life when she led Will Riker to her unconscious body just seconds before the Genesis Wave hit the planet. The counselor considered the young Bolian to be a good-luck charm, and vice-versa. After all, Troi's combadge, pinned on Dezeer by her dying mother, had been the child's own salvation. But how many other children had not been so lucky? Despite their monumental efforts, the death toll had to be in the thousands, maybe millions. They wouldn't know for sure until the Romulans went back, and that might be a grim and pointless journey.

She gave Dezeer a wan smile as she watched her play, although the child's preternatural calm continued to disturb her. Dezeer was about the size of a human eight-year-old, but Troi had quickly discovered that she had the mental development of a five-year-old. She might be an exceptionally large child, even for a Bolian, or she might be suffering from some sort of disability. The girl had spoken very little since losing her parents to suicide and nearly losing her own life on Myrmidon. It had only been a couple of hours, and Troi wasn't going to push her. She had left her alone for short periods, but she wasn't going to let Dezeer be shipped off at the first port with the other evacuees. She considered the child to be her personal responsibility.

Her combadge chirped, and a familar voice said, "Picard to Troi."

"Troi here," she answered, rising from the couch and walking out of earshot of the child. Anything she said in these trying days was liable to be disturbing.

"Dr. Haberlee says that Beverly and the others are out of danger," began the captain. "In fact, he says he can wake her up and let us question her."

"Is that wise?" asked Troi with concern. "She's been very ill."

"If it wasn't for our missing crewman, Ensign Paruk'N, I wouldn't be taking these measures. But we have to find out what happened over there . . . and what might happen here."

"Yes, sir," answered Troi, knowing he was right. "When are they going to awaken her?"

"As soon as possible. I'm on my way to sickbay now."

"Yes, sir." Deanna lowered her voice and said, "I have to leave my patient with a Bolian family, then I'll meet you there."

"Thank you, Counselor. Picard out."

With a sigh at the unpleasantness facing her, Deanna turned back to her young patient. Mustering a smile, she strode toward the girl and leaned over to look at her doll. "I think Miss Barbara is ready for her party. Are you ready to meet some more people?"

The blue-skinned girl shrugged and continued working on the doll. "It doesn't matter . . . my mommy's here."

Troi frowned, her smile fading. "Your mommy is on board the *Enterprise?*"

"I've seen her." Dezeer picked up the doll and carefully put it in a duffel bag Troi had given her, as if she didn't have a care in the world.

Deanna hated dashing the child's illusions, but accepting reality was part of getting well. "Dezeer, your mother isn't on board the *Enterprise.* We picked up very few passengers on Myrmidon."

The blue-skinned being looked with pity at Troi, as if *she* were the one who was delusional. She put her fingers to her lips and made a hissing sound—the traditional sign for a secret. Then the child bounded off her seat and headed out the door, forcing Troi to rush to catch up with her.

At least, thought the counselor, this delusion was giving the child some peace. Dezeer remained calm, if quiet, when Troi dropped her off at the quarters of the Hutamps, a Bolian couple whose own children were grown and living elsewhere. Dezeer didn't say anything to them, but she complied with their wishes. Most important, Deanna was able to leave the child there and head to sickbay, as per the captain's orders. Still she felt guilty about deserting her charge even temporarily.

When Troi reached sickbay, she found Captain Picard, Dr. Haberlee, and Nurse Ogawa conferring in the anteroom. Through the windows, she could see the sick crew members from the *Neptune,* and the security guards hovering over their beds.

"Hello, Counselor," said Picard. "I'm just getting up-to-date on their condition. You were saying, Doctor?"

The young man cleared his throat and looked very serious. "Dr. Crusher is quite weak, but the fungal infection is in remission. Her lungs are clear, and she can breathe on her own. But she's not leaving that bed for a while. The others are in the same condition, a little behind or ahead of her."

"When would she wake up on her own?" asked Troi.

"That's hard to say—in a day, maybe in an hour," replied the doctor. "Since the fungus has infected her brain, we're leery about this comatose state. We would probably bring her out of it, anyway."

Ogawa nodded in agreement. "Yes, it's the right thing to do. I'm sure Dr. Crusher would want to take the risk."

"What risk?" asked Picard, his eyes narrowing.

Dr. Haberlee cocked his head and looked apologetic. "Although we've done lots of scans and don't see any major damage, some things may have escaped us. The fungus entered through the bloodstream, and possibly the nostrils and ears, and we don't know exactly what it's done to her. It could be safer to wait until all trace of the fungus is out of her system, but that could be a few more days."

"There are only four days until the Genesis Wave reaches Earth," said Picard grimly. "The Romulans will arrive any moment to conduct a rescue mission to Myrmidon, and we're their only support. We have to function at peak efficiency, and we can't do that with this illness hanging over our heads. We need answers. Proceed, Doctor."

"Yes, sir," answered Haberlee hoarsely. The young doctor nodded to Ogawa, his beseeching eyes asking the veteran nurse to take over the procedure.

Ogawa led the way toward the row of examination tables in central triage, where all seven patients lay unconscious. An empty bed at the end of the row, plus the presence of a half dozen security guards, reminded Deanna that Beverly's crew was in serious trouble as well as being seriously ill.

Troi thought about all the millions of people—even billions—whose lives and homes were being destroyed as they talked. Yet their attention was riveted upon these seven people, and the eighth who had mysteriously disappeared within the bowels of the *Enterprise*. It was just one more horror in a chain of horrors, which showed no sign of letting up.

Shaking off her fretful reverie, Deanna turned her attention to Ogawa. The efficient medical worker disconnected nourishment tubes while an orderly applied restraints to Beverly's pale limbs. Her good friend looked as wan and ill as she had ever seen anyone, and Troi had to gulp back her conflicted emotions. Part of her wanted to beg the captain to let Beverly heal before she had to be interrogated, but the other part knew that time was their most immediate enemy.

Ogawa took some tricorder readings, checking them with the overhead display. When she was satisfied with the status of her patient, she lifted a hypospray and carefully loaded it with a fresh vial. "Synaptic stimulant ready," she told Haberlee.

The young doctor nodded, looking grateful for having Ogawa at his side. "Go ahead."

The nurse pressed the instrument to Crusher's neck. After delivering the injection, she immediately passed the hypospray to an orderly and took up her tricorder. The security officers pressed forward, as did Deanna, and the captain motioned them back. "Give them some room to work," he said calmly.

Troi returned her attention to the troubled face of Beverly Crusher. Beverly's furrowed brow looked troubled, and she puckered her mouth as if she were tasting something sour. Deanna started forward, disturbed by these involuntary muscle contractions.

"She's not in pain," explained Ogawa to the observers. "This is a typical reaction. Look, her limbs are moving, too."

They all glanced down to see her arms struggling weakly against the restraints, and she moaned softly as if coming out of a dream. "If she falls into normal sleep," Dr. Haberlee said, "I won't use another stimulant to wake her up. Even in a semiconscious state, she may be able to answer your questions."

"Mmmm," said Beverly, her tongue darting over her lips, her eyelids fluttering. "Need to stop them . . . the attack . . . target their bases." Her voice was a croak, barely audible, but her instinctive struggle against her bindings grew more intense.

Captain Picard leaned over the doctor and gently brushed the hair from her right temple. "Beverly, what do you see down there? Why are you firing at the planet of Myrmidon?"

"The Dominion," she answered hoarsely. "We've seen them. Starfleet told us . . . to watch . . ." Crusher shook her head and seemed to run out of energy as she slumped back onto the table. Deanna Troi let out a nervous breath, hoping she was okay. She wanted Beverly to be allowed to rest, but she doubted if that would be the case.

"Vital signs unchanged except for brain activity," said Ogawa, monitoring the readouts carefully.

Without warning, Crusher's eyes popped open, and she stared wide-eyed at her companions, seeming to recognize them for the first time. "Wesley? Is Wesley okay?"

"Your son?" asked Deanna uncertainly. "Wesley's not here, but you're safe, Beverly. You're back on the *Enterprise*."

Crusher screwed her eyes shut and wept quietly. "But he was on the ship with us. I *saw* him." She struggled involuntarily against the straps on her wrists.

"Can't we take her restraints off?" asked Captain Picard.

"Certainly." Dr. Haberlee loosened the restraints, and Beverly finally relaxed, letting her body sink into the bedding.

"Wesley?" she asked again. "Is he okay?"

"I'm sure that Wesley is just fine," said the captain soothingly. "He's . . . not here now, though."

Crusher nodded, and her eyes closed as she seemed to drift off to sleep. "Yes, he's gone . . . I can tell he's gone."

After a moment, Nurse Ogawa reported, "She's asleep."

"I don't think Wesley would have told her to attack her own shipmates," said Troi. "For whatever reason."

"I don't believe Wesley was ever on that ship," answered Picard. "It must have been part of her hallucinations—along with the Dominion and everything else she mentioned. Has she talked about him lately?"

Troi nodded. "We talked about him just a few days ago, as we often do. She misses him a lot, and the strain of their separation—without any word at all—is beginning to show. But I didn't think it was serious. In fact, it's normal."

"Not anymore," muttered the captain. "The question is, what if these aren't delusions?"

"If her crew thought the Dominion was down there, wouldn't they have contacted us?" asked Troi.

"Perhaps they were all having delusions . . . some kind of mass hysteria," answered Dr. Haberlee. "Maybe they didn't know *we* were here."

Silence followed, as everyone in the room considered the possibilities, all of them troubling. The captain's combadge sounded, and a familiar voice broke in, "Riker to Picard."

"Yes, Number One."

"We've been contacted by the Romulans, who should arrive in about fifteen minutes."

"Give my regards to Captain Tomalak," answered Picard absently, his attention still on Beverly Crusher.

"It's not the *Terix* but the *D'Arvuk* that's coming," answered Riker. "We'll be dealing with Commander Jagron. He was the young one, as I recall."

Now the captain frowned and looked away from the sleeping woman. "Yes, that's right. I hope nothing has happened to Tomalak."

"This is a dangerous mission," conceded Riker. "They sent their youngest—let's hope he's their best."

"Alert me when they're in transporter range," said the captain, his gaze returning to Beverly. "I'd like to be left alone until then. Picard out."

Dr. Haberlee looked as if he had been thinking hard during their conversation. "I'd like to run more tests before I bring any more of them around. I don't think you're going to get much more information than you've already gotten."

"Do you think she has further brain damage?" asked the captain.

"I don't think so." Haberlee turned to Ogawa, who was busy checking her tricorder. "Did you catch anything, Nurse?"

"We have a lot of data to analyze," the sickbay veteran answered, "but I don't see anything offhand. It's natural for her to be disoriented. In truth, she's doing as well as can be expected, and I hope to have her up and eating very soon."

"I hope so," said the captain. "If any of them should wake up and want to talk about what happened, make a log of it, and notify me as soon as possible."

"Yes, sir," answered Dr. Haberlee, still massaging his sore neck. "Just to be on the safe side, we'll get started on making a vaccine for the fungus."

"Make it so," ordered Picard.

"I'll stay for a bit." Troi gave her captain a look of confidence she didn't entirely feel.

"What do *you* sense?" he asked, looking pointedly at his half-Betazoid counselor.

The question shouldn't have surprised her, but Deanna appeared stunned for a moment as she considered her answer. The truth was, she didn't have an answer. It was as if her empathic skills were clouded.

"I haven't sensed anything yet," she said with puzzlement. "Maybe my senses are overloaded . . . with all the death, uprooted families, and misery."

"Don't forget your head injury," Dr. Haberlee added . "You probably are a bit foggy. You really ought to take the spare bed on the end."

"No, thank you," answered Troi. She shivered, thinking that she *did* sense an emotion, one which had been prevalent lately: fear. Only she wasn't sure if the fear emanated more from those around her—or herself.

"Keep me posted." Captain Picard lowered his head and strode toward the door. From the stiff angle of his shoulders, Deanna could tell he was tense, and she could think of no way to console him. At this point, giving him the merest word of encouragement seemed like offering false hope.

Captain Picard stood in Beverly Crusher's quarters, scrutinizing the tasteful surroundings. In her choice of furnishings, Beverly revealed a romanticism that she didn't show in her everyday demeanor. There was the delicate oil lantern on the antique desk and the embroidered pillows on the settee, arranged just so. He noticed gifts he had given her, a Regulan horned beetle encased in amber and a collection of nested dolls from Ogus II. It was the kind of room that showed its owner to be meticulous yet sentimental and playful—a person like Beverly Crusher.

Normally he wouldn't have taken the liberty of letting himself inside a crew member's private quarters, even one he had visited many times; but this was an exceptional case. Beverly was facing a court-martial, demotion, or worse for her actions, unless they could come up with a justifiable explanation. Picard wasn't sure what he could possibly find in her quarters to exonerate her, but he was determined to spend a few minutes looking.

The captain paused at her vanity to view three holographic photos he had seen many times before. One featured Jack Crusher on a fishing trip, grinning and holding up a freshly caught trout. Beverly's husband had been his best friend, and Jack's death was still a painful wound after twenty years.

As a third wheel to the Crushers, Picard had spent so many years hiding his feelings for Beverly that he still couldn't quite bring himself to admit them. If she had only met him before she met Jack, how different their lives might have been.

The second photo was of Wesley, looking impossibly young and fresh-faced. Of course, there were no recent photos of him, and he had to be a man by now, with the glow of innocence gone. Picard shook his head, thinking that Beverly must have been in agony for years now, wondering if her only child was safe. They hadn't been callous about Wesley's absence, but they hadn't given her much solace either.

The third photo showed Beverly snuggling on a couch with Jack, while cuddling Wesley in her lap. The boy was little more than a toddler. Beverly looked achingly beautiful and deliriously happy in the photo, which only produced a deeper pang in the captain's heart. There was much to be said for devoting one's life to serving others, but delirious happiness wasn't usually the result. With planet after planet falling to the Genesis Wave—and Earth in the direct path—all of their sacrifices felt oddly hollow. Instead of a family to protect, he had the *Enterprise*. The ship was important, but somehow it didn't seem as important as the happy grin on Beverly's face in that photo.

Would anything ever make her that happy again?

"Captain?" said a voice. Startled, Picard whirled around, almost expecting to see one of the ghosts from the photos, but instead he saw Data, standing in the doorway. The android looked curiously at him, having never quite understood the tendency of humans to daydream.

"Yes, Data," said Picard. "Is something wrong?"

"No, sir," answered Data. "You asked to be left alone until the Romulans arrived, and they have arrived."

"Yes, of course," said the captain apologetically. "What is our status?"

"Commander Jagron is transporting over to meet with you, and Commander Riker suggested I accompany you to the transporter room." The android glanced around the tasteful stateroom. "Have you discovered any cause for Dr. Crusher's actions?"

"Perhaps." Picard looked wistfully at the photo of Beverly, Jack, and Wesley in happier days. Tugging on his tunic, the captain shook off his nostalgia and said, "Shall we go?"

"Yes, sir."

Walking in silence, the captain followed his second officer to Transporter Room Two, where Chief Rhofistan remained on duty.

"Hello, Captain," the dour Andorian said. "Coordinates for Commander Jagron have been laid in."

Picard nodded. "Energize."

Two swirling columns materialized on the transporter platform and swiftly coalesced into two slim Romulans, the young commander

Picard had met earlier and a statuesque female. With grace typical of their race, the visitors stepped down from the platform to greet their hosts.

"Captain Picard," said Jagron with a stiff bow. "I am pleased to meet you again."

"You, too, Commander. This is my second officer, Data."

Jagron raised a curious eyebrow. "Yes, the android—how interesting. This is Lieutenant Petroliv, my intelligence officer."

Petroliv smiled charmingly at Picard. "I'll need to go to your bridge and check your sensor readings, to see if they correspond with ours. We don't want to return to Myrmidon prematurely."

"No, we don't," agreed Picard. "Commander Data can take you to the bridge."

The android gave the attractive Romulan a cockeyed smile, while Picard turned his attention to the young commander. "I hope that your presence here doesn't mean that some problem has befallen Commander Tomalak and the *Terix*," said Picard.

Jagron looked mildly annoyed, but he answered, "Both were fine when I last saw them. Commander Tomalak is a hero to us, something like yourself, and his presence was needed closer to home."

"I can understand that," answered Picard. "We are having our own problems—with a fungal disease that's infected several members of our crew."

Petroliv looked alarmed. "Is it under control?"

"It's confined to sickbay, but I'd like to keep contact between our crews to a minimum. There's no reason to share crew, is there?"

"That depends," answered Jagron. "I had hoped that *you* would join us for this expedition. We don't know what to expect, so we should have an observer from the Federation on board . . . someone who can make decisions on the Federation's behalf. For example, suppose we could save only a few hundred survivors? Who should they be?"

With a thoughtful nod, the captain considered the request, seeing the logic in it. If Admiral Nechayev and the others were dead, Starfleet would want his confirmation. He preferred to stay close to Beverly, but he was almost too close. Even if she and her crew recovered fully, he might never find out what possessed them to act as they had, except for the vague effects of a fungus.

"I'll return with you to Myrmidon," promised Captain Picard. "When do we go?"

"As soon as we get the sensor readings and have time to study them," the hawk-faced Romulan answered.

Captain Picard had a sudden inspiration, and he motioned to the android at his side. "I'd like to bring Data with me. He's very useful in places that may be dangerous for biological beings."

Jagron's eyes narrowed as if he didn't like the idea, but he still bowed and said, "If you wish. I shall return to my ship, while Lieutenant Petroliv consults your sensor readings on the bridge."

"Thank you, Commander," said the captain sincerely. "Your help in this dire situation is more than we could possibly expect."

"More than you deserve," the Romulan replied with equal sincerity.

# five

Geordi La Forge sat on a large red boulder—at least it looked and felt like a boulder—and watched Dolores Linton weave a crude net from vines she had collected. There was no shortage of raw material on Myrmidon, but it was all extremely raw: gruesome mires, overgrown thickets, mammoth trees covered in grayish moss, slimy pools, and pulsing geysers. They were only about two hundred meters from their base at the riverbed, but it seemed as if they were two hundred kilometers from another living soul. A foul mist, which wreaked of ammonia and sulfur, hung over the dense forest, and Geordi shivered from the chill, even in his expedition jacket.

Dolores, meanwhile, was in her element in this forest primeval. Most of the survivors were sitting around in a stupor back at the riverbed, unable to grasp the horrible metamorphosis of their world. But in the last few hours, Dolores had gathered driftwood and debris from the unaffected part of the riverbed, explored the woods, and hacked her way through a mass of vines with an improvised knife. Now she was patiently weaving her vine cuttings into a net, for what purpose Geordi had yet to fathom.

"Will you ever tell me what you're going to do with that?" he asked. "You're not making a tree house, are you?"

"I'll show you in just a minute," she answered playfully. "Are you ever going to get off that rock?"

Geordi shook his head. "No. I feel safe up here—and unsafe when I'm walking around down there."

"The ground is okay, if you look out for sinkholes and quicksand." As Dolores talked, her strong fingers continued to ply the thick strands.

Something which looked like a large newt slithered up to her boot, and she shook it off without even glancing away from her work.

Geordi shivered again and looked around at their gloomy surroundings. The tall trees, which were shrouded in hanging moss, blocked out all but a minimal amount of sunlight. Nevertheless, the misshapen thorn bushes and treacherous vines continued to sprout like weeds without direct sunlight. Despite the incredible growth, the new planet was eerily quiet; Geordi could hear the vines scraping together as Dolores worked them with her hands.

He was reminded of the aftermath of a hurricane, an avalanche, or some other great disasters he had seen on away missions. Only in those cases, there were usually a few birds left to chitter and chirp in the rubble. On Myrmidon, there was no rubble, and no birds left to disrupt the silence.

He looked up to see the geologist tying a fist-sized rock to one corner of the net, but he knew better than to ask her why. Her forearm muscles bulged as she pulled the knots tight. He did feel guilty for not pitching in more, but he couldn't shake off his gloom. Leah had been right—this wasn't the kind of place anyone would want to live. To rebuild, the Bolians would have to be awfully determined. The worst had happened, but there was no sign of any relief. They could be in survival mode for years to come.

His thoughts returned to Leah, the real root of his misery. She was gone again from his life—just like that—and he hadn't even put up a fight to keep her. Instead, he had guaranteed they would remain apart by sticking himself on Myrmidon. All for spite.

"There!" exclaimed Dolores, jarring him out of his gloomy reverie. He looked up to see her tugging on the center of her net, testing its strength. There were now rocks tied to two corners of the net; stretched out, it was about three meters by two meters.

"That ought to work," she said with satisfaction.

"Are you going to tell me what you're doing?" asked Geordi.

"Oh, you're going to get a close look, because you're going to help me."

"I am?" he replied in a scratchy voice.

She nodded sweetly and batted her eyelashes. Grumbling, Geordi climbed down from the safety of his red rock and stepped gingerly over the mushy ground to her side.

"There's a good one," said Dolores, striding to the slippery edge of a brackish pool. Scum floated on top of the black water, and life-forms teemed under it, producing ominous ripples on the surface.

Geordi grimaced in disgust, then his implants widened with alarm. "Wait a minute! You aren't thinking about using that net in *there*. I'm an engineer, not a fisherman."

"That's too bad, because at the moment, we've got an opening for a fisherman but none for a warp-core engineer." Although Dolores said it in a kidding tone, there was the backbone of truth in her words. With a sigh, Geordi picked up one corner of the net. "Okay, what do I do?"

"Just a second." Dolores drew her improvised knife and chopped a path all around the teeming pool. "There, now we have room to maneuver."

She had left loops of vine on the upper corners of the net, to be used as handles, and she handed one of them to Geordi. "Just drag it along your side of the bank, and I'll go along my side. We'll see what we end up with."

Geordi moved slowly, aping her movements as much as he could. As soon as he got close to the edge of the pool, he sank into mud up to his ankles. Dolores did too, but she somehow kept moving, doing a sort of shuffle through the muck. They finally got close enough to the pond to lower the weighted end of the net into the murky water, which smelled like a combination of tar and dead fish. The rocks dragged the net down quickly.

"Go slowly," ordered Dolores.

Geordi nodded, and once again, he mimicked her as he carefully dragged the net along the bank. About halfway across the small pool, the net got heavy and hard to pull, while the water churned with unseen life. Dolores grabbed her handle with both hands and told him, "Keep pulling, we're almost done!"

Slipping and sliding, getting covered with stuff that looked and smelled like sewage, Geordi tried to match her stride. He was only a few paces behind her when they finally got to the end of the pond. Dolores immediately began pulling her catch out of the water, and he strained with all his might to get his end out. As they pulled, a gruesome collection of flopping, wriggling creatures spilled onto the bank, and La Forge nearly gagged at the sight of them. There were tentacled white slugs, squirming lampreylike fish with toothy suckers, and things which looked like newts and tadpoles. Some of them were a half meter long, and a few were misshapen and half-formed, as if they were unsuccessful mutations.

His mind off his work, Geordi slipped in the mud, and his feet flew out from under him, landing in the squirming mass of life. He yelled as the creatures latched onto his legs and curled around his ankles.

Within seconds, Geordi felt strong hands reach under his armpits, dragging him from the wriggling morass. He gripped Dolores desperately, and she made a quick decision. "Get your boots and pants off!" she ordered.

La Forge didn't wait to be told twice, because many of the gruesome creatures still clung to his legs. With Dolores's help, he finally squirmed out of his pants, and she held the infested clothing at arm's length. With powerful strides, she walked back to his red boulder and beat the pants on the rock until the life-forms went flying. With her bare hands, she carefully wiped off the crushed tentacles and teeth.

Geordi felt light-headed and probably would have fainted, except that he was freezing to death. His bare knees knocked together as he tried unsuccessfully to cover his thighs with his jacket.

"Nice legs," said Dolores with a smile. She tossed him his pants.

Even though he was cold, Geordi hesitated before putting on the filthy pants. Instead he looked at the mass of life writhing in the mud, grimaced, and asked, "Please don't tell me you're going to eat those."

"Well, I'm going to cook them first," she answered. "That's why I gathered firewood. But I might try them raw, too. Who knows? Someday these things may be considered a great delicacy."

Geordi laughed out loud at the absurdity of it all. "I wonder what kind of wine goes best with them."

Dolores started giggling, too. Geordi figured the sight of a freezing man in the wilderness with no pants, cackling insanely, *was* funny.

After their laughter died down, La Forge caught Dolores admiring his legs again, he quickly pulled his pants back on, trying to ignore the glaze of slime all over them.

She gave him a smile and looked off into the woods. "I have a feeling that food won't be a problem, but it's going to get damp and cold at night. We can heat rocks with our phasers for warmth, but that's only temporary. We need to think about permanent shelter. We might have to phaser down a few of these big trees and hollow them out."

The engineer grabbed his boots and walked gingerly to the red boulder, where he found a dry spot to sit. He sighed and gazed up at the moss-covered trees. "I knew we might have to stay here for a while—without help—but I never thought about what it would be like. There won't be any quick rescue, because every ship in the Federation is occupied."

Nodding her head, Dolores sat down beside him. "This is really Genesis all right—it's like Adam and Eve."

"Except this isn't exactly paradise," replied Geordi as he poured rancid water from one of his boots.

She looked frankly at him with wide brown eyes. "It could be."

Geordi didn't feel very romantic, but anyone who had just saved his life deserved a kiss. Their mud-splattered faces came close together, and their lips met in a tentative kiss that probed for some kind of meaning in this madness. Finally Geordi gave in and let himself be swept away by her passion and vitality.

When their lips finally parted, he gulped and said hoarsely, "Yes, let's think about getting some shelter."

"What can we use?" Dolores rose to her feet and surveyed the dark canopy hanging over their heads. "There is a ton of that moss . . . mistletoe, or whatever it is. I wonder if we could press it into building blocks."

With his superior hearing, La Forge caught voices in the forest— angry voices, coming closer. "There's somebody headed our way," he said, jumping to his feet.

Dolores grinned. "It's a good thing you got your pants back on."

"Commander La Forge!" came a shout. "Where are you?"

"Over here!" he called. They kept shouting at one another until a search party of about a dozen people staggered into view. Geordi recognized the Bolian doctor and one or two others who were local dignitaries.

"Has something happened?" he yelled. "Is the admiral okay?"

"She's recovering," answered the doctor, panting heavily as he made his way toward them. "We just had to talk to you. What are you doing way out here?"

"Take a look!" said Dolores, pointing proudly at her pile of wriggling food.

"Oh, my!" the doctor exclaimed, with a grimace of disgust. Several members of his entourage looked away, their blue faces turning a mottled shade of purple.

"This is what I have to talk to you about," the doctor grumbled. "We can't stay out here, living like animals. We want to go to the neighboring village of Quonloa."

"Uh, there's no village left," replied Geordi.

"We know that," said the doctor testily. "But they put the interphase generators inside the sanctuary, so the sanctuary is still standing. At least they have a roof over their heads."

"But there's likely to be sixty thousand people crammed inside one of those places," Dolores countered. "We can *build* shelters, if we just fell a few of these big trees and collect some moss—"

"You do that, and you eat these disgusting animals, if you want. We're not going to." There were grumbles of agreement to the doctor's words, and he went on, "A lot of us feel that things must have gone better at the sanctuary . . . in the village."

"Things went fine in the riverbed," said La Forge defensively.

"You call losing ninety-three people doing fine?" snapped the doctor. "We've got nothing in this place—it's a hopeless wilderness."

"The whole planet is like this, or worse," Dolores said.

"We're going to the village!" shouted a woman in the crowd. "You can't stop us!"

"I won't stop you," Geordi said, with resignation. "I'd advise against it, because we don't know what's between here and there. I don't think you're going to find a lot of shelter."

"Anything has got to be better than this," the doctor muttered, to more shouts of agreement. "Do you want to come with us?"

"We can't," La Forge answered, "because this is where Starfleet is coming to look for us."

The woman cackled derisively. "Do you think Starfleet is coming back for you? They're too busy trying to save Earth and everywhere else. We're on our own."

"More reason to stick together," Dolores said, softly.

"Which way is the village?" demanded the doctor, cutting to the point of their visit.

Geordi took his tricorder from his belt and consulted it. "Almost due east from here, about twelve kilometers. If you backtrack to the riverbed, you'll have to go a bit northeast."

"Can we have that tricorder?" the doctor insisted.

"No, I need it." La Forge rose to his tiptoes on the red boulder, peering east and looking for a landmark that could guide them.

"Do you see that big geyser out there?" Geordi asked, pointing to a plume of steam rising over the treetops. "That's due east from here. Once you get there, I'd say you're close."

The doctor scowled. "All right. You won't change your minds?"

"No, but if you meet up with anyone, try to use the combadges, or send a runner back to tell us. Let's try to keep in contact."

"All right," agreed the doctor, his belligerence softening. "I know you told us this would happen, but . . . seeing the destruction . . . it's mind-boggling."

"I know," said Geordi. "I'm sorry. Good luck to you."

Chatting among themselves, the party turned and trudged back through the jungle the way they had come. Geordi and Dolores sadly watched them go.

"Now it really does seem like Adam and Eve," said Dolores. "Only this must be after they got kicked out of paradise."

The engineer nodded solemnly, feeling as if he should have done more to hold them together. But what could he offer them, besides slugs to eat? If Admiral Nechayev were well, maybe she could inspire them to stick together. But probably not. They were determined to see for themselves what was beyond the horizon, even if logic said it was the same foreboding wilderness as this.

"We'd better get back," said Geordi. "Let's fill up the net with as many of these slugs as we can carry."

Dolores mustered a wan smile. "We need to find a better name for them if we're going to convince people to eat them."

"Why don't we call them 'hot-fudge sundaes'?" asked Geordi.

"Works for me," Dolores said, with a laugh. "Before we leave, I want to check the depth of this pond."

She lowered one of the rocks to the bottom of the pond, noting how far the net extended into the water. Geordi watched absently as she took the measurement, and he noted how the water had gotten clearer now that most of the life-forms had been removed, allowing the sediment to settle. The water acted like a prism to distort the portion of the vines that were underwater.

*Water bends light waves,* he thought to himself. *Waves can be bent.* He suddenly remembered the testing back on the *Enterprise* before they had deployed the interphase generators on Myrmidon. He could never get the protomatter beam lined up with the target, because the protective force field kept bending it. He finally had to turn the force field off to complete the test.

He muttered aloud, "If the protomatter beam can be bent, maybe the Genesis Wave can be bent and redirected. If it passes through a convexo-concave lens, it can even be narrowed!"

"Pardon me?" asked Dolores.

He jumped up, grabbed the geologist, and kissed her excitedly on the mouth. "I think I know how to stop it!"

"What?" she asked, still in a daze from the kiss.

"I know how to stop the wave!" he exclaimed. "We've got to get back to the ship!"

"Geordi—"

He pounded his palms on his forehead. "I can't believe I didn't see this before! But there was so much going on, and we were committed to the phase-shifting. I've got to see if the subspace radio works!"

He jumped off the rock and landed in knee-high mud. After a few seconds of lurching helplessly in the muck, Dolores had to reach down to pull him back to safety. "Nobody rushes on this planet, Geordi. Just slow down, take your time."

"No, we haven't got any time!" he shouted. "I've got to get back. Right now!"

She gave him a wistful smile. "So much for paradise."

# six

Will Riker scowled and considered doing something he hated to do—
argue with Captain Picard. He had long ago given up the notion of fulfilling one of a first officer's primary duties, that of keeping the captain
on the ship and out of danger. But even Riker had limits. Since they
were in the privacy of Picard's ready room, the commander plowed
ahead.

"Captain, I've got to disagree with your decision," he began, rising
to his full height and looking down at the smaller man. "Even if you
ignore the danger, which I can't, our command staff is already deci-
mated with La Forge gone and Crusher out of commission. With you
and Data gone, we'll really be shorthanded on the bridge."

"You'll have to press Troi into service for your relief," the captain
said evenly as he stepped behind his desk. "I'm sorry about this, but I
don't expect Data and I will be gone for very long."

"There's a good chance you'll never come back," the first officer
said, with exasperation. "Do you remember what the residue of that
wave did to our torpedo module?"

The captain sat down and studied his computer terminal. "We
weren't in a cloaked ship with phase-shifting. I'll admit, there's danger, but Commander Jagron is right when he says that someone from
the Federation should go along. I'm a logical choice, and so is Data.
I'll note your objections in my log, Commander, but this discussion is
over."

Riker heaved a sigh and put the brakes on a half dozen other good
arguments. That was the prerogative of being the captain—*you*
decided when the discussion was over, and who won. Besides, he
wasn't sure he could even bring up the point that bothered him most—

he was worried about Deanna taking over the bridge. She had gone through hell both on Myrmidon and Persephone V, getting a head injury in the bargain. If the situation weren't desperate, she would be recovering in sickbay.

These words passed through his mind, but he said instead, "If you'll excuse me, sir, I think I'd better take a dinner break before you go. I'll alert Troi to come to the bridge."

"Very well, Number One." The captain looked up and gave his first officer a sympathetic smile. "You know, I've appreciated the freedom I've had to leave the ship—a luxury many captains in Starfleet don't have. It's all because of you, knowing the ship is in such excellent hands."

Riker's scowl lightened a bit. "Fleet scuttlebutt has it that you're going to take over the whole evacuation if Admiral Nechayev doesn't make it. Is that true?"

Now it was Picard's turn to scowl. "I'm afraid so. That's why I'm personally going to bring her back. Get some dinner and as much rest as you can, Number One. That's an order."

"Yes, sir." The tall first officer strode from the ready room onto the bridge. "Data," he said as he passed by the android's station, "do you have any idea when you and the captain will be leaving?"

Data checked his screen. "The Romulans have indicated that they wish to leave at nineteen-hundred hours, providing they are satisfied with the latest sensor readings."

"Then I have about forty minutes for a meal break," said the first officer. "You have the bridge. I'll send Troi up here in case you leave sooner than that."

"Yes, sir."

As he strode toward the turbolift, the commander tapped his combadge. "Riker to Troi."

"Troi here," said the counselor. "Did I forget a date for dinner?"

"No," Riker answered with a smile as he stepped into the turbolift. "Computer, deck eight."

After the doors snapped shut, he went on, "The captain and Data are leaving the ship to return with the Romulans to Myrmidon. I'm not thrilled with this decision, but—"

"You were overruled."

Riker sighed. "Let's just say, you are now my only relief on the bridge. I'm taking a dinner break, so report there as soon as possible."

"Yes, sir. There's not much going on here in sickbay, anyway."

"How is Beverly?"

"Sleeping peacefully," answered Troi. "They say she's getting better, but I don't see any change in her condition. None of the others have regained consciousness, but they're talking about bringing them around."

"That investigation is going to have to be put on the back burner for a while," the first officer grumbled. The turbolift came to a gentle stop, the doors opened, and he stepped briskly into the corridor.

"I would like to spend some more time with Dezeer," said Troi.

"After the captain and Data leave, I'll take over for you." Riker passed a crewman who was stopped in the corridor, studying a map of the ship on the public display. The ensign glanced at the commander, giving him a blank look, then he turned back to the display. If Riker hadn't already been involved in a conversation, he would have offered to help the man, but he kept walking.

"I'll let the Hutamps know they have to keep Dezeer for a little while longer," said Troi.

"I hope they're getting along." Riker stopped at the doorway to his quarters and placed his hand on the wall panel, which instantly read his palm print and opened the door. "I'd better let you go," he said. "Just alert me when the captain and Data are ready to leave."

"Eat something healthy. Troi out."

With that admonition in mind, he headed toward the replicator, walking past his trombone, music stand, and old record player. Riker rubbed his eyes for a moment, deciding what to order. "Computer, give me a large bowl of Chinese stir-fried vegetables over brown rice, easy on the soy sauce."

A steaming bowl of food appeared in the receptacle, and he took it and placed it on his dining table. Then he returned to the replicator and added, "Green tea, iced."

After that, all he needed were chopsticks, a napkin, and some reading material. For that, he picked up a padd containing a report on the just-completed repairs to the forward torpedo module. He ordered up some Benny Goodman instrumentals for background music and sat down to his dinner.

Riker was about halfway through his reading and his Chinese food when his door chimed. He quickly wiped his mouth and gulped down a mouthful of food before he replied, "Come in."

The door slid open, and a shapely figure entered. It took him a moment to focus his eyes and realize it was Deanna. He leaped to his feet, a smile on his face. "What are you doing here?"

"I contacted the bridge, and they're not leaving right away." She walked toward the table, sniffing the air. "Mmmm, that smells wonderful." But it wasn't the food she was looking at with hungry eyes, it was *him.*

She lifted her hand to stroke his clean-shaven jaw, as she gazed longingly into his eyes. "Oh, Imzadi, you mean so much to me. Why can't we ever fit in some time for ourselves? Why can't we get away and forget about everything else?"

"I'd whisk you right away," he replied in a husky voice, "if Earth and half the Federation weren't about to disappear."

"Well, just a minute or two won't make any difference," she whispered, her lips drawing closer to his.

He suddenly noticed something odd about her forehead—the bruise from her injury was gone. Before he could think any more about that, her lips clamped onto his. Her kiss, which was always wonderful, tasted extraordinarily delicious.

Riker was so engulfed by her kiss that he surrendered completely, and he didn't even know when he lost consciousness and slumped to the deck. He never realized that the creature he had kissed was not even remotely humanoid. With a shudder, the being pulled hundreds of loosely hanging strands of moss into the semblance of two legs, two arms, and a torso. It was a rough approximation, but that was all the parasite needed to be ambulatory in its waking state. A cloud of fungus, so small as to be invisible to the naked eye, floated around the amorphous gray figure.

A branchlike tendril reached down and plucked Riker's combadge from his fallen body, absorbing the small device into its wispy recesses. Then the cryptogamic creature shambled to the door and exited into the corridor.

On a makeshift cot in the moist sand of the riverbed, Alynna Nechayev lay sleeping. At times the admiral would moan or twitch, but she was still under the influence of the drugs the Bolian doctor had given her. She wouldn't wake up for hours. Geordi La Forge stood over the admiral, marveling at the signs of recovery. Not only wasn't there any scarring or discoloration, but the healed skin looked fresh and young. She would probably have to have cosmetic surgery to age the new skin to match her unburned skin. He just hoped there were no side effects from his desperate application of the soil while it was still mutating. Even if there was, he had done what he had to do to save her life.

La Forge wanted to wake the admiral up and tell her about his plan to stop the Genesis Wave, but she was in no position to help. None of them were. They were totally dependent upon the Romulans.

At his insistence, he and Dolores had rushed back to the riverbed only to find that they didn't even have enough juice left in the gel packs to power their portable subspace radio. All they had were their combadges, which didn't work because of the electromagnetic interference. No communications worked, except for screaming really loudly, which was what Geordi felt like doing.

"There they go," said Dolores Linton sadly.

La Forge looked up to see a mass exodus of Bolians trudging out of the riverbed, dragging their meager belongings and their bawling children and animals with them. It seemed that no one was going to stay with the three Starfleet officers, who had saved their lives. At least the survivors were headed east toward the geyser he had pointed out, Geordi noted with satisfaction.

The unruly mob got bogged down immediately when they hit the underbrush, bumping up against the advance party, who were supposed to be clearing a path with clubs and tools. Children were crying, animals were baying and struggling against their ropes, and some of the adults were complaining loudly. La Forge fought the urge to run over and help them get organized. When the Romulans came back to get them, he realized, none of these people would be able to leave. Perhaps it was just as well that they were showing their independence and determination, because they would need it.

Still he wondered how the people in Quonloa would react when fifty thousand more people showed up on their one and only doorstep.

"At the pace they're going," he observed, "it will take them days to get there."

"I don't feel right about letting them go out there alone," muttered Dolores. "I think I'm going to go with them."

"What?" Geordi asked with alarm. "You can't go with them. When the rescue party comes looking for us, they won't know how to find you! If our combadges aren't working, we will have no way to contact you. Yours will be just one of millions of life-signs!"

The attractive geologist gave him a shrug. "You're doing what you have to do by running back to the *Enterprise*. What if those people hit quicksand or sinkholes? They don't know what to look for, but I'm beginning to understand the geography of this place. Basically, they need a scout, and I'm the best one for the job."

Geordi's shoulders slumped, and he tried to think of some way to dissuade her. But he could see from the determination in her eyes that she wanted to be useful, and they did need her.

"If you don't get back in time, I'll try to convince them to look for you," he said. "But I can't promise anything."

Dolores gave him an affectionate smile and gently touched his cheek. "You save the Federation, Geordi, that's your job. I just want to save this group and take a look around this crazy planet."

She lowered her eyes and kicked at the sand. "If I don't get back in time, and you can't find me, do what you have to do. Don't worry about me—I'll survive."

"But—"

She stared at him with her dazzling dark eyes. "Geordi, you try to be happy, because that's one area where you don't try hard enough. If that means chasing after Leah Brahms, then chase after her. But when you find her, make sure you tell her how you *feel*."

Geordi opened his mouth to protest—to say that he didn't feel anything special for Leah anymore—but both of them would know that was a lie. Instead he grabbed Dolores. Her brawny arms wrapped around his back and came close to crushing him, while her body melted against his.

When their lips finally parted, she grinned at him and said, "*That* will get me back here quicker than a bunch of Romulans showing up. Take care, Geordi."

He didn't really trust himself to say anything, so he watched in silence as Dolores joined the throng making its way through the misty woods. He heard her voice ringing above the others, telling them to watch out for quicksand and sinkholes. They probably didn't realize it, but their luck had just taken a dramatic turn for the better.

*What about* my *luck?* Geordi thought glumly. Without that beautiful geologist, would his life take a turn for the worse?


"Picard to bridge," said the captain as he stepped upon the transporter platform. Data joined him, bearing two satchels full of their belongings and copious records about the Genesis Wave and the location of the shelters on Myrmidon.

"Troi here," came a crisp response.

"Hello, Commander," said the captain, mildly surprised. "Riker not there yet?"

"He sent word that he's on his way," she replied. "Said in his message he fell asleep."

"I'm sorry we had to wake him. I just want to make sure there were no further messages from the *D'Arvuk*."

"No, sir, they're expecting you, and they hope to leave immediately."

"Very well. Maintain your position and wait for us." Picard would have preferred to have the *Enterprise* tracking them on sensors, but there was no chance of doing that while they were under cloak. "Picard out."

The captain had a moment of doubt, when he wondered whether he should leave the ship under such clouded conditions. He could only hope that the journey would be as swift as he envisioned, and as productive; but in reality, they had no idea what they would find on Myrmidon.

"Coordinates are laid in," reported the transporter operator, probably wondering why the captain was delaying.

Picard nodded and said, "Energize when ready."

"Yes, sir."

A moment later, the human and the android disappeared in two sparkling pillars of displaced molecules and refracted light.


"Stay close together!" shouted Dolores Linton to the ragtag band, which was strung out behind her for what looked like a half kilometer. To her right, a murky waterfall plummeted downward with a roar. Its origins were lost in the mist above the towering treetops, and it plunged into a jagged basin and promptly disappeared. The ground underfoot had the consistency of gelatin and smelled like reptiles pickled in formaldehyde.

"Stick to the path—no stragglers!" Although she kept yelling, Dolores doubted whether many of her charges could even hear her, and soon they wouldn't be able to see her either. It was getting dark in the cold, gloomy forest. The geologist couldn't tell if the gloominess was due to nightfall or the massive trees overhead. Here the hanging moss was so thick that it was like a shroud, and she was worried about stragglers falling behind and getting lost.

At least, thought Dolores, the underbrush was more sparse where the moss grew in abundance, and that made clearing the path easier. She had given up the idea of scouting ahead, because there was no chain of command. She had no one to pass information to, no one willing to make the unruly mob work together. With her tricorder, she was the only one who had a compass. In this power vacuum, Dolores was forced to do everything—from guiding the pathcutters to haranguing the stragglers to keep up. She had shown the advance party what the sinkholes and quicksand looked like, and so far they had avoided serious mishap.

"Tighten up there!" she bellowed, wondering how long her voice would hold out.

As she surveyed the horde spread out behind her, Dolores was reminded of crowds leaving sports stadiums in her native Ohio. By the downcast faces, lowered heads, and muttered complaints, it looked like a crowd that had seen the home team lose the game. They were stunned, wondering how in the universe this could have happened to them. The endless canopy of misshapen trees, dripping with moss, did nothing to cheer their souls, and the waterfall sounded like the roar of the victorious team.

*We'll have to stop for the night,* she thought gloomily. Most of them still had enough freeze-dried rations and water not to starve, but it was already damp and getting colder. Now Dolores wished she had forced them all—somehow—into making shelter instead of undertaking this mad trek.

A voice ahead of her shrieked, and the geologist whirled on her heel and peered into the gloom. She reached for her tool belt, grabbed a flashlight, and shined a beam into the shadows. At first, she thought it was snowing heavily, because puffs of darkness were falling from above. With a start, Dolores realized it wasn't snow but the moss that was falling; a second later, a wispy tendril brushed along her hair and face, and she suppressed a scream.

She looked up, squinting. For some ungodly reason, the trees were shedding layer after layer of the thick moss, and it floated downward like a gossamer net. Dolores quickly drew her knife and calmly sliced through the stuff as it cascaded down, but others around her screamed and tried to flee.

"Stay calm!" she shouted. "You can cut right through it!"

All of a sudden, Geordi La Forge appeared in front of her, staring into her eyes as if he had never seen a human being in his entire life. His ocular implants glowed like two orbs of ectoplasm, and his arms reached out for her. From his gaping mouth came the homey smell of her mother's rhubarb pie baking in the oven.

"Geordi!" she muttered, overcome by a combination of confusion and relief. "What are you doing here?"

"I love you," he answered, sounding the wrong inflections, as if he were speaking for the first time in his life. He wrapped his arms around her, only they weren't entirely arms, because part of his limbs felt like a prickly thorn bush.

Instinctively, Dolores brought her knife upward in a slashing motion, ripping through Geordi's gut. The being in front of her turned into clumps of moss, which fell apart like a poorly built scarecrow. Instantly, another Geordi La Forge rose up from the forest floor, leering at her with a demented smile.

Now Dolores screamed. Gasping for breath, she tried to run, but more of the gray shroud engulfed her as it floated downward. She stumbled and fell over others who were underfoot, and the weeds and slush became a quagmire of terrified Bolians. With horror, she stared at a woman who was smiling and cooing while she fondled a pile of the smothering moss.

Dolores struggled to get to her feet, but it seemed as if every breath she took only made her weaker. She slashed ineffectually with her knife at the clinging tendrils, but they engulfed her like a downy comforter. As the seconds crawled past, Dolores forgot why she was struggling, when sleep would be so welcome.

"We're only going to rest for a few minutes," she said to no one in particular. Darkness descended over her mind and the misty forest at the same time, as blankets of moss continued to float down.

# seven

"Myrmidon," said Commander Jagron, motioning to the elaborate viewscreen on the bridge of the Romulan warbird *D'Arvuk*. "The dark areas are swamps; the lights you see are not cities, but volcanoes."

Captain Picard gazed at an olive-colored planet peeking through a haze of ominous gray clouds. The ugly globe looked as if it had been splattered with gobs of ochre, which meant it had swamps the size of oceans. Glowing embers of light sprinkled the primitive landscape, and there was a ring of volcanoes around the equator. The poles looked like frozen whitecaps shrouded in clouds. Jean-Luc Picard had seen a lot of planets in his life, but few more foreboding than this one.

"Are there any life-signs?" he asked.

The Romulan commander turned to the officer standing at the science station, and he pursed his lips. "The magnetic poles have yet to stabilize, and electromagnetic interference is making identification difficult. But there are many life-signs—the planet is teaming with life."

Data stepped closer to the science station and gave the display a look. The Romulan officer promptly angled his back, cutting off the android's view of his screen.

"Thank you, Commander Jagron," Picard said with sincerity. "You've fulfilled your promise and have gotten us back here without incident. I'm extremely impressed by your technology."

The cadaverous Romulan continued to stare at the dusky planet on the viewscreen. "And I'm impressed by your technology."

"Unless I am mistaken," said Data, "you cannot operate transporters while cloaked. How will we effect rescue?"

"You are mistaken," said Jagron with a smile. "We can't operate *normal* transporters, but we have a special transporter setting that is synchronized with our interphase generators. We can only transport one person at a time, over short distances, but we can get you to the surface and back."

"Is the planetary atmosphere stable?" the android asked.

"As a matter of fact, it is," answered Jagron. "That's an interesting feature of the Genesis Wave matrix—the planet returns to normal quicker than the surrounding space. If we had a low enough orbit, we might be able to launch a shuttlecraft."

"You've learned a lot about the Genesis Wave," said Picard, impressed.

"I'm a quick study." Jagron turned to a phalanx of six guards wearing skull-hugging metal helmets. "With your permission, I'd like to bring this security detail with us to the planet's surface."

Picard blinked in surprise at the tall Romulan. "You're coming down there with us?"

"Yes," answered Jagron. "My government wishes to know what's down there, too."

Data cocked his head. "Since combadges may not work, and we can only send one person at a time, I suggest that I go first. Then you can transport me back to deliver a report."

The commander put his hands behind his back and considered the request. "Very well. But we won't be able to identify anyone on the planet, so we'll have to set up a blind transporter pad. Anyone who steps onto the pad will be beamed back automatically."

"That solution represents security problems," observed Data.

Jagron smiled and motioned to his six brawny centurions. "That's why they're going."

"We'll need warm clothing," said Captain Picard.

"It's all in our main transporter station. Shall we go?" With a regal wave of his hand, Commander Jagron led the procession off the bridge of the Romulan warbird.

Geordi La Forge shivered, even though he was sitting a meter away from a pile of hot, glowing rocks. Admiral Nechayev slept peacefully beside him, covered with both of their emergency blankets. La Forge picked up his phaser and shot a beam at the rocks in his pile, heating them back up to white-hot. But it made very little difference in the way he felt, and he finally decided that it was the oppressive darkness that was making him shiver.

Their lanterns didn't penetrate far into the gloom, and they only had a circle of light about twenty meters across. Beyond this fragile pool of light, the darkness wrapped around them like the feathered wings of a great vulture. Cloying fog drifted across the riverbed, carrying odors that brought back memories of the misshapen creatures dwelling in the mires. Although Geordi could have sworn the forest was quiet during the day, at night it was a cacophony of dripping, slurping sounds.

Their banishment to this place was an odd reward, he thought, for the people who had saved the population, if not the planet. For the sake of irony, though, it made sense. Leah Brahms had warned him repeatedly that no one could live on Myrmidon after the Genesis Wave, and now he was forced to prove her wrong. Or right.

*Will I ever see Leah again?* he wondered. With a start, he realized that she wasn't as important to him now as she had been yesterday. He had found her, held her in his arms, and made sure she was alive. In doing so, he had finally seen the woman with her shields down. Who knew her marriage was a sham? Who knew she had to struggle for happiness and balance in her life, like everyone else? No longer was Leah Brahms the ideal lover, companion, and brilliant physicist all in one beautiful package. She was just as prone to bad luck and bad decisions as the rest of them.

She was just a human being.

Dolores Linton, on the other hand, *was* a superior human being. That much he now realized. Of course, she also had a wanderlust, a craving for adventure, and an unfortunate aversion to spaceships. She wasn't the answer to all his prayers, but he sure longed to have those strong arms wrapped around him right now.

With a sigh, Geordi stared off into the velvety darkness, in the direction where Dolores and fifty thousand survivors had trudged off hours ago. He kept expecting them to return, saying they had been to the village, and it wasn't any better than the riverbed. Unfortunately, that fantasy wasn't going to happen, because they probably wouldn't reach Quonloa until tomorrow, even with Dolores as their guide. He doubted whether any of them would want to make the return trip right away.

So he listened to the night. La Forge wasn't sure when the random sounds emanating from the blackness shifted into a pattern—a kind of rhythm. But they did. As he listened, Geordi began to think he heard marching . . . or, rather, the shuffling of feet. A great many feet. He lifted his lantern and waved it at the darkness, but it was like trying to light all of space with a flare gun.

That's when he saw *them*. La Forge grinned and leaped to his feet.

They had returned! Wave after wave of humanoid shapes came plodding through the forest, shuffling their feet. It was hard to make them out clearly, and he wondered if his ocular implants were malfunctioning somehow. *That's all I'd need,* he thought ruefully, *to have my vision go on me.*

"Over here!" he called, waving his lantern as if they couldn't see the only light in the forest. Wordlessly, the strange shapes kept marching toward him, the lantern light glinting off their bald, blue heads. As they drew closer, he saw one in the lead who wasn't a Bolian—it was a shapely female with tresses of auburn hair falling to her shoulders.

"Dolores!" he called, happiness and relief mixing with worry. "You've come back. . . . Is everything all right?"

She moved into the light, dragging her feet as if she was very tired. The others slowed down and finally stopped altogether, just outside the circle of light. It didn't matter, because Geordi's attention was riveted on the beautiful geologist.

He rushed forward to meet her and gripped her in his arms, while she gave him a tender hug back. She nestled her head on his shoulder. It didn't matter that they were surrounded by thousands of people in the middle of a bizarre wilderness.

Geordi lifted her chin to kiss her, and she purred, "I love you."

Without warning, a phaser beam streaked from the darkness. Dolores exploded, chunks of her flying in every direction, and a scream froze in Geordi's throat. His initial horror was replaced by utter disbelief, because her blasted corpse looked like a piñata full of shredded newspapers and confetti, fluttering down.

"What the—?" he gasped, whirling in the direction of the shot. To his astonishment, he saw Data standing there with a calm expression and a drawn phaser. The android turned and leveled the weapon at the crowd of Bolians who were creeping forward from the darkness. To Geordi's astonishment, they stopped and stood perfectly still, and their chemical composition seemed to change before his implants. Standing as still as hedgerows, now they looked more vegetable than animal.

"I am sorry to have startled you," said Data. "You were under attack, were you not?"

Geordi hurriedly wiped his mouth and spit. "Yes, I guess I was. But I thought it was Dolores Linton!"

The android cocked his head. "You have been without a girlfriend for too long."

"No, seriously, I thought it was a human being!" insisted Geordi. "It was a shape-shifter, or I was hypnotized . . . or something."

"Its shape never shifted," Data said with certainty. "Its mass changed after I shot it, but it remained some sort of animated vegetable matter."

Data picked up a sprig of the mistletoelike plant from the ground. "I will analyze this, but right now, we must leave. I see that Admiral Nechayev is injured."

"Yes," said Geordi, leaning protectively over the admiral. "She almost died, but she's—"

"Put down that phaser immediately," ordered a voice that sounded exactly like Captain Picard.

The captain was suddenly standing in front of Geordi, and just as suddenly, Data blasted the apparition to pieces. "You are in grave danger," he said. "You must transport up immediately."

With a rustling sound, the horde of Bolians stepped toward him, and La Forge blinked, trying to clear his vision and his mind. Something grabbed him by the back of his neck and lifted him off his feet. It wasn't until Geordi opened his eyes that he saw it was Data, holding him like a bag of garbage.

"You are leaving now," said the android, striding toward a glowing disk in the distance. Several of the Bolians shambled into his path, but he pulverized them with his phaser. A few others he clubbed into piles of rubbish.

"But I can't leave!" insisted Geordi. "The admiral needs help . . . and Dolores Linton is out there somewhere! They're all in danger!"

"I know," said the android, never slowing a step or pausing in his slaughter of the creatures, which looked like Bolians. "We can only transport one at a time, and you will go first. Tell the captain that Admiral Nechayev will follow you, and I will come last. I believe both of you will need medical attention."

"But—" There was no further discussion, as Data placed him on a glowing disk set into the ground, surrounded by gel packs. The engineer was instantly transported to an unfamiliar room, and he staggered from a transporter chamber to be caught by a brawny Romulan. The guard wrinkled his nose at the human's frightful appearance and smell, then dropped him to the deck.

"The admiral is coming next," La Forge managed to blurt out. "She's unconscious."

"Step aside," ordered Captain Picard, muscling his way through the helmeted and regally bedecked centurions. "Good to see you, Mr. La Forge."

"Thank you, sir." Geordi breathed, just as a slight figure wrapped in blankets appeared on the transporter platform. She tumbled into the captain's arms.

Picard cradled the admiral and laid her on the deck, then looked up at his Romulan hosts. "She needs medical attention."

A Romulan commander stepped forward, tapping an insignia that joined two of his opulent belts. "Commander Jagron to the Medical Center. Send a medteam to the main transporter station. Situation: urgent."

"Thank you," said Picard, his eyes steely cold. He turned to look at Geordi. "Are you all right?"

The engineer nodded weakly. "Physically, I'm okay. I'm shaken up . . . over something that just happened."

"And Data?"

"Yes, he should be coming soon. But he's immune to them."

"Them?" Picard asked warily.

La Forge nodded slowly, still unable to believe what he had seen. "There are creatures on the planet—they can hypnotize you into thinking they're people. One of them looked like *you*, Captain. It's some kind of plant that can move around, like Piersol's Traveler. I'm afraid for everyone left down there."

The captain nodded gravely and looked down at the fragile figure of Admiral Nechayev, still sleeping peacefully on the deck. Geordi could tell from the captain's puzzled expression that he had noticed the smoothness of her healed skin.

"What happened to the admiral?" he asked.

Before Geordi could fashion an answer, there came a flash, and Data appeared in the Romulan transporter. The android stepped down, holstering his phaser. "I suggest you turn off the automatic transporter pad."

"At once," Jagron answered, nodding at the operator.

"Are you well, Geordi?" asked Data.

"I'm okay," answered the engineer. "Thanks for saving me. But there are so many others down there! *You* saw those creatures . . . they looked like Dolores Linton and Captain Picard! How could they do that . . . how did they *know?*"

"They may be telepathic, capable of reading your mind." The android turned to Captain Picard. "I have a theory about what happened to Dr. Crusher and her crew."

"Go ahead," the captain answered gravely. La Forge saw Commander Jagron lean into the conversation, to make sure he didn't miss a word.

"I took some tricorder readings before I left," Data began, "and the creatures exude the same fungus that infected Dr. Crusher and the crew of the *Neptune*. I believe this fungus rapidly infects the brain, producing the hypnotic effect that Commander La Forge has described. It produces delusions, too. In fact, it may produce whatever mental state the creatures desire. They may be parasitic in nature, using this euphoric effect to control the host organism."

"Dolores!" Geordi exclaimed, jumping to his feet. "Captain, we've got to go back down there."

Before Picard could reply, a Romulan medical team barged into the transporter station. They looked to their commander for orders, and he motioned to Nechayev. The admiral was soon taken from the captain's care and loaded onto a gurney.

"Are we going to have to quarantine my ship?" asked the commander, sounding quite calm about the possibility.

Captain Picard looked frankly at his counterpart. "We're just starting to learn the truth about our enemy. My ship is already infected, and this may explain what happened to a missing crewman of ours."

"What happened to Dr. Crusher?" asked La Forge, trying to get control over his emotions. It was suddenly clear that they couldn't send rescue parties back to the planet, unless they had an army of inorganic androids, like Data.

Briefly, the captain explained about the *Neptune* and its unexpected attack on the planet. Commander Jagron's eyes narrowed, and his jaw worked furiously as he listened.

"Ah, so that's what happened to Admiral Nechayev," said La Forge. "She was a casualty from that attack." He explained what he had done to keep her alive during those first terrible minutes after the Genesis Wave had swept across Myrmidon.

"How did they get there?" asked Commander Jagron. "These parasites."

Data answered, "I believe they were created as part of the Genesis matrix. They were programmed to be grown on the planet, along with an environment to serve them. It is a rather cost-efficient way of colonizing."

"Procreation and colonization in one easy step," said Picard, his lips thinning in anger. "Our enemy has achieved the ultimate use of Genesis, but they can't plan for everything. The Bolians weren't supposed to be there after the wave swept through, so now they have to deal with them."

La Forge let out a troubled sigh. "Since our shelters were successful, there must be millions of people stranded on Myrmidon with those things. We have to save them!"

The engineer snapped his fingers and staggered to his feet. "What about environmental suits? Unless we breathe this fungus, we won't be infected, right? Can't we go down there in suits and be safe?"

Data shook his head. "I would not risk it. It is my theory that the fungus enhances the effect of their telepathic abilities, so an environmental suit would not offer full protection. Furthermore we have no idea how numerous they are—they could number into the billions and have a telepathic group mind. The *D'Arvuk* has a limited number of crew and the ability to transport only one person at a time. Searching and clearing huge tracts of forests of an ambulatory plant is an undertaking that would require years, even with unlimited resources."

"But we can't just leave them down there!" countered Geordi. He began to pace, remembering why he had wanted to be rescued so badly. "Captain, I've got something else to tell you."

"Go on."

La Forge gulped and spoke the words that would probably end this rescue mission and doom Dolores and the others to their fate. "I think I know how to stop the Genesis Wave."


The Sanctuary of the First Mother looked like a golden pillow dropped into an overgrown weed patch. A lone blue-skinned figure could be seen walking around its perimeter, chopping back the greedy underbrush just enough to get past. He wielded a kind of Bolian scythe called a *purka,* which made short work of all but the thickest branches. Even though he was working hard to keep the path clear, Mot still shivered and had to pull his jacket more tightly around his shoulders. It would be dark very soon, he thought with trepidation.

Solely because of his casual connection to Starfleet, the barber had become the de facto leader of this dispirited throng of forty-five thousand souls. He was setting an example by taking the night's first patrol around their perimeter, although the worst threats seemed to be hunger and depression. He was afraid that many of his fellow Bolians would resort to suicide if they grew too despondent.

Some of the animals were stuck outside with him, tethered and crying forlornly. A few of the younger and hardier survivors had ventured off on their own, trying to find someplace better. Mot didn't know about that, but he was sure they could find a place less crowded. It was even more chaotic inside the sanctuary, with the Mother who was ostensibly in charge more worried about protecting the Crown than her congregation. In fact, she had run off into the forest to hide the relic. At least, thought Mot, he had used his status to get his parents private quarters in a closet off the attic. He couldn't do much else for them.

With his scythe, he hacked at the thickets and vines, releasing sticky sap that smelled like black hair dye. "Damn this stuff," Mot cursed, panting heavily. "It's worse than cutting a Tellarite's beard!"

He began to get discouraged when he found himself battling the same brush he had cut back only an hour ago. The rampant growth was determined to claim the sanctuary, and he had no doubt that it would, given time. Already moss-laden trees towered over the dome, and vines were crawling up its golden inlay.

"Where's Starfleet?" he wondered aloud. The unfortunate and obvious answer was that they were probably setting up more shelters on other endangered planets. Those poor souls had no idea what was in store for them. If they knew . . . the suicide count would be in the billions. His mind wandering, Mot wasn't paying attention, and his sleeve got caught in a mass of thorns. He cursed loudly as he tried to extricate himself, but the vines seemed to have eyes as they pricked his limbs and snared his clothing.

"Just relax, Son," said a soothing voice.

Mot looked up to see his roly-poly mother, smiling benignly at him. "Mama! What are you doing out here?" He tried to restore some dignity to his pose, but that was difficult while caught in a thicket.

She moved toward him, shuffling slowly, as anyone would in this godforsaken place. Smiling fondly, the elder Bolian reached up and tweaked his cheek. "Oh, you're so funny, my little Teeko Bean."

He blushed, his blue skin turning purple. "You haven't called me that in years."

"Give us a little kiss," she cooed, standing on her tiptoes and puckering her dark-blue lips.

This moment of tenderness seemed to be wildly inappropriate under the circumstances, but how could he refuse his mother? Everyone was going a little crazy out here, including him and his parents. Besides, the shivers had finally left him, and Mot felt oddly warm in his mother's presence.

"That's a good boy," she said, pulling his face closer to hers. His mother smelled like powder scented with lollo blossoms, a scent he always associated with her. Mot took a deep, heady breath, and he was soon lost in her comforting embrace.

# eight

"Mr. Mot!" called a voice, barely breaking into the barber's consciousness. "I apologize for this."

The first phaser beam struck the Bolian in the back, and he dropped to the ground like a big blue avalanche. Data stepped closer, adjusting the setting on his phaser pistol, and the moss creature flinched just before he blasted it into confetti with his second shot. As he holstered his weapon, gray tendrils floated down from the dark sky like feathers.

The android glanced around the ragged path that surrounded the dome, but he saw no more of the shambling plants, or any survivors. A quick tricorder reading assured him that most of the survivors were safely ensconced inside the domed sanctuary, although there were some animals at risk by the front door. Data picked up the big Bolian and slung him over his shoulder as if he were an old coat, then he took several tremendous leaps along the path and arrived at the front entrance.

As Data had feared, moss creatures were draped all over the domestic animals. Some animals were standing, some were lying on the ground, snoring, but all seemed to be in bliss. The android set Mot on the ground, propped him up against the building, then drew his phaser. With pinpoint accuracy, he drilled the parasites until there was barely enough left of them to brush off with his hand.

By that time, he heard a groaning sound, and Data turned to see the Bolian coming to his senses. "Mr. Mot," he said, kneeling beside his shipmate, "I am sorry I had to stun you, but I have discovered that a mild stun works as a sort of reset for humanoids. When they regain consciousness, the hypnotic effect of the fungus has been alleviated."

"What?" asked Mot, blinking puzzledly at the android. "What fungus?"

"That was not an acquaintance you were kissing—it was a creature native to this new planet. A very dangerous creature." Data took a padd from a bag on his waist and handed the electronic device to the startled barber. "I do not have time to explain, but all the information we have is there. Barricade yourselves inside this building and do not allow anyone to enter, no matter *who* you think they are."

"But . . . but we've got people out there!" Mot pointed helplessly into the gloom.

Calmly, Data placed his phaser pistol in the Bolian's outstretched hand, then he handed him a bundle of three more phasers. "If you are in doubt, shoot them with a mild stun. A true humanoid will fall unconscious for a short period but will not be harmed. If the stun has no effect, increase the phaser setting. These parasites are the enemy, probably the ones responsible for the Genesis Wave. Do you understand?"

His mouth hanging open, Mot nodded. "Right . . . parasites are the enemy."

Data rose to his feet and concluded, "Excuse me, I have many shelters to visit and only one shuttlecraft for transportation. Take heart, Mr. Mot, because you have not been deserted."

The android tapped his combadge and disappeared in the shimmering halo of a transporter beam. Mot looked warily at the foggy woods, the sleeping animals, and the sprigs of moss scattered on the ground. Clutching the padd and the phaser, he lumbered to his feet and dashed inside.


First officer Maltz eyed the star chart on the battle display, which was centrally located on the bridge of the *HoS*. The three-dimensional hologram showed an undistinguished stretch of space with no class-M planets and vast pockets of asteroids and dust. In distant epochs, those celestial graveyards had been stars or giant planets, thought Leah Brahms. It was an old part of space, and it looked it—used and worn out.

"Magnification by four," ordered Maltz, and a young officer at the tactical station hurriedly made the adjustment from his console. Leah was surprised by how little the Klingons used the ship's computer. It was as capable as those in Starfleet, but it seemed to be an adjunct to hands-on operation. Almost every system on the ship could be operated manually, including hand-pumped hydraulics to keep life-support going on the bridge. No wonder Klingon ships were notoriously tough to bring down.

A fist encased in a studded gauntlet jabbed into the middle of the display. "There it is," growled Maltz, "Lomar, class-L. According to our records, the last time it was explored by anybody of note was two hundred years ago. We have it lumped in with a million other planets nobody wants."

Leah frowned at the chart hovering in the air. "It doesn't look very promising, does it? But it's not far away from the Boneyard. Only two light-years."

"It's not too late to change course and go to the Boneyard," the crusty Klingon said. "We wouldn't lose much time."

Leah realized that once she made a decision, she had to stick with it, unless she was proven dead wrong. She couldn't give this crew even the slightest opportunity to question her orders. However, they did deserve an explanation.

"I've been thinking about the whole issue of the wave's origin," she began. "I wonder if we haven't been operating from a misconception. This doesn't have to be a continuous wave beamed from a fixed point, as we've assumed. It could have been launched with one massive burst. Then it would be like a tidal wave. It passes through and leaves behind refuse and wreckage, but life resumes."

"Some cowardly form of life," grumbled Maltz.

"Yes, they're cowards," agreed Brahms, "so they've probably covered their tracks by now. I doubt if there's anything left to find in the Boneyard, and that's why we don't see anything on our sensors."

Maltz's rheumy eyes narrowed. "Then what happened to the task force Starfleet sent there?"

"I don't know, but I do know one thing—*I'm* not going to blunder into danger like they did." Leah Brahms leaned over the chart and studied the unfamiliar legends in an alphabet she was just starting to understand. "We need to gather information before we go there. What's the closest inhabited planet or outpost? Maybe somebody nearby knows something about Lomar."

"Here," said Maltz, running his hand across a membrane keypad and shifting the view to a neighboring solar system. "There's not much, except for this dilithium mining colony, Protus. It's on the biggest asteroid in the sector—a planetoid. Freighters from Protus used to stop at Hakon, and I know there are freelance miners and prospectors there. Perhaps some of them have taken side trips to Lomar."

"We need more information than what's in this database," Brahms said with frustration. "I'm not comfortable with just showing up at this planet."

Maltz scratched his stubbled white beard and narrowed his eyes at her. "Captain, you know that every minute we delay, the more of your worlds and people die."

"I'm aware of that," Leah Brahms answered, her blue eyes growing as cold as comets. Once again, she tried to muster the resolve and confidence of Admiral Nechayev. "If we fail, their deaths will be in vain. I can't be sure that anyone else will have a chance to stop them, so it's up to us. You have your coordinates, Mr. Maltz."

"Yes, sir." The old Klingon turned toward the row of consoles behind him. "Helm, prepare to change course."

"Change course now," ordered Commander Riker, sitting imperiously in the command chair at the center of the *Enterprise* bridge.

"Yes, sir," answered the officer on the conn, a female Antosian. "Course laid in for Lomar."

Deanna Troi lay huddled in a corner of the bridge near the door to the captain's ready room, shivering, and feeling violently ill. For over an hour, ever since Will Riker had strode confidently onto the bridge, she had been sick and bewildered. It was as if she had an instant allergic reaction to him . . . her Imzadi! But it was worse than that—it was as if neither her mind nor her body could function in his presence.

Deanna realized that she had been feeling mentally fogged ever since her concussion . . . especially after the *Neptune* crew were brought aboard. When Troi pried open her eyes, she could barely focus on Riker anymore—he looked blurry and indistinct.

Despite the heaves in her stomach and wracking cramps, she tried to remain still, so they wouldn't know she was awake. Not that she posed much of a threat to this person who had calmly taken over the ship. Just looking at him gave her a severe headache. Her reaction was the complete opposite of the rest of the bridge crew however; they were prepared to follow him anywhere.

He had shut down the ship's internal and outside communications, locked all doors and turbolifts, secured everyone and everything where they were, and had done so with enormous efficiency. Why Will had to do this was a puzzlement, because he was already acting captain of the *Enterprise*. In fact, she doubted if anyone in the crew knew anything was wrong. There were variations of red alert, where the bridge crew assumed command of every system and locked everything down. They were just dutifully following orders . . . orders that made no sense to

Troi. Maybe she had misunderstood, but why should they go to a planet named Lomar?

The others kept talking, but she could barely hear them for all the pain and fuzziness that filled her head. Still she knew she had to do something. Just beyond the door to the ready room, which had been sealed along with the others, was an access panel to a Jefferies tube. Those crawl shafts would be the only means of getting around the ship until normal operations were resumed. But getting there, opening the panel, and crawling out seemed impossible to Deanna, who could barely lift her head off the deck.

Thinking and analysis seemed to clear her head a bit, and she decided that most of the damage being inflicted upon her was mental, not physical. His effect on the others was complete control, but she had the opposite reaction—revulsion, physical and mental. If they were in control of their minds, she reasoned, wouldn't they question having a senior officer cowering in the corner? But they didn't even seem to notice her.

While the bridge crew was busy making the course change, which seemed to take them longer than usual, Troi tried to quell the roiling in her gut. *I'm in control,* she told herself. She wanted to strike back mentally, but she didn't want to alert him. He was occupied for the moment, and it had been a long time since any of the rest had paid much attention to her.

Mustering all her strength and resolve, Troi rose to a crouch and leaped toward the access panel, grabbing the handles and ripping it open as she skidded past.

Riker leaped to his feet and pointed at her. "Tactical, stop that woman! Use your phaser."

Troi crawled into the opening just as the officer drew his weapon and fired. The phaser beam struck the top of the hatch, bombarding her with flaming sparks of molten metal, but she pulled herself through and dropped feetfirst into the tube. As she bounded down the ladder, Troi heard shouts and commotion above her, but her pursuers weren't fast enough to catch her. She reached the next level, kicked the access panel open, and tumbled into a corridor.

To her relief, the farther away from the bridge she got, the faster both her head and her nausea cleared. Troi was feeling hungover but almost herself when she rounded a corner in the passageway and ran into two shipmates. They were security officers, and she recognized them immediately. "Help me!" she pleaded. "They've taken over the ship. It's not Commander Riker up there . . . something is wrong. But we can retake the ship—"

A hulking security guard glowered at her and took a step forward. "That's what the commander said . . . a mutineer."

"Apprehend her," his comrade answered, drawing his phaser.

Without thinking, Deanna put a palm strike right in the chest of the closest officer and sent him sprawling into the one with the phaser. She dashed down the hallway and squeezed around the corner just as a red beam streaked past. Stretching flat-out, Troi dove headfirst toward the open access panel and gripped the opening with her fingertips as she slid past. Hearing footsteps behind her, Deanna ducked into the Jefferies tube just as her pursuers rounded the corner and squeezed off another beam.

Now she dropped faster than ever through the bowels of the ship, not stopping until another phaser beam streaked past her from overhead, barely missing. Without knowing where she was, Deanna jumped into an adjoining passageway, heading horizontally through the ship. *How far does his control reach?* she wondered in a panic. *Where can I go to find help?*

The more her mind cleared, the more absurd the whole thing seemed. Why was Will Riker commandeering the ship, when he had control of it, anyway? The answer was that he wanted to do something so out of character that the crew would resist his orders. Deserting the captain and Data to go to Lomar—wherever that was—certainly qualified.

At the moment, she couldn't face the more serious question—whether that really was Will Riker on the bridge. The answer might mean that her beloved was dead, or seriously injured, or he'd been possessed by some alien intelligence. Still, Troi knew she had to discover the truth, and the place to start would be Will's quarters. He had been normal when he left the bridge to go to dinner, and he'd been poison to her after his return.

Panting heavily, Deanna removed her combadge so they couldn't find her with the ship's computer. Then she stopped to listen—to see if anyone was following her. No one could scramble up and down these ladders without making noise, although she didn't hear any. Of course, even without her badge, they could use tricorders to find her, but they couldn't get around any quicker than she could, unless they reactivated the turbolifts. The worrisome thing was that she had no idea how many crew members had fallen under Riker's spell. Was she the only one who had an odd kind of immunity?

While stopped, Troi looked around to get her bearings. She finally found a plaque on the wall of the tube that identified it as serving deck nine. That was a small piece of luck; Riker's quarters were not completely out of reach from this part of the ship. She plowed onward until she found a tube leading up, then she began to climb.

Troi figured that she could get to Riker's door, but how could she get it open? She would need a phaser to disable the circuitry, and then something to pry the door open. Her arms and legs aching, she climbed until she reached the access panel on deck eight. She lunged for it, just as it popped open in her face.

Deanna instantly collapsed against the ladder, expecting a phaser beam to streak out of the opening, but instead a tentative voice called, "Hello? Who's down there?"

It might be a trick, thought Troi, but they had her in point-blank range, and there was no need for them to use tricks. She waited breathlessly until two blue antennae bobbed over the edge of the opening. Finally a long, blue head followed the antennae, and the saturnine face of Rhofistan, the transporter operator, peered curiously at her. "Counselor Troi?"

"Yes," she said, letting out her breath. "Are you . . . are you aware that the ship is headed to Lomar?"

"Lomar?" asked the Andorian. "Where's that? And why is everything locked down?"

"Help me out," she said with relief. "The ship's been taken over . . . by an intruder, I think."

"That would explain much," said the Andorian, lowering a long arm to her.

After pulling her out, the two of them stood in the corridor, looking around, trying to catch their breath. Troi noticed the phaser on his belt.

"Good, you're armed," she said, "and we need that."

"We must fight other members of the crew?" he asked in alarm.

"No, we have to get into a door."

"I'd like to get into a transporter room and several other places," said the Andorian, "but there are only crew quarters on this deck. Nothing vital."

Deanna frowned and brushed back a dark lock of hair. "That's probably why there are no guards down here yet. He's got command of everyone on the bridge, but not the whole ship."

"Who has control?"

"Come with me," ordered Troi. She led the way down the corridor, scanning the bulkheads for any tools or weapons they could use. Spotting an emergency panel, she opened it and grabbed a first-aid kit, a tricorder, and a small tool box full of spanners and wrenches.

A moment later, Troi paused in front of a turbolift, which didn't open at her approach. "We can't get in there," Rhofistan said glumly.

"I know." Troi continued to study the support frame surrounding the door. The long, slim pieces of metal looked awfully strong to her.

"May I have your phaser for a moment?" she asked, placing her other articles on the deck.

"Certainly, Commander." His blue fingers drew the weapon and handed it to Troi.

"Stand back." With pinpoint bursts, she sheared off two metal slats about two meters long from the door frame. Rhofistan gathered them up as they clattered to the deck.

"Come on, we're almost there." Troi handed the phaser back to the Andorian, picked up the other articles, and charged down the corridor. When they reached Riker's door, she flicked on the tricorder and checked for life-signs. To the relief of her thumping heart, she found one weak life-sign inside.

Deanna pointed to the control box to the left of the door. "Do you think you could disable that?"

"Yes, sir." The Andorian drew his phaser, checked the setting, and swiftly demolished the control box in a shower of sparks. A Klaxon sounded, and Troi looked around, knowing this forced entry wouldn't go unnoticed on the bridge.

Troi grabbed one of her metal rods and used it like a crowbar on the door. Grunting and groaning, she didn't make much progress until Rhofistan grabbed the other slat and slammed it into the door jamb. The big Andorian was about twice as strong as a human—almost as strong as a Vulcan—and he quickly opened a slit of several centimeters. As the siren continued to howl overhead, both of them gripped the door with their fingertips and pulled in opposite directions. With a cracking sound, the door finally broke loose and slid freely.

"Will!" cried Deanna, rushing into the room with the first-aid kit in hand. She found Riker sprawled on the deck, barely breathing, his skin clammy and hot as if a fever were raging. Her first instinct was to call sickbay for help, but then she realized that wasn't an option in the absence of her combadge. Not that calling sickbay would help in any case, at least until the imposter was exposed. As Rhofistan took up position at the door, phaser drawn, Deanna opened the first-aid kit and pulled out a hypo full of lectrazine, an all-purpose stabilizer.

"Hang on, Imzadi," she whispered. "I knew that wasn't you up there."

She administered the hypospray to his neck and held her breath, waiting for a reaction. Will looked as sick as Beverly and her crew, but she was hoping that she had caught him before he slipped into an actual coma.

Without warning, a phaser beam streaked down the length of the corridor, and Rhofistan returned fire. As more phaser beams criss-crossed the air, the Andorian was forced to duck into the stateroom. "They're coming!" he warned.

Deanna grabbed Will's shoulders and lowered her ear to his chest, but all she heard was his ragged breathing. "Come on, Will, wake up! Get better!"

Rhofistan shrieked, staggering back from the door with a nasty phaser burn on his thigh. Troi fumbled in the first-aid kit for anything that could bring Will around, but she heard the pounding of boots coming closer. She thought about picking up the phaser, which had fallen to the deck along with the Andorian, but she couldn't win a shoot-out with security officers. Instead she lifted Will's head and cradled it in her arms.

"Don't move!" shouted a voice, and Troi looked up to see gold tunics crowding the broken doorway, and phaser rifles aimed directly at her.

# nine

For a moment, confusion reigned in the confines of Will Riker's quarters, as a security detail confronted what they thought was a band of mutineers. Deanna Troi could tell from their startled expressions that they didn't expect one of the renegades to look exactly like the acting captain they had left on the bridge.

Troi stared at the man she had punched in the chest a few minutes earlier, and he muscled his way past the others. He glowered at her, while his phaser barrel stayed pointed at her chest. "I . . . I don't know what's going on here," he murmured, "but you're going to the brig."

"*This* is Commander Riker!" Troi insisted desperately. "He's ill. We have to get him to sickbay. Believe me, I *know* Will Riker, and that's an impostor on the bridge!"

The officer's face showed a flash of doubt, but he finally stiffened his spine and waved to his comrades. "Arrest them all, and get them to the—"

"Johnson, don't be a horse's ass," croaked a voice. Deanna felt a rumbling in her breast, and she realized with joy that it was Will, talking and awake. She hugged him even tighter.

"I told you in your last review," Riker continued, his voice gaining strength, "that you react without thinking. You're a good man, but you want to get control of that temper of yours. There's always time in any situation to *think.*"

Johnson looked really confused, and he backed out of the room, shaking his head. "I don't know . . . I don't feel well either."

"Help me sit up," Will whispered, smiling weakly at Deanna. She rose to her knees and pushed him forward, noting that his skin still felt clammy.

Riker gazed from one officer to another—they numbered four now that Johnson had run off—and they gripped their phasers nervously. "We're in no shape to hurt you," said the commander, "so you can lower your weapons and talk to us."

Hesitantly, glancing at one another, the officers lowered their phasers. The commander nodded and went on, "We're even, because I don't know what's going on here either. But I know one thing—when Ensign Paruk'N disappeared, we realized there might be an intruder onboard. We discussed that, remember?"

They nodded at one another, looking more accepting of the idea. Riker coughed and took a raspy breath, but he plunged on. "We also know I'm sick . . . and that you may be next. It's probably the fungus . . . the same thing that got the *Neptune*."

Troi hugged him protectively and said, "You have to go to sickbay. You got a strong dose of it."

He frowned worriedly at her. "You didn't come in when I was eating dinner . . . and kiss me? Did you?"

Deanna looked up at the dinner dishes left on the table and shook her head.

"I didn't think so," Riker answered, his body shivering. "I *know* where I got it."

"We can get him to sickbay through the Jefferies tubes," said a Deltan officer, reaching an arm down to Riker. He sounded convinced that it was Riker.

"Chief Rhofistan, too." Troi motioned to the wounded Andorian, who nodded appreciatively.

The four guards helped the first officer and the transporter operator to their feet and guided them into the corridor. Deanna retrieved Rhofistan's phaser from the deck and tucked it into her belt.

"Are you coming with us?" called the Deltan officer as they helped Riker lower himself into the Jefferies tube.

Troi waited until her beloved was out of earshot, and she answered, "No, I've got to go back to the bridge."

"We could go—"

"No, you can't come with me," she insisted, gripping the phaser in her belt. "I'm the only one who can face him."


"The *Enterprise* is not there," said Commander Jagron, pointing accusingly at the elaborate viewscreen on the bridge of the *D'Arvuk*.

"What?" Captain Picard asked, taking a step toward the display and staring at it. He had heard Jagron give the correct coordinates for the barren stretch of space where they had left the *Enterprise*. He had personally given his crew orders to wait for their return. What had happened?

"Maybe it's the infection," suggested La Forge, standing at his side. "You said the *Neptune* also did unpredictable things."

"Yes." The captain frowned thoughtfully, then added, "Or perhaps they were called away by Starfleet."

Jagron sneered. "What is more important than this mission—to see if your shelters even work? Besides, the *Enterprise* is under quarantine, like us."

"All right, they're gone," said Geordi. "Can't we go back to Myrmidon and try to search for more survivors?"

"Before we do anything," answered Picard evenly, "we have to broadcast a subspace message, explaining your theory. All the parties have to know there's a chance that the Genesis Wave can be bent or narrowed by force fields. Do you have those notes I asked you to compile?"

"Yes, sir." La Forge took an isolinear chip out of his pocket. "I think we could use tractor beams on a massive scale to form a kind of convexo-concave lens."

"Let's get the word out." Picard looked expectantly at Commander Jagron, who scowled and led the engineer to a communications console.

*Where would they go?* the captain wondered to himself as he stared at the empty region of space. *If our enemy has captured the* Enterprise, *wouldn't they use it to help their cause?*

He walked to the console and looked over Geordi's shoulder. When the transmission was almost complete, he added, "Two more things: Let Starfleet know that Admiral Nechayev is alive, and put everyone on alert for the *Enterprise*. If they see it, they are to use caution and allow no person-to-person contact. Anyone who sees the *Enterprise* should contact the *D'Arvuk* immediately."

"Do you really think it will be that easy?" asked Jagron.

"No," answered Picard, working his jaw as furiously as La Forge worked the communications panel.


Using her mind like a homing device, Deanna Troi crawled through the Jefferies tube under the bridge, trying to find the false Riker. From the pain and nausea that overwhelmed her, she determined that he was sitting in the command chair, right where she had last seen him. He was pumping out telepathic energy like a generator. No wonder he had to sit and remain still. For her part, she tried to remain calm and keep a clear head while she waited in the cramped crawlspace. That meant fighting down bile churning up from her stomach, but Troi managed to maintain her position.

One of her patients was a member of the maintenance crew for the bridge, and he had described how odd it was to be working in the access space under the bridge, and to have your hand in the center of the captain's chair or the ops console. She could envision that now, and she had no trouble finding the circular compartment under the command chair.

Still Troi had to wait, fighting the revulsion, until she decided that her foe wasn't going to move or react to her presence, if he even knew she was there. They were on course to wherever, and they didn't seem to be worried about anything. That was all Deanna needed to know. She wanted to open the compartment, crank her phaser to overload, and stick it in a strut inside the command chair. The resulting explosion would put this creature out of commission. Permanently.

But tempting as the plan was, it wasn't an option, at least not one she could live with. So with a quick yet careful shot with her phaser she began to saw her way through the deck itself. If she could just talk to this being for a moment perhaps they could reach some sort of—
Alarms went off, and the lighting in the passageway changed to red-alert status.

Guess he's not in the mood for a chat, she thought, as she continued drilling the deck with her phaser. Ducking back into the Jefferies tube, Troi narrowly avoided a collision with Captain Picard's chair as it fell through the fresh hole in the bridge's floor. Phaser reset to full stun, she popped up through the hole and fired before the imposter or crew could react.

What followed seemed to surprise the rest of the bridge crew almost as much as it surprised Troi herself.

Nothing happened at all.

Riker had been looking over the shoulder of the science officer when Troi aimed at his side. He didn't even seem to notice, much less react, when the beam first struck him. Finally, when he realized that his crew was staring at him dumbfounded, he began to draw his own phaser.

"Didn't I tell you to take care of her?" he said, apparently irritated, but at no one in particular. Troi's head pounded and she felt faint. She reset her phaser.

"Stop." Her voice sounded to her own ears like it was emerging from the end of a long tunnel. "Please don't make me kill you." The imposter continued to raise his weapon.

Whoever you are and whatever you want, I'm sorry I have to do this, she thought as she watched the form of the man she loved disintegrate under her fire.

When the acrid smoke surrounding the panel behind Riker cleared, Troi looked around at the bridge from an angle she had never expected to see. Scattered everywhere were sprigs of gray vegetation—like mistletoe—along with the pieces of the chair and deck. The bridge crew gaped at the wreckage and the bizarre remains of their commander. One of them bent over and dropped to his knees, vomiting. Deanna knew how he felt, although her own nausea was fading.

She dragged herself out of the jagged hole. "That was not Commander Riker. The real Riker is in sickbay by now."

She crossed to the ops station, trying to sound confident and collected. "Computer, turn off red alert!" she ordered. The noise instantly stopped, and the lighting returned to normal.

Deanna breathed a loud sigh of relief. "Let's get communications going, and all systems back to normal. Conn, bring us to full stop."

When they just stared at her, the counselor resorted to her most sympathetic tone. "It's all right, none of you are to blame. The ship is infected by . . . something. We'll get things squared away in no time." She hoped that would be true.

Pacing the bridge, Troi stopped at the conn and noted that they were still on course to a planet she had never heard of. "Do any of you know why we're headed to Lomar?"

Still stunned, the young officers looked at one another and shook their heads. It was as if they had collective amnesia and couldn't remember being under the sway of a clump of moss, which was now scattered around the deck.

"Okay," she said, "at least put out a distress signal, and do it now." That order was simple enough that the tactical officer, the same one who had fired at her earlier, managed to tap his board. "Distress signal going out on all channels."

"Full stop," reported the conn.

"Unlocking transporters, doors, and main hatches," the officer on ops said.

Troi nodded slowly and smiled. "Thank you. Get a repair team up here, too." She looked around at their stunned expressions and added, "And call relief for yourselves. I think all of you could stand a visit to sickbay."

While the crew numbly obeyed orders, Deanna's gaze traveled to the viewscreen and its panorama of star clusters and distant nebulas. Somewhere out there was a vile enemy, dangerous beyond belief, which wasn't above using biological warfare in its most horrible permutations.

"Tactical," she ordered, "bring up everything we know about our last destination . . . Lomar."

"Admiral, good to see you!" Captain Picard said heartily, mustering more cheer than he felt. He strode up to Nechayev's bed in the tasteful medical center aboard the Romulan warbird. La Forge was a step behind him, but the engineer couldn't muster a smile. Dozens of worlds stood at the verge of destruction, and La Forge remained concerned about the two women caught up in the tragedy. Picard supposed that was the hallmark of a true crisis, when one's priorities shifted in unforeseen directions.

"Captain Picard," Nechayev said, squirming in her bed. "Why am I cooped up here? I feel perfectly fine!"

The captain sighed. "You nearly died on Myrmidon."

"From what?" she demanded. "If I'm still here, that means the interphase generators worked as planned. Either that, or La Forge here is a ghost. Hello, Commander."

"Hello, Admiral," the engineer said with a respectful nod. "The interphase generators *did* work, and I'm not a ghost. Don't you remember the attack just before the wave hit?"

"No, tell me about it."

Nechayev scowled thoughtfully as La Forge and Picard related the story about the *Neptune*'s treachery. Coupled with the discovery of the fungus, at least they had a probable explanation for what had happened to the task force. It would also explain the sudden disappearance of the *Enterprise*.

"That's not all," said La Forge. "When the dust cleared, we weren't alone on Myrmidon." When he described his experience with the moss creature who impersonated Dolores Linton, the admiral cringed.

Picard went on, "Since Data is immune to the effects of the fungus—and the creatures who spawn it—we left him behind, to warn the survivors."

"Why did you have to leave Myrmidon so suddenly?" asked Nechayev.

La Forge lowered his head modestly. "We have a theory on how to stop the Genesis Wave."

After hearing the details, Admiral Nechayev tried to jump out of bed. "I'm alive, and we've got lots to do. Let me tell the captain we need a shuttlecraft."

Picard steadied her arm, although he wished she would return to bed. From nowhere appeared a gray-haired Romulan doctor, who sneered at his patient. "You will lie quietly until I release you from that bed, or I'll put you in the brig. Perhaps this is a good time to show you a mirror."

From behind his back, the doctor produced an ornate looking glass, which he thrust into Nechayev's hands. The startled woman took the mirror and slumped back onto the bed. She stared at her reflection, marveling that one side of her face was perfectly smooth, like a teenager's cheek, while the other half showed the wrinkles, folds, and spots she had so richly earned.

"Somebody did a great . . . half a job," she muttered.

"That would be me," Geordi answered sheepishly. "You were dying, and I used the mutagenic soil while it was still active . . . applied it directly to your burns. I reasoned they would help you heal, and they did."

"Am I infected with this fungus, too?" she asked.

"No," answered the doctor. "As far as I can tell, you're not. You seem to be very healthy . . . for an elderly human."

She blinked at the Romulan, but Picard could see her tense anger fading to a warm glow. "Thank you for helping me, Doctor. By all accounts, I should be dead twice over, but I'm not. So I'm not going to complain. However, if I'm healthy now, I presume I will be allowed to leave your care."

"I suppose," he said. "But you should be under observation, in case there are unexpected consequences of your unorthodox treatment."

"Believe me, when I get back, I'll be under observation," said the admiral, looking again at her two-sided reflection in the mirror. "Let me get back and help save both of our worlds. I've faced the Genesis Wave head-on, and it's a part of me now. I won't have to explain its power—I'll just point to my face. I'll also prove that we can stand up to it and *win*."

"Go on," muttered the doctor. "I don't think you will ever be a satisfactory patient."

Nechayev leaped to her feet and wrapped the sheet around her slight form. "I need a new uniform. Where's your replicator?"

The doctor scowled. "Do you think we can just replicate Starfleet admiral uniforms? That we have them in our data bank?"

"Please," said Admiral Nechayev, her eyes narrowing. "Time is precious."

The Romulan doctor grunted his disapproval and stood ramrod straight. "I will see what I can do."

When he marched out of the room, Picard tapped his combadge. "Captain Picard to Commander Jagron."

"Jagron here," came the disdainful voice. "How is the admiral?"

"She's well, and your doctor is going to release her. She'd like a shuttlecraft—to get back to the front and put La Forge's plan into effect."

"She'll have to leave immediately," answered the commander. "Because we have a new destination."

"Where is that?" Picard frowned, dreading to hear that they had been ordered to Romulan space or some other hot spot.

"The *Enterprise*," answered Jagron. "We've received her distress signal, and we're the closest ones to her. They're halfway to the origin point."

La Forge lowered his head, a crestfallen look on his face. Both of them knew they weren't going to return to Myrmidon any time soon. Picard wanted to tell him to trust Data, but Myrmidon was a bewitched and unpredictable place. He feared that the *Enterprise* was also compromised.

"We shall depart as soon as the admiral is off the ship. Jagron out."

Picard turned to Admiral Nechayev, still huddled in her sheets, and asked, "Admiral, can you get some help to Myrmidon?"

"Yes, Captain, I will," she promised.


"Fire!" barked Mot. Nobody did, and the barber shouted again, "Fire phasers! They're not our people—they're not people at all. Fire!"

Still his small cadre of soldiers nervously gripped their weapons and stared at the advancing horde of Bolians, shuffling toward the front door of the sanctuary. They looked like people they knew—relatives, lovers, children, old friends. It was extremely eerie, because reason told them that these people were not on Myrmidon. Or if they were, they were far away with no means to get here. Still the onslaught of friends and relatives, shambling out of the forest, was enough to paralyze anyone.

Mot shook off his malaise and grabbed a weapon from a startled youth. He raked the front line with phaser fire, and nothing whatsoever happened. "That's on stun," he said. "See, they're not *us*. We can't let them get too close."

The big Bolian cranked up the setting and his courage, and his next volley of beams cut the advancing party into shreds. His cohorts were horrified, and there were angry shouts all around him; more than one phaser was pointed at Mot.

"Look at them!" he shouted. "Look at the dead ones!"

There weren't any dead ones, they discovered to their shock, just leaves and sprigs caught in the underbrush. Some of the creatures in the back took on the identities of the ones who had disappeared, and they kept shuffling forward.

Mot stuck the phaser back into the boy's hands and growled, "Fire!"

He did, and soon all of them were wantonly firing phasers. The primeval woods lit up with blazing streaks, felling trees and foes alike. Clumps of moss came tumbling out of the sky, and smoke swirled everywhere. It was like shooting up a row of hedges that kept advancing in unison. The hulking shapes no longer tried to disguise themselves—they just looked amorphous and menacing.

The intrepid band kept firing, but there was no relief and no end. The faceless shamblers kept pouring out of the dense woods, their ranks never diminishing. They were crowding into the clearing. "Fall back!" Mot shouted, discouraged. "Into the sanctuary!"

With tears in his eyes, he hustled his frightened squad into the nebulous safety of the golden dome, and bolted the door behind him. Mot cried because of all that had been lost—an innocence as well as a civilization and a home. The might of Starfleet and the resources of the Federation had always protected them before, even from the Borg and the Dominion. But Starfleet crumbled in the face of this heinous weapon and the demons who sprang from the slime.

# ten

"Welcome back," said the smiling face of Beverly Crusher as Captain Picard stepped off the transporter platform onto the deck of the *Enterprise*. The captain beamed at his companion and gripped her by the shoulders. That was when he noticed the hypospray in her hand.

"Oh, this is an official greeting," he said with disappointment.

Beverly grinned and lifted the hypospray. "This is my first official duty since getting well, and I requested it. Believe me, you'll be glad you got this inoculation against the fungus." The doctor administered the hypo with her usual efficiency.

Picard nodded with appreciation. "Good work on the vaccine."

"I had nothing to do with it, except for being one of the guinea pigs," she admitted. "It was all Dr. Haberlee. He's still a little nervous but he held sickbay together. We don't need the security detail anymore."

"It sounds like we needed them on the bridge," muttered Picard.

Another sparkling column appeared on the transporter platform, and Geordi La Forge stepped down. The engineer still looked gloomier than usual. "Sorry it took so long," he said. "The Romulans are still cloaked and are only sending one at a time."

"Taking precautions, are they?" Crusher asked, moving toward La Forge with a loaded hypospray. "They needn't worry—we've got a vaccine now."

"We won't get sick?" asked Geordi with relief.

"You'll be okay with the fungus, but you're still susceptible to their telepathic abilities. It was Troi who finally got rid of the moss creature who infected our ship . . . and the *Neptune*."

Crusher looked pained and apologetic at the memory. "On the

*Neptune,* it pretended to be Wesley. I thought he had come back to help us. Here, it pretended to be Commander Riker, and it nearly killed him."

"How did Troi stop it?" asked the captain, moving toward the door.

Beverly frowned for a moment. "Uh, you'll see as soon as you get to the bridge. We're lucky that Troi got an allergic reaction to it, not the euphoria . . . the willingness to believe that affected the rest of us."

"Why is it some people get violently ill," asked Picard, "while others can resist for days, or never become sick?"

"The creatures are cryptogamic parasites," she answered. "They don't want to kill you—not right away—they prefer to keep you alive to do their bidding. When they're done with you, they can give you a fatal dose of the fungus that will kill you within hours. The toxics and chemicals in that fungus are quite an evil brew. We think the fungus might even be a symbiotic plant growing within the moss—it's a complex creature."

Picard nodded grimly as he stepped into the corridor. "Make sure you get the formula for the vaccine to Starfleet Medical. We have to send it to every ship and port in the Federation."

"We have," she answered wearily. "But immunizing everyone is a massive undertaking . . . along with everything else that's happening."

Picard straightened his tunic, trying not to be overwhelmed by everything that needed to be done, at once. They were only one ship, and he was done playing defense—he wanted to go on the offensive. "How is Riker doing?"

"Still recovering. He should be out of sickbay in a day or so." Crusher headed off in the opposite direction. "If you'll excuse me, we've got to inoculate everyone on board."

"Beverly," said Picard with compassion, "I'm sorry that Wesley didn't come back."

"Me, too." The doctor nodded sadly, then lifted her chin and charged off down the corridor.

Picard and La Forge took the turbolift to the bridge, and the captain found out what Beverly meant when she said he would know what had happened to the intruder. There was a giant, scorched hole in the deck where his command chair used to be.

"Hmmm," said La Forge, "interesting decorating decision. Very bold."

Counselor Troi lowered her head, looking chagrined. "I'm sorry, Captain. The repair crew is replicating what they need to fix it. I had to use the Jefferies tube to acess the bridge so I could confront that . . . being."

"Quick thinking, Commander," said Picard with an appreciative nod. "I don't think I'll be doing much sitting, anyway. Where was the intruder taking the ship?"

"To a planet called Lomar," Troi answered, bringing up a chart on the main viewscreen. "It's old and mostly barren, but it bears a resemblance to the worlds created by the Genesis Wave. Captain, do you know . . . what those creatures are like?"

"Yes, Myrmidon was infested with them. Terraforming is only a part of what they're doing—they're using the Genesis Wave to colonize and procreate."

Troi grimaced. "We've got to stop them."

"We will." The captain's stern expression softened a bit. "Now that I'm back, Commander, why don't you take a break. Go check on my first officer."

"Thank you, sir!" With a relieved smile on her face, Deanna hurried to the turbolift.

The captain strode behind the ops station. "Ensign, find out how close the Boneyard is to a planet named Lomar."

"Yes, sir," she answered, working her board furiously. "They're close, about a light-year away from each other. The Boneyard is closer to our present position."

Picard nodded, making a decision. "Tactical, alert Starfleet and the *D'Arvuk* that we're headed to the Boneyard. Following that, we'll be going to a planet named Lomar."

From the tactical station, a young Deltan announced, "Captain, Starfleet has recalled all ships to Earth . . . for the final evacuation."

"There won't be an evacuation," vowed Picard. "We've got a plan to divert the wave. Contact Starfleet and tell them that we're on a mission approved by Admiral Nechayev. She'll back us up."

"Yes, sir." The young ensign worked his board for a few moments, then he reported, "Messages sent. The *D'Arvuk* is replying . . . they request permission to accompany us."

"Tell them we don't expect to come back until the enemy has been defeated." The captain's lips thinned.

The young officers on the bridge exchanged nervous glances, then quickly turned back to their consoles. The Deltan sent Picard's message, and a few seconds later, he reported, "That is acceptable to the Romulans."

"Thank them for their courage, and send them the coordinates for the Boneyard." Picard paced the deck, carefully avoiding the gaping hole. "Conn, set course for the Boneyard, maximum warp."

*   *   *

Carol Marcus shook herself awake and stretched her arms luxuriously in the coolness of her bed, a lilac scent priming her senses. With her illness fading, she could smell again, and she noticed the fresh vase of flowers on her nightstand. For what seemed like the first time in days, her body wasn't consumed by wracking coughs and pain, and her mind was clear. Everything seemed normal—except for the pink string tied around her finger, slightly pinching it. At first, Carol couldn't remember why she had tied that string there, then it all came rushing back to her.

*They're not human,* she told herself. *David and Jim are dead. Those creatures out there are not my loved ones.*

Carol primped her flat and dirty white hair, thinking that she felt strong enough to take a shower. They would be coming to see her again, now that she was almost recovered from the fever. Although the old woman despised her captors, she found herself looking forward to their contact once again. She then shuddered with self-disgust at that desire. If she hadn't been so lonely, she wouldn't have been such a prime candidate for their deception.

But she had to admit they did a good job impersonating David Marcus and Jim Kirk. Of course, they certainly had plenty of raw material to work with, all of it dredged from her own mind. She longed to see them again, even though she knew they were imposters. Quite excellent imposters.

*If they can read my mind,* she thought suddenly, *won't they know that I'm onto them?*

*I'll have to act, too,* she realized. *My surface thoughts can't betray me. I'll have to play this game of pretend, too.*

Some forty years ago, she'd had a yoga expert for a bodyguard, and she had trained extensively with him. She would have to use all of her powers of meditation and concentration to fool them, but she could do it. She would *have* to do it. Her life—and countless other lives—depended on it. It was important for her to present a facade of normality.

The old woman sat and practiced her yoga for a long time—how long, she didn't know. Finally she was satisfied that she could face them without her thoughts giving her away. Now that she was mentally prepared, it was time to make herself physically presentable. She rose to her feet and walked toward the bathroom.

Although the door and windows to her bedroom were locked as

tightly as a vault, she still had access to her bathroom. Like everything else, it was a replica of the one in her home on Pacifica. Now Carol could see that the sunshine beaming through the skylight overhead was artificial, not the hot island sun. This house had many conveniences, she thought ruefully, such as being close to Regula I, a space station that had blown up ninety years ago.

Where had they been when she was on vacation at her family home on Earth? *Probably right here,* came the answer. *Wherever* here *is.*

She turned on the shower and climbed inside. At least the warm water felt real, as did the smooth, tiled walls of the stall. She decided that her bedroom and bathroom had to be real buildings, albeit replicas. They had remained solid all through her illness, even after her captors had backed off.

*Of course these walls are real,* she thought disgruntledly. *They have to function as a prison cell.* As Carol washed, she was very careful not to disturb the string tied around her finger. Getting out of the shower, the old woman toweled off and put on a fresh jumpsuit from the closet. She felt a bit weak and hungry, but otherwise fine.

As if somebody had read her mind, a transporter beam flashed, and a tray of food appeared on her vanity table.

"Thank you," she said cheerfully as she crossed to the table and grabbed a slice of toast. She lifted the cover off a bowl and smelled the contents. "Ah, oatmeal with cinnamon. My favorite!"

"You feel better?" asked a disembodied voice, which sounded vaguely like Jim Kirk.

She told herself it was Kirk. "Yes, Jim, I feel much better. My compliments to the doctor who took care of me. He did a great job."

"Yes, he did," agreed the voice. "Your vital signs look excellent."

"How does the project go?"

The fake Kirk hesitated before he responded, and Carol tried to keep a cheerful disposition while she waited and ate.

"Not so well," said the voice. "There have been some complications with the initial wave. We'd like to do another discharge."

*And wipe out how many more planets?* Carol thought briefly. She purged that thought from her mind and concentrated on how delicious the food tasted, even if it came from a replicator.

"Whatever you say," she answered with her mouth full. "I'm always ready to go to my lab."

"There's just one thing," said this Jim Kirk, who suddenly didn't sound as confident as before. "You'll see us, but we still can't come into close contact with you. It's not safe."

*How interesting,* thought Marcus. *For whom isn't it safe?* she wanted to ask. Instead she concentrated on a problematic equation for the Genesis matrix, so they would think she was working.

"No kisses or fooling around for a few days," he added.

Carol tried not to let her stomach disgorge all the food she had just gulped down, and she forced a laugh. "I just want to see some people—I'm tired of being cooped up in here."

"Of course, my darling," he answered, sounding chipper again. "Sorry, but it was necessary. You were very sick. And we wouldn't want a relapse, would we?"

"No, you took good care of me," answered Carol, injecting a note of truth into the conversation. There was a hint of apology in Kirk's words, as if they were responsible for getting her sick . . . by accident.

"Anyway, too much kissing isn't good for anyone," she said offhandedly.

Suddenly her bedroom door clicked, then it creaked open a few centimeters. Carol polished off another couple of bites, wiped her mouth with her napkin, then rose to her feet. She walked briskly out the door, anxious to see what was out there with sober eyes.

The first thing she noticed was the darkness and the outdoor breeze, damp and sulfurous smelling. She had never noticed that smell before. Her island might be out there—or a facsimile of it—but all she could really see were a few dark shapes outlined by a canopy of stars. It looked like every star in the universe was out; she had never seen such a vivid night sky before. On the other hand, she seemed to be on a world bereft of life or light.

"We're going to be staying on Regula I from now on," said a cocky voice. She turned to see the fake Kirk standing about twenty meters away. A pang of love drove deep into her heart, and she was overwhelmed by all her old feelings for the dashing young officer. For a moment, she was certain that she had to be mistaken. Surely, Jim was real!

Then Carol looked at the thread around her finger, and her memory returned. The Kirk in front of her grew a bit indistinct to her eyes, and she instantly turned her mind to neutral thoughts.

"Is David on the station?" she asked.

"Yes."

"Then it's all right with me if we stay there." She smiled wistfully. "I've spent plenty of nights there, I can tell you."

"That's good," said Kirk with relief.

"What went wrong with the project?" Marcus asked innocently. "The last I heard, it was going better than the simulations."

"So it was." He turned away from her and looked at the brilliant starscape, his face covered in shadows. "The transformation was incomplete on some of the targets. There was interference—a kind of phase-shifting. But we've isolated it, and we need your help to make the carrier wave immune to it. We thought we would try again, in a different trajectory."

"I'd like to see your scans, the raw data," replied Marcus, feigning concern.

"Patience, my darling, we have time to fix it." The fake Kirk opened an old-fashioned communicator and spoke with his familiar clipped tones. "Kirk to Marcus. Beam us up, David."

Carol Marcus tried to maintain a benign smile on her face as her molecules were rearranged and then whisked off to a place that hadn't existed for ninety years.

Data stood in a dismal forest, surrounded by towering trees, the sunlight obscured by layers of thick, hanging moss. The android checked his tricorder, then gazed at the trees. Very deliberately, he took a stride forward. At once, clouds of moss came fluttering out of the treetops, bombarding him with fluffy gray tufts. In a few seconds, the moss draped over him like an old ragged overcoat, but it slipped off at his slightest touch.

"Interesting," Data said aloud, recording his voice on his tricorder. "Apparently they are alerted to the presence of prey by vibrations." Even more clumps of moss fluttered down, and he watched them fall like filthy snow. "They are also alerted by sound. Even though I can attract the moss creatures, they do not recognize me as a host animal."

Stepping lightly, Data walked a bit farther into the woods, coming upon a black, soupy swamp. There he found several moss creatures being dragged through the mire on the backs of ugly amphibians. The slimy white animals were about two meters long and looked like giant newts.

Data followed them for a bit, plodding through the muck and recording his log: "I have also observed the moss creatures feeding upon mobile amphibians. These would seem to be their preferred host species, as they were programmed into the Genesis matrix to be abundant."

Suddenly, his tricorder beeped, alerting the android to a preset condition. He stopped, standing chest-high in filth, and checked the readouts. To his surprise, he was picking up a huge group of humanoids—tens of thousands of them—moving in his direction.

Since he had programmed the tricorder to alert him to the presence of survivors, Data turned and sloshed off in that direction.

A few minutes later, he strode out of the swamp and was once again slogging through thickets and thorn bushes. There was no doubt that the huge crowd of humanoids was headed in his direction, almost as if they, too, were following a tricorder.

He looked forward to meeting more survivors and finding out how they had fared in this bizarre new world. At last he saw a wall of blue-skinned figures, tromping through the woods. They were unusually quiet for humanoids—he heard breathing, but no talking. Mixed in among them were a few humans and other species, but the vast majority were Bolians. Data quickened his step, and so did they, until he was almost on top of them.

At that moment, it was too late. He didn't see the moss draped all over their backs, growing into their ears, noses, and mouths until they were on top of him. Although Data was as strong as fifty humanoids, he was surrounded by thousands of them, all crawling over the others to get to him. They beat and ripped at the android—with bare hands, knives, or whatever tools they had. Some sunk their teeth into his body in a frenzy of destruction.

With great struggle, Data just barely managed to stay on his feet. Five beefy Bolians had a hold of each limb, while a wild-eyed human bounded over the others, flattening them. With disappointment, he recognized the female with the auburn hair and thick muscles, although her vine-covered face and bloodshot eyes were barely recognizable.

"Mission Specialist Dolores Linton!" he snapped. "Attention!"

Dolores twitched for a moment and stared at him, while moss curled around her head and entered her ears, plugging them tightly. Opening her mouth wide, showing fungus growing over her teeth and gums, she lunged viciously at the android's face.

# eleven

"The moss creatures are able to control their hosts' mobility . . . and drive them to attack," said Data into his tricorder, speaking until the device was ripped from his hand by one of the thousands of mindless Bolians who were trying to tear him apart.

Dolores Linton was gnawing at his face, but he was able to hold her at bay; still the others kept coming in their mindless attack. Fortunately, the android had been prepared for this exigency. With a superhuman effort, he wrenched an arm free from the clutching Bolians and drew his phaser pistol, which he had modified. As soon as he pressed the trigger, the weapon emitted a stun field instead of a single beam, and the attackers closest to him collapsed to the ground, unconscious. He caught Dolores Linton as she went down, then he retrieved his tricorder.

Outside the stun field, about ten meters away, the infected Bolians kept coming; but Data finally had room to take a leap. With Dolores Linton and a pile of moss in his arms, the android bounded upward and sailed in a mighty arc over the advancing horde.

He barely missed landing on two of the Bolians, and the others shifted direction to chase him. Carrying Dolores as if she were a large pillow, Data dashed between the disorganized humanoids and the trees, moving much faster than they could. Although the possessed Bolians were formidable in numbers, individually they were slow to react. Jumping and leaping through the forest, Data was able to get far away from the mindless throng.

As soon as he was able to find a clearing, he laid Dolores on the ground and began ripping the moss from her ears, nose, and other orifices. Pulling thorns and suckers from her skin, he detached the moss from her back and cleared away all of it that he could see. Data was concerned that the sudden separation from the parasite might harm her, and that she would become ill from fungal infection, but he wasn't going to leave her in this condition.

As soon as he cleared her trachea, she gasped and with difficulty began to breathe. "Please wake up," he said, gently shaking her, but she refused to comply.

He held her tightly with one hand. With his other hand, he tapped his combadge, sending a signal to the waiting shuttlecraft orbiting the planet. A simple signal was the best communication he could manage, but it worked. The two of them immediately disappeared in the blazing swirl of a transporter beam.

Mot sat perched on the top of the sanctuary, not feeling too confident about the makeshift scaffolding that supported him. The tiled dome was still a slippery slope, although enough vines were creeping upward from the ground that he could probably catch hold of one if he slipped. What he wouldn't give for a level balcony and a folding chair, thought Mot, as he gingerly shifted his weight.

Using the sanctuaries as shelters had been a good idea, Mot decided, but using the sanctuaries as forts against the demons outside wasn't such a good idea. The sanctuaries weren't built securely, and they had no good vantage points. The survivors finally had to smash out the skylight and use a ladder to climb out onto the roof. Then two house painters had built the scaffolding for him.

As usual, Mot felt indebted to be the first one to try the new watchtower, because of his limited experience on the *Enterprise*. "I'm a barber, not a security officer," he muttered to himself, but in truth he didn't resist.

*Maybe,* he thought glumly, *I'm trying to escape responsibility by always being the first one to volunteer to go outside.* It was getting rank inside the sanctuary, both in odor and in civil discourse. There were constant arguments, complaints, and recriminations, especially against Starfleet.

The survivors couldn't say that Starfleet had sold them a bill of goods, exactly. It had all happened so fast—the warning, the panic, then the destruction—that they hadn't had time to consider what they were getting themselves into. The Federation had done what they said they would do, which was save lives, with no thought as to what would happen afterward. Although most of them had lived, their planet had died a grisly death—to be replaced with a cold, smelly mire of horror.

Thus far, no one who had entered the gruesome forest had ever returned, and no one had visited them, except for Data. They seemed to be all alone, abandoned on this quagmire of a planet.

And there was nothing Mot could do for his charges. All the good cheer and brave words he had employed in the beginning now sounded deluded. There was no happy spin he could put on the situation, not · after what they had seen coming out of the trees.

All in all, he had good reason to hide up here on the roof. It was almost better to face the monsters than forty thousand embittered Bolians. What could he tell them? That Starfleet was on their way, ready to ride to the rescue? No, they knew Starfleet had one android and a handful of technicians on the planet, and that was all they were going to get for the foreseeable future.

When a clump of moss floated down from the trees, Mot lifted his phaser and blasted it into gray confetti. Something moved in the thick brush below him, and he took a long look and decided it was more moss, which he disintegrated with one blast. The barber was getting good at destroying the vile plant, but what good did it do? The moss was all around them, hanging from every branch; it seemed to mock him as it waved in the damp breeze. Only a raging forest fire could get rid of all of it.

*Hmmm,* Mot thought to himself, *a forest fire.* That was the way the enemy had fought, with their dastardly Genesis Wave. Why should the survivors show them any mercy? They hadn't shown any to the inhabitants of Myrmidon.

Suddenly a head popped out of the hole behind him, startling Mot. He nearly fell out of his perch, but he managed to grip the ropes and hang on, clattering noisily on the golden tiles.

It was his father, looking very worried. "Son, you had better get in here. Ten of our number have hung themselves in the rectory."

Mot gasped, hoping his father was mistaken; but the elder Bolian was a practical man, not given to exaggeration. Mot sighed and lumbered back into the hole, stuffing the phaser into his father's hand. "Stand guard on top."

"But I . . . but I don't know what to do!" protested the elder.

"Neither do I, but I'm trying anyway," answered the barber. "Just keep watch and let me know if anything unusual happens. A few moss creatures aren't unusual, but thousands would be. If there's any sign of Starfleet—"

"Right," said his father, not sounding very confident about that prospect.

"Where did you say they are? The rectory?"

The old Bolian nodded, and Mot climbed down the ladder to the main attic, which was crowded with surly, frightened people, including his mother. Even children were hanging from the exposed rafters that bolstered the dome. The barber said nothing—what was there to say?—as he brushed past them and descended a flight of stairs, which was packed with people at every step.

Finally he made his way to the rectory, which had been the humble dwelling of the Mother in charge of this Sanctuary. On the first day, she had fled into the woods with the Crown of the First Mother tucked under her arm, never to return. So they had given her little apartment to ten people to share.

Holding his breath, Mot pushed open the door, and it thudded against something heavy. Pushing hard against the door, he managed to squeeze inside, but he wished he hadn't. They hung from the rafters like blue punching bags in a gymnasium.

He bumped into a child at the door, and she peered curiously into the room.

He pushed her back and said quickly, "No, little girl, I don't think you should look at this."

Big black insects hovered around the bodies, and the smell was like the sweat and waste in the rest of the building, but with a sickly sweet smell added in.

"Are we going to eat them?" asked the little girl. "My mother says that when we run out of food, we'll have to eat each other."

"No," muttered Mot through clenched teeth. "Nobody will be eaten."

"What are we going to do about this?" cried another voice. The outer hallway quickly filled with grumbling.

Mot squeezed out of the room and closed the door behind him. "We're going to cut them down, then vaporize them."

"After that?" snapped his interrogator. "If you don't *do* something, more of us are going to choose the path of no suffering."

Mot frowned and looked at the closed door. "I don't know if strangling to death is a 'path of no suffering.' "

"What *are* we going to do?" shouted someone else, and a sea of angry countrymen pressed toward him.

Mot stammered, trying to find some words that would mollify them. "I . . . I have a plan to kill all the monsters . . . and clear the forest."

"What?"

"How?"

"We're going to burn it down!" vowed Mot, righteousness surging in his veins. "I don't know what we're going to use for fuel, or how well it burns, but I'm tired of that ugly forest and the foul beasts within it!"

"Right! Burn it!" bellowed the man who had interrogated him.

Soon everyone took up the chant, and the dome reverberated with the cry of "Burn it down! Burn it down!"

People began running around like children on a hunt for treats, and Mot soon realized they were looking for articles that would burn. Rags, oil, perfume, trash—it was suddenly a monstrous scavenger hunt.

The barber recoiled, a bit startled from the frenzy he had unleashed. His mouth dropped open as he realized that they were going to carry out his vengeful idea right now, without any further discussion.

"Wait a minute! Just a minute!" he shouted, waving his hands in the air. But no one was listening to him now.

A weeping woman stuck a large knife in his hands and said, "Can you cut them down?"

Mot gulped, realizing that he had lost control of the situation, even as he had finally given the distraught survivors a reason to live.

"Cut them down," begged the woman, her hands wrapping around his hands, encircling the knife handle.

He nodded solemnly. "Yes."

It was almost with relief that he sought the company of the dead inside the rectory. In truth, Mot envied them. They were the only ones not making demands, not girding for revenge, not eaten with fear and doubt. They were the only ones at peace.

However, they were also defeated—failures, nothing but unnamed casualties of war. Maybe they could have been saved if he had just been stronger, or wiser. The barber shook his head miserably; he felt like a failure, too.

The woman ducked her head into the door, looking distraught. "There are no stools—they've taken all the furniture outside!"

"Stay here," ordered Mot. "I'll get the phaser."

He stepped back into the hallway and climbed the stairs to the attic, which was now empty and completely devoid of furniture. His father was descending the ladder from the roof.

"Son!" he called with relief. "I was just coming to get you! What are they doing? They're dragging furniture, clothing, everything they own outside! And the moss creatures are active."

"I need the phaser," said Mot glumly. "Go on back up and keep watch. They're starting a fire in the woods—let's hope they start it far away from the building."

"A fire? Are you sure that's wise?"

"I'm not sure of anything anymore." Once again, Mot descended the stairs, which were also clear for the first time since the wave struck. He returned to the rectory to find nothing changed, except that the woman who had given him the knife was sitting in the corner, weeping softly.

"Which one is yours?" asked Mot, staring numbly at the suspended corpses.

"That one," she rasped, pointing a trembling finger at a large male.

"I'm just going to vaporize them here," said Mot, "with your permission."

"The words?" she said hopefully, twisting her hands together. "Who will say the words?"

"I don't know the proper chants," said Mot. "If the Mother had returned to us . . . but she hasn't."

Seeing her flooded eyes, he took a deep breath and plowed onward. "Let us say this about these brothers and sisters who now swim in the Vein of Mystery: they were spared suffering. They died with their minds calm."

The woman wept even louder, and Mot checked his phaser. Starting with her loved one, he vaporized the hanging bodies, until there was nothing left in the room but a sickly smelling fog, and the buzzing insects.

His shoulders hunched in dejection, the barber climbed the stairs and then the ladder, to join his father on the roof of the dome.

It was bedlam all around the building, with numerous groups trying to start fires, some succeeding, most failing. A few were way too close to the building, and others were so far away that Mot feared for their safety. All of them made a great deal of noise, whooping and hollering. There was something so primal and satisfying about starting a fire that he couldn't resent their elation. Fire represented warmth, relief, and sovereignty over their environment.

Smoke drifted upward, polluting the haze. He saw two moss creatures stumbling through the underbrush, already on fire. They burned like walking torches. Where the flames were spreading, the underbrush shook with the movement of unseen animals trying to escape.

"What is happening to us?" his father asked. "Now we're the destroyers."

"As in most wars," Mot said, miserably, "we have sunk to the level of our enemy."

They continued to watch the smoke curl upward through the moss-covered boughs, while flames consumed the underbrush and licked at the tree trunks.

\* \* \*

Data held Dolores Linton's body against his shoulder. She was coughing and gagging, and she had about as much control over her bodily functions as a baby. But she was still alive, against considerable odds. Undoubtedly, a doctor in a fully equipped sickbay would be able to do much more for her, but Data had at least nursed her through the initial stages of her withdrawal from the parasite and its deadly euphoria.

Without warning, she groaned, followed by rasping words. "Where am I? And why are you carrying me like a sack of potatoes?"

He let her down gently into a seat on the Romulan shuttlecraft. "You are coherent."

"No, not really," she murmured, wiping her mouth. "I feel like I ate a compost heap."

Data motioned to a few sprigs of moss he had saved in a sample bag. "You were covered by a moss creature. They are cryptogamic parasites, and they use a symbiotic fungus as well as telepathy to control the host organism—"

"That's enough," grumbled Dolores, grabbing her stomach. "Are you saying . . . I was a host organism? To a bunch of moss?"

"I am afraid so," said Data. "Humanoids are very susceptible to their powers. You do not recall falling prey to them?"

She rubbed her head. "Oh, I remember walking in the woods . . . it was getting dark, and I was trying to keep everyone together. The moss fell out of the trees. Was Geordi there?"

"No, but perhaps a facsimile of him appeared to you."

"Is Geordi all right?" she asked with concern.

"By now, he is aboard the *Enterprise,* along with Admiral Nechayev," answered Data, checking his instrument panel. "That is odd—the forest on the surface of the planet is burning in several regions."

"Because of volcanoes?" Dolores asked, rubbing her neck. Her fingers gingerly touched the sucker and thorn scabs where the creature had attached itself.

"No, these fires appear to be spontaneous, close to several shelters." The android peered curiously at his readouts. "The pattern of the fires is odd, unless they were set deliberately."

"By these moss creatures you talk about?"

"No, they have no reason to set the forest on fire, since it has been grown to their specifications. In fact, they have the most to lose, since they could not outrun a moderately moving blaze. I am most concerned about the flammable gases extant on the planet, such as methane, hydrogen, and methyl formate. Those swamps may be highly flammable. We should return to the surface."

Dolores sat up wearily. "Before I see other people . . . is there anyplace on the vessel for a girl to freshen up?"

Data pointed to the rear. "Yes, there is a fully equipped 'fresher, plus clothes are available from the replicator. This Romulan shuttlecraft, *Raptor*-class, is quite well appointed, and it is eleven percent faster than our fastest shuttlecraft."

"But we're not going anywhere, are we?" asked Dolores, rising unsteadily to her feet.

"No. My orders are to remain here and assist the survivors until I am relieved. Besides, it is uncertain that we could leave the planet's atmosphere without being destroyed. This craft is not equipped with phase-shifting."

Dolores grimaced as she stretched her back. "Yeah, but the planet's got hundreds of interphase generators lying around."

"That is true," allowed Data with a cock of his head. He filed that observation away for later use. Dolores Linton was one of the most practical humans he had ever met.

The geologist shuffled off, then she stopped and looked back at Data with a grateful smile. "Thanks for saving me. All those other people with me—"

"I have only the resources you see here," answered Data, motioning around the gaudy but cramped shuttlecraft. "We will have to hope the infected survivors will be able to live until help arrives. I believe the moss creatures will want them for their mobility . . . if they hope to avoid the fires."

Dolores shivered and pulled her filthy, ripped jacket around her body as she stared at the mottled planet taking up most of the main viewport. In a quavering voice, she asked, "What did we do to this place?"

"It was not us," answered Data. "It was a species who used our technology as they use everything else—without thought."

"Humans were once like that," murmured Dolores.

"Yes, I have often wondered what change occurred in your history to set you upon a different course," said the android with honest curiosity.

"We had to hit bottom—the last big war." Touching the scars on her neck, Dolores shuffled to the aft compartment.

"Our enemy has not hit bottom," said Data to himself.

*   *   *

Behaving like her personal valet, Commander Jagron carefully removed the heeled boots worn by his intelligence officer, Lieutenant Petroliv. Bending over like a toady, he massaged the statuesque Romulan's feet, until she lifted a foot and kicked him onto his back. Jagron rose quickly, trying to maintain some of his dignity, but it was difficult when he was so hungry for his lover. It had been days since they had been able to escape to his quarters.

"My Lady, I haven't cleaned your uniform yet," he said apologetically.

Petroliv looked at him with pity and held out her arms. "You may remove it now."

With extreme care and tenderness, he lovingly undid every button on her intricate uniform, allowing himself to get close enough to smell her astringent odor. Petroliv kept herself very clean.

She sighed with impatience as he took his time. "I need that sonic shower. I've had a difficult day."

"I know." Jagron gave her a sympathetic bow. "Before we departed, did you check the bomb you planted on their bridge?"

"Yes!" she snapped at him. "Unlike *some* on your staff, I follow through on my projects. The device is still responding to signal, and its miniature phase-shifting is working well."

"I worried that the android might detect it," said the commander, "but he is gone now." With trembling hands, he slid one of her sleeves down her bare arm and over her wrist, and he watched her fine black hairs rise to the cool air of his quarters.

Jagron ran his hand over her arm, and she slapped it sharply. "Are you getting familiar with me, Servant?"

"No, Mistress," he responded, giving her a respectful bow. The commander was careful not to touch the back of his hand where it stung.

"Just remember who runs this ship," said Petroliv, eyeing him disdainfully.

"I tremble at your command." Jagron dropped to his knees and prostrated himself before the haughty woman, who towered over him, half undressed. "I accept your punishment. I am unworthy."

"I know," she answered with a sneer. "Don't worry, you will still become the youngest Senator in the Star Empire. Just make sure you obey me."

# twelve

Protus was an oblong asteroid that looked like a burnt potato that had started to sprout. Its appearance belied its enormous size—it was a planetoid with the lazy orbit of a comet. As the *HoS* drew closer, Leah Brahms could see that what looked like sprouts were in reality drill sites, huge light poles, communication arrays, solar collectors, and docking bays. The darkest spots were actually tunnels with monorails and conduits running into the depths of the gigantic asteroid. Dilithium freighters scooted back and forth in a monotonous pattern.

"Things look normal here," said Leah.

Beside her, Maltz scowled. "Yes, they are groveling for money as usual. The mining companies are mercenaries, and so are the free-lancers. They'll sell to anyone with enough latinum. The Federation is supposed to be in charge here, but this colony predates the Federation—and the traders know how to get around their restrictions. On Hakon, we had traders who bought dilithium legally from Protus and sold it illegally to anyone. They would claim it was for domestic use, or for approved customers, but it was not."

"Why, Maltz, I'm shocked," Leah said with a smile.

"I wasn't responsible," the old Klingon protested. Then his shoulders slumped, and his leathery face took on a few more wrinkles. "But I turned my back on what was happening. I let the documents go through my office and took the fees. This is what I was reduced to—a money-grubbing civil servant."

"Have you ever been to Protus before?" asked Brahms.

"No," answered Maltz, "but I have heard they do not like people coming here unless they have business. We should have a reasonable story." He grinned slyly. "Let us say we want to buy dilithium for the Cardassians, who are not approved but need it badly. With Hakon destroyed and our usual sources gone, we were forced to come here directly."

"Then why do we need to ask about Lomar?" Brahms queried.

"We want to use Lomar as a secret dilithium refining station. We need a planet that's out of the way but near here." Maltz beamed with delight at his own cleverness. "I am almost as devious as a human."

"If you say so," answered Leah. "Helm, contact their operations and request permission to dock."

"Yes, sir."

A moment later, the young officer reported, "They wish to know our business."

Leah looked at Maltz and shrugged. "We're dilithium buyers. We normally go to Hakon, but it doesn't exist anymore."

The officer relayed the message, then listened intently to his earpiece. "We have been cleared to dock—bay seventeen."

The captain and her first officer watched with interest as their helmsman piloted the Klingon cruiser between two sparkling metal gantries that extended a kilometer from the dark asteroid. A sophisticated system of blinking lights guided them into a force-field bumper, and giant clamps emerged from the structure to secure the ship. A moment later, a giant tube snaked outward and connected to their main hatch.

"You and I should go, Captain," said Maltz, "plus some security."

"Is the security really necessary?" asked Brahms.

"We are Klingons in Federation space," Maltz reminded her. "Besides, I don't trust these people."

Leah nodded. "Very well."

There were five of them waiting to disembark when the main hatch opened. Leah led the way into the giant tube, which functioned as a gangplank, and she saw a tow rope moving at a slow speed over her head. She grabbed the rope, as did the four Klingons, and they were soon moving weightlessly down the length of the tube.

In due time, they reached the end of the gangplank, which opened onto a monorail car with artificial gravity. With relief, Leah took a seat in the sleek conveyance, as did her entourage. Soon they were hurtling along a dark tunnel into the bowels of the giant asteroid. Every so often, they caught a glimpse of mining operations.

The Klingons looked a bit out of place riding in such luxury, but Leah enjoyed it. This was the first time since losing her husband and coworkers and fleeing from the Genesis Wave that she felt relaxed. It wasn't peace exactly, but it was rest. Leah sat quietly, turning off her mind and letting the monorail do the work.

With a shudder, the conveyance came to a stop, jarring her from a light sleep. The Klingons rose to their feet, looking anxious about being so deep inside this Federation rock, and Maltz motioned them to the door. "Look lively," he growled. "Remember, we are Klingons. Honor with discipline."

They all nodded, except for Gradok, the hulking weapons master. He grinned. "Do they have ale here?"

"I hope so," said Maltz, "or we're going to smash the place up." His fellows grunted their approval at that sentiment.

Leah shook her head, thinking that she couldn't be in safer company, or more dangerous company. But they hadn't come to Protus to have fun—they had come here to find out about Lomar. Anything else that happened was immaterial.

She led the way off the monorail into a bustling underground city. The high ceilings gave her the impression that this was a hollowed-out mine converted to public use. Much to the delight of her entourage, there were bars, taverns, and restaurants everywhere, as well as storefront offices with signs proclaiming, PUREST DILITHIUM, BEST PRICES. And CURRENCY BROKER—PRECIOUS METALS ACCEPTED. Plus the ubiquitous, MINERS WANTED. INQUIRE WITHIN.

The low gravity inside the asteroid gave her step a definite bounce, but it also reminded Leah of her lab back on Seran-T-One. She tried to shake her melancholy, but it was difficult to see this happy, humming city when her own world had been reduced to a foul swamp. She tried to concentrate on their fact-gathering mission, but they weren't exactly inconspicuous. Although there were representatives of numerous races among the inhabitants, there were no other Klingons. People glanced suspiciously at them and gave them a wide berth as they strode through the underground complex.

"These people act like they've never seen a Klingon," muttered Gradok, casting an appraising eye at a Bajoran female, who hurried away.

"We're a long way from Klingon space," answered Leah.

"How well I know that," replied Maltz. "I've lived in this region for ten long years—never saw another Klingon myself."

Leah looked at him with newfound sympathy. "That must have been difficult."

He shook his head. "No. Being imprisoned on my own ship ninety years ago—*that* was difficult. Ever since then, being an outcast has been my life. It came easily."

"Can you ever redeem yourself?" asked Gradok.

Maltz nodded forcefully. "I will redeem myself when I wash my hands in the blood of Carol Marcus."

"We have to find her first," said Leah, trying to keep their minds on the task at hand. "What's that?"

She pointed into the distance, where a golden fountain was shooting a beautiful plume high into the air, almost to the roof of the great cavern. Leah altered course to head toward the fountain, and as they drew closer, she saw it wasn't water but golden glitter shooting upward. Force fields or magnetic fields must have controlled the golden flow, because it rippled back into a pool of gold in a varying array of patterns. Leah felt like she had never seen anything more beautiful in her entire life, and she was drawn to the fountain as if to a magnet.

"Isn't it lovely?" Leah said breathily, staring at the massive piece of art.

"If it were ale, that would be lovely," Maltz said to the appreciative laughter of his fellows.

"They're flecks of gold-pressed latinum," explained a voice behind her. "Ostentatious, but it shows how rich we are."

All five of them turned around to see a short, chubby human dressed in gaudy plaids that would do a Tellarite proud. He held his hand out to Leah and said, "Welcome to Protus. I'm the chief administrator, Colin Craycroft."

"Hello," she answered, "I'm Captain Leah Brahms, of the *HoS.* We just got in—"

He chuckled and held up his hand. "Oh, I know that. Word came down that a Klingon ship had docked, and I frankly couldn't believe it. And now you tell me that *you're* the captain?"

"You have a problem with that?" grumbled Maltz, eyeing the smaller man ominously.

"Oh, by no means, no," Craycroft answered swiftly. "I take it . . . you're not part of the Klingon fleet?"

"No, we're independent traders," answered Leah, feeling funny about lying. But they needed information, and if they could get more information by pretending to be dilithium traders, then so be it.

"This is my first officer, Commander Maltz," she said, giving her comrade a field promotion. She went on to introduce Gradok and the rest of them, priding herself on having finally learned all their names.

"You're a long way from home," observed Craycroft.

"We were on Hakon and barely escaped when it was destroyed," Brahms answered, injecting a bit of truth into their story.

The administrator shook his head and clucked his tongue. "Yes, terrible tragedy that. So many planets gone—I hear Earth is next."

"I think Earth still has a few days left," answered Brahms, "although not many. Maybe someone can do something."

"We're lucky it passed us by," Craycroft said with a shiver. He glanced again at the quartet of strapping Klingons. "I don't suppose any of you would like to work as miners for a few weeks? The pay is excellent."

"Work in a hole in the ground? That is not the life for a warrior." Maltz rubbed his lips and looked around. "Do we have to stand out here and talk?"

The little man smiled. "Of course, you must be thirsty and hungry after your narrow escape. Let me introduce you to my favorite place, the Pink Slipper."

Gradok grimaced. "I'm not sure I want to drink in a place called 'The Pink Slipper.' "

"They have fifty different types of ale," answered Craycroft.

"Why didn't you say so!" exclaimed Maltz, wrapping his arm around the little man's shoulders. "Where is it?"

"Nearby." The administrator led them around the fountain and across the plaza toward a large establishment that beckoned with the sounds of laughter and music. Catching sight of the tavern, Maltz said warily, "Maybe we should check it out, Captain?"

"Go ahead," she answered. The Klingons surged ahead, leaving Leah Brahms and Colin Craycroft to bring up the rear.

The little man gazed at her. "You must be quite a remarkable woman to lead a band of Klingons."

"They're a good crew," she answered, "and people don't usually try to cheat us."

He chuckled. "No, I wouldn't think so. I don't believe I've ever heard of Klingons who were dilithium traders."

Leah said nothing in response to that, and they strolled into a large but dimly lit tavern with several gaming tables, dining tables, and an old-fashioned bar. But the main attraction seemed to be scantily clad men and women swinging on trapezes suspended from the high ceiling. Seeing the performers' footwear, Leah knew where the Pink Slipper got its name. Although their acrobatics were quite tame, the novelty of having these artists flying overhead was apparently enough to fill the place.

Maltz and the other three Klingons had already commandeered the bar, shoving the other customers aside. Leah began to wonder whether bringing all of them along had really been a good idea, but they were here now. The sooner they got out, she decided, the better.

Bluntly she asked Craycroft, "Have you ever heard of a planet called Lomar?"

He gazed at her thoughtfully. "I believe I've heard of it, but I can't recall any details. Is it near here?"

"Not too far, only a light-year away. I thought you might know something about it."

"There can't be any mining there," said the administrator, "or I'd know about it."

"Maybe some freelance miners know the place," Leah said hopefully.

Now Craycroft looked curious. "Why? Are there precious metals there? Fuel crystals?"

Leah shook her head, thinking this was pointless. She meant to grill *him* about the place, not the other way around. With Craycroft in tow, she wandered toward her crew, who were laughing loudly and hoisting mugs. By the time she got to the bar, Maltz had already drained his first mug and was calling for a second.

She rose on her tiptoes and whispered in his ear, "Go easy there— we're here on business."

"I know. I'm just trying to fit in." He pounded a beefy fist on the table. "You! Barkeep!"

Gradok suddenly leaped high, swiping giant hands in the air, and Leah realized that he was trying to snag one of the trapeze artists as she flew past.

"Gradok!" she snapped. "Honor with discipline."

The weapons master looked dumbly at her, then his craggy face broke into a smile. "Sorry, Captain. It's been a long time since we were in port."

"I know, but we've got business." Leah glared pointedly at him.

"Right." Loudly he bellowed, "Does anybody here know anything about Lomar?"

Leah cringed, thinking there was a reason why Klingons didn't make very good diplomats, or spies. The tavern suddenly grew quiet, and the only noise was the whooshing of the trapezes over their heads. After a few moments of this uncomfortable silence, the conversation and gaming began again.

From the shadows crept a bent old man—a Tiburonian, judging from his giant, elephantine ears. He shuffled up to Gradok, barely coming up to the Klingon's chin, although he must have been taller in his youth. "You want to know about Lomar?" he asked in a gravelly voice.

Leah inserted herself into the conversation. "Yes, we do," she answered. Unless someone demanded to know why they were curious about Lomar, she wasn't going to use their cover story.

The grizzled Tiburonian licked his thick lips. "I don't suppose you could give an old miner a little drink."

"Gladly!" exclaimed Maltz, shoving a fresh mug into his hands. "Have you been there?"

The old miner nodded. "Yeah. Only once." He took a long chug of ale, as if the memory of Lomar made him thirsty . . . and afraid.

"What's your name?" asked Leah, trying to cut the tension between them.

"Krussel," he answered hoarsely.

"Why did you only go to Lomar once?"

He stared at her with haunted black eyes. "Because that's a bad place."

"What do you mean?"

"I mean, most people who go there . . . never come back." Krussel took another long swig, and he set the mug on the bar with a trembling hand. "More, please."

"A man after my own heart!" Maltz bellowed, slapping the old miner on the back and nearly knocking him over. "Barkeep, two more here!"

Leah rubbed her eyes, hoping they had enough latinum to pay for all of this. She also noticed that Mr. Craycroft had not gone away; instead he was lurking behind her, trying to be inconspicuous while he eavesdropped on the conversation.

"What's so dangerous on Lomar?" she asked.

"Evil, ugly place. Nothing of worth there," answered Krussel. He lowered his voice to add, "There are carniverous plants on Lomar."

Maltz laughed heartily. "A true warrior is not afraid of any plant."

"Then you're a fool," said the old miner.

Before Leah could blink, Maltz had grabbed the Tiburonian by the collar and lifted him off his feet. "Who are you calling a fool?"

"Maltz!" barked Leah. "Put him down—he's trying to help us. Besides, there *are* carniverous plants in the universe."

Delicately, Maltz set Krussel down and brushed off his clothing, but the old miner spent several seconds coughing. "I apologize," said the Klingon. "I got carried away. Here, let me buy you another ale."

"No, no!" The miner tried to escape, but Gradok swiftly grabbed him and held him in place.

"You do not refuse a Klingon when he wants to show you hospitality," the weapons master said sternly.

Sandwiched between and Maltz and Gradok, the old Tiburonian had little choice but to nod helplessly. "Y-yes, another one, please."

The bartender, who had barely had a moment to deal with his other customers, quickly rustled up more mugs of foaming ale. Leah Brahms tried not to roll her eyes and look discouraged, but she felt as if they were getting nowhere . . . but drunk.

She felt a tug on her sleeve, and she turned to see the administrator, Colin Craycroft, who had been all but forgotten in the interrogation. The rotund little man smiled at her. "Why don't you and I go to a private booth and discuss business?"

Leah knew they were already discussing the business she had come here to discuss, but she couldn't say that. Maybe it would be good to get away from her boisterous entourage. With a sigh, she answered, "All right."

She look pointedly at Maltz. "I'll be right back. Behave yourselves."

"Always," he answered with a lopsided grin.

Once again, Leah tried not to roll her eyes. She let Craycroft take her arm and lead her away from the laughter, music, and trapeze artists to the back of the tavern, where it was even darker. Giggles wafted from secluded compartments hidden by red curtains. Suddenly she wished she were back on the *HoS,* plowing blindly ahead. Perhaps this detour had not been such a good idea.

Craycroft nodded to a tall Andorian waiter lurking in the shadows, and a silent communication passed between them. The waiter drew open the red curtain on one of the booths and motioned them inside, then he quickly hurried away.

The booth was uncomfortably intimate, with luxurious lounge chairs and a small antigrav table, which floated in the air and could easily be pushed aside to make more lounging space. As she slid into the compartment, Leah was glad that she had four hulking Klingons outside, willing to protect her, although Colin Craycroft didn't look particularly dangerous.

He folded his hands and smiled pleasantly at her. "How many cubic meters do you want?"

"Pardon me?"

"Dilithium. You did come here to buy dilithium, didn't you?"

Brahms had her lie carefully prepared, but it suddenly seemed pointless to lie when time was so precious. They were already on Protus and couldn't be turned away, so this was no time to mince words.

Still she surprised herself when she blurted out, "We don't need any dilithium. I really came here to find out about Lomar."

"Why? The old miner said it had nothing of worth."

"That's not *our* information," Leah answered cryptically.

Craycroft clapped his hands on his thighs. "Well then, why don't we organize an expedition to find out what's there?"

"Um—" Leah tried to think of a good reason to head off this idea. Before she could reply, the curtain parted, and the Andorian waiter appeared with an open bottle of champagne and two fluted glasses.

"This isn't really necessary," Leah said with embarrassment.

"Why not?" asked Craycroft, grabbing the bottle and glasses and doing the pouring himself. With a wave, he dismissed the waiter. "This is champagne . . . from Earth. You'd better enjoy it, because there may not be any more where this came from."

Leah couldn't dispute that grim assessment, so she took the proffered glass and put it to her lips. The fizzy beverage tasted incredibly delicious—tart, fruity, and alive—and she felt herself relaxing as it coursed down her throat. Still there was a feeling of guilt, as they lounged in this opulence while millions died or were left homeless.

"You were saying," said Craycroft, "there is something of value on Lomar?"

Brahms opened her mouth to deny it, but she suddenly felt lightheaded and extremely tired. Her mind tried to form a quick lie, but her mouth betrayed her—speaking slowly and deliberately, she answered, "The Genesis Wave . . . comes from Lomar."

Craycroft peered at her and snapped his fingers. "Rakber, get in here!"

Through a blurred haze, she saw the Andorian waiter stick his head through the curtain. "Yes, boss?"

"I want you to listen," he said. "Her speech is getting slurred, and I don't want to miss anything."

The Andorian slid into the seat beside her and gently took her hand. "Just relax," he said in a deep, soothing voice.

*Oh, I'm relaxed,* she wanted to say. *I'm about to pass out.* She could see and hear them, but she felt like she wasn't really there—as if her body were floating above them, looking down. She understood everything they said when they spoke directly to her, but their conversation with each other came in fuzzy pieces.

"I . . . gotta . . . go . . ." Leah tried to rise to her feet, but the muscles in her legs refused to work. She tried to shout, but her voice came out a hoarse whisper. "Maltz—"

"Your friends are doing fine," Craycroft assured her. "They're very happy, and they want you to tell me everything you know about the planet named Lomar."

"Lomar . . . source of Genesis Wave . . . maybe."

They waited for her to say more, but she didn't seem to know anything more. Leah felt like a video lens—able to see and hear . . . but unable to react or participate. She had to concentrate to understand what they were saying, and she still got only the gist of it.

"That's all she knows?" Rakber asked in amazement.

"Well, it's something," said Craycroft thoughtfully, "although what it is, I'm not sure. What are the Klingons doing?"

"Drinking," answered the Andorian. "So far, the drug hasn't had any effect on them. Or very little effect."

"See if you can pick a fight with them," said Craycroft. "We need to have them arrested."

The Andorian gave him a sidelong glance. "You don't pay me enough to pick fights with Klingons."

"Go tell them that you saw the two of us leave through the back door," the little man said with a smile. "That should keep them drinking for a while. I'll take her downstairs."

Rakber shook his head doubtfully. "Remind me to ask you for a raise." The dour Andorian slipped out of the booth and through the red curtain.

Craycroft gripped Leah tightly around the shoulders. Although she wanted to scream and slap him, she was unable to do either one. "I'm not really the chief administrator," he said apologetically. "But I'll take you to him, if you cooperate."

He reached behind the couch and pressed a panel. At once, the wall behind her slid open, and the booth began to rotate. The soft cushions dropped away beneath her, and Leah felt herself falling into darkness. This time she screamed involuntarily.

# thirteen

Through a hazy fog and blaring music, Maltz thought he heard something troubling—a scream. He looked around the Pink Slipper, but he wasn't able to focus on anything in the dimly lit tavern—not the laughing patrons or the grinning trapeze artists floating overhead. It was all a fuzzy blur.

The old Klingon had been drunk many times in his life, especially the last few years on Hakon, so he knew the feeling well. This wasn't it. With a lunge, he slapped the mug out of Gradok's hand, and it went banging across the bar into a row of bottles, resulting in a loud crash.

"Watch it!" the weapons master bellowed, his words slurred. "Why did you do that?"

"There's something wrong," muttered Maltz. He looked around, blinking to clear his eyes. "Where's the captain?"

Gradok snorted. "Oh, she went off with that popinjay. When it comes to mating, she must prefer smooth-heads. *jIyaj.*"

Maltz looked around more thoroughly, and he spotted the Tiburonian, Krussel, lying at his feet, blissfully passed out. Their two younger comrades, Kurton and Burka, were leaning over the bar, semiconscious.

Angrily, Maltz grabbed Gradok and whirled him around to face his fallen comrades. "Have you ever seen two Klingons get drunk so quickly? Have *you* ever gotten drunk so quickly?"

Gradok gave him a smile that was missing several teeth. "Good ale!"

"No, *bad* ale! Drugged ale." Now he looked around for the bartender, who had suddenly disappeared.

At that moment, a gangly Andorian approached them, an insincere smile plastered to his narrow face. "I bring word about your captain. She has gone off with Mr. Craycroft to see the—"

In a flash, Maltz whipped out his knife and shoved the point under the Andorian's chin, while gripping his antennae with his other hand. "I've never gutted an Andorian before," whispered Maltz. "Are your intestines as blue as your skin?"

"I . . . aghh . . . I can't talk this way," complained the waiter, trembling.

"I bet you can, and speak the truth," hissed Maltz. "What is in these drinks?"

"Regulan ale."

Maltz pressed the knife point home, drawing a drop of blue blood from the Andorian's quivering chin. "I'll tear off your antennae with my bare hands, so help me Kahless. Where is our captain?"

With a trembling finger, the Andorian pointed to the back of the tavern. Gradok removed the knife from his chin and prodded the Andorian's back. "Lead the way. One false move, and it's the last move you'll ever make. Gradok, wake up those two children. Bring the Tiburonian, too."

The big Klingon picked up the remaining mugs of ale and dumped them over the heads of Kurton and Burka, who jumped up sputtering and swinging their fists. *"Qeh!"* he barked, then he grabbed the old Tiburonian and tossed him over his shoulder like a sack of *targ* food.

With the terrified Andorian in the lead, the wary party of Klingons stalked to the back of the tavern. By now, it was very quiet inside the Pink Slipper; the blaring music and gambling tables were stilled, and customers scurried out of their way.

"Watch our backs!" Maltz told the younger Klingons, never taking his eyes or his blade off the Andorian. When they reached the rear of the tavern, they could hear the giggling coming from the curtained booths. Gradok dumped the Tiburonian onto the floor and began throwing open the curtains, eliciting many shrieks and much scrambling for clothes.

"Which one?" snarled Maltz, letting his knife make his point for him.

"This one," said the waiter, pointing to the only booth that had been empty. "There's a secret panel behind the cushions."

Suddenly, there was a commotion and a stampede of footsteps coming from the front of the tavern. "Security!" shouted a deep voice. "Nobody move!"

"Help!" screeched the Andorian. With a quick thrust, Maltz made sure it was the last sound he ever made.

Maltz shoved the body headfirst into the emtpy booth and motioned to his comrades. "Hurry—in here! Grab the Tiburonian! Lay down cover fire!"

Gradok picked up the old miner, while Kurton and Burka drew their disruptors and sent scarlet beams streaking across the tavern. The place erupted in screams and chaos, and trapeze artists tumbled out of the air onto the advancing security guards. That gave the two younger Klingons time to duck into the crowded booth with their comrades. They closed the curtain behind them and waited to fire the moment anyone opened it.

Maltz was busy ripping cushions away from the walls. "If that worm was lying, I'll kill him again!" Finally he uncovered the panel and pressed it without a moment's hesitation.

At once, the plush booth turned into a carnival ride, swirling around and dumping all of them—four Klingons, a sleeping Tiburonian, and a dead Andorian—down a long chute into the darkness.

A wild howl erupted form Maltz's throat, but it was silenced with a thud when he and his comrades landed in a sea of soft cushions. Flickering artificial candlelight barely illuminated a circular chamber; pillows covered the floor, and lewd paintings of debauchery covered the dark stone walls. There was a bar, a viewscreen, the chute they had fallen down, and two doorways, but no sign of Captain Brahms or Colin Craycroft. Both doorways led to rustic passageways carved from the black rock and lit by more flickering lights.

"Get up!" Maltz growled at his men. "Kurton, Burka—cover the chute and the doorways. Gradok, hide that body in the cushions."

The weapons master quickly burrowed through the pillows and cushions to the floor beneath, where he deposited the dead Andorian. Grabbing handfuls of cushions, Gradok wiped the pale-blue blood off his thick chest and his pitted metal sash, then he tossed the stained cushions over the body.

Meanwhile, Maltz went to the viewscreen and pressed buttons until he activated the device. The view on the screen showed the empty trapeze above them, and he pressed more controls until the scene switched to a sweeping view of the central tavern, now lit up. Security officers were clearing out the customers and searching the place, to no avail. They apparently didn't know about the saloon's secret passageways.

Maltz hurriedly tapped his combadge. "First officer to the *HoS*.

Come in, Kurok!" There was no answer. *"taHqeq!* We are too deep inside this infernal rock to contact the ship."

"We told them to leave at the first sign of trouble," answered Gradok.

"I hope they are able to leave," said Maltz. The old Klingon continued to bang on the controls of the viewscreen, cycling through various other sights until he found a plush bedroom with a woman lying prone on the bed. It was difficult to tell, but it looked like Leah Brahms.

"Which way?" he bellowed, now wishing that he had kept the treacherous Andorian at least partially alive. Maltz drew his disruptor and motioned to his younger comrades. "Burka, Kurton—you take the left-hand passage and look for this room . . . where they hold the captain. If you find her, try to contact us via communicator, and we will do likewise. If we can't communicate, try to make your way back to the ship. If that's impossible, return here. Do not allow yourselves to be captured."

The two young Klingons nodded in acknowledgment and hurried down the assigned passageway. Maltz motioned to the old Tiburonian, who was snoring peacefully, and Gradok heaved a sigh and picked him up.

With a worried frown, Maltz leveled his disruptor and led the way down the right-hand corridor. They hadn't walked far when they heard whining, grinding, and clanging sounds. Ahead of them, it appeared that the corridor widened, but it was hard to tell in the flickering light. Maltz slowed his pace and motioned Gradok against the wall, which was a difficult maneuver for the big Klingon burdened by the unconscious Tiburonian. Cautiously, Maltz made his way toward the rhythmic noises in the distance.

Within a few paces, the corridor expanded into a much larger chamber, with gleaming walls of yellowish crystal, buttressed by shimmering force fields and narrow walkways at different levels. Flashes startled him, and the Klingon dropped into a firing crouch; a moment later, he saw that the flashes were industrial, robot-controlled phasers carving their way through the glittering crystals.

Workers in lightweight environmental suits and hoods manned these weapons and other more primitive tools, like grinders, airhammers, and saws. Most of them wore green suits, but a few of the bosses wore white. Although the walls appeared to glisten like solid facets, Maltz could see that many of the cuttings were waste. Harried miners had to physically chop and grind the rubble in order to find crystals large enough to be saved. These crystals, about the length of a

Klingon's hand, were carefully placed in pressurized conduits, which whisked them away. Other workers shoveled the debris left by the process into biofilter bins, where the inert black rock disappeared, to leave only dilithium chips. All of these materials were carried away in conduits.

Portable light stands lit the cavern all too brightly, making Maltz nervous. He slipped back into the shadows of the tunnel and motioned Gradok to go back the way they had come. After a moment, Maltz stopped to listen.

"Are you sure where you're going?" the weapons master asked, dumping the Tiburonian onto the ground.

Maltz shook his head. "Who can tell? Was the captain transported somewhere? There's a busy mine this way, so we have to backtrack. Pick him up."

"Why can't we *wake* him up?" The brutish Klingon reached into his belt and removed a small capsule, which he broke under the old miner's nose. At once, the Tiburonian gasped and waved his arms feebly.

Maltz reached down and pulled Krussel to his feet. "You're all right, be calm. They drugged us in that evil place . . . the Pink Slipper."

"*Me?* I've never been drugged in there before. You must be *very* important." Krussel sniffed the air and looked around the rustic passageway. "Where are we?"

"Near a dilithium mine." Maltz scowled at the bent old miner. "They drugged us, kidnapped our captain, and tried to arrest us. Since they outnumbered us, we fought until we could make an escape."

The Tiburonian trembled. "Oh, dear, what have you gotten me into! Don't you know you'll be sentenced to the *mines?* It will take you twenty years to work off your sentence!"

The grin faded from Gradok's face. "What are you talking about?"

Krussel motioned toward the noise coming from the depths of the artificial cavern. "*Listen* to them—a lot of them are prisoners leased out to the mines. That's where you're going to go! Work makes the time go faster, and you can earn a little money while you're in. But I don't want to go back! You made a big mistake . . . because Colin Craycroft is the *owner* of the Pink Slipper. He's a powerful human around here."

Maltz grunted in anger. "I'll kill him later. First we must find the captain. Back to the pillow room." Pushing the other two ahead of him, the grizzled Klingon stalked down the corridor.

They hadn't walked far when the Tiburonian froze and held out his hands, his big ears twitching. Maltz almost ran over him, but he was able to catch himself. Then he reached out a long arm to catch Gradok.

"What is it?" asked Maltz.

"Voices," whispered the old miner. "Ahead of us, not the way we came."

"Stay here." Maltz motioned both of them to remain while he scouted ahead. It took several moments of stalking through the shadows, but he finally heard the voices, too. They were angry, busy, and officious—security voices. It sounded as if they had found the Andorian's body, which they could have done with a tricorder. If they had tricorders, they would soon investigate the corridors, too. Maltz hurried back down the corridor.

Into his communicator, he whispered, "Maltz to Kurton. Kurton, respond." He waited, but there was no answer, which didn't surprise him. Plunging ahead, he reached Gradok and the Tiburonian. "The authorities are back there. We have to think like humans."

"Oh, do we try to talk our way out of it?" asked Gradok.

"No. We use human subterfuge." Maltz pointed back down the hallway toward the distant sounds of mining. "I know . . . what about those environmental suits the miners wear?"

"They're actually more like cleanroom suits," said Krussel, "to keep the crystal from being contaminated."

"They will disguise us," said the Klingon. "Where can we get some?"

"Off their backs," Gradok answered with a shrug.

"Better yet, from the clothing bins or the locker room," Krussel said, craning his neck to look around the corner. "They should be nearby."

Maltz leveled a jaundiced eye at the old miner. "Are you going to help us get out of here, or are you going to betray us?"

Krussel snorted. "If I'm in your presence, I'm in as much trouble as *you* are. We need a diversion."

Suddenly they heard voices behind them—loud enough for anyone to hear. Maltz reached into his sash and pulled out a tiny chunk of pliable explosive, which he affixed to one of the flickering artificial candles.

"Go ahead of me," he ordered. "Walk slowly, as if you belong in there. Find suits and disguise yourselves, then look for me. Move."

Gradok pushed the old Tiburonian down the corridor, while Maltz backed away from the charge he had rigged. He rounded the corner and stopped at the farthest distance he could go and still see the light fixture, then he aimed his disruptor. The moment the guards appeared, he shot the light with a narrow beam. The guards ducked, but it didn't help them. The explosion blew out a ton of rocks and rumbled through the caverns, filling the passageway with smoke and dust. Lights went out the length of the corridor, plunging it into merciful darkness.

Somehow the explosion ricocheted along the power lines into the main chamber, where several light standards exploded, causing even more panic. There was chaos on the narrow catwalks, and one or two miners fell off their perches as a third of the mine was plunged into darkness. "Cave in! Cave in!" sounded the cries.

Maltz emerged into the larger room to find total confusion, with miners discarding their tools and rushing for the staircases and turbolifts. He didn't waste time getting a disguise—he hid in the smoke until a miner passed by, then he jumped out and clubbed him with his disruptor. Maltz dragged his unconscious victim into a shadowy corner and ripped the hood off his head.

He emerged a few moments later, looking like all the other panicked miners, except that he carried a Klingon distruptor in his hand. After making sure the security guards were still delayed by the explosion, he crept along the wall, looking for two miners who were not running as fast as the others. He noticed them lurking in the doorway of a small closet—a towering hulk who strained the material of his suit and a bent one who barely filled his out.

He motioned with his disruptor, and they waved back. Soon all three started in the direction of the mad rush. They had to practically carry the old Tiburonian, he was trembling so badly.

"You there!" someone shouted. "If he's injured, get to the emergency transporter!"

It took a moment for Maltz to realize that the white-suited boss was talking to them, thinking the Tiburonian was wounded and they were assisting him. "Thank you!" he muttered, turning away. Although the hood completely covered his head and the suit his body, the faceplate was transparent.

The figure in white pointed impatiently, and the trio scurried in the indicated direction. They got into a line with other miners waiting to enter a large tube. At first Maltz was worried that they would be whisked away in some kind of pressurized conduit like the crystals; then he saw two wounded miners enter the tube ahead of them and disappear in the swirl of a transporter beam. It was probably a short-range transporter, he decided, which wisely avoided passing through the dilithium-loaded rock.

While they waited, Maltz tried to ignore the alarmed shouts all around them, thinking that the miners weren't very disciplined. Of course, working underground was conducive to panic, especially when tunnels began mysteriously collapsing and exploding. He had already decided to go down fighting rather than risk being slave labor in this glittering hole.

Nevertheless, he hid his disruptor from view and told Gradok, "Limp. Pretend to be injured."

Finally they reached the tube, where the operator waved all three of them aboard. With relief, the trio stepped upon the transporter platform, only to have their molecules scrambled and reassembled at an unknown destination.


Still groggy, Leah Brahms was hauled rudely to her feet, and she looked longingly at the soft bed she had just left. Then she realized that she didn't know where she was. She blinked at the little man in the plaid jacket who had dragged her to her feet; she knew him, but she couldn't place him. The details of his identity were lost . . . somewhere in the cobwebs of her brain.

"Wake up!" he said urgently, shaking her by the shoulders. "We have to get out of here! The tunnel alarm has been set off."

Leah mumbled something in agreement, but instead she dove back onto the soft bed, curling up with a silky sheet. "No!" shouted Craycroft. "Oh, to hell with you. What do I care if you get arrested? I'll beat you to Lomar."

Suddenly Leah was left alone . . . nobody tugging on her arm, nobody yelling in her ear. Still she could hear the Klaxons and sirens at an indistinct distance, and she knew waking up in a strange bedroom was never good. The guy who had been shaking her was no good either—that stood to reason.

Despite all attempts to go back to sleep, her analytical mind took over, and Leah Brahms slowly accepted the notion that she should be awake and coherent. At least for a while. In her condition, she wanted to reserve the right to go back to sleep.

She rolled over and tried to find the floor with her feet. *Oh, this is bad,* she realized. *Whatever landed me in this state . . . in this place . . . had better be worth it.* There were lewd paintings on the walls, and the room was decorated with mountains of lacy pillows and billowing curtains. The curtains hid only small air vents, not windows. Despite its posh accessories, the bedroom had the feeling of being homemade, like a spare room in someone's basement. Maybe it was the lack of windows that gave it such an eerie quality—it was definitely a hideaway.

The bed lay between two doors at opposite ends of the room; they were solid metal, and both were ajar. Brahms had her choice of exits . . . or of not leaving at all . . . but a vague feeling of urgency propelled her to her feet. She knew she couldn't wait around to answer questions. Swaying unsteadily on her feet, she closed her eyes; when she did, gnarled, grizzled faces floated in her mind's eye.

The Klingons! *My crew.* A rush of memories came flooding back, giving her such a headache that she slumped back onto the bed. That was when she heard loud voices and hurried footsteps near the door to her right.

Flashes of light slashed into the metal door, ripping it apart in a hail of sparks. Two figures collapsed against the metal debris and tumbled into the room. To her horror, Leah witnessed the final seconds of life for the young Klingons, Kurton and Burka. They died in a conflagration of crisscrossing beams, and their bodies disappeared in a sizzling red haze.

Leah had no time to do anything but hurriedly pull the covers around her and cower in the bed. Phaser rifles leveled for action, a detail of four security guards burst into the bedroom. They instantly focused their attention and their weapons on her, and she pulled the covers up to her chin.

"Out of the bed!" ordered the one with the most stripes on his sleeve. He pointed his weapon at her head. "Hands up!"

"I am naked!" she pleaded, letting them see only her face. Luckily, Leah had long ago mastered the innocent-but-sexy gamine look, and she had no problem mustering real tears after seeing two of her crew killed. "The *awful* things they did to me . . . the *animals!* You wouldn't believe—"

The hardened guards looked sympathetic but still wary, and she added, "There were *two* more Klingons! They went out the other door. If you hurry, you can catch them!"

The ensign looked back at a subordinate, who was carrying a padd. "That's the report," she said. *"Four* Klingons."

Leah felt for the small hand phaser she kept on her belt. It had been part of her tool kit ever since Gradok had cornered her in the bowels of the ship. She forgot where in her travels she had picked up the phaser, and she hoped it was set on stun.

Doubt left the leader's eyes, and he barked, "Squad, continue pursuit! Keep alert, and use your tricorders. Lady, when we leave, you get dressed and wait here for us. We have questions for you."

Leah relaxed and gave him a warm smile. "Thank you, sir. I look forward to seeing you again . . . soon."

He flashed her a quick grin, then signaled. "Move out!"

Seconds later, the security detail was gone, passing through an unfamiliar door that led to parts unknown. At least they were unknown to Leah. She assumed they were still on Protus, but that was all she knew—although she had a strong feeling that she shouldn't wait around to be questioned. She hoped she hadn't inadvertently sent them after Maltz and Gradok, wherever they were.

Throwing off the covers, Leah rolled out of bed, her head still groggy. She would have to come to her senses on the run, she decided, so she staggered toward the door where her young crewmen had died. After all Leah had witnessed, she ought to be immune to the effects of death, which had chased her over half the quadrant; but she was terribly saddened by the loss of these two. They had been young, eager to follow orders, and dependent upon superiors to use them wisely. It was her idea to come here, and they had probably been trying to rescue her when they died. Leah had forgotten that humans were often the worst predators.

Then again, Burka and Kurton had gone down fighting—their fellows would say they had achieved honorable deaths. Leah wasn't ready for that yet, because she wasn't done fighting.

Taking a deep breath and getting her wobbly feet under her, she plodded out the door into a narrow tunnel carved from black stone. Dim lights flickered along the length of the winding tunnel, and Leah tried to combat a pounding headache as she walked. Finally she picked up her pace, noting the pits in the wall and the scattered pebbles where the recent phaser battle had left its mark.

She wracked her brain. *What do I remember? What do I know?*

*Nothing about this place or how I got here,* came the answer. *No matter how hard I try to forget, I remember too much about Seran, Hakon, Myrmidon, and the other planets that have already died.* Leah plunged onward into the gloomy passageway, certain only that she needed to survive and keep moving, just like before.

# fourteen

Maltz, Gradok, and the feeble Tiburonian, Krussel, inched toward a huge underground chamber that was outfitted with at least fifty beds, a hundred blinking displays, and two dozen medical workers. Still disguised in green mining suits with hoods, they had been shepherded into this line the instant they stepped off the transporter platform. There was no apparent way to escape from the underground chamber. The corridor went straight from the transporter tube to the trauma center, and it was awash in a sea of blithering humans and their allies, all convinced that they needed medical attention.

There had to be a lot of mining accidents on Protus, thought Maltz, because they were prepared for a large influx of patients. He fought the temptation to fight or run from the close-pressed horde, because the Klingons were outnumbered and stuck inside this subterranean labyrinth. They would have to wait for an opportunity, but they couldn't wait long. Despite hanging back as much as possible, the threesome were being pushed toward the medical workers. Soon they would have to take off their hoods to be examined, revealing their identities.

*Think!* he ordered himself. *What would a devious human do?*

When he couldn't come up with an idea, he merely looked around. The workers in the center were extremely calm as they dealt with the influx of patients. Did they even know or care what kind of emergency it was? Escape would be much easier, he decided, if the people on this level were in a cowardly panic like the miners below.

With a smile under his disguise, the cagey Klingon bent down to the old Tiburonian. "Krussel, take off your hood and shout as loud as you can that the Genesis Wave is going to hit Protus."

Krussel threw his head back and gasped. "Is that true?"

"Yes," he lied, thinking the old miner was either addle-brained or still drugged. "The collapse in the tunnel was just the beginning."

"Oh, my! I'll tell them." With difficulty, the Tiburonian pulled the hood over his big head and floppy ears. Then he shrieked at the top of his lungs, *"Doom!* Doom is here! The Genesis Wave is headed toward Protus!"

"What? Where! Says who!" bellowed the workers, most of whom were already frightened by the explosion, smoke, and dust below in the mine. Maltz grabbed his confederate, Gradok, and pulled him away from the mob that was starting to collect around the ranting coot.

"The Genesis Wave is going to hit Protus!" the Tiburonian shouted, believing it more thoroughly each time he said it. "That's what's causing the tunnels to collapse!"

Worried cries erupted in the medical center, and Maltz decided that panic was a very good weapon indeed. The combination of the Genesis Wave and collapsing tunnels was an effective rumor on Protus, judging by the reaction. He was sorry that they had to desert the old miner, but escape was crucial.

While most of the people in the corridor surrounded the Tiburonian and bombarded him with questions, the two Klingons plowed against the current of bodies. Maltz was bound for the only visible exit, the transporter tube on which they had arrived. Keeping their hooded heads low, they approached the transporter as two injured miners limped off.

"What's going on down there?" asked the transporter operator, craning his neck to see over the surging mob.

"Word just came down that the Genesis Wave is going to hit us!" answered Maltz, trying to sound like a worried human. He nodded to Gradok, who stepped behind the operator.

"What? Are you kidding me?" the worker exclaimed. "Says who?"

"Look! You can see for yourself." Maltz pointed into the chaos at the door of the medical center. While the human was distracted, Gradok brought a heavy fist crushing down on the back of his head, and Maltz caught the man as he fell.

"Taken ill," said Maltz in case anyone was watching. But no one was. He dragged the human behind the transporter console and propped him up as best he could, while Gradok bent over the controls. The human must be nicely thick-headed, thought the Klingon, because he was still breathing.

"There are many preset destinations," Gradok said with confusion as he studied the complex board. "No time to look up coordinates."

"What destinations are there?" the elder Klingon asked, rising wearily to his feet.

"There they are!" cried an agitated voice. Maltz whirled around to see that the Tiburonian had spotted them and was pointing in their direction. "They can verify it! They're the ones who told me about the wave coming!"

"Pick a place!" Maltz shouted, leaping into the transporter tube.

Gradok punched the board a couple of times, then he jumped into the transporter just as their molecules were collected in a spinning flurry of light.

Once the tingling of the transporter beam had stopped, Maltz warily opened his eyes; he found himself in a sumptuous booth that was decorated with lacy curtains and golden tassels. Gradok peered curiously at him, but neither one of the Klingons could offer a guess as to where they were.

With dread, Maltz pushed open the curtain, and he and Gradok stumbled out of the booth into the middle of a lady's lingerie shop. A fashion show was in progress, and both the models and the customers gasped at the sight of two hooded miners in their midst.

"What is the meaning of this?" demanded an indignant matron, as the models bounced off the stage and rushed for cover. "You're not supposed to be on this level!"

Wide-eyed, Maltz stared at the women. "Everybody, run for your lives! The tunnels are collapsing! The Genesis Wave is headed toward Protus."

That brought even more abrupt gasps from the audience. Maltz considered pulling out his disruptor and trying to destroy the transporter booth, so no one could immediately follow them; but he had created enough havoc already. They had to slip away unnoticed, not draw any more attention.

Gradok was craning his neck, trying to locate the scantily clad females, and Maltz grabbed his collar and barked, "We have to keep moving!"

"Why?" muttered the weapons master with disappointment.

People in the crowd peppered them with questions and demands, but Maltz just shoved his way through them, while keeping a close eye on Gradok. Running, the Klingons quickly outdistanced their pursuers and exited the clothing shop into the busy subterranean mall. Maltz whirled around as they walked, searching for the Pink Slipper, but he didn't recognize any landmarks. Even the golden fountain wasn't in sight—there was no telling where they were in this maze of an underground city.

The old Klingon looked around for signs, easily reading the Federation tongues he had learned during his dipomatic career. Finally his eyes lit up behind his clear faceplate. "Look! There's a sign for the space docks."

"You want to return to the ship without our captain? Our men?" Gradok gaped at him.

The old Klingon glared at his comrade. "Remember this well, the Blood Oath is more important than any one of us. If the others are worthy, they will find their way back to the ship."

Maltz slapped his comrade on the back of his tight-fitting suit. "But we will do what we can to help them. Perhaps we should continue to spread panic."

The climb was slow and laborious, because Leah Brahms had to stop every meter or so to burn more handholds and footholds with her phaser. Then she wrapped rags around her hands in order to endure the heat of the handholds. In this tedious fashion, she continued to scale the metal slide she had found in the pillow room. She could vaguely remember plunging down this slide to reach the plush chamber below.

It helped that the gravity was light inside the asteroid, so she could make good progress up the metal incline once she got started. Still it was slow having to carve footholds as she went, but it had to be done. If she ever lost her hold on the slippery slope, she'd slide all the way down to the bottom and would have to start again.

Only a hint of light trickled down from above, but it seemed to be getting brighter the higher she climbed. Leah was also relieved that her memory was coming back to her—now she recalled entering that secluded booth in the Pink Slipper. That was really the last thing she remembered clearly, other than drinking champagne, making mindless conversation, and riding down the slide.

With determination and patience, the engineer climbed to the top of the metal incline, where she found a shattered wall with a hole big enough to climb through. She emerged into the same private booth she had visited before, only now it was torn apart. With the pillows and curtains ripped to shreds, she could easily inspect the mechanism of the tilting booth and its attached chute. The gears and springs looked ancient and grimy, and she wondered if the slide was really an old piece of mining equipment, discarded then put to a use for which it was not originally intended.

As she caught her breath, Leah noticed something even more unusual—silence. Earlier, the Pink Slipper had been full of raucous noise and behavior, but now the tavern was eerily quiet. Bright lights illuminated every square centimeter of the place, which gave the garish decor a sickly pallor. She stepped out of the booth and looked around, verifying that the huge chamber was deserted. Several of the gaming and dining tables were overturned, and empty trapezes hung like dead vines from the cathedral ceiling.

Leah strolled through the abandoned playground, which looked phony and tawdry in the glaring light, and she wondered what could have cleared it out so totally. Then she remembered that she had left four Klingons behind, and two of them were dead. Maybe all four of them were dead, she thought with a pang of remorse. They had probably caused a commotion while looking for her.

*It's all my fault,* she decided gloomily. *I brought them here. All this time, I was worried about* their *conduct, when* my *conduct was what endangered the crew and the mission.*

Still distracted, Brahms reached the front door of the Pink Slipper and nearly crashed into it when it didn't open automatically. She pushed on the door, but it refused to budge. Peering out the smoky-glass windows of the tavern, Leah discovered that the door was locked from the outside with a blinking contraption. She was locked in!

When she saw three people run past the tavern in a panic, Leah wondered what was going on. The mall itself seemed to be deserted, or at least in the process of getting cleared out. Gone were all the amiable shoppers and merrymakers, and most of the businesses appeared to have closed their doors.

It was tempting to stay in the relative safety of the empty tavern, but she had to return to her ship . . . and hope she still had a crew. Leah stepped back and aimed her phaser at the window. The beam was already set to melt solids, and she had no problem carving a hole in the window big enough to crawl through. An alarm went off, but it only added to the surreal atmosphere in this part of the subterranean city.

A moment later, Leah was loping through the mall alongside members of the populace. She singled out a woman, who appeared to be a Coridan by her distinctive hairstyle. "Where is everyone going?" asked Leah.

"You haven't heard?" asked the Coridan in amazement. "We're all getting out of here. The tunnels are collapsing, and the Genesis Wave is supposed to hit us any minute!"

"We're not in the path of the Genesis Wave," declared Brahms. Even though she knew that to be true, just the idea panicked her. "Lots of planets are in danger, but not Protus."

"What makes you such an expert?" The woman picked up speed, pointedly running away from Leah.

The engineer stopped jogging and stepped into a recessed alcove, so as not to be run over by the stampede. She pulled out her communicator badge and barked, "Brahms to the bridge of the *HoS*. Come in! Kurok, are you there?"

When there was no response, she scowled and put the device away. It wasn't going to be that easy to get out of here, but she had to keep trying. Studying the signs overhead, Leah saw that most of the riot was headed the same way she was—to the space docks.

As she walked, the underground city looked oddly familiar—like a hundred space stations—yet it was alien and unfamiliar, too. Leah had no idea where she was, so she just had to follow the trickle of frightened citizens.

That trickle became a sluggish throng as they neared the monorail station. She was soon bogged down in the crowd and could do no more than move with the flow, trying to listen and stand on her tiptoes to see. Through the bobbing heads, she got a glimpse of security officers surrounding the monorail track, where a train waited. They were wearing riot gear and gas masks. Not a good sign.

Angry shouts rose over the anxious murmur of the crowd, and she could make out a few phrases: "The monorails are overloaded! Go back. There is no emergency!"

Just as loudly came the responses: "Then why can't we get on board? I've got to get back to my ship! Let us go!"

Like a wave sloshing toward the shore, the crowd pressed forward, and Leah found herself carried along. With a feeling of dread, she turned and tried to fight her way against the tide, but it was futile. Once again, she was sucked into the frenzy. Although this had to be a false alarm, the panic was just as real as it had been on Hakon. Besides, thought Leah, for all she knew, the tunnels really were collapsing—this much chaos didn't happen in a vacuum.

The verbal exchange between the guards and the mob became heated, when suddenly a projectile came lofting over their heads. It landed amid the crowd, and a big plume of red smoke went up, followed by cries of alarm. But the people nearest the red smoke sat calmly on the floor looking blissful. Despite the innocuous effect, the shouts turned to shrieks, and everyone in the crowd tried to run in a different direction. Leah held her breath and kept low, managing to avoid the fumes; still her eyes watered. *Dazzle gas!* She had heard of it, but she never thought she'd ever see any.

Brahms fought the temptation to drop to the floor and curl into a ball. Instead she jumped upon some poor soul's back and tried to peer over the choppy sea of heads. Now the security guards were arguing with each other as well as the rabid crowd, and pushing and shoving broke out. Another gas canister lofted over the crowd, exploding in a burst of colorful smoke, and the screams reached a higher pitch.

It was like the guards were inciting the riot, thought Leah. *What idiots!* Without warning, she was dumped off the broad back she had been climbing, and she barely landed on her feet. Finally the crowd had figured out that they could only escape from the dazzle gas by going in the opposite direction, away from the monorail station. Exhausted and bruised, Leah joined the sluggish flight.

Using her elbows and shoulders, she worked her way over to the wall, looking for an access panel, a ladder, anyplace where she could gain a handhold and pause in this mad flight. She heard a burst of screams as another canister was lobbed into the crowd, raising the panic level. Leah pushed toward her objective; her step quickened when she saw the familiar black and yellow colors of a fire hose box.

Fighting against the press of the mob, she lunged for the handle of the box and gripped it as she flew past. With a click, the door opened, and she swung back on the hinges into the wall. Leah didn't quite get the breath knocked out of her, but it took all her effort to hold on and keep from blacking out.

Finally she was able to squeeze against the wall and use the open door as a shield. It was a good thing she was small. Some of the overzealous guards in their gas masks were fighting their way through the crowd. For what purpose? she wondered. Everything they did just made things worse.

Leah glanced inside the box on the wall and saw a lever beside the coiled fire hose. She had an irrational urge to fight back against the heavy-handed security officers and their dazzle gas. Besides, if she got arrested, maybe she could tell her story to someone in charge. So she grabbed the nozzle of the hose. Her actions did not go unnoticed, and two of the masked security guards veered off from the others and headed in her direction.

Angry over the way she'd been treated—and the way all these people were being treated—Brahms reached inside the box, grabbed the lever, and pulled it down. At once, the recoil from the fire hose slammed her against the wall, but she gripped the nozzle and managed to maintain control of a powerful jet of fire-fighting chemicals. The stream blasted the advancing guards, who slipped to the ground. It also knocked down a few frightened citizens, but they were no worse off than when they were fleeing from the tear gas.

While Leah was watching, she lost track of the guards. One of them jumped to his feet right in front of her and tried to grab the hose from her hands. She fought with all her might to hold on, but he was strong, almost berserk, in his determination. When his partner gripped her wrist, she was helpless to stop them from wrenching the hose from her hands.

"You come with us!" ordered a gruff voice, and she was pinned rudely against the wall.

# fifteen

Leah Brahms was certain that she was about to be arrested—or beaten—in the sodden mall deep inside the asteroid named Protus. To her surprise, the two guards who had assaulted her suddenly let her go, and the one with the hose turned it back upon his fellows, several of whom were trying to advance to their position.

"It's *us,* Captain!" barked a voice in her ear.

Leah whirled around to stare at the snaggle-toothed face under the gas mask and hood. "The hose was a brilliant idea!"

"Gradok?" she asked in amazement.

He nodded. "First officer Maltz, too."

She looked at the wiry warrior manning the fire hose, keeping dozens of locals at bay. "Have you seen Kurton and Burka!" he shouted over the din.

"Yes . . . they're dead!"

"How!" roared the Klingon.

"I'll tell you about it later," she answered. "Can't we get out of here?"

"Yes! Follow me." Using the powerful jet as a battering ram, Maltz surged into the crowd, cutting an impressive path with the water bolt.

When a few phaser beams streaked over their heads, Gradok drew his disruptor and returned fire in deadly fashion. At least three of the guards dropped, and the others were soon in retreat. It seemed as if they didn't want to fire for fear of hitting the onlookers, but Gradok had no such compunction.

They fought their way toward the monorail station until the length of hose ran out. Maltz let it go, and it snaked around violently, whipping a stream of chemical spray into the cascade already pouring down from above.

Disruptors blazing, the Klingons ran toward the closest empty monorail car. Brahms could do little more than try to keep up with them. She realized they were shooting to open a hole in the conveyance. Their bold actions were lost in the general pandemonium, and no one rushed forward to stop them. However, the car began to move.

"Hurry!" yelled Maltz.

Shooting on the run with his disruptor, Gradok drew a crude oval on the side of the car, then he crashed into it at full speed. The Klingon and a chunk of the car fell into the cabin with a crash, and Maltz and Leah dove in after him—just as the monorail picked up speed and tore out of the station.

"We can't stay here!" shouted Brahms. "We'll lose pressure and oxygen!"

She charged toward the front of the car, which was connected to another car; and she grabbed the wheel to open the hatch just as a sudden rush of air yanked her off her feet. It almost sucked her backward out the gaping hole, but Maltz steadied her. Gradok took the wheel, twisted it easily, and opened the hatch. They ducked into the air lock and slammed the door shut behind them just as the last of the air rushed out of cabin.

Calmly, regaining his composure, Maltz opened the door to the next car. It was full of what looked like dignitaries, the rich and beautiful people of Protus, who all turned around to stare in amazement. Maltz stepped into the cabin, leveled his disruptor with one hand and pulled off his gas mask with the other. At the sight of the crusty old Klingon, there were audible gasps among the thirty-or-so passengers.

Maltz sneered. "We are taking a slight detour."

A well-dressed human frowned at him. "Are *you* the ones who have thrown this entire operation—the whole asteroid—into an uproar?"

"None other," said Maltz with a sense of accomplishment. "So imagine what we could do to this one car if you don't cooperate?" Without taking his eyes or weapon off the passengers, he nodded toward a console at the front. "Captain, you might want to see if you can get us back to our ship."

"Right," answered Leah, striding down the aisle, ignoring the looks of contempt from the passengers. "We didn't treat you people any worse than you treated us," she muttered to no one in particular.

While Leah settled in at the controls of the speeding monorail, she heard Maltz say, "Do any of you know Colin Craycroft, owner of the Pink Slipper?"

Now came vehement words of disgust, and more than a few people observed, "Of course you would know *him!*"

"Tell Craycroft to make his peace, because he will die the next time I meet him," replied the old Klingon.

That somber proclamation brought much of the conversation to a hush, and Brahms was finally able to concentrate on the readouts. She located dock seventeen and found that she could reroute the monorail to get there.

She heard Maltz say, "I need crew. Who wants to sign on?"

Now there were disbelieving looks all around, followed by nervous tittering. Someone asked pleasantly, "Where are you going?"

"To find the fiends who created the Genesis Wave and kill them." That brought the muttering to a complete stop, and the only sound to be heard was the whisper of the rail overhead.

It took a while, but finally a human youth stood up. "I'll go," he said shakily.

"Herbert, sit down!" shouted the woman with him, probably his mother. She clutched his arm. "They'll kill you!"

"No, boredom will kill you," declared Maltz. "Step out here, young human."

The lad gently pulled away from the woman's clutches. He looked down at her with sympathy and love, but also with the coldness that comes with a streak of youthful independence. "Aunt Patricia, I'm old enough, and this is what I want to do. Please don't stand in my way."

"To go off with these—" She glared at the Klingons, then lowered her head and sniffed. "If your parents were alive—"

"Well, they're not and it's because that thing, that Genesis Wave, killed them and destroyed our home. I'm not going to let the same thing happen here. Good-bye, Aunt Patricia." The lad stepped forthrightly into the aisle, and Maltz and Gradok sized him up. He looked like a well-groomed teenager, with a slight build, sandy hair, about sixteen years old.

"A little skinny," said Gradok with a frown.

"I'm a good rock climber," declared the boy proudly.

"We accept you," answered Maltz, slamming a beefy hand onto the lad's scrawny shoulder. His aunt shrieked and tried to charge up the aisle, but her friends wisely stopped her.

Leah turned back to her board, and she made a decision, too. "There's a maintenance station coming up," she reported. "It's empty, and I think we should stop and let everyone out there."

"Except the lad," said Maltz.

"Crazy volunteers exempted," Brahms said with a glance at the boy. "Just don't expect a long career and a pension." She wanted to slap him and tell him he was insane, but they needed the crew. The rest of his life might be short, but it would be exciting.

"Captain," said Maltz hoarsely, "how did Kurton and Burka die? Was it a warrior's death?"

"Oh, yes," she answered. "There was a fantastic battle in the tunnels. They were trying to protect me, but they were outnumbered. They went down in a blaze of phaser fire."

"Their bodies were not desecrated?" asked Gradok.

"No. In fact . . . they were vaporized by all the phaser beams."

"Let's announce them to *Sto-Vo-Kor*," Maltz said with a tear in his rheumy eye.

The Klingons threw back their heads and roared to the heavens with frightening howls. The passengers shrunk back and covered their ears at the unearthly sounds. It went on for such a long time that even Leah grew edgy, and she finally decided that the only way to accept it was to join in. She cut loose with a gut-wrenching shriek, which only caused Maltz and Gradok to yell all the louder, until their voices collided in an anguished chord.

When they stopped at the maintenance station, the passengers bolted off without being told, while the howling went on. Herbert's protesting aunt was dragged off by the friends, and Leah glanced back to see if their newest recruit was still aboard. He was.

"Last chance!" she shouted over the din. He stood perfectly still, rooted to the spot, and Leah shrugged and put the monorail into forward motion. She no longer cared who lived and died anymore, as long as the ones responsible for the Genesis Wave were on the rolls of the dead.

*This is quite an impressive hologram,* Carol Marcus mused as she gazed around her spacious laboratory on Regula I, with its 360-degree view of the stars and an impressive collection of nebulas beyond. One of them was the Mutara Nebula, which shouldn't exist in this timeframe.

*No wonder all of it seemed so familiar—they dredged it up from my mind, warts and all.* The old woman looked at a scratched microscope screen, which she had always meant to replace. She remembered how she had made that scratch ninety-five years ago with a pair of dropped tongs; in many respects, her memories had never been clearer.

Her captors had spared no effort in producing this recreation for her benefit. Still, parts of the lab were undoubtedly real, such as the computers and test chambers; other areas had to be fake. This whole space station couldn't exist—*didn't* exist—in the current year. Besides, she was convinced that they were on a starship. There was something in the familiar sounds and sensations—delicate whirs, the vague sensation of motion—that conveyed the impression they were headed somewhere.

As always, Marcus was able to compartmentalize and put all other considerations aside while she worked. It had felt wonderfully sinful to be immersed again in her Genesis discoveries and designs, all returned home to roost in her mind like long-lost children. But she no longer had to imagine the most soulless and evil purpose to which Genesis could be put, because she saw it outlined in front of her. *The doomsayers had been right for once,* she thought miserably. *Imagine that.*

*Keep working,* she ordered herself. "Computer, activate personal log."

"Log activated," said the officious voice.

She rubbed her eyes and continued: "Dr. Carol Marcus, general notes for Genesis Wave, test two. The goals are to implement three improvements over the first discharge. One will be a solar analyzer built into the matrix; this will analyze suns in the path faster and more accurately than before. Suns meeting criteria will undergo mild conditioning instead of drastic conditioning. These two improvements should cut down on the losses of otherwise suitable planets when their suns were altered too hastily."

Carol shivered, trying not to think of how many worlds had been destroyed and then wasted when they couldn't exist with their new mutilated suns. She hurriedly went on:

"The third change is increased resistance to phase-shifting, as found in non-Federation cloaking devices. Stage two will incorporate a random pattern of tachyons, which are known to disrupt temporal fields. Although this theory should work, we lack both the raw data and the time needed to test it, even in a simulator. I believe we have about a fifty-fifty chance of success."

Carol paused, wondering who had circumvented the original wave with phase-shifting. Romulans? Some other race? How many races had they destroyed in the deluge of horror she had helped unleash?

"End log." Sniffing back her emotions, Marcus tried not to grieve too much for the millions, probably billions, who had perished. She couldn't afford to—as far as she knew, she was the only one standing in the way of a second Genesis Wave, worst than the first.

There were ways she could sabotage this new trial, but she knew they could read her mind. She had to be honest with them whenever possible, which meant not attempting to keep a secret. Yet in their own way, they were as wary of her as she was of them. There was something in her captors' makeup that was oddly dependent . . . nothing like the real David Marcus or Jim Kirk. It seemed as if they would do anything to keep her alive, solely because she was useful.

*I'll have to do something spur-of-the-moment,* she decided, *and I'll probably have only one chance. Until then, I'll pretend they're my loved ones, while we all go through the motions.*

The door whooshed open, and Carol quickly turned back to the schematic of a tachyon cannon, wondering how they could mount it inside the emitter array. The fake Kirk swaggered in, wearing the protective cleanroom suit he wore almost all the time now. That suit was designed to protect the environment from the wearer.

"Do you like the new suits?" he asked rhetorically, reading her mind as easily as she read the screen. "I'm just giving it a test—see how it wears."

"I don't care what suits you wear, darling," she answered, peering at her instruments. "However, I would like to figure out how to time the tachyon burst with the variable speed of the wave."

Jim cocked his head under the pale yellow hood and stepped closer. "I thought you had that figured out."

"In theory," she answered, "the carrier wave will force the tachyon stream to keep pace, but I have to adjust for the drag coefficient when we're in active mode on a large celestial body. I mean, there's no way to try the changes before the test, so we'll have to live with the results. I'm also worried about matrix degradation, because this wave is already carrying a lot of data."

Innocently, she added, "If we could delay the test—"

"Impossible," snapped Kirk. He immediately softened his stance, and she could see a youthful grin behind his faceplate. "Hey, this test will tell us if the tachyons work or not, so let's just do it. There's no point in having *two* tests, now is there?"

"We *are* having two tests," she answered truthfully, "and it would help if I could see all the figures from the first test. Where are the long-range scans you and David were talking about?"

"You heard us talking?" said Kirk with surprise. "Your hearing is very good for—"

"An old lady?" Carol finished his sentence. But she was thinking about something else . . . that she had picked up their thoughts *mentally.* Unless they were talking to each other for her benefit, which they often did, they had no reason to communicate in audible sound. She couldn't have heard them making verbal communication—she knew that for a fact.

"You're not old," said Kirk, mustering some of the tenderness with which he had enthralled her. With a gloved hand, he touched her cheek. "You know what you're doing here, don't you?"

"Getting a second chance," she answered, knowing that was true in more ways than they ever considered.

"You're worried about the target planets," Kirk said with mocking good humor. "I told you, we've taken great pains to avoid inhabited planets. We are doing this quadrant a tremendous service, terraforming useless rocks into a chain of beautiful paradises!"

Plastering a smile onto her face, Carol squeezed his hand in return and tried to concentrate on pleasant memories, of which there were many. "Believe me, I've been thrilled to see you again, darling . . . and to work with you and David. Whatever magic you used to make this happen, you won't get any complaints from me."

She turned back to her instruments with a sigh. "I'm sure you know what you're doing when you keep data away from me, but I warn you that my results may be less than perfect."

The fake Kirk held his palms up. "The data is . . . confusing. We just didn't want to confuse you."

"But you're also confusing the algorithms for the solar analyzer," she replied. "Those variables are dependent upon raw data, and we could use some more data for the simulations."

"You'll get the raw data," said Kirk, as if coming to a decision. "Let me go to the computer room and fire up the sensor logs. Quick thinking as ever, sweetheart." When he playfully tweaked her cheek, she tried not to grimace.

After the creature left the room, the elder scientist let out a sigh and gripped her console for support. It was draining—keeping up her guard while working around-the-clock at a high level . . . for a nefarious cause. But she had learned something valuable today—that the mind games seemed to be working *two* ways now. They had nearly killed her by accident, but their cure had left her with something of theirs. She had a feeling that she would only be seeing the two ghosts when necessary.

*The worst of the damage has been done,* Carol Marcus told herself, *both to me and the galaxy. The only thing left is to stop it from happening again.*

# sixteen

All across the mottled plains, forests, and swamps of Myrmidon, massive fires burned out of control. Watching from orbit in the Romulan shuttlecraft, Dolores Linton thought it looked like a newly born sun trying to break out of its crumbling shell. Where the dense smoke and clouds allowed visibility, the forests blazed like glowing lava, and it was impossible to tell the chain of fires from the chain of volcanoes. In their zeal to fight the moss creatures, the Bolians had turned Myrmidon into an unholy inferno.

After taking a few sensor readings, she could tell that the smoke was winning the battle against the clouds to rule the blackening atmosphere.

"All readings getting worse," she told Data, who sat beside her at the controls of the Romulan shuttlecraft.

The android cocked his head and replied, "If current trends follow my predictions, most of the survivors will be dead in thirty-eight hours, when the air becomes unbreathable. However, the moss creatures will be neutralized."

"Small consolation," Dolores said miserably, as she looked out the viewport at the smoldering planet. "I feel like I'm a part of that place—I don't know why. It feels like *I'm* dying inside."

"You were a part of the natural order," answered Data, "before I rescued you."

"Yeah, and I can't thank you enough. But after all we tried to do . . . to lose all those people is hard to take."

"Perhaps they are not lost," Data said thoughtfully.

"What do you mean?"

"There may be a fleet of rescue vessels just waiting to come to

Myrmidon," said the android. "Certainly the Federation must be very interested in the outcome here, since we have been unable to communicate. But this hypothetical fleet will not be able to come here unless they know it is safe to cross the residue of the Genesis Wave."

"How will they know that?" asked Dolores, already dreading the answer.

"We will have to pilot this uncloaked shuttlecraft back to unaffected space."

Dolores shifted nervously in her seat. "But I've already told you, there are interphase generators lying all over the planet!"

"However, using phase-shifting will not be a viable test. To assure the admiralty that a normally equipped fleet of starships can fly safely to Myrmidon, we need to accomplish the feat in a normal craft."

"But . . . but if the residue is still active, we'll be dead!"

"That is correct," answered Data.

"Do you have a Plan B?" Dolores asked hopefully.

"No, I do not," answered Data. "I suppose we could rescue a few more Starfleet personnel, five or six at the most, and wait until someone eventually contacts us."

"And everyone on the planet will be dead?" asked Dolores.

"There will be a small percentage who find a way to survive," answered the android. "Three-tenths of one percent, by my calculations."

Dolores laughed with frustration and disbelief. "You know, I thought I would get used to your cold way of talking about this stuff, but I can't. Don't you *care* what happens to anyone? Even yourself?"

"I have an emotion chip," Data said with some degree of pride. "Would you like me to activate it?"

"Yeah, go ahead."

Once again, the android cocked his head slightly. His eyes widened in complete horror, and his frantic face went through every emotion known to humankind—joy, terror, rage, fear, hope, and about fifty more—in a few seconds. Dolores got exhausted just watching his rubbery face.

He turned to her with a look of complete panic. "What is the *matter* with you? We must save these wretched souls on Myrmidon! We must get *help!*"

Then Data trembled with fear. "But what if you are *right*? What if the effect has not dissipated? We will *cease* to exist. I am too young to cease to exist! You will have to make a decision!"

"First of all, turn off the emotion chip!" she cried.

"Done," he answered with a nod, his becalmed self once again. "I apologize—I seem to have many pent-up emotions concerning this issue."

"All right," muttered Dolores. "Set your course. I never expected to live forever, anyway."

"We should know very quickly," Data assured her as he worked his board.

"Well, that's a relief."

"I want you to know that you have been very good company these last forty hours."

"You, too," said Dolores, "although I wish I could hear you play the violin once more . . . before I go."

Data glanced to the back of the shuttle. "I do not believe the Romulan replicator is equipped to produce Terran musical instruments, although it does offer Starfleet uniforms."

"I'm wearing one," said the geologist with a smile. "I'll just *imagine* the violin music while we head off into space."

"I could hum for you," said Data.

"Just make it quick, like you promised." The geologist stiffened in her seat and screwed her eyes shut. A moment later, she felt them banking as the shuttlecraft pulled out of orbit.

She waited stiffly, but she felt nothing unusual. Shakily she asked, "Tell me when it's going to happen."

"Nothing happened," answered Data.

"We're alive?" whispered Dolores. She opened her eyes to see nothing but a beautiful sprinkling of stars floating in the darkness. It didn't look as if this sector of space had been ravaged by the Genesis Wave.

"Enough time has passed for the effect to have dissipated," said Data, "although communications are still unresponsive. Our destination is the rendezvous point where we met the Romulans."

The android rapidly worked his console, then reported, "Going to warp drive."

Dolores Linton sat back and breathed her first relaxed breath in what seemed like weeks, but she didn't feel relaxed. There were too many people in danger, too much to do, too much undone. People were spread out all across the quadrant, battling this scourge. Where were Geordi La Forge, Leah Brahms, Admiral Nechayev, Captain Picard, and all the others? She didn't bother to ask Data, because she knew he didn't know. Even if they had survived a risky gamble, they were still just two beings who had been left behind to witness a disaster. She tried to shake the fear that Myrmidon was a lost cause—a planet that should be left to fester and die alone.

"We have arrived," said Data, pulling Dolores out of her melancholy.

With excitement, she sat up to look out the viewport, but all she saw was a nondescript array of stars and distant dust clouds. No ships.

Dolores looked down at her sensor readings, but Data was way ahead of her. "There are no ships in the vicinity. We will have to use delayed subspace to communicate."

"Where the hell are they?" muttered the geologist, banging her fists on the console.

"Unknown," answered Data. "If I were to make a supposition, I would say Earth."

"Earth?" echoed Dolores. Feeling spent, she slumped across the console, her head resting on her brawny arms. "It's hard to imagine Earth being gone."

"Not for another twenty-three hours," said the android.

"Are we going there now?" Dolores asked wearily.

"No, we could not reach Earth in time to be any help. We will follow the *Enterprise* and the *D'Arvuk* to the Boneyard."

"What about all those people on Myrmidon?"

"We are one small shuttlecraft," said Data. "I will send a report via subspace, but their fate is out of our hands."

"Damn," muttered Dolores, dropping her head back onto her arm. "This thing just stays messed up, doesn't it?"

"Yes, it does," agreed the android.


As seen from Earth, a band of bright stars and glowing nebulas swept across the night sky. Near the Southern Cross, this dazzling belt of light was interrupted by a jagged hole—a black nebula called the Coal Sack. Not a true nebula, although there were plenty of opaque dust clouds in its depths, the Coal Sack was a huge chunk of space that was relatively empty. Compared to the brilliant starscape surrounding it, the Coal Sack was a desert. It was a good place to put something you didn't want, thought Admiral Alynna Nechayev.

Standing alone in the stellar cartography room aboard the *Sovereign,* the admiral had her choice of viewing any known object in the heavens, from any angle. She moved a tiny jumpstick on a device in her hand to enlarge her view of the Coal Sack. Her feet clacked across the raised platform as she inspected the contents of the dark nebula.

In its mysterious heart floated an even darker body—the Furnace. This opaque object was classified as a nonstandard quasar, as if there were such a thing as a standard quasar. Its pronounced redshift on the spectrum made early Terran astronomers think it was much farther away than it had turned out to be. It put out enormous amounts of radio and electromagnetic interference, and some said it should be classified as a pulsar. Whatever it was, the Furnace obliterated anything that came too close, including most varieties of light waves.

For Nechayev, it was the ultimate incinerator, and she was assigning the dirtiest garbage to it. That is, if the La Forge theory worked and their forty thousand starships did their job.

If the plan didn't work, a certain planet named Earth would not exist—as anyone recognized it—by this time tomorrow. And they would probably be at war with the Romulans.

Nechayev tried never to second-guess herself, but she couldn't help but wonder if she could have done anything differently. After all, she knew Carol Marcus had been kidnapped, and she should have been ready for some deployment of the Genesis technology. But she wasn't expecting something of this immense scope.

Should she have sent more ships to find the source? Nechayev had thought the task force of *Defiant*-class vessels would be enough, but they had disappeared without uncovering anything. After that, her dependence on a defensive strategy of evacuation, shelters, and now the Ring of Fire had necessitated hanging on to all the ships at her disposal. She was still mired in the ramifications of that quick decision.

It was clear by now, thought Nechayev, they were fighting more than the Genesis Wave itself. There were signs of a ruthless, clever enemy behind all of this. By now, a dozen ships had reported back from the Boneyard, and no one had found anything unusual. The enemy had covered their tracks, as any sensible foe would do, and sending more bloodhounds wouldn't be useful. By dealing with the wave, she felt they were attacking the most immediate threat to the Federation. If their homeworlds were wiped out, what did vengeance or justice matter?

*After so many failures and partial successes, we finally have a plan to neutralize the wave,* Nechayev assured herself. *I still don't see what I could have done differently, except to protect Carol Marcus better.* As in so many games of war, the early mistake is often the most costly one.

The door whooshed open, mildly startling her. The admiral turned to see her main attaché, Lieutenant Kelly, stride into the domed room.

"I have the latest dispatches," he said.

She nodded brusquely. "Make it fast—we only have an hour."

Her subordinate nodded and consulted his padd. "Commander

Data has sent word that the forests of Myrmidon are on fire. He says the devastation is almost total. There's a detailed report in your inbox, but the gist of it is that the survivors have set most of the fires themselves—in an attempt to drive out the moss creatures."

The admiral's face hardened, and she said nothing. Her subordinate cleared his throat and went on, "Commander Data requests aid for the survivors within the next thirty-eight hours, maximum. He says we can navigate the space around Myrmidon safely now—the effect is over."

"That's good," Nechayev said simply. "Adjust the orders for the Klingons, so that they'll go to Myrmidon as soon as we release them. Make sure *all* orders for the cleanup stage get out as soon as possible."

"Yes, Admiral," the young lieutenant said, making a note on his padd. "The *Enterprise* reports that it has almost reached the Boneyard, but sensors don't find any sign of the Genesis Wave or its origin."

"Not surprising," answered the admiral. "Go on."

Kelly glanced down at his padd, and a smile crept over his youthful face. "I don't know what to make of this one. The mining colony on Protus says that they were invaded by Klingons."

Nechayev laughed despite herself—an unexpected release of tension. Her face and tone quickly turned somber again. "I don't see how. Every Klingon ship is here with us."

"I know, sir," Kelly answered, scrolling to the end of the report. "They haven't furnished many details either, except that the commercial district and mining operations were destroyed."

"I've been to Protus," said Nechayev. "I don't blame them one bit. Ask for more details—in triplicate. We are sending Klingons in that direction, so maybe they're just repeating a rumor they heard."

"That's probably it," agreed the lieutenant. She looked up and caught him gazing at her face, and he quickly diverted his eyes. Half of Nechayev's face was wrinkled and full of character, while the other half was youthful and smooth—a result of having been treated with mutagenically active soil on Myrmidon.

She would get it fixed when there was time—until then, she was a walking billboard for the power of the Genesis Wave. As usual, Alynna Nechayev didn't mind grabbing attention—that was how she got things done.

"Anything else?" she demanded.

"The Romulan third fleet reports that they're in position," answered Kelly.

"Good thing. They're only an hour and five minutes behind schedule." The admiral stared at a blazing ring floating in the middle of the three-dimensional holographic representation of the region. She had dubbed it the Ring of Fire—forty thousand starships, assembled from all the powers and fleets in the Alpha Quadrant.

"It's an extraordinary feat," said Kelly. "Just getting them all here."

She scowled. "That's just issuing orders and having them followed. The feat is yet to come. If I'm wrong, it will be the greatest failure in the history of the Federation, and Earth."

Kelly started edging to the door. "I'll be on the bridge. Are you . . . are you going to stay down here alone?"

"For the duration," answered Nechayev, regarding the celestial charts hovering in midair. "Do you remember my telling you that, as a commanding officer, you must never say 'Oops!' And you must never let your forces see you cry?"

"I remember that," Kelly answered, forcing a smile.

"Well, I intend to heed my own advice. Just tell the captain to keep feeding data to my charts. Dismissed, Lieutenant."

"Yes, sir." The young man nodded, then bolted for the door.

After he left, the admiral's shoulders slumped, and she let her guard down. Wearily, she walked away from her charts to sit at the master console, where a small viewscreen cycled through various views of the forty thousand warships under her command. Great Romulan warbirds, massive Klingon birds-of-prey, starships of every class and description, freighters, scows, and junks—it was the greatest fleet ever assembled. Like their enemy, they hoped to be victorious without firing a shot.

But the wave was now four million kilometers wide, and it took no prisoners and gave no quarter. The idea of stopping it with a ring of ships and a network of force fields was almost absurd. *But it has to bend,* she told herself. *Everything has to bend eventually, doesn't it?*

Allowing herself the luxury of a yawn, Nechayev realized how weary she was. Stress, lack of sleep, and an abbreviated recovery period from her injuries had all led to bone-deep exhaustion. She would like to sleep, but she couldn't—she had one more chore to do.

"Computer, take a memo. To Admiral Brud'khi, Chief of Starfleet Command, San Francisco." She paused, thinking that there might be no San Francisco by the time this message was delivered. "Computer, correct address to fleet at large," she went on.

"Admiral, with deep regret, I hereby tender my resignation from Starfleet, effective immediately," Nechayev said, her voice cracking. "If you have received this, then our strategy to divert the Genesis Wave away from Earth was a failure. I take full responsibility, as I have from the beginning. I let the genie out of the bottle, and it was my duty to recapture it. I tried every way I could in the time allotted, but I made decisions that might have been wrong. If I have failed, then I have failed the uniform, the honor, and the purpose of Starfleet. Sincerely, Alynna Nechayev."

She caught her breath, then went on, "Computer, hold this message for forty-five minutes, then send with my approval only."

"Acknowledged," answered the computer. Her viewscreen went back to revolving views of the ships waiting for action. Each was so distant from the others that the ring was indistinct—there was no video log big enough to capture it.

Nechayev glanced back at the holographic representation of the Ring of Fire—a massive circle of vessels and space stations, anything that could be towed or flown into position. Every vessel had to be capable of producing a force field or tractor beam. Young Kelly had been wrong—assembling the ships had not been the hardest part of the operation—matching the strength and synchronizing the timing of the beams had been the hard part. There was no room for error—if one ship was off, the entire network would fail.

She wondered if the Romulans and Klingons realized how vulnerable the Federation was at this moment. It was lying in front of them, its throat uncovered—but that was just one more leap of faith they would have to make. The admiral wished they'd had time for at least one test, but the last segments of the circle had just fallen into place. There was no dress rehearsal, only the real thing.

To her surprise, Nechayev actually drifted off to sleep—or at least she was in a drowsy state when she heard the voice of the captain addressing the ship. "To all hands, the Genesis Wave has been spotted and is still on trajectory with an ETA of twelve minutes, twenty seconds. It's available on your viewscreens, and should be rather impressive as it passes through the Hag's Head Dust Cloud in ten seconds."

Nechayev shook her head with exasperation, thinking that captains always had to inject more drama into a situation than was already there. She had lived through the Genesis Wave once—barely—but she couldn't remember a thing about that experience. With reluctance, she turned to her viewscreen.

Moments later, she was grateful that Alvarez had drawn their attention to the sight, because the Genesis Wave truly was a marvel to behold. Like a primal force, it came roaring through the big multicolored dust cloud, exploding it like a dandelion blasted by the wind. Just as quickly, the debris coalesced into an amorphous, pulsing body, trying desperately to become a planet. It succeeded in becoming nothing but a stomach-churning oddity as it twisted in the grimy detritus of the Genesis Wave. Nechayev found herself recoiling from the sight, even though it was just inert rock and dust being mutilated. The smooth side of her face tingled with the memory.

"Beginning ten-minute countdown," added Captain Alvarez. "All stations, maximum synchronization."

Nechayev gripped the arms of her chair, and she didn't let go for the next ten minutes.

# seventeen

"Ten, nine, eight, seven, six, five, four—"

Admiral Nechayev rose to her feet and began to pace the stellar cartography room, unable to watch the moment of truth on the viewscreen. She also turned away from the holographic images on the charts floating overhead. She would know if they succeeded—she'd feel it in her soul.

"Three, two, one. We have contact with the intruder," said the computer's voice. Nechayev held her breath. Against her will, she looked at the Ring of Fire circling the wave's target; at that moment, it illuminated brightly. Did the lights in the room dim, or was that her imagination? This ship, as well as all the others, was being taxed to its limits by the power demands of the force fields.

On the simulation, a red beam entered the Ring of Fire, and the admiral held her breath again. The image flickered for a moment—probably the real moment when the wave hit the ring—then the red beam went streaking off at a different angle. It blinked as it headed toward the dark desert in the sea of stars, the Coal Sack.

Still Nechayev didn't let out her breath, because these were only simulations—the real wave may not have behaved that way. She rushed back to the master console. Before she even sat down, the captain's voice sounded on the shipwide intercom:

"Mission achieved. The Genesis Wave has been diverted. Earth is saved!"

With a grin, Nechayev slumped into her seat, hearing in her mind the cheers that went up all over the ship—in every ship. The Romulans probably looked smug and rolled their eyes, but she was certain the

Klingons were cheering. They loved a victory against overwhelming odds, and they loved the moment when the tide turned in battle.

She banged on her console and said, "Nechayev to Tactical Command, Ring of Fire."

"Yes, Admiral," came the prompt response. "Admiral Horkin here. Congratulations, gutsy call. Maybe they'll let you retire now."

"Don't count on it," she snapped. "Is the wave past, or is it continuous?"

"Sensors show it's past—nothing left but the residue we've seen before."

"Good, then we can start the cleanup. I know we diverted the wave, but did we also narrow it?"

"Affirmative on that," answered her fellow admiral. "It's on course to the Furnace, and we've diverted all traffic from its path. Worked like a charm."

"That's enough patting ourselves on the back," said Nechayev brusquely. "Get those fleets dispatched—lots of survivors need them."

"Yes, sir. And now you'll check yourself into sickbay, and get the care you need?" he asked hopefully.

"Not yet," answered Nechayev. "I've got a comrade out there, and I'm going to help him. Picard and I have had our differences, but if anybody is going to find the root of this evil, he will. It's time to go on the offensive. Nechayev out."

With a smile, she added, "Computer, cancel message to Admiral Brud'khi."

"Acknowledged."

A satisfied smile on her face, Admiral Nechayev rose to her feet and considered the holographic charts gleaming overhead, especially the red streak that represented the Genesis Wave. Without warning, the red beam went dim and faded away. Nechayev rushed back to the master console just as her combadge chirped.

"Nechayev here," she answered impatiently.

"This is Admiral Horkin again. I don't know if you noticed, but—"

"I did."

"Okay, then you won't be surprised to learn that the Genesis Wave just died."

"Died? Be more specific."

Horkin's words spilled out. "We've got the top minds here, including a Vulcan who has seen this wave before, and she feels that the Genesis Wave has expanded to its utmost potential. It weakened to the point where it dissipated, except for the unpleasant residual side effects we've seen."

Nechayev gulped and sunk down onto the chair. "Are you telling me that all of this was for *nothing?* That the wave was going to dissipate, anyway?"

"That's the way it looks," said the admiral, "although our actions may have hastened it. Alynna, that residual could have wreaked a lot of damage on Earth. You still did the right thing."

"I wonder," rasped the admiral. "Have I left them hanging out there all alone?"


In Beverly Crusher's research laboratory off sickbay, Captain Picard studied a clump of moss growing on a miniature willow tree. The moss didn't look deadly, but it was ensconced in its own octagonal growing chamber, transparent and totally self-contained. He could inspect the soil and the root system of the tree, thinking they looked healthy, but the moss hung on the branches like an evil fog. It took some intestinal fortitude, but Picard lowered his head close enough go nose-to-nose with the innocuous-looking plant.

"Go ahead, it won't bite you," said Beverly Crusher with a smile. "The chamber is protected by biofilters and force fields. In fact, we've updated all the ship's biofilters for the moss, the fungus, and the spores."

"It's hard to imagine that this little plant nearly brought the Federation to its knees," said Picard with amazement. "Where did you get it?"

"It's a sample that Data picked up on Myrmidon," answered Crusher. "I don't know if it always grows this quickly, or whether accelerated growth is a by-product of the Genesis Effect—but a day or so ago that plant was just a little sprig the size of your finger."

The clump of moss moved slightly, causing Picard to jump back. Beverly chuckled and tried to wipe the smile off her face. "I should have warned you about that. In its waking state, the plant is ambulatory. It's nurtured by a tree until it's the equivalent of an adult, then it goes searching for a meatier host. I don't need to tell you, that's when it's dangerous. I think it's warming up to go hunting for a new host."

"I'd like to post a guard on it," said Picard. "Around the clock."

Beverly frowned. "You know, I'm not real fond of having security in sickbay, but in this case—"

"They'll be here as soon as I leave." Picard bent closer to the plant, still keeping his distance. "Can it read our minds now, do you think?"

The doctor shook her head. "I don't know. Everything this creature does is parasitic—for its own survival, no one else's. The fungus, the telepathy, they're very impressive; but I don't know how much is learned behavior and how much is instinctive. You would think that an individual who could infiltrate a starship, posing as a crewman, would have undergone special training. In our culture, they would have to."

Crusher gazed at the twitching parasite. "Then again, maybe it's born with enough skills to dig into your mind and impersonate a loved one."

Picard smiled sympathetically at Crusher. "You weren't the only one who was fooled. In order to develop these specialized traits, it must have preyed on humanoids and large animals for millions of years."

"Enslaved them, then preyed on them," said Beverly somberly. "I don't think they're handy with tools, but they could easily enslave a whole population of humanoids to do their bidding. I'm very worried about the survivors on Myrmidon . . . and anywhere else we've left these things."

"However, when they created their dream world, they didn't program humanoids into the matrix," Picard said curiously. "From all reports, the animal life was decidedly sluggish and low level."

Crusher's jaw clenched, and she gazed with hatred at the plant. "I think they consider humanoids to be decidedly sluggish and low level."

"How do they reproduce?" asked Picard, trying to change the subject.

"I know they don't grow from a seed. Probably a spore. Of course, this one's mommy was the Genesis Wave."

Picard frowned at the captive. "When it gets larger, what are we going to do with it?"

"What do we always do with alien life?" asked Crusher. "We should try to communicate with it. Telepathically."

The captain looked at her. "Do you mean Counselor Troi?"

"We don't have any Vulcans on board," she said with a shrug. "Besides, I wouldn't allow anyone else to touch it or breathe the same air. But imagine, Jean-Luc. These creatures had the means to imprint billions and billions of their offspring with whatever they wanted them to know. What is that knowledge? Until a week ago, we didn't even know they existed, yet they stole our technology and used it against us."

Beverly's eyes grew distant as she stared at the moss. "On Myrmidon, people are burning them up . . . for their own survival. It makes you wonder who's the parasite, and who's not."

"We never would have used the Genesis technology the way *they* did," answered Picard. "Then again, who's to say what we would do under desperate circumstances? Maybe the council was right ninety years ago when they tried to keep it secret. This technology is not safe in anyone's hands."

"It really is playing God," agreed Beverly, her gaze returning to the innocuous clump of gray moss. "Right down to making the inhabitants in your own image."

The captain's combadge chirped, and a voice said, "Riker to Picard."

"Picard here."

"We've reached the Boneyard, Captain," said the first officer. "The *D'Arvuk* is coming out of warp right behind us."

"Short-range scans?" asked the captain.

"There doesn't appear to be anything unusual, but it's a big asteroid field."

"I'm on my way to the bridge," said the captain. "Send a three-person security detail to the research lab in sickbay. The doctor is growing one of the moss creatures there, and I want it watched. Picard out."

He headed for the door, then glanced back at Beverly and the octagonal chamber. "I'll talk to Troi about helping us communicate with it, but I won't take any unnecessary risks where these creatures are concerned."

"Understood," said Crusher. "See you at dinner."

After the captain left, Dr. Crusher picked up her tricorder and began checking the health of the willow tree. For a host plant, it wasn't doing badly, she decided; it might even live if the moss left it to pursue another host. But the young tree would certainly die if left alone with the growing parasite.

She looked up from her tricorder and gasped with shock, dropping the handheld device to the deck. Inside the chamber, it wasn't a tree and a clump of moss anymore—it was an innocent baby hanging by intravenous tubes! Unmistakably, she recognized the helpless infant trapped inside the chamber.

"Wesley!" she cried, pressing her face against the transparent case. Finally she shook her head and pulled away, knowing she had to be hallucinating. With a tremendous force of will, Beverly Crusher rushed out of the room and banged a wall panel to shut the door behind her.

As she was catching her breath, three security officers entered sickbay, asked for directions, and were sent her way. Crusher had a moment to compose herself before the security detail reached her.

"Dr. Crusher," said the ranking officer, "Lieutenant Kraner at your service."

She pointed to the door. "Guard this laboratory. Nobody goes in or out without *my* personal approval. That includes *you*."

The young lieutenant gulped. "Why, is something dangerous in there?"

"Yes." Crusher shivered as she looked back at the door. "By the way, don't let *me* go in there alone. If I want to go in there, insist upon accompanying me."

"Yes, sir," the lieutenant answered uncertainly.

"Don't worry, I'll be sleeping here in sickbay," said Beverly, striding toward her office. "I won't be hard to find. Don't let that door open."

"No, sir, we won't." The young lieutenant glanced at his comrades and gulped. "You heard what the doctor said. Look alive."


Geordi La Forge sat back in his seat, grinning broadly. Dolores Linton's face was on his screen at his desk in engineering, and the muscular geologist was talking a kilometer a minute. "So, Geordi, there I was, with this stuff growing all over me—yuck!—and Data comes along and saves my life!"

"Actually," Data said, sitting beside her on the shuttlecraft, "you were trying to bite my face."

"I'm sorry," she replied, "but I was having a really bad day. Anyway, this stuff was growing everywhere, and I was like a zombie. But Data brought me back. For once, I was glad to get off solid land and onto a creaky ship."

"Data saved *my* life on Myrmidon, too," replied Geordi. "He's a handy fellow to have around."

The android smiled modestly, then turned serious. "Unfortunately, there are millions we could not save. I hope help arrives in time. Do you know about the fires on Myrmidon?"

La Forge nodded. "I haven't had much to do except to keep track of dispatches back and forth. I'm sure glad the Genesis Wave faded, whatever part we had in that."

"An ironic end," observed Data. "But is it over? There is always the possibility our enemy may deploy the wave again."

"That's why we need you back here, Data," said the android's best friend. "The captain says we're going to wait at the Boneyard until you get back, but no longer. When is your ETA?"

"Three hours and fifty-two minutes," Data answered precisely.

"Geordi," said Dolores, leaning forward, "have you heard anything about Leah Brahms?"

He shook his head and tried not to show how concerned he was. "No, not a peep. She's not on a Starfleet vessel anymore. I've heard she's on a Klingon privateer, which is supposed to be in the area. If that's true, she's on her own. But if we hear from her, I'll let you know."

"Good to see you, Geordi," Dolores said with heartfelt sincerity.

"Look me up as soon as you get on board," said La Forge. "Out."

His screen reverted to a Starfleet logo, and the chief engineer sat back in his chair, frowning. If Leah was somewhere in the area, he sure wanted to find her. It was a big relief that Dolores was safe again, because he felt responsible for leaving her on Myrmidon . . . or letting her out of his sight. He wished he could've kept Leah Brahms in sight, too, but he had no control over her. If only he could see Leah one more time, maybe he would finally get it through his skull that she didn't love him, that they weren't going anywhere.

"Sir, here are the recalibration reports on the forward impulse thrusters," a nasally voice said, breaking him out of his reverie.

La Forge looked up to see a young ensign, a Benzite named Mahzanor. "You requested these as soon as possible," the ensign insisted, thrusting the padd toward him.

"Thank you." La Forge mustered a courteous nod, took the padd, and tried to read the missive. But he couldn't concentrate. He tugged at his collar. "I'll get back to you later. What's the temperature in here?"

The Benzite peered curiously at him. "Are you feeling all right, Commander?"

"Not entirely." La Forge rose to his feet at the instant that the ship was rocked by what felt like a strong jolt. He staggered to stay upright, although Mahzanor seemed to have no such trouble. The ensign reached out to steady La Forge, but Geordi's legs suddenly lurched out from under him. The office was spinning all around his ocular implants, and La Forge pitched to the deck with a dull thud.

# eighteen

Roaring talons of flame curled upward from the tops of the trees, sending billows of black smoke hurling into the befouled atmosphere. The stench on Myrmidon was wretched, the air was as thick as a sandstorm, and the heat was like a blast furnace. The underbrush burned with an ethereal white flame, aided by geysers of methane covering the ground like a foggy napalm. Nothing could live in this inferno except for the scattered handfuls of Bolians who crawled into the cesspools, fighting the salamanders and lizards for shelter from the flames.

Mot grabbed one of the squirming monstrosities by the gills and slammed it onto the bank. With fury and primitive rage, the big Bolian throttled the man-sized amphibian until he broke its neck with a loud snap. The flapping tail and limbs finally went still. Behind him, he heard his mother weeping, while his father tried to comfort her—but that wasn't easy when they were submerged in a murky swamp full of squirming horrors.

There were more shouts and shrieks as the others in their wretched party battled with the rightful denizens of the swamp. One of the females had a slithering thing wrapped around her throat, another was trying to pry it off, while a third bashed its head with a stick. They finally pried the thing loose and heaved it into the blazing bushes. With the rage of the dispossessed, the Bolians battled the amphibians, either driving them away or killing them, until they finally took possession of the dank pool.

The leeches and sucker fish still plagued them, eliciting the occasional scream, but the largest of the beasts were gone. The flames and heat were so intense that they could see each other's blistered blue faces as if it were daylight, but the sky was as dark as the blackest night. They cowered in the brackish water, barely opening their eyes to watch the conflagration. They didn't need to see it—they could *feel* it. Mot hugged his parents as they all gasped for breath, trying to steal some oxygen away from the inferno.

Like a slow version of the Genesis Wave, the snorting fire finally moved on, leaving behind a dark, mutated version of what been there before. Instead of the towering trees, now there were just spindly, black sticks, denuded of branches, leaves, and the moss. The underbrush was completely blackened, and the crunchy remains crumbled into ash at the slightest touch. Smoke continued to swirl over the devastated forest, blocking out all light and making it so dark that it felt like the end of the world.

"That should suit those monsters!" muttered a woman, whose voice quickly degenerated into a coughing fit. Some of the other survivors managed raspy, hoarse laughs of appreciation, but Mot could only wheeze. For the second time in a week, Myrmidon had been destroyed in order to save it. They seemed to have been successful, but that didn't afford him any consolation.

Gingerly, Mot let go of his parents, who still clung to each other in wide-eyed shock. Like him, they were amazed just to be alive. The sight of the charred forest and smoldering ground only added to the surreal sense of *déjà vu*. It was hard to tell if this sooty winter was better or worse than the gloomy forest it had replaced. It still seemed like one big nightmare.

Mot's lungs were sore from breathing smoky air—what little there was of it—and he wondered how long the planet's oxygen would hold out. One thing was certain, they couldn't breathe methane.

Coughing and wheezing, Mot dragged himself out of the mire and pulled his muddy body across the ash and stubble until he flopped with exhaustion on top of a rock. The rock was covered in black soot, and it only added to the bedraggled mess he was—a pathetic creature without enough strength left to pull a leech off his cheek.

He heard muffled crying and moaning. With great effort, Mot lifted himself up on his elbows and crawled back to the slimy pool. First he pulled his mother out, then his father; and they lay flopping in the ashes like two fish in the bottom of the boat, gasping for breath. Moments later, others crawled out of the muck and lay on the ground, barely half alive.

*Is there anything left?* he wondered. *Probably even the sanctuaries are gone now.* The big Bolian began to weep.

After a moment, he felt a hand on his shoulder—it was his father.

"Don't cry," breathed the elder. "We are still alive . . . still together. There's always hope."

"No!" rasped Mot. "I should have talked you into going with me on the *Enterprise*. Captain Picard said he would take us. What a fool . . . what an idiot I am! The ones who chose suicide are smarter than I." Tears spilled out of him and ran down his blistered flesh, burning like the fire.

"There's still time for suicide," his father said helpfully. "I wouldn't mind that either, as long as we are all together."

"I think trying to live here *is* suicide!" groused one old man, who might have been a young man under his scars. There was wheezing laughter at that remark, and even Mot had to chuckle.

"The First Mother taught us to suffer," said Mot's mother. "Maybe we were too comfortable."

The laughter died away as they considered that remark, and Mot began to sniff back his tears, wondering what they should do next. Surely these idiots weren't still depending upon him for leadership? When it had been *his* idea to burn up the forest! He consoled himself that somebody else would have come up with that bright idea, once the awful nature of the threat was known. There were certain ways a Bolian would be quite happy to die, but hosting a parasite while living in a swamp wasn't one of them.

"So, Son, where are we off to next?" asked his father, while the air still hung with ash and soot.

Mot shook his head and gasped for breath. "I'm fresh out of ideas . . . maybe that's a good thing."

When no one else had the energy to speak, he went on, "You know, the humans I serve with always think you can 'get a break.' Something good will happen if you just hang in there."

"What a stupid idea," his mother said, aghast.

"Not born out by the facts," grumbled his father.

Mot wheezed. "I know, but I've seen it happen on the *Enterprise*. Let's test it . . . imagine that something *good* will happen next . . . like the First Mother will appear in front of us and guide our weary souls to safety!"

In a bright flash, a dark, towering creature appeared in front of them, dressed in studded black armor and a pointed hood, and holding a disruptor rifle with bayonet. As smoke swirled around the frightening apparition, he stepped forward, his rifle aimed at Mot. After a moment, he lifted the weapon.

"If you're still alive, raise your hand!" he demanded, his voice booming from his hooded head. Through the faceplate, dark eyes glowered at them.

Mot did as he was told, along with every other member of his tiny party. The mammoth figure suddenly jerked to the right, plunging his rifle toward the ground. Mot heard a squishing sound, and the armored man brought up a huge, squirming salamander, speared on the end of his weapon.

"Ah, good hunting here," he said with satisfaction. With a heave, he tossed the creature into a swirl of smoke behind him. "Krombek to main transporter, nine to beam up from these coordinates. I will look for more."

Then he waved to the survivors. "The accommodations on a Klingon ship are not much, but they're better than this. *"HIjol!"*

Mot could do nothing but weep with joy and hug his parents as their molecules were whisked away to a ship orbiting high above the smoke and flame.

A mammoth tree towered above him—it seemed to be the ancestor of all trees—majestic, thick with bushy leaves, and unspeakably ancient. Its trunk was as wide as his engineering room, and the aged plant seemed to be just as complex and intricate. The forest itself was primordial, unsullied by civilization. Still, sunlight trickled cheerfully through the thick bows of the regal tree, illuminating a forest floor of delicate wildflowers and tiny ferns.

Geordi La Forge had never been much of a biologist, and he couldn't identify the mammoth tree, except to know that it had to be the grandest tree in all creation. He touched its weathered, flaky bark and felt himself in communion with growing creatures all over the universe. La Forge could feel the life-force in the tree, pulsing with as much raw energy as any antimatter reactor under his command. He realized without being told that this tree was the pinnacle of life—the wellspring from which all good things flowed.

He heard a slight crunching in the leaves on the ground, and he turned to see an ethereal figure in a flowing white gown padding toward him. Her head was lowered, in deference to the tree; when she looked up, her radiant face was bathed in a shaft of golden sunlight. It was Leah Brahms, looking impossibly beautiful, her soft mane of brown hair encircled by a garland of yellow flowers.

Geordi's already soaring heart went into warp drive at the sight of his beloved. Grinning broadly, he took her hands knowing that she had joined him in the forest—before the magnificent tree—in order to become his mate for all eternity. His throat was speechless at the sight and promise of her beauty, but his face and eyes blazed with unrestrained happiness.

A shriveled black leaf tumbled from the tree and drifted before his eyes, dispelling his giddy sense of joy. His mind uncovered a tiny shred of reality, and La Forge asked himself, *How am I seeing this so clearly? Where are my ocular implants?*

Geordi knew what normal vision was like, ever since their visit to the planet of the Ba'ku, where his eyes had miraculously begun to function. Once again, he was seeing through real eyes, but they had to be someone else's eyes.

Desperately fearful he would lose Leah, he gripped her hands all the more tightly until she winced with pain. Leah mustered a brave smile for him, and her voice whispered in his ear, "Not yet, but soon."

She touched his eyes—only they weren't his eyes, they were thick, bulging scabs! Now everything was black, and Geordi had no vision whatsoever—not even the artificial impulses he had come to depend upon. In the black ink, he flailed his arms, trying to touch something . . . anything . . . to find out where he was.

Strong, unseen limbs struck from the darkness, grabbed his arms and legs, and pinned him to the ground. He struggled, but he knew he was as good as captured—he was so helpless. Geordi had experienced temporary bouts of blindness before, but for some reason this was more terrifying. Maybe it was because he was anxious about Leah, and he couldn't do anything to help her in this condition.

"Calm down, Commander. You're among friends," said an authoritative but compassionate voice. Hearing her say his rank brought him back to another reality—that he was a Starfleet officer. Before he panicked, he always tried to remember that his job incurred unexpected hazards—he just had to live with the risks. Geordi let his shoulder muscles relax, and he tried to lower his hands to touch his face. There was some resistance by his captors to let his arms go.

"Let him feel the bandages," said the female voice. With trembling fingers, La Forge touched the thin, rubbery appliances over his eyes—they felt like a second layer of skin.

"Good," said the voice. "I didn't want to give you a hypo. It's Dr. Crusher, and you're in sickbay. I can't tell you how sorry I am that you can't see, but it's temporary."

"What's wrong with me?" asked Geordi. "Was the ship attacked?"

"Not in the usual sense," answered Beverly testily, "but the assault by that damn plant goes on. You're infected with the fungus."

"But how can I be infected?" he asked with alarm. "I had the vaccine."

"Originally, *you* weren't infected. It was the bionic component of your ocular implants that became infected. This fungus is bad and it's persistent—it looks for any opening. You got a strong exposure on Myrmidon. Although you passed through our biofilters and took our vaccine, your ocular implants were bypassed. I'd guess that the fungus lodged in the mechanical portion of the implant, where it was protected, then it migrated into the biological receptors, where it got to the rest of your body. Since there wasn't a creature involved to control it, the fungus ran wild. I'm going to have to revaccinate everyone on the ship."

"But how long will I be without sight?" asked La Forge, getting to the heart of the matter.

"The infection is centered in your eyes," Crusher explained. "Even if you were a sighted person, your eyes would be covered, and I wouldn't let you use them for forty-eight hours. We'll replicate you another set of implants, but I can't install them until you're well."

He held up his hand, and she jumped in. "Don't even ask. You're too sick to wear your old VISOR. The only break you get is that we caught this really early, and you shouldn't be sick for long. Your fever is already gone.

"Go get his visitors," she said, apparently talking to someone else in the room. He heard footsteps clacking away, and he tried to relax. *It's temporary . . . I'm in good hands.* Geordi wanted to tell the doctor about his dream, but that seemed so inane with all that was going on. *Let her deal with my illness, not my love-life.*

A moment later, he heard loud footsteps charge into the room, and his bed moved slightly as people sat beside him. Someone who smelled very good and very earthy planted a wet kiss on his cheek, and a cold hand grabbed his.

"Geordi, I am perturbed to see you ill," said a polite voice, shaking his hand.

"Thank you, Data," answered Geordi warmly. "Dolores, could I have another kiss?"

"Sure," she purred, this time pressing against him as she did the honors.

"Don't get my patient too excited," warned Crusher. "He's got to rest. I'm kicking you out in a few minutes."

He heard Crusher walk away, and he called out, "Thank you, Doc!"

"I hope we've seen the last of this," she muttered.

Dolores squeezed his shoulder and moved closer. "They say you'll be fine in a couple of days, Geordi, and I'm not going anywhere. But I don't know why *I* haven't gotten sick yet."

"You were taken over by an entire plant in a much cruder but quicker-acting form of symbiotic relationship," answered Data. "The inexperienced plants on Myrmidon treated the humanoids as they did the trees, whereas experienced individuals can indulge in elaborate ruses to gain a humanoid's trust. That is when exposure to the fungus is the most intense. I believe there may be numerous levels at which humanoids and these moss creatures can interact."

"Okay, Data, okay," said Dolores good-naturedly. "Sometimes you take all the pleasure out of asking dumb questions."

"Thanks for coming to visit," said La Forge, trying to muster some enthusiasm. "I wish I could enjoy this reunion more, but I'm really out of commission. Has anything happened since I've been in here?"

"I don't know," answered Dolores. "We just got back twenty minutes ago. But it doesn't sound like much has happened."

"I take it we're on our way to that planet . . . Lomar?" asked Geordi.

"We have not yet left the Boneyard," answered Data. "Our departure is under discussion. I believe your illness had caused some concern to our Romulan escort."

"I don't blame them," said Geordi glumly. He barely listened to what else they said in the mixture of scuttlebutt and small-talk. At Dolores's urging, Data agreed to do another violin concert, to lift the crew's spirits.

Dr. Crusher was true to her word and returned to throw them out. La Forge accepted more sympathy and another kiss, then was left alone . . . in the dark. Even though he was a blind man, darkness was something he seldom experienced, thanks to the devices he usually wore. The engineer didn't care for it one bit, although it certainly made him notice his other senses. He could smell the antiseptics and hear the slight whirs and gurgles in the equipment. Distant, muffled voices were audible but maddening—in that he couldn't make out distinctive words. *Maybe with a little more effort,* he thought.

Geordi's hands rubbed nervously against the bedding, which felt course and clammy—much like his emotions. Just when he was getting over Leah, she had to return in that startling and wonderful dream. Of course, that didn't mean that he would ever see her again in real life, or that she cared if she ever saw him again. The dream was just his subconscious telling him he hadn't gotten over her at all.

*I have to be practical and really try to forget her,* he told himself, *and give Dolores a chance. Why couldn't I have met Dolores sometime when Leah was nowhere around?*

Leah was unfair competition, at least for *his* heart. Geordi tried to forget about all of it and go to sleep, while his body and the medications fought the fungus. It was ironic to become ill from an eye infection, when his eyes were normally no more useful than his appendix or his tonsils. Still, they were a part of his body, and he had to accept that they were still his weakest part.

So La Forge lay there in the darkness, his sightless eyes swathed in bandages, urging sleep to make the darkness less frightening.

Captain Picard sat at the desk in his ready room, trying not to let anger creep into his neutral expression. He knew he had to undergo this tirade if he wanted to come to any kind of agreement at all.

The narrow, scowling visage of Commander Jagron of the Romulan warbird filled his computer screen. "Captain, I simply cannot believe that you are unable to control this fungal disease infesting your vessel. Perhaps you need some of our doctors to attend to your patients, as your medical staff seems woefully incompetent."

At that, Picard bristled. "Our medical staff is perfectly competent, and we only have one patient. It was a bionic component of his that became infected. I hope for your sake that your ship continues to avoid infection . . . and the moss creatures."

"Certainly it behooves us to keep our contact with *you* at a minimum," the Romulan said snidely, "but we can't ignore the fact that we are wasting valuable time. The one good thing that came from your ship being infiltrated by the enemy is that we have the name of a planet. It may not be their homeworld, but it's a start. So now we are off to Lomar, correct?"

Picard took a deep breath and replied calmly, "All of our indicators say that the source of the Genesis Wave is here, in the Boneyard."

The Romulan rolled his eyes. "We've had twelve hours to run sensor scans and have turned up nothing."

"We could run sensor scans for twelve *years*—"

"I know," said Jagron with a conciliatory gesture. "This asteroid field is immense, and I agree with you that one of us should stay here and continue observation. So I propose that we split our forces, and I will take my ship to Lomar. You are the logical choice to stay behind, while you fight your ailments. If this is agreeable to you, we leave immediately."

Picard almost replied that he never asked for the Romulans to come along, anyway. Instead he smiled and said, "Good hunting."

"Thank you, Captain. Jagron out." The lanky Romulan nodded, and the screen went blank.

Captain Picard sighed and sat back in his chair. Although their enemy was despicable, he wasn't sure if they deserved to have the Romulans turned loose against them, without any supervision. There was no doubt that the Romulans could be unusually cruel in their own right. Nevertheless, the *Enterprise* couldn't be in two places at once, and both the Boneyard and Lomar required investigation. He took some consolation in knowing that more Starfleet ships were on the way.

He leaned forward and tapped the companel. "Picard to bridge."

"Riker here," came the familiar reply. "I see the Romulans are leaving."

"Yes, they're on their way to Lomar. We're going to stay here and investigate. You know what we're looking for. Have Data put together a plan that will make the most of our resources."

"Yes, sir," answered Riker. "Counselor Troi is waiting to see you."

"Send her in."

The door opened a moment later, and the dark-haired Betazoid entered the captain's ready room. "You wanted to see me, sir."

"Yes, Counselor," he answered, rising to his feet. Picard searched for words for a moment, then explained, "Essentially, we've captured one of the enemy, and we need to interrogate it. Did you know that Beverly is growing one of the moss creatures in her lab?"

Deanna's already pale expression lightened two more shades. "Yes, I knew before anyone told me. I went down to visit Geordi, but I couldn't get two meters inside sickbay before I started to feel nauseated and dizzy."

The captain frowned. "Then you couldn't help us communicate with it?"

"No," said Troi emphatically. "I get violently ill around that creature. It's really incompatible with our kind of telepathy."

Picard nodded understandingly. "Then we'll just have to find some other way."

Deanna's dark eyes flashed. "We could always do what I did with the other one—strap an overloaded phaser to it."

"I'm sure you could find many people who would support such a solution," said the captain dryly. "However, I must say I'm a bit surprised to hear the suggestion from you. I don't believe I've ever seen you in such a vengeful mood."

Her jaw clenched for a moment, but then she seemed to will the tension away with a sigh. "Telepathy should be used as a tool, not a weapon to deceive and kill. I can't even begin to describe what I saw on Persephone V, what it tried to do to Will—"

"All right, Counselor, I get your drift."

"I have a bad feeling this war is not over," Deanna Troi said grimly.

# nineteen

Lomar looked like a planet captured in ancient black-and-white photography, thought Leah Brahms. Every bit of color and life had been drained from its jagged features. Gray and foreboding, it looked like an oversized moon with a wispy white halo of sickly atmosphere. Its own moon, although distant, appeared to be half as large as the aged planet itself. Lomar had towering peaks and dingy gray poles. The forbidding terrain would have given the planet majesty had it not been for the great black bogs that pocked the ashen landscape.

The black holes were tar, concluded Leah, checking her readouts at the science station on the *HoS*. It was natural asphalt, like the sticky detritus in the La Brea Federation Park. Geysers of methane, ammonia, and other noxious gasses leaked from the putrid surface.

No one said anything as they assumed standard orbit. The mood aboard the *HoS* had been stark since the deaths of Kurton and Burka. With a small crew, the loss of two was devastating, even if they had picked up one young, raw recruit. But Herbert was human, like Leah, and that was suspicious in the light of the events at the Pink Slipper on Protus. Worse yet, they had lost two crewmen while gaining no information about Lomar, except that they had carnivorous plants. From this distance, it didn't appear the place had any plants at all.

For the first time, she sensed some real hostility from the Klingons; even Maltz was a bit distant. None of this could be serious, she thought, because Klingons tended to exhibit their emotions openly. Then again, perhaps they were beginning to question their captain's decisions and qualifications. She couldn't blame them, because she was searching blindly for the enemy, making decisions by the seat of her pants. Coming here could be a huge waste of time, worse than going to Protus.

"Herbert," she asked her newest crew member, "there are supposed to be carnivorous plants down there. Do you see anything that looks like vegetation? Plant life?"

The sixteen-year-old bolted to attention at his console, where he was tracking a chemical analysis sensor. He was looking specifically for chlorophyll, chloroplasts, magnesium, and other signs of plant life. "Yes," he said, his voice squeaking. "A little vegetation in those bogs, if I read this right. Not much."

Leah frowned in frustration. In the records, Lomar had looked like one of the planets created by the Genesis Wave. Close up, it seemed to be a dead version of that model—desiccated and all used up. She continued to search for energy sources, cities, anything that resembled civilization, but it seemed pointless.

"Maybe this *was* the enemy's homeworld," said Maltz. "A long time ago."

Gradok, the weapons master who was now on tactical, called out, "There is a shuttlecraft on the surface!"

Maltz jumped down, and Leah hurried from her station to tactical. They peered over Gradok's shoulder at what was unmistakably a vessel, nestled in a relatively level and dry crater. "Federation, civilian class," said Gradok. "Speed-rated for warp two."

"Colin Craycroft," muttered Leah Brahms, shaking her head.

"What?" snarled Maltz. "From the Pink Slipper?"

"Yes, I remember now—he said he was going to beat us here. And he did."

"What is *he* looking for?" asked Maltz.

"He thinks there's treasure here, given our interest in the place." Brahms shook her head with confusion. "I wish I could remember our conversation better."

Maltz rubbed his hands together. "Good, we will kill him and be done with it before we go on. Ready away team." The old Klingon glanced around at his sparse crew and lifted an unruly gray eyebrow. "Gradok and Herbert, you come with me."

The lad looked startled, as if he hadn't expected such an assignment. "Yes, sir!"

"I'll go, too," declared Brahms.

The old Klingon lowered his head. "As you wish, Captain, but we won't be talked out of killing him."

"I'm ordering you *not* to kill him," responded Leah. "If we find him, we have to question him. Then I—and only I—will decide what to do with him."

Maltz narrowed his eyes and scratched his stubbled chin, but he answered, "Yes, sir."

Gradok lifted a beefy fist clad in leather and shook it at his board. "Give me the word, Captain, and I'll destroy his shuttlecraft right now! A small torpedo will do it."

"Is there anyone on board?" asked Brahms.

"No. No life-signs in the area," the hulking Klingon answered with disappointment.

"For all we know, it's a wreck, abandoned," said Leah. "It may not belong to Craycroft at all. But it's the only interesting thing we've found so far, so let's inspect it." She looked pointedly at Maltz, as if telling him to get his landing party moving.

"Kurok, you have the bridge. Keep shields up except when transporting. Use caution."

"Yes, sir," answered the second officer, a quiet sort who did as he was told.

"Away team, follow me!" growled the old Klingon. As they filed off the bridge onto the turbolift, Leah fell in beside the youth, Herbert.

"We're going to have to wear environmental suits," she said.

He nodded several times. "I've done that before—I can do it."

"I don't know what to tell you to expect," Brahms said with sympathy. "Just follow orders, and you'll be fine."

The lad wrung his hands together nervously. "But I *know* Mr. Craycroft. He's a family friend."

"Good, then you can kill him," Maltz said as the turbolift door slid shut.


Carol Marcus pretended to be sleeping on her laboratory cot. She had left the newest algorithms for the solar analyzer on her screen, without sending it to her captors, and she was fairly certain they would want to see the solutions immediately. It was an impressive piece of work, if she said so herself, and it would undoubtedly increase the number of custom-made planets and organisms they were able to spread across the galaxy. Try as she might, the old woman couldn't do anything less than her best, and that was pretty damn good.

Unfortunately, Jim and David were closer than ever to discharging the Genesis Wave a second time—in a different direction—and she still had no idea how to stop them. They had done their best to stay away from her, except to compare notes and talk business. Neither side made an effort at tenderness anymore. She was still a part of the team, turning in good work, so they let her live while they concerned themselves with the biological portions of the matrix.

Still Carol sometimes had the sense that they considered her to be indispensable, like a good-luck charm. At times, their neediness was palpable and a bit chilling.

The scientist felt them in her mind before she heard the door to the lab open. As she had practiced in so many naps, she tried to become a receptor—putting out nothing, giving them nothing to suspect, taking in everything. She was an old woman; they were used to her naps. Thanking the fates for all those yoga classes she had taken some forty years ago, Marcus managed to clear her mind.

They stole into the room, anxious needs filling their thoughts. Sometimes she could hear them speaking words as plainly as day, like two people sitting at a table behind her in a restaurant. Other times, she felt only impressions and emotions. They weren't cold and impassive, as she had thought, but hungry and desperate—it was like the center was missing from their lives.

Still dressed in their cleanroom suits, the two of them shuffled like old men to her computer station, which was about fifteen meters away. Eagerly they began poring over her results, and she felt their excitement.

"This will work," said the phony Kirk. "We must incorporate it immediately."

"Is she asleep?" asked the one she knew as David.

Carol willed herself into an empty-headed meditation. "Yes," answered Kirk. "We are ready now."

"But the test area is guarded by that ship," said David. "We can go no closer."

"Then we must discharge from here."

"No, the preparations will attract their attention. Please do not worry—we have other means." As if frightened by their argument, the verbal exchange degenerated into a lot of touchy-feely camaraderie between the two, and Carol almost felt a stirring of sympathy for them. But not quite.

They shuffled out of the room as laboriously as they had shuffled in, and Carol waited until the door closed—then a few heartbeats more—before she started thinking again. It was clear, a ship was stopping them from docking in the ideal position to discharge the second Genesis Wave. Perhaps that would buy her some time, thought the scientist, but she had better do more than simply eavesdrop. She had to break out of this hologram and see the rest of the ship—where they really were.

Four figures shrouded in dark suits that resembled armor, and hoods that looked like horned helmets, appeared in a flash in a barren crater on Lomar. Wispy ammonia fog with ammonia sleet swirled around them, and it was hard to believe this had once been an almost breathable atmosphere. Leah Brahms stepped forward to inspect the shuttlecraft, which sat in a black scorch mark at the bottom of the crater. Half-covered in frozen sleet, it was hard to tell how old it was. The craft looked dark and lifeless, and her tricorder gave no indication of activity inside.

Maltz motioned them all back while he cautiously approached the shuttle, disruptor leveled for action. From the way he scrutinized the ground, Leah got the idea he was looking for tracks. When he found what he was looking for, he bent down and inspected a booted tread mark in the slush.

The old Klingon's voice was amplified in her ear. "I say they saw us coming on their sensors and ran like the cowards they are."

"I see only one track," said Gradok, peering over the elder's shoulder.

Maltz looked around, verifying for himself how many tracks there were. Without another word, he headed off in a northerly direction, bent over like a crab. Gradok fell in behind him. They were evidently hot on the scent.

Leah looked at Herbert and motioned him to follow. For some reason, she didn't mind bringing up the rear. The lad, armed with no more than a tricorder and a knife, padded carefully after the Klingons, and Brahms moved fast enough to keep up with them.

She really wanted to take readings and spend some time analyzing them, but slow and deliberate wasn't her crew's method of doing things. She pitied Colin Craycroft if they caught him, but not much— as long as they didn't lose sight of the mission. Of course, this excursion could be the second dead end in a row on which she had led them, and she might face a mutiny. On top of that, the shuttlecraft was probably a diversion they didn't need.

She checked her readouts and said, "Maltz, I don't see any life-signs on my tricorder."

"It wasn't a ghost who made these tracks," barked the old Klingon.

"Sensors found a lot of kelbonite in these ridges, so your readings may be masked. Trust nothing but your eyes."

The party slowed down as they climbed a ridge with silty, ashen soil underfoot. It was a slippery ascent, especially in the sleet, and the Klingons forged ahead. Fortunately, Herbert was a good climber, as he had claimed, and he hung back to give Leah a hand. When they reached the top of the crusty ridge, everyone stopped to stare at the foreboding landscape beyond.

Spread before them was a vast black bog of natural asphalt, with seething bubbles shooting little puffs of smoke into the murky air. Around the edges of the bog were a few plants that looked like cattails, and in the center of the bog was a blackened tree trunk surrounded by brackish scum. At least, it looked like the remains of a tree, thought Leah, but one that had died eons ago.

Maltz and Gradok were stopped at the edge of the bubbling pitch. They would be scratching their heads if they could reach them, thought Leah. "The trail ends here," said Maltz, his gravelly voice booming in Leah's helmet.

She and Herbert reached the bank a moment later, and she glanced at her tricorder, even though Maltz had dismissed its readings. Signaling to each other, the two Klingons split up and went opposite ways along the bank, while Leah collected readings.

The lad stepped closer to her and asked, "What are we looking for?"

"Originally, it was the bastards who set loose the Genesis Wave," answered Leah. "But now it seems to be Colin Craycroft and the owners of that shuttlecraft. They beat us here, so maybe they know something. You have a pack of photon flares, don't you?"

"Yes," he answered uncertainly. "I'm not sure how to use them."

"Give me one," she said, holding out her hand. Behind her faceplate, she granted him an encouraging smile, but Herbert still looked shell-shocked by his extraordinary change of fortune. Finally the lad reached into his pack and pulled out a squat pistol with a large barrel, which he gently placed into her gloved palm.

She studied the device for a moment, gripped its awkward stock, then fired a bright stream of photons over the tar-encrusted bog. The dismal scene lit up like an amusement park on the Fourth of July, then a stream of live photons sprinkled down over the bog, which shimmered with strange energy surges. The tree trunk lit up like a Christmas tree in the glowing fallout, and it appeared to be a spiral staircase, not a tree at all. Some kind of boat or craft floated at the base of the tree.

"Holy cow!" said Herbert.

Brahms saw the two Klingons standing stock still, staring at all she had uncovered, and she couldn't resist broadcasting to all of them, "It's a holographic cloak. Sometimes you need more than your eyes."

"Is that a *boat* out there?" asked Maltz, jogging back to her.

"Hovercraft," she said, checking her tricorder. "A small one, probably two-person."

"How are we going to get there?" Gradok asked, dashing along the bank.

Leah pressed a button. "I just sent the coordinates to the ship. I think they can transport us there—one by one. Who goes first?"

"May I have the honor?" asked Gradok.

She contacted the ship and gave the order, and the weapons master was transported to the tree in the center of the tar bog, about seventy meters away. He had his knife drawn with a disruptor for backup, and as soon as he arrived on the tiny island, they saw his flailing silhouette fighting something invisible to them.

"Gradok, what is it?" demanded Maltz.

"A blasted net!" he grumbled. "Must be the holographic cloak!" There was a vivid burst of sparks, and they could make out Gradok kicking something on the ground. From the shore, they could see nothing but vague outlines and sparks, which finally died down to the normal gloom.

"Fine now," he muttered. "I see the hovercraft. Want me to bring it over? There's not much room to stand here."

"Do you see the staircase?" asked Brahms.

"I see a hatch. I think we can blast it."

"Belay that," ordered Brahms. "Don't destroy anything until we see what it is. We'll keep transporting over. *You* climb into the craft to make room for us."

"Yes, sir," grumbled the weapons master.

In an orderly fashion, they transported to the tiny island around the old tree trunk in the asphalt bog. Gradok had indeed destroyed a holographic mesh that covered the boat and the hatch. The cloak didn't do much but mirror the surrounding textures, but that had been enough in this gloomy place.

"I think visitors put this cloak up," Brahms said, holding the shimmering fabric between her gloved fingers. "Because the hatch was hidden without it."

"Craycroft!" said Maltz, seething. "How did *he* get in?"

The two Klingons scrutinized the small hatch at the base of the tree. Both of them tried their brawn on it, but there was nowhere to get a grip. The smooth, domed surface looked like it had to be opened from inside.

"Let me try," said young Herbert.

Glowering doubtfully beneath their hoods, the two Klingons stepped into the sticky tar to make room for the lad to approach. He peered intently at the dull hatch for several seconds, then he peered upward at the burnt tree trunk. With a quick move that startled Leah, the lithe youth jumped up and caught the burnt stump of a branch. When the branch tipped downward, the hatch opened like a camera lens. In the dim light, Leah saw a spiral staircase winding downward into darkness.

"How did you know to do that?" Maltz asked suspiciously.

"It just made sense," answered the lad. "If someone came over here in that hovercraft, he must have been able to let himself in."

"What if it's a trap?" asked Leah.

"Then it's a good one," said Maltz. "They have captured *my* curiosity. The honor is still yours, Weapons Master."

Gradok grunted and flicked on a light atop his helmet. Disruptor rifle leveled for action, the hulking Klingon tromped down the staircase, with Maltz on his tail. Leah nodded brusquely to Herbert, who took up the next position in the descent. She didn't know why, but she had a feeling that this was too easy, too convenient. Craycroft hadn't had that big of a lead on them. How had he found this place?

Before she could answer that or any other questions, Leah Brahms was clomping down a slippery metal staircase, plunging into the bowels of the dank planet. At this point, it seemed as if they had stumbled upon nothing but a pit under the tar bog, and she momentarily wondered if it was an excavation pit, maybe an archaeological dig. The walls of the stairwell seemed to be as hard and black as obsidian, and she figured some kind of process had been used to harden the asphalt.

Using the light on her helmet, Leah kept glancing at her tricorder as she descended. "There's oxygen down here," she told the others. "It's not breathable air, but it's getting close to it."

"There is more than that," said Gradok. Brahms leaned over the rail of the spiral staircase and looked down into the depths, where she saw the Klingons' lights. They had stopped descending and were standing motionless outside an open doorway, illuminated in a flickering light. Their weapons were ready for action, but they weren't firing.

When the two humans reached their position, Leah finally saw what had given them pause. Lying in the doorway, surrounded by his own dying light, was the old Tiburonian, Krussel. Gradok lowered his head to shine his beam at the frail Tiburonian, and Leah gasped out loud.

His face was frozen in a grimace of sheer terror, as if he had died of fright, and his fingers were curled into grasping claws. It might have been lack of oxygen that produced such terror, Leah told herself, because his headgear lay about a meter away from his paralyzed hand.

"Is that . . . the old miner?" she asked, just to make sure.

"Yes," answered Maltz. "He was going to be our guide, and he must have become Craycroft's guide instead."

Young Herbert turned away from the sight, while Gradok lifted his light into the blackness beyond. Leah turned to her tricorder, trying to get an estimate of how long he had been dead.

"Maybe it's the conditions in this pit," she reported to the others, "but he hasn't decomposed much. I don't think he's been dead long."

Gradok kicked the body out of the way, and he and Maltz continued plunging into the darkness. Herbert stood petrified on the stairs, as stiff as the dead Tiburonian, and Leah had to squeeze past him. "You can stay here if you want," she told the youth.

"No, no, I'll go," he insisted. "Captains first."

She rolled her eyes at him. "Thanks."

Brahms only gave the Tiburonian's body a passing glance as she walked by, concentrating on the uneven floor and her tricorder readings. They were in a dark tunnel that had also been carved from solid tar. This tunnel was different only in that some kind of moss grew on the walls at intervals, along with thick vines underneath it.

Brahms checked her tricorder but didn't note anything unusual about the plant growth—it was probably a natural occurrence from the dampness and the increased oxygen. These types of plants, including the fungus she was picking up, didn't need much sunlight. They may be getting sunlight from the surface, she surmised; maybe these were the roots of the cattails above.

"We see him!" said a sharp voice in her ear.

Leah jogged in her heavy suit to catch up with Maltz and Gradok. She instantly knew it was bad, because the Klingons were backed up against the mossy walls of the cavern. Her eyes followed their light beams to a frail form sitting on a rock, and the being turned around and gazed at her with blurry, indistinct eyes.

To her horror and amazement, it was the old Tiburonian, Krussel! Only this time, he was alive and grinning contentedly at them.

# twenty

A phaser beam struck the grinning figure of Krussel and blew him apart in a haze of green confetti. His body floated down from above like a feather pillow torn apart in a pillow fight. Instantly, the Klingons dropped to a firing crouch, their disruptors aimed, looking for the source of the phaser blast in the dark tunnel. Leah glanced at Herbert, half-expecting that *he* was the one who had fired the unexpected shot, but the lad was cowering from the remains of Krussel, which were still floating down.

They didn't look like parts of a body, thought Leah, that was for sure. Unfortunately, there was only pitch blackness in the tunnel, and their pitiful lights did little to dispel it.

"Don't shoot! Don't shoot!" screeched a voice. From the blackness ahead of them, a phaser skittered across the floor, and Leah bent down to grab it. Then a figure emerged from the inky blackness, wearing civilian clothes and waving his hands frantically in the air.

"That wasn't Krussel!" shouted Colin Craycroft. "That wasn't *real!*"

Maltz kicked at the remains of the old miner, which looked like dried leaves, then he leveled his disruptor at Craycroft. His voice boomed from his helmet. "What in Klin was it? Speak fast, or I'll kill you!"

"Yes, go ahead and kill me! I beg you!" The crazed human opened his shirt and showed them his flabby chest.

Leah quickly stepped between them. "Hold your fire, mister. I have some questions for Mr. Craycroft here."

The old Klingon lowered his weapon and glowered at Craycroft. "Yes, I have some questions, too."

Brahms turned to the tavern keeper. "First of all, there's air in here? You can *breathe?*"

"Yes! No!" he answered confusedly. "Yes, there is air, but no, don't take off your helmets. They'll confuse you, like they did with Krussel. Listen, come with me, and I'll show you."

The little man rushed off down the corridor, and Maltz and Gradok were quick to follow. Brahms gave Herbert a shove, and they both made a wide path around the pile of leaves that had looked like a humanoid a few seconds ago. Leah could well understand the boy's fear; but this was a volunteer mission for him, so he had no reason to complain. Hearing a discussion ahead of her, she hurried to catch up with Maltz, Gradok, and their new guide, Colin Craycroft.

"You can't con a con artist!" Craycroft said with a satisfied chortle. "I knew they were fake. For his own protection, I sent Krussel back to the shuttlecraft, but then he picked up your ship on sensors. He panicked . . . forgot to put on the camouflage. But at least he told me where to look. Wait 'til you see it!" He skipped ahead of them down the gloomy corridor.

"Don't get out of my sight," warned Maltz.

But they needn't have worried about that, because they soon emerged into a vast, well-lit engine room. Huge, gleaming crankshafts and rods churned away, and massive silos towered dozens of meters into the air, turning slowly, gurgling softly. It was difficult to tell what kind of energy they were producing, or storing, but this was well-maintained equipment. Nevertheless, there were piles of dead leaves scattered around the expansive floor.

"What is this place?" asked Maltz suspiciously.

"I don't know, but I claim salvage rights!" Craycroft said, giggling. He dashed through the cavernous chamber, pointing at the piles of dead vegetation. "Don't worry, it's safe. I killed them all!"

"What has this got to do with the Genesis Wave?" demanded the old Klingon.

That stopped the crazed human in his path. "Genesis Wave? I thought that was just a rumor you were using to keep away the competition. This is a secret production facility—for what, I don't know. But if they want to remain secret, they've got to pay *us* to go away. And then a little stipend every now and then to keep quiet. Either that, or I file salvage claims . . . to these ruins."

"These aren't ruins," insisted Brahms. "And according to you, this place was inhabited . . . before you killed all of them."

"Besides, we're going to *kill* you." Maltz aimed his disruptor at the agitated human.

"Wait!" begged Craycroft, holding up his hands in supplication. "I *saved* your lives! I led you to this place! It wasn't just Krussel—I have sophisticated mine detectors on my shuttlecraft, and *I* was the one who spotted this underground complex. And I killed these creatures in self-defense!"

"Hold on," Brahms said quickly. She interceded with the old Klingon. "I said we're taking him prisoner. We could use his shuttlecraft, and he might be worth a ransom to someone."

Maltz scowled behind his faceplate, but he finally said, "Yes, sir." Pulling a coil of rope from his sash, he strode toward Colin Craycroft and grabbed him by his wrists. When the human put up a struggle, the Klingon smashed him in the mouth, drawing blood. After that, Craycroft went silently and allowed Maltz to tie him to a pole with his hands behind his back.

"This is a death sentence!" shouted Craycroft, spitting out a tooth. "You'll see. You *need* me!" He kept babbling, but it was incomprehensible.

"I've had enough of this." Without hesitation, Brahms drew a phaser—she now had two of them—and set it for stun. Then she drilled Colin Craycroft with a bright beam, and he slumped into a pile at the bottom of the pole. The cavernous chamber was much quieter without his ranting.

The Klingons again signaled to one another and started forward, inspecting the braces that held up the vats, looking for hidden enemies. At least the gleaming silos looked like vats to Brahms, and her tricorder indicated that they contained an unidentified liquid. From a quick glance at the chemical components in the vats, she guessed it was fertilizer. Leah wanted to find a computer terminal, or other high-level processor, so she concentrated her tricorder search on power sources and electromagnetic impulses.

Herbert walked around, gazing up at the ceiling, which was covered in a thick growth of moss.

"This place is the key!" crowed Maltz, his loud voice sounding deranged in her headgear. "I know they were here—I can *feel* them. This is the lair of the enemy."

"This complex is big—goes back a long way," Brahms said, amazed at the readings she was getting. "We could spend a week searching it."

Gradok suddenly ran to the wall and began ripping away the vines and moss. Slowly he uncovered a sealed metal doorway. The big Klingon tugged on the door and beat it with his fists a couple of times.

"Youngster!" he called. "Do you have a way of getting this door open?"

It took Herbert a moment to realize that he was being addressed, and he stumbled forward. "Let me look at it." To her surprise, the lad didn't use his eyes but instead used his tricorder. On her tricorder, Leah was picking up impressive circuitry behind the door, and she was all in favor of getting it opened.

Before the young human could work any magic, they heard a gruesome scream from behind them. The mangled cry was enough to make them all whirl around. It had to be Craycroft, thought Leah, but their prisoner was too far away—behind too many poles and braces—for them to see him.

"You should have used a longer stun," said Maltz.

"Was *that* Mr. Craycroft?" asked Herbert. "It didn't even sound human."

"I'll go look," volunteered Gradok, lifting his disruptor rifle and trudging off toward the entrance to the mammoth cavern. A moment later, he disappeared in the forest of machines and silos.

"If we contact the ship," said Leah, "maybe they can transport us to the other side of that door. We're not that deep inside the crust."

Maltz nodded thoughtfully, but before they could act on the suggestion, they heard startled shouts; and disruptor beams flashed across the empty spaces of the cavern. A moment later, the entire complex was plunged into darkness, and all they had were the insufficient light beams on their helmets.

"Gradok!" Maltz shouted, trying to raise his comrade. "Gradok, respond!"

"Sir!" cried Herbert, pointing a trembling hand into the darkness, where a row of ghostly shapes had suddenly materialized and were slowly advancing upon them.

Brahms didn't wait to see more of this; she aimed her phaser and raked the front row of attackers. But the stun setting had no effect on them, and she cranked it up to full. This time, both she and Maltz cut loose with withering beamed fire, blasting the front row of attackers into flaming confetti. Lit up like a mobile bonfire with flames leaping off their backs, the mysterious enemy kept advancing.

Within seconds, Leah, Maltz, and Herbert were backed up against the door they had uncovered. Leah drew her second phaser and blasted away with both weapons at the advancing horde, while Maltz clubbed them to shreds with the butt of his rifle. Still the enemy kept coming from the blackness, reforming into ranks from the flaming debris.

Just when there was no place left to go, the door behind them creaked open, and a strong hand grabbed Leah and yanked her into the darkness. Herbert and Maltz wasted no time following her, as they ducked into the unknown.

Geordi La Forge bolted upright in his bed, sweat streaming down his face. His stomach was knotted, and his clothes felt clammy. For a moment, he was totally disoriented by all the alien sounds and smells—not *his* normal sounds and smells—and he was even more confused by the unfamiliar darkness.

*I'm blind,* he reminded himself. *I'm in sickbay, not engineering. No, I don't belong here, but this is where I am. But damn, that dream was awful.*

Before he had a chance to stop it, the dream replayed in his mind's video log. He was a prisoner in a transparent cage in a laboratory, which he could see much more clearly than his ocular implants should allow. He wanted out of this crystal cage in the worst way, because he could *imagine* a giant tree where he belonged. The great tree towered above him, offering sanctuary, shelter, nourishment, along with Leah Brahms and everything else that gave him comfort in life. The longing to escape his cell was the strongest urge he had ever experienced, and he felt totally bereft without that tree.

*The tree—the answer to everything—was behind a door.* He *knew* that. The object of his desire was behind a closed door that was very near—Geordi could feel it like the heat radiating off a fire.

After a moment, he lay back in his bed, trying to shake off the beautiful but disturbing images. Geordi didn't know which was worse—being a prisoner or feeling helpless. He supposed they were both related. At the same time that he saw things more clearly in his dreams than he ever had, he couldn't see at all in real life. Where was the door he was supposed to find? He felt its presence very near at hand.

Leah blinked in amazement, because in the bobbing light of her headlamp stood Gradok, half-naked with his suit and hood gone—but grinning broadly. She heard scuffling, and she turned to see Maltz and Herbert struggling to shut the door Gradok had opened for them. She leaned into the oblong metal hatch, but the forces on the other side were also determined. Thick vines crept around the side of the door and lashed at their arms, while a concerted force pushed against them.

It wasn't until Gradok muscled into the fray that they got the door closed and latched, chopping off dozens of branches, which fell to the earthen floor.

Panting so loudly it echoed in her own ears, Leah Brahms turned around. She didn't think she had enough breath in her lungs to gasp, but gasp she did. She was standing outdoors, with a starlit sky sparkling above her head—the stars looked like loose diamonds sprinkled on black velvet. In the distance, a ghostly horizon bathed in mists and lit by Lomar's huge moon beckoned with the enchantment of a fairy land. The tar bogs glistened like black pools of forgetfulness.

"How did we get outside?" she asked.

"Don't trust your eyes," said a voice as a hand thrust a tricorder into her view. She looked down to see energy readings leaping across the tiny screen, then she looked up at Herbert's youthful face. "It's a holodeck," he said.

"Gradok, how did you get in here?" Maltz asked with suspicion.

He pointed toward the door they had just closed. "Those creatures . . . they surrounded me, but I managed to cut a hole in the wall with my disruptor. It was just big enough for *me* to get through, not my suit. They took the suit, and I barely got out of it in time. Then I ran along the wall until I found the door."

"So a hole is open, and they're coming through?" asked Brahms.

"The hole is small," answered Gradok, "but we should keep moving."

"What happened to Mr. Craycroft?" asked Herbert with concern.

The big Klingon flinched at the memory. "Those plants were growing all over the human. He must be dead."

"Good riddance," muttered Maltz.

"You can take your suit off," suggested Gradok. "The air is good in here."

"Belay that," said Brahms. She lifted her phaser and shot a beam straight into Gradok's chest, and he promptly slumped at her feet, unconscious.

Maltz whirled on her. "Why did you do that?"

"To see if he was real," Leah answered. "Remember, the *two* Krussels we saw, and what Craycroft told us? They're shape-shifters . . . or something. He'll come to in a few seconds. Until we need to take our suits off for a specific reason, we leave them on."

The engineer began wandering through the starlit scenery, checking her tricorder. "Herbert, if this is a holodeck, then there's got to be a computer running it. Use your tricorder to help me find it. Maltz, cover us."

"But, Captain, we've got to get more people—explosives!" protested the old Klingon. "We've got to *destroy* these evil creatures." "First of all, we don't even know if these beings set off the Genesis Wave," answered Brahms. "We've got to find proof, and I haven't seen any. If this is a conventional holodeck, then maybe they have a computer, which we can access. Until then, *we're* the intruders, and they've got every right to attack us."

"Yes, sir." Grumbling under his breath, the grizzled Klingon jogged back to his fallen comrade, Gradok. The weapons master sat up, slowly regaining consciousness.

Brahms shouted loudly, "Computer, end simulation!" Nothing happened, and the two humans continued to explore in the darkness for several minutes. Without warning, there were flashes of disruptor fire behind them, followed by Klingons howling in victory. Leah tried to suppress her fear and concentrate on the task at hand.

Herbert called excitedly, "Captain Brahms, there's a strong energy source over here!"

She rushed toward the youth, monitoring her own tricorder readings as she ran. Herbert had stopped at the edge of a cliff overlooking a rather picturesque black bog; it seemed likely that no one would progress much beyond this point. Leah could easily make out the energy surges that had attracted the lad, but she suspected it was an energy coupling or a conduit, not a computer station. That would be a start.

"Step back," she ordered, drawing one of her phasers. The boy didn't wait to be told again, and he scurried away. Without worrying about accuracy, Leah cranked up the phaser to a destructive setting and turned it loose on what appeared to be a methane mist floating over the bog. The mist started to shimmer, and sparks flew out of nowhere.

Leah stopped the phaser barrage. When the smoke cleared, she saw that she had wreaked enough damage to reveal a black-and-gold grid where there had been a distant horizon. After a few more flickers, the entire scene switched to a beautiful copper beach, complete with gently waving palms and a quaint beach house in the distance.

The Klingons staggered toward her, shielding their eyes from the sun-drenched scenery. "What is *this* supposed to be?" demanded Maltz.

"An island . . . on Earth. Or Pacifica." Brahms frowned. "Pacifica? Why should that mean something?"

She was startled out of her musing by the sharp buzz of her Klingon communicator. *"HoS* to away team!" called a frantic voice. It was

Kurok, sounding more perturbed than she had ever heard the second officer.

"Brahms here," she answered for the team. "What is it?"

"A large Romulan warbird has just shown up, and they are demanding to board us."

"No!" bellowed Maltz. "Tell them to take their shoulder pads and stuff them up their—"

"Belay that!" cut in Brahms. "They're supposed to be our allies. Tell them we have an away team on the surface."

"I did," answered Kurok. "They are demanding that we transport to their vessel and turn over all records to them. They act as if they want to take us prisoner, but I have yet to lower shields."

"They want all the glory!" yelled Maltz in rage. "I am not leaving until I fulfill my blood oath. Listen to me, Kurok, do *not* lower shields to transport us. Or for any other reason. Get out of there as fast as you can! The Romulans won't pursue you."

Brahms caught her breath, wondering if she should override Maltz's rash orders. But she realized two facts—she didn't want to lose her ship to the Romulans, and she wasn't ready to leave this planet yet. "Go on, Kurok, get away from here. Come back when they're gone."

"Yes, sir," answered the second officer.

Herbert flapped his arms, looking incongruous in his bulky environmental suit on the sunlit beach. In a squeaky voice, he asked, "Captain Brahms, are you sure you want to defy the Romulans?"

"We've come too far to let anyone stop us," the engineer declared with grit in her voice. She drew one of her phasers and handed it to the young man. "Here, you may need this."

# twenty-one

"Commander!" called the centurion standing at the tactical console on the bridge of the *D'Arvuk*. "The Klingon vessel is powering impulse engines. Shall I open fire?"

The cadaverous Romulan commander turned to his ornate viewscreen and saw the outdated Klingon cruiser suddenly veer away from the ugly planet. "Are their shields still up?" asked Jagron.

"Yes, sir."

"Then don't bother. Unless we destroy them, it might cause an incident." The commander of the mighty warbird returned to his planetary sensors. "It is interesting that they would leave a landing party on the planet, unless that was a lie. Do we sense any life-forms?"

"No, sir," answered the centurion on tactical, "but it will take us several hours to complete a scan. Lomar would appear to have very little life . . . only a few plants."

"Hmmm, what kind of plants?" asked Jagron with interest.

"Unknown from these scattered readings. Shall we prepare an away team?"

"Prepare *ten* away teams," answered Commander Jagron, glowering at the gray, misty planet. "We are going to search every centimeter of Lomar. But use caution, and make sure everyone is vaccinated against the fungus. The creature that took over the *Enterprise* wanted to come here, and so did the Klingons. There *must* be something here."

"Sir," said the centurion with urgency, "I have just detected a shuttlecraft. Civilian Federation design."

The corners of Jagron's thin lips curled into a smile. "For a deserted planet, there's considerable traffic here. I will lead Team One myself."

* * *

Cautiously, Leah Brahms approached the front door of the quaint beach house just off the glittering copper beach. Neither one actually existed, because this was a holodeck; but the simulation had been done with considerable detail. If time were unlimited, she would have preferred to linger by the sparkling lagoon, watching the mysterious black shapes glide under the turquoise water. But she knew she had to access some real technology if she was going to learn anything.

As her gloved hand touched the doorknob of the front door, the knob suddenly turned from rustic wood to a glittering chunk of faceted crystal, and she found herself standing on the porch of an antebellum mansion. The scenery behind her also switched from the tropical isle to a flower-laden garden in the center of a quaint city, like New Orleans. On the other side of a hedge of flaming bougainvillea, she saw and heard pedestrians strolling by, filling the air with pleasant chitchat. Their voices only added to the rich sounds, which included birds and the gentle buzz of the bees as they darted among the colorful daffodils and petunias.

Disruptor beams suddenly tore into the strolling crowd, who completely ignored them and continued on their way.

"Don't fire!" she ordered, turning to see Maltz and Gradok, ready for action. "They're not real—they're part of the program. As much as I'd like to look around here, this holodeck is unstable. We need to get out of here."

"Holodecks," grumbled Maltz, his voice filled with disdain. "I know some Klingons use them for exercise and battle drills, but I never liked them."

"Holodecks are a favorite pastime among humans," agreed Brahms, walking across the porch and stopping at a setting of old-fashioned wicker furniture. "And this one is decidedly human. I would say this is a scene from Earth."

"And who do we know from Earth?" Maltz proclaimed triumphantly. "Dr. Carol Marcus!"

"It's incriminating, but it's still not proof," said Leah. "We need to find something definite to link this complex with the Genesis Wave."

"Captain Brahms!" Herbert's high-pitched voice said loudly in her headgear. "I think I may have found another exit."

It took her and the Klingons a moment to locate the lad, who was in a far corner of the garden, standing over what looked like a wishing well, complete with hand-cranked bucket and overgrown vines. Beside the well stood some small, weathered statues of garden gnomes. The wishing well was the only feature in the otherwise cheerful garden that looked at all foreboding.

Herbert stood over it with a tricorder. "According to my readings, this is a real hole," he declared. "Before the scenery changed, it was a sinkhole near the lagoon. If we want to explore it, I think the rope will support us." He gave the rope a forceful tug, and it didn't fall off the crank.

Maltz leaned over the well and aimed the light from his helmet into the pit. "It looks dark down there. And wet."

"I think the water is an illusion," answered the boy hesitantly.

"You *think?*" replied the Klingon. "Then you go first." He shoved the boy forward, and Leah said nothing. She was too busy watching a commotion on the other side of the hedges. The happy pedestrians were suddenly bustling about in agitation, running into each other, but she couldn't see the cause of the problem through the thick bougainvillea.

"Hurry!" she urged them.

Without hesitation, Gradok slung the disruptor onto his back and leaped into the well, grabbing the rope on his way down. He disappeared into the dark water without a splash, and Maltz shoved Herbert toward the opening. The lad hurriedly stowed his tricorder and phaser before he took hold of the rope and leaned over.

A rustling sound alerted Leah, and she whirled around to see the bougainvillea split asunder by a wedge of thick boughs. She wondered if the hedges had been programmed to move, until she realized that a horde of moss creatures were trying to break through. A disruptor beam sliced into them, cutting the shrubbery to shreds and filling the air with debris. At once, Herbert flung himself into the well with surprising agility in the bulky suit.

"I've got you covered, Captain!" insisted Maltz, laying down more fire. Moving seemed the prudent thing to do, and Leah rushed for the hole, swinging her legs over the side of the stone wall. As the bougainvillea completely disappeared—to be replaced by the inside of a physics laboratory—Leah grabbed the rope and plunged feetfirst into the watery hole.

Her feet hit the shimmering surface with absolutely no sensation. As she passed through the illusionary water, the rope disappeared from her hands, and Leah plummeted into darkness.

Strong arms caught her and yanked her out of the way, just as Maltz tumbled down from above, landing headfirst on the hard floor and smashing his lamp to pieces. The only light they had was from Herbert's helmet, and he tried to sweep the room while Gradok rushed to help Maltz.

The old Klingon sat up, shaking his head. He stared at the weapons master, who shrugged apologetically and said, "I could only catch one of you."

"Where are we?" grumbled Maltz, gazing upward at the dark hole he had fallen down.

"I don't know, but it's cold in here," answered Gradok, his scarred body shivering.

"It's another storage area, I think." Leah turned on her light and directed the beam upward into the rafters, where what looked like sides of beef were hanging. That was her first impression, but the reality brought a gasp to her lips. They were not sides of beef but hundreds of naked humanoids in all shapes and sizes. They were encased in transparent bags, which expanded and contracted at the rate of normal breathing; the poor souls appeared to be in some kind of suspended animation.

As Leah looked more closely, her stomach tightened, because the bodies were being fed by vines and clumps of moss, snaking everywhere among the dark rafters.

"Holy cow," murmured Herbert.

"Do I see Klingons up there?" asked Maltz in rage.

"All kinds . . . all kinds of humanoids." Brahms guided her light to two small forms in a single bag, fed by twin stalks. "Look, there's a pair of Bynars."

"Are they still alive?" asked Gradok, his teeth chattering from the cold.

"Yes, according to the tricorder," answered Herbert.

"What fiends these are!" seethed Maltz. "If I were convinced the Romulans would do a good job, I would beg them to raze this planet. But they would more than likely befriend the devils and turn the Genesis Wave on *us*."

"We still don't know who *they* are," insisted Brahms. "Like the old miner said, this planet is riddled with weird plants, but who's in charge? Could a bunch of plants have built this complex? I don't think so. These beings, who are hanging in stasis until they're needed again, could have built this place. The question is, are they captives, or are they here of their own free will? This could be some kind of cult, or a conspiracy against the Federation."

"No Klingon would live like *that!*" shouted Maltz, shaking his fist at the gently breathing bodies hanging above them. "I say we cut one down and ask him."

They were hanging so low that Maltz reached a lanky arm upward and grabbed the foot of the closest encased humanoid. With his other hand, he drew his disruptor.

"Maltz, be careful," warned Leah. "I don't want a murder on our hands."

The Klingon nodded, then with pinpoint precision, he shot a beam into the vines and sheered them off around the head of the suspended captive. When the vines snapped, they spewed a vile, greenish sap all over the bag as it tumbled down. Gradok rushed to help Maltz catch the fallen dead weight, and he got the sap all over his bare skin.

"Aiyyagh!" howled Gradok, slapping at his skin as if it were on fire. That left Maltz to lower the body to the floor by himself, and he did so with surprising gentleness. Both Leah and Herbert moved forward, shining their lights on the naked humanoid in the bag, who was gasping for breath.

"Open the bag," ordered Leah.

The old Klingon reached for a small slit in the top of the bag, which was over the man's head. That feat alone wasn't easy, because the suddenly lively corpse was struggling for air and fighting blindly. Nevertheless, Maltz braved the onslaught long enough to get his fingers into the hole and rip it downward, tearing the squirming package open like a ripe banana.

"Oh, God!" croaked Herbert, turning away. The lad's action resulted in only half the light being cast on the afflicted man, but that was just as well, decided Leah. She cringed in horror but kept her eyes focused on the poor creature, whose mouth, ears, nose, and other orifices were plugged with moss and leaking vines.

Meanwhile, Gradok rolled around on the floor, writhing in pain. Brahms was glad that she had told the rest of them to keep their environmental suits on. She took a step toward the weapons master, but he motioned her away. "I will live," he said hoarsely. "A warrior can survive discomfort."

"Let me know if you need help." She turned to Maltz and motioned to the being he had cut down. "You've gone this far, so finish the job. Pull that stuff out of his mouth, so he can talk."

With a grimace that was clear even behind his faceplate, the grizzled Klingon bent down and began yanking weeds from the man's face. As he worked, Leah stepped closer to give him more light, and she tried to look beyond her disgust to see what species he was. From his high forehead and his black hair pulled into a severe ponytail, she assumed he was Antosian.

"Do you still think he's an accomplice, or a victim?" asked Maltz, panting from the exertion of clearing the man's windpipe and nostrils of the ubiquitous moss. "Even an Antosian is not so stupid as to agree to *this*."

Leah leaned in a bit closer to the afflicted man. As his breathing came more easily, he relaxed and stopped his struggles, slipping back into a comatose state. From a pouch on the side of her environmental suit, Brahms took out a small first-aid kit and quickly assembled a hypospray.

"What are you going to give him?" asked Maltz.

"A stimulant. We haven't got time to wait around here for him to wake up, do we?"

"No," agreed the Klingon. He gazed upward at the disturbing contents of the cold chamber. "Hurry, Captain."

Squelching her disgust at the slimy, naked body, Brahms bent down and stuck the hypo in his neck. Instantly his body twitched to life, and his eyes opened, staring around with shock and horror. Before the Antosian could focus his eyes on the frightening figures in dark armor, Leah said softly, "Try to relax, you're among friends. We're here to *rescue* you—to help you."

"Huh? Erghh?" His lips moved, and he seemed to want to talk, but the motion skills were just not there. "Mouth . . . sore," he finally croaked, working his jaw.

"That's a start," she said encouragingly. "Do you know where you are?"

He shook his head and looked around, then he curled into a fetal position and shivered. Brahms pulled out her phaser and shot it at the floor, heating a small area to a red-hot temperature—enough to warm both the Antosian and Gradok, who huddled near the spot.

"Captain Brahms," said Herbert with concern. "According to the tricorder, his vital signs are abnormally high, as if his system was racing."

She bent down in front of the Antosian, trying to get his attention. "What do you remember about being here? What did they make you do?"

He looked at her with confusion and puzzlement. "I . . . I thought I was somewhere else . . . my homeworld. My job . . . I did my *job!* I was never so happy."

"What is your job?" demanded Maltz.

"Biomolecular physiologist," said the Antosian, his eyes flashing with remembrance as he stated his title. "Where are my wife and children? They were here, too!"

Leah grimaced, because she didn't think his wife and children

were here. At least she *hoped* they weren't. "Do you know what you
were doing? What was the project?"

"Programming . . . theoretical." He shook his head. "We had syn-
thesized several genomes into a matrix that could be exchanged over a
carrier wave."

"Exchanged?" asked Maltz suspiciously. "Exchanged with
whom?"

The Antosian shook his head. "Listen, I need some clothes . . . I
need to get out of here!" He tried to stand, but his legs were none too
stable, and he collapsed back to the floor.

"Do you *know* a way out of here?" asked Herbert, moving forward. "We'll be glad to save you."

With a trembling hand, the Antosian pointed into the darkness. "I
remember . . . that way . . . I think."

Then he clutched his throat and began coughing and wheezing for
breath. Leah moved to his side, as did Maltz, but they were too late.
With a massive seizure that shook his whole body, the Antosian cried
out in pain, then he went limp. The color drained instantly from his
flesh, and he looked as if he had been dead for days.

Herbert spoke up, his voice cracking. "He's dead. He was dying
even while he was talking to us."

Gradok leaped to his feet, rubbing his arms to keep warm. The
Klingon jogged off into the darkness. "He said this way—come on."

As they followed, Maltz fell in beside Leah, and Herbert brought
up the rear. "It sounds to me like he was working on the Genesis
Wave," said the old Klingon.

Brahms nodded. "But the question is—what do we *do* about it?
We're four strangers, lost inside this planet, with no ship and a Romulan warbird circling us."

"There is Craycroft's shuttlecraft," answered Maltz.

"If we can get to it," answered Brahms.

As they walked, the room began to narrow, and there were no
longer bodies swinging over their heads. With Gradok leading, they
moved quickly but warily, casting light ahead to look for dangerous
plants in the shadowy corners. Soon they were inside a tunnel that
appeared identical to the one they had passed through to reach the
room with the crankshafts and silos. Moss grew at intervals, and vines
snaked the length of the dark passageway. Although none of this vegetation was moving, it didn't look innocuous anymore, and they eyed
the moss warily as they passed.

Brahms had the disturbing feeling that they were walking in cir-
cles when they saw light shining ahead of them. A few seconds later,

they came upon a gleaming chamber with closed metal doors—it looked like some kind of secure portal. There was a small console standing at the side of the doorway, and Leah went straight toward it.

Herbert tagged along, still reading his tricorder. "It doesn't look like a hologram. It's giving off energy readings."

Leah shook her head and squinted at the small, unfamiliar console, which blinked at her with a cyclopean eye. She finally pressed the eye, and the door slid open. The inside of the chamber blinked and beeped invitingly.

"Maybe it's a turbolift," suggested Maltz. "Or a transporter."

"Or a disposal unit to disintegrate the bodies," said Herbert.

After a moment, Leah asked, "Are we going in there or not?"

For once, Gradok did not immediately volunteer, and Brahms didn't blame him. There was something unsettling about this gleaming metal compartment at the end of the dark tunnel, not far from where hundreds of helpless beings hung in suspended animation.

"If we only had some way to test it," said Brahms.

Without warning, a huge explosion sounded behind them, shaking the undergound passageway and causing dust to cascade down. The two Klingons and two humans whirled around and shined their lights down the corridor, where all they saw was smoke. Leah instantly drew her tricorder from her pouch and checked for life-signs, finding dozens of them about a hundred meters away.

"What in Klin was that?" snarled Gradok.

"The Romulans," answered Leah. "They're in the chamber with all the bodies, coming closer."

"Romulans!" snarled Maltz, making it sound like an expletive. He lifted his disruptor rifle and assumed a firing crouch. "I am not going to be captured by Romulans."

"They're *our* allies!" said Herbert, his voice a strangled squeak. "Can't we make a deal with them?"

"There is no dealing with Romulans," answered Maltz. "I will not jeopardize my blood oath to please Romulans. In this narrow passageway, we can hold out against an army."

Another explosion ripped through the underground chamber, rocking the passageway again, but still there was no sign of the Romulans. Herbert drew his phaser, gripping it nervously. Without warning, the teenager turned and shot a beam that struck Gradok, and the big Klingon slumped to the floor.

"Traitor!" shouted Maltz. He fired his disruptor, but Herbert anticipated that action and ducked out of the way of the deadly beam. Then he scrambled down the dark tunnel, moving awkwardly in the bulky suit.

"Don't kill him!" ordered Brahms.

Maltz reluctantly lowered his disruptor rifle and just scowled instead. Then he turned on his heel and dove through the open door of the portal. No sooner had the Klingon entered the gleaming compartment than his body disappeared in a blinding flash.

Leah was about to follow him when another beam streaked from the darkness and struck her in the back. That was the last thing she remembered before she collapsed to the floor beside Gradok.

# twenty-two

Maltz floated out of the chamber at the other end of the transporter link and gaped in awe at his surroundings. He was inside the most monumental space dock he had ever seen, a sphere containing literally hundreds of ships from every corner of the galaxy. As far as the eye could see were rows upon rows of sleek metal hulls, floating on moorings that expanded outward like spokes from a glowing central hub.

As he looked more closely, he realized that some of the vessels were centuries old, and others were partially disassembled, as if they had been salvaged for parts. But some starships looked brand-new and in perfect working order, such as the four squat *Defiant*-class vessels closest to him—no doubt the missing task force from Starfleet.

The old Klingon tried to turn around but couldn't do so while floating weightlessly, so he drew a small harpoon gun from his pack and shot it behind his head. After hearing a satisfying clink, he tugged on the rope and found it taut. Now he had an anchor with which to pull himself around. The effort was worth it, because the view behind him was no less remarkable. Through a somewhat clouded but expansive viewport, he could see a gray, foreboding planet, as close as if he were in orbit . . . or slightly farther out.

"I'm inside the moon!" he croaked to himself with amazement. He was at the outer edge of a hollow sphere that was easily as big as Lomar's moon, and he was looking through a camouflaged viewport. Like every other discovery, this one only reinforced his certainty that the enemy deserved no mercy.

"I am left alone . . . alone to destroy these monsters. It is my destiny." His blistered lower lip quivering and his rheumy eyes filling with tears, Maltz went on, "I will *smash* the wicked weapon and *kill* the woman who birthed this monster. If no living soul knows my glory, the heroes in *Sto-Vo-Kor* will know! Redemption will be mine . . . at last."

Maltz breathed deeply, trying to calm his war spirit for the immense task ahead. He looked again at the ugly planet in the window, thinking that if he watched long enough, he might see the hated Romulans cruise past. He chuckled with delight. It was funny that the overconfident Romulans were completely ignorant of this treasure trove of starships right under their noses. It had to stay a secret—at least until he made his escape.

Maltz let go of the rope to grab his disruptor rifle, which he aimed at the sleek transporter chamber. He unleashed a barrage of blazing beams, ripping the circuitry to shreds. Within seconds, the chamber exploded in a dazzling aurora, and the concussion propelled him backward, spinning at slow speed.

The Klingon flailed his arms for a moment, to no avail, until he realized that he would soon hit one of the vessels. The lanky warrior stetched his legs out straight, trying to time his collision, and he stuck feetfirst to the hull of a shiny *Defiant*-class small cruiser. After swaying on his feet for a moment, Maltz thanked Kahless for the magnetized soles of his boots.

The Klingon clomped across the saucerlike hull of the freshly minted vessel, looking for the gangway hatch. He finally found it on the underbelly of the ship, and he was relieved to see that the hatch had been left open. That was very careless of the enemy, but he loved it when an enemy was overconfident. They thought they had nothing to fear from these humanoid races they had fooled for countless centuries, but the Klingon would teach them otherwise.

Maltz opened the hatch and clomped inside the spacecraft, turning himself rightside-up in the process. Once inside the vessel, he carefully closed the hatch and looked around, the beam from his helmet the only light. He appeared to be in a storage area with photon torpedoes stacked all around him.

The Klingon found an access panel, which opened to a maintenance tube with a ladder leading upward, and he began to climb. He reasoned that he was down, and the bridge had to be up. It wasn't a large ship, and he found the heart of the vessel with no difficulty. The bridge had an efficient layout, with most of the stations facing forward as in Klingon vessels.

"Computer," he said loudly, "resume life-support."

At once, the lights blinked on, and the whir of air circulation sounded in his ears. Ah, it was wonderful that Starfleet engineers were such trusting souls, thought the old Klingon. Years of living in a Federation stronghold had taught him most of their terminology and technology, and he assumed he would have no trouble turning this discovery to his advantage.

He noticed a plaque on the bulkhead, which gave the name of the ship as *Unity*. That was ironic, thought Maltz, considering it now had a crew of one. The Klingon strolled up to the main viewscreen as he removed his helmet. It felt good to breathe freshly manufactured air again.

"Computer," he said with authority, "on main viewscreen, show me the most recent video log of activity on the bridge."

"Now displaying most recent log record before system shutdown," said the female voice of the computer. With that, the large screen came to life, showing images of a harried crew running around. Maltz sat in the pilot's seat, disturbed by the padded, contoured feel of a chair built for pampered humans, not for Klingon warriors. He stiffened his back, trying to make himself less comfortable, as he watched the drama unfold on the screen. Finally he would learn what had happened to the ill-fated task force, and he hoped to learn more about the enemy in the bargain.

Leah Brahms shook her head and painfully opened her eyes—only to focus with difficulty upon a pair of intense black eyes gazing down at her through a green-tinted faceplate. Slowly the cadaverous face pulled away from her, and she realized that she had been nose-to-nose with a Romulan, even though her own helmet had been removed.

"No lasting damage," said a voice behind her. "She will recover fully."

"Hello, Dr. Brahms," said a cultured voice. "Or should I call you *Captain* Brahms?" The hawklike face regarded her with mild amusement.

"Did you shoot me?" she asked hoarsely.

"No, that would have been our operative."

"Your operative," she echoed. "You mean . . . Herbert?"

The slim figure shrugged in his gleaming green environmental suit. "Yes, he is not actually human, nor is he young," answered the Romulan. "He was an agent we put on Protus for just such an emergency. We were very fortunate that he was able to join your crew when he did, or your refusal to cooperate would have resulted in casualties."

Leah gritted her teeth and sat up, anger flashing in her green eyes. "Where is Herbert now?"

"Aboard our ship, being debriefed by my intelligence officer. So is the Klingon we apprehended." The Romulan smiled like a snake. "I am Commander Jagron of the *D'Arvuk,* and it's imperative that you cooperate with us. That is why we kept you on the planet—to help us. Where is the other Klingon?"

Her jaw worked furiously in anger, and she finally spit out, "I wouldn't tell you that, even if I knew."

"I see." Jagron's eyes narrowed into dangerous slits, and he motioned to the ornate chamber at the end of the narrow tunnel. "We know he went into this device, but our attempts to operate it have failed so far."

He gave her a pained smile. "I would hate to have to leave you here . . . now that you've been exposed to the fungus."

"Are you threatening me?" snapped Brahms. "I've been through more than you could possibly imagine! We didn't get here much before you did, and I'm sure your spy already told you how we found the shuttlecraft and a couple of crooks from Protus. Then we started exploring, and *this* is as far as we got. If you're here, then you've seen everything *I've* seen! So take your ridiculous threats and go some-where else."

"Living with Klingons hasn't done much for your disposition." Jagron frowned under his hood and turned to the minions waiting behind him. "Team leaders, have all your teams concentrate their search in this complex. Tell them to exterminate the moss creatures as needed."

With nods of acknowledgment, several of the suited Romulans withdrew into the darkness, and Jagron turned to shake a fist at Leah. "If you've been lying to me, you will *pay.* Tell me how this chamber works."

"I don't even know what it does," she answered. "Maltz could be dead, for all I know. Why don't you walk in there and see?"

"I have," replied Jagron as he strolled into the empty chamber and turned to glower at the human. "Are you saying you haven't learned anything about the Genesis Wave from this place?"

Leah shook her head with frustration. "While you're standing here asking me stupid questions, maybe the enemy is getting away. Did you ever think of that? Or maybe they're planning another attack with the Genesis Wave. I don't care if you leave me here or not, as long as you *do* something."

"I feel we are closing in on our prey," Jagron said as he stepped from the empty chamber. "You'll be taken to our medical center and examined." He motioned to two more centurions, who hustled forward and picked Leah up.

Leah thought about saying something snide and spitting at this arrogant, two-bit potentate. But he was wearing an environmental suit, so it would be an empty gesture. Now that she thought about it, maybe this whole quixotic search had been an empty gesture.

Maltz sat back in his pilot's chair, his mouth hanging open at the image on the viewscreen. It was an oblong, brownish asteroid, which wouldn't have been remarkable except for one thing: It was fake! One after another, the other ships in the task force had been absorbed into an immense opening in the side of the asteroid, and the mostly human crew of this ship, *Unity,* were preparing to go next. They were total zombies, under the sway of several moss creatures, which lounged in the background, occasionally stepping forward to talk to the crew.

In those instances, the humans' faces registered absolute bliss when they talked to these monsters. It was sickening, but the video log wasn't fooled by their mind-clouding powers, unlike the weak-willed humans.

When it was over, Maltz checked the console where he had captured crucial data from the log. He had the warp signature of the fake asteroid, and he knew the exact location where they had captured these ships. It was incredible, but any force that built this fake moon could have done the same thing with an asteroid. It wasn't much different from a Dyson Sphere.

The Klingon had a burning certainty that Carol Marcus and the fiends behind the Genesis Wave were aboard that false asteroid. He was also certain that it was the location of the emitters that sent the wave on its genocidal onslaught. He would end the destruction and bathe in their blood.

Maltz rubbed his hands together and gazed at the Starfleet instrument panel. All of the security safeguards had been disabled, much to his advantage. Maybe he could use the ship's sensor to locate a Klingon ship in this mothballed fleet, and then transport over to it. That seemed unlikely, however, because they were awfully far from Klingon space, as he well knew. Better to use a shiny new Starfleet craft than a rusted hulk from bygone days. A more logical use of the sensors would be to find the exit from this immense cage, although he could always blast his way out if he had to.

*That might be more fun.*

Commander Jagron cringed behind his green-tinted faceplate and turned away from the desiccated, vivisected corpse they had found in what appeared to be a medical laboratory. It might have been a sickbay, but if so, it was one of the coldest and most heartless medical facilities he had ever seen. What had they been doing to this poor humanoid when they cut him up? Were they in such a hurry that they had to leave him here, opened up and drying like a carcass at the side of the road? Even for a man who could stomach a considerable amount of cruelty, this was a bit much.

"I'm detecting some of the fungus," said a science officer using a tricorder.

"I would imagine," answered Jagron distastefully. He turned to the specialists he had working on a computer terminal in the laboratory. "Have you retrieved anything?"

"Not yet, Commander," answered a gray-haired centurion. "They are using a high-level Federation encryption program, which we hope to crack in a few minutes."

The slim Romulan scowled, thinking that all this effort had better pay off soon. The complex was fascinating, but its infrastructure was clearly devoted to maintaining itself, not the Genesis Wave. Half of his crew was occupied with exterminating the enemy, and the other half lagged behind them, often exploring areas that had been damaged. If they weren't careful, they might be here for days, sifting through the layers of this eerie operation. In all they had seen, there was no direct evidence of the Genesis Wave.

"Bridge to Commander Jagron," said a familiar voice in his helmet. It was Petroliv, his lover and most trusted officer, and she sounded agitated.

"Go on."

"Commander, a Starfleet ship has appeared out of nowhere, and then has gone quickly into warp."

"Out of nowhere?" he asked doubtfully.

"We think they may have been hiding on the moon—or behind it," she explained. "From its warp signature, it's a *Defiant*-class small cruiser. There are some anomalies around the moon that we should investigate. What should we do?"

Jagron cursed under his breath. "I would pursue this ship, but we can't get everyone back on board quickly enough. Put long-range scanners on it and try to track it. We may have to leave personnel here, with shuttlecraft for support, while we rejoin the *Enterprise*. What have you learned from our prisoners?"

"Nothing," she answered. "Even though they arrived before us, they don't possess any significant knowledge. Our operative confirms everything they say. Leah Brahms lost her husband and colleagues on

Seran-T-One, so this is a personal matter with her. The Klingon we're holding is just a soldier. The Klingon who got away, Maltz, was at the Genesis Planet ninety years ago—he saw the original device."

"So he may have special knowledge," said Jagron thoughtfully. "And where did he go? This becomes frustrating, staying here. Ready two shuttlecraft for launch, and begin withdrawing the away teams. Start with my team. We'll decide quickly how many people to leave on the planet."

With disgust, the Romulan looked around at the cold laboratory, then at the gruesome, sliced-up corpse. "I am ready to leave Lomar."

"Commander," said Petroliv in the tone of voice she used when she was about to suggest something naughty, "I have an idea for our two visitors, Brahms and Gradok. They can't tell us anything, and they're really no threat. To return them to the *Enterprise* would only result in a lot of questions. Why don't we leave them here on Lomar, where we found them? We'll have a sizable force, and they'll be safe. Certainly Brahms can help our people with encryption and codes."

"Very well," answered the Romulan commander. "As always, I like the way you think. No one's government can squawk that we mistreated them, since this is where they wanted to be. Ready the prisoners for transport."

Geordi La Forge stared at a vast meadow with its gently waving grasses and shiny pools dimpling the landscape, all of it bathed in the golden glow of sunset. If this sight weren't magnificent enough, in the center stood a perfect, towering tree—the refuge he had always sought. At the base of the tree stood Leah Brahms in a flowing white dress, waving happily at him. He saw the gleaming meadow as clearly as he had seen sunset on the Ba'ku planet, when his eyes had functioned normally. Logic told him he shouldn't see this or anything at all without his ocular implants—or being immersed in a dream—but he was wide awake.

The engineer knew he had to rise to his feet and walk up that hill to the tree. Although it looked like a simple matter, a sickness had weakened him, and he knew it wouldn't be easy. It would require all his will and a major physical effort—he was certain of that. He gripped the sides of his bed, which was resting on the edge of the meadow, and he threw his legs over the side and climbed out.

At first, his legs were wobbly from spending too much time in bed; but since Geordi was normally on his feet all day his legs were strong. He willed himself to walk forward. His reward was a big smile from Leah Brahms, who waved encouragingly from the root of the tree. He could see her face vividly, too, for the first time, and he gasped at her angelic beauty.

There were unexpected obstacles in the way—trees and bushes that sprung up almost at the touch, blocking his passage. As much by feel as eyes, he guided himself around these obstacles, until he was again on a straight path to the proud tree. Geordi had heard the term "old oak" but still didn't know exactly what an old oak looked like, but he knew it represented something large, solid, and lasting. That described this big tree, beckoning like a lighthouse in the darkness. Its boughs were laden with fruit, leaves, and dew-covered moss, which glittered like emeralds.

As Geordi struggled up the hill, his legs weak from his sickness, gnarled vines erupted from the ground to block his way. As he struggled against these new obstacles, the vines wrapped around his arms and legs, catching him in place.

"But I'm so close!" Geordi shouted as he struggled. One vine rapped him on the jaw, knocking him to the ground. From there, the vines converged upon him—and that was the last thing he remembered before he blacked out.

When La Forge regained consciousness, the bed he was lying upon was much harder than his other bed, and the voices and hubbub were much louder. He reasoned that he was lying upon one of the examination tables in the outer triage, not the nice private area he'd had before. Geordi had to deduce where he was, because he was once again enshrouded in darkness.

"Hi, Geordi," said a familiar voice. "Do you know where you are?"

"Yes, Doctor," he answered, "I'm in sickbay . . . trying to get well."

"Is that all you remember?" asked an authoritative voice that he recognized as Captain Picard's.

La Forge shook his head, wondering why he felt as if he had holes in his brain. "Do you mean the dreams? I was having dreams."

"And walking in your sleep," added Dr. Crusher.

"I was?" asked Geordi with confusion. "I got up out of bed?"

"You certainly did," answered Crusher. "You got up from your bed, walked freely through sickbay—even though you're not wearing your implants—and then attacked three security officers who were stationed outside my research laboratory."

"I did?" asked La Forge in amazement. "I don't remember that—it wasn't in my dream."

"Security reports that you wanted to get into the laboratory very badly," said Picard, "and that you acted like you were awake. What did you think was in there?"

"A tree," answered La Forge, suddenly remembering—even if the image wasn't as vivid as before. "I know that sounds silly, but I could see a tree . . . at the top of this gentle hill with long grass and little puddles." He left out the part about Leah Brahms, because he knew she wasn't on board the *Enterprise,* which meant that his memories were more dream than reality.

Crusher's soothing voice broke into his thoughts. "You could *see* it? Don't you usually dream in your regular vision, from your implants or VISOR?"

"Yes, but I *saw* this. It was like seeing with eyes, which is an experience I'm familiar with." He didn't mean to sound defensive, but he was a bit weary from the questioning. Can't a sick, blind man have his dreams?

"Commander," said the captain sternly, "there is *something* behind the door that you were trying so hard to enter. One of the moss creatures is growing in there, and you seem to have made telepathic contact with it. It's grown to maturity now, and it's probably trying to find a new host."

Geordi recoiled in the darkness and pulled his bedding around him. He had never felt so helpless. "Why me?"

"It may be a residual effect of the fungus," answered Dr. Crusher. "The fungus enhances the telepathic connection, making the victim even more susceptible to suggestion. We thought we had everyone placed at a safe distance from it, but we were wrong. I myself can't go in the lab, because it has immediate control of my mind, offering more images of Wesley."

Crusher sighed, sounding like she was pulling herself together. "Your visions have probably been conjured up from your own mind, plus what it *wants* you to see. The fungus-telepathy combination has proven very effective on the rest of us, but you have an advantage over us. When you *see* something, you should know automatically that it's false. You can't physically see at the moment."

La Forge gulped, wondering what they wanted him to do. On one level, he would miss the beautiful visions if they stopped, but every fiber of his being urged him to battle these chimeras. Lovesick, blinded, recovering from an illness—he already felt helpless and vulnerable. Now one of those horrible plants was trying to control his mind.

"It's a disturbing organism," said Captain Picard, "but it's obviously intelligent. We'd like to find a way to talk to it. Perhaps more than that. Over what distances can they communicate with each other? Where is their base, where they launched the Genesis Wave? So far, these creatures have managed to manipulate *us,* and I'd like to return the favor. Will you help us, Commander?"

Geordi nodded forcefully. "Yes, sir, I will."

# twenty-three

The more Carol Marcus saw of the fake Jim and David on the equally bogus Regula I space station, the more she hated them. Perhaps it was their condescending glances when she turned in her work, like a person looks at a cute puppy who has done a clumsy trick. They obviously didn't want to make her sick again, so they conferred with her infrequently, always encased in their cleanroom suits. Lately they had resumed making the occasional joke in character, and she could sense that their dark mood had lifted. This could only mean that they were close to unleashing the Genesis Wave again . . . and time was running out.

In her solitude, the old woman had figured out the basics of what she needed to do. She had to incapacitate Jim and David and get out of this holodeck long enough to sabotage their plans. Her only weapons were that she had been left with the power to read their thoughts, and she knew the real Regula I like she knew the rummage of her own brain. This simulation was impeccably accurate.

Ninety-two years ago, she had accidentally turned off the artificial gravity on Regula I by overloading the main superconducting stator with gravitons—an improvement that didn't work out. Although the holodeck program undoubtedly had safeguards built in, the lack of gravity wasn't life-threatening. The program should allow it to happen, she reasoned.

Ninety-two years ago, a chrylon gas leak had followed the gravity disruption a couple minutes later, but she was going to speed that up. She also intended to mix reality with illusion, as her captors had. Marcus had collected enough solvents, acids, propellants, and other chemicals to make a fairly noxious smoke bomb combined with an aerosol herbicide, the same kind she had used sparingly on her garden on Pacifica.

She had collected huge chunks of raw meat from the food replicator, which her jailers didn't seem to monitor, and she had stuffed one of the cleanroom suits with the slimy material. That suit full of dead meat was going to play *her* in the little scene she was directing; while she wore a lightweight environmental suit and stayed behind the curtain.

The preparations in her mind had taken days, but the old woman knew that the execution had to take seconds. There could be no hesitation. She had to perform each step precisely, never giving her captors a chance to realize that *they* had been fooled. For once.

If she were going to be stopped, fortunately, it would be at the very beginning—if the artificial gravity failed to go off inside this combination holodeck-laboratory. It was a good bet that these beings were more rooted to gravity than a spry old lady, and the weightlessness would affect them more.

As soon as she fastened her environmental suit shut, Carol Marcus leaned over the computer board and upped the graviton feed from the EPS conduits to the laboratory gravity system. With satisfaction, she watched the readouts—just like ninety-two years ago, then she stepped briskly away from the console toward the test chamber.

Carol reached the chamber just as the gravity actually cut out, forcing her to activate the magnets in her boots. That was cutting the timing a bit closely, and she sounded realistically out-of-breath when she hit her combadge.

"David! Jim! Help!" she implored them. "We've lost gravity in the lab! There's an overload in the superconducting stator!"

She pulled a melon-sized, papier-mâché ball from the chamber and lit the fuse with a lab burner. Within seconds, greenish yellow smoke billowed from the sputtering ball and flowed around the circular lab, obscuring the starscape in the surrounding viewport.

"And . . . and . . . now there's a chrylon gas leak!" she cried with alarm. "I'm . . . I'm losing consciousness . . . help me, David!"

Under cover of her crude smoke bomb full of homemade herbicide, Marcus reached into the test chamber and pulled out the cleanroom suit stuffed full of meat. She gently pushed the dummy, which was now weightless, into the center of the smoke. It was exactly like the kind of suit *they* had been wearing for weeks, and she had a feeling the meat would attract them.

With the curtain up and the action underway, it was time for the director to get off stage. So Carol grabbed the retractable pulley she had rigged to the door of the lab, hunched down, and waited.

The door whooshed open, and the two suited figures stood there, transfixed by all they saw. She cleared her mind as she had been practicing for many days, making them depend on their other senses, which were weaker than telepathy. Jim and David were loathe to enter a weightless room full of smoke, but they also knew this was a holodeck, where things were not as they appeared. They had to assume they could make this room go back to normal with a simple command.

However, the body floating in front of them was very real, and Carol could sense their worry and distress over the likelihood that she was dead. In unison, they made up their minds. They didn't rush into the room—they slithered in, keeping close to the floor, under some of the smoke, and using their hands like crawling vines.

It was slow, awkward going in their suits, and Carol held her breath, knowing that the cleanroom suits pulled air out of the atmosphere and filtered it. Even if they didn't remove their suits, they would still get a dose of poison.

When the fake Jim Kirk finally did remove his helmet, and she saw what was underneath, Carol tried not to gasp. But her mind reacted with horror, alerting both Jim and David. She turned off the magnetism on her boots, tugged on the retractable line, and flew across the room and out the door.

Her feet landed in a corridor with gravity, and she promptly turned around and grabbed the door of the hatch. Before she shut it, she saw Kirk shrivel up like a dried bush in a forest fire. Still wearing his suit and coping unsuccessfully with a lack of gravity, David crawled toward her, using his hands and legs like clawing vines.

Daggers of outrage and misery assaulted her mind. "Mom! Why are you hurting me?" screamed a voice, sounding exactly like David when he was little, getting a scraped knee bandaged. "You're going to leave me to die, just like you did before!"

That accusation cut deeply, and a pang of guilt tore at Carol's insides. Then she gritted her teeth and slammed the door shut on the creature who slithered toward her. Pulling down the latch, she closed the airtight seal, trapping her tormentors inside—one already dead, the other dying.

"Mom, don't leave me!" screeched a voice.

Covering her ears, Carol Marcus shouted to the stars, "You're dead, David! You're really, really *dead!* Killed by a Klingon blade . . . and nothing will ever change that. I can't see you again . . . not in this life."

Sniffing back tears, the old woman shuffled down the corridor, taking heart from the fact that she had been right—this *was* a starship.

Now she was certain of it. Although it lacked specific signage, it seemed very much like a Federation vessel, or at least a vessel designed for humanoids to operate. It was very efficient, right down to the . . .

Blinking red lights and loud Klaxons that suddenly blasted and blared all around her. "Intruder alert!" warned a deep voice. "Go to red alert! Intruder alert!"

The creatures must have lived long enough to sound an alarm, thought Carol with frustration. If they were looking for an intruder, her only hope was to look like she fit in. She quickly shed her environmental suit and stuffed it behind a bulkhead joint, then she straightened her uniform, which she had pulled out of the replicator. Carol Marcus hurried down the corridor and rounded a slight bend just as a doorway to her left opened. When half-a-dozen people stepped into the blinking red lights, she realized she had stumbled upon a turbolift.

"Thank goodness, you're here," said Marcus, trying valiantly to hide her disgust at their appearance. They were all young humans in battered Starfleet uniforms, but they looked sick and malnourished. Still it wasn't their vacant-eyed expressions that chilled her—it was the greenery growing on their backs and necks like a lion's mane. In addition to this rich pelt of vibrant moss, tentacles reached into their noses, mouths, and ears. She caught an insignia on a shoulder that read, "Fifth Task Force Starfleet."

"There's been an explosion in the holodeck. There are casualties. Down there!" Marcus pointed down the corridor, where indeed there was smoke.

The afflicted officers just stared at her, dumbfounded, and she quickly reasoned they they were waiting for telepathic confirmation from their masters. She had learned to receive telepathically—could she send, too?

*Believe this woman,* she broadcast over and over again with her mind. *She is one of us. One of us. Trust her.*

They stared at the sincere elder, and the pathetic soul who was in charge snapped out of his stupor. "Thank you, ma'am. It might be dangerous here. Will you go up to the control room?" He motioned to the turbolift.

"Indeed I will," she answered, backing into the turbolift. "Thank you." She shivered as the doors closed tightly.

Going to the bridge was tempting, but it seemed to her that there might be more plant monsters on the bridge, keeping their deluded crew in line. She was free, and the main objective was to stay that way until she learned more. "Up one deck," she ordered cautiously.

The door opened abruptly, making her jump. When Marcus stepped out of the turbolift, she still found strobing red lights and sirens, but there was no one in view. In fact, she seemed to be in an unfinished part of the vessel that was now used for storage. The vast room was divided into aisles by rows of raw materials, disassembled modules, and starship components. She noticed a row of particle emitters exactly like those that would be used for the Genesis Wave. Marcus walked past thickets of cables and conduits until she reached the bare bulkhead, and she turned to look around. They had enough stuff here to double the strength of the Genesis Wave.

Without warning, the strobing red lights and Klaxons stopped, and the large storage room reverted to normal ambient light. Maybe they had stopped looking for her, thought Carol with relief; maybe they had even accepted her fake body as real. With any luck, it would take them a while to recover and inspect the meat in the suit, plus they had to cope with the untimely deaths of the creatures who called themselves Jim and David. She hoped that would be a crippling blow to their plans.

It was tempting to stop here and rest a while, but Marcus knew she couldn't stand still and wait for them to find her. She had to keep exploring the ship. Judging by the size of this empty deck, the vessel had to be rather large and an odd shape. As the scientist walked down an aisle lined on both sides with shiny new equipment and components, she looked for anything she could use as a weapon, or a bomb.

Her eyes lit upon a portable force-field generator, such as the kind erected outside an encampment for protection, or inside a cave to fortify the walls. If they had this kind of equipment, she thought with excitement, maybe they had gel packs to power it. Her heart thumping, Marcus rummaged through row after row of components until she found a case that was the right size. After prying the latches open, she lifted the lid and looked with delight at two deep stacks of gel packs and the fittings and tools needed to hook them up to just about anything.

Now she could turn this place into a fortress—or maybe turn herself into a walking fortress. But she had to work quickly.


"All right," said Geordi La Forge uncertainly, "can we go over exactly what you want me to do?"

"Yes," answered Captain Picard, sounding very patient and very serious. "So far, the mental exchange with these creatures has been very one-sided, with them probing our minds, stealing what they want, and regurgitating it back in a pleasing form."

"I know all about that," said Geordi. He grimaced as he recalled how one of them had kissed him while it was impersonating Dolores Linton. If Data hadn't saved him on Myrmidon . . . he tried not to think about it while he waited in the dark prison of his sightless eyes. Geordi wasn't even certain what room they were in, although his chair was comfortable enough.

"Dr. Crusher assures me that you've been cured of the fungus," the captain went on, "although you're still receptive to their telepathic overtures. Of all people, Mr. La Forge, you ought *not* to be fooled by their visions and falsehoods. You can contact them with a clear head, knowing nothing you see is real."

Picard took a breath as he seemed to collect his thoughts. "Since this plant is a young individual without much experience, we think you could even control the exchange. They have imparted a lot of false information to us, and we feel we can do the same to them. Counselor Troi has a few thoughts on the matter."

"You're doing my job for me," said the ship's counselor, "because I can't go anywhere near that thing without becoming physically ill. It's like a beacon that is always left on—putting out signals, trying to pick up signals. From what you've told us of your visions, you have invented a kind of symbolic language to speak to this creature. The tree isn't really *your* symbol—it's the moss creature's symbol of yearning. It's outgrowing its enclosure, and it wants a tree in which to roost. This is all it knows . . . for now."

"I know where you're going with this," said La Forge somberly. "You want me to give false information to this creature, instead of the other way around."

"That's right," said Picard. "For two days, we've scanned this asteroid field with sensors, and we could spend a lifetime doing that without success. We need to draw the enemy out . . . make them think it's safe to emerge from hiding. They're here somewhere—all our models show that the Genesis Wave originated in the Boneyard. But where?"

"The tree," said Geordi with realization. "You want me to tell this creature that the tree it searches for is here. And you think it will mentally contact other creatures nearby?"

"We're ready to try it," said Picard. "The evidence from Myrmidon is that they communicate with each other telepathically. They've lied to us with impunity, and now it's time to even the odds.

But this is a controlled situation where we've minimized the danger to you as much as possible."

La Forge nodded solemnly, not relishing the idea of having to perform counterintelligence, but this ruthless enemy didn't leave them much choice. He was the logical one—if he could just remember that he was blind.

"Are you ready?" asked Deanna Troi. "Do you want some rest first?"

"No," said Geordi, rising slowly to his feet. "Let's go."

"Good luck," said Deanna, squeezing his arm. "I can't get any closer than this, but Dr. Crusher will be monitoring you by tricorder."

"Should I go into the room . . . with this thing?" asked Geordi.

"That's up to you," answered the captain. "The force fields will remain on, so it can't have physical contact with you. We'll be watching all the time. Remember, we want it to think it's safe here—that help is at hand."

In the captain's firm grip, Geordi allowed himself to be led from the room and down a long corridor. Before they even reached the laboratory, he felt the yearning and longing swell upward from unseen depths, striking him like a wave. Truly, it was the longing he felt so often—an emptiness that could be met by only one thing. For him, it was Leah Brahms; for the creature, it was an idealized tree. Not just any tree, Geordi knew, but a home where every need would be met.

He hardly felt the captain's hands on his arm or the voices talking to him, because his perfect sight had returned. In the golden meadow stood the majestic tree, and he knew instantly that he had to seize control of the exchange at this instant, before his opposite could dictate terms.

Instead of passively seeing, Geordi began to imagine. He imagined a tree even more wonderful than the creature's idealized tree, adding his own special impressions of a healthy infrared aura, coolly pulsing veins, and a vibrant electromagnetic glow. He had no trouble visualizing his favorite fruits—ripe and dripping with juice—along with plump leaves and vegetables. He also envisioned the hordes of moss creatures he had seen on Myrmidon, shuffling forward, claiming the entire planet as their own.

La Forge imagined an entire propaganda log for the benefit of their prisoner, extolling the wonderful day when hordes of moss creatures would cover the heavenly tree . . . all living in bliss.

With tears streaming down his eyes, Geordi pressed his face against the door, feeling the abject longing swell within him, then slowly dissipate. He knew instinctively that his message was getting through, and he joined the unseen creature in its unbridled joy at the idyllic outcome. The human had no trouble imagining a wonderful ending to their long, long search—he just had trouble making it happen for himself.

La Forge shook off this lapse of negativity, while he imagined the *Enterprise* giving up and departing. He played that scene over and over again—that they were safe, and all the enemies and bad times were gone. He imagined seeing the *Enterprise* zip into warp drive with such clarity that he knew it was his opposite regurgitating the visions he had fed it. They weren't so different, he and the creature, which didn't see in conventional fashion either. The parasite only saw through the eyes of others, which Geordi found tragic in a way. When it controlled others, it saw itself through a warped mirror.

Growing weak, the human slumped against the door and fell to the deck. Once again, he tried to concentrate on the beautiful tree, combining his unique vision with the brilliant clarity of the plant's view, creating the mightiest tree that had ever grown in rich soil and perfect climate.

Then his correspondent doubled the intensity, and the massive tree glowed with unearthly light. It put out wave after wave of warmth and nourishment, which washed over him like a cleansing rain. Geordi groaned with a mixture of ecstasy and fear. He could see himself turning into one of the moss creatures, with sprigs and vines spouting from his empty eye sockets.

Abruptly all vision and sensation ended, and Geordi felt himself being carried off on a gurney. Darkness reclaimed his world, and he struggled to return to the light. A hypospray softly kissed his neck, and his anxieties melted away.

"You're fine," said Dr. Crusher, whispering in his ear. "But you were getting agitated, so we ended it. I'm not sure what happened to you, but your brain waves were very active."

"I lied to it," he said hoarsely. "But I think it told me the truth."

"What do you mean?" asked Captain Picard, his voice coming from the other side of the gurney.

"I think," said Geordi hesitantly, "that they're going to release the Genesis Wave again."

"What makes you say that?"

"Because they *showed* it to me," La Forge said with wonder and dread. "It's the only thing that can save them."

"Are you sure about this?" asked Picard.

La Forge shook his head helplessly. "You're asking me to describe an illusion inside a dream," he answered. "I believe I did as you ordered, sir."

In the silence that followed, Dr. Crusher remarked, "I think we can fit you with a new pair of implants, after you've rested."

"That's a relief," said the engineer, although he knew he would miss those vivid images of Leah Brahms waving to him from the golden meadow.

He heard the beep of a combadge, followed by the efficient voice of Data. "Bridge to Captain Picard."

"Picard here," came the response.

The android went on, "An asteroid on the inner part of the Boneyard has just changed positions and is emitting unusual energy readings."

"I'm on my way. Picard out." Geordi felt a squeeze on his shoulder. "Well done, Commander."

"I hope we're in time," answered La Forge worriedly.


Glancing at his instrument panel, Maltz suddenly bolted upright and lifted his unruly gray eyebrows, deepening his rugged head ridges. The asteroid he had been tracking had suddenly moved . . . when none of the asteroids around it were moving. It also gave off readings like a starship powering up weapons. The old Klingon watched with growing alarm as the huge oblong rock rose above the other asteroids in the Boneyard, giving it a clear line of sight in almost every direction.

"Come on, you Starfleet scow . . . *move!*" He pounded the board, taking the *Defiant*-class *Unity* from warp five to maximum warp, overriding the safeties. Even so, he knew it would take about a minute to reach the suspicious asteroid, and he began targeting photon torpedoes.

Without warning, the *Unity* was slammed by powerful beamed weapons, and the craft shuddered but stayed at warp speed. "What pathetic shields!" bellowed Maltz upon seeing that his defenses were already down thirty percent. Checking sensors, he verified that the barrage had come from the mysterious asteroid, which was humming with power.

The *Unity* couldn't take much of that kind of pounding, thought the Klingon, unless he took evasive maneuvers. "Blast evasive manuevers!" he roared. "Full speed ahead!"

Maltz diverted all power to shields and set course for the center of the asteroid. He knew that enemy fire would cripple the shields and bring the ship out of warp before he got there—he just hoped he would get close enough. The Klingon gathered up his weapons and gear, sticking as many disruptors, phasers, and tricorders as he could carry in his sash and belt. Then he dashed to the transporter room just off the bridge. As the *Unity* hurtled toward its doom, Maltz punched coordinates into the transporter console—coordinates deep inside the fake asteroid.

As the ship was again rocked by enemy fire, the Klingon yelled, "Hold together, you sand bucket!"

Quickly he entered a five-second delay into the transporter settings, knowing he was either going to be beamed off or blown to smithereens in that length of time. Another barrage slammed into the *Unity*—the lights dimmed, and sparks burst from burning consoles all over the ship. The computer issued a verbal warning, but Maltz knew without being told that the shields and warp drive were gone. He could only hope there was enough left of the impulse engines to get him in range.

As smoke and flames engulfed the dying ship, the old Klingon leaped onto the transporter platform and vanished in a brilliant flash.

A second later, the *Unity* disintegrated in a hail of silvery shards, which rained harmlessly against the craters and pits of the massive brown asteroid.

# twenty-four

Maltz's eyes were scrunched tightly shut in anticipation of materializing inside a bulkhead or a vacuum. When he took a gasp of air and pried his eyes open, he found himself standing in the middle of a curved corridor—and he was still alive! The old warrior let out a groan of relief and slumped against the wall, but he allowed himself only a moment of self-congratulation.

Clomping footsteps alerted him, and the Klingon whirled around with a disruptor in each hand. Sirens sounded, and a strobing red light bathed the corridor, forcing him to concentrate on his aim. He couldn't see the foes clearly when they came tearing around the corner, so he relied on overwhelming firepower. His disruptor beams cut down the first row before they even spotted him. Although they looked humanoid, if they were in the service of these monsters, they were the enemy.

Roaring with rage, Maltz charged into the enemy lines. His foes were numerous but badly organized and slow, and he ripped them to shreds before they could even take aim. One of their lucky shots singed his mane of white hair, and he pounded that one to the deck with his disruptor. As he hit the being's face, sap exploded onto his hand and wrist, burning like the fires of *Gre'thor*. This only increased Maltz's rage, and he drew his knives and tore into the dumbstruck horde.

When he was done, Maltz stood panting over ten bodies lying in the scorched smoldering corridor. Bathed in ominous red light, the bloodied Klingon threw his head back and howled with victory, but he kept his celebration short. As long as this fake asteroid existed, the enemy had a base for their murderous ambition. He had to find its heart and destroy it.

With a grunt, the old Klingon jogged off down the corridor.

\* \* \*

"Sorry, Number One, to disturb your rest period," Captain Picard said as he and Will Riker stepped into the turbolift.

"It's okay, I got almost two hours of sleep," the first officer answered, suppressing a yawn. "What's the emergency?"

"One of the asteroids in the Boneyard suddenly moved and started putting out unusual energy readings. We think it may be their hidden base. Through La Forge, we fed them misinformation to bring them out of hiding."

"Really?" Riker asked, impressed.

"Destination?" queried the computer.

"Bridge," answered Picard.

"Acknowledged."

The captain felt the slight sensation of movement, although he gave no thought to how fast they might be going. That is, until an explosion shook the conveyance, nearly throwing Picard and Riker off their feet. The turbolift stopped with a jerk and the lights dimmed, then turned blinking red. The computer intoned, "Red alert! Red alert!"

The captain slapped his combadge. "Picard to bridge! What is going on?"

"Data here," said a calm voice. "Captain, I regret to inform you that the bridge has been badly damaged by an explosion. Possibly a bomb, given the circumstances. No senior officers were present, but there are many casualties among the relief crew. In fact, I am the only one who is unharmed."

Picard breathed a sigh of relief at the news that Data was fine, but it was small consolation for the other casualties. "A bomb? Who had the opportunity to plant a bomb on our bridge?"

"The log shows that Romulan officers from the *D'Arvuk* were on the bridge to exchange information after the Genesis Wave hit Myrmidon," answered the android.

"Damn!" Picard cursed, slamming a fist into his palm. "Has the *D'Arvuk* returned?"

"Unknown," answered Data. "We are unable to use sensors at present, and they may be cloaked. Excuse me, Captain, but I must tend to the wounded until medical teams arrive."

"Of course," answered Picard. "Riker and I will go to the auxiliary bridge."

"I would not hurry, sir," said Data matter-of-factly. "The ship is badly damaged, and the hull may be compromised. We will not have mobility for several hours."

Picard's shoulders slumped. They were dead in space. "We'll still go to the auxiliary bridge. Picard out."

He turned to see Riker scowling as he inspected the access panel near the door. "I'm not so sure we'll be going anywhere. We were almost at the bridge when that explosion hit. We're at a lateral position maybe sixty meters to port. There's been damage this far out, and the safeties have kicked in."

"We're stuck," Picard agreed.

The first officer looked doubtfully at the strobing red light. "The ship is on red alert with major damage to the bridge. I figure everyone within five decks is stuck where they are . . . for now. What do the Romulans hope to gain from this?"

"Project Genesis," Picard said with realization.

The captain frowned as he looked around at the seamless interior of the turbolift. "Any chance we can get out?"

"I wouldn't try it, sir. If the turbolift came on suddenly, we could be beheaded, or cut in two."

The captain nodded grimly. "You talked me out of that notion. What about transporting out?"

"If we've lost hull integrity . . . ," muttered Riker, not finishing his dire thought. The big human rose slowly to his feet. "I think we'll be here until a repair crew reaches us, and they make sure this area is safe. As for the *Enterprise*, we could open the shuttlebay doors manually if we had to. We could muster a dozen shuttlecraft to investigate."

"To go up against a Romulan warbird?" the captain asked skeptically. "A warbird that is undoubtedly cloaked. No, I won't risk any more lives. If Jagron wants to play this hand alone, then let him."

Picard's eyes narrowed. "I just hope he knows what he's doing."


"I never gave you orders to detonate that bomb!" shouted Commander Jagron, shaking with rage as he stood before his subordinate and lover, intelligence officer Petroliv. He could speak his mind, because they were meeting in his private retreat near the bridge.

The lithe Romulan smiled seductively and touched Jagron's cleft chin. "I was just taking the initiative, darling. Isn't that what *you* were supposed to do? The enemy has shown themselves—opportunity is upon us." She pointed toward a small trapezoidal viewscreen, where an immense asteroid floated by itself in space. "We don't need the *Enterprise* getting in the way."

"They'll know it was *us*," he said, sensing that he was beginning to whine, a weakness that always delighted Petroliv. "This isn't a game—this is my *career,* perhaps the future of the empire."

"You know, you're quite attractive when you fret," the intelligence officer said, amusement dancing in her dark eyes. "Everything is a game of strategy. How are we going to get away from here with the Genesis Device unless we cripple the *Enterprise?* Now we can easily destroy her, if we have to."

Jagron shook his head, feeling his authority slip away, layer by layer. He loved this woman—or at least was obsessed with her—but he realized for the first time how dangerous it was to have this overloaded warp coil so close to him.

"Now we *will* have to destroy the *Enterprise,*" said Jagron testily. "I was hoping we could get the Genesis data without the Federation knowing about it. The human scientist, Dr. Carol Marcus, is the key."

"Is she in there?" asked Petroliv, pointing to the asteroid on Jagron's viewscreen. "From our energy readings, we know something is happening."

"We could destroy them in a matter of seconds," said the commander. "Too bad that's not an option. Whatever we do, we have to take action before any more Starfleet ships arrive. Do they have shields?"

"Not that we've seen," she answered. "But they have weapons. They destroyed that *Defiant*-class ship without any problem. Many areas of the asteroid are hidden from our sensors, but they act as though they have nothing to fear."

"Since we're cloaked, they don't know we're here." The commander paced a few strides, then stopped abruptly, having made a decision. "We'll get so close to them that they can't fire weapons. I want you to lead an assault team. Board that fake asteroid and take it over."

"Me?" she asked with amusement. "Why me?"

"Because you're the only one I can trust to steal the Genesis secrets," Jagron answered with an encouraging smile. To himself, he added, *with any luck, you'll be killed in the process.*

Carol Marcus gaped in awe at the last thing she had expected to find on this ship, or whatever it was. Using a portable force-field generator taken from the storage room, she had broken through a locked door, hoping to find a central computer or some other crucial system. Instead she had entered a small greenhouse dominated by a single living tree.

Marcus set down the force-field generator, which stood on a tripod, and took out her tricorder. Although the tree stood a good fifteen meters tall, it was not an altogether healthy specimen, according to the readings. The grow lights and hydroponic system did not seem to be meeting all of its needs. Undoubtedly, the tree would be much happier outdoors, growing in real soil with sunlight and fresh air; its very presence in this bizarre place was something of a miracle.

Carol walked slowly around the tree, inspecting it with her tricorder. The plant was being housed with all the splendor of a visiting dignitary, yet it remained sick and frail—much like herself under the same kind of benign imprisonment. The old woman felt an instant kinship with the tree, and she wondered if it served the same purpose she did—a combination good-luck charm and crucial cog in their war machine.

"I wish I could set you free," she told the tree, picking a shriveled leaf off one of its lower branches.

This pathetic plant only reinforced her impression of her captors. They seemed to have everything going their way and were on the verge of remaking the galaxy to their own specifications, yet they were also desperate, missing some crucial part of their being. She didn't know why, but she knew that destroying this tree would wound them deeply, perhaps fatally.

It would also create the diversion she needed, and maybe it would reveal their weaknesses.

The old woman looked around for something that would burn, and she found it in the dried leaves scattered all over the greenhouse. She quickly assembled a pile of leaves around the spindly trunk, and she produced the small laboratory burner she had kept on her person. Marcus didn't have the sense that she was killing the tree—she was freeing it from this unnatural imprisonment. Feeling no sorrow, she lit the pile of leaves. Flames quickly rushed up the trunk and spread to the dried branches.

By the time Carol stepped back, the sick tree was ablaze. She barely had time to crouch behind a stubby bush when an unseen door at the back of the greenhouse whooshed open. At once, a dozen plant-like creatures shambled into the greenhouse, and she cleared her mind so as not to attract their attention.

She needn't have worried about that, because their attention was riveted upon the burning tree. The creatures milled around nervously; a few brave ones tried to put out the flames. For their efforts, they were set ablaze. Their panic screamed in Carol's senses.

Forgetting caution, she leaped to her feet, grabbing the force-field generator, and rushing out the door from which the creatures had entered. To her astonishment, she found herself inside a bustling control room, with row upon row of consoles facing a large viewscreen. The consoles were manned by humanoids afflicted with the moss, who scarcely noticed her as she entered their midst. Carol's attention was riveted upon the screen, where she saw a vast array of emitters and dishes.

She watched with alarm as immense space doors opened and the emitter array lifted toward the stars. A computer voice intoned, "Sixty . . . fifty-nine . . . fifty-eight . . . fifty-seven—"

*They're getting ready to discharge the Genesis Wave!*

The first thing she did was set up her force-field generator at the door she had just entered. This stymied the moss creatures who attempted to return to the control room, and she felt their frightened emotions screaming in her mind. Trying to block them out, the old woman staggered into the room, uncertain what she could do to stop the countdown.

"Stop! Stop it!" she yelled at the collected zombies. "You're *humans!* You're destroying the Federation!"

They paid her absolutely no attention, and she grabbed the closest human and shook him by the collar. He stared blankly at her, but the the moss extending from his neck, mouth, and ears twitched slightly.

"Thirty-eight . . . thirty-seven . . . thirty-six—" intoned the computer's voice.

Mustering all her strength, Carol Marcus grabbed the man and threw him out of his chair, then she sat at his seat and began to scan his readouts. There had to be a way to *stop* this countdown! Or maybe the entire vessel had a self-destruct sequence.

*Kaboom!* An explosion nearly knocked Carol out of her seat. Debris filtered down from the ceiling, and the giant viewscreen shimmered for a moment. But the countdown continued. Marcus looked toward the other side of the control room, where smoke and sparks billowed from a shattered door. Through the smoke strode a terrible apparition from the past—a heavily armed Klingon with a weapon in each hand, blasting anything and everything in his path.

Strafing the humanoids at their consoles, killing indiscriminately, the Klingon strode into the room like a messenger of death. He caught her eye and grinned fiendishly as he approached her.

"Carol Marcus!" he crowed with triumph, aiming his weapons at her. "Prepare to die!"

# twenty-five

"Fifteen . . . fourteen . . . thirteen—" intoned the computer voice as hundreds of emitters on the viewscreen began to throb with pulsating energy.

"Go ahead! Kill me!" Carol Marcus shouted at the enraged Klingon. "But *stop* the countdown! Can't you see—they're going to discharge the Genesis Wave!"

The old Klingon's resolve faltered for a moment as he listened to the countdown. Then he looked around at dozens of mindless technicians he hadn't killed, all working their boards as if nothing were amiss. He whirled on the viewscreen with his disruptors and blasted it into silvery shards, then he turned on the rest of the workers and began methodically shooting up their consoles.

Marcus had never seen such a ruthless rampage in all her life, as the wild-eyed, wild-haired Klingon completely obliterated the control room. Sparks and flaming embers shot into the air, along with severed limbs and chunks of moss.

Finally the computer voice croaked a strangled, "Four . . . three . . . two—" then stopped.

Carol glanced at her board and breathed a sigh of relief—the discharge had been aborted. When she looked up, there was a disruptor aimed directly at her head.

"I can't let you live," said the old Klingon, who looked vaguely familiar.

"I know you can't." Marcus peered curiously at him. "You're . . . you're the one who survived all those years ago."

"Much to my shame," said the grizzled Klingon. "But I have redeemed myself, and the name of Maltz will no longer be spoken with contempt."

As he lifted his weapon to fire, the computer's voice broke in, "Intruder alert. Decks six and seven."

"Are there more in your party?" said Carol.

"No, I am alone."

No sooner had the words left his mouth than four figures materialized in the flash of a transporter beam. Maltz whirled around and fired before they even had a chance to get their bearings. A split-second later, four dead Romulans lay sprawled on the deck among the rest of the carnage.

"Romulans!" seethed the Klingon. "You know what *they* will do if they get their hands on the Genesis Wave?"

"No one will ever use Genesis again," vowed Marcus as she returned to the only console still working. "This vessel *has* to have a self-destruct sequence."

"How do I know that is truly what you're doing?" Maltz asked suspiciously.

"I was under their influence, but not now. Just watch both of those doors. I've got a force field on one of them." Carol Marcus began to work furiously, hoping that the enemy hadn't made self-destruction too difficult. They had been careful to base all of their systems on Starfleet technology, keeping it simple, knowing that humanoids with diminished capacity had to use the equipment.

Maltz dutifully checked both doors, the one from the greenhouse, and the one he had entered. He recoiled in horror from the moss creatures lined up pathetically at the greenhouse door, blocked by a simple force-field device. Many of the creatures were on fire, and the room was filled with rancid smoke.

As he approached the second door, a female voice called from the other side, "Hold your fire! We want to negotiate!"

He glanced back at the elder human, who replied, "I found it! Just give me a few more seconds."

Disruptors leveled for action, Maltz edged toward the door and said in a gruff voice, "We're in charge of this place now. Any more attacks, and I destroy the Genesis database. What are you offering?"

"A ship! A full pardon! Riches beyond your wildest dreams!" came the answer. "Just turn this facility over to us—intact. You can't resist us. At this moment, a Romulan warbird is docking with this fake asteroid, and hundreds of soldiers are boarding. They will join us in a minute."

That brought a smile to the old Klingon's blistered lips. "How fortunate for you. I must confer with my comrades. No false moves, do you understand?"

"You have five minutes," came the reply.

Maltz backed slowly toward the remaining console, where Carol Marcus was completing her preparations. The old woman looked at him and nodded, then she rose wearily to her feet.

In a voice too soft to carry more than a few meters, the computer said, "Self-destruct sequence initiated. Two minutes until detonation."

"You had better get away now," Marcus said urgently.

The old Klingon grinned. "I have no escape plan. Besides, I am going where I want to go."

"Me, too," replied the human, shivering.

"Come here, woman." The Klingon wrapped a strong arm around Carol Marcus and held her tightly as the countdown continued. "Death is not to be feared. It's an old friend who has waited patiently for us."

"Five . . . four . . . three . . . two . . . one. Self-destruct sequence activated."

Carol was very glad of the strong arm around her shoulders, holding her up as the deck began to tremble under her feet. At long last, the end was near.

"What are you doing?" screamed the female Romulan as she charged through the doorway.

"Dying in glory!" roared the old Klingon.


There were thousands of mammoth, misshapen asteroids in the Boneyard, but only one of them suddenly exploded like a balloon full of flaming hydrogen. Halos of fire soared outward, consuming the sleek Romulan warbird docked alongside. The emerald-green warship erupted with another momentous blast that tore the starscape asunder, causing a chain reaction among the closest asteroids. Twisted metal, scorched rocks, and flaming embers spread outward in a shimmering ripple of debris and gas.

On the bridge of the *Enterprise,* Data had just gotten an auxiliary viewscreen to work, and he cocked his head with interest at this extraordinary sight. Fortunately, their position was a hundred thousand kilometers away from the concussion wave, so they were in no danger.

The android tapped his combadge and said, "Bridge to Picard."

"Picard here," came a weary voice. "We're still stuck in this turbo-lift. Any sign of the Romulans?"

"Captain," said the android calmly, "the *D'Arvuk* has been destroyed, and so has the enemy's hidden base. I cannot tell you the cause of their destruction, but I can say with certainty that there are no survivors."

# twenty-six

"I'm leaving now, Geordi," said a soft voice.

Geordi La Forge turned away from the railing on the gangplank that overlooked the bustling central mall of Starbase 302. He saw Dolores Linton and several more members of her geological team, dressed in traveling clothes and carrying their luggage. Forty-eight hours after the events that had ended the threat—events still not fully understood—the *Enterprise* had limped into Starbase 302 for repairs. Some members of the crew were being reassigned, including Dolores's team, which had never gotten to perform their survey on Itamish III.

Geordi looked apologetically at the party he was with, which included Captain Picard, Commander Riker, Counselor Troi, and Data. The captain smiled encouragingly and said, "Go ahead, Mr. La Forge, we still have a few minutes before the admiral arrives."

"Thank you." Geordi quickly shepherded Dolores out of earshot of the others, and they stopped in a secluded corner of the starbase, while travelers and Starfleet officers bustled past them.

"Um . . . so you're leaving?" asked Geordi. Even after all they had been through, he was still a bit tongue-tied in the presence of the attractive, young geologist.

Dolores smiled with fondness and brushed his cheek with her hand. "It's all right, Geordi. I heard that they found Leah Brahms on Lomar, and she's on her way here. But it was time for me to go, anyway. You know I'd rather be on solid ground, even if it's not so solid, than the classiest starship in the fleet. Besides, I know you don't love me."

"Dolores," he said, cupping her hand in his. "I . . . I really wish—"

"You've always been totally honest with me, Geordi," said Dolores, tears welling in her soft, brown eyes. "You're the most decent man I've ever met, and you're a great catch. But I didn't catch you."

"Dolores," he said helplessly, grasping for words. "Will you . . . will you stay in touch?"

"You bet!" Dolores answered bravely. "And you had better not make this sacrifice of mine go for nothing! You tell that lucky girl that you *love* her. And if she ever treats you badly . . . well, I've got an extra hammock in my duffel bag."

With that, Dolores grabbed him in a forceful bear hug, and he could hear her sobbing against his chest. When she let him go, she rushed away without even looking back.

La Forge stood on the busy gangplank for a moment, unable to move, or think. He was still staring into space when he felt a firm hand on his shoulder. He turned to see his best friend, Data.

"Your tear ducts are active," said the android.

That fractured observation brought a smile to Geordi's lips. "I'm still terrible with women, even when I'm not so terrible."

"That remains to be seen," said his friend.

"Now arriving at dock one, the *U.S.S. Sovereign,*" announced a voice over the speaker system.

Geordi took a deep breath and composed himself before he and Data joined the others. Deanna Troi gave him a sympathetic smile, as did Captain Picard. Both of them knew that the course of love was seldom smooth. As the pipes sounded, announcing the arrival of a high-ranking officer, the entire company from the *Enterprise* came to attention.

Down the gangplank strode Admiral Nechayev, accompanied by Leah Brahms. La Forge gulped, somewhat shocked at their appearance. The admiral's burns had healed, but with unusual results—half of her face was as smooth and youthful as a teenager's, and the other half reflected her age. Leah looked drawn and haggard, as if she had been fighting a war at the front, which she had. He had never noticed gray in her hair before, but now he did. Still Leah was the most beautiful woman he had ever seen.

Despite her startling appearance, Admiral Nechayev seemed energized as she rubbed her hands together. "Thank you for meeting us. We only have a few minutes, but I felt that the crew of the *Enterprise* deserved to get a face-to-face briefing before I returned to Earth to address the Council. Do you mind talking here?"

"No," answered Captain Picard with a smile. "We have several questions."

"I'm not sure I'll be able to answer all of them," said the admiral. "If I can't answer, perhaps Dr. Brahms can. She uncovered their operations on Lomar. The planet appears to be deserted, but there are extensive underground facilities, where the moss creatures held thousands of humanoids in stasis. They apparently used them as slaves. In their moon base, they had a very impressive collection of hijacked starships, shuttlecraft, freighters—just about any kind of vessel you could imagine. It's safe to say that these creatures were preying on our shipping lanes for centuries before they launched their offensive with the Genesis Wave."

Geordi listened in amazement and horror as Admiral Nechayev described what they had found on Lomar. His eyes drifted toward Leah, and she gave him a wan smile. And he thought *he* had been through hell.

"We've turned over Lomar to a consortium of scientists from all the great powers of the quadrant," explained Admiral Nechayev. "However, the Romulans destroyed all of the creatures and a great deal of the complex before we got there. We're working to revive as many of the slaves as we can, but that has proven difficult. We found indications that Dr. Carol Marcus was there, but we didn't find her."

"Were there records of the Genesis Device?" asked Picard worriedly.

"No. There were fragments of data, but nothing anyone could use to re-create it. We can only surmise that all the records and equipment were destroyed in that explosion in the asteroid field."

"Why did they do it?" Riker asked bluntly. "If they were cruising along for centuries, without anyone knowing they existed, why did they feel the need to destroy so many planets?"

"Because they were dying," answered Leah Brahms. "They had lost the ability to reproduce. We found ancient records and physical evidence that Lomar had once been a garden planet, with many different species, including humanoids. It must have taken millions of years for the parasites to move from the trees to animal hosts, but that's when they developed their telepathic abilities. As they multiplied, they must have killed all the humanoid, animal, and plant life—they turned Lomar into a wasteland. That's when they went underground. Apparently, they needed the trees in order to reproduce."

"So they resorted to the Genesis Wave," said Picard. "Colonization and reproduction in one easy step."

"It may have been more complex than that," said Brahms thoughtfully. "I've been trying to figure out why there aren't any humanoids on the planets they created. Manipulating humanoids may have become something of an addiction to them. I believe they grew to resent it, and hate themselves for it—but they didn't know any other way of life. In those worlds they created, they were also trying to create a generation that wasn't dependent upon enslaving humanoids. In a strange way, they were trying to give up their bad habits . . . and get back to nature."

"At our expense," grumbled Riker. "Now instead of one homeworld, they have dozens."

"Not for long," said Admiral Nechayev, "but we're not going to wipe them out either. It will require Council approval, but my plan is to leave them one planet—probably the planet formerly known as SY-911, which was a lifeless rock before the Genesis Wave. It seems to be the most stable of their planets, and nobody has any claims on it. Needless to say, it will be declared off-limits to everyone. On that planet, hopefully, they will never know what it's like to enslave a humanoid."

There was a moment of silence while everyone digested this knowledge, and Leah Brahms finally spoke up. "I have a question for you. Have you seen Maltz, the old Klingon who was on my shuttlecraft?"

The *Enterprise* officers looked at one another, but no one could offer any information about the sole survivor from the original Genesis Planet. "No," answered Picard. "We haven't seen anything of Carol Marcus either."

"Maltz was determined to find her," Leah said softly. "Maybe he did."

Admiral Nechayev scowled. "The Romulans are demanding more information about how the *D'Arvuk* was lost. I don't suppose—"

"We don't know anything," answered Picard. "As I reported, a very suspicious explosion on our bridge put us out of commission. I would personally like to ask the Romulans more about *that.*"

"Perhaps some mysteries are best left unsolved," said Nechayev with a wry smile. "If there's nothing else, Dr. Brahms and I have to return to Earth. But I believe we have one passenger to return to you."

There was a sudden noise behind them, and they all turned to see a stout, blue-skinned Bolian hurrying down the gangplank, carrying half-a-dozen large bags with difficulty.

"Mr. Mot!" exclaimed Picard with delight. "We had all but given up on seeing you back on board the *Enterprise.*"

"And you don't know how close I came to fulfilling that dire prediction," said the barber breathlessly. "If it hadn't been for Mr. Data here . . ."

While they exchanged harrowing war stories, Geordi tugged on Leah's sleeve and whispered, "Can I talk to you for a second?"

"Sure." She walked away from the others, and Geordi followed, screwing up his courage with every step.

When she turned to gaze at him with those beautiful hazel eyes, he blurted out, "Leah, I love you."

She smiled sweetly and touched his lips with her fingers. "Geordi . . . you mean so much to me, but I can't—"

"I don't want you to say or do anything right now," said La Forge quickly before he lost his courage. "I know you're not ready, and I know you've been through hell. Ten months from now, there's a conference in Paris on theoretical propulsion. I'm going to be there, and I'd like to see *you* there."

She nodded slowly, as if coming to a decision. "Ten months from now . . . Paris. I'll put it on my calendar. Until then, Geordi, don't ever change."

"Dr. Brahms," said Nechayev, stepping away from the *Enterprise* officers, "we have to be going. The *Sovereign* is on a tight schedule. Is there anything else you want to say?"

"No," answered Leah, smiling at Geordi. "I think we've said it all."